THE
PRODIGAL
MAGE

Books by Karen Miller

Kingmaker, Kingbreaker
The Innocent Mage
The Awakened Mage

The Godspeaker Trilogy
Empress
The Riven Kingdom
Hammer of God

Fisherman's Children
The Prodigal Mage

Writing as K. E. Mills

The Rogue Agent Trilogy
The Accidental Sorcerer
Witches Incorporated

THE PRODIGAL MAGE

FISHERMAN'S CHILDREN
BOOK ONE

KAREN MILLER

www.orbitbooks.net

New York   London

Orbit
Hachette Book Group
237 Park Avenue, New York, NY 10017
Visit our website at www.HachetteBookGroup.com

First Edition: August 2009

Orbit is an imprint of Hachette Book Group. The Orbit name and logo are
trademarks of Little, Brown Book Group Limited.

The characters and events in this book are fictitious. Any similarity
to real persons, living or dead, is coincidental and not intended by the
author.

Library of Congress Cataloging-in-Publication Data
Miller, Karen.
    The prodigal mage / Karen Miller. — 1st ed.
        p. cm. — (Fisherman's children ; bk. 1)
    ISBN 978-0-316-02920-9
    I. Title.
    PR9619.4.M566P76 2009
    823'.92 — dc22   2009018136

        10 9 8 7 6 5 4 3 2 1

                    RRD-VA

Printed in the United States of America

To Kim Manners, director, producer and storyteller extraordinaire.
A man of wit and wisdom, who left us far too soon.

PROLOGUE

The first time Rafel told his father he wanted to travel beyond Barl's Mountains he was five, sailing towards six. When Da said no, Meister Tollin's expedition didn't need any little boys to help them, he cried... but not for long, because he had a new pony, Dancer, and Mama had promised to come watch him ride. And then, ages and ages later, the expedition came back—which was a surprise to everyone, since it was declared lost—and he was glad he hadn't gone with Meister Tollin and the others because while they were away exploring, four of the seven men sickened and died, wracked and gruesome for no good reason anyone could see. Not even Da, and Da knew everything.

Once all the fuss was died down, some folk cheering and some weeping, on account of the men who got buried so far away, Meister Tollin came to tell Da what had gone on while they were over Barl's Mountains. They met in the big ole palace where all the grown-up government things happened, where the royal family used to live once, back in the days when there was a royal family.

He knew all about them grand folk, 'cause Darran liked to tell stories. Da said Darran was a silly ole fart, and that was mostly true. He was old as old now, with an old man's musty, fusty smell. His hair was grown all silver and thin, and his eyes were nearly lost in spiderweb wrinkles. But that didn't matter, 'cause the stories he told about Lur's royal family were good ones. There was Prince Gar, Da's best friend from back then. Darran talked about him the most, and blew his nose a lot afterwards. There was the rest of the royal family: clever Princess Fane and beautiful Queen Dana and brave King Borne. It was sad how they died, tumbling over Salbert's Eyrie. Darran cried about that too, every time he remembered...but it didn't stop him telling the stories.

"You're young to hear these tales, Rafel, but I won't live forever," he'd say, his face fierce and his voice wobbly. *"And I can't trust your father to tell you. He has...funny notions, the rapscallion. But you must know, my boy. It's your birthright."*

He didn't really understand about that. All he knew was he liked Darren's stories so he never breathed a word about 'em in case Da fratched the ole man on it and the stories went away.

He especially liked the one about Da saving the prince from being drownded at the Sea Harvest Festival in Westwailing. That was a *good* story. Almost as good as hearing how Da saved Lur from the evil sorcerer Morg. But Darran didn't tell him that one very often, and when he did he always said not to talk about it after. He didn't cry, neither, after telling it. He just went awful quiet. Somehow that was worse than tears.

When he overheard Da telling Mama about Meister Tollin coming to see him, in the voice that said he was worrited and cross, Rafel knew if he didn't do a sneak he'd never find out what was going on — and he *hated* not knowing. The trouble with parents was they never thought you were old enough to know things. They praised you for being a clever boy then they told you to run away and play, don't bother your head about grown-up business.

He got so cross when they said things like that he had to hide in his secret place and crack stones with his magic, even though Da would wallop him if he found out.

Of course he knew perfectly well he wasn't supposed to do a sneak. He wasn't supposed to do *any* kind of magic, not just stone-cracking, not unless Da or Mama was with him. Or Meister Rumly, his tutor. Da and Mama said it was dangerous. They said because he was special, a *prodigy,* he had to be very careful or someone might get hurt.

He thought they were boring and silly, all that fussing, but he did as he was told. Mostly. Except sometimes, when he couldn't hold the magic in any more, when it skritched him so hard he wanted to shout, he danced leaves without the wind or made funny water shapes in his bath. Only playing. There was no harm in *that*.

The time when Da said he and Meister Tollin were going to meet and talk about the failed expedition, that was when he was s'posed to be in his lessons. But the moment Meister Rumly left him to work some problems on his own, and took himself off for a chinwag with Darran, he did the kind of earth magic that helped Mama creep up on a wild rabbit she wanted for supper and fizzled away to the white stone palace. He had to wait until there weren't any comings and goings through its big double doors before he could hide in the tickly yellow lampha bushes beside the front steps. Waiting was hard. He kept thinking Meister Rumly would find him. But Meister Rumly didn't come, and nobody saw him scuttle into the bushes.

Da and Meister Tollin came along a little while after, and he held his breath in case they didn't choose to talk in the palace's ground floor meeting room where Da and the Mage Council made important decisions for Lur.

But they did, so once they were safely inside he crawled on his hands and knees between the lampha and the palace wall until he fetched up right under that meeting room window.

There, hunkered down on the damp earth, yellow lampha blossom tickling his nose so he had to keep rubbing it on his sleeve in case he sneezed, and got caught, and landed himself into wallopin' trouble, he listened to what Meister Tollin had to tell Da about his adventure, that Da didn't want anybody else to hear.

The lands beyond the Wall were dark and grim, Meister Tollin said. Weren't nothing green or growing there. No people, neither. All they'd found was cold death and old decay. Mouldy bones and abandoned houses, falling to bits. There wasn't even a bird singing in the stunted, twisted trees. That sorcerer Morg had killed everything, Meister Tollin said. Might be Lur was the only living place left in the whole world. It felt like it. On the other side of Barl's Mountains it felt like they were all alone, in the biggest graveyard a man would ever see.

Meister Tollin's voice sounded funny saying that, wobbly and hoarse and sad. Rafel felt his eyes go prickly, hearing it. *All alone in the world.* Meister Tollin was using tricky words but he understood what they meant. Most every day Mama told him he was too smart for his own good, but he didn't mind that kind of scolding because in her dark brown eyes there was always a smile.

Next, Da wanted to know why Meister Tollin and the others had broken their promise and not contacted the General Council through the circle stones they took with them. They couldn't, said Meister Tollin, sounding cross. In the dead lands beyond Barl's Mountains their magic wouldn't work. Not gentle Olken magic, not pushy Doranen magic. They tried and they tried, but they had to do everything the hard way. Just by themselves, no magic to help out.

Rafel felt himself shiver cold. No Olken magic, the way it was before Da saved Lur? That was nasty. He didn't want to think on that.

Then Da wanted to know more about what happened to the four men who died. Three were Olken, and two of them were his friends, Titch and Derik. They'd been Circle Olken, and helped him in the fight against Morg. Da sounded sad like Darran, saying their names. It was horrible, hearing Da sad. Scrunched so small under the meeting room's open window, Rafel tried to think how he'd feel if his best friend Goose died. That made his eyes prickle again even harder.

But before he could hear what Meister Tollin had to say about those men getting sick for no reason, Meister Rumly came calling to see where he was. His manky ole tutor had a sneaky Doranen seekem crystal that Olken magic couldn't fool. Meister Rumly was allowed to use it to find him. Da had said so.

It wasn't *fair*. There were rules about that for everyone else, about using Doranen magic on folk. There were rules for pretty much *everything* to do with magic and big trouble if people broke them—but sometimes they did and then Da had to go down to Justice Hall and wallop 'em the way grownups got walloped. He hated doing that. Speaking on magic at Justice Hall got Da so riled only Mama could calm him down.

Remembering his father's fearsome temper, Rafel crawled his way out of the lampha bushes and scuttled to somewhere Meister Rumly could find him and not cause a ruckus. If there was a ruckus Da would come out to see why and his tutor would tell tales. Then Da would ask what he'd been up to and he'd say the truth. He'd have to, because it was Da. And he didn't want that, because when Da said *"Rafel, you be a little perisher too smart for his own good"* he hardly ever smiled. Not with his face and not in his eyes.

So he took himself off to the Tower stables and let Meister Rumly find him hobnobbing with his pony. Knowing full well he'd been led on a wild goose-chase, his tutor wittered on and on as they returned to lessons in the Tower. And all the long afternoon, bored and restless, he wondered and he wondered what else Tollin told Da.

That night at supper, sitting at the table in the fat round solar where they ate their meals, his parents talked a bit about Meister Tollin's expedition. They didn't mention any of the scary parts, because his stinky baby sister was there, banging her spoon on her plate and making stupid sounds instead of saying real words like Uncle Pellen's little girl could. He wished Da and Mama would send Deenie away so they could all talk properly.

"So that's that," said Da, who'd called Meister Tollin a fool for going, and the others too, even though Titch and Derik were his friends. "It's over. And there'll be no more expeditions, I reckon."

"Really?" said Mama, her eyebrows raised in that way she had. "Because you know what people are like, Asher. Let enough time go by and—"

Da slurped down some spicy fish soup. "Fixed that, didn't I?" he growled. "Tollin's writin' down an account of what happened. Every last sinkin' thing, nowt polite about it. I'll see it copied and put where it won't get lost, and any fool as says we ought to send more folk over Barl's Mountains then Tollin's tale will remind 'em why that ain't a good idea."

Mama made the sound that said she wasn't sure about that, but Da paid no attention.

"Any road, ain't no reason for the General Council to give the nod for another expedition," he said. "Tollin made it plain—there ain't nowt to find over the mountains."

"Not close to Lur perhaps," said Mama. "But Tollin didn't get terribly far, Asher. He was only gone two months, and most of that time was spent dealing with one disaster after another."

"He got far enough," Da said, shaking his head. "Morg poisoned everything he touched, Dath. Ain't nowt but foolishness to think otherwise, or to waste time frettin' on what's so far away."

"Oh, Asher," Mama said, smiling. Da's grouching nearly always made her smile. "After six hundred years locked up behind those mountains, you can't blame people for being curious."

Six hundred years. Rafel could hardly imagine it. That was about a hundred times as long as he'd been alive. Mama was right. Of course people wanted to know. *He* wanted to know. He was as miserable as she was that Meister Tollin and the others hadn't found anything good on the other side of Barl's Mountains.

But Da wasn't. He gave Mama a look, then soaked his last bit of bread in his soup. "Reckon I can blame 'em, y'know," he grumbled around a full mouth. That wasn't good manners, but Da didn't care. He just laughed when Mama said so and was ruder than before. "You tell me, Dath, what's curiosity ever done but black the eye of the fool who ain't content to stay put?"

Rafel saw his mother cast him a cautious glance, and made his face look all not caring, as though he really was a silly little boy who didn't understand. "Tollin and the others were only trying to help," she murmured. "And I'm sorry things went wrong. I wanted to meet the people who live on the other side of the mountains. I wanted to hear their stories. And now we find there aren't any? I think it's a great pity."

With a grunt Da reached for the heel of fresh-baked bread on its board in the centre of the table. Tearing off another hunk of it, he glowered at

Mama. Not angry at her, just angry at the world like he got sometimes. Da was never angry with Mama.

"I tell you, Dathne," he said, waving the bread at her, "here's the truth without scales on, proven by Tolin—there ain't no good to come of sniffin' over them mountains. What price have we paid already, eh? Titch and Derik dead, it be a cryin' shame. Pik Mobley too, that stubborn ole fish. And that hoity-toity Lord Bram. Reckon a Doranen mage should've bloody known better, but he were a giddy fool like the rest of 'em. They should've listened to me. Ain't I the one who told 'em not to go? Ain't I the one told 'em only a fool pokes a stick in a shark's eye? I am. But they wouldn't listen. Both bloody Councils, they wouldn't listen neither. And all we've got to show for it is folk weepin' in the streets."

Sighing, Mama put her hand on Da's arm. "I know. But let's talk about it later. Supper will go cold if we go on about it now."

"There ain't nowt to talk on, Dath," said Da, tossing his bread in his empty bowl and shoving it away. "What's done is done. Can't snap m'fingers and bring 'em all back in one piece, can I?"

Da was so riled now he sounded like the cousins from down on the coast, instead of almost a regular City Olken. He sounded like the sky looked with a storm blowing up. Even though stinky Deenie was a baby, three years old and still piddling in her nappies, she knew about that. She threw her spoon onto the table and started wailing.

"There now, Asher!" said Mama in her scolding voice. "Look what you've done."

Rafel rolled his eyes as his mother started fussing with his bratty sister. Scowling, Da pulled his bowl back and spooned up what was left of his soup and soggy bread, muttering under his breath. Rafel kept his head down and finished his soup too, because Da didn't like to see good food wasted. When his bowl was empty he looked at his father, feeling his bottom lip poke out. He had a question, and he knew it'd tickle him and tickle him until he had an answer.

"Da? Can I ask you something?"

Da looked up from brooding into his soup bowl. "Aye, sprat. Y'know you can."

He felt Mama's eyes on him, even though she was spooning mashed-up sweet pickles into the baby. "Da, don't you want anyone going over the mountains? Not ever?"

"No," said Da, and shook his head hard. "Ain't no point, Rafe. Every-thin' we could ever want or need, we got right here in Lur." He looked at Mama, smiling a little bit, with his eyes all warm 'cause he loved her so much. Da riled fast, but he cooled down fast too. "We got family and friends and food for the table. What else do we need, that we got to risk ourselves over them mountains to find?"

Rafel put down his spoon. Da was a hero, everyone said so. Darran wasn't the only one who told him stories. Da hated to hear folk say it, his face went scowly enough to bust glass, but it was true. Da was a hero and he knew everything about everything . . .

But I don't believe him. Not about this.

Oh, it was an awful thing to think. But it was true. Da was wrong. There *was* something to find beyond the mountains, he *knew* it—and one day, he'd go. He'd find out what was there.

Then I'll be a hero too. I'll be Rafe the Bold, the great Olken explorer. I'll do something special for Lur, just like my da.

PART ONE

CHAPTER ONE

❈

It was a trivial dispute...but that wasn't the point. The *point,* as he grew tired of saying, was that dragging a Doranen into Justice Hall, forcing him to defend his use of magic, was demeaning. It was an *insult.* Placing any Olken hedge-meddler on level footing with a Doranen mage was an insult. And that included the vaunted Asher of Restharven. His mongrel abilities were the greatest insult of all.

"Father..."

Rodyn Garrick looked down at his son. "What?"

Kept out of the schoolroom for this, the most important education a young Doranen could receive, Arlin wriggled on the bench beside him. And that was *another* insult. In Borne's day a Doranen councilor was afforded a place of respect in one of Justice Hall's gallery seats—but not any more. These days the gallery seats remained empty and even the most important Doranen of Lur were forced to bruise their bones on hard wooden pews, thrown amongst the general population.

"Arlin, *what?*" he said. "The hearing's about to begin. And I've told you I'll not tolerate disruption."

"It doesn't matter," Arlin whispered. "I'll ask later."

Rodyn stifled his temper. The boy was impossible. His mother's fault, that. One son and she'd coddled him beyond all bearing. A good thing she'd died, really. Undoing ten years of her damage was battle enough.

Justice Hall buzzed with the sound of muted conversations, its cool air heavy with a not-so-muted sense of anticipation. Not on his part, though. He felt only fury and dread. He'd chosen to sit himself and his son at the rear of the Hall, where they'd be least likely noticed. Aside from Ain Freidin, against whom these insulting and spurious charges were laid, and her family, he and Arlin were the only Doranen present. Well, aside from his fellow councilor Sarnia Marnagh, of course. Justice Hall's chief administrator and her Olken assistant conferred quietly over their parchments and papers, not once looking up.

Everyone was waiting for Asher.

When at last Lur's so-called saviour deigned to put in an appearance, he entered through one of the doors in the Hall's rear wall instead of the way entrances had been made in Borne's day: slowly and with grave splendour descending from on high. So much for the majesty of law. Even Asher's attire lacked the appropriate richness — plain cotton and wool, with a dowdy bronze-brown brocade weskit. This was Justice Hall. Perhaps Council meetings did not require velvet and jewels, but surely this hallowed place did.

It was yet one more example of Olken contempt.

Even more irksome was Sarnia Marnagh's deferential nod to him, as though the Olken were somehow greater than she. How could the woman continue to work here? Continue undermining her own people's standing? *Greater?* Asher and his Olken brethren weren't even *equal*.

Arlin's breath caught. "Father?"

With a conscious effort Rodyn relaxed his clenched fists. This remade Lur was a fishbone stuck in his gullet, pinching and chafing and ruining all appetite — but he would serve no-one, save nothing, if he did not keep himself temperate. He was here today to bear witness, nothing more. There was nothing more he could do. The times were yet green. But when they were ripe... oh, when they were ripe...

I'll see a harvest gathered that's long overdue.

At the far end of the Hall, seated at the judicial table upon its imposing dais, Asher struck the ancient summons bell three times with its small hammer. The airy chamber fell silent.

"Right, then," he said, lounging negligent in his carved and padded chair. "What's all this about? You're the one complaining, Meister Tarne, so best you flap your lips first."

So that was the Olken's name, was it? He'd never bothered to enquire. Who the man was didn't matter. All that mattered was his decision to interfere with Doranen magic. Even now he found it hard to believe this could be happening. It was an affront to nature, to the proper order of things, that any Olken was in a position to challenge the rights of a Doranen.

The Olken stood, then stepped out to the speaker's square before the dais. Bloated with too much food and self-importance, he cast a triumphant look at Ain Freidin then thrust his thumbs beneath his straining braces and rocked on his heels.

"Meister Tarne it is, sir. And I'm here to see you settle this matter with my neighbour. I'm not one to go looking for unpleasantness. I'm a man who likes to live and let live. But I won't be bullied, sir, and I won't be told to keep my place. Those days are done with. I know my place. I know my rights."

Asher scratched his nose. "Maybe you do, but that ain't what I asked."

"My apologies," said the Olken, stiff with outrage. "I was only setting the scene, sir. Giving you an idea of —"

"What you be giving me, Meister Tarne, is piles," said Asher. "Happens I ain't in the mood to be sitting here all day on a sore arse, so just you bide a moment while I see if you can write a complaint better than you speak one."

As the Olken oaf sucked air between his teeth, affronted, Asher took the paper Sarnia Marnagh's Olken assistant handed him. Started to read it, ignoring Tarne and the scattered whispering from the Olken who'd come to point and stare and sneer at their betters. Ignoring Ain Freidin too. Sarnia Marnagh sat passively, her only contribution to these proceedings the incant recording this travesty of justice. What a treacherous woman she was. What a sad disappointment.

Condemned to idleness, Rodyn folded his arms. It seemed Asher was in one of his moods. And what did that bode? Since Barl's Wall was destroyed this was the twelfth—no, the thirteenth—time he'd been called to rule on matters magical in Justice Hall. Five decisions had gone the way of the Doranen. The rest had been settled in an Olken's favour. Did that argue bias? Perhaps. But—to his great shame—Rodyn couldn't say for certain. He'd not attended any of those previous rulings. Only in the last year had he finally, *finally*, woken from his torpor to face a truth he'd been trying so hard—and too long—to deny.

Lur was no longer a satisfactory place to be Doranen.

"So," said Asher, handing back the written complaint. "Meister Tarne. You reckon your neighbour—Lady Freidin, there—be ruining your potato crop with her magework. Or did I read your complaint wrong?"

"No," said the Olken. "That's what she's doing. And I've asked her to stop it but she won't." He glared at Ain Freidin. "So I've come here for you to tell her these aren't the old days. I've come for you to tell her to leave off with her muddling. Olken magic's as good as hers, by law, and by law she can't interfere with me and mine."

Arlin, up till now obediently quiet, made a little scoffing sound in his throat. Not entirely displeased, Rodyn pinched the boy's knee in warning.

"How ezackly is Lady Freidin spoiling your spuds, Meister Tarne?" said Asher, negligently slouching again. "And have you got any proof of it?"

Another hissing gasp. "Is my word not enough?" the potato farmer demanded. "I'm an Olken. You're an Olken. Surely—"

Sighing, Asher shook his head. "Not in Justice Hall, I ain't. In Justice Hall I be a pair of eyes and a pair of ears and I don't get to take sides, Meister Tarne."

"There are sworn statements," the chastised Olken muttered. "You have them before you."

"Aye, I read 'em," said Asher. "Your wife and your sons sing the same tune, Meister Tarne. But that ain't proof."

"Sir, why are you so quick to disbelieve me?" said the Olken. "I'm no idle troublemaker! It's an expense, coming here. An expense I can't easily bear, but I'm bearing it because I'm on the right side of this dispute. I've lost two crops to Lady Freidin's selfishness and spite. And since she won't admit her fault and mend her ways, what choice do I have but to lay the matter before you?"

Asher frowned at the man's tone. "Never said you weren't within your rights, Meister Tarne. Law's plain on that. You are."

"I know full well I'm not counted the strongest in earth magic," said the Olken, still defiant. "I'm the first to admit it. But I do well enough. Now I've twice got good potatoes rotted to slime in the ground and the market price of them lost. That's my proof. And how do I feed and clothe my family when my purse is half empty thanks to her?"

The watching Olken stirred and muttered their support. Displeased, Asher raised a hand. "You lot keep your traps shut or go home. I don't much care which. But if you *don't* keep your traps shut I'll take the choice away from you, got that?"

Rodyn smiled. If he'd been wearing a dagger he could have stabbed the offended silence through its heart.

"Meister Tarne," said Asher, his gaze still sharp. "I ain't no farmer, but even I've heard of spud rot."

"Well, sir, I *am* a farmer and I tell you plain, I've lost no crops to rot or any other natural pestilence," said the Olken. "It's Doranen magic doing the mischief here."

"So you keep sayin'," said Asher. "But it don't seem to me you got a shred of evidence."

"Sir, there's no other explanation! My farm marches beside Lady Freidin's estate. She's got outbuildings near the fence dividing my potatoes from her fields. She spends a goodly time in those outbuildings, sir. What she does there I can't tell you, not from seeing it with my own eyes. But my ruined potato crops tell the story. There's something unwholesome going on, and that's the plain truth of it."

"Unwholesome?" said Asher, eyebrows raised, as the Olken onlookers risked banishment to whisper. "Now, there's a word."

Rodyn looked away from him, to Ain Freidin, but still all he could see was the back of her head. Silent and straight-spined, she sat without giving even a hint of what she thought about these accusations. Or if they carried any merit. For himself...he wasn't sure. Ain Freidin was an acquaintance, nothing more. He wasn't privy to her thoughts on the changes thrust so hard upon their people, or what magic she got up to behind closed doors.

"Before it was a Doranen estate, the land next door to mine was a farm belonging to Eby Nye, and when it was a farm my potatoes were the best in the district," said the Olken, fists planted on his broad hips. "Not a speck of slime in the crop, season after season. Two seasons ago Eby sold up and she moved in, and both seasons since, my crops are lost. You can't tell me there's no binding those facts." He pointed at Ain Freidin. "That woman's up to no good. She's—"

"That woman?" said Ain, leaping to her expensively shod feet. "You dare refer to me in such a manner? I am Lady Freidin to you, and to *any* Olken."

"You can sit down, Lady Freidin," said Asher. "Don't recall askin' you to add your piece just yet."

Young and headstrong, her patience apparently at an end, Ain Freidin was yet to learn the value of useful timing. She neither sat nor restrained herself. "You expect me to ignore this clod's disrespect?"

"Last time I looked there weren't a law on the books as said Meister Tarne can't call you *that woman*," said Asher. "I'm tolerable sure there ain't even a law as says he can't call you a *slumskumbledy wench* if that be what takes his fancy. What I *am* tolerable sure of is in here, when I tell a body to sit down and shut up, they do it."

"You *dare* say so?" said Ain Freidin, her golden hair bright in the Hall's window-filtered sunlight and caged glimfire. "To *me?*"

"Aye, Lady Freidin, to you," Asher retorted, all his Olken arrogance on bright display. "To you and to any fool as walks in here thinkin' they've got weight to throw around greater than mine. Out there?" He jerked a thumb at the nearest window, and the square beyond it with its scattering of warmly dressed City dwellers. "Out there, you and me, we be ezackly the same. But in Justice Hall *I* speak for the law—and in this kingdom there ain't a spriggin as stands above it. Barl herself made that plain as pie. What's more, there's a way we go about things when it comes to the rules and how we follow 'em and you ain't the one to say no, we'll do this your way."

Enthralled, the watching Olken held their breaths to see what Ain Freidin would say next. So did Arlin. Glancing down at his rapt son, Rodyn saw in the boy's face a pleasing and uncompromising contempt. So he was learning this lesson, at least. Good.

Asher picked up the summons bell's small hammer. "If I use this, Lady Freidin," he said, mild as a spring day now, and as changeable, "the hearing'll be over without you get to say a word in your defence. D'you want that? Did you come all this way from Marling Vale to go home again a good deal lighter in your purse, without me knowin' from your own lips how Meister Tarne lost his spuds to rot?"

"I cannot be deprived of my right to speak," said Ain Freidin, her voice thin with rage. "You are *not* the law here, Asher of Restharven. One act of magical serendipity hardly grants you the right to silence me."

"I don't want to silence you, Lady Freidin," said Asher. "I want you to answer Meister Tarne's complaint. What are you up to in them outbuildings of yours?"

"That's none of your business," Ain Freidin snapped.

"Reckon it is, if what you're up to means Meister Tarne keeps losing his spuds," said Asher. Still mild, but with a glint in his eye. "Folks be partial to their spuds, Lady Freidin. Boiled, mashed or fried, folks don't like to be without. Last thing we need in Lur is a spud shortage."

"So *I'm* to be blamed for the man's incompetence? Is that your idea of Barl's Justice?"

Asher idled with the bell's hammer. "Answer the question, Lady Freidin."

"The question is impertinent! I am not answerable to you, Asher of Restharven!"

As the watching Olken burst into shocked muttering, and Ain Freidin's family plucked at her sleeve and whispered urgent entreaties, Arlin wriggled on the bench.

"Is she right, Father?" he said. "Does she not have to say?"

Rodyn hesitated. He'd told the boy to be quiet, so this was a disobedi-ence. But the question was a fair one. "By the laws established after the Wall fell, Lady Freidin is wrong. We Doranen must account for our use of magic."

"To the *Olken?*"

He nodded. "For now."

"But—"

Rodyn pinched his son to silence.

Ain Freidin's family was still remonstrating with her, their voices an undertone, their alarm unmistakable. They seemed to think she could be brought to see reason. But Asher, clearly irritated, not inclined to give her any more leeway, smacked the flat of his hand on the table before him.

"Reckon you be tryin' my patience, Lady Freidin," he announced. "Impertinent or not, it's a question as needs your answer."

"I am a mage," said Ain Freidin, her voice still thin. "My mage work is complex, and important."

"There!" said the Olken farmer. "You admit it! You're up to no good!"

Ain Freidin eyed him with cold contempt. "I admit you've no hope of comprehending what I do. I suggest you keep your fingers in the dirt, man, and out of my affairs."

"You hear that, sir?" said the farmer, turning to Asher. "She says it herself. She's doing magic in those outbuildings."

"That ain't breaking the law, Meister Tarne," said Asher. "Not if the magic's in bounds."

"And how can it be in bounds if my potato crops are *dying?*" cried the Olken. "Meister Asher—"

With his hand raised to silence the farmer, Asher looked again to Ain Freidin. "Aye, well, that's the nub of this dispute, ain't it? Lady Freidin, Barl made it plain to you Doranen what magic was right and what magic weren't. So...what mischief are you gettin' up to, eh?"

"*You* can no more comprehend the complexities of my work than can this—this—*clodhopper* beside me," snapped Ain Freidin. "Olken magic, if one can even *call* it magic, is not—"

"I'll tell you what it ain't," said Asher. "It ain't why we're here. And I reckon I've heard more than enough." He struck the bell with the hammer, three times. "I declare for Meister Tarne. Lady Ain Freidin is fined twice the cost of his lost potato crops to cover Justice Hall expenses, five times their cost in damages plus one more for disrespecting Lur's rule of law, payable to him direct. *And* she's to pay a hundred trins to the City Chapel, seein' how Barl never was one for proud and haughty folk of any stripe. Also she'll be frontin' up to the Mage Council on account of there being a question raised of unwholesome magic. Unless—" Leaning forward, Asher favoured Ain Freidin with a bared-teeth smile. "She cares to have a friendly chat in private once the business of payin' fines and charitable donations is sorted?"

For a moment Rodyn thought the foolish woman was going to create an unfortunate scene. He found himself holding his breath, willing her to retain both dignity and self-control. Ain Freidin intrigued him. There was something about her, he could feel it. She had power. Potential. She was someone he'd do well to watch. But if she forced Asher's hand...

As though she could hear his thoughts, Ain's braced shoulders slumped. "A private discussion is agreeable," she said, her voice dull.

"Then we're done," said Asher. He sounded disgusted. "Lady Marnagh will see to the details, and bring you to me once you've arranged payment of your fines."

Rodyn stood. "Come, Arlin."

Leaving Ain Freidin to her fate, and the Olken rabble to cavort as they felt like, he led his son out of Justice Hall. Standing on its broad steps he took a deep breath, striving to banish his anger. A Doranen mage answerable to Asher of Restharven? The notion was repellent. Repugnant. An affront to every Doranen in Lur. But as things stood, there was nothing he could do about it.

As things stood.

It was past noon, but still enough of the late winter day remained to send messengers to discreet friends, call a meeting, discuss what had happened here.

And it must be discussed. The situation grows less tolerable by the day. I know how I would like to address it. The question is, am I alone?

He didn't know. But the time was ripe to find out.

"Come, Arlin," he said again, and started down the steps.

"We're walking back to the townhouse?" said Arlin, staying put. "But—"

He turned. "Are you *defying* me, Arlin?"

"No, Father," Arlin whispered, his eyes wide. "Of course not, Father."

"Good," he said, turning away. "That's wise of you, boy."

"Yes, Father," said Arlin, and followed him, obedient.

Sat at the desk in the corner of the townhouse library, tasked to an exercise he found so simple now it bored him to tears, Arlin listened to his father wrangle back and forth with his vistors over Lady Ain Freidin and her hearing in Justice Hall.

"There's no use in protesting her being called to account by an Olken, Rodyn," said Lord Baden, one of Father's closest friends. "The time to protest is ten years behind us. When Lur came crashing down around our ears, *then* we had the chance to mould the kingdom more to our liking. We didn't. And now we're forced to live with the consequences."

"Forever?" said Father. "Is that your contention, Sarle? That we meekly accept our portion without question until the last star in the firmament winks out?"

Arlin flinched, tumbling his exercise blocks to the carpet.

"What are you doing, boy?" Father demanded. "Must I interrupt my business to school you?"

On his hands and knees, scrabbling under the desk to retrieve the scattered blocks, he fought to keep his voice from trembling. "No, Father."

"Get off the floor, then. Do your exercises. And don't interrupt again or you'll be the sorrier for it."

"Yes, Father."

The training blocks cradled awkward to his chest, he caught a swift glimpse of sympathy in Sarle Baden's pale, narrow face. Father's other visitor, Lord Vail, eyed him with a vague, impatient dislike. Cheeks

20

flushed with embarrassed heat he got his feet under himself and stood. In the library fireplace, the flames leaped and crackled.

Lord Baden cleared his throat. "Rodyn, my friend, I think you need to be a trifle less circumspect. Are you suggesting we foment social unrest? For I must be honest with you, I doubt the idea will be met with anything but distaste."

"I agree," said Lord Vail. "Life is comfortable, Rodyn. What Morg broke is long since mended. The royal family's not missed. We've suffered no hardship with the fall of Barl's Wall. I strongly doubt you'll get anyone to agree with stirring trouble."

Arlin held his breath. Father *hated* to be contradicted. The blocks he held in his hands hummed with power, fighting against their proximity to each other. He subdued them, distracted, and waited to see what Father would do.

Father nodded. "True, Ennet," he said, with a surprising lack of temper. "Nothing's changed in Lur. Unless of course you count the Olken and their magic."

"But I don't," said Lord Vail, sneering. "You can't say you do, surely? You can't even say it's magic, Rodyn. Calling what the Olken do magic is like calling a candle-flame a conflagration."

Contradicted again, and still Father did not snap and snarl. Bemused, Arlin set the blocks on the desk and sat once more in his straight-backed chair. The blocks jostled before him, their energies tugging fitfully at each other. With a thought he calmed them, smoothed them to amity. Then, picking up the foundation block, he let his gaze slide sideways, beneath his lowered lashes, to see what happened next.

Instead of challenging Lord Vail, Father looked at Lord Baden. "Sarle, what do you know of Ain Freidin? Didn't you court her cousin?"

Lord Baden laughed. "Years ago, without luck. And Ain was a child then."

"What did you make of her?"

"Make of her?" Lord Baden stared at Father, surprised. "She was a *child,* Rodyn. What does one make of a child?"

"Whatever one needs," Father murmured, smiling faintly. Then he

21

frowned. "Was she precocious, when you knew her? Was she inclined to take risks?"

"Risks?" Lord Baden tapped a thoughtful finger to his lips. "I don't know, but now that you mention it, Rodyn...she was certainly *bold.*"

"In the hearing she was accused of destructive magics."

Lord Vail grimaced. "You'd take the word of an Olken?"

"Never," said Father. "But I can't deny it's likely she was caught out in some mischief. She accepted the adverse ruling and the fines without fighting them and was quick to avoid explaining herself to the Mage Council. That says to me she had something to hide."

"It's your opinion she's been...experimenting?" said Lord Baden, after a moment. "If that's so, then she's grown more than bold." He glanced over. "But perhaps this isn't a fit topic of conversation. Young Arlin—"

"You needn't concern yourself with Arlin," said Father. "My son knows how to hold his tongue."

"It's not his discretion I'm concerned with, Rodyn. He's a boy, yet. I don't care to—"

"And *I* don't care to be lectured, Sarle," Father snapped. "Arlin cannot learn soon enough what it means to be Doranen in this new Lur of ours."

"For the life of me, Rodyn, I can't see what you're getting at," Lord Vail complained. "Lur hasn't changed. *We* haven't changed. All is as it was, aside from the Olken and their dabblings and as I keep telling you, they don't count. They weren't important before and they're not important now."

Father leaned forward in his comfortable leather armchair, elbows braced on his knees, his expression keenly hungry. "That's my point, Ennet. As Sarle so rightly has said, the destruction of Barl's Wall and the fall of House Torvig—the end of WeatherWorking—that was a moment when our lives could have changed. *Should* have changed. But we allowed ourselves to be overcome by the upheaval. We permitted ourselves to be paralyzed with guilt, over Morg, over Conroyd Jarralt, and Durm. Instead of seizing our chance to become more than what we are, we stepped back. We abased ourselves before the Olken. Instead of consigning that mongrel Asher to Olken oblivion we stood aside and countenanced his elevation to Lur's hero. *Worse* than that—some of us even championed the brute."

Lord Vail and Lord Baden exchanged uncomfortable glances. "Well, to be fair, Rodyn," said Lord Baden, "he did save us from Morg."

"And if he did?" said Father. "I think you'll find he was merely saving himself. It was chance he saved the rest of us along with him. But even so, should we now, ten years later, continue to afford him authority over our lives?"

"Are you looking to challenge this latest ruling in Justice Hall?" said Lord Vail. "For I don't see how you can. If Ain Freidin was indeed experimenting then she's broken Barl's Law of Magics. That's nothing to do with Asher—or any Olken. Any one of us sitting in judgement would have ruled against her."

"True," said Father, and sat back. "Ennet, that is quite true."

"This isn't about Asher, or the Olken, is it?" Lord Baden said quietly. "This is about Barl's magical prohibitions. This is about what we can and cannot do as Doranen. Am I right?"

Instead of answering, Father got up from his chair and crossed to the cabinet that held his liquor and costly crystal glasses. Arlin busied himself with his blocks, pretending he wasn't listening. Pretending he didn't care, or understand. It was always better when Father forgot his presence.

"Barl's Law of Magics," said Father, pouring brandy for himself and his friends. "I freely concede it served a purpose, once. When we were ruled by a WeatherWorker it served a purpose. Magical restraint was paramount in those days. Nothing could be permitted to disturb the balance lest the Wall be brought down."

"And now there is no Wall," said Lord Vail. "So it follows there's no need for such restraint? That's your contention, Rodyn?"

Smiling, Father handed his friends their drinks. "Is it so outrageous a notion?"

"You want to experiment, is that it?" said Lord Baden. "Like Ain Freidin? If indeed she has been experimenting. She's not admitted it."

"Not in public," said Father, returning to his armchair with his own glass. "I'll know what she admitted to Asher in private once the Mage Council next meets."

"Rodyn, my friend, I sympathise with your frustration," said Lord Baden. "I do. But I can't bring myself to think there's anything but danger in the notion of abandoning Barl's prohibitions against experimental magics. It was Morgan and Barl's unwise meddling that set our people on the road to ruin. Would you steer us into a second Mage War? When this tiny kingdom is the only untainted place we know, would you risk it for no better reason than you're bored?"

Father tossed back his brandy in one angry swallow. "*Bored?* I invite you to my home that we might discuss the future of our people and you call me *bored?* Sarle, I'm insulted."

Wincing, Arlin abandoned the training blocks. Lord Baden shouldn't have said that. He was Father's friend. Didn't he know better? Perhaps he thought Father wouldn't shout because they were both men.

"I'm sorry you feel that way, Rodyn," said Lord Baden. "It wasn't my intent to insult you. And I can't fault you for feeling frustrated, or slighted, but—"

Father banged his emptied crystal glass on the wide oak arm of his chair. "*Slighted?*"

"Now, now, Rodyn, there's no profit in working yourself into a temper," said Lord Vail. He sounded uneasy. "And there's no need to take umbrage when Sarle says you're feeling slighted. Barl knows *I* do. And I warrant Sarle feels the same way. What you say is true. We did make a mistake in the weeks after Morg. We let that Asher and his woman and the rest of the Olken ride roughshod over us. But it happened, and what's done is surely done."

"*No,*" said Father. "What's done can be *undone,* if we have the will and the courage to undo it. Do you think Ain Freidin is the only Doranen tempted to explore forbidden magics?"

Father's friends stared at him. "Rodyn," said Lord Baden, his voice husky. "Surely you're not admitting—"

"I've broken no laws," said Father. "I'm not such a fool. I'll do nothing to jeopardise my place on the Mage Council. Someone needs to keep a close eye on Asher. But that doesn't mean I don't think — *dream* — of a different future. It doesn't mean I don't envisage a time when our people are freed from the cage Barl made for us."

Lord Vail sipped his brandy. "You think you're the man to turn the key in its lock?"

"I think I'm the man who's noticed there *is* a lock," said Father. "*And a cage.*"

"Then why do you need us?" said Lord Baden. "Why summon us here?"

Father smiled. "As I said, Sarle, I'm no fool. I can't do this alone. I need good men, like yourselves, who'll help me make the dream a reality."

Father's friends exchanged another look, guarded this time. "And what is it you dream?" said Lord Vail. "These vague hints do you no credit, Rodyn. Come. Speak plainly, since we are your friends. What do you want us to help you make real?"

Father turned his head. "Arlin."

He jumped a little in his chair, then slid to his feet. "Father."

"Come here," said Father, beckoning.

Was it the blocks? Had he done something wrong with the blocks? But he hadn't, he knew he hadn't. They were stacked perfectly now, their competing energies correctly aligned. Nothing would scatter them. Until he released them they would stand tall and strong.

"*Arlin,*" said Father, his eyes narrowed, and snapped his fingers.

Doing his very best to conceal his trembling, he crossed the library to stand before his father. "Sir."

Father handed him his emptied brandy glass. "Transmute it."

"What?" said Lord Baden, startled. "Rodyn, the boy's *ten*. He's not old enough to —"

"Show him, Arlin," said Father. His eyes were glittering. "Make a liar out of my dear friend, here."

"Yes, sir," he said.

With an apologetic glance at Lord Baden, he balanced Father's empty crystal glass on his carefully flattened palm. The brandy-smell lingered, smeared in traces of amber. It tickled his nose. Teased him almost to sneezing. He didn't like its sharp taste in his throat. But that wasn't important. Pleasing Father was important. He let his eyes drift half-closed, and coaxed his idled powers to life. They answered him readily, pliant and supple, and he understood why he'd been set to working with the blocks. They were a limbering exercise. One trotted a horse before galloping. This was no different.

Transmute the glass. Into what? Father didn't say, so the choice must be his. A bird, perhaps. He liked birds. He envied them their wings, and the sky.

The transmutation incant flowed as easily as Father's brandy. The sigils were in his fingers, waiting to be released. He felt the air ignite in brief fire. Felt the crystal warm, and melt, and remake itself as he commanded.

"Amazing," said Lord Vail, and laughed. "Rodyn, that's *amazing.*"

Arlin willed his power to sleep then opened his eyes. Cooling and perfect on the palm of his hand, a crystal falcon. Curved beak open, wings mantled in defiance, it sparkled in the light from the library's glimfire chandelier.

"He's only ten," said Lord Baden. He was staring at Father, the strangest look on his face. "He can do this at ten? As I recall, you struggled with that incant when you were—" He stopped, and cleared his throat. "What else can the boy do?"

"This and that," said Father, his eyes still frightening. "He's not without promise. But what good is promise, I ask you, when he is chained by the past? When he is bound by outdated prohibitions? Strangled by the fears of inferior men? My friends, I've sired a mage who could rival Barl herself and who will ever know it?"

"This is your dream?" said Lord Vail. "To free Arlin?"

Father stood. "To free all of us, Ennet. For six hundred years we've cowered like field mice in the wheat, terrified of every shadow that flies overhead. But Morg is dead and all danger died with him. I say the time has come to stop cowering. I say we stand tall and proud in the sun and reclaim our heritage. We are *Doranen,* my friends. No more shame. No more apologies. No more fear."

Lord Baden was frowning. "Stirring words, Rodyn. But what do they mean?"

"Sarle," said Father, "they mean whatever we want them to mean. It is for us to decide. The future of our people is for us to mould, not the Olken. And not Barl either, six hundred years dead. So. Are you with me? Will you help me unlock the cage so our people might be set free?"

"I don't deny I'm tired of answering to Olken," said Lord Vail. "And I won't pretend I've not had my own dreams of unfettered magic. Very well. I'm with you, Rodyn — provided we act within the law and provoke no violence."

"No violence," said Father. "A firm resolve only. Sarle?"

Lord Baden stared at the crystal falcon. "I have doubts, Rodyn. I think this will not be as easy as you imagine."

"I don't imagine it will be easy," said Father. "But I believe it is right."

"Right," Lord Baden murmured. "Well. Time will tell, I suppose." He nodded. "But I'm with you. We've deferred to the Olken long enough."

"Excellent," said Father. "Arlin, you can go. And toss that thing in the fire. Crystal baubles are girlish."

There was no point protesting. "Yes, Father."

As he passed the fireplace on his way to the library door he threw the falcon he'd made into the greedy flames. Perhaps one day he'd make another. When he was older, his own man, and Father could no longer tell him what to do.

He was very, very careful to close the door quietly behind him.

CHAPTER TWO

❊

The feeling rolled through him as he wandered the cherry orchard Dathne had seen planted in the palace grounds. Not that there were any cherries to steal yet—the trees hadn't even started to bud. But winter was waning: the merest hint of springtime warmth in the sunshine kissed his cheek. That meant the cherry trees would soon be bursting blossom pink and swelling with fruit. It was a cheerful thought, and he'd escaped out here to be cheered. To be alone. Just a snatch of peace and quiet in the fresh air, beneath the milky blue sky, before the demands of both Councils and Justice Hall dragged him under again.

And then the sickening surge of wrongness struck him, and he had to clutch at the nearest gnarled tree-trunk to keep his feet. Had to spit saliva to the damp, tangled grass, bent almost double, and hope he didn't lose his lunch. This was bad. *Bad*. The worst yet. The first time he'd felt it when he weren't asleep and trapped in dreams. And that meant he couldn't pretend any more. Couldn't shrug the feeling aside and call it too much apple pie and spiced cream close to bed. This time he had to face the awful truth. Something weren't right in their small jewel of a kingdom.

Heart thudding, belly roiling, Asher closed his eyes and waited for the surging sickness to ease.

"Sink me," he muttered, cautiously straightening at last. "Bloody sink me."

It was a long, long while since he'd felt this afraid.

Wiping his mouth on his jacket-sleeve, he looked around. He was still alone, but since he'd told folk where he'd be it most likely wouldn't stay the case. That ole trout Darran weren't never happier than when there was something to nag about. He needed somewhere he could think this through. Somewhere he'd not be found. That nobody would ever imagine he'd be. But that were easier said than done. Being who he was — who he'd become, against his will — such a place weren't so easy to find.

The answer came to him with a nasty jolt.

Barl's Weather Chamber.

Of course. Not only 'cause it were quiet, but...

His mouth still sour, his heart still thudding, he abandoned the sweet and peaceful orchard and made his way to the one place he'd thought never to set foot in again. The place where one Asher had died, and another was born.

Panting a little, brushing dead leaves and forest cobwebs off his wool coat, he stood in the mostly overgrown clearing and stared at the Chamber. So long since he'd been here. The day after Morg had brought down Barl's Wall, he'd come, and never once after.

Ten years now, just gone. Sink me... it's been that long?

Yes. That long. Because Rafel was ten now and that was how he measured the length of his life: his yardstick wasn't Gar's death, or the Wall's ruin, but the miracle of his first child's birthing. The promise of a future untainted by prophecy. A future he'd not been sure would come to pass.

In the days and weeks following Morg's destruction, after the fall of Barl's Wall, when feelings and fears were still running a mite high, there'd been folk who called for this Weather Chamber to be torn down brick by stone by timber by nail, to be splintered and smashed and burned to rubble and cinders. Ripped from memory, from history, as though it had never been. But he'd not agreed to that. Tear this chamber down, and in years to come folk might say it were only a story. The chamber, the magic, the way weather ruled in Lur. Folk might say none of that ever was. Things get made up, they might say. That ain't nowt but a lullaby for spratlings.

And that was the time when old mistakes got made fresh.

In the raw aftermath of the kingdom's desolation, with the royal family gone and life turned topsy-turvy, he'd had his way. He was Asher of Restharven, who'd slaughtered Morg the sorcerer. Anything he'd wanted he'd got without a fuss. The folk who'd bayed for his blood and then owed him their lives were eager to show him how bygones were bygones. No hard feelings. All friends now, eh?

"Don't hate them," Dathne had told him. "They were weak and afraid, Asher, but they're not evil. Not like Morg."

Which was true enough. And besides, who was he to point fingers and complain with Gar dead to save him and all those harsh words between them never put right? So he'd pushed aside his resentment, the most bitter of his memories — *rotten eggs, cruel jibes, crueler pikestaffs jabbing* — and done his best to see the kingdom restored to an even keel. Had succeeded, with the help of folk like Dathne and Pellen Orrick and those in the Circle who'd not been lost along with Veira.

And now here he stood, staring at the Chamber's rough-hewn blue stonework, at the glass dome atop it, knowing in his bones Lur was in trouble, again.

Fighting down misery, sick with resentment, he stamped his feet to warm them...and then stamped inside.

The domed chamber was ezackly as Morg left it the day he died, with its circular wall still covered in charts and scribblings, legacy of that lost time when Barl's will had ruled every life in Lur. Her magic map of the kingdom still took up most of the scuffed floor-space, too, nearly all of it spoiled by Morg's vicious meddling. Hard to stomach, that was. Of everything Barl made, her Weather map was the most beautiful. It had enchanted him even when he'd been bludgeoned to moaning stillness by her Weather Magic...but now only a few scraps of its beauty remained.

Even though he'd come here to worrit and brood, he smiled at the spacious, grass-covered Dingles and the scattering of tiny untouched towns and villages. They were frozen, of course. Trapped between heartbeats, a forever reminder of the moment Barl's Wall fell, and how that fall sundered the ancient marriage of weather and world.

He reached down to touch the Weather map's nearest edge. Just to give thanks. To acknowledge Barl and all she'd done. For six hundred years she'd kept them safe and well. What happened ten years ago weren't her fault. His fingertip made contact, lightly — and a sparking of power leapt through his blood where the Weather Magic slept fast, undisturbed for years.

Shocked, he pulled his hand back.

No. That ain't possible. Barl's magic died. Didn't me and Dath and the rest of us feel her magic die? Didn't we see it die when Morg brought down her Wall?

Heart thudding hard again, blood woken and singing, he touched the Weather map a second, cautious time. Let his fingers rest there as he held a long, deep breath. Yes. He could feel something. Barl weren't quite dead yet.

Or . . . was it nowt but an echo? A taunting from the past, from a brief time when he'd been lord of this place, Lur's weather, its magic — a king in everything but name.

Not that I ever wanted that, mind. Not that I did it for myself.

No. He'd done it for Gar, a good man. For their unlikely friendship. To thwart a man he didn't like. For reasons that mayhap didn't matter any more. He'd done it and he'd paid the price. And unlike some others, he'd lived to never tell that tale.

Oddly, the desperation of those dark days had mostly faded. He could remember being terrified. He recalled how trapped and put-upon he'd felt. There'd been panic. Confusion. An endless wail of *why me?*

Of course, he'd been young then. Fractious and bloody-minded. He was older now. A married man, a father twice over, reluctant head of Lur's Mage Council and sought-after voice on its General Council. Defender of the law in Justice Hall. He'd never wanted to be a leader, but ten years on still nobody asked what he wanted. Didn't matter he never cared for it, he had the knack of bein' in charge. And after the Wall fell, and folk were so fratched and disordered, even the Doranen, they needed someone to boss 'em. To chivvy 'em down the road in the right direction. Besides...after how he'd saved 'em no-one wanted to let him go. They refused to believe they could get along without him. So he'd stayed in Dorana City, even though he was desperate for the clean ocean. It was the only way he could think of to make his amends to Gar.

But it don't make me king, no matter what that ole fart Darran says.

Any road, it weren't a bad life. How could he call it a bad life when he had Dathne and Rafel and little Deenie to love? When he had good friends like Pellen Orrick, and a purpose worth serving? An ungrateful bastard he'd be, if he sat on his arse whingin' on how he didn't have the whole world his own way. That'd make him no better than that dead seaslug Willer.

And if ever he woke from dreams of snowstorms, of gentle rain falling and the turbulence of sprouting seeds, of Weather Magic like boiling wine scouring his veins, well...no life got itself lived without there weren't some small regrets.

Beneath his resting fingers Barl's map whispered and hummed. Not just an echo, but a real sizzle of power. Breathing out a slow sigh he drew back his hand a second time, then closed his eyes. Time surged like stormswell, and surging with it a single, searing memory: his first WeatherWorking.

He watched his shaking fingers draw the sigils as a voice he scarcely recognised recited the raincalling incantation. Watched the sigils burst into fiery life. Saw blue flames dance up and down his arms. Felt magic's wind rise, gently at first, then stronger, and stronger still, till it buffeted him like stormbreath racing inland over the open sea. His blood bubbled with a power that remembered the ocean. He couldn't have stopped even if he'd wanted to.

Barl save him. He didn't want to.

The air above the map begin to thicken. Darken. The power he'd raised gave tongue in rumbling thunder and tearing cracks of light-

ning. He was hot and cold all at once. Shaking and utterly still. His body tingled, like the kissing of a hundred pretty girls. His hair spat sparks, and his fingers, and all the world shimmered bright and blue.

Then the rain burst forth...and the world washed blue to red in a heartbeat as his blood exploded through the confines of his flesh, poured burning from his eyes, his nose, his mouth. And everywhere he turned there was pain.

Shouting, heart banging his ribs, Asher staggered back from the map. There was sweat on his face, running hot down his spine. He touched his nose, his eyes, then stared at his fingertips, expecting to see them daubed with blood.

They were clean.

Blotting his forehead on his woollen sleeve, he paced around the room, carefully not looking at Barl's ruined map. Slowly, too slowly, the woken pains in his body slunk away to hide. His breathing eased. The vivid, wrenching memory receded.

All done now. All done. I ain't livin' that madness any more.

"Sink me," he muttered, listening to the uneven thud of his boot heels on the scratched parquetry floor. "Don't do that again, y'gawpin' great fool."

His voice sounded shocked and ragged, breaking the silence. And then he heard swift footsteps on the Chamber's stone spiral staircase.

"Asher? Are you up there? Asher!"

Dathne.

She came through the open doorway and stopped short, seeing his face. "Jervale's mercy, are you all right?"

He could cross Barl's bloody Mountains himself and vanish in the shadows, fall into an endless, lightless abyss, sink himself to the bottom of Westwailing Harbour—and he reckoned she'd still find him. She'd come to drag him home. She *was* home, and always would be.

"I'm fine, Dath," he said, halting. *Don't tell her. No need for her to be scared. Not yet.* "I'm just—just hidin' from Darran."

Dathne's gaze was keen. "Darran and Rafe are book-buying down in the City."

"Ah," he said. "Good. I'm safe a while, yet."

Still Dathne stared at him, skeptical. "Hmm."

Ten years and two spratlings later, she hadn't changed a whit. Sometimes, caught looking at her, he thought he'd see Matt any moment, so like her younger self did she seem to his eye. The Dathne of Dorana's Market Square, that first day, and the Dathne who frowned at him now, they were the same woman. Small and lean and lithe, dark hair long and careless, clothes careless too. An important Olken she'd become, but you'd never know it to look at her. She wore silk like tired cotton and laughed when he gave her jewels.

"Asher..." Dathne crossed the empty space between them and rested her palms against his chest. Tilted her head back to stare up into his face. "This isn't about Darran."

A strand of hair escaped from braided confinement tickled her sharp-boned cheek. He curled it round his finger and tugged, gently. "Course it is."

"Asher," she said, pinching his chin between her thumb and forefinger, "don't treat me like a fool. No-one comes to this Weather Chamber. Not any more."

"You knew where to find me."

She smiled. When she smiled like that she near melted his bones. "Well...yes. I'm Jervale's Heir, remember?" Lightly her fist punched above his drubbing heart. "Or used to be." Her glorious smile faded, leaving her face and eyes sombre. Shimmering with fear. "So no more games, my love. I know why you came here."

And she did, he could see it. Feel it. But he didn't want her to say it aloud. Once the words were spoken, what he'd felt in the cherry orchard, in his dreams, would be true—and he didn't think he was ready to face this truth. Ten years of peace, they'd had, and continued prosperity.

Ten years ain't long enough. We deserve longer than that.

"Something's stirring in Lur," she said, a hint of sudden tears in her voice. "Something—not right. It's been making you restless at night. And a little while ago—that same sense of unease, stronger than ever. Don't tell me you didn't feel it too, for I won't believe you."

As always, she stole his breath. Was there any part of him that stayed hidden from this woman? From before he'd even laid eyes on her she'd known more of him than he ever knew of himself. But he hadn't realised she'd been feeling things too. That were irksome. How come she could always hide from him when he almost never managed to hide from her?

"If you been feelin' this, Dathne, why ain't you said so?" He sounded accusing, and didn't much care. Mayhap if they fratched a little they'd not talk about what frighted him.

"I wanted to be wrong," she whispered, turning away. A breath caught in her throat, a small, stricken sound, and she turned back. "I'd give anything to be wrong. But I knew from the first I wasn't. What's causing it? Do you know?"

Since the day he killed Morg — and Gar — he'd hardly ever used the power in him, that he'd never asked for or wanted. There was no need for it. What he did in both Councils and Justice Hall, that were thinking and talking and wheedling folk to see things sensible. A man didn't need magic for any of that.

But lately, it felt like his magic was stirring anyway.

Wakin' up in a sweat in the small hours. Feelin' the earth groan. Knowin' Lur's earth-song's gone and changed its tune — that, too. All of it's magic, whether I like it or not.

"I ain't sure, Dath," he said. "That's the truth."

She was frowning. "It's not the Doranen, is it? It's not that arrogant Ain Freidin still thinking she's another Barl?"

"I don't reckon so. The fuddlin' she were up to, that couldn't upset the earth. And she swore blind to me her lesson was learned. Besides, I ain't heard from Farmer Tarne that he's lost any more crops and it's been nigh on a month since the bloody woman was found out."

"Still…" Dathne hugged her ribs. "Don't stop watching her, Asher. She's not to be trusted."

"I know," he said. "I ain't recalling our man just yet."

Even though that didn't make life on the Mage Council with Rodyn Garrick any easier. They'd already had sharp words, Garrick making it plain he didn't care for an Olken taking a Doranen to task over magic.

When he learned Ain Freidin was being *watched* he near frothed himself into a spasm. But the rest of the Mage Council had over-ruled his objection.

What's Garrick's game? I can't work him out. Formal hearings in front of the Mage Council mean trouble for everyone. No keepin' that quiet. Is that what he's after? Folk buzzin' about Doranen magic just when Lur's pretty well stopped nightmaring about Morg? Why?

It was a good question, with no answer to it. But Rodyn Garrick weren't his only worry. He was starting to worry about all the Doranen. Now that there was no Weather Magic to keep folk sensible, how many more Ain Freidins were out there, sneakin' off to muck about with dangerous incants? Breaking Barl's Law? Ain Freidin was lucky. A few slimed spuds on her conscience, no real harm done. But what about next time? Next time, could be, someone might get hurt. Or die.

"I wish Matt was here," said Dathne, sorrow shadowing her face. "He'd know who or what was causing this. He was the best I ever knew at feeling things in the world."

Aye, and so did he wish it. Not a day went by he didn't wish for Meister Matt. Couldn't walk into the Tower stables without remembering. Feeling grief. Seeing him shoeing a stallion, mending a blanket, stirring his smelly horse porridge on the tack-room's old stove. Time was supposed to heal wounds, soften loss. Grass was supposed to grow green over a grave.

But not his grave. No, nor Gar's. I'm as wounded today as I was when they fell. And not even Dathne can bind those hurts.

"I'm sorry," she said, watching him closely. "I didn't mean to stir up—" She sighed. "I'm sorry. You never talk of it, so I forget sometimes..."

"Ain't nowt to say, is there?" he said, shrugging. "We can't unmake the past."

"And wouldn't if we could," she whispered, arms folding again to her ribs. Thinking not only of Matt, but Veira too, that bossy, managin' ole besom. And the folk from her Circle who died before she knew them. "Even if it hurts us."

Because her pain hurt him, because he couldn't kiss it away, he turned back to Barl's Weather map. "No," he agreed, reluctant. "We wouldn't."

Dath shook herself. "So let's not think on it. We've a problem here and now to solve and no matter who or what's behind it, with luck there's still time to fix things before it's too late."

Despairing, he shook his head. "You reckon?"

"I reckon it's time we told each other what little we know. For we'll have *no* hope if we keep secrets," she said sharply. "Didn't we promise each other there'd be no more secrets?"

Aye. They'd promised that. And they'd kept the promise for ten years... because there'd been no secrets to keep. He shoved his hands in his pockets, brooding.

"I thought it were over, Dath. I thought once I killed Morg your sinkin' prophecy was dead too, and Weather Magic put behind me for good. I thought Lur was free of all that."

She took a deep, unsteady breath. "It is. Asher, it *is*."

"No, Dath, it ain't," he said, and nodded at the Weather map. "'Cause that bloody thing ain't dead."

"Not dead?" she echoed. "Asher, what are you talking about? *Look* at it. Morg destroyed Barl's map when he brought down the Wall."

"I wanted to believe that. But Dathne, I'm tellin' you, there's power in it still. I can feel it. And that can't be good."

Dathne circled the blighted Weather map, her eyes wide and trepidatious. "How can there be power in it? There's no more Weather Magic in Lur. Morg—"

"I know that's what we thought," he said wearily. "But we were wrong. Looks like Doranen magic don't die so bloody easy. Could be it don't die at all. It's fierce, Dath. It burns. It wants to—to *live*."

It wasn't a truth he'd ever shared with her before, knowing it would steal her hard-won peace of mind. It weren't a secret, not ezackly. Just a little something he'd kept to himself, for her sake.

Halting behind the Weather map, Dathne lifted her gaze to him. Her face was disquietingly pale. "You feel it? After so long, you still feel it?"

He nodded. "Aye."

For countless nights after his blood-filled confrontation with Morg he'd gone to bed terrified he'd conjure in his sleep, in his nightmares, those fell battle-beasts of Doranen warfare he'd learned from Barl. The wereslags and the horselirs and the gruesomes, monstrosities of myth and murder. Had been terrified he'd wake in his bed to find Dathne clawed to bloody shreds beside him. In the end, exhausted and desperate, he'd turned to Pother Nix. The Doranen physick had drugged him and muttered over him, wrapped his tired mind in spells and soothings. Taught him how to seal away the dreadful words he knew, that meant he could kill with a thought. And he'd found in that teaching a rough measure of peace.

But the words were still there, still buried inside him, just like the Weather Magic. Not even Nix could take them away. Barl's magic had branded him, altered him, and there was no going back. There was only going forward, understanding what he'd become.

Dathne's face was crumpled into grief. *"Asher..."*

"It's all right. Don't fret on me. We got this to fret on now."

With another deep breath, she banished pain. Stared at the map. "So if the Weather Magic hasn't died, what does that mean for Lur?"

Joining her, he slid his arm around her narrow shoulders. As she leaned against him he felt the chill of foreboding ease, just a little. "I don't know," he said, resting his cheek against her jasmine-scented hair. "All I can be sure on is somehow, what we been feeling is tangled up with this bloody Weather map."

"Asher..." Her fingers drummed against his chest. "How long have you been feeling unsettled?"

"Ha," he said, tightening his arm. "You tell me."

"Four days. You?"

Nine. "Close enough."

"I'm sorry I didn't say anything." Her fingers tightened on his jacket and shook him. *"You* should've said something."

He kissed her. "Aye, well. Since we're both wrong, there be no blame. What is it you've been feeling, ezackly?"

"A change in the air," she said, her voice low. "A change beneath my feet. A sour note on the edge of hearing. Only a whisper, until today." She shivered. "It shouted today."

Aye, it bloody well did. "You ain't had a vision? Nowt's come to you in your dreams?"

"Not for years. Not since before the Wall fell. I'd have told you if it had."

"You didn't tell me this."

"I thought you said there was no blame!"

He kissed her again. "Sorry."

"I didn't want it to be true," she said, her voice shaking. "We've been so happy, my love. We weathered the storm of the Wall's falling, the revelation of our true magical natures. We've forged a new Lur from the ashes of the old and what troubles we've had we've dealt with, swiftly. Olken and Doranen have managed to keep the peace, most of the time. I can't bear to think of our new lives tumbling around our ears."

Neither could he. But worse than that, he couldn't bear to see her distressed. Pulling her closer, he held on tight. Needing the comfort of her warmth in his arms.

"Who said they're tumblin', eh? We don't know that, Dath. Not for sure. But even if they are, fratchin' ourselves won't help. Whatever trouble this is come knockin' on our door, we'll survive it. After what we've lived through, Dath? You and me, we can survive anythin'."

He felt her shudder. Then she stepped out of his embrace and started circling the Weather map again, revulsion and yearning clouding her face.

"So this thing's not dead after all." She chewed her lip, thinking hard. "But what does that *mean?*"

"Well..." He started prowling the map with her. "We had ourselves six hundred years of Barl's Weather Magic, Dathne, soakin' into Lur's bones. And this map were a big part of that."

"And if it's not dead, like we thought, then—" She gasped, her eyes opening wide. *"Asher..."*

He nodded, feeling sick. Knowing they were thinking the same awful thought. "I reckon some of that magic was still workin' even though the Wall came down. Keepin' this map just a little bit alive."

"Leftover Weather Magic," she murmured. "That would explain the ten years since Morg. No floods. No drought. No famine. Lur's not been much different from when we had a WeatherWorker. I'll admit it, I've been surprised."

He'd been surprised too—but he was more surprised now, to hear her say so. He stopped his prowling. "You never said that. When folk asked, you said there were no reason to think the weather would turn topsy-turvy."

"So did you," she retorted, halting opposite him, "and we both know why. Because keeping folk calm was our most important task."

"Aye," he said, troubled. "But I believed it, Dathne. I thought you did too."

Uncomfortable, she hugged her ribs again. "When the Wall came down I feared those storms would never end. And then they did. And I thought—I hoped—it meant that nothing had changed after all. That nothing *would* change. That Lur's trials and suffering were brief, and over. I was a fool. I should've known better."

"Why?" he demanded. "This ain't your fault, Dathne. How were you s'posed to know? How was any of us s'posed to know? It ain't like this has happened before."

She managed a small, unhappy smile. "I can't help it. I'm Jervale's Heir. The kingdom's always been mine to protect."

And mine. But he didn't say that aloud. Didn't even like thinking it. *Nobody asked me if I wanted the bloody thing.*

Dathne was once more frowning at the Weather map. "So if the earth is stirring now—if we can feel something's wrong—" She looked up, a horrified understanding clouding her eyes. "Jervale save us all."

He didn't want to believe it either. The thought made his skin crawl. But—"Don't reckon there's another explanation, Dath. The Weather Magic's runnin' dry at last, and Lur's feelin' it." He swallowed. "*We're* feelin' it. And I reckon what we're feelin' might just be the start."

Her face was stark with anger and fear. "So the cataclysm we dreaded ten years ago is come upon us *now?*"

"Could be." He shoved his hands in his pockets. "And if it is…"

She inhaled, sharply. "*Asher.* You *can't.*"

"I might not have a choice, Dath."

"There's always a choice!" she snapped. "*No more Weather Magic,* you told me. How can you think to undo that decision?"

"How can I *not* think it? There's a bloody kingdom at stake!"

"But Asher, you lied to both Councils. To everyone in Lur. You said killing Morg burned the Weather Magic out of your blood. If you *tell* them you lied then trust will be broken. And once it's broken—"

"There's worse things than trust as could get broken here, Dath," he said. "I lied so Lur could start over. Leave the past in the past. But the past's just gone and sunk its teeth in our arse, ain't it?"

"Asher, if you bring back WeatherWorking you could *die*. It could *kill* you!"

"I never said I wanted to bring it back!" he protested. "Believe me, Dath, it's the last bloody thing I want. I never took a breath without it hurt me, all the time I was doin' Gar's job for him. Every day it was like walkin' on knives. Breathin' glass. Breathin' fire. It's behind me, and good riddance. I don't want them poxy days back again. But—"

"What?" she said. "But what?"

His belly was churning. They were fighting. They never fought. Not like this. Not over poxy *magic*. "You know what, Dath. If we've spent the last ten years livin' on Barl's leftovers...if the wrongness you and I are feelin' is just a taste of things to come...what do we do about it? What do *I* do? If I'm the only man standin' between us and ruination? *What do I do?*"

"Who says you're the only man? Lur's a land of magicians now, Asher. Throw a stone in any direction and you'll hit three on the head."

She was trying to protect him. There'd been a time, once, when she'd tossed him headfirst into danger...but that was before. She might look the same, but she was a different Dathne now.

Question is, I reckon, am I a different Asher?

"Aye, mayhap, but they'd be the wrong kind of magicians, Dath," he said, knowing the answer. Feeling the weariness rise in him like a bloodstained tide. "There ain't a man or woman in Lur to do the Weather-Working aside from me. I'm the only one livin' with that magic inside.

41

And there ain't a way of passin' it on. Not any more. You know that. You bloody *know* it."

Pointed chin arrogantly tilted, eyes glittering, she glared at him across Barl's troublesome map. "Then forget about the Weather Magic. We'll find another way to fix things, if it turns out they're broke. But you can't go back to those days of blood and pain, Asher. I won't have it. You're a father. Your children need you. *I* need you."

"Oh, Dath..." Warmed anew by her fierce love, chilled by his fears, he shook his head. "It ain't never been about what we want. What Lur wants did always come first. You're the one said I was born to save it."

"And you did save it," she said. Tears trembled on her lashes. "That's done."

"What if it ain't done? Eh? What if Lur needs itself savin' again?"

The tears spilled. "Then somebody else can bloody save it! There's no prophecy I know that says you have to save it twice!"

He went to her. Folded her within the shelter of his arms. "Not a prophecy, no. More powerful than that, I reckon. You said it, Dath. I'm a da. You think there's nowt I won't do to keep Rafe and Deenie safe from harm?"

"I know there's not," she whispered. "But I won't have you risk yourself—risk all that we've worked for—on nothing more certain than feelings. D'you hear me? *I won't.* This is too important. This is our lives."

Aye, but she were a stubborn, slumskumbledy wench. She knew it weren't so simple. She knew this were about the lives of every man, woman and child in Lur. Again. That they depended on him, again, when all he'd wanted was peace.

"Dath, Dath..." He was aching with regret. "Ain't no use hiding under the blankets on this one. The trouble's real, we both know it, and chances are we ain't the only ones to feel it. There's powerful sensitive Olken in Lur. Folk who be woken to ezackly who and what they are. And if they start stirrin' round about the place and we ain't ready to settle their fears? That'll mean strife, the kind that spreads itself fast."

She nodded reluctantly, shivering. "I know. But you can't risk yourself on guesses and mayhaps. We need to know for certain what's happening."

"Aye, but—"

"The Circle can help us," she said, pulling free. "What's left of it. I'll reach out to the best of them—Fernel Pintte, and Jinny of Hooten Creek. One or two others. I'll ask them to the City. We'll see what they know. And *then* we'll decide what's to be done. Agreed?"

He sighed. "Aye. Agreed."

Her pointed finger stabbed him hard in the chest. "And that means no Weather Magic in the meantime, Asher. No meddling until we're sure there's nowhere else to turn. Promise me that. *Promise.*"

"I promise," he said, because what else could he say? He didn't want to fight with her. He didn't want to make her cry.

She kissed him. "Good. Now let's get out of here. I never liked this Chamber. It makes me want to throw up."

CHAPTER THREE

※

In worried silence they walked hand-in-hand back from the Weather Chamber, by privy pathways that meant they'd meet no folk wandering the public parts of the palace grounds. Coming in sight of home at last, Asher felt Dath's fingers tighten painfully around his. Pother Kerril was standing lonesome on the Tower's distant steps, neat and tidy in her green physick's smock. Waiting for them, it looked like.

"What now?" Dath said, and let go of him. "Please, not Rafel. Not again." She hurried ahead.

Asher wanted to hurry with her, but he made himself walk slowly, casually. Not because he didn't care, but because he knew he cared so much. And because he wasn't comfortable letting all and sundry see how deep he loved his son. That were private. That were his heart, for him to know and no-one else, save Dath. But if Rafe had tumbled into fresh trouble, hurt hisself so soon after his last heedless scrape...

He'll be the death of me, that boy. I'm goin' grey afore my time.

As he reached calling distance from the Tower steps, Dath turned from Kerril. "It's all right. It's not Rafel."

Praise Barl. He didn't need to ask if it was Deenie. His daughter weren't rambunctious like her big brother. Deenie was his little brown mouse, who startled at a loud sound and eyed boisterous Rafel askance.

But in the wake of relief he felt a pinching of worry. Beneath Dath's smile was something heartstruck, and dreadful.

"What?" he said, climbing the wide stone steps to join her and the pother. "What's amiss, Dathne?"

Instead of answering, Dath looked to Kerril. A tall Doranen woman with a calm face and kind eyes, she'd taken over from Nix on his retirement to the coast. Royal physician in everything but name, she was, with a keen and constant interest in the health of her patients.

She nodded, a brisk greeting from one authority to another. "Asher. I'm sorry . . . it's Darran."

He felt his heart thud hard, just the once. *Darran.* Silly ole fart. Thorn in his side. Enemy then ally. Family, of sorts. "He's dead?" he asked, and heard the roughness in his voice.

"No, he lives," said Kerril. He wished her eyes held less sorrow. "But he's sinking. A palsy."

"Sinkin' how fast?"

"I wish I could tell you, Asher. I wish I had better news."

And if wishes were fishes then no-one would starve.

"So do I," he said. "How'd this happen, any road? Ain't he just had you breathin' down his neck for an ague in his chest? You standin' there tellin' me you never noticed he had a palsy brewin'?"

He knew he sounded angry, as though this was all Kerril's fault. As though somehow, by coming to tell him, she'd made it happen in the first place. He knew he wasn't being fair. But he couldn't help himself. This after the cherry orchard? And the Weather Chamber? It was too much.

Dathne clicked her tongue. "Asher, that's hardly—"

"No, it's a reasonable question, Dathne," said Kerril, her grave expression unchanged. If he'd hurt her, or angered her, he'd never know. She wasn't like Nix, who'd blustered and fussed. "I physick your family, you need to know I know my task." Hands clasped before her, she frowned before answering. "Palsy often strikes without warning, Asher. A man can be fiddle fit one day and drop dead in his doorway the next. There's no rhyme nor reason, alas. It kills the young and the old, men and women both. I doubt Darran's ague had a thing to do with it. He was mostly over that, just a little cough remained."

"And now he's dyin'." Grief surged, unexpected, stealing his breath. In the djelba trees surrounding the Tower courtyard, nightbirds flapped their wings. Day's end approached and they were waking from sleep.

"Asher..." Dathne rested her hand on his forearm. "Kerril says Rafel was with Darran when the palsy struck."

He stared. "What? Where is he?"

"Indoors," said Kerril. "He took no harm. He called for help then stayed with Darran comforting him. He was a brave boy, I'm told."

Of course he was. He was Rafel. Exasperated, he turned to Dathne. "And we're out here flappin' our lips instead of seein' to our son 'cause—"

"Because he doesn't need us smothering him," she snapped. "Because a space of time and silence are as healing as soft words."

He loved her so much that he forgot, sometimes, how hard she could be. Her years as Jervale's Heir had marked her. She were more comfortable than she used to be, but the core of her remained unchanged, stronger than iron.

"He can have both, Dath," he said. "Ain't no need for him to choose."

He looked past her and Pother Kerril, through the Tower's open double doors and into its circular marble-floored foyer—and saw his son on the spiral staircase. Rafe's knees were pulled close to his chest, dark hair flopping over his lowered face, small hands clutching his shinbones tight.

"Can I see the ole man?" he asked Kerril, his eyes not moving from that slight, still body on the snail-shell stairs.

"He's asking for you," said Kerril. "Stay as long as you like. I've eased him as much as I can, and left an elixir. If the shaking takes him again, a spoonful should help."

With an effort, he wrenched his gaze from Rafel. "Will he see sunrise?"

"As I said, these things can't be predicted," Kerril replied gently. Then she sighed. "But there's a good chance he won't."

"Go," said Dathne. Her dark eyes were full of quiet misery. An iron core, she had, aye... but a lot more besides. "If business arises I'll see to it. Don't fret on that."

He nodded, suddenly unable to trust his voice.

"If you've need of me, send to my infirmary," Kerril added. "I have possets and so forth to see to. I'll be working late into the night."

"My thanks, Kerril," he said. Shamed that he'd lashed out at her, looked to hurt when all she'd done was help. *I know better than that. I'm me, I ain't my brother. Zeth hurts folk heedless. I'm better than Zeth.* "There be no pother in Lur could've cared more for Darran, I reckon. He's old and wore out, that's the sad fact of it. And I'm thinkin' he's walked a long road. Longer than most."

"Indeed," she replied. "Though that's small enough comfort."

It were no comfort at all. Barl save him, he was sick to death of death. With a nod for Kerril, and a small smile for Dathne that was all pain and no pleasure, he left the women on the Tower's front steps and trudged inside.

Hearing his footsteps, Rafel looked up. With the evening drawing in, the foyer had been lit with glimfire. Sconces glowed against the circular wall, throwing shadows. Their warm light found the tears in Rafel's eyes, that the boy was too proud to let fall. His face was grimy, his short black hair streaked with dust. Rafe charged through life as though it was a race, heedless of skinned knees and bruises, never frettin' if he fell. Why would he? He'd find his feet all right. He always did.

"Da," the boy said. His bottom lip quivered. "The ole fool's dyin', I reckon."

"Aye," he said, and sat himself on the stair beside his son. "Reckon he is. But don't call him that, eh? He's got a name, Rafe, and enough years in his dish you can respect him by usin' it."

Rafe twitched one skinny shoulder. "You call him an ole fool. You call him worse, I've heard you."

"Aye, but that's me," he said, and draped an arm round his son. "What I call him be our business, Rafe. Mine and Darran's. You know the ole man and me got history. You're a spratling yet. You ain't earned the right."

"I never will, if he's dying," said Rafe, and his voice broke in a small sob. "He's my friend, Da. I don't want him to die."

"I know you don't, Rafe," he whispered, and pulled his son close. "Nobody wants their friends to die. Friends is what makes the world worth livin' in, even when it's falling in flames around your ears. But you got to remember, Rafe, men don't live forever. No-one lives forever."

He felt Rafe's thin, wiry body tremble. "Like Dancer?"

"Aye," he said gently. "Just like Dancer. He had a good long life and Darran has too. There ain't nowt to be sad on for that. But don't you go lettin' your ma hear you measurin' the ole fart to a pony. She'll clip you round the earhole for that."

"And she'll clip you for calling Darran an ole fart," said Rafe, swiftly smiling. He looked like his mother then, quicksilver mischief, their dark eyes the same.

"Aye, mayhap she will," he said. "So that be our secret, eh?"

Rafe heaved a deep sigh. "Da..."

"Aye, Rafe?"

"Can't — can't you live forever?"

The plaintive question plunged through him like a harpoon meant for a shark. Breached his heart and stole his breath. Bleeding tears on the inside, for he'd not ever let his son see a weeping father, who should be strong, he shook his head.

"No, Rafe. But there's nowt to fret on, I promise. I ain't goin' nowhere for years and years and years."

"Morg lived forever," Rafe said, his voice still broken and soft. "Nearly. He would've, 'cept you killed him. Can't you..." He sniffed. "You know."

Stricken, Asher stared through the open foyer doors. Dathne and Pother Kerril still stood on the Tower steps, gossiping like women did, praise Barl. For if Dath were here, and caught Rafel in such a question...

He tightened his arm hard around his son's slight frame. "No, Rafe. *No.*" Fear had him by the throat, squeezing it almost closed. "We talked on this before, remember? That kind of magic is *wrong*. And it don't exist any road. Not any more."

48

"Maybe. But Da, you're a great mage," said Rafe. He was stubborn, so stubborn, he never knew when to leave well enough alone. "You could find it. You could never die."

Swamped, Asher hauled his son closer still, wrapped both arms around him and hung on for grim life. "I told you, sprat, I ain't dyin'," he said, muffled against Rafel's dusty, disordered hair. "I know you're fratched 'cause of Darran, but that's *him*. That ain't *me*. Now, you put that kind of magic out of your head, you hear? It ain't never to be spoke of again. Not to me, not to your mother, not to a living soul. Understand?"

Rafel nodded. "Yes, Da."

Leaning back, Asher stared into his son's vivid face. "You just sayin' that, Rafel? Or are you hearin' me? Do you promise? Is this your proper word, given man to man, and no breakin' of it for nowt?"

The tears Rafe had held back were sprung free now, and sluicing his cheeks. "Promise," he said, choking. "My word, Da. Man to man."

"All right then," he said, still terrified because Nix, who knew such things, had told him and Dath seven years ago that Rafel, their precious son, had magic in him like his father. No tame Olken mage, this boy, but a child of both worlds who could scorch as well as soothe. "All right. So that's your word sworn to me, and we'll not speak on this again."

"No, Da," Rafel whispered. "Da, I was just asking. I didn't mean to do wrong."

And there was another wave crashing over him, stealing his breath again. "I know. I know. You're a good sprat. I know."

He felt Rafel's arms curl round his neck. Felt his son's wet, grimy cheek press against him. His own da had been a good man, a kind man, a man to love with all his heart. But fishing were a hard life; he never was one for hugs and kisses. Love was food on the table, a bed to sleep in, and no leaky roof.

Ma had hugged him, but Ma died young. He'd had to wait until Dathne to feel that loved again. And as he'd stood by her bedside ten years ago, as he'd watched her hold their squalling newborn son, indignant and outraged, still sticky with birthing blood, he'd promised himself:

He won't doubt me. He won't wonder. He'll have hugs and kisses every day.

"I got to go, Rafe," he murmured, holding on tight. "I got to see that ole fart up there, that ole man what's dyin'."

"Can I come too?" said Rafel. "Darran and me, we never finished our game. We couldn't find a good book to buy so we were playing hop-poddle and I was winning, for real."

"Mayhap you can see him later," he said. "For now there's words as need sayin' between him and me and no-one else."

Sniffing, Rafe wriggled free. "What if there ain't a later, Da?" he said, and dragged a grubby sleeve across his woeful face. "He might die of a sudden. Goose's ma went like that."

"If I reckon he's goin', I'll say somethin' for you," he promised. "What should I say?"

Standing on a lower step, head down so his eyes and his slow tears were hidden, Rafel shrugged. Then he looked up. "Tell the ole fool I love him, Da. Tell him thank you for his stories."

He tousled his son's hair, then pushed to his feet. "I will. Now go find your ma, Rafe. I'd say she's worrited for you."

But instead of leaving, Rafel stared up at him, so solemn. "I'm sorry, Da. It ain't fair, how your friends die."

"Don't you fret on me, Rafe," he said at last, when he could trust himself, so close to breaking. "I got you and your mother. I got your sister. You're my best friends, you are. I be fine."

Rafel's smile broke through the grief and tears. It was his own mother's sunlight smile, found its way to his small son's face. "Don't you fret on me neither, Da. I ain't leavin' you. I ain't goin' no place."

He watched Rafel bound down the foyer stairs, leap lightly across the marble floor and run to Dathne, alone now on the Tower's sandstone steps. He watched them embrace, and for a hurting heartbeat saw Dana and Gar, who'd loved one another the way Dath and Rafel loved.

And then he turned and trudged his way up the Tower's spiral staircase, sorrow a dreadful weight bowing his spine.

*   *   *

Pother Kerril had left glimfire burning in Darran's chamber, and scented tapers so the air smelt of spring. The curtains were drawn against the window, dark blue velvet echoing a summer night sky. Darran had slept in this small space for more than ten years. It was the room he took when Jarralt—Morg—banished him to exile here with Gar. When that business was done with, and Lur had been saved, he'd been offered the whole floor of the Tower where Gar used to live, the king's privy chamber and his study and his library too.

Shocked, offended, Darran had refused. That floor was Rafel's now. And Darran lived here, a chamber less than one-quarter of a single floor, so simple and spare. No fancy tapestries and folderol for Darran, who dressed in black every day of his life. He'd sleep in black nightshirts, if that were something that got done.

But it weren't, so there he was beneath his blankets, white nightshirt buttoned to his scrawny throat. His lank hair on the pillow was pure silver, the echoing colour of old Cygnet's mane and tail. His hands, their skin gauze-thin and wrinkled, blotched with spots, fingers gnarled, rested on his toast-rack chest; he'd never got fat, not by an ounce. He still looked like a stork. He still scolded and sighed. His breathing barely stirred the air as his palsied face spasmed and ticced.

Asher eased the door closed and crossed to the bed. A plain chair stood beside it. Sitting, he reached for Darran's thin hand. It was icy cold, as though winter's grip on Lur hadn't loosened and he'd been outside with no gloves.

"Hey there, ole man," he murmured. His eyes burned. His throat felt tight. "Lazin' about like there ain't no work to do. What kind of example is that to set, eh?"

Looking more closely, he saw that glimfire shadows hid the worst of Darran's twisted left cheek, his drooped eyelid, his sagging mouth. Spittle dribbled down his grey-stubbled chin. Letting go of Darran's hand, he took the cloth from its bowl of water on the bed's posset-crowded nightstand, wrung it to dampness and wiped the old man clean. Then he put the cloth back and took possession of Darran's hand again, hoping his own warm blood would warm this dying man's frail flesh.

"Asher," said Darran, his eyes still closed, his voice slurred, and so soft. As though speaking were as hard a task as calling down the rain. "Have . . . some respect."

He tightened his fingers, just a little. "Oh, aye. Like you've earned it, eh, you ole crow?"

"Reprobate," said Darran. His eyelids lifted, painfully. Beneath them his clouded eyes swallowed the light. "Rapscallion. Ruffian."

"Aye," he said, scowling. "Reckon I be all those things, do you?"

Darran's fingers tightened, no stronger than a baby's. "All those and more." He frowned. "What's the matter?"

Nigh on twelve years ago now, he'd met this man. In nigh on twelve years they'd danced a dance or two. Hated each other. Hurt each other. Wept in silence side by side.

"What's the matter?" he echoed. "What d'you reckon, you ole fool?"

"Yes, I'm dying," said Darran, acerbic, not even frailty able to sweeten his tart tongue. "But I'm not such . . . an ole fool I think . . . you're grief-struck because of it. There's . . . something else, don't . . . deny it. I've lived . . . my whole life watching . . . great men of power. I know when aught's amiss, and setting them . . . on edge."

Great men of power. *His palsy's addled him.* "You're wrong," he said quietly. "I ain't pleased to see you go."

"Asher . . . Asher . . ." Darran managed a lopsided smile. "You'd keep me here, in this . . . faded, failing body? That's cruel . . . even for you."

He looked away until he was certain he could speak without letting loose words he'd come to regret. "You want to die? Is that it?"

"I want you . . . to tell me . . . what's wrong," said Darran, still slow, still soft — but with as much iron in him as Dathne. Dying hadn't rusted him, that much was clear. "Perhaps . . . I can help you. I'd like . . . to think I can. One last service . . . for the kingdom. I think . . . you owe me that much."

There was no repaying what he owed this persnickety Olken. No undoing of past mistakes, no healing old wounds.

But how can I tell him what me and Dath think? His light's goin' out.

He deserves an easy death, not doubt and fear and frettin' over what he can't help.

"Asher..." Darran closed his eyes, just for a moment, then dragged them open again. "If I make it...my last wish? If I beg you? Shall I...beg?"

"Why d'you want to know?" he said roughly. "There ain't nowt you can *do*."

"I can listen," said Darran. "And whatever...you tell me, I can...take it to my grave. I'll do that...best of all."

Sighing, he let his chin drop to his chest. The ole man weren't entirely wrong...and he could say things to Darran he couldn't say to anyone else. Not even Dathne. Especially not Dathne. She was brave, she was so brave, but he'd kill her, saying this. He'd given her a promise, knowing that he lied.

"Asher," said Darran, his fingers tightening a little more. "If this is about...the kingdom's safety...you can't spare me. You can't...spare yourself. Gar *died*...for Lur. Will you sit there...and not speak?"

The ole *bastard*, skewering him like this. Twisty, sneaky, bringin' up Gar.

Bitterly he stared at Darran. "Since when did I spare m'self, you manky ole man?"

"Never," Darran whispered. "So...don't start...now."

Sink me. Sink me. I ought to walk away. I ought to keep my mouth shut. If I don't say it then it ain't true.

"You're not...a coward," said Darran, relentless. "Barl knows you've...more faults than a cur dog...has fleas, Asher, but..." He broke off, his breath catching in a cough, that ague in his chest not done with him yet. "A problem...denied is a...problem unresolved. Borne's father...taught me that. A lesson...well learned."

He stared at his fingers. If he closed his eyes he might think he could still feel that sizzle of power in them, from touching Barl's map. If he closed his eyes he'd feel the flogging might of her magic...

"*Asher,*" said Darran, his voice tight with pain. "Is Lur...in danger? Is that your dread?"

On a gasping breath, he nodded. "Aye. Feels like it. And if it is...could be I'll have to do somethin'. Somethin' I don't want to do, as might cause as much trouble as it'll fix."

"Ah," said Darran, a long slow sigh of regret. "WeatherWorking... you mean?"

Startled, Asher stared at him. "I never said that. Why d'you think that? Ain't no such thing as WeatherWorkin' no more, Darran."

So feeble, the ole man was now. His eyes sunken, his colour bad, the palsy dancing in his cheek. A fresh thin thread of spittle crept down his chin. Weakly he swiped at it, then weakly snapped his fingers for the damp cloth. Wouldn't take help in cleaning himself, this time.

"No...such thing?" he said, handing the cloth back. His clouded eyes couldn't mask his temper, or the disgust he felt at his body's slow decay. "Of course...there is, Asher. You never...lost that power. You just...lied and said...you did. For the...greater good, of course. Because Lur needed...to hear it. I always...knew better." Blinking slowly, he pressed withered fingertips to the flickering muscle beneath his cheek's lace-thin skin. "But what makes...you think now...our kingdom might need to hear otherwise? Is it the...uncertainty you're feeling...in the sleeping...earth?"

"What?" he said, choking. "How'd you know that? You ain't—you said you felt nowt of Olken magic in your blood. Were *that* a lie, Darran? You been lyin' to me?"

"And if...I was?" Darran retorted, an echo of his younger, vigorous days sounding in his voice. "About myself? About something...so personal...and private? Whether or not...I was born gifted, is that any...business of...yours? I don't think so. I think—" He broke off, coughing again, sunk too low for indignation.

"Here, here, you ole crow," he said, and helped Darran sip from a glass of water. "Best you stop flappin' your lips now, I reckon. Best I leave you be, to rest."

Darran only swallowed twice, with awful difficulty, tiny mouthfuls, then turned his face away from the glass. Asher eased him back to his pillows, returned the glass to the nightstand and started to rise. But Darran's hand stopped him, with a strength born of desperation.

"I feel...nothing," he said harshly, every indrawn breath a fight. "It was...Rafel. Rafel told me. He said the earth...feels wrong."

Rafel? Asher sat again, thudding hard onto the chair. "My son told you that?" *You, and not me?*

"He's...a boy," said Darran, smiling. "Boys have...their secrets, Asher." The smile faded. "And you're...strict with him, you know. Over magic."

"If I am, I got to be!" he said, stung. "You know what Nix said of him, Darran. You know what it might mean."

"I know you've...never trusted your own...gift," said Darran gently. "You never...wanted it. You resent it. You blame...magic for every...loss."

"Why shouldn't I? Don't you? Don't you blame magic for who it killed?"

"It wasn't...the magic that...killed him, Asher," said Darran sadly.

Pricked to his feet, Asher stamped to the window and drew the heavy curtain aside. This side of the Tower looked out over the home field beside the stables; in the fast-falling dusk he caught the pearly gleam of Cygnet's thick winter coat as the doddery horse, without a halter, followed Jed to the gate. Good ole Jed, as kindly as ever, grown more childish with the passing seasons. Not even Nix or Kerril could help that. The blow to his head all those years ago had damaged him in ways that could never be undone. Kerril said there'd come a time when Jed wouldn't be safe around the horses. Kerril said there were a good chance his friend wouldn't make old bones.

Death, greedy and hovering, in here, out there, no escape. No reprieve. Rafel, keeping secrets. And now this old wound, reopened.

Gar.

"I know what killed him, Darran," he said harshly, keeping his back turned. "That were me. I killed him. Think I need you to tell me who I killed? I don't. Don't need you tellin' me you hate me for it, neither."

"Hate you?" said Darran. "I don't hate you. If there's...any hating, Asher, you're...doing it. You're the one...who won't forgive."

He turned. "What are you witterin' about, you stupid ole fool? I don't hate him! I never hated him. He were my friend."

"I know," said Darran. His clouded eyes were full of tears. "You loved him...like a brother. But you did...hate him...a little bit too, Asher. Don't try to...deny it. I'm dying, but...I remember. We...both do."

Aye, he remembered. He wished he didn't. He'd thought he'd found peace in the months after Gar's death. While Rafel grew in Dathne's belly he thought he'd found a way to live with what happened. Turned out he was wrong. Turned out some wounds were just too deep to heal proper. And now, feeling the changes beneath Lur's green and growing skin, all he could think was it had all been for *nowt*.

"Why are we talkin' on this?" he said. "It don't matter now. Gar's gone. You'll be gone soon. What are you doin', Darran? Makin' me pay one last time, while y'still can?"

Panting, Darran straightened against his pillows. "I *never*...blamed you, Asher," he said with dreadful effort, the chamber's sweet air thick and rasping in his throat. "I know...it wasn't your...fault. Gar...went his own way. He never...told me what he planned but...I knew there was...something. Hadn't I been...watching him...from the moment...he was born? I *knew* him, Asher, better even than...his own flesh-and-blood. I knew...he was keeping...secrets. I...could see it...in his eyes."

Ten years since that moment in Dorana City's Market Square, before the steps of the great Barl's Chapel, and the pain was still so raw. The words of UnMaking blasting through him. Gar falling dead as stone at his feet. Ten years and so much silence. He and Darran had wept over Gar's coffin and never talked of it after. Not even once. Not even nearly.

"You ole *bastard*. Then why didn't you *say?*" His hands were fists, and they wanted to *pound*. "Why did you let him throw his life away like that? The magic was *mine*, not his. The prophecy was for *me*."

Strength spent, Darran slumped. "You...know why," he said, almost too faint for hearing. His palsied cheek writhed. "Because...he'd not have...forgiven me. Because he was...my king. Because you might...have loved him, Asher, but you...were still blind. *I* wasn't. *I* could see it. And I was...sworn to serve him. Not...my will, but...his."

Rage was a storm, battering him near to sightless. "*Blind?* What are you talkin' about? What did you see I didn't?"

"That not...dying for Lur...would have...killed him," whispered Darran. "That what he...did to you, breaking his...oath to you, handing you over...to Jarralt—to Morg—what was...done to you...by that monster...*was* killing him." Darran coughed again, his lungs heaving for air. "He never...wept for himself, Asher, but he...wept for you."

"Don't you tell me that," he said, turning aside. "Why tell me that? It's over, it's in the past. Why drag it up now?"

"Over?" said Darran. His fingers plucked at the blankets. "It will *never*...be over. Not while you...remember him. Not if Lur is...in peril. He left...his kingdom...in your hands, Asher, to keep...safe. But if you turn from...your gift...how is it...safe? How is that...loving...him?"

"I never said I wouldn't keep Lur safe. But that don't have to mean WeatherWork. Ain't no surety in that!"

Darran's laugh was breathless, and wry. "Ain't no...surety...for Lur...if...you won't do...what's...needful."

"How would *you* know what's needful, you silly ole crow?" he said, nearly choking on outrage. "How would you know *anythin',* with nowt a drop of magic in you? Fussin' and bossin' and tellin' me what to do! Tellin' me what to think! What to *feel!* All that's over now, d'you hear me? We ain't goin' back to them magic days, Darran. We ain't goin' back to hoity-toity Doranen and us Olken bendin' our knees. This ain't the old Lur, that old Lur's dead like Gar. And I ain't about to kiss its corpse awake, I ain't about to—"

"*Asher!* What are you *doing?* Have you taken total leave of your senses?"

Dathne, shocked and staring in the open doorway.

Somehow he swallowed his unspoken, angry words. "Dathne, you—"

"Oh, be quiet, be *quiet*," she said, stepping inside and pushing the door shut behind her. "Darran—here, take some posset—"

Numb, he stood with his back to the wall and watched as Dathne tipped spoonfuls of Kerril's elixir into the ole fool's mouth, as gentle and as loving as though he were one of her babes, or her da. She eased the blankets around the ole fool and chafed his cold hands, smoothed the tarnished hair from his mottled forehead and smiled.

"Don't be angry . . . with Asher," Darran whispered. "You know . . . how it is . . . with us. I . . . fratch him, Dathne. There's . . . no harm . . . done."

"You let me judge that," said Dathne, her voice kind, her flicking glance furious. "And rest. Be easy. Guard your strength, Darran. We don't want you to go."

There were tears in her voice. More tears in Darran's eyes, tipping onto his twitching cheek. "I know," he said, trying to smile even as the spittle ran down his chin. "But I'm going." His gaze shifted. "You should . . . talk to your son . . . Asher. You need to know his secret."

"No, you tell it me," he said, scowling. "Darran—"

Darran's eyes closed. "Remember . . . your friend, Asher. Remember . . . Gar. Don't . . . waste . . . his sacrifice. He died . . . for you."

The room blurred, and Darran with it. Dathne dropped onto the bed beside the old man.

"I can't stay here," he muttered. "I ain't stayin' here. I need air."

"Asher!" said Dathne, turning. "Asher, wait, where are you—"

Haunted, hunted, he left her and the ole crow behind.

CHAPTER FOUR

✳

Nonplussed, Dathne stared after her impossible husband. Beside her, in his bed, Darran wheezed and dribbled. Barl's *tits*. The dear old man deserved a death with dignity after his lifetime of unselfish service to the crown, and Lur's people. Without Darran there'd *be* no Lur. At least, not a land anyone living now would recognise. Instead it would be burned and blasted, reduced to blight and stinking evil miasmas, just like the lands beyond Barl's Mountains. Lands they'd visited once and would never tempt again.

We owe him so much. And now he's dying and Asher's fighting with him? I could smack him, Matt, I could smack him so hard.

An old habit, that was, talking to Matt. Sometimes she thought she ought to break herself of it. Talking to a dead man? Not a good idea, surely. But she missed him, as much now as ever she had in the days after his death when she could not understand his absence, could not turn to him for counsel or comfort, and felt herself entirely alone without him. Her friend. Her brother. Her conscience.

What would you say, Matt, if you were here? I wish you were here. I wish—I wish—

"Dathne," said Darran, the feeble fingers holding hers tightening a hairsbreadth. "Don't...fret. And don't...weep. Not...for me."

That was when she realised her cheeks were wet, her throat hot and tight. She lifted Darran's hand and pressed it to her lips.

"I'm sorry," she whispered. "He'll come back. He will."

"Mayhap," said Darran, who never used that country word. "You must...have a care...for your ruffian, my dear."

She frowned at him. "I do. You know I do. Darran, why were you and Asher fighting? What's this about a secret?"

Darran's eyes drifted closed. The palsy in his cheek had worsened, the wasted flesh beneath his skin leaping and twitching. "Ask Rafel."

"Why?" she said, her heart thudding with dread. "Darran, what do you know? *Darran?*"

He didn't answer. Sleep had claimed him, the torpor of a failing spirit. She let go of his hand and roamed his small chamber, suddenly sickened by the burning tapers' sweet smell. It was too much. *Too much.* Finding Asher in the Weather Chamber. The fear in his eyes. Hard on its heels, this awful news of Darran. And now Rafel? Her Rafel?

What secrets can a child have, that matter enough to hasten an old man's slow dying? To disquiet his last hours with such discord?

Oh, she wanted Asher. But she couldn't leave poor Darran to go chasing after him. Besides, who could find sense in him when he was in a tearing temper? Older he might be, but not so noticeably wiser. Still a hot-head, still quick to take offence. Always digging in his heels.

No. No, I'm not fair. He's afraid. The things he feels, that I feel, whose meaning we fathom all too well. They frighten him. They frighten me. We thought peace was well-earned and paid for. We thought life was good and would not change.

But wasn't that precisely what the people of Lur had thought before the coming of the Final Days? Only she, Jervale's Heir, had known truth for a lie. And the Circle, who'd relied on her to guide them blindfolded in the dark.

The thought of reconvening the Circle made her feel ill. Not for seeing her friends again, but for what such a calling meant. More strife for Lur, more suffering for its people.

Oh Jervale, if you can hear me, let Asher and I be wrong. Let this be nowt but a phantasm, a boggle of the mind.

But beneath her feet, she felt Lur shift and groan . . .

"Mama," said a small voice, and she spun round to hear it.

"Rafel! What are you doing? I told you I'd come back to you by and by."

Escaped from the family's privy apartments, where he and Deenie were eating their early supper, Rafel stood clean and miserable in the doorway. And Deenie stood with him, tempted sometimes — like now — to follow her brother into mischief, when he wasn't chasing her away for being a tiresome girl.

"I wanted to see Darran," he muttered, his lower lip pouting. Oh, he did not care to be scolded. So like his father, proud and spirited. Hands clenching to fists at the least provocation. "Da said I could."

"Your father said you'd be called if Darran was in the mood for visitors," she retorted. "Truth's not an ivy-plant, Rafel, to be grown any shape that suits you. And you, Deenie," she added, frowning at her daughter. "You've run off from Cluny too? For shame."

Deenie was small for her eight years, slender like a poplar sapling, a child of thistledown and whispers. Eyes as round as pansies in her narrow, secret face. Where scolding made her brother cross, she wilted under the mildest scrutiny.

"Sorry, Mama," she said, her voice hiccupping with dismay. "I only wanted to say goodbye, like Rafel."

Dathne felt her heart break. *No, no, she's too young.* "What do you mean, goodbye? What a nonsense that is."

Deenie glanced up at her brother, fingers twisting in her bright blue cotton smock. "Rafe said—"

"Tattle-tale!" Rafe spat at her, and shoved his shoulder against hers. "Hold your tongue, I told you. Now look what you've done, Mama's fratched!"

So Rafe had told Deenie the old man was dying. Anger nipped at heartbreak's heels, that he'd so carelessly shatter his small sister's innocence.

Rafel's chin was up, his brows knit together in a belligerent scowl.

61

And oh, it was his father's face he was showing her now, all bark and bite, their tempers two bright mirrors reflecting each other.

"No-one said not to tell," he muttered. "Da never said I weren't to tell."

And neither had she said it, never dreamt she'd have to. She glanced sideways at the bed, at Darran, and saw that he was roused from drowsing and watching her from beneath half-lifted eyelids. His sunken eyes, age-fuddled and dimmed with his slow dying, still reflected a gentle amusement. Oh, he loved her children. If she hadn't discovered an exasperated affection for him before Rafe was born she'd have lost her heart to him after, in his doting on her child. On both her children, who loved him for his kindness and his stories and the way he poked gentle, impolite fun at their father.

"Dathne..." Darran's voice was the threadiest whisper. "You'd ease me...if you let...them stay."

She wanted to deny him, but only because she would shield her children. Yes, Rafe and Deenie had both encountered death, but it had been the small deaths of animals. This death was not small. Darran had grown to be a loving part of their lives. She feared so much the wounds his dying would inflict upon her son and daughter.

Did I mean to let him become so important? Did I not notice how we all grew to lean on him, even Asher? When did I start to love him? When was the first time Asher turned to him as a friend?

She couldn't remember. She only knew it was true, that this ole man, this ole fart, ole scarecrow, ole trout, was part of her family. And that his death would cause her beloved Rafel and Deenie pain. But she couldn't protect them, she knew that. No mother could, though she gave her own life to save their innocence from harm.

"Please, Mama," said Rafel, so stubborn. He never once let go of a coveted thing, not even in his cradle. "I want to stay."

She looked at her son. Saw with a pang, with grief-sharpened eyes, that he wasn't a little boy any more. Ten years old and growing fast. Sturdy, like his father. A promise of charming good looks contained within the childish framework of his face.

But his eyes are far from childish. He knows things. He feels them. Pretending he doesn't makes no difference to the truth. We've cursed him, Asher and I. When we made him, we gave him power.

It galled her, to think that Darran knew things about her son that she didn't. That Asher didn't. That she needed to be told by a dying old man that her son had a secret which was causing him hurt.

"Please, Mama?" said Rafel. "Don't make me go." He glanced sideways at Deenie and pulled a little face. "Can't we stay?"

If Asher were here she was almost certain he'd say no. Not to spite Darran, but to protect his children.

And he would be wrong.

"Yes, Rafe," she said, feeling her eyes sting. "You can stay . . . and say goodbye." Then she shifted and looked down at the old man. "But you mustn't be long."

"Thank you, Dathne," Darran breathed. "I'll not . . . keep them."

She nodded at her children, then stepped back from the bed into pooled shadows, as Rafe and Deenie moved to Darran's side. At the old man's smile Deenie clambered onto the blanketed mattress and took his withered, age-spotted hand in hers. Rafel, scorning such babyish scramblings, echoed his father with thrown-back shoulders and a fearsome scowl and stayed standing.

"Rafel," Darran whispered. "Deenie. Shall I . . . tell you a . . . story?"

Still scowling, Rafe shrugged. "S'pose. If you want to. I don't care."

But Dathne, watching, knew that he did. He was desperate for a story. He loved Darran's tales. So did Deenie. Asher never looked back, not even for his children. Darran's stories taught them about their father, who loved them beyond all things but kept so much of himself a closed book.

Darran gestured to the chair at his bedside. "Make yourself . . . comfortable, then, Rafe," he invited. His rheumy eyes looked feverish now. She could see he was burning the last of his guttering candle for her children's sake. She should in conscience send them away.

But I can't. I can't. They need this. And so does he, I think. And so do I.

Rafe dropped onto the chair beside Darran's bed. Trying hard to be brave, though his small heart was breaking.

"Your father," said Darran, his gaze shifting from Rafe to Deenie and back again, so much love in him she could feel it like a furnace, "is a rowdy...and a ruffian...and the bravest...man I ever...knew. Braver...even than our dear...late king, and Gar...had courage enough...for twenty men."

The bravest man? Braver than Gar? Dathne heard her heartbeat drumming in her ears. He'd never said that before. He'd praised Asher, yes, but never once above his precious prince, the boy he'd looked on as a son.

"Rafel, I know...I've told you...before," said Darran. His voice was raspy, the chamber's scented air wheezing in his throat. "The story of...how your father...saved Gar's...life. But...I've not told...your sister. I think...I think..." His gaze drifted to the shadows. "It's time...for Deenie...to hear this one."

Dathne folded her arms against a sudden shiver. Deenie knew her father was counted a hero of Lur. How could she not know it? But they'd kept her sheltered from the details. She was still a little girl. She had the rest of her life to discover Lur's harsh, recent past.

Except...there was something important about her hearing such stories of her father from Darran. For one thing, Asher would never tell them. He squirmed and scowled when anyone tried to praise his doings. Not only because he'd never relished public acclaim, but because his victory over Morg was tainted by those other deaths. By Gar's death especially, which quietly haunted him and robbed him of peace.

But Deenie, like Rafel, was entitled to know his worth. And there was something special about stories that were told not by a mother and a wife, but an outsider. She understood that. She knew what Darran's stories meant to Rafel. Coming from the old man, the tales were somehow more — more *true*.

And Deenie deserves that truth no less than her brother. She deserves to know her da's a great man.

Darran was watching her, his gaze anxious. Eager. He wanted to gift her children with one last story and his time was dwindling. How could she refuse?

When she nodded, his pale, palsied face flushed with pleasure. A tear escaped his drooping left eye to trickle down his twitching cheek. Deenie pulled a kerchief from the pocket of her smock and gently patted his face dry.

"Thank you, Deenie," Darran whispered, when he could speak again. Then he smiled. "Deenie. Gardenia. Do you know...Dathne...when I said...you should call...a girl-child that...I was teasing."

She nodded. "We knew."

"Ah," he said, and didn't speak for a moment. Then he turned again to her children. "Very...well. A story. This happened...when your father...was a brash...young man. The...old king, Borne...was unwell. He sent...his son...the prince Gar...to Westwailing in his stead..."

After walking off the worst of his temper, Asher made his way to the Tower stable yard. The lads were bustling about evening stables, doors rattling, the water pump's handle groaning, filled pails sloshing, glim-fire lanterns gilding the air and throwing shadows. Though he were fratched, he smiled at the horses' impatience, whickers and snapping teeth, and hooves banging and scraping. The cool air smelled of hot horse porridge and fresh manure. He found Jed in the feed room, painstakingly counting carrots into seven waiting feed buckets. Seeing Asher, his oddly young and unlined face split wide in a smile.

"See?" he said, pointing proudly. "See?"

"Aye," he replied, and clapped his boyhood friend on the shoulder. "I do see. You be a great help, Jed."

Jed nodded, tongue-tip held fast between his teeth. The cruel, dented scar in his forehead caught the glimlight, flatly shining. "Great help. Great help."

The lingering embers of Asher's resentment died. Poor Jed. So much lost to him. So much stolen by bad luck. Now he was about to lose

Darran, who fussed over him like a hen with one chick. Who'd have thought the ole fool had so much love in him, eh?

Not me. I never thought it. Sometimes I reckon I never knew him at all.

After a quick stir of the horse porridge, pungent steam stinging his face, he perched on the edge of the oat-bin, arms folded. "Jed. Jed. Are you listenin' to me, Jed?"

Jed nodded, industriously counting carrots. That blow to his drunken head hadn't stolen all his life. Just most of it.

"Jed, I got to tell you somethin'. About Darran."

Jed's face lit up. "My friend Darran. Ole crow. Ole fart."

"Yeah, the ole fart," he said, pain like a vice crushing his chest. "Jed...come along, you got to listen to me."

Beyond the almost closed feed-room door, the lads whistled and laughed. On their own tonight, with Meister Divit away to Crackby for a family funeral. More death. More despair. People ought to live forever. Jed was counting carrots again, lost in his misty mind.

"Jed!" he said sharply, and kicked one heel against the oat-bin. "Bloody *listen,* would you?"

Jed startled at his sharp voice and the boom of the oat-bin, carrots tumbling from his fingers. "Sorry. Sorry."

Abruptly remorseful, Asher dropped to a crouch before his addled friend and took hold of his wrists. "Ain't no need for sorry," he said gently. "You ain't done a thing wrong, Jed. I just need you to listen."

Wide-eyed, his untidy dark hair streaky grey, his cheeks and chin stubbled grey and black, Jed nodded. "I be listenin'."

He couldn't say Darran was dying. Even if Jed understood, the words would only fratch him. "Darran's goin' away for a bit, Jed. He asked me to say goodbye for him."

"Away?" Jed said vaguely. "Where?"

Good question. Who knew if the Barlsmen were right? Who knew if there was a life beyond death? "To the countryside, Jed."

Jed frowned. "Can't I go? I like the country."

"I know you do," he said. "Only not this time. Another time, mayhap."

"Another time. Aye. Aye." Jed stood. "I have to look at Cygnet's water," he announced. "That's my job. I look after Cygnet."

The feed-room door banged closed behind him. Asher stayed crouched on the brick floor a moment longer, a hot pain pulsing at his temples. Then he pushed to his feet and started dishing out the evening feeds, scoops of oats and chaffed hay dropping into the feed buckets. Taking refuge in a task that had once meant so much.

"A sad night," said a familiar voice.

Bloody Pellen. Stealthy like a cat he was, even with one good leg and one carven-wood stump, to take the place of the shin and foot he'd lost to Morg.

When he could trust his face, he turned. "Aye. How'd you know?"

Ten years of mayorin' Dorana had left Pellen Orrick grizzled and inclined to sharp-tongued sarcasm. Fatherhood had warmed him. Buryin' his wife had lined him deeper. Two years on and he still grieved. Of course he did. He'd loved Ibby with his whole heart, a heart that never thought Lur held a woman for him.

Good thing he's got little Charis, I reckon. Reckon he'd have followed his Ibby into the ground elsewise.

Leaning against the feed-room's doorjamb, his brass-buttoned blue and crimson guard uniform long since given way to sober, respectable brown wool, Pellen cleared his throat.

"Dathne sent word. Seeing Darran's importance, she thought I should know."

Trust Dath to think of it. He'd been too angry. Too sad. "She were right. You should."

"Hard to believe we're losing him," said Pellen. "Seems he's as much a part of Dorana as the palace itself."

He nodded. "Aye."

"You don't talk of it, but I know you and the old man have grown close, these past years," Pellen said quietly. "I'm sorry, Asher."

Drat the man and his bloody sympathy. *Go away, Pellen. Did I ask you to poke your nose into how I feel? Did I?* "Aye. Well, that's the way of things, ain't it? Nowt lasts forever, though you reckon it will."

Pellen's hatchet-face stilled, its kindness freezing. "Asher? What's going on? It's not just Darran, is it? There's something else rubbing at you."

Sink it. First Darran, now Pellen. That was the trouble with having friends. They saw things. Worse, Pellen had been a guardsman and then a captain more than twice the time he'd been a mayor. Those keen instincts never left him, which was why he was still mayor. Nobody wrangled the guilds and the Doranen and every last fratchin' Olken in the City the way Pellen did.

Oh well. I were always goin' to tell him.

He shrugged. "I been...feelin' things. Changes. In the air. In the earth."

Pellen looked at him in silence, fear churning behind his eyes. Pellen Orrick afraid: now, there was a thing. "In the weather?"

Of course he'd guess that. There were four of them left now, him and Dath and Pellen and Darran, who knew close and personal about Jarralt and Morg. Just the four of them still standing, who'd stared evil in the face and breathed its foul breath. The rest of Lur, reprieved, and after living it at a distance, had marched on. But not them. They were burdened with memories, weighed down by the past. That was the price they'd paid, so Lur *could* march on. And now Darran was dyin' ...

"Mayhap," he muttered. "You ain't felt nowt?"

"Me?" Pellen shook his head. "No. Whatever magic we Olken possess, it's thin in my blood. You know that." He sighed, the lines in his face deepening. "Ibby was the one with the gift."

"You ain't heard folk whisperin' in the City?"

"No," said Pellen. "I didn't know I should be listening for them. I'll listen now, if that's what you need."

Asher glanced past Pellen out to the yard, where his friend's horse whickered hopefully in the spare stable. All the mucking out and watering and rugging-up was done. Any ticktock now the lads would be barging in, looking for the evening feeds. The Tower horses were banging at their stable walls and doors even louder than before. He turned back to the feed-bins, to finish the task of doling out oats and chaff.

"I ain't sure what I need. 'Cept the horse porridge. Fetch me the pot, eh? And the stirrin' stick."

So the Mayor of Dorana turned his hand to horse care, and together they finished preparing the evening feeds. Just as he worked the last dollops of steaming barley and linseed through the chaff and oats the lads wrangled into the feed room, laughter hiccupping to surprise as they saw grand Pellen Orrick with bits of porridge on his sleeve.

"Here you go then," said Asher. "Feed's done, with an extra for His Worship's nag." He turned to Mizzil, the senior lad. "You be in charge till Meister Divit's home again, remember. Don't let me be seein' owt amiss, or we'll have words."

As Mizzil and the other lads swore blind there'd be no trouble, Asher caught Pellen's amused eye and led him into the yard, where twilight had at last surrendered to night.

"You want to see Darran, then?" he said, as the lads bustled out of the feed room with their buckets of porridged oats and chaff. "Afore..."

Pellen nodded. "Can I?"

"Kerril said there weren't no harm," he replied, and headed out of the yard. "Ain't nowt she can do to stop him leavin' us."

"Then I will take a moment," said Pellen, following. "But first, tell me what you're going to do about—this other business."

"Well, Dath's for meeting with a few of them Circle Olken. Reckon she's prob'ly right. Aside from her they be the best mages we got."

"No," said Pellen, with quiet intensity. "You're our greatest mage, Asher."

Trust him to mention it. "I ain't any kind of mage, Pellen. Not any more."

"I know you like to think so," said Pellen. "But I'll not fight with you about it. Not tonight."

They'd reached the wooden door in the stable yard wall, that gave onto the meandering garden path to the Tower. Opening it, Asher waved Pellen by him then tugged the door closed behind them. A short walk away, the Tower blazed with glimlight, so warm and inviting. No hint of the sorrow gathering beneath its tiled roof.

"You can't summon these Circle members here openly," said Pellen, as they continued. His gait was rolling and uneven, the path's gravel echoing his lack of two flesh-and-blood feet.

Asher looked sideways. "Why not?"

"Because more than likely they'll be recognised. If you're not wanting to make a fuss about this—"

"What do you mean? I reckoned on shouting our troubles from the roof of Justice Hall."

"Very funny," said Pellen. "But by all means, bite my nose off till there's nothing left of it, my friend, if that'll ease you."

The only thing that would ease him was finding this day were nowt but a dream. And since *that* weren't likely...

"You can't go to them, either," Pellen added. "It's meant kindly enough, but even though you live your life circumspect nowadays, folks still take a keen interest in your doings."

And that were true, sink it. He shoved his hands in his pockets. "How do we meet with them, then?"

"With a little sleight-of-hand I think we can bring these mages to Dorana without raising suspicions," said Pellen, after a thoughtful pause. "And we can talk matters over at my home. That is, if you're certain the risk is worth it. If you really believe..." He sighed. "I so want you to be wrong."

They were almost at the Tower. Its double doors stood wide open, glimfire washing over its wide steps and the courtyard's raked blue and white gravel. Asher put his hand on Pellen's arm and tugged him to a halt.

"And you reckon I don't?" he said, his voice lowered again. "You think I ain't standin' here, quakin' in my boots?"

Despite his worry, Pellen smiled. "You? Quaking? That'll be the day."

Once Pellen had risked everything, his livelihood, his life, turned his back on his solemn captain's oath and leapt blindly to his aid, all because Gar had asked it of him. Because he was a good man who couldn't bear to think that his mistake had caused an innocent man to suffer. A friendship had grown out of that...as true, in its own way, as those friendships with Gar and Matt.

Asher let his fingers tighten on Pellen's arm. "This ain't funny, Meister Mayor. It ain't—" He let his hand fall and took a moment to breathe, just breathe. "If we celebrated too soon..."

"You think we did?" said Pellen, his eyes hooded, his mouth tucked tight. "Do you think—is it possible—can it be Morg?"

"No," he said swiftly. "Me and Gar UnMade him. He's dead. But that ain't to say his mischief got UnMade the same way. Remember what Tollin found over the mountains? Blight and misery and nowt good anywhere. Killed him in the end, didn't it? And them who came back with him. Took 'em slower than the others, aye, but it still took 'em. Reckon Morg left a legacy what's poisoned near the whole world."

"And us along with it?" said Pellen, openly dismayed. "Asher—" He cleared his throat. "Can you fix this? You—you know what I mean."

Aye. He did. Like Dathne, he'd told Pellen the truth about his Weather Magic. He could lie to the kingdom, but he couldn't lie to them. Not after what they'd sacrificed for him. And any road, he'd needed them to keep an eye on him, in case something with the magic went wrong one day, what with him being Olken and never meant to wield it.

"I don't know, Pellen," he said. "First I got to find out if I'm guessin' right. And then, if I am..." He scowled. "Reckon I'll cross that bridge when I reach it."

"*We'll* cross that bridge," Pellen retorted. "You'll not tackle this alone, Asher. Not while I'm Mayor of Dorana and on both Councils, with an oathsworn duty to keep City and kingdom safe."

"Fine," he agreed reluctantly. "But this ain't for talkin' on willy nilly, Pellen. You and me and Dath can know there's trouble. No-one else."

"Asher, I can agree with not telling the General Council anything, at least not yet," said Pellen, frowning. "But the Mage Council has a right to—"

"No, it bloody don't. Think I'll trust Rodyn Garrick on this? After how he fratched at me about Ain Freidin? Don't reckon I'd trust him to tell me the bloody time!"

Pellen sighed, gustily. "Then what about Barlsman Jaffee and Sarnia Marnagh and—"

"*No*, Pellen," he snapped. "It ain't safe. What they don't know won't cause us ructions."

"I don't like it, Asher," Pellen muttered. "I'm not comfortable with these kinds of secrets."

"Then you bloody *get* comfortable, Pellen. I can't sort this with the Mage Council breathin' down my neck!"

"This—this *change* you've been feeling," said Pellen, after a moment. "Who else can feel it, do you think?"

Rafel. But he couldn't tell Pellen that. He could hardly bear to think it. He and Dath had done what they could to shield their son from the magic that was in him—but was it enough? At only ten, still a sprat, was he outgrowing that protection?

No. No. Don't let it be that.

"Don't know," he said. "But if it gets any worse there'll be a lot of folk feelin' it."

"If that happens you can forget keeping secrets," said Pellen, and ran a hand over his face. "From the Mage Council *or* the kingdom. How long do we have before this becomes common knowledge?"

"Don't know that, either."

"Is there anything you *do* know?"

Biting his tongue, Asher half-turned away. Brawling with Pellen, on account of they were both frighted and heartsore, weren't likely to help things.

"I know I need you to stand by me, Pellen. I need you to trust I can find us a way out of trouble."

"Don't be a fool!" said Pellen, stung. "Whatever's gone wrong, I know you'll put it right."

There were no doubting his friend's sincerity. But suddenly, instead of helping, Pellen's faith was a fearful burden.

What if he's wrong? What if I can't? It's been ten years and I ain't stirred my magic hardly at all since Morg. What if I can't make it do what's needful? What if I don't know the right words?

Pellen took hold of his shoulder. "Asher, don't worry. When the time comes—*if* it comes—you'll know what to do. And whatever help you need to do it, just ask. I'll not turn my back."

"Good," he said, and heard his voice rasp. "That's good, Pellen."

And since there weren't nowt else to say, he started again towards the Tower. Pellen walked with him. They climbed the sandstone steps and went inside, then tramped the spiral staircase to Darran's quiet, sweet-smelling room. Pother Kerril was there, bending over the ole man. Dathne too, at the foot of the bed.

"He's failing fast," she whispered, greeting them at the open door, then managed a trembling smile for Pellen. "I'm sorry. He wore himself out for the children."

Asher frowned. "You let Rafe and Deenie—"

"Yes," she said, her voice sharpening. "My decision, Asher. You were too busy sulking."

He didn't want to fight. And Rafe had said he wanted to say goodbye. But *Deenie?*

"I let Charis say goodbye to her mother," said Pellen, his voice low. "It pained her, but it was the right choice. Your Deenie's a quiet child, Asher, but she's resilient. Not saying goodbye would be harder, I think."

Pellen knew Deenie well. She and his Charis were good friends, thick as thieves. Only a year between the girls, with Deenie the younger, living in each other's pockets like peas in a pod.

Asher glanced at Dathne, whose eyes were tear-washed. His heart, which he was guarding, cracked a little for her pain. "I ain't fratchin' you, Dath. You're their ma, you know what's best."

"Can I take a moment with him?" said Pellen. "I'll not stay long."

"Of course," said Dathne, and stroked a hand down Pellen's arm. "It's good of you to come."

As Pellen crossed to the bed to say his goodbyes, Dathne wiped her wet cheek with the back of one hand. "The dear old man told the children one of his stories. The storm at Westwailing. He said you're the bravest man he ever knew. Oh, *Asher...*"

Each word was a hammer blow, cracking his heart wider still. *That ole fool, that ole scarecrow, that manky ole man.* He couldn't speak.

Pellen rejoined them. "I'll leave you," he said, his voice rough with sorrow. "Send word when — send word. Between us we'll see he's treated right. Lur owes him a debt he never would let us repay."

On tip-toe, Dathne kissed his cheek. "Thank you, Pellen."

Asher nodded. "Aye. Thanks."

Pother Kerril released Darran's wrist, straightened and turned. "I'm sorry," she said, heedless of Pellen's departure. "It's doubtful he will wake again."

As the pother gathered up her bits and pieces, Asher opened his arms. Dathne leaned into him, sobs choking in her throat. "You should sit with him," she said at last. "I'll go to the children. They shouldn't be without one of us."

"You're right," he said, and kissed her brow.

Dathne stepped back. "He told the children he loves you. Make your peace with him while you can."

She and Kerril left after that, and he was alone in the sweet room with the old dying man. Taking hold of the chair beside the bed, he bumped it closer and sat.

"Why'd you make me yell at you, ole crow?" he whispered, reaching for Darran's ice-cold hand. "Ain't I got enough regrets in my life, you make me yell at a dyin' ole fool?"

The palsy in Darran's face had quieted. He looked peaceful, and painless, breathing so slowly, so shallowly, it was hard to tell that he breathed at all.

"You want me to say it, don't you?" he demanded. "You want me to say it so you can throw it back in my face." He dragged a silk forearm across his burning eyes. "Fine, all right, you persnickety ole codger. I love you. You happy now? You got your last laugh? Come on, you meddlesome mugwort. Let's hear you laugh. Let's hear it. Come on."

The silence deepened, muffling as snow.

"Aye, well, that'd be right," he said. "Got to have the last word, eh? Got to put me in my place." He tightened his fingers. "When Gar died, I didn't hate him. You hear me, Darran? Are you listenin'? You see him, you tell him that. You tell him that from me."

Deeper silence again. A breath held...a waiting...and then, like a blessing, the cold fingers in his moved.

But while he was weeping, Darran stole away.

CHAPTER FIVE

❊

After three days of folk saying how sorry they were he'd died, they put Darran in the royal crypt next to Da's best friend King Gar.

Staring at the marble effigy on top of the tomb, Rafel couldn't believe it wasn't ole Darran magically turned to white stone. He didn't know which was more shocking: that the effigy was so perfect, or that Da had made it. Da *never* used magic. Only glimfire, and that didn't count. He never talked of it, even. And if anyone tried to make him, well...that wasn't a good idea.

Only once he'd ever been frightened of Da, and that was the day he complained because other boys' fathers did magic, so why wouldn't he? It wasn't fair. The boys he knew from the City, from school—Doranen boys like Arlin Garrick—they laughed at him and said mean things. Why didn't Da care?

Afterwards, Mama sat with him and let him cry a little bit into her lap. He'd been eight, too big for tears, but Da had been so fearsome angry he couldn't help it.

"If those boys laugh again then you walk away," she'd told him, cuddling him close. "Stupid boys, what would they know? Magic's a solemn thing, Rafe. It's not for boasting, or for playing like a game."

"Goose plays," he'd muttered, sniffing. "And that Arlin, he shows off all the time."

Mama flicked the end of his nose. "You're not Goose, or Arlin Garrick. This family's got its own rules when it comes to magic. Rafe..." She tightened her arms. "I hope you're being a good boy. I hope you remember what Da and I said. *No-one* can know there's Doranen magic in you. Not yet. Not until we tell you it's safe to say."

He hated being told that. Why did he have to be a *secret?* Why did it matter he could do Doranen things? And he could. He *did*. And not just cracking stones, either. For three weeks now, safe on his lonesome, he'd been doing Doranen magics pinched from Arlin Garrick and his poxy friends, and getting the incants and sigils right *every time*.

He'd had to do it. The itching in him that only magic could scratch got so bad it kept him awake. Got so bad that cracking stones made no difference. The first time he did it, broke his word to Da and Mama, he nigh on wet his trews from fear. Half-expected to die, or be found out. But he didn't. He wasn't. The Doranen magic worked. He turned his white-painted woodcarved pony jet black and *nowt terrible happened*.

Almost a dozen Doranen spells he'd pinched since then, and not *once* had things gone wrong. So *why* was he meant to stay a secret? It wasn't *fair*.

"Rafe," said Mama. "Are you listening?"

"Yes, Mama," he said, nodding. Feeling so bad to be lying. Knowing he could never tell her the truth.

"Oh, Rafel," she said. "There's more to life than magic. It doesn't make you brave, or good, or strong. You wouldn't be any happier, I promise, if Da and I let you run about the place casting spells from sunup to sundown. Believe me."

She was wrong, but he had to pretend she was right. "Yes, Mama."

"Yes, Mama," she echoed, smiling, but her eyes were sad. "You're a big boy, Rafe, but you're not grown-up yet. There are things your Da and I know that you don't. You'll have your magic when it's time, and not before."

Later that night, when he was tucked up in bed, Da had come to see him. In the warm summer darkness he'd sat beside him, his arms safe and strong and holding, his cheek scratchy with stubble.

"Sorry I shouted, Rafe," he said, his voice gruff. "Sorry I scared you. You're only eight, a spratling. You don't understand."

"Is magic bad, Da?" he'd asked. " 'Cause I got magic. Does that mean *I'm* bad?"

"No," Da said, and crushed him so close it was hard to breathe. "But you got to be careful, Rafe. Magic's deep and dark and dangerous, especially for you."

And there was Da hinting, just like Mama. They were always hinting, they never came out and *said.* " 'Cause I'm like you, Da? Why is that dangerous?"

Da sighed. "That be a small question with a sinkin' big answer, sprat. When you be a mite older we'll try talkin' it through. But for now you got to trust me and your ma to know what's best."

Everything was about when he was older. But he wanted to know *now.* This was his life, not theirs. And anyway, they were wrong. His Doranen magic wasn't dangerous. It was the best thing in the world.

Da kissed the top of his head. "Feels mean, don't it, sprat. Feels poxy unfair. But I never said life was fair, did I? Never promised you that."

No, he never did. He shook his head against Da's broad chest. "Nuh-uh."

"And I will tell you, Rafe," said Da. "One day. When you be ready to know."

Though it was dark in his room, not even glimfire, just a little moonlight spilling between the drawn curtains, he'd looked up, struggled to read his father's face. Thought he saw in it truth, and sadness, and memories he didn't want to share.

"Really, Da? You promise?"

"My word, Rafe," said Da, nodding. "Man to man."

Da always kept his word. Always. But still... "How much older, Da?"

"Just older," said Da, in the voice that said *enough.*

He was ten now, and still waiting for an answer. For a little while after that, 'cause he felt so guilty, he'd stopped pinching Arlin's magics. But only for a little while, 'cause the itch grew too strong and he had to scratch it. Just like before, nothing went amiss. So he stopped feeling guilty. He was right and Da was wrong. Magic *wasn't* dangerous, at least not for him.

But he still wanted to know what Da wouldn't tell him.

Not long after his ninth birthday, tired of waiting, he'd asked Darran. "Why doesn't Da like magic? Why's it make him so fratched?"

The ole man had sat at his desk for a long time in silence, counting trins out of one open lockbox and into another. "I could answer that," he said at last. "But I'm not sure I should."

"I won't tell," he'd said. "Promise."

Darran pursed his lips, clinking trins with his fingers. The office door was closed. It was just the two of them alone. "Magic's not been kind to your father, Rafel," he said at last, so softly. "It's been used to hurt him. And he's used it to hurt. He had to, you understand. Your da's a good man. We're only safe today because of him. But he never asked for his power. He never was comfortable being important. He never will be."

But why? "I think magic's grand," he muttered. "Da should be happy he's got so much of it."

"Is that so, young man?" said Darran sharply. "Then you've not been listening to a word I've said. Trust me when I tell you that power is not a promise of happiness. Haven't I lived my long life among men of power? Be guided by me, my boy: for every man it makes happy, it makes another three miserable."

Darran didn't understand. How could he? He was an ole man, and he had no power at all. "I've got power, and I ain't miserable, Darran."

"You?" said Darran, his straggly grey eyebrows shooting up. "You've got nothing of the sort. You've some talent for magic, and more talent for trouble. *That's* not power. Nor is it a combination to set a father's heart at ease." He'd peered then, suspicious. "I hope you're not playing games with your magic, Rafel. You know the rules."

That made him feel all fratched. Bloody ole man, scolding. Who asked him, eh? Wasn't his job to scold. He wasn't Da, or Mama.

"I know, I know," said Darran, crossly amused. "I should mind my own business. But you started this conversation, Rafel, not me. If it's not turned out to your liking, well, that's hardly my fault."

Squirmy, he'd scowled at the floor. "Huh."

"Rafel, I shared a confidence with you, which I'd like you to keep," said Darran, still snappy. "And I'd like you to remember this: if you're kept on a leash, and you find it fretsome, consider that your parents have only your best interests at heart. For it's true, you do have power. But you're not old enough to wield it or comprehend what it means. Trust your father to know. Trust your father."

"I do!" he'd protested. "I *do* trust him, Darran."

But the ole man didn't look like he believed him, and that had made him so cross he'd stormed off to his secret place and cracked so many stones there he had to make a hole and bury them, after.

When that was done, and he sprawled face-up on the ground panting and sweaty, something Darran said had floated back to him like dandelion fluff on a breeze.

Magic's not been kind to your father, Rafel. It's been used to hurt him.

He'd never heard that before. He could hardly believe it. Someone hurt Da? With *magic?* How could they? Da was—was—a *hero.* He was the saviour of Lur. Darran was a stupid ole trout, what did he know? He had to be wrong. Hurt Da with magic?

As if anyone could.

"Rafel. *Rafel.*"

Blinking, he pulled free of the past and looked up into his father's solemn face. They were alone in the crypt now. Mama and Deenie and Uncle Pellen had gone outside. Da looked so sad, glimfire making his eyes too bright. He reached out his hand and Da's fingers closed tightly around his, a little muscle leaping along his jaw.

"It's a good effigy, Da. It looks just like that ole fish."

Da nodded. "The magic took, that's a fact."

He stared again at cold, stone Darran. "You did it with Doranen magic, didn't you?"

"Aye," Da said at last. "Gar taught it me, a long time ago."

He looked at King Gar's stone likeness. "Did you make his, too?"

Da nodded again. "I did."

He couldn't believe it. They were talking *magic*. He and Da hardly *ever* talked magic. Maybe there were some kind of spell on the crypt. "I'd like to do that. I'd like to make a marble picture of Mama's face, when she's smiling."

Da's holding fingers twitched. "Mayhap you will, sprat. One of these days."

"Only if you teach me, Da. Only if you let me do real magic."

"Real magic?" Da snorted. "Doranen magic, you mean."

"So?" he muttered. "It's more fun than earth-songs and flowers."

"*Rafe*—" Da let go of him. "Only reason you think that is 'cause you ain't got any idea what Doranen magic be about."

He wanted to shout, *"Yes I do!"* He wanted to show Da here and now the things he'd taught himself, pinching Arlin Garrick's magics. But he couldn't. The *trouble* there'd be, if he did that.

So he scuffed his boot-heel on the crypt floor, feeling hot and sulky. "I would if you'd tell me."

"And I *will* tell you, Rafe," Da said, snappish. "Just not today. So don't go on at me."

"I ain't," he protested. "I only — Da, I want to make faces in marble, like you do. 'Cause it's beautiful."

Even though he was fratched, a reluctant smile tugged at Da's lips. "Beautiful, eh? You tryin' to wheedle me, sprat?"

"No, Da," he said, earnest and dutiful, though of course he *was* ... and both of them knew it. "I'm just saying my druthers. Couldn't you tell me the words? Couldn't you show me how they go? Just this once?"

He wanted it so badly there was a pain in his chest. Him and Da together, doing magic. No need for telling tales, no need to hide. Him and Da doing magic, out in the open.

Da let loose a slow sigh. "You ain't strong enough, Rafe. Once Doranen magic gets in your head you can't get it out again. It sits there like a toad. It changes you, sprat, and there ain't no changin' back after, not even if you want to."

Now Da looked worse than sad. Dumbstruck, Rafel folded his arms.

That ain't true, Da. I'm not changed. I haven't got a toad in my head.

"Rafel," said Da, and dropped to a crouch before him. "Listen. I got to ask you a thing. I got to ask, and you got to answer me straight."

He nodded, slowly. Fright made his mouth suck dry. *Does he know? Has he found out?* "All right, Da. I will."

"What did you tell Darran, that you ain't told me or your ma? About magic. About...feelin' things in the earth."

Fright flashed to indignation. *That ole fart. That ole trout. He promised he'd not tell.* Betrayal hooked him like a fish, left him gasping for air.

Da fastened strong fingers to his shoulder. Shaking him a little, his eyes fierce, he scowled. "No use fratchin' at Darran, Rafe. He's dead, he ain't listenin'. And I need to know what happened. When did you come over funny, sprat?"

"Week afore last," he said, his voice small. Glaring at stone Darran from underneath his lashes. *You promised. You promised.*

"And what were you doing? Were you doing magic?"

He had to look at the floor again, afraid his guilty secret would show in his eyes. "No, Da. Only working with the blocks."

The blocks Pother Kerril had told him he needed for practise, so his Doranen magic didn't fizz up his blood. Da didn't like it, not one bit, but Kerril said it had to be. Kerril said it was dangerously foolish to go on pretending his magic didn't exist. He'd not said a word, he'd been so scared his guilty secret would show then, too. But it didn't. And ever since, for nearly five months, he'd practised with the blocks Kerril gave him. She was right. They did help scratch his itches. But—but—

"Da!" he said, his heart jumping. "Was it—was it *my* fault? Did I—"

"*No!*" said Da, almost shouting. "Ain't none of this your fault, sprat."

Giddy with relief, he nearly blurted it all out. Nearly told Da *everything*—then swallowed the words just in time. Da could never know. Neither could Mama. Neither of them would ever understand.

"Rafe," said Da, gently now. "Tell me what you felt. It's all right. You ain't in trouble."

Not so long as he kept his secret, he wasn't. "I felt a funny skritching, all over."

"Like ants havin' a picnic 'neath your shirt and trews?"

Dumbly, he nodded.

"And then," said Da, "a kind of rumble and rollin', like someone put you in a pepper pot and shook you all about?"

"Aye, Da," he whispered. "And then the air—the air—"

Da sighed. "It felt like the air got its neck wrung, like a chicken?"

A tiny sobbing gasp escaped him. "Yes. Did you—"

"Aye. Me and your ma. We felt it too. How many other times have you felt it, Rafe?"

"Once. The day Darran got sick." To his shame, his voice broke. He felt his eyes sting, and his lips quiver. He wanted to bawl like Deenie, left behind because boys don't play with girls.

Da pulled him close in a tight hug. "Why didn't you tell me and your ma?" Letting go, he sounded hurt. "Why did you tell that ole fool Darran and not us?"

"I never meant to tell him, Da," he said, feeling like he'd stuck a knife in Da's heart. "Only he came looking for you when I was practicing the blocks, and that's when I got the feeling, and he saw." Another hot rush of anger. "He said he wouldn't tell."

"He only told 'cause he knew he were dyin'," said Da. "And he thought we should know. Rafe, why'd you keep it a secret?"

He scuffed the floor again. "Thought I might be comin' down with an ague," he muttered. "Thought you might say I couldn't go with Goose and his da to see the brewery in Banting."

"And the second time?" said Da—then shook his head. "I s'pose, with Darran poorly..."

He nodded. And even though Darran poorly had really been Darran dying, even though they were stood right in front of his coffin, he still felt rankled. 'Cause Darran had *promised*.

"Rafe," said Da, noticing. "The ole trout's dead. You forgive him, eh? You'll feel better if you do."

He wasn't so sure on that, but it was Da asking, so he turned to the coffin and kissed the ole man's stone brow. "I forgive you, Darran. Reckon you thought you were doing what was right."

"Rafe," said Da, after a moment, sitting himself on the crypt's cool floor. "You believe me, don't you, that it weren't you practisin' your blocks as made things go awry? 'Cause it weren't your fault, no more than bein' able to do Doranen magic be your fault."

Did this mean they were going to talk about it, at last? Suddenly hopeful, he bumped himself down beside his father. "Then why won't you let me learn more magic, Da? If I ain't doing anything wrong, why won't you?"

Da shook his head again. "'Cause it ain't that simple, sprat. A thing don't have to be wrong for it to be the wrong thing to do. There be a time and a place for you and Doranen magic, but we ain't there yet."

"But—"

"I *told* you, Rafe. Doranen magic sneaks up on you. And you don't see what it really means until it's too bloody late."

Da didn't sound hurt any more. Now he sounded angry, like he wanted to take out his magic and punch it.

"Da," he said, his voice small. "I—I don't mind it...all that much."

"You don't?" Da said. He sounded almost puzzled. "It don't fright you?"

He shook his head, feeling bad. As though not hating his magic was the same as not loving Da. "No."

"Not ever?"

Remembering how it felt to crack stones, and dance leaves, and make his bathwater leap into frogs and dogs and horses—remembering all the other wonderful things he'd done—he stared at his knees. He could always lie. He could say it *did* fright him sometimes, and that might make Da feel better. But he didn't want to. He didn't know why, but he knew that would feel even worse than not confessing his terrible secret.

"No, Da. It don't fright me. Not even a bit."

"Rafe, Rafe," said Da, sighing. "What am I s'posed to do with you, eh?"

More than anything he wanted to say, *"Let me be a mage."* If he'd been born Doranen he'd be learning Doranen magic. He'd be like Arlin

Garrick, magicking all over the place. If he was like Goose, just an ordinary Olken, he'd be doing Olken magic and nobody would think twice.

But I ain't one thing or the other. Same as Da, I'm both. And he thinks 'cause he don't like it then I shouldn't either. And that ain't right.

But he couldn't tell Da that. He was just a sprat. He went hot, feeling his prickly crossness rise.

"Rafe," said Da, "you got to tell me and your ma if you feel that skritchiness again."

"I will, Da." He chewed his lip. "Da...what does it mean?"

Da grabbed hold of King Gar's tomb and hauled himself to his feet. The crypt's glimfire danced shadows over his face as he walked round and round between the coffins, staring at the peaceful marble people without ever seeing them proper.

"I felt it, Da, so you ought should tell me," he said, so daring. Nobody bossed Da about. Well, nobody save Ma. Da shot him a sharp look, but didn't scold him on it. He was scowling, like he did when all his thoughts were tangled. "Tell me, Da. Please? I won't tattle, my word, man to man."

Da looked like he wanted to swear. *Really* swear, lots of bad words, the ones Mama wouldn't let him say. "It's complicated, Rafe. You be a spratling, and this ain't spratling business."

Prickly cross, prickly cross. "Maybe not, Da. But I felt what you and Mama felt. I never asked to, but I did. It ain't fair if you don't tell me."

Da stopped circling the crypt. Halted at King Gar's marble feet and brooded into his cold white stone face. It was a nice face. Sad, and understanding. So young. Hard to think of Da that young, the same age as King Gar when he died. He wasn't exactly old now, not as old as Uncle Pellen, say, but he looked old. Not in a wrinkled way. In a sad way. A tired way.

I never saw that before. I never saw he looked tired. I never saw that made him look older than he is.

He felt odd, all of a sudden. Standing on the outside, looking at his da. Thinking these strange thoughts. Noticing things.

"I were your age when my ma died," Da said, very quiet. "She got sick and no pother could help her. Just like that, I weren't a spratling no more. My da were lost without her. My brothers…well…" His face pinched. "Weren't no love lost there. I learned things, Rafe. I learned 'em too soon." He nodded at King Gar's effigy. "So did he. Weren't no reason for us to be friends, you'd think. He was royalty. I weren't. But he learned things young too, and they made him sad. I knew what that felt like. That's how we were friends. He lived sad, and he died sad. He never had a chance. Rafe, you don't need to know what's going on. Not yet, any road. When you do I'll tell you. My word, man to man. But you stay a sprat for now. You'll grow up soon enough."

Staring at him, Rafel knew he'd waste his breath complaining. Just like with his magic, he wasn't allowed a say. All right, if he was honest, the upset in the earth *did* fright him a tiddy bit. He'd told himself it were nowt, he just had an ague, but down deep he'd known different. Down deep he'd known something was wrong. And without ever saying so, Da had told him he was right.

He can't pretend I'm ordinary forever. One day he'll have to stop treating me like a sprat.

"Rafel," said Da. His voice was stern. It was the voice he used when what he said was as good as a law. His Justice Hall voice. "This be serious business. What you felt ain't to be talked on. Have you told it to Goose, or any other boy or girl?"

He'd been thinking to tell Goose. He told Goose most everything. He'd just been waiting till he felt not so wobbly. "No, Da. I only told Darran."

"Huh," Da grunted. "That's somethin', any road. So you don't tell Goose, you hear me? No teasin' him on what you felt, and no askin' if he felt it. You don't tell *anyone*. I got your word on that?"

He nodded, smothering disappointment. He hated keeping secrets from Goose. "Aye, Da."

Da's face relaxed. "I know it don't seem fair, Rafe. I know you be fratched 'cause you ain't got your answer. But you'll get it, by and by."

He sighed. His father kept on saying that, but it was getting harder to believe him. "Aye, Da."

"Good sprat," said Da. "Now we'd best be on our way, or your ma will be thinkin' we've turned to marble in here."

Side by side they left the crypt, the glimfire snapping to darkness behind them, and walked out blinking into the Garden of Remembrance. Every time he came here he stopped to look at the statue of the man he was named for, who died a hero in the war against Morg. He didn't exactly know how it happened. Darran never told him that story. But every time he stood here with Da, and he looked at Da's face, he knew it was a sad tale.

Other straggling folk were here and there in the garden, because everyone loved the flowers and the trees, but nobody tried to speak to them, on account of the whole City knowing Darran was being put in the crypt today. They got stared at, though. One ole biddy was weepin'. Da noticed, but he didn't say a word.

"Come on," he said, after they'd stood there a goodly while, looking at the statues of Rafel and Veira and Matt. "There'll be supper waitin' for us in the Tower, and your ma with a wooden spoon to wallop us 'cause we ain't sat at the table on time."

That made him giggle, even though he was mixed up, prickly cross and sad. "Not you, Da. Mama ain't going to wallop you."

Da rolled his eyes. "Ain't no-one your ma wouldn't wallop, Rafe. She ain't got a fear in her, that wench. Make certain sure you find a woman to marry what's like your ma. Life'll be sweet, that road."

He grinned. "You called Mama a wench."

"Wash out your ears," said Da, grinning back. "I did no such thing. Now stir your stumps, sprat. It's time to go."

On a shared smile they turned their backs on the garden and wandered home to the Tower, companionably silent. Overhead a ghost moon winked at the sliding sun, and the waking nightbirds sang in the djelba trees. Nightbirds never stopped singing, and they never sounded sad.

Rafe swallowed a small sigh. Wherever Darran was, he hoped the ole man could hear them.

Naked and sated, Asher smoothed Dathne's tangled hair from her face and kissed the corner of her mouth. Her lips moved beneath his, curving into a smile, and she slapped his arse lightly.

"Get off me, you lump."

Obliging, he rolled to her side and scooped her against him with one arm. Their skin stuck moistly together; she smelled of roses and apricots. Heaving a contented sigh, his head comfortable on their pillows, he dropped a hand to cover her breast. Her hand covered his, and they lay for some time in sighing silence.

"The ole fart reached a goodly age," he said softly, at last. "A better age than my da did, Barl rest his bones."

Dathne's fingertips traced idle patterns on his belly. "I wondered if you'd thought on that. But you never said, and I didn't want to pry."

He snorted. "First time for everythin', eh?"

"Rogue," she said, pinching him. "So. You made your peace with the dear old man?"

She'd not asked, before. It was one of the many things he loved about her, the way she could sit silent and wait till she knew he were ready to talk on things that mattered.

"Aye," he said, feeling again Darran's cold fingers in his hand. "We settled things."

Her lips pressed against his chest. "Good. You travelled a strange road together, you and that persnickety fellow. You hurt each other on purpose, and not...but even so..."

It were funny, how she was so much harder than him but could still easily touch matters close to the heart, when he couldn't.

"Don't worry," she added. There was a smile in her voice. "I ain't about to get maudlin on you, Meister Asher."

He thanked her with another kiss, slow and considering. She laughed, amusement whispering, and stroked her hand down his back, fingertips bumping from scar to scar.

"You spoke to Rafe?" she said, head settling on his shoulder. "I hope you did. I took Pellen and Deenie out so you'd have a moment with him alone."

"Aye," he said. "I spoke to him."

"And?" she prompted, after a moment.

He sighed. "And he don't much like bein' held back, Dathne."

"You think that's news to me?" she said. "He's wanted to run before he could walk ever since he snapped his fingers and called glimfire when he was barely a year old. What did you tell him?"

"I told him not to fret on what he felt. That it were important, but you and me, we were mindin' it 'cause that's our job, not his."

"You know..." The gentle fingers scoring his skin ceased their movement, leaving him bereft. "We can't hold him back forever. We don't dare. The power in him will find its way to the surface, no matter how deeply we try to keep it buried."

He felt his heart pound. Felt his hot blood flow cold, thinking on it. "I never said forever, Dath. But he's a *spratling*. He's *ten*. He's got his whole life for magic. It can wait."

"Can it?" she said, and wriggled until she was up on her elbows looking down at him. Moonlight turned her sharp face to silver, and shone mysterious in her dark, solemn eyes. "Asher, you and I, we're children of the old kingdom. He's a child of the new. Magic is his birthright. It's the birthright of every Olken, if they choose to embrace it. And he's made his choice, my love. He wants what he was born with, Olken and Doranen magic both. What we want...what *you* want...that's not important. Child or not, we can't ride roughshod over him."

"Speak for y'self," he retorted. "*I* bloody can. He's my son. I'm his father."

She let herself drop back to the feather mattress, and their blankets. "When you say things like that, Asher, I think you must sound like your brothers."

The words stung him, as she knew they would. "That ain't fair, Dath. I ain't like Zeth and the rest of 'em. I don't use my fists, and my belt, and I don't scream at him neither. I don't use him up and spit him out. No, and I ain't like my da was, neither. He let grief turn him blind to what were goin' on under his nose. But me, I ain't blind, Dath. Rafe's my life, you bloody *know* that. Ain't nowt I won't do for him."

"Nowt but let him be himself," she said gently. "Asher, he's not you. He's not—"

"Not what? Go on, Dath. Don't say your tongue's fallen out now."

She lay quietly beside him, her moonlight face darkened with shadows. "Not afraid," she said at last. "Not bitter. He's living *his* life, not yours. And in his life magic's a thing to be celebrated, not — not kicked aside."

Her words stole his breath.

"My love, you can't protect him," she said, letting her hand rest atop his busy heart. "Not from this. Barl save us, Asher, we *tampered* with him, and he still felt what we felt. Like it or not, that's the truth we have to swallow once and for all. Rafel's a mage of power with Doranen magic in him. And nothing we can do will save him from that."

He closed his eyes. "You ain't never called me coward before. Not once. Not even at Veira's cottage, and I was frighted to death then. You sayin' I be a coward now 'cause I want to keep my son safe?"

"Being afraid and being a coward aren't the same thing and you know it," she snapped. "Don't try to fratch me into a fight, Asher, just so you won't have to talk about this. And he's *our* son. Not yours alone."

"Aye, he's our son," he said, sitting up. Her hand fell away from him but he didn't feel the lack of it. "And there ain't a body in this kingdom knows better than us what harm being a powerful mage can do. Do you want that for him? After what we lived through? What we dream on, ten years later? Is *that* what you want for him?"

"I want what you want," she said. "Rafe happy. Lur safe."

He flinched as her warm hand came to rest between his shoulder blades. "He reckons he's hard done by, but he's a spratling. He knows *nowt*. We let him muck about with magic, Dath, he'll learn quick smart what unhappy's about. He will. I swear — if I could rip his magic out of him with my bare hands, I would."

A creaking of the bedboards as she sat up beside him. A caress of warmth, as she sighed across his bare skin and slid her arms around his ribs. "Oh, *Asher.*"

"Mayhap that Kerril can brew up a potion," he said, staring through the chamber window at the moon, fat and full and boldly shining. "Some way of smotherin' what's bubblin' in him, past — past what we've kept locked away safe. He's too young for it, Dath. He ain't ready for what it means."

"I thought you were over this," she murmured, her cheek resting against his spine. "Ten years is a long time. I thought...I hoped...Will you never accept who you are? *What* you are?"

"And what am I, Dath? A fisherman who ain't allowed the sea. A fisherman brimful of magic, who never once asked for it. A da who can't protect his son from pain. A da who gave him that pain, who bloody *poisoned* him with—"

"Asher, *stop* it!" she said, and tightened her arms till his ribs creaked. "This is grief talking. This is your nerves on edge because of what you felt in the Weather Chamber. Your imagination's run rampant, dreading the worst with no good reason. You're being foolish. It's not like you."

On a deep breath he turned, and pulled her into his arms. Buried his face in her hair, buried his fears in the feel of her, soft yielding flesh over bones of diamond and gold.

"Hush, my love, hush," she murmured, her warm hands gentling him. "We'll be all right. Rafe will be all right. Whatever we're facing we'll survive it. You're the Innocent Mage, my love. You were born to prevail."

Because he loved her, because she ruled him, he showed her his face. "You sure on that? You promise?"

Tears shimmered in her eyes. "I promise."

They made love again, not tenderly. And afterwards, spent and panting, waited a long time for sleep to claim them.

"You called them Circle folk here yet?" he asked, hearing his voice slur. "We got to get things sorted, Dath."

Her unbound hair tickled his skin as she slowly shook her head. "Tomorrow," she said, drowsy. "I'll send word to them tomorrow. With Darran at rest I can think clearly now."

He hadn't meant to nag. "Right. Tomorrow."

"You mustn't fret," she whispered, on the brink of sleep. "They'll come, and we'll sit down together and see what's what. There's an answer to this mystery and they'll help us find it."

Drowsy himself, he drifted his fingers to the old faded scar on his chest. Felt the shard of Circle crystal he still carried within him, that he could've had cut out a hundred times over... but didn't.

"Aye," he said. "Aye, we'll find it."

And didn't know if he believed that, or not.

CHAPTER SIX

꽃

Heart thudding, Rafel closed Da's library door behind him. He wasn't meant to be in here. Not without Da or Mama. He wasn't meant to know what Da kept in the big trunk under the window. And he *definitely* wasn't s'posed to faddle with it.

But here he was. Alone in Da's library where he wasn't meant to be. 'Cause it was in his head like a worm in an apple, to have a looksee in that trunk full of books and scrolls on Doranen magic.

Two days after they put Darran in the royal crypt he'd overheard Da talking to Uncle Pellen on some bit of Doranen magic or other he had to rule on in Justice Hall, saying as how he'd been studying what Durm said on it in the privy diaries the master magician had left behind. Uncle Pellen had muttered how the thought of those magics being writ down to fall into the wrong hands made him awful nervous. And *Da* had said how Uncle Pellen weren't to fret, for they were kept safe and tight in his library trunk where no eyes but his would ever see 'em.

That was all he'd overhead, 'cause Da and Uncle Pellen had started walking down the Tower stairs again on their way out to the stables. But he'd not been able to forget what was said. Could hardly sleep for wondering what more he could learn about Doranen magic, that he couldn't pinch off Arlin. That Da wouldn't tell him, even though he *ought* to.

Every time Da wouldn't, he felt better about his terrible secret.

Then, a week after he overheard Da and Uncle Pellen talking their business, out of the blue came this one chance to have a looksee for himself. With Da and Mama gone early to visit Uncle Pellen, and Deenie spending the day with Charis, Cluny to mind them, and no more stickybeaking Darran in the Tower, Barl rest him, and this his one day of the week let out of school, he could sneak into Da's library and have a rummage through that trunk of magic. 'Cause the spells he pinched from Arlin, they were all right but they weren't *big* spells. And he really, *really* wanted to try a big spell.

So even though he knew this was bad, he waited till no-one was nearby and slid into Da's library like an eel into waterweeds. And if a teeny tiny part of him felt ashamed of doing this behind Da's back, when Da trusted him? Well. He wasn't going to think about that. What was one more secret? Besides. He wouldn't have to sneak, would he, if Da would keep his promise, and talk magic.

The mysterious trunk had a lock on it.

Not an ordinary lock, neither, with a brass key to turn it. No, this lock was made of Doranen magic. He could feel its buzziness in his mind, behind his eyes, where he always felt it. Scowling, Rafel thumped to the carpet in front of the trunk. Not one spell he'd ever pinched off Arlin would do the trick.

Sink it.

He closed his eyes. Sat very still and quiet. Let the buzziness in his mind tell him what the lock looked like...and maybe how it could be undone. Inside his head he saw it as a big ball of string, looped and knotted and stuck through with thorns. But if he tugged *this* bit — then *this* bit — and got it loose and wiggly right *there* —

With an odd kind of springiness, the trunk's Doranen-magic lock gave way. Shocked, Rafel opened his eyes. He'd *done* it. All by himself, without even one of Arlin's pinched spells to help him. And the feeling of it, the way the magic made his blood thick and hot, the way it made him feel strong and — and — *invincible*. Not one of Arlin's spells had ever made him feel like *this,* like a *real mage*. He was Rafel of Dorana, and he'd fuddled Da's lock.

If Da finds out he'll bloody fuddle me.

But he was too cockahoop to fret on that right now. Hurrying, 'cause chances were one of the Tower maids would get down to dusting this floor pretty soon, he lifted the trunk's lid and gazed greedily at its contents.

All the books! And the scrolls! All the secret Doranen magic!

Careful, since Da would notice if the trunk's contents were messed about too much, he poked and prodded his way through the forbidden treasure. Read a bit here, a bit there, understanding some of it. Not all. Not most of it. Feeling the buzziness in his mind stir stronger and louder. Feeling his fingers *itch,* wanting so much to play.

But he didn't dare. If something went wrong...

Goose said once, when they were talking on magic, that a lot of Durm's books had ended up in the General Council library. His da, who'd been a councilor then, could've brought some home if he'd wanted. Only he had no interest in Doranen magic, which had nowt to do with hops and ale, and Goose said he didn't want a clip over the ear for asking, thanks.

But compared to *these* books of magic, those others were nothing. He didn't care any more that he couldn't get his hands on them. These books, with Durm's name scrawled and faded on the flyleaf, they were *special.* And one day he'd read them and learn every spell. One day he'd do every last bit of magic in them. And then he could feel like a real mage *every* day.

But not today. He couldn't stay in Da's library any longer. Through the closed door he could hear Biddy singing, loud and out of tune like always, as she dusted her way down the Tower staircase. If she found him in here there'd be such a ruckus...

Reluctantly, he started to close the trunk's lid. Then his eye caught sight of a fat scroll tucked down the side. It looked much newer than the other scrolls he'd rummaged through. Holding his breath he eased it out, undid the ribbon keeping it closed and let it unroll just enough to see.

His heart thumped so hard it nearly leapt out of his chest. *Tollin's account of his expedition over Barl's Mountains.* He felt like dancing. Like shouting. Like laughing out loud. Not caring any more that Biddy was dusting closer, he let the scroll unroll itself properly.

And it turned out there were three copies of the same account bundled together. The writing was small and cramped and squiggly, so that Tollin's memories would fit front and back on one long sheet of parchment.

Rafel stared at his discovery, feeling sweaty sick. Everything he ever wanted to know about Tollin's adventures, that Da and Mama would never ever tell him, that not even ole gossipy Darran would tell him...

I could take one. I could. Why'd they need three for? They don't need three. And if I keep it proper hidden, no-one will find out.

All those books and scrolls of magic. All the truths Da wouldn't share. The magic that was kept from him. The things he didn't know.

Da shouldn't keep secrets. Not about me.

Quickly he took one of Tollin's scrolls, folded it over and over and shoved it inside his shirt, down the waistband of his trews. Then he rolled up the other two, tied the ribbon tight round them again, shoved them back into the trunk then closed its lid with a soft thump.

And then he realised—he had to lock it again.

Oh.

With his eyes closed and his mind still, feeling that lumpy folded parchment slowly warming against his skin, he picked up the undone ends of Da's lock and...put them back the way they were. Not sure how he was doing it, knowing only that he was. That he could feel exactly which bit went where, and how, so Da would never know what had happened.

When he was finished Rafel opened his eyes, shaken and blinking as the buzziness in his mind faded. The trunk was locked again. It was time to go. He and Goose were meeting at the City gates to spend the day on horseback. If he didn't hurry he was going to be late.

Closing Da's library door behind him, he heard Biddy's clomping footsteps on her way down the staircase. Any ticktock she was going to find him.

He bolted.

"Hey! Hey! Race you!" Goose shouted as soon as they were safely through the City gates, and dug his heels into his pony's ribs. Eyes rolling, ears flattened, the pony swished its tail and bolted.

Rafel stared after him, mouth dropped, then let out a bloodcurdling yell. Stag needed no more urging. With a snort and a kick-behind he pounded after Goose's pony. Lucky thing the road into the City was empty just then, for between them they'd have easy run a fancy carriage into the ditch.

Laughing, breathless, the wind whipping his face, Rafel galloped after Goose. Heels drumming, elbows flapping, lurching left and right in his saddle — Stablemeister Divit called his best friend a sapster — Goose veered off the roadway and across the open meadow towards the river where it pooled and puddled near Dragonshead Bridge.

Goose's pony was a game one, but Stag was bred down on the Dingles, on the horse farm King Gar started when he was a spratling prince. The best bloodlines in Lur came from Kingsfarm: Cygnet, and poor dead Ballodair, and every horse in the Tower. His first pony, Flea. Then Dancer. Now Stag.

Standing in his stirrups, knees gripped tight to Stag's barrel ribs, he buried his fisted hands in the pony's black mane and shouted into one turned-back ear. "Go on! Catch him, Stag! Catch him! Go on!"

He felt the pony stretch out long and low beneath him and saw clottings of green turf fly past, dug loose by Stag's hard shod hooves. They were gaining on Goose…gaining…gaining…there was the bridge…there was their favourite patch of flower-scattered meadow…there was the deep riverpond, known to locals as the Dragon's Eye…

"Ha!" he shouted, triumphant, as Stag surged past Goose's wallowing beast. "Beat you, Goosie! Beat you! Ha!"

Goose's wail of defeat made him laugh and laugh. Which was mean, he knew it was mean, but he couldn't help it. He liked to win.

Their race over, they let the hobbled ponies graze the grass and flowers, kicked off their boots and socks and sat on the pond's low grassy bank dangling their bare feet above it. Nearby flowed the Gant, wide and slothful. The snow up high hadn't melted yet, so the springrace was still a few weeks away. A long stone's-throw distant stood Dragonshead Bridge, and the sound of the river slipping and sliding around and past its stone supports was sleepy and comfortable. The Eye sparkled in the sunshine, early dragonflies dancing across its still, mirror surface.

Rafel breathed out a huge sigh of satisfaction. Aside from practising his magic, there was no better way to spend a free day than with Goose and the wide blue sky, nowt else. What with Darran dying and all, it felt like years since he'd been let loose to amuse himself.

And there's Tollin's adventure inside my shirt. I got such a tale to tell.

"One of these days," said Goose, his long black hair flopping, "I'm going to win a race agin you."

"Y'reckon?" he said, grinning.

Goose slumped. "Prob'ly not."

"Prob'ly you're right," he said, still grinning, and idly kicked Goose's knobby sockless ankle. "Get yourself a Dingles-bred pony, you might stand a chance."

"Don't you spit on Taff," said Goose, firing up. "He's a good pony, he is."

Rafel looked sideways to where Stag and Goose's pony were tearing at the meadow, their slipped bits jangling, nudging and jostling jealously over the sweetest bite of grass. Stag's dark brown coat gleamed ripe with dapples. Beside him, Goose's muddy cream pony looked a lot like a nag.

Goose, seeing it, stayed loyal. "Any road. Even if my dad did believe in paying Dingles money for a pony, I wouldn't push Taff out. We're friends, him and me."

"I know." He didn't want a brangle with Goose. Not when the sun was shining and the day was theirs to play with. Not with Tollin's parchment snug tight against his skin. "You're right. He's a good pony."

After a hard look, just to make sure he wasn't being joshed, Goose reached beneath his laced-up leather jerkin. There was a clinking, and some wrestling, then two bottles of beer sat on the grassy bank between them.

Impressed, Rafel stared. "That for us?"

"No," said Goose, going cross-eyed. "For Taff and Stag."

"That your da's brew?"

"It is," said Goose. "His best strong beer, from the bottling that won him the last guild gold medal." A quick, shy smile. Goose was proud of his da. "Put hairs on your chest, that will."

Did he want hairs on his chest? They'd be a bit hard to explain... Chewing his lip, Rafel frowned at Goose's folly. Beer, eh? He'd never drunk a whole bottleful before. Sometimes Da gave him a mouthful from his own tankard. He didn't care for it overmuch but he never told Da that, because sharing a brew was manly important. He wasn't about to tell Goose, neither. Not with his friend all puffed up for bringing it.

"Your da catches you pinching his prize beer, Goose, you'll get walloped right into next week," he said. "He notices his prize beer gone missing, you won't sit down three Barlsdays running."

Goose hooted. "Notice two bottles gone? My dad won't notice that. He's got so much beer in the pantry there's no room for spuds. You should hear my ma. Trust me, Rafe, I'm safe."

Prob'ly that was true. These days Goose's da was Meister of the Brewers' Guild. Near to all the back yard of his City house in Brewers' Corner was taken up with a hops-oven and a malting hut and the smelly vats where he made his homebrew beer. Breathing at Goose's house was like swimming in the stuff, yeasty and eye-tickling. He always went home from Goose's smelling like an alehouse, so Mama made him wash even when he was still clean.

Goose held out one bottle. "Drink up."

He took it. There was a little gleam in Goose's eye, as though he knew this was a kind of dare. As though he knew he could make up for losing another pony race. Ha. Rafel unstopped the bottle with his teeth, spat out the spongewood stopper and tipped his head back. Beer swilled, blood-warm and heady, over his tongue and down his parched throat. The taste was strong and earthy, a punch to his belly. A rush to his head. It didn't taste anything like the beer Da liked to drink.

"Good, eh?" said Goose, smacking his lips. He'd been raised on beer, and ale, and watered-down wine. He was going to be a brewer when he was a man growed. Not because his da said he had to, though he did, but because he wanted it.

And what'll I be? I don't know. I want to be an explorer, 'cept there ain't nowt left to explore in Lur. And we can't get past the reef and there ain't no more going over the mountains, so that doesn't leave me much save Council work, and who wants that? I don't.

"Keep drinking," said Goose, not noticing. "You let beer sit too long, all the bubbles burst. You shouldn't let it sit too long once you've unstopped it, Rafe. All the goodness is in the bubbles."

He gave Goose a sideways look. "Practising to be Guildmeister, are you?"

Goose shrugged. "No. It's just you got to drink beer proper, Rafe. You got to respect it."

Respect it? It was *beer.* But there was Goose looking to get all hot and bothered, so he shrugged and swallowed another mouthful. Didn't want Goose thinking he was a girl, did he? It tasted even better this time. He swallowed again. Burped. Laughed.

Goose was eyeing his own bottle sadly. He'd nearly drained it dry. "Should've brought more."

He nodded, grinning. This was good beer. Worth its gold medal. "Aye."

"I will, next time," said Goose, slumping his chin to his chest. "Two each. Dad won't notice. He never notices what I do. He says I won't be interesting till I'm old enough to shave."

Rafel pulled a face. Poor ole Goose. Still, the beer was good. Swallow by swallow, his stolen bottle emptied.

Below their dangling bare feet, gaddies chased away the dragonflies and whizzed in dizzy circles above the riverpond's quiet surface. A stir, a splash, and a fat silver-scaled carp hurtled into the air and swallowed a mouthful of gauzy wings. Goose hooted again, finger waving. "Lookee that! Lookee!"

Goose was tall and gangly for ten, lots of space in him to fill out. His da was a big man, and he'd be big too. So it always seemed funny, that he could giggle like a girl. Like Deenie and Uncle Pellen's Charis when they played silly dolls together.

Rafel snatched a handful of grass and threw it at him, haphazard. "It's a fish, Goose. You ain't seen fish before?"

"Sure I seen fish," said Goose. "But these are *funny* fish, Rafe."

Beneath the riverpond's surface more silver carp thrashed and jostled. The water seethed . . . then fell silent.

"Oh," said Goose, disappointed. "Where'd they go?"

"Somewhere," he said, and tipped the last of the warm beer between his teeth. In his head a warm buzz, like the droning of summer bees. Like Doranen magic. "Want 'em back, do you?"

Goose tip-tilted his own beer bottle, gurgling the dregs. "Yes, but they're gone."

Poor Goose. His da hardly noticed him and his pony wasn't Dinglesbred. It'd never run faster than Stag, not even if it had two extra legs. Rafel tossed aside his emptied purloined beer bottle then tugged the folded parchment out from under his shirt.

"Here," he said, flipping it to Goose. "Mind that. No peeking."

Goose fumbled the catch. "What is it?" he said, picking up Tollin's scroll from the grass.

"A surprise, for later," he answered, then scrunched himself right to the edge of the riverbank. Slid a little further, then dropped down into Dragoneye Pond.

"Rafel!" said Goose, his voice squeaking. "Rafe, don't be daft! Don't go in there. You want to drown?"

"I ain't going to drown," he said, the cool water lapping at his leather belt. Cutting him in half. Beneath his bare feet sludge squished and pebbles bruised. "I could swim before I could walk." Well, almost. Near enough. Him and Deenie both weren't frighted of the water, Da had made certain sure of that. They'd even been swimming in the ocean, down on the coast. "But don't you try it, Goose," he added, and jabbed a pointed, warning finger. "You're a City Olken through and through. *You'd* be drownded in no time."

"Aw, come on, Rafe, come up from there," Goose begged. "What if you slip? What if I can't pull you out?"

"Tosh," he said. That was one of ole Darran's little words. *Tosh*. It meant, don't be a doddlehead. Saying it, remembering, he felt a sharp sting of pain. But just as quick he squashed it hard like a bed bug, because fretting on Darran wouldn't bring him back to life.

"Rafe," said Goose. He was almost wailing. Stretching the sound long, like a piece of string. Gangly tall Goose-egg, all fratched and frighted. *Tosh*.

Ignoring him, Rafel rested his gaze on the riverpond's sun-sparkled surface. The darting gaddies had darted away. He could see the blue sky reflected, and skittish lamb-clouds. He could see his own face. Rafel of Dorana, the hero Asher's only son. There was Da in there, and Mama. Bits and pieces of folk he'd never know. He was in there. They were his eyes.

That's my face. That's me. But who's me?

In his blood there was beer, its bubbles bursting. In his blood there was power, that could crack stones and whirl leaves and do all kinds of things. That could unpick magic locks he'd never come across before. Because of his power he felt oddness in the earth, just like Da.

A mage. That's who I am. That's what I want to be.

With his mage eyes he looked deep into the pond. Saw the fish. Saw right into them, and felt their little lives. Then he looked into his thudding heart. Into his blood, which held his magic.

If Da finds out what I've been up to, there'll be so much trouble. Da hates his magic, so I have to miss out.

Hot crossness prickled him. He was tired of missing out. Tired of being a secret. Goose knew a little bit, but he didn't know it all. He trusted his friend like he trusted his own hand, or his foot, but it was safer that way.

"Goose," he said, not looking up. "If I show you something, you have to promise not to tell."

"I promise," said Goose. "Show me what? Rafe, what's going on?"

"Hush up," he said dreamily. "I need to think."

"Rafe!" said Goose, close to wailing again. "You're making me nervous. Come out of there. Please?"

He shook his head, grinning. "No. Just you watch this."

"Watch *what?*" said Goose. "Rafe, what are you *doing?*"

Instead of answering, he dabbled his fingers across the riverpond's sleeping surface. "Come on, little fishies," he crooned under his breath. "You ain't going to hide from Goosie, are you? Come on. You come back now. Rafel says come back."

The stolen beer was all swallowed, but he could still taste it on his tongue. He could feel it in his belly, warm and sloshing. He could feel it in his head, softly buzzing. He could feel his magic buzzing, the way it sang without words, sang a tune only he could hear. The rest of the world was deaf. Da was deaf.

Da doesn't want to hear.

One by one Goosie's little fishes came back.

Doing his lessons with Meister Rumly, he was made to keep so calm. So tame. Little bits of Olken magic. Teeny tiny drips. *Never* anything else. Even when he broke the rules on his lonesome, cracking stones, dancing leaves, all that silliness in his bath, the spells he pinched from Arlin, he was always careful not to do too much, only a smidgin bit, in case someone noticed. In case Da felt it and came storming to find him.

But this was his free day and Goose's stolen beer was in him, and Da was a long ways away back in the City. He felt big and restless. Bold and reckless. He'd undone a magic lock. That was something, that was. Sink him sideways, he wanted to *play.* He wanted to show someone what he could do. And why shouldn't he? After all, this was Olken magic and he was Olken. He wasn't doing anything wrong. So he called the Gant's fat silver carp, enticed them from their shadows, enticed them to the shallows, and made them leap for joy. This was Darran's story of the Sea Harvest singing. How many times had he heard that story? How often had he seen that seething harbour in his head?

"Lookee! Lookee!" Goose was shouting, his face flushed with beer and delight. "Look at them fishes dance! Woo hoo! Woo hoo!" Then he faltered, and stopped his bouncing on the riverbank. "Rafe, is that you doing that?"

Words were a nuisance. He didn't want to speak. So he flapped a hand at Goose, glaring, saying *aye* and *shut up* and *leave me be* all at once.

Goose's eyes bloomed round, like two new-minted trins. *"Rafe,* I never knew you could do magic like *that.* How are you doing it? Can you show me?"

He wasn't sure he could. There weren't any words, he was just—just *feeling* it, feeling the fish in the water, feeling their fins and their tails, feeling the silver wriggle of them leaping into the warm almost-spring air. He wanted them to dance for Goose, so they were dancing. It was as simple and as terrible as that.

Why doesn't Da want this? This is—this is grand.

The silver carp leapt. The riverpond seethed. Like his bathwater in its tub it started foaming into shapes, barking dogs and prancing ponies. Barl's Mountains, towering high. He could feel his magic burning, churning, the beer bubbles in his blood turning bright gold.

"Rafe..."

"What?"

Goose wasn't laughing now. He'd stopped his bouncing, and his fingers clutched his knees. "Rafel, maybe you should stop," he said, sounding nervous. "You know you're not s'posed to."

Impatient, he pulled a face. "You weren't s'posed to steal that beer, but you did."

"That's beer," said Goose. "That's not magic. Rafe, you better stop."

"Quit fratching at me," he said, hardly paying attention. "You've seen me do magic before."

"Not like this, Rafe," said Goose, as the riverpond boiled silver and fat fish leapt over Barl's watery Mountains. "Come on—you should stop—Rafe—"

Rafel flashed his friend a grin. "Tosh to you, Goose-egg. I'm fine. Don't witter."

Splashing and leaping, the riverpond's carp obeyed his eager summons. The magicked water sloshed around him, surging into his face. Soaking his blue cotton shirt, his close-cropped hair, running rivulets down his cheeks, like tears. But he wasn't weeping, oh no. He was laughing. *Laughing.*

And then he shouted as something ripped through the air. Ripped through the earth and the sludge between his toes. He sucked in a shocked breath, sucked in pondwater with it. Stale and stagnant, it drowned the sweet taste of Goose's pilfered beer. The sweeter taste of magic, burning in his blood. The leaping fish fell and didn't leap again. He felt them flee to the pond's shadows, released from his spell.

"Rafe!" Goose yelled. "Rafe, what's wrong?"

Bewildered, knocked sideways, he lost his footing and plunged to his knees. The riverpond's water closed over his head. His eyes were open but he couldn't see. His mouth was open but he couldn't scream, though he wanted to. He couldn't breathe, neither. Everything felt *wrong*. His head was spinning. The earth and air of Lur were in *pain*.

Da—Da—help me, Da!

He flailed his way to the riverpond's surface, a silver carp called Rafel leaping for the sun.

"Rafe! Rafe! Grab my hand here, Rafe!"

That was Goose, with his voice like crying. He was face-down on the riverbank, his arm stretched out and his fingers reaching. He couldn't swim. He was a City Olken. Bloody useless, the lot of 'em. That's what Da muttered on the days he missed the coast, when he'd been cooped up in Justice Hall telling people what to do. As everything spun about behind his eyes, the pain in the earth and air a pain in him, too, Rafel plunged towards Goose's hand and anchored himself there, finger to finger.

"I got you!" Goose panted, helping him scramble up the grassy bank. "I got you, Rafe! Don't let go! I got you!"

Escaped from the stinking riverpond, Rafel crawled to the top of the bank, abandoned Goose's hand and spewed up every last mouthful of beer and water he'd sucked down. He could feel Goose beside him, all fretted and cross.

"I told you, Rafe. Didn't I? I told you to stop! Rafe? Rafe! Say something! Rafe! Are you drowned?"

His belly emptied, his mouth foul, he rolled onto his back and squinted at the sun. His shirt and trews clung soggy to his flesh. And now that he could think straight he could feel that itching skritching under his soaked skin. Horrible. But the screaming pain from the earth and sky was fading, like a dream. That was something, any road. He needed that to go away.

Blinking, he looked at his friend. Goose was on his feet now, hovering. "How can I be drownded, Goose? Ain't I just puked out my guts?"

"Rafe!" Goose's eyes were so wide they looked near to popping from his skull and his face was pasty pale, like he wanted to puke too. "You should've stopped when I said. Didn't I say stop?"

Goose was a funny one. All bold and beer stealing one minute, fretting himself ragged the next.

"Pie-face to it, Goose," he said. "Stop wittering at me."

"I ain't *wittering*," said Goose, offended. "You nearly drowned, Rafe. What *happened?* Did you—did your magic do that?"

He'd promised Da not to talk on this, but how could he stay silent now? Goose was here, he'd seen it. He had to explain. And any road, Goose already knew his biggest secret, about him having Doranen magic.

"I won't tell, Rafe," said Goose. "You know I won't."

Aye, he did, 'cause he and Goose swore the swear. Two years ago they did that. Another secret. He'd cracked a stone and they'd cut each other's hands. Mixed their blood and promised friends forever. Not magic. Not really. Just a promise, was all. A promise Goose had kept.

Besides. He was tired of this secret. It was like a hot coal in his head. Da wouldn't talk of it. Neither would Mama. *Wait till you're older.* But it was burning him *now.*

"Rafe?" Goose said, not wheedling, but worried. It felt good. Family cared 'cause they had to. Goose cared 'cause he *wanted* to. That made a difference, even if he wasn't sure why.

So I don't care if I ain't s'posed to talk on this. It's Goose. Not trusting Goose is like not trusting myself.

And he needed to talk on it. He needed someone to listen when the burning got too bad. Like now. Didn't Da used to have King Gar to talk to? And didn't he have Mama? And Uncle Pellen?

How is it fair, that he's got folk to talk to and I ain't s'posed to say a word?

Tucking his knees close to his chest, Rafel pulled a face. "It ain't my magic doing it, Goose."

"Then what is?"

"I don't know. Just... there's something wrong."

"What kind of wrong?" said Goose, his eyes all big and round again.

Goose's Olken magic gave him a good touch for growing things. Goose's da said that was what made a meister brewer, being able to sing the hops and croon the brewing. But did that mean he could feel the earth's pain, too?

"You ain't felt it?"

"I don't know," Goose said cautiously. "What did you feel?"

It was hard to say out loud. Made him all skritched again, hot and tickly under his skin. *I ain't frighted. I ain't.* "Like the ground hurts. Like the air's crying."

"I ain't never felt that," Goose whispered, shocked. "What is it, Rafe? Is it Doranen magic gone wrong?"

He dug his fingers into the riverbank grass, tugging. "D'know. Might be."

A little bit of silence, while Goose thought on that. Grazing close by, Stag stamped at the droning flies. The river slapped itself against the bridge. A louder bang, as a floating tree branch smacked it. Yonder, along the distant City Road, a carriage-horn tooted. Its music was a faint sound blown on the breeze. The warm air sang of summer, coming.

"You told your dad?" Goose said at last. "You should tell your dad."

"He knows." Rafel tugged more grass free. Smelled the crushed green stems and the spring-damp soil. Felt his clammy shirt drying sticky on his back. "But he won't say what's what."

"Why not?" Goose hesitated, breath hitching. "Not 'cause he don't—"

"No," he said quickly. "Course not. My da knows everything. Just—he reckons I don't need telling."

"Well, that ain't fair," said loyal Goose. "You can feel it. He should say."

"Aye," he said, nodding. "But he won't. And I can't make him tell me, Goose."

Goose sighed. "Being a sprat's hard." His face crumpled a bit, and his bottom lip wobbled. "What do you think, Rafe? Why's the ground hurting? What's making the air cry? I wish you'd tell me. I really want to know."

CHAPTER SEVEN

✠

Rafel swallowed. Goose sounded so frighted he was sorry he'd said anything. Sorry he'd made the fishes dance, and the riverpond make shapes, and told his friend his burning coal secret. "I don't know. Prob'ly it's nowt, Goose. Prob'ly I'm being a girl."

"Prob'ly," said Goose, and tried to laugh. But it didn't work. He tugged some grass, too, and stared down the sloping riverbank to where Stag and his pony stood in the meadow side by side, rump to nose, dozing and swishing each other's biting flies.

Just like us. Best friends.

"Rafe..." Goose whispered. Still staring someplace else. "What you felt. It's real, isn't it?"

He nodded. "Aye."

"And—and it means Lur's in trouble?"

For the first time ever, he was sorry he could feel things. "I ain't sure, Goose. Prob'ly."

"You frighted?" said Goose, letting his tugged grass slip through his fingers.

"No!"

Goose rubbed his eyes. "Me too."

"I ain't!" he insisted, and banged a fist on his knee. "Ain't nowt to be frighted on. My da, he'll fix it. That's what he does."

"I could help," said Goose, almost a whisper. "I could try feeling it. If you want, Rafe. Then we could—"

Rafel scrambled to his feet. "No, Goose. Don't you dare. You might do yourself a mischief."

"You don't have to say that," said Goose, glaring up at him. "You don't have to be like that. I know I can't crack stones, like you can, or make fish jump into the air just by thinking. But I've got magic, Rafe. I can do things. I can—"

"*No!*" he said again. *Sink me, if I get Goose hurt…*"I told you, Goose. It feels bad. You'd hate it. *I* hate it. I wish—" But he didn't want to say that. "You might feel it one day, Goose. By chance. When you're doing your own magics. But don't you go looking for it. Reckon that'd get us both walloped, if my da or yours found out."

Goose sighed. He almost always gave in when they fratched. "Don't bite, Rafe. I only wanted to help."

"I know." Then he frowned. "Goose, if you want to help, swear you won't tell anyone about this. Not ever."

"I swear," said Goose. "But are you going to tell your parents?"

"I have to," he said, nodding. "I promised. Only—not all of it. I won't tell them you know. That's got to be our secret."

"Our secret," said Goose, all solemn. "I swear."

Relieved, he flopped himself back onto the riverbank. "And I swear I'll never tell about the beer."

Fizzy with relief, they grinned at each other.

"Hey," said Goose, and again dug his fingers inside his leather jerkin. Pulled out the lumpily folded parchment he'd been safekeeping. "Want this back?"

Tollin's adventures! He'd clean forgotten, what with the earth crying out and nearly getting himself drownded. "Thanks."

"What is it?" said Goose with a wicked snicker. "A love letter from Charis?"

Ever since he once saw Uncle Pellen's Charis making google-eyes at him, Goose thought it was funny to niggle on it. Rafel used his Doranen magic to push his friend flat on his back.

Take that! "No. It ain't."

Goose howled in protest, kicking at the sky. Then he sat up. "So what is it?"

Finished unfolding the parchment, he laid it flat on the grass and smoothed out its wrinkles, gently. There was prob'ly Doranen magic to make it good as new, but he didn't know it. He would one day, though. One day he'd know it all.

He looked up. "It's the story of what Tollin and the others found when they crossed over the mountains."

Goose's mouth dropped open. "It never is!"

"Is too."

"Where did you get it?" Goose breathed.

He almost told. Almost. The boasting words were tickling the tip of his tongue. But then he swallowed them. "Best I don't tell you, Goose," he said, his sly smile dying. "Not 'cause I don't trust you!" he added quickly, as Goose's face fell. "It's just ... best you don't know."

Goose's eyes opened so wide he looked like a string-puppet. "Oh, Rafel. What did you do?" He swallowed. "Something ... Doranen?"

He stared at the uncrumpled parchment spread on the grass, feeling the fizzy triumph of breaking Da's lock. Feeling the stir behind his eyes where his Doranen magic lived. He wanted to tell Goose so bad ...

'Cept I can't. Ain't nobody meant to know about that trunk and what's in it. That's Da's secret. It ain't mine to tell.

"It doesn't matter," he said. "What counts is I found the parchment. And I'll read it to you, only —"

"Rafel," said Goose solemnly, "I won't never, ever tell. Not ever. Not even if Arlin Garrick pokes me full of pins."

He scowled. Arlin Garrick was the kind of Doranen who'd do worse than poke pins if he thought he could get away with it. "You better not, Goose. This has to be just ours."

"It will be!" said Goose. "Catch me telling Arlin Garrick anything."

True. They might go to the same City school, him and Goose and Arlin Garrick and the other Doranen boys, but that didn't mean nowt.

Didn't mean they had to *like* each other. *Which is good. 'Cause we don't.* He'd never pinch spells from a boy he liked.

"So what's it say?" said Goose eagerly, nudging the parchment. "Start reading. And when you're done, we can be explorers!"

Being explorers was one of their favourite games. "You still want to do that?" he said, leaving the parchment where it was. "When you're growed up? Ain't you going to be a brewer, like your da?"

"No law says I can't be both," said Goose. Then he grinned. "When I'm growed up I'll brew the best beer and ale in Lur and take it over the mountains to sell. I'll be the richest brewer in Lur, I will. No, I'll be the richest Olken in Lur. The richest *man* in Lur. That'll be me. I'll be so rich, that Arlin Garrick, he'll have to bow when I ride by."

"Ha!" he said. "Only way you'll get Arlin Garrick to bend in the middle is if you kick him in the chestnuts."

Goose's grin got wider. "I could do that, too. Wearing boots made of solid gold."

The thought was so naughty they crowed and rolled around on the grass for a bit. Their amusement startled the ponies, and that made them laugh even harder. But the laughter dribbled dry eventually, until it was just them sprawling silent under the warm sun. Slowly but surely, the fear of what he'd felt faded.

"So go on, then," said Goose, breaking the hush. "Read it. 'Cause I want to know what really happened to Tollin and the others. I want to know why most likely I never will get to sell my beer and ale on the other side of the mountains."

His clothes gently steaming, his damp hair full of grass, Rafel reached for the stolen parchment. Held it up between his face and the sky, so he wasn't squinting into the sun.

And started reading.

Tired of waiting for the kettle to boil a second time, Pellen Orrick was sorely tempted to ask Asher if he'd stir the water along. Just a bit. But he refrained, because asking Asher for a frivolous use of his magic would do nothing to sweeten his friend's sour mood. Three hours this morning, they'd spent, he and Asher and Dathne, thrashing through the dangers that may or may not lie in wait for the kingdom, reaching no firm conclusions or decisions, certain of only one thing: that should the worst come to pass then surely every man, woman and child in Lur—Doranen as well as Olken—would look to Asher of Restharven for rescue.

And is he sour because he resents the assumption... or because he knows he has no hope of saving us?

He'd not asked the question, though it did crowd his thoughts. He was ashamed of himself for thinking it. Ashamed that despite knowing what he knew, knowing the sacrifices Asher had already made, he could even consider asking for more. And perhaps, if he only had himself to worry about, he wouldn't be ready to ask. Wouldn't have the thought in his head at all.

But I'm a father now, and that makes the difference. There's nothing I won't do to see Charis kept safe.

Once he'd believed his devotion to Dorana City, and to Lur, was the fiercest thing he would ever feel. And now he knew that devotion was water-weak compared with the fury that rose in him at the thought of harm coming to his only child.

The kettle boiled, at last. But as he poured the steaming water into the second teapot, refreshments for his newly arrived guests, he heard Asher suck in a sharp, pained breath—and looked up.

"What? Asher, what's amiss?"

Stood by the kitchen window, brooding through the open curtains at Ibby's run-to-seed garden, Asher shook his head and pinched the bridge of his nose between tight thumb and forefinger. A grunt of discomfort escaped him, and he hunched over a little as though tormented by a belly-gripe.

Pellen put down the kettle. "Asher, are you sick? Should I call for—"

"Asher," said Dathne, hurrying into the kitchen from the parlour, where she'd been talking with those four members of the old Olken Circle who'd travelled to Dorana circumspect to meet with them. "Did you feel that?"

Asher nodded, his eyes slitted against whatever ailed him. "Aye. Nasty."

"We all felt it," said Dathne. "Asher—"

Pellen raised a hand. "I didn't feel a thing. Are you talking about—"

"Aye," said Asher. "What I told you in the stable yard. That wrongness in the earth. It's back."

"Oh."

Sometimes, over the years, as he watched his fellow-Olken discover their long-buried powers, watched them revel in Olken magic, he'd felt a pang that their joy was denied him. Not often. Just sometimes. But now, with Asher and Dathne so clearly distressed, he found himself grateful that magic, for him, was little more than a fizzle. He'd lived for years without it quite happily. He didn't need it to make him a whole man.

Dathne gnawed at her bottom lip. "Rafel, Asher. Do you think he—"

"Prob'ly," said Asher. "He's felt it othertimes. We'll ask him at supper."

He blinked in surprise. *Rafel* could feel whatever was going on, too? Asher had kept that quiet. But Rafe was just a boy, barely tutored in magic. And if *he* could feel it...

Charis's night-terrors. What if I'm wrong? What if it's not Ibby she's missing after all? What if—

With an effort he strangled his leaping imagination. If he wasn't careful he'd smother his daughter. Little ones had bad dreams. No need to alarm himself into conniptions.

"At supper?" said Dathne. "I'd rather ask him now." Fretting, she wrapped her arms about her narrow ribs. "But we've let him romp off on his pony for the day, without a care in the world. I hope he's all right. If this is going to keep happening, if we can't know when or where this feeling will strike, he might not be safe. Asher—"

"Hush," said Asher, and pulled her to him. "Can't keep Rafe cooped up in the Tower, Dath. Can't stop him racin' about the countryside with his friends. He's a boy. He's got to *be* a boy."

She tugged free of his embrace. "But he's not just a boy, is he? Not an ordinary boy, at any rate."

"He is for now," said Asher, insistent. "He is so long as we don't start treatin' him different."

"He *is* different, Asher!" Dathne retorted. "And you not wanting it to be so doesn't change a thing."

Asher's face darkened. "He's only different if we let him be, Dath. Only if we think on him that way. And I won't do it. I ain't about to ruin his spratlin' days with fuss and malarkey and makin' him feel that he ain't like his friends. Pushing him to do magic that he ain't ready for. That he don't need."

A reluctant eavesdropper, Pellen looked away. There was such pain in Asher's voice. Nothing to do with whatever trouble threatened Lur, and everything to do with being Rafel's father. Pain in Dathne too, and fear. So much of it they'd forgotten where they were. That he was listening. But what did they mean about their son being different? This was the first he'd heard of it . . .

His guardsman curiosity reprehensibly piqued, he cleared his throat. "Ah — friends —"

Startled out of acrimony, they stared at him. Then they exchanged mutely horrified looks. Asher, his discomfited dismay forgotten, cleared his throat.

"Pellen —"

And suddenly he was ashamed again. He had no right to expect confidences. After all, he'd not told them about Charis, had he? "Never mind," he said. "No explanation's needed. Family business is family business."

"It ain't that we don't trust you," said Asher, suddenly awkward. "You know better than that. It's complicated, is all."

"But we will explain," Dathne added. "We never meant to keep it from you forever. As Asher says — it's complicated."

Their assurances warmed him. In the wrenching aftermath of Ibby's loss, ill-equipped to deal with grief and a baby and every grand dream smashed to jagged pieces, he knew he'd been in danger of foundering completely. Dathne and Asher had eased him. Sheltered him. Saved him, in truth, from too much strong drink and silence.

He shrugged. "When you're ready. Let's leap one hurdle at a time, eh? I'm not as spry as I used to be."

He'd long since come to terms with the loss of his leg. But Asher never had, and seeing him wince at the joke was a jabbing reminder of that. *Fool.*

"So, what you both just felt," he said hastily, with a glance towards the parlour. "You and those Circle folk in there. You're sure it's more of the same trouble?"

"Yes," said Dathne, nodding. "And whatever it is, I fear it's getting worse."

"But why is it happening at all? That's the question we've yet to answer."

"You want to hold the rest of our meetin' in here?" said Asher. "Only I don't reckon this kitchen of yours be big enough for us and them Circle folk too, Meister Mayor."

"You're right, it's not," he said. "So let's go through to the parlour and get started. I want this problem nipped in the bud. I've enough on my mayoral plate as it is. I don't need more headaches."

"You might not need 'em, but you've got 'em, I reckon," said Asher. "Now, you done makin' that tea like an ole besom?"

He was deeply worried, but still he had to smile. In a life full of upheaval one star remained constant: Asher was Asher, and would surely be himself without fear or favour until the end of his days.

"Besom yourself," he retorted mildly. "I could use another pair of hands."

He and Asher carried the brewed tea into the parlour, with Dathne bringing the tray of cups, milk, sugar and biscuits. They might well be here to discuss death and destruction but there was no reason to do it parched, or on an empty stomach.

The four summoned former Circle members sat eggshell-anxious in his parlour. Two women and two men, only one of them younger than fifty, and all of them schooled in the mysteries of Olken magic. Sensitive, as Asher and Dathne and now, it seemed, Rafel—and maybe

Charis — were sensitive to the subtle shiftings beneath Lur's placid, well-ordered surface.

"You know I can't feel this trouble," he said, helping Dathne to hand round steaming cups of tea, "but I don't doubt it's real. What we must decide, here and now, is what's to be done about it."

"If anything *can* be done," said Polly Marsh from Wynford, on the far side of the Saffron Hills. Plump as an apple puff, surprisingly dressed in baggy trews and even baggier shirt, with her salty dark hair clipped boyish short, she stirred three spoonfuls of sugar into her tea. "For it seems to me we're at the mercy of chance. We had no warning that the earth was troubled. And there's no hint of what's causing it. We're in the dark."

"Polly's right," said the man beside her on the couch. Beale Lafton, who'd travelled the furthest to be here. All the way from Tamwold, he'd come, right close to the coast, near Salting Town. His hair and beard were silvered through, his face as crumpled as an old linen kerchief. But despite his great age his voice was energetic, his manner brisk. "Whatever's stirring in this kingdom now, I fear we're powerless to stop it."

"Nonsense," snapped Dathne, and dropped onto a footstool. "What kind of thinking is that, Beale?"

Beale eyed her narrowly from beneath extravagantly bushy brows. "The kind that comes from reading the earth for more than sixty years, young lady."

"I don't disagree this is — uncomfortable, Beale," Dathne said, colour washing her sharp cheeks. "But to call ourselves *powerless?* That's giving up before we've even started."

"And what would you have us do, Dathne?" Jinny of Hooten Creek asked softly, her blind, gentle eyes darting side to side. She'd lost her sight during the battle with Morg, when the Circle's binding link with Veira was severed. "We Olken might have our magic restored to us, but it's no more than it ever was. We can't bully nature. We can't dominate with our powers, like the Doranen."

Pellen, content to stand by the parlour's cold fireplace and observe, watched Dathne flick a glance at Asher. He was perched on the edge of the room's deepest windowsill, arms broodingly folded, his rough-hewn face set in that familiar, defensive scowl.

"I know that, Jinny," Dathne said. "I'm not suggesting we try."

"Then why send for us?" demanded Fernel Pintte, quarrelsome. Youngest of the four, somewhere in his thirties, and smoothly handsome. Nothing gentle about him, his manner was impatient and curt. "We dropped our lives and came running to you, Dathne, out of respect for who you once were. But—"

"Who she still is," said Asher, stirring. "Jervale's Heir. Mind your tone there, Fernel. Ain't got much patience with them as disrespect my wife."

Fernel put his cup down on the wooden arm of his chair. Some of his easy belligerence faded, and a wary look crept into his eyes. "There's no disrespect here, Asher. I'm puzzled." He glanced around at the other Circle members. "We're all puzzled. And I think we're owed an explanation for why we've been summoned."

"You're here to tell us what, if anything, you feel," said Dathne. "And when you started feeling it. You're here so we can work our way through what these stirrings mean, and how we can protect Lur if indeed it is in danger again so soon after Morg."

Knowing that Asher and Dathne depended on his silent scrutiny, Pellen kept watching closely. Saw that dreaded name stab the Circle members. They breathed deeply, quivering, and briefly looked away.

"Of all the Circle that's left now," Dathne added, "you four are the strongest. You have the keenest senses, the sharpest intuitions. Between us, you four and me and Asher, I'm certain we can unravel this mystery."

"And if we do unravel it?" said Polly, hands clasped to hide their trembling. "What then? Jinny's right. We can't forge new chains for Lur."

"Not without making bargains with the Doranen," added Fernel. "Is that what you're thinking, Dathne? That we dance that sorry dance again?"

"That *sorry dance* saved us from Morg and his domination," said Dathne, annoyed. "Remember?"

"What I remember is living twenty years of my life in terror of being discovered," Fernel retorted. His narrow face pinched cold, and he reached for his tea-cup again as though he needed to hold on to something warm. "I remember twenty years of secrets and lies, of holding my breath every time I crossed paths with a Doranen, certain they'd sense the magic in me and cry *traitor*. I remember hearing of Timon Spake's execution and weeping at the thought his death could be mine."

On the outskirts, on the windowsill, Asher stirred. "Timon Spake's dead and buried. You ain't here to talk on him."

Pellen, with his own memories, met Asher's bleak gaze. Saw in his friend's face a reflection of his own sickness, his own memories, never quite overcome or forgotten.

"We were all of us afraid, Fernel," said Polly, and reached over to the armchair to pat his white-knuckled hand. "But it does no good to dwell. The bad times are behind us." She sighed. "At least, those bad times are."

Dathne, on the low footstool, rested her elbows on her knees and propped her chin in her hands. "Fernel, I don't know how to answer you. It could be that whatever is wrong can only be put right by the Olken and the Doranen melding their magics again. I hope that's not so. I want to look forward, not back. You think I can't see how fraught with dangers such a choice would be?"

"Do they know?" said Beale. "About these... shiftings?"

Dathne shook her head. "I'm sure they don't. We've said nothing to the Doranen on the General Council. Or the Mage Council. Nothing to any Doranen we know. And nothing has been said to us. But I think it's only a matter of time before they realise — or learn — that something's brewing. Our two peoples may still live mostly separate lives, but if what we're feeling grows any stronger —"

"If it begins to reveal itself, you mean?" said blind Jinny. "If something odd starts to happen with the — the weather?"

And with that one word, all eyes turned to Asher.

"Ain't no call to think it'll come to that," he said flatly. "Ten years without WeatherWorking we've had, ain't we, and the rain's come as needful. Snow and ice in winter, enough for the icewine vineyards and pond skating, but not so much folk find 'emselves buried. There's food aplenty, no threat of famine. I don't reckon there's cause to start thinkin' that'll change."

He sounded confident but Pellen saw something flicker between him and Dathne. Some misgiving, unshared. He knew them too well. His belly tightened, and his throat.

Lie to them if you must, but you'll not lie to me. When we're done with these four the three of us will keep talking.

"Asher's right," said Dathne, her chin lifted in the way that dared anyone to contradict. "This isn't about the weather. Let's not fright ourselves for no reason."

"Then what is it about?" said Jinny. Her blinded brown eyes were wide open, as though she could see things the rest of them were denied. "What is causing the earth's disquiet?"

"And are we going to tell the Doranen?" Fernel added. "Before the earth does the telling for us, and we're accused of dreadful things?"

Like thunder on the horizon, the memory of fear teased the air. Ten years in the open wasn't a long time, not after six hard centuries of secrecy.

"It ain't your concern, Fernel, what they're told and when," said Asher. "That's for me and Pellen to decide, seeing as how he's Mayor of Dorana and we both be on the Mage Council."

"Not my concern?" Fernel laughed, unpleasant. "Don't be a fool, Asher. It's every Olken's concern. Until the day comes when the last Doranen leaves our land we've got to live with them. We've got to live with their magic, which overpowered ours once and easily could again."

"No, it can't," said Dathne. "There are laws, Fernel, binding laws that keep us safe. And doesn't Asher preside over Justice Hall, to make certain?"

"I feel Fernel's not so misguided, to worry," said Beale, gnarled fingers kneading at the arm of his couch. "It's their own goodwill that keeps the Doranen bound to decency, not any fear of reprisals from us.

They know we have none. Nor have we any guarantee that their decency will last."

"You bloody have, y'know," said Asher. "You got *me*. Reckon I'll sit idle if a Doranen tries any funny business on one of us? Took care of that bloody Ain Freidin, didn't I? Trust me, I ain't forgot what I learned killin' Morg. And I'll use it quick as a fly's fart if any Doranen breaks them laws we all agreed to."

"And if they decide that us keeping secrets from them is a breach of law?" countered Polly. "What then?"

"Ain't said we will keep it secret, Polly," said Asher, almost snapping. "But I don't see any use flappin' our lips till we know what we be flappin' about. Do you?"

Polly's round cheeks tinted deep pink. "I'm sure there's no need to be rude, Asher."

He threw up his hands. "I ain't *rude*. Why do folk always bleat that I'm *rude?* I'm just *sayin'*—"

"Perhaps a smidgin forcefully," said Pellen, swallowing a bark of laughter. Asher's lack of tact and his genuine bewilderment never failed to amuse. "Though I think the point is fair." He nodded at Polly, letting her see his sympathy. "I understand your concern, madam, but after ten years as Dorana's mayor, rubbing shoulders with the Doranen every day, I can promise you they'll not take kindly to us talking about any kind of magical trouble without proof or a reasonable explanation."

"They can hardly bring themselves to admit that what we have and do *is* magic," said Dathne sourly. Then she shrugged. "I suppose it's not surprising. Compared to them we're glowing coals to their bonfires."

Fernel snorted. "We're subtle. They're brash. It's not the same thing. Shame on you, Dathne, for disparaging your own people."

"She ain't disparagin' anyone," said Asher, a dangerous edge to his voice. "Fernel, what be your problem? Eh? Mayhap you and I should step outside and talk on it private, like."

"You'll do nothing of the sort!" said Dathne, leaping to her feet. "I don't need you thumping Fernel or anyone else on my behalf. Fernel—"

"I speak my mind," Fernel retorted. "It's not my fault if you don't care for what I —"

"Please, let's not fight," said Jinny, a little breathless with distress. "We've gathered here to talk of Lur's troubles, not start new battles amongst ourselves."

Pellen cleared his throat. "She's right. Would you have me pull out my old Captain's uniform and play City Guard beneath my own roof? Asher?"

"No," Asher muttered.

"No," said Fernel, his jaw tight with temper.

"Then *leave be*," he said firmly. "*Both* of you. We've plenty to talk about without reopening old wounds, be they Timon Spake's death or what life was like as a Circle member or what the Doranen did hundreds of years before we were born. None of that matters. All that matters is *now*."

Asher and Fernal looked at each other, tomcat unfriendly, but held their tongues.

Letting out a sharp breath, Dathne dropped again to her footstool then nodded at Polly. "You go first. Tell us what you've been feeling in the earth."

Taken aback, Polly shifted a little beside Beale, plump fingers fluttering to the pale pink stone hung on a chain about her neck. "I don't know," she said, almost whispering. "It's hard to explain." Then she half-laughed, half-sighed. "You'll think I'm just a foolish old woman."

"No, we won't," said Dathne, leaning forward. "I asked you here to share your impressions, Polly." She swept her sharp gaze across everyone's face. "Nobody will mock you, no matter what you say."

Polly's fingers tightened on her pink stone pendant. "The only way I can describe it is to say ... it feels to me as though the flowers are crying."

"The *flowers?*" said Fernel. "Oh come now, Polly. How can flowers —"

"I don't know!" Polly cried, turning on him. "I told you it would sound silly. But I'm a gardener, growing things is my gift, and I tell you that when I'm planting seeds or tending bulbs, when I'm pruning or weeding or watering, I'm one with the earth and the flowers are *crying!*"

Beale took her hand and gave it a small, reassuring shake. "It's all right, Polly. We believe you."

"What about you, Beale?" said Dathne. "What have you been feeling?"

The old man sat silent for a time, holding Polly's hand. Then he stirred, and let his eyelids droop half-closed. "When the Wall fell," he said, his voice a hairsbreadth from trembling, "it was a dreadful shock. The air itself was torn and bleeding. The earth was bleeding, in my heart. But it healed. In time, it came to feel whole again. But lately . . . lately . . ."

"What?" Dathne whispered. "Beale, please. The truth now, no matter how difficult."

Beale opened his eyes. They were red-rimmed with unshed tears. "This will sound foolish and fanciful, just like Polly. But I imagine we're living inside an hourglass, Dathne. The sand is running out . . . *it's running out* . . . and I don't know why. I only know that when it *does* run out — may Jervale have mercy on this poor kingdom of ours."

Pellen shifted his gaze to Asher, and what he saw in his friend's face nearly stilled his heart. *He knows. He knows what Beale's talking about.* For a moment he was so angry it felt like he was breathing fire. Asher, sensing it, looked at him . . . and then looked away. Shadowed swiftly in his eyes, a shamefaced regret.

Dathne, caught up with Beale, hadn't noticed. "Please, Beale, don't fratch yourself," she said. "Whatever it means, I'm sure we'll be all right."

The old man nodded. "Yes. Yes." He managed a painful smile. "With the Innocent Mage to fight our battle, I've no doubt we'll prevail."

If the Innocent Mage agreed with him, he wasn't saying so. Asher's scowling face was shuttered tight. Unfathomable to anyone who didn't know him. But Pellen, who knew him so well, who had seen him in every extremity: rage and agony and despair and blinding grief, knew that what he saw now was fear.

Damn you, Asher. What do you know?

CHAPTER EIGHT

Y our turn, Jinny," said Dathne. Sweet, fragile Jinny of Hooten Creek
sighed, fingers pressing against her pale lips. They all looked at
her, expectant. It was held that those who'd lost their sight gained in
other ways. Would she prove it now?

"Jinny," said Asher. "It ain't easy to talk on, I know, but...can't one
of us hide from this, much as we want to."

Shoulders slumping, Jinny pinned her hands between her knees. "I
feel sick with nerves, all the time. As though I'm waiting for bad news.
As though a messenger is bringing it, and he's riding just out of sight.
Even when the sun feels hot on my face, underneath the heat there's a
bitter cold. *Dread.*" Her next breath caught in her throat. "That's what it
is. I feel dread."

"Dread," said Fernel. His scorn could've etched glass. "Crying flowers. Hourglasses. *Listen* to yourselves. If Veira were here she'd slap the
three of you silly. And she'd slap you too, Dathne, and you, Asher, for
encouraging them. The explanation for this unease is obvious, if only
you'd wake up from your dream."

"And what dream would that be, Fernel?" said Asher. Instead of belligerent, dangerously polite. Pellen saw Dathne brace herself, and felt
his own muscles tense.

Careful now, careful. Let's all of us keep our heads.

But either Fernel Pintte didn't know Asher well enough to take heed — or he didn't care. "The dream that tells you we can keep walking the road we're on without consequence." His hostile glare swept all their faces. "The earth is off-kilter. Doranen magic has been poisoning Lur for centuries. *I* fear our home is succumbing at last. I fear that if we don't put an end to the Doranen taint, our land will sicken until it *dies*."

"What do you mean, *put an end to the Doranen taint,*" said Dathne, staring at him. "They live here, Fernel."

"Only because we've not sent them away," Fernel retorted. "When the Wall was destroyed we should have told them to leave. Lur is not their home. It's *our* home, and they *stole* it. When the Wall was destroyed we should have taken it back."

Dathne was shaking her head. "And sent the Doranen *where?* Across the mountains? Thousands of them? All the mothers, with their babies? Children scarcely old enough to walk? The elderly and infirm too? Fernel, are you *mad?*"

"They came here over the mountains," said Fernel, his face red now. Ugly. "They could've left the same way. Or they could've taken boats and sailed off. Just so long as they left and never came back."

"Ain't no sailin' beyond Dragonteeth Reef," said Asher, watching the man carefully. "Every sprat in Lur knows that. Them sinkholes and whirlpools the dyin' Weather Magic left behind won't let any sized boat through to open water. Not even a dinghy. It's suicide to try. We got enough dead fools buried in fishing village graveyards to prove that even to you, I reckon."

"*I don't care!*" said Fernel, his teeth bared, his eyes narrowed to slits. "Let them drown, every one. I'll not lose a wink of sleep. Lur will *never* be clean until it's free of the Doranen."

Dathne pushed to her feet. "I don't believe what I'm hearing," she said, sounding dazed. "How long has your hatred been festering, Fernel? Did *Veira* know you felt like this?"

"No," Fernel snapped. "I never told her. Why would I? What business was it of hers? My duty was to safeguard Lur, and you, and the Circle, and at the risk of my own life that's what I did. You expect me to apologise for hating the interlopers who made that life a misery? Who forced me to live a lie? Who to this day *sneer* at me, because I'm not one of *them?*"

Dathne threw up her hands, as Polly and Beale stared at the man and blind Jinny kneaded her fingers in her lap. "Fernel, Fernel, there's nobody *sneering* at you!"

"Course there is, Dath," said Asher, and slid off the windowsill. "We got scores of Conroyd Jarralts in Lur. Rodyn Garrick and his cronies, for starters. Folk born blond and magical and better than everyone else. Leastways, that be what *they* reckon. Now you and me might reckon they're wrong, but it don't matter. It's only thoughts. And folks can think what they like. Fernel here, he can think we ought to toss every last Doranen over the mountains or into the ocean. I won't do it. And I won't let him do it, neither. But he can think on it all he likes, if that's what makes him happy."

Fernel stood, hands fisted at his sides. "I'm not alone, you know. I'm not the only Olken who thinks it's high time Lur was returned to its rightful owners. With the Wall destroyed, all that keeps the Doranen here is greed, and their habit of believing that what is ours belongs to them."

"Fernel, there is nothing for the Doranen beyond those mountains!" said Dathne. "You *know* what Tollin's expedition found. Blight. Corruption. Lingering death. We'd be no better than *murderers* if we threw them into that!"

"That was years ago," said Fernel. "Thanks to our cowardly General Council, we don't know what's there now. For all we know those lands have grown green and fertile these past few years, Dathne. For all we know Tollin lied. Got cold feet and *lied*. Or killed those men with incompetence, then brought back a nonsense tale to cover it up!"

Pellen had known and liked Ryn Tollin. "And then sickened himself and the other survivors to death, I suppose, to be certain no-one doubted their story? Shame on you, Pintte, for slandering men who can't defend themselves."

As Fernel Pintte sneered, Dathne turned to Asher. "He's mad," she said, helplessly. "I had no idea. I doubt Veira knew, or she never would've have brought him into the Circle. He's an insult to her memory."

Asher shook his head. "Dath—"

Ignoring him, Dathne rounded on Polly and Beale. "Did *you* know? Have you heard any of this—this vile spewing before?"

"I knew he had no love for the Doranen," said Beale heavily, after a moment. "But then neither do I."

"Polly?"

Plump Polly Marsh fingered her pendant, looking away. "I've nothing against them personally," she murmured. "Some of them are quite nice. I suppose."

Despairing, Dathne turned again. "Jinny? Jinny, tell me you don't agree with Fernel. *Please*."

"Not agree, no," said Jinny, reluctantly. "Though I understand his anger."

"But you two agree with him?" Dathne demanded, staring again at Beale and Polly. "You think the Doranen are a taint? A poison to Lur?"

"Not quite so far as that, perhaps," said Polly, blushing. "But they did take what was ours, Dathne."

"They saved us from Morg!" Dathne retorted. "The best way they knew how. It might not have been a perfect solution but we never *suffered*. We *prospered*."

"Tell that to Timon Spake," spat Fernel. "And Maura Shay, murdered before him. As for Morg, the Doranen *created* him. It was their *duty* to save us from him and then leave us alone!"

"Oh, this is ridiculous," said Dathne. "*You're* ridiculous. You need the help of a good pother, Fernel. Even if you're right about Barl and the first Doranen who came here, the Doranen living in Lur today are innocent of any crimes *they* committed. Our Doranen didn't ask to be born here any more than we did. Fratching ourselves over what happened six hundred years ago changes *nothing,* you fool. All we can do is worry about *now*. And *now* we have a new challenge before us; and if we don't meet it, more Olken—and Doranen—might well die."

Fernel folded his arms. "I've told you what the problem is," he said curtly. "And I've told you what must be done to fix it. If you choose to disregard my advice, well, I can't stop you. But I don't have to stay here and listen to you, either."

Alarmed, Dathne looked at Asher then back at Fernel. "What are you going to do, Fernel? Forswear your Circle oath and speak of what's been discussed here?"

Fernel raised one scornful eyebrow. "What Circle oath? The Circle's broken, Dathne. You broke it yourself eight years ago, remember? You said it was no longer needed. If you recall, I disagreed with your decision. But you knew best. You always know best, don't you? You're an arrogant one, Dathne. In fact, you're a lot like a Doranen. Perhaps that's why you champion their cause. You always thought being Jervale's Heir made you better than the rest of us."

Dathne took a step back, as though he'd struck her. "What? I *never*—Fernel, that's not true."

Asher cleared his throat. "Well," he said, considering. "It's a *bit* true, Dath. Bossy you were back then, and bossy you are now. Ain't much changed, that road. Still. You got a point." He nodded at Fernel. "Broken Circle or not, Meister Pintte, you swore blind you'd do everything in your power to protect Lur. I reckon once an oath like that's made you don't get to take it back."

"So I'm answerable to *you* now?" Fernel demanded. "Is that it?"

Asher's smile was deceptively genial. "I s'pose you could look at it that way. *I* don't. But you could."

"I'd rather not," said Fernel Pintte, his lip curled in another sneer. "I'd rather leave. So if you'll excuse me—"

Sickened, Pellen looked at Asher. He'd restrain the hateful fool if he had to, find some pretext or other that would see him cooling his heels in the City Guardhouse for a day or so. After all those years a captain, and his rule book not forgotten, he could trump up something or other that would give them a moment to breathe.

I might well hate myself, but I'd do it. We've lost too much already to throw the rest away.

Fernel Pintte was almost at the parlour door. Asher, looking after him, released an irritated sigh. Pointed a finger and said, very softly, *"Drego."*

Fernel Pintte froze in mid-stride, turned stone-still with one word.

As Beale and Polly cried out a protest, and blind Jinny gasped, and Dathne dropped back to the footstool, pale with despair and staring at the carpet, Asher wandered over to Fernel and frowned into the man's rigid face.

"There now, see?" he said, sounding mildly peeved. But Pellen, who knew him, could hear the killing fury beneath the words. "You made me use magic on you, Fernel. I ain't fond of usin' magic on folk. It makes me feel manky. And I don't like feelin' manky. So just you lissen a bit while I tell you what's what."

Dathne looked up. "Asher..."

He lifted a finger at her, never taking his cold gaze from Fernel Pintte's wide, unblinking eyes. "I meant what I said, before. You can think what you like. I ain't about to stop you. You be a free man, in a free land. But if I hear you rousin' up other folk to hate, Fernel? If I hear you agitatin' of an evening down your local alehouse, how Lur'd be better off if all them pesky Doranen got 'emselves tossed over the mountains or beyond Dragonteeth Reef? And you know I will hear, Fernel. You know I hear everythin', sooner or later. Well, if I hear owt of that I reckon I might be a bit fratched. Reckon I might have to come pay you a visit." He leaned close. "Fernel? You don't want me payin' you a visit. You don't want me gettin' *riled*. The last man who got me riled were Morg. Didn't end well for him. Reckon you might not want to make his mistake."

Pellen swallowed, feeling ice slide through his veins. The cheerful parlour crackled with menace.

"Vardo," said Asher, and took a step back.

Sickly white and slicked with sweat, Fernel Pintte stared at Asher in silence. Tried to speak. Could only stutter.

"Well?" said Asher. "What you waitin' for? Off you go."

Fernel Pintte ran.

*   *   *

"He's not a bad fellow, really," said Beale at last, breaking the taut silence. "He just takes things to heart. Always has."

Pellen exchanged a raised-eyebrow look with Asher, then turned to the old man. "How well do you know him?"

Beale sighed. "Well enough to know he's mostly talk and very little action."

"And we're to take your word on that, are we?" Dathne said dully. "We're to trust him? After what he's said?"

"Fernel only said what some of us think," Polly snapped. "Perhaps if you spent less time in the City and more time talking to regular Olken you'd not be so surprised."

"And what's *that* supposed to mean?" said Dathne, stung.

"It means we're shocked and upset," Jinny said, before Polly could answer. "Please, we didn't gather here to talk of Fernel's obsession with the Olken people's lost heritage. Our concerns are far greater than that. What are we to do about this—this *wrongness* in the earth? The imbalance we feel must be put right. I fear a calamity for everyone in Lur if we don't."

"You assume it *can* be put right, Jinny," said Beale, and looked at Asher. "Can it? Or are we just spitting in the wind?"

"I don't know," said Asher, shrugging. "Reckon all I aimed for in meetin' you here was to make sure I ain't been imaginin' things. Didn't reckon you'd expect me to snap m'fingers and fix whatever's the matter this time." He snorted. "Like magic."

"It pleases you to be *snide?*" said Beale, his lined face lining deeper with displeasure. "When this poor land of ours is groaning in pain, you think—"

"He doesn't mean it like that, Beale," said Dathne quickly. "He's just being Asher. Of *course* he's worried about—"

"Don't reckon I need you speakin' up for me, Dath," said Asher, frowning again. "Reckon I'm growed enough to speak for m'self. Any road, ole Beale here's just fratchin' at me 'cause he's scared spitless we got more trouble."

"And why wouldn't I be afraid?" Beale demanded. "When you can make light of what's happening? Our lives were built on faith in you. On believing that you'd save this kingdom from destruction. Fernel might be misguided, but he wasn't entirely wrong. A lot of good people gave up any hope of true peace, true happiness, so you might fulfill your destined purpose. Years and years of sacrifice, Asher. Years that did not leave us untouched."

"Years I never bloody asked you for!" Asher spat at the old man. "So don't you go throwin' 'em in my face! Sink me bloody sideways, you think *I* wanted any of this? *I* had a life! *I* had plans! But you and your bloody Circle, that ole besom Veira, you had *other* plans. And I did what you wanted. I saved the bloody kingdom. Killed my best friend to do it, too. So don't you sit there on your skinny ole arse waggin' your finger at *me!* Not when you be expectin' me to save Lur *again!*"

Silence, ragged and raw. Pellen, heartsick, watched as Asher turned his back on the room, his breathing harsh. Dathne pressed her fingertips to her closed eyes, trying to contain tears. Polly, not trying, took a kerchief from her purse. Blind Jinny smoothed her green wool skirt over and over her knees. Then, neatly, precisely, she folded her hands in her lap.

"You've yet to tell us what you've felt, Asher," she said softly. "Like it or not, you are the Innocent Mage. The most powerful Olken magician in Lur. What has the earth been whispering to *you?*"

Asher hesitated, then turned round. Shoved his hands in his pockets, his face settling into that familiar, belligerent scowl. Pellen looked from him to Dathne. Her lips were pressed tight, her arms folding as though to contain some bitter pain within her belly. He felt a fresh wave of unease flood through him.

Whatever they know, it's very, very bad. I wonder if I'm strong enough for the truth?

"Asher?" said Beale. Awkward with age he levered himself to his feet. In his chaotically lined face, a dawning suspicion. "That's a fair question. Why don't you answer it? What do you feel?"

"I'm thinkin'," said Asher, his voice still edged. "Some things ain't easy to put into words, Beale. I ain't no Fernel bloody Pintte. I ain't never had the slickest of tongues."

131

"What about you, Dathne?" said Polly. Tears dried, her plump, soft sorrow had hardened into a brittle wariness. "As Jervale's Heir you were gifted with visions. What have they shown you? What do *you* believe is happening in Lur?"

"I've had no visions since before Morg was killed," said Dathne. "I'm Jervale's Heir no longer. Not in that sense. Like you I'm an Olken mage with ties to the land. But I never had the greatest reading of it. All I know is what you all know, that Lur has been peacefully sleeping for the last ten years . . . and now it stirs to waking."

"Waking to what?" Jinny whispered. "I thought the fear and destruction of the Final Days were behind us. Was I wrong? Is the worst yet to come?"

"*Asher,*" said Beale. "Slick or not, it's time you wagged that tongue of yours. When you needed the Circle, the Circle was there for you. Some of us, like Jinny here, like poor Veira and her kinsman, Rafel, and your friend Matthias, paid a dreadful price for their help. Here's your chance to repay that debt. Tell us what you know. Tell us what you *think* you know and what your intentions are. Honour the sacrifices we made for you."

Asher flinched as though Beale had struck him. No outburst of anger this time, no flood of furious words. Dathne choked out a small cry of protest, seeing the pain that lit up Asher's eyes like lightning in an inky sky.

"You want me to say any ole thing?" he said, holding Beale's accusing stare. "Say what'll ease you, be it honest or not?"

"Of course not!" cried Polly, and pushed herself to stand close-pressed beside Beale. "What we want is your respect. You asked us to come here and we came, without question or care for how inconvenient it's been. You asked us to tell you what we've felt, and we told you. Now it's your turn."

"And if you won't tell us," said Jinny quietly, as she too found her feet, "we'll leave. And the next time you need our help you'll ask for it in vain."

It was a long time since Pellen had seen Asher looking cornered. Uncomfortably reminded of days he thought he'd thrust well behind him, he took refuge in staring at the floor. Dared one upwards glance, at Dathne, and saw that she too could not bring herself to witness Asher's pained dismay. Her gaze was fixed unwavering to her knees.

Then Asher sighed. "You reckon I got all the answers just 'cause once upon a time I fit the shape of your bloody prophecy? Sorry, Jinny. It don't work like that. Somehow, and I ain't got the first clue why, I can do a few Doranen tricks. Don't make me all-knowing. Don't bloody make me Barl."

"I don't recall any of us saying it did," Beale said.

Asher snorted. "Maybe not. But I reckon you been thinkin' it." He shook his head. "Look. Ole man. I can feel what you feel. Somethin' ain't right. But that's *it*. Don't you reckon if I had all the bloody answers I'd have left you alone? You reckon I don't know what I owe you three? And aye, Fernel Pintte. You reckon there's a day goes by I don't say sorry to Veira and Rafel and Matt, that they had to *die* for me? You reckon I *wanted* that? That I wanted Pellen, here, to get hisself crippled?"

Pellen looked up sharply. "I was Dorana's Captain of the Guard. I fought for my City and our kingdom. I don't regret that. And I don't need your regret, either."

Startled, Asher stared at him. "Pellen —"

"Oh, be quiet," he said. "Sometimes you make me very tired, Asher." He looked at Beale. "You three — four — were asked here today because we needed your insights. You've shared them with us and we're grateful to you. As Mayor of Dorana I extend my official thanks. And I ask that you keep what we've discussed here privy."

"We know how to keep secrets," said Polly dryly. "And our Circle oaths still stand. But it's almost certain there'll be others who've felt things and they're bound by no promises to keep those feelings to themselves."

Pellen nodded. "I know. But unless I've badly misread the situation, I think we've a little time before private misgivings turn into widespread public panic. We'll use that time wisely, I promise, to discover the cause of these ructions you've felt."

"And that's an official promise, is it?" she said, sniffing. "From the Mayor of Dorana?" Her gaze flicked sideways. "And the Innocent Mage?"

He nodded. "Yes."

With a sigh, Dathne at last rose from the footstool and let her weary gaze touch their three visitors' faces. "You're probably cursing me for dragging you here. For playing on past loyalties and making you face a darkness you'd hoped was nothing but your imagination. I'm sorry. I am. More than anything else I don't want this to be true."

"None of us does," said Beale. "But Prophecy never covered this possibility, did it?"

Dathne sighed, so sad. "No, Beale. It never did."

"You hadn't a choice, Dathne," said Jinny. "You had to call us. And we had to come."

"But Jinny's right," added Polly, a warning glint in her eyes. "We won't be taken for granted."

"I never meant to do that," said Asher, scowling again. "This business...I be rattled. I thought I were done with prophecy. I thought it were done with *me*. Don't much like thinkin' on the chance that ain't so."

"None of us much like it, Asher," said Beale, holding out his hand. "We're fighting the same fight. Best we not fight each other as well."

Relieved, Pellen watched Asher cross the parlour and take the old man's hand in a firm clasp. "No, Beale. Best not." He let go. "So. If we are lookin' to fight another battle, can I count on you?"

As Beale and Polly exchanged looks, Jinny nodded. "Of course," she said firmly. "We were born to the Circle, Asher, and we'll die in its service. Just as one day you'll die the Innocent Mage, even though you never wanted that and resent what it means with every breath you take."

"Thank you for coming," said Pellen. "Thank you for trusting us."

"We have to trust each other, Pellen," said Polly, her lips trembling. "We have to trust there's a way out of this. I can't believe we defeated Morg only to see Lur crumble so soon after. I can't believe that's what Jervale had in mind."

"It's not," said Dathne. "Perhaps it's just..." She cleared her throat. "Perhaps we relaxed too soon."

"What of the Doranen?" Beale asked. "We can't leave them ignorant forever."

Asher shrugged. "They be my problem, I reckon. You leave 'em to me."

"And Fernel?" Pellen added, frowning at the Circle members. "I know he's your friend. I know you're loyal to him, and why. Believe me, I don't wish to come between you. But what he said here today, well, I'll not deny it disturbs me. I've a nose for trouble...and troublemakers. Your friend doesn't strike me as the type to keep his grievances to himself." He glanced at Asher, then looked back. "Even though he was warned."

"I know Fernel best," said Polly. "We're less than a day's cart ride distant from each other. I'll hear soon enough if he's stirring up mischief. But I can't honestly believe that he'd—"

"You'd best believe he might," said Asher. "Pellen ain't never wrong about this kind of thing." Then he pulled a face. "Well. Almost never."

And that was a sly dig at their own complicated past. Pellen, sparing him a pointed look, offered Polly a smile. "I hope you're right. But if you should feel uneasy, or hear anything untoward..."

"Yes," said Polly, unhappy. "I'll send word."

"All of you should stay vigilant," said Dathne, looking from Jinny to Polly to Beale. "Not only about Fernel. We need to know as soon as you hear word of unrest, or misgivings, or folk whispering about what they've felt in the earth."

The three remaining Circle members nodded.

"Thank you," she said. "And if I've been high-handed, or bossy, or made you feel—feel *slighted,* I beg your forgiveness. I never meant to. I've been worried too. And I'm no better at being worried than Asher is."

She kissed each of them then, and afterwards Pellen escorted them to the front door. Blind Jinny held Polly's arm, steadfast and composed.

He watched Beale shepherd them courteously down the path to the gate, then drew back into his home and returned to the parlour.

"Sink me, Pellen," said Asher, looking up. "What a bloody great mess that turned into."

"Oh, I don't know," he said, dropping gratefully into the chair Jinny had used. "Things might've got a bit heated here and there, but you got what you wanted. You learned what they knew . . . and pulled the wool completely over their eyes."

Asher stared at him, nonplussed. "Eh? Pellen, what are you—"

"Don't even bother trying to deny it," he snapped, and fixed Asher with his best Captain of the Guard glare. "Because we both know you know more than you revealed to those three Circle members. But you *are* going to tell *me* the truth, Asher. Every last syllable of it. Starting right now."

Instead of answering, Asher looked at Dathne. Pellen, watching their silent communion, thought *Ibby,* and felt his heart thud. Oh he missed her, he *missed* her, and the thoughts they could share with a single, fleeting glance.

"You have to, Asher," said Dathne, sighing. "He has a right to the truth."

Stifling a groan, Asher returned to the window and hitched himself once more onto the deep sill. As though he found some kind of strength, or solace, in the sturdy timberwork around him.

"I know that," he grunted. "Reckon I don't know that, woman?"

Dathne's eyebrows shot up. "*Woman*? Careful. Innocent Mage or not, I can still—"

"Oh, *enough,*" said Pellen. "After all we've been through do you think the pair of you can divert *me?*"

They fidgeted, silenced.

"And I want to know about Rafel, as well," he added, still curt. "If he's sensing things—" His throat closed, fear stifling the words.

"Pellen?" said Dathne. She could read him almost as well as Ibby ever did. "What is it?"

With a wrenching effort he laid his unclenched fingers on the arm of his chair. "Charis."

"She's sensing things too?"

"I don't know. I think so. I have my suspicions." He had to blink hard, to hold back the stinging fear. "So whatever's troubling this kingdom we have to fix it. Because she's my little girl and she's suffering. She's suffering, Dathne, and I can't help her. I'm her father, it's my duty to protect her, keep her safe, but—"

Dathne dropped to a crouch beside him and took hold of his forearm with both hands. "Pellen, don't fret yourself. You're a *wonderful* father. Charis adores you. The way she looks at you sometimes, with her heart in her eyes? She'd drown you in love if she could. You've not failed her. You'll *never* fail her."

"Dath's right," Asher said gruffly. "You be a grand da, Pellen. Ain't no call for you to be doubtin' yourself on that."

Touched, comforted a little, he looked first at Dathne, then at Asher. "This—this wrongness in the earth. How did you explain it to Rafel?"

"I didn't," said Asher. "Not ezackly. I told him not to be frighted. I told him it weren't nowt to worrit on. I told him I'd explain what it meant when he were older."

"Oh," he said. "And he accepted that?"

"Course he did. I'm his da, ain't I?"

Well, yes, except . . . "He's very much your son, Asher. He's a stubborn lad. The kind of boy who likes real answers when he asks a question."

"Weren't no point fillin' his head with tales of Weather Magic and suchlike," said Asher, pulling a face. "He don't never need to know about any of that."

Need to? Of course he didn't. But Rafel was the kind of lad who'd want to. Surely his parents knew it? He was their son. They weren't blind to him, were they?

"Rafel's fine," said Dathne, retreating to the couch. "And I'm sure Charis will be, too. Let's not worry about them now. This problem in Lur, Pellen—we're determined to fix it. Quickly, so Rafel—and Charis—and all of us in the kingdom—can go about our lives untouched by shadows."

A sentiment with which he heartily agreed. But—"Fix it how, Dathne? Come on. The time's come for you to empty your purse on the table."

"Aye," said Asher, and let his head fall against the window's embrasure. Turned his gaze to the garden beyond, so his eyes were hidden. "You're right. You got to be told. So, any road, here's what I know..."

With increasing alarm, Pellen listened to his friend reveal dreadful, close-kept secrets. So many times waking at night, tormented by a nameless dread. The knots in his gut that grew tighter, never easing, as Lur's underpinnings tilted, unbalanced. The growing suspicion that terribly, fantastically, Barl's Weather Magic was somehow involved.

The Weather map, for ten long years believed to be dead.

"Alive?" he said, horrified. "With *power* in it? How can that be?"

Asher shrugged. "I don't know, Pellen. How am I s'posed to know? I didn't invent the bloody thing, did I?"

"But you said it was *dead.*"

"That's 'cause I thought it was!" Asher retorted. "Now it looks like I were wrong. You want to lock me up for makin' a mistake?"

"No! I want you to tell me what this means! I want to know what's happening, what's gone awry!" *I want you to fix it!* But he didn't say that. He knew better than to say that, after today.

Except Asher, being Asher, heard his unspoken words. "Sink me, Pellen. Not you too."

"I'm sorry," he said, stricken. "Asher, I'm sorry."

Asher pulled a knee to his chest and let his forehead drop to it, hiding his face. Skewered with guilt, Pellen watched him wrestle fear, wrestle despair, fight his never-ending battle against what was asked of him, who he was, that he'd never asked to be. The self he couldn't deny, because he was a good man.

"I am sorry," he said again. "Truly." He breathed deeply, hesitating... then surrendered to his own fear. "But it's *Lur,* Asher. And we've no place else to go."

Asher lifted his head. His eyes were bleak with resentful acceptance. "I know. Pellen, I know what I am. The Innocent Mage. And like it or not, Lur's last livin' WeatherWorker."

Weather Magic. Remembering what it looked like, he winced. "You were WeatherWorker once. But must you be that again?"

"I might."

"No, you mightn't," said Dathne sharply. "We'll find another way."

"And if there ain't one?" said Asher, so weary. "What then, Dath?"

"I don't know! And I don't care!" Dathne leapt up. "I nearly lost you to the Doranen's magic once, Asher. If you think I'll lift a finger to help you risk yourself again—"

"Fine!" Asher banged a fist on the windowsill. "So this time I sit on my arse and do nowt. And what—Lur perishes? Then what were the point of savin' it the first time, Dath? What were the point of Gar dyin', Matt dyin', your precious bloody Veira dyin', and her Rafel, if I do nowt to help when there's more trouble stirrin'?"

"I'm not saying don't help! I'm saying *find another way!*"

Pellen, uncomfortable, considered a loose thread in his blue trousers. He'd have to pinch it safe with a stitch or three, later. Glancing up, he caught the anguish on Dathne's face, the grim endurance in Asher's, and felt his own heart break a little.

"Please. Don't fight. We're this kingdom's caretakers. Its guardians. How can we help it if we're battling each other?"

Dathne dropped back to the couch. "And how can you ask me *not* to fight for him, Pellen? He's my life."

"Just as you're his. But he's right. If we aren't going to save Lur this time we might as well have given it to Morg."

"Besides," said Asher, striving for lightness. "You be the one who started this, Dath, with your prophecy and your Circle and suchlike."

"Oh, don't remind me," she said bitterly. "As if the thought doesn't make me sick at heart, Asher. *Sick.*"

Asher slid out of the embrasure and went to her. Sat beside her on the couch and drew her close to him, kissing her hair. "Don't feel too sick. It were prophecy brought us together, remember?"

She sagged against him. "Well, now I want it to leave us alone!"

"You're certain, are you," said Pellen, "that the solution to our problem will come down to WeatherWorking?"

"Certain?" Asher shook his head. "Ain't nowt certain about any of this, Pellen. But I got my suspicions."

"And if what you've all felt is connected with the WeatherWorking? With Barl's Weather map? What then? We don't truly know how the map's magic works, do we?"

"No," said Dathne. "Not beyond what little Gar told Asher. And I don't think he understood it. I don't think even Durm did. Or Borne. Barl was the expert, and she left no instructions behind."

Frustrated silence. Then Asher cleared his throat.

"As it happens, Dath . . . that might not be true."

CHAPTER NINE

Pulling away from him, Dathne stared into her husband's apprehensive face, her dark eyes hollow with misgivings. "The *diary?*" she said at last. "Asher, are you saying..."

"Do you mean Barl's diary?" said Pellen, as she and Asher held each other's molten gazes. "Asher, you said that was destroyed. To keep Lur safe from the magics it contained, Gar burned the diary to cinders, you said."

Asher shrugged. "Aye, well. I lied."

"To me!" cried Dathne, and wrenched herself off the couch. "Asher, how *could* you?"

Jaw stubbornly set, Asher shrugged again. "I promised Gar I'd keep it safe, didn't I?"

"And what about keeping Lur safe?" Dathne demanded, hands on her hips. "You said it yourself—for all the equality that now exists between the Olken and the Doranen there are still mages like Rodyn Garrick who consider themselves superior. Who pine for the old days. Let the brute magic in that diary fall into his hands, or the hands of a mage like him, and—"

Asher shook his head. "That ain't goin' to happen."

"You *hope* it won't happen!" she retorted. "But in matters of Doranen magic *I* prefer certainty to hope. You *should've* burned that diary, Asher. You had no business keeping it. You had no right to lie!"

"Look," said Asher. "I'm sorry. You weren't never meant to find out the diary ain't destroyed. But—"

"And why isn't it?" Pellen asked. "You and Gar, of all people, you both knew how dangerous it is."

"'Cause Gar—" Asher sighed. "It sounds daft, I know, but he...I reckon he went a bit soft on Barl, there at the end. Translatin' bits and pieces of that bloody diary, I reckon he—and he was goin' to *die!*" He scrubbed his hand across his face. "It were his dyin' bloody wish, weren't it, that I keep the diary safe so there'd be somethin' of her left in the world. How could I say no?"

Stony-faced, Dathne stared down at him. "You could've said yes, then burned it after."

"Gone back on my word to him?" said Asher, his own stare just as hard. "I don't bloody think so. And if you reckon that's the kind of man I am, Dathne, then—"

"I don't know what I *reckon*," she said coldly. "Not any more. After all, until a few moments ago I *reckoned* you'd never lie to me."

"Sink me bloody sideways!" said Asher, close to shouting. "I *owed* him, Dathne, and I—"

"And what of your debt to me?" she said, tears threatening. "Your wife. The mother of your children."

"Aye, well, as I recall there were one or two truths *you* forgot to mention along the road, Dath," said Asher, well and truly fired up now. "So mayhap you'd best not start flingin' mud, my fine lady, seein' how—"

"All right," said Pellen, as Dathne stalked to the parlour window. "Please. Let's everyone take a deep breath. The last thing we need is to say something we'll soon enough come to regret. Asher—"

"*What?*" said Asher, his scowl ferocious. "You got a knife you feel like stickin' in me too, Pellen?"

"No. No, of course not," he said, as soothingly as he could. "But I can't help wondering—Asher, did you think you couldn't *trust* us with the truth?"

Asher looked at him as though he'd lost his wits. "Don't be bloody stupid, Pellen. I reckoned you'd be happier not knowing, is all. Happier thinkin' there weren't no chance of a Doranen gettin' their hands on the sinkin' and usin' old Doranen magic ever again. I know I'd be bloody happier thinkin' that!"

Remembering his nightmares of that battle in the Market Square, of seeing Morg transform helpless men and women into foul, slaughtering beasts...remembering the terrifying creatures Asher had summoned from thin air to defeat them, he nodded. "I'm sure you would."

Asher's eyes were grim. "Sometimes I wake up at night, frighted on what's in that diary," he said, his voice almost a whisper. "Frighted on what could happen if some of them spells got loose. Think I want that for you and Dathne?"

"Oh, well I'm sure it's very considerate of you," said Dathne, icy. "But perhaps that's the kind of decision we should've been left to make for ourselves!"

"Don't you be bloody stupid either, Dath," said Asher. "Once I told you then you'd know, wouldn't you? There ain't no takin' it back after, is there?"

Dathne opened her mouth, then thought for a moment. "That's not the point," she muttered. "The point is I don't appreciate being treated like a child."

"I didn't treat you like a bloody child!" he snapped. "I treated you like the woman I love best in the world. I was tryin' to protect you, Dathne. And you, Pellen. Any road, you know now the diary ain't burned, so let's not fratch on it, eh? What's done is done."

As Dathne breathed hard, subduing her temper, Pellen frowned. "So...where's it hidden?"

"Ha." Asher's lips quirked with brief, wry amusement. "Gar's got it."

He stared. "What? You don't mean—"

"Aye. It's in his coffin. Ain't nobody goin' to footle about in there."

"That's disgusting," said Dathne.

"Why? He won't mind," said Asher. "Means he's still safeguardin' his kingdom, don't it? Reckon he'd smile on it, if he knew."

"Asher—"

Pellen raised a calming hand. "Peace, Dathne. He's right. What's done is done. And what we need to do now is decide what's to be done next. Is the diary even any use to us? We know there are warspells in it, but is there anything else? Anything that can help us now?"

"Gar translated some of it," said Asher. The lingering amusement in his face died out, leaving him sorrowful. "But I never read nowt 'cept the warspells. And after I killed Morg... after Gar..." He shook his head. "Never wanted to lay eyes on the bloody thing again, did I?"

"So it is possible," he persisted, "that somewhere in that diary is an explanation for what's happening here. Maybe even some kind of spell that can—can *heal* Lur before even the least sensitive Olken among us realises something is wrong, or someone tells the Doranen, or they notice it themselves."

"If there is, and Garland translated it, we could avert widespread panic," said Dathne. Arms folded, eyes brooding, she flicked a glance at Asher. "We could save Lur without anyone else having to know it needed saving at all. *Without* WeatherWorking."

"I could live with that, I reckon," said Asher. "Ain't like I be champin' at the bit to start that malarkey again."

Pellen considered him, uneasy even though this was their best hope for averting disaster. "So you'll retrieve the diary?"

"Soon as I can," Asher replied. "My word on it."

He nodded, feeling strangely comforted. If there was a way out of Lur's new trouble his friend would find it.

"Good."

Asher frowned. "Pellen, don't you go gettin' your hopes up. There ain't no surety I'll find an answer in that diary. And even if I do, could be I ain't good enough to use the magic. I ain't trained and there ain't a Doranen I can ask for help. I mean—I'll try. I'll do my bloody best. But I can't promise you nowt."

It wasn't fair, what they were asking. What they expected. Stung with guilt, he tried not to see the fear beneath Asher's customary brusque exterior. "I know you can't," he said, trying to smile. "It's all right."

"Ha," Asher muttered. "It ain't all right, Pellen. It's just the way it is."

An uncomfortable silence fell then, as they lost themselves in their separate thoughts and separate fears. At last, afraid of letting himself drown in the doldrums completely, and niggled by one last piece of unfinished business, he looked up. Reluctant to mention it, though he did badly want an answer.

"What?" said Dathne.

He felt his face warm. *She knows me too well.* "Nothing. Sorry. Only . . . you were going to tell me about Rafel."

"Rafel," sighed Asher. "Aye." He rubbed his chin. "The thing is, seems Rafel's like me."

"Like you," he said blankly. And then he realised what Asher meant. "A *mage* like you? He can wield Doranen magic?"

"Aye." Asher didn't look pleased about it. His eyes were bleak, his mouth pinched. "Which ain't what me and Dath were after."

Of course it wasn't. Who knew better than they did, the kind of complications such a talent wrought? "Who else knows?"

"Well, Rafe knows," said Asher, with a kind of grim humour. "Ole Pother Nix. And Pother Kerril, as he's retired. And Darran knew."

"No-one else? Not any member of the Mage Council?"

"No," said Dathne, as troubled as her husband. "And we want to keep it that way."

" 'Cause the last bloody thing we need is Rodyn Garrick and his poxy friends gettin' the wind up over Rafel," said Asher. "Bad enough they still look sideways at me. I don't need 'em lookin' that way at my son."

"And what of Deenie? Is she—"

"We don't think so," said Dathne. "She's shown no sign of it so far."

"So cross your fingers for us she never does," said Asher, scowling again. "My little mouse don't need Doranen magic."

Thinking of Charis, and how he'd feel were he to find she was blighted like Rafel, he frowned. "No." And then the implications of this news began to stir. "Rafel knows, does he, how important it is that he not—"

"Aye," said Asher. "Me and Dath, we've told him."

Looking closely at his friends, Pellen could see his own unease reflected in their tight faces. Saw more than unease, and felt his nerves jump. "Ah—just how powerful is he?"

Asher and Dathne exchanged guarded glances. Then Dathne sighed. "Powerful enough that we—took precautions when he was still small," she admitted, reluctant. "With Nix's help we've hobbled him so he can't do himself or anyone else a mischief."

"Does he know?"

Asher shook his head. "Tell Rafe that and like as not he'd see if he could unhobble himself. Gets easy fratched over not bein' able to magic as he pleases, does our Rafe."

That didn't surprise him. Asher and his boy had so much in common. "Thank you for telling me," he said, feeling oddly formal. "Of course I'll not breathe a word."

After that there seemed nothing left to say. As he saw Asher and Dathne to his mayoral home's front gate, Charis returned from her play-time at the Tower. The maid who'd brought her back let go of his daughter's hand, bobbed a curtsey to him, then Asher and Dathne, accepted a silver trin in thanks and went on her way.

"Dadda! Dadda!" Charis squealed, flourishing a sunflower. "Look what I grew!"

Snatching his daughter up in his arms, he buried his face in her frothy black curls. Love was a battering storm within him. "I see it! Who's a clever puss, then?"

Wriggling, Charis flashed a smile at Asher and Dathne. "Deenie grew one too, but mine's bigger," she said proudly. "And Meister Rumly didn't help me *one bit*."

"You had lessons with Meister Rumly?" he said, and shook his head at his friends. Not because he minded her learning to use her magic, Ibby's gift, but because the Olken mage charged handsomely for his tutoring and neither Asher nor Dathne would countenance him paying part of the fee whenever Charis joined in Deenie's lessons.

Dathne dropped a kiss on Charis's head. "It's a beautiful sunflower, Charis."

"Aye," said Asher, smiling. "You be the queen of sunflowers, poppet."

Pellen squeezed his daughter tight. "No, she's the queen of the tub. Come along, little gardener. Bath-time for you. Asher—Dathne—"

The smile died out of Asher's eyes. "We'll talk, by and by."

"Good," he said, and let his voice snap, just a little. "No more secrets."

"Secrets?" said Charis. "What secret, Dadda? Who's got a secret?"

Ah, Barl save him. Children. "I have," he said, turning away from the front gate, and his friends. "And I'll bet you never guess what it is."

"I will! I will!" she said, pouting. "I can guess, Dadda. I can!"

Laughing at her vehemence he took her inside, closing the door on the world and its troubles. Letting himself pretend, for the last sweet time, that they were safe, and Lur was safe, and bad times were nothing but stories from the past.

Leaving behind the leafy residential district where the wealthiest Doranen and Olken lived, and Pellen lived for as long as he was mayor, Asher and Dathne made their unspeaking way into the commercial district so they could wander along the high street up to the palace, and home. With the weekly markets still four days away, the City's streets were only moderate busy. A few ridden horses. A handful of carts and carriages. Some folk trudging, wearing out their shoe leather. Dorana's inhabitants, well-used to seeing them out and about on foot, did nowt more than nod and smile as they passed. Sometimes not even that, if they were Doranen.

The sun was starting its long, slow sink, gilding the brightly coloured buildings' walls and tiled roofs. With afternoon's shadows lengthening, some shops were starting to close their doors and shutter their windows. Asher felt himself frown at that. He and Dath had lost nearly the whole day to Lur and its troubles, yet they were still no closer to solving them. Instead they'd piled more strife onto their plates, what with dratted Fernel Pintte and his foaming hatred of all things Doranen, and Polly's unwelcome opinion that his resentments were widely shared.

Chewing on that news, not liking the taste of it one little bit...not liking either the thought of digging up Barl's bloody diary...he let the heavy silence drag on until he and Dathne reached halfway to the Tower. Then he took her hand in his, possessively, and tugged her a step closer.

"Come on, Dath," he wheedled. "You know you can't stay fratched at me forever."

She snorted. "I can try."

"Mayhap it weren't right I never told you about the diary...but I didn't hold my tongue 'cause I don't trust you."

He felt her fingers relax. Heard her release a long, slow sigh. "I know," she said. Sounding like she did when she wanted to be fratched with him, and couldn't. "But that doesn't stop me wanting to slap you."

"Y'can do more than slap me after lights out," he suggested. "Y'can have your wicked way with me, woman, and I won't try to fight you."

Another snort. "You're impossible."

"Aye," he said, grinning. "It's why you love me, I reckon."

A third derisive snort. "Who says I love you?"

Heedless of anyone who might be watching he halted, swept her to him and bent her over his arm to plunder a breathless kiss. "I do."

Blushed bright red, she beat a small tattoo against his chest. *"Asher!"* she protested, as Olken passers-by whispered and giggled. "What are you *doing?*"

He raised an eyebrow. "Practisin' for lights out."

And she laughed, just like he knew she would. Hand in hand they kept walking up the sloping High Street.

"Asher..." said Dathne, breaking the brief silence. "About Fernel Pintte..."

He squeezed her hand. "Don't you go fratchin' yourself on him, Dath. Reckon I put that fool straight."

"You scared the daylights out of him, is what you did," she retorted. *"And* me."

"Didn't mean to," he said, surprised. "Not you, any road. Him I meant to bloody terrify. Stupid bastard. What's he thinkin' on, eh, wantin' to stir up that kind of trouble?"

Dathne chewed at her bottom lip. "Asher, what if it's true? What if some Olken are as unhappy as he and Polly claim?"

"Dath, I ain't heard that kind of claptrap from a single Olken I know. You let him rattle you, is all."

"Just because people aren't saying things doesn't mean they're not thinking them."

"And what if they are? You said it, Dath. We can't kick the Doranen out. There ain't no place for 'em to go. So if there are more stupid Olken like Fernel Pintte and that biddy Polly, they'll have to face facts, eh? 'Cause ain't nowt going to change. The Doranen be in Lur to stay, just like us Olken."

She sighed. "Oh, *Asher*..."

"Dath, you can *Oh, Asher* me into the middle of next bloody week. I'm right, and you know it." He squeezed her hand again. "Don't fret. Once we got the earth settled again, everythin' else will settle too. You'll see."

Lapsing into friendly silence, they left the city behind and entered the palace grounds. Strolled the wide, djelba-lined carriageway towards the Tower, nodding and smiling at the visitors who'd been paying their respects in the Garden of Remembrance. A few times they stopped to chat, pretending all was well, because it was expected of them. They weren't Lur's royal family — but they were its next best thing.

At last they passed through the gates that kept their privy grounds safe from the public...and saw their grubby son sitting cross-legged on the grass beneath a sheltering tree. When he saw them he leapt up, hands fisting by his sides.

"Da. Mama." Rafe's lower lip jutted, a sure sign he expected trouble. "We got to talk."

Last thing before bedtime, every night 'less he were sick, or in trouble, Rafel padded his way downstairs and out to the stables to give Stag an apple for his supper. Even on winter's coldest nights he did that. It made him feel warm inside, knowing the pony wouldn't go to sleep until they'd had their whispering moment.

The dimly glimfired yard was hushed, all the lads and Jed in their dormitory over the stables where once upon a time Da used to sleep. In their snug stables the horses made sleepy night sounds, straw shifting beneath them, hooves clinking on the bricks. There was a lamp burning in Stablemeister Divit's privy quarters above the feed room, and a shadow flickering against his drawn curtains that said he was safe in there, minding his own grown-up business.

Stag looked out over his stable door, ears pricked, head tossing up and down. His pony way of saying *hurry up, hurry up*. Rafel clicked his tongue and Stag whickered, deep in his throat, so it sounded like he was laughing. Pleased to see him. Greedy for his apple.

"There you go," said Rafel, stroking the pony's warm brown neck as it crunched and slobbered, white apple-foam dripping. "You did good today, running faster than Goose's nag. You're the best pony in the kingdom."

Stag snorted, agreeing. Rafel rested his forehead against Stag's cheek, fingers reaching to scratch behind the pony's ears, where it sometimes itched. He heard the funny flap-flap-slap of Stag's droopy lips, the sound the pony made when his fingers found the right spot.

"I'm frighted, Stag," he whispered. "Da and Mama say what I felt in the riverpond was Lur rolling over in its sleep, that's all, but that ain't true. I *know* it ain't true. And I reckon Da's gonna try and stop what's really wrong. But what if he can't, Stag? It's bad. It's really *bad*. What if Da—what if he—"

He couldn't say the words out loud. He felt dizzy to *think* them, even.

He smeared his sleeve across his face, angry at himself for being frighted Da might die. Angry at his father for lying. For still treating him like a sprat.

I ain't Deenie. I'm old enough to know.

Stag nudged his arm, asking for more apple.

"Sorry," he said. "I only brought one. I only ever bring one. Reckon you ought to know that by now, you ole trout."

Stag snorted again, nose wrinkled, and stuck out his long tongue. Because it was their game, and it wasn't Stag's fault he was frighted,

Rafel grabbed the pony's tongue and tugged it, but only a few times. He wasn't in the mood for playing.

"Night, Stag," he said, and patted him goodbye. "See you in the morning."

He walked back to the Tower, feeling the cloudy night stretching dark and quiet around him. Even the nightbirds' singing was soft, as though they couldn't not sing but were afraid of waking something. Bright light burned in Da and Mama's parlour window. It was far too early for them to be asleep. Halfway up the Tower's wide stone steps he slowed, then stopped. He was meant to go straight to bed now, that was the way it worked. One apple for Stag then upstairs to sleep. Except...

How am I s'posed to sleep when they won't tell me the truth? They should tell me the truth, after what I felt today.

But there was no point arguing on it, even though he surely wanted to. He'd already tried once. Made Da all fearsome, so Mama had to soothe him down. She was good at that. She got a lot of practise. But seeing Da fearsome made him glad he hadn't told his parents everything. He'd told them what he'd felt at the riverpond with Goose, but he left out the part about calling the silver carp. It wasn't Doranen magic, but even so...they'd be fratched. Last thing he needed was for Da to be fratched. When Da was fratched he noticed things.

And if he figures out what else I've been doing when he's already riled...

Feeling guilty and scared, and twice as prickly because of it, he stamped into the Tower and up the winding staircase to the blue floor, which was all his. Maybe he'd feel better for reading Tollin's adventures again. They were fearsome too—he and Goose had near wet themselves, reading that parchment—but in a funny way it was a good kind of fright. A ghost story fright. They'd played explorers the whole afternoon after reading it, and pretended to die dozens of lingering, gruesome deaths. But as he rode home he'd remembered the riverpond...and his happiness had fizzled. Cheering himself up with Tollin's parchment was sure to help. Except—

Deenie was perched on the middle of his bed, waiting for him.

"What do you want?" he said, slamming the chamber door behind him, his heart slamming just as hard. If she'd been snooping...if she'd found the hidden parchment... "This is *my* room. You ain't allowed in here."

Knees pulled up to her chest, arms wrapped around them, her long nightdress glowing pinkly in the bedside lamp's glimfire, Deenie looked at him. Her eyes filled with tears.

"Snivel, snivel, snivel," he added, feeling savage. "You're such a *girl*, Deenie. Go back to bed."

She sniffed, not budging. "What happened today, Rafe?"

That made him blink. "Nowt. Why? What d'you mean?"

"I felt something," she said, hugging her knees even harder. "I felt—I felt *you*."

"You did not," he retorted. "You're just a sprat, Deenie. You can't feel *nowt*."

"Yes, I can," she said, nodding hard. "You did a big magic, Rafe. And then you got all scared and upside-down when the earth went funny. I felt it."

"No, you *didn't!*" His mouth was dry, his belly churning. "And if you tell Da and Mama you did, I'll—I'll—I don't do big magic!"

Her chin was all wobbly. "Yes, you *do*. Today you made the fish jump. And other times you crack stones and you dance leaves and you do silly things with your bathwater." She was breathing all hiccupy now, her eyes glitter bright. "You do trickier things too. And—and this morning you did something *really* tricky."

She could feel him doing the spells he pinched from Arlin? She'd felt him picking Da's Doranen lock? Shocked breathless, he stared at his sister. And then he shoved her hard with both hands so she tumbled backwards onto his pillows.

"If you tell Da or Mama any of that I'll—I'll *spit* on you!" he panted, nearly cross-eyed with fright. "With magic in it! See if I don't!"

Deenie scrambled to the floor, putting the quilt-covered bed between them. "I won't tell. Why would I tell? Don't spit on me. Please don't spit on me, Rafe."

Suddenly he felt horrible, like the worst person in Lur. Deenie's eyes were so wide. She was a bratty sprat, his little sister, a *girl,* but she was family. And there she stood staring at him with her wide eyes dribbling tears, because of him. He'd done that. He'd made her afraid.

"I won't," he said, hot with sudden shame, and dropped onto his bed. "I won't, Deenie. I promise."

Sniffing again, she clambered up beside him. "Why'd you go all upside-down, Rafe?"

"I ain't sure," he said, and held out his arm for her to snuggle against him. "It's hard to explain. How come you know when I do tricky magic, Deenie? Not even Da knows that."

Safe and soothed beside him she shrugged, a tiny wriggle of her shoulders. "I just do," she whispered.

"Aye, but how?"

Another wriggle. "I feel it," she said. "In here." She poked a finger into her nightdress-covered chest. "Like a tickle."

He'd never heard of such a thing. Pother Kerril had never said anything on it. Neither had Da or Mama. "Who knows you feel magic?"

"No-one," she said. "Just you."

"Da doesn't know? Or Mama?"

She shook her head. "No."

"You ain't even told Charis?"

"Rafe—"

"Why not? You tell her everythin' else," he said. "You're always whisperin' and gigglin', you two."

She wriggled right out from under his arm. "We are not! Anyway, you and Goose are the same. 'Cept you don't giggle. You snort. That's boy's giggling, Charis says."

"Charis," he sneered. "She's a frilly sprat, she is."

"She is *not!*" said Deenie. "Anyway, Goose is a—a—*goose.*"

"He ain't no such thing!"

"Is too!"

"Is not!"

"Is too! He—he—"

"You hush up, Deenie," he said, fist raised. "This is *my* room, and Goose is *my* friend. So you don't get to call him names."

Flushed and teary again, Deenie slid off the bed and put her hands on her hips. "You're mean, Rafel. You're a — a — bossy ole *fart!*"

He rolled his eyes. "I'm *ten*, Deenie. I ain't bloody *old*."

"*Oooh!*" she said, and slapped a hand to her mouth. "You said *bloody*, Rafel. You said a *swear*."

He smirked. "So did you. So we're even. So *there*."

"It's not the same!"

"Is too."

"Is *not!*"

Frustrated and furious they glared at each other. Then Deenie giggled. He tried to stay cross with her, tried to keep his scowl from slipping, but he couldn't. So they giggled together, Deenie scrambling back to his side again, knees scrunched tight to her chest the way she liked best.

And then he didn't feel like giggling any more, because he remembered what she'd said. Like probing a sore tooth with his tongue, he couldn't leave it alone. "You really felt me call those fish?"

Solemn, eyes round like an owl's, she nodded.

"And after that? You felt — you felt —" He couldn't say it. Whenever he thought about Lur's groaning earth he went trembly sick inside.

"Mmm," said Deenie, and her eyes filled with more tears. Deenie was a watering pot, she cried all the time. She was such a *girl*. "Everything went funny," she whispered. "Crackly and crinkly. The air smelled wrong. And you were so *scared*."

He wanted to say, *I was not!* But he knew she'd argue. Funny how she described it. *Crackly and crinkly*. It wasn't the way he felt things, but Pother Kerril said every mage was different.

He frowned at his bratty, spratty sister. "Have you told Da or Mama about you feeling the earth go funny?"

"No," she said, and seemed to shrink into herself. "Don't you, either."

That surprised him. "Why not?"

Instead of answering, she drew pictures on his quilt with one careful finger.

"Deenie, why not?"

She shrugged. "Da's fratched. He doesn't like magic."

Deenie was too young for Da to talk to her man to man. So how would she know he was fratched? "Is that you feeling things again?" he said, suspicious.

"I can't help it," she said, her voice wobbling. "I just do."

He didn't like it, but he s'posed he couldn't blame her. "Why ain't you told Charis?"

"'Cause," said Deenie slowly. "She gets all bouncy and she can't keep a secret. She doesn't mean to tell, she just does." She sighed. "Did you tell Goose?"

"Course I did," he said, scornful. "*He* ain't bouncy. He knows how to keep his trap shut. Not like a girl."

"It's not 'cause she's a girl! It's 'cause she's Charis. But she's still my bestest friend." Deenie's cross face turned wistful. "She grows beautiful sunflowers. Better than me."

Rafel nudged his sister gently with one knee. "Maybe. But she can't feel things like you do."

"I think she might." Now Deenie traced a fingertip up and down one of the quilt's fat blue stripes. "I'm not sure. I haven't asked her. But I think she knows something's wrong, too."

Rafel thought about that. He knew. Da knew, and Mama. Deenie knew. And now Charis? Da wanted to keep it a secret, but how could he? Maybe lots of people knew. And if they did then soon they'd come clamouring at him. That's what people were like. They'd make a fuss, expecting him to fix things like he did before 'cause he was the Innocent Mage. Fear surged again, hot and hungry and crowding into his throat.

He ain't got King Gar to help him this time. He's got Mama, but it's not the same. It ain't fair. This is all the Doranen's fault. They started it. They should fix it. What if Da can't fix it on his own? What if—what if—

"Rafel?" said Deenie. Her voice was nearly a whimper. "Rafel, what's the matter? What—"

And then the chamber door opened, and Mama was standing there with *such* a look on her face.

"Rafel? Deenie? Jervale's mercy, what do you think you're doing?" she demanded. "Do you know what time it is? Back to bed at once, young lady. And you, Rafe! You should be in bed too. There'll be no more supper apples for that pony if *this* is how you carry on!"

Deenie tumbled off the bed, swallowing a sob. She never could help snivelling if ever a voice got raised at her. "Sorry, Mama."

"I should think so. And you, Rafe?" said Mama, as Deenie squeezed past her on bare, scurrying feet. "Are you sorry too?"

No, he wasn't, but if he said that, Stag wouldn't get his supper apple for nigh on a week, most like. So he ducked his head. "Aye, Mama."

"Ha," said Mama. She was a tough one to fool. "A likely story."

She still sounded cross, but not *too* cross. So he looked up again. "Mama..."

"What is it?" she said, and came properly into his chamber. "Rafe? What were you and Deenie talking on? You didn't tell her anything, did you? About what happened today?"

No, Mama. She told me. But he couldn't say that, either. "Course not. You said not to say."

"Good," she said, and sat on the bed beside him. Smoothed her hand over his hair. "Because she might be bright as a button but she's still a little girl. A shy little girl, Rafe. She's not rough and tumble bold, like you."

Rough and tumble bold. Mama had never called him that before. He liked it. "Deenie's a watering pot," he said, pulling a face. "Boo hoo hoo, all the time."

Mama's fingers pinched his ear. "That's not nice, Rafe. Big brothers look after their little sisters. They don't call them names."

"Yes, Mama," he said, like a good boy, because he didn't want her taking away his nightly visit to the stables. "Sorry, Mama."

"Wheedler," she said, half-smiling, half-scolding. "As bad as your father. Now into your nightshirt, my fine fellow, and bed."

"All right," he said. "I will."

This time she kissed his forehead. "Good boy."

"Mama..." he said, as she stood. "Da—Da—"

"What about Da?"

Can he save us? Will he save us? But he couldn't get the words past the lump in his throat. Mama dropped to a crouch, and took his cold hands in hers.

"Rafel, you're not to fret," she said softly, her eyes hard and bright. "Nowt bad is going to happen. Your da won't let it. Your da is the strongest, bravest man in the kingdom. We're safe as safe, all of us. I promise."

He nodded, feeling his eyes sting, seeing her face blur. He hadn't snivelled once when he was telling her and Da about what he'd felt in the riverpond . . . but now he couldn't help it.

"Hush, now," Mama said. "And into bed. When I come back I want to find you fast asleep."

"Yes, Mama," he said, gulping a bit.

As she closed the chamber door behind her, he kicked off his boots. Yanked off his socks. Stripped off his shirt and trews and smalls, leaving them draped all anyhow over his chamber chest, and slithered into his nightshirt. Dove beneath his blankets and doused the glimfire lamps with a finger-snap.

Your da is the strongest, bravest man in the kingdom. We're safe as safe, all of us. I promise.

Hugging Mama's words tight, his fears banished for now, and not needing Tollin's parchment, he drifted to sleep.

CHAPTER TEN

✷

Asher hadn't thought to find himself back in the royal crypt so soon. After leaving Darran to sleep here, he'd thought he were done with the place. It prodded him in old, half-healed wounds he needed to leave alone. Not just for his sake, but for everyone else's too. It was those closest to him, the ones he loved best, Dathne and the sprats and Pellen, who suffered when a black mood came on him like a southeast winter sea storm.

"But since when did my druthers get noticed, eh?" he asked Gar's still, stone face. "Never, I reckon. So nowt much has changed."

Glimfire, flickering, seemed to reveal Gar's lips quirking in a wry, reproving smile.

Asher, Asher. Petulance doesn't become you.

Startled, he looked around. Thought for a moment he'd see Gar standing behind him, warm, living flesh instead of cold white marble. But no. He was alone.

"Petulant?" he said, and snorted. "I ain't petulant. I'm *fratched*. And I reckon I've a right, Gar. This were s'posed to be *over*. You and me, I thought we ended it."

No reply. He didn't expect one. Gar was dead, and the dead did not speak.

For a long time he stood there, brooding. Dathne had offered to come with him so he didn't have to face without her what was hidden in Gar's coffin. But he'd said no, because he had no idea how long he'd be here. And her coming with him would've meant leaving Rafe and Deenie in the Tower with only Cluny to call on if Rafe woke from a bad dream, tormented by the uneasy earth. Remembering his son's tale of the river-pond, Rafe's wide eyes and pinched face, he felt his belly gripe tight.

I got to stop this. I got to. It be hurting my boy.

Reluctant, resentful, he used a Doranen spell of compulsion to ease aside the coffin lid, with its effigy, just far enough for him to fit his hand and arm within. He held his breath as the lid shifted, fearful of being assaulted by something foul, the heartbreaking stench of decay and corruption... but instead he caught the faint, sweet scent of flowers. Pamarandums, best favoured by Nix in the rooms of the dead. Holze and Pother Nix between 'em had done right by Gar. He was whole. He was clean. Time had left him alone.

Closing his eyes, feeling his heart's dull thud within his broad ribcage, he eased his hand into Gar's burdened coffin.

Mayhap hidin' that bloody diary in here weren't such a crackin' good idea after all.

When his fingers brushed against Gar's linen wrappings—against Gar—he felt his belly heave in revolted protest. Had to press his fisted left hand hard to his lips, his teeth, to keep the surging bile at bay. Where was the sinkin' bloody thing? It had to still be here. No-one knew what he'd done. It couldn't not be here.

On a sharply indrawn breath, almost a sob, the sweet pamarandum scent turning sour in his throat, he scrabbled blindly for the diary, skinning his knuckles on the coffin's smooth side and floor as he poked and prodded and slid his fingers into places he couldn't bear to think on closely.

Come on—stop hiding—come on—

He nearly shouted when at last he touched the diary's ancient leather cover, smooth and cool after ten years in the dark. Snatching it hard, he pulled, desperate to be done with this. Grunted in pain as he banged and bruised his hand on the coffin lid dragging Barl's secrets into the light.

Sweating, breathing harshly, he stared at the small, unremarkable book that in Durm's arrogant hands had seen a prophecy fulfilled and a kingdom brought perilous close to destruction. Seen lives ruined. Villages smashed to bits and pieces. Seen the helpless innocent made widows, widowers and orphans, and bodies piled high in the streets like corded firewood.

So much death. So much ruin. All 'cause one man couldn't leave well enough alone.

But it were done, and couldn't be undone, and Barl knew Durm had paid a terrible price for his pride.

Easing himself backwards until his shoulder blades and spine touched Fane's cool, quiet tomb, he beckoned a hovering ball of glimfire closer and started leafing through Barl's diary. Not to read the actual entries, because to his Olken eye they were nowt more than chicken scratchins in the dirt. But Gar's scribbled translations were still stuck between its pages, so he read those. Well, some of them. He didn't need to read the translated warspells. Didn't even want to look at them. Instead, for the first time, he read the other bits and scraps, memory stirred by Gar's neatly fluent penwork.

Remembrances of the Doranen's battle to cross over the mountains...the lands they travelled through, the peoples they encountered. Grief at the loss of friends, of children...relief at finding such a pliable people, the Olken...the fateful bargain they'd struck. The words of Making and UnMaking—*sink me, I bloody remember that*—and the spell that had let Durm see through the Wall, that brought Morg into the kingdom, sealing their fates...

Page after page, and no mention of the Weather map or how the Weather Magic worked its will. Eyes hot and gritty, feeling as though sand were trapped under their lids, Asher read and read...starting to feel desperate as the scraps of Gar's scribbling mounted up, with no answers. There hadn't been time to translate every last page of the diary, true, but surely, *surely,* if he'd been able to translate the history, which didn't matter a bloody damn, then Gar would've bothered to translate the *important* bits, the *magic.* It weren't like he didn't know the magic mattered most.

Except it looked ezackly like that, 'cause eventually he got to the last hastily scrawled page and he'd not found a single useful word.

Disbelieving, despairing, he let the diary drop into his lap. Stared at the stone effigy he'd created with such care. "Gar, Gar, you *fool.* You bloody *barnacle.* Why didn't you realise I'd *need* that magic one day!"

Gar, being dead, or canny, had nowt to say for himself.

Muscles cold and stiff, his joints seized up, Asher levered himself to his feet, groaning, letting the diary tumble to the crypt floor, and stamped about relieving his temper with unbridled bad language.

When he was calm enough to think clearly he dropped onto the edge of Darran's coffin, taking mild pleasure in knowing it'd make the ole trout curse and cuff.

"All right, then," he said, glaring at Gar's silent effigy. "You weren't the only bloody scholar in Lur, were you? There's other Doranen studied the kind of claptrap you liked. Old books and poems and the way you folk used to talk. Barlsman Jaffee, he's nigh on cross-eyed from readin'. I could show him the diary, couldn't I? I could trust him with it, don't you reckon? He's a bloody Barlsman. All that piety. If I swore him to secrecy he'd have to keep his word, eh? Wouldn't he?"

He wanted to think so. But then, Durm had been Borne's Master Magician, hadn't he? The most powerful, most important mage after the king. Nobody knew better than Durm the dangerous muck in Barl's diary. And what did he do with it? He let Morg in through the back door.

So no. He didn't dare even trust Barlsman Jaffee. Which meant he'd have to try and sort the problem on his own. Bloody wonderful. As if he had the first idea what to do... He scowled at Gar's serene stone face.

Don't know where you are, or if you can hear me, but just in case? A bit of help about now wouldn't go astray.

Silence. Shadows. The dull beating of his heart.

"Right," he said. "So that's that. Lucky me, eh?" He shook his head. "All I ever bloody wanted was a fishin' boat of my own..."

He returned the diary to its hiding place. Magicked the coffin lid back where it belonged. Took a moment to honour Borne and Dana and pull faces at Fane. Tweaked Darran's stone nose, just 'cause he could. Then, with a final frown at Gar, he doused all but one ball of glimfire and left the royal crypt without it bobbing overhead.

The earlier high cloud cover had cleared, leaving a night full of stars and a fat moon. They'd not had rain in nearly three weeks. He stared at the humped darkness of the mountains. Even after all this time he sometimes found himself surprised that the golden wash of Barl's Wall was absent. If he closed his eyes he could see it, that curtain of magic cutting Lur off from the rest of the world.

If someone had asked him, scant weeks ago, whether he was sorry it was destroyed he'd have said *Are you bloody daft? Of course not.* Without thinking twice. Because until a few weeks ago he'd believed life was good, and they were safe, and the future smelled sweet. But that were a few weeks ago. Now the land was losing its balance... men like Fernel Pintte were stirrin' trouble round the edges... and the safety of a kingdom sat fair and square on his shoulders. Again.

And if bein' fratched on that means I be bloody petulant, then fine. I can live with bein' petulant, Gar. But I ain't sure I can live with not bein' able to fix what's gone wrong with Lur.

And on that bleak thought, he doused the glimfire and headed back to the Tower.

Dathne woke to the cold kiss of snow on her face.

"Asher," she whispered, rolling towards him. "Asher, wake up."

He didn't stir. The moonlight shafting through the partly curtained window glittered silver on the flakes of ice falling gently from the grey cloud he'd created, dreaming, beneath their bedchamber's frescoed ceiling.

"Asher," she said again, as the delicate snowflakes danced and drifted and tangled, melting in her hair. *"Asher."*

The first time this happened, in her bedroom above the bookshop, it had changed her life in a heartbeat. Since then the power in his blood had stirred to life many times in his sleep. In dreams he had no defences against it...and Weather Magic was the most powerful of all. Waking he could deny it, and did, no matter how hard that was.

But it would not—could not—be denied forever.

She rested her hand on his tense shoulder. "Asher. It's snowing. You need to wake up."

He flinched at her touch, his head restless on the pillow. Glinting beneath his tight-closed eyelids, a hint of fresh blood. She had to be careful. She couldn't wrench him awake. Once, she'd done that, and had hurt him so badly he'd stayed painwracked and bedridden for two long, dreadful days.

"Asher...can you hear me?" she whispered, and stroked her fingertips down his cheek. "Come back now. Come back to me. Let it go. Come back."

Her voice always roused him. He always came back, hearing it. At least he always had before. But he wasn't hearing her this time. Even as she watched, she saw his moonlit face twist. Heard his breathing harshen, and deepen, and saw his fingers clutch at their blankets.

"*Asher,*" she said, concern sliding towards fright. "Please, my love. Please. *Wake up.*"

A gust of cold air swirled round the chamber. The falling snow swirled with it, stinging as it struck her face and lashed her eyes.

And then she nearly screamed, because around their comfortable bed the air was starting to shiver. Something dark and terrible was sliding over her skin. She'd felt this before...she'd seen it...ten years ago...

"*Asher!*" she cried, and thumped him with both fists, desperate. "Asher, you're calling warbeasts! *Asher, wake up!*"

Cruelly wrenched from magic, Asher came clawing awake. No mere hint now, the blood dripped freely from both eyes and his nose, too, splattering the white sheets and fouling his face.

"What? What?" he said, flailing. "I can't see! What's amiss?"

As the air curdled around them, thick with snow and fire, crowded with monstrous shapes taking slow, writhing form, she clapped sharply, twice, and brought thought to life. Flooded their chamber with glimfire, then seized his face between her hands.

"Look, Asher! *Look!*" she said, and forced his gaze where she needed it. "Stop this. You're awake now. *Stop dreaming.*"

On a choked cry of pain he jerked free of her tight grasp and sat up. Stared in horror at the warbeasts he'd unwittingly summoned.

"Luk rana! *Rana!*" he commanded hoarsely, waving one arm. *"Rana!"*

The warbeasts vanished, taking the wild snow with them.

Groaning, he fell back to the pillows. Pressed both hands flat to his bloodied face, shaking, each shuddering breath hurting him like knives.

Just as shaken, Dathne slumped beside him, one hand on his shoulder, the other pressed to her heart. Pound any harder and it would pound right through her thin chest.

"You all right, Dath?" said Asher, muffled, still hiding behind his hands. "Those things didn't hurt you?"

"No," she whispered, and was shamed to hear weeping in the word. "Asher...what happened? You've never done that before."

"That bloody diary," he said, and let his hands slide. Beneath the smeared blood his face was chalk-white. "Reading it stirred me up good and proper, I reckon."

Threading her fingers through his sweaty, disordered hair she bent down and kissed him. Tasted iron and salt, his blood on her tongue. "It wasn't your fault."

He shook his head, squinting in the bright glimlight. Seeing that, she dimmed it. Ashamed of herself because less light brought relief. Meant his pain and fright were shadowed. Hidden. She couldn't bear to see him hurting and scared. She'd been so fierce and strong, once...but love had made her soft. Sometimes she thought the old Dathne, who'd had the visions, who'd planned to poison Timon Spake, who'd sacrificed everything and everyone in the service of prophecy...sometimes she thought that Dathne was a dream.

"Course it be my fault," Asher said, always so unforgiving. "I called the bloody things, didn't I?" Then he grunted, a small sharp sound of pain. "Feels like my head's goin' to blow right apart."

"Oh, Asher..." She kissed him again. "I'm sorry. I tried to wake you gently but—"

"You did right. What were needful." He looked at her, and broke her heart. "Always feared I might do that some day. Call them warbeasts out of the past. They're in me, Dath. They're in me and I can't rip 'em out. What if I call 'em again? What if I can't stop 'em next time?"

"Don't," she said, and pressed her fingers to his blood-smeared lips. "You're tormenting yourself for *nowt*. You're strong enough to keep the magic under control. You are. This was one time. *One time.* There won't be another."

Groaning, he sat up. Wrapped his arms tight around her and buried his face against her neck. Tremors ran through him, born not just of pain, but fear as well. She held him with all the strength in her body, poured all her love into him.

"It's all right...it's all right..." she murmured. "Asher, it's all right."

The chamber door flew open, and Rafe barrelled in. "You gotta come!" he panted. "Quick! Deenie's having a conniption!"

"Really," said Lady Marnagh, frowning at her neatly interlaced fingers, "I don't have any objection to the proposal, in principle. In principle it seems sensible, and practical, and would certainly ease the workload on the Justice Hall staff. And it does seem to be in keeping with the other changes we've made these past years." She turned a little in her chair. "Do you see any spiritual obstacles to the General Council's suggestion, Barlsman Jaffee?"

Pellen, comfortably sprawled in his own council chair, kept part of his attention on the elderly Barlsman, who never answered a question quickly when slowly was a choice, and kept the rest of it on Asher. Instead of taking his own place at the table he was slouched at a window, brooding into the palace gardens beyond. Had hardly spoken a word through this entire Mage Council meeting, even when their talk had turned to the Bibford fleet's over-fishing of the waters between Lur's west coast and Dragonteeth Reef.

Something was wrong. Something new? From the look an Asher's face, he thought so. Just what they needed...another crisis to be dealt with.

Jaffee's wheezing, worse now than it had been a few months ago, sounded loud in the hushed meeting chamber. The Barlsman fingered his long, thin braid of devotion, the gold holyring on his thumb catching fire in the sunlight. Thady and Eylin, seated side by side at the wide Council table, exchanged resigned looks and dropped their chins to their chests. Two years each they'd been Olken representatives on the Mage Council. They knew there was no point trying to hurry Jaffee along.

Rodyn Garrick drummed his fingers on the arm of his chair. Of middle height for a Doranen, and less lightly fleshed than most, his pale blue eyes rarely showed warmth. Not a City-born Doranen, he'd been elected to the Council from his country estate near Fiddler's Green, where his family grew grapes for icewine.

"This is a temporal matter," he said, in his typically clipped way, clearly tired of waiting for Jaffee. "The guidelines laid down six centuries ago *clearly* mandate that any dispute between a Doranen and an Olken must be satisfied in Justice Hall. I see no reason to alter the arrangement."

"Can't say I be surprised to hear that, Rodyn," said Asher, not turning from the window. "But think on this, why don't you? For six hundred years, justice for Olken folk fratchin' with the Doranen has been decided in a place the Doranen built. Crammed floor to ceilin' with statues and paintins and whatnot of Barl. Now, there's folk as think it be past time we let go of habits as seem to favour the Doranen over the Olken — and I reckon they might be right."

"Given that you ruled in favor of that Olken farmer and against Ain Freidin," said Garrick, "I find *that* comment laughable."

Pellen swallowed a groan. *Not again.* "Rodyn, please. Ain Freidin was in the wrong and she admitted as much. Let's not sidetrack ourselves into pointless dispute. If we could perhaps —"

"I'm sorry, but I must protest too," said Lady Marnagh. "As Justice

Hall's administrator I am responsible for its conduct of business. To suggest there has been *any* unfair dealing is to question my integrity."

Asher flicked her a glance over his shoulder. "I ain't sayin' that, Sarnia."

"Then what are you saying?"

"I'm sayin' a lot of things were a bloody sight easier when we had a royal family. Borne, or Gar, they made their rulin' in Justice Hall and nobody said boo about it 'cause—well—we was all used to 'em layin' down the law. Life ain't so tidy now. That's what I'm sayin'."

"It will only get untidy if we *allow* it to get untidy," said Garrick. "My objection stands. I see no good reason for any change."

Turning away from the window, Asher fixed the Doranen lord with an incredulous stare. "Rodyn, be you blind? There's been nowt but change since the Wall came down. And like it or not, change ain't done with us yet. Not by a long shot."

Garrick's thin lips pinched. "What are you suggesting? That we discard every last tradition? Abandon centuries of established legal precedent and turn Lur into a judicial free-for-all?"

"Course not," Asher snapped. "But we got to face facts, Rodyn. Your good ole days be dead and gone. We got *these* days to think on now. And I reckon if one of yours and one of mine get 'emselves in a brangle, whether magic be involved or not, there ain't no harm in 'em tryin' to sort it out first and foremost on their own doorsteps, like good neighbours. If they can't I'll sort the problem for 'em in Justice Hall, same as always. But we ought to give 'em first crack, I reckon."

Before Garrick could voice an opinion, Jaffee stirred and cleared his throat. "Yes, that seems fair," he pronounced, his voice weak and wavering. "Blessed Barl never desired to ride roughshod over the Olken people."

Pellen looked at Thady and Eylin. "Your thoughts?"

They exchanged glances, then Eylin shrugged. "I suppose it depends on what you mean, Asher, by sorting it out on their own doorsteps. How certain are we that the Doranen will accept any ruling from an Olken district court?"

"A ruling agin them, you mean," said Thady dryly. "Can't see them complaining about a judgement in their favour."

"And you think that's likely, do you?" Garrick retorted. "An Olken court ruling for a Doranen against one of its own?"

Dismayed, Pellen slapped his hand flat to the table. "For shame! In this chamber we are sworn to uphold justice for *everyone*."

"True, Pellen, that's our aim," said Eylin. "And in this chamber we might, for the most part, be able to forget which of us has dark hair and which of us is blond. But beyond these palace walls, well...it isn't always so cut-and-dried."

"She's right," Thady added. "I know a mort of folk who believe us Olken won't never stand toe-to-toe with the Doranen until the Doranen yield a time or two."

Folk like Fernel Pintte. Churned with disquiet, Pellen stared at the table. *What has been festering in our towns and villages, that I've not seen? That neither of Lur's Councils have seen? Just how many Fernel Pinttes are out there?* He tried to catch Asher's eye, but Asher had turned back to the window. It was clear, at least to him, that the Innocent Mage did not want to be here.

Rodyn Garrick was staring at Thady as though the City's most prosperous innkeeper, and one of its best mages, had grown another head. "Are you serious?" he said at last. "How have the Doranen not yielded to you, man? Barl save us, we've given back land, we've changed certain laws, we let you do magic, we —"

"*Let* us?" echoed Eylin. "You *let* us? When the magic was always ours? When without Olken earth-singing Barl *never* would've been able to —"

"Now, now," said Jaffee, raising both hands. "I see little advantage in raking over the past. Can we not simply agree that —"

"Yes, Barlsman Jaffee, we certainly can agree," said Eylin. A farmer from the Hawshore district, used to wrangling bulls, she had no fear of Barlsmen or any other lofty Doranen. "We can agree that while it's doubtless difficult for your people to see yourselves knocked off your lofty perches, you'd best accept it. As we accepted losing our sovereignty when first you came upon us."

"The Doranen saved your lives!" spat Garrick. "You seem quite eager to forget *that* small fact."

"Tell you what I be eager for," said Asher, mildly enough. "I be eager for the lot of you to shut your bloody traps."

Pellen covered his mouth so the others wouldn't see his smile. They looked so *shocked*. Which was silly, really. *How* long had they known Asher?

Asher favoured them with his most jaundiced stare. "You be talkin' claptrap, every one of you. Think I ain't heard all this before? When the Wall came down, as we were pickin' up the pieces after? Think you be the first folk to try rakin' over what's well dead and buried? Six bloody centuries this kingdom rubbed along just fine, pretty much. And now ten years after Morg you want to tear it to pieces?"

"Of course we don't," said Thady, glowering. "But—"

"But? But? Ain't no *but*," said Asher, glowering back at him. "Choice is simple, Thady. We get along or we don't. We pull together or we bloody pull apart. Take your pick."

As Thady subsided, silenced, Asher turned on Garrick. "As for you, Rodyn. Know who you sound like? Conroyd bloody Jarralt, that's who."

Pellen winced. *Low blow, Asher.* Further along the table, Sarnia Marnagh paled. Barlsman Jaffee kissed his holyring. And Garrick looked like he'd just swallowed a hedgehog, whole.

"You've no right to say such a thing to me," he said, his voice tight with fury.

"Don't be daft," said Asher. "I got every bloody right. You want I should show you the scars Conroyd left me?"

Garrick's fingers clenched bloodless. "That wasn't Jarralt. That was Morg."

"It were both of 'em," said Asher. "I worked alongside Conroyd Jarralt for more than a year. I *knew* him. He despised us Olken and he enjoyed what Morg did to us. To me. They were cut from the same cloth, them two. Are you cut from it, Rodyn? Are you the kind of Doranen as thinks us Olken are nowt but cattle?"

"No, he's not, Asher," said Barlsman Jaffee, surprisingly firm. "He, Sarnia and I are all Barl's children, as devoted to Lur as any Olken, I assure you, and wholeheartedly committed to the causes of unity and peace. Whatever you doubt, I urge you not to doubt *that*."

"Them's pretty words, Barlsman," said Asher, his gaze not leaving Rodyn Garrick's cold face. "But I reckon they'd be prettier if I'd heard 'em out of Lord Garrick."

Pellen held his breath. Garrick was haughty, true, like most Doranen, but was he really another Jarralt? *I hadn't thought so ... but could be I'm wrong. Barl save us all. Fernel Pintte on our side, Rodyn Garrick on theirs. Are we doomed, then? Is peace beyond us?*

Garrick cleared his throat. "I regret if I misspoke myself," he said stiffly. "Barlsman Jaffee has the right of it. Of course I accept the Olken as equals in this land."

"Good," said Asher, his eyes so watchful. "Reckon I be mighty pleased to hear it."

"But I want an admission from you, Asher," Garrick added. "I want you to admit that an Olken is as capable of bias — of fault — as any one of *my* people. Can you deny that?"

"Deny it?" said Asher, eyebrows lifting. "When every day for a bloody year I had that sea-slug Willer Dryskle snappin' at my heels? Course I don't deny it, Rodyn. Ain't neither of our folks hold all the cards when it comes to bein' bloody stupid."

"No," said Garrick. "No, they do not."

Asher nodded. "Then I'd say we be fine, Rodyn." He looked at Thady and Eylin. "Don't you reckon?"

Thady and Eylin nodded, murmuring assent. With that, the almost unbearable tension in the council chamber eased. Pellen looked down to hide his surprised relief, then reached for his quill and notepad.

"So," he said, as brisk and as businesslike as he could contrive, "we're agreed, are we, that the petition for the altering of judicial pro-tocols shall be approved and returned at the next session of the General Council?"

They were agreed. And since the petition was the last item listed for discussion, they were also done. But just as he took a breath, ready to declare the meeting adjourned, Barlsman Jaffee raised a cautioning hand.

"Forgive me," he said. "There is a matter I would like to mention. What it means, I'm not entirely sure. Perhaps you will call me alarmist, a foolish old man, but I feel it's my duty to speak."

"Then speak," said Pellen, as his insides hollowed. "What's concern-ing you, Barlsman?"

Jaffee steepled his knobby-jointed fingers before him, tapped his lips and half-closed his eyes. "As you know, my duties as City Barlsman do not end with conducting services in the Chapel. I am called upon to hear secrets and private misgivings, to ease the burdened among us and share with them Barl's peace. During this past week I have heard whis-pers, my friends. Alarming whispers. Four different Olken have told me the same tale. Without betraying names, I would tell you what they said . . . for I confess, I'm at a loss."

Pellen didn't dare look at Asher. "Please, Barlsman. Continue."

"All four told me they've been disturbed by vivid, frightening dreams," said Jaffee. "And terrible feelings that something is wrong. In the earth." He shrugged. "I know that sounds odd, but it's how they put it. *Something wrong in the earth.* Of course, being Doranen, I could not share their concerns. I've prayed for enlightenment, but alas, enlight-enment eludes me. They are my spiritual children, and look to me for guidance, and I have none. I don't know what to say. Asher . . ."

Pellen dared look at him this time, along with everyone else. Asher's face betrayed nothing. As he still stood by the window, his expression showed only courteous interest.

"Aye, Jaffee?"

"Do you know what they meant? Have you felt anything odd these last few days? Or you, Pellen? Thady? Eylin? Earth-singing is an Olken gift. Have *any* of you sensed this disturbance?"

Only his former life as a City guardsman let Pellen keep his own face strictly schooled. He felt sick. "I haven't," he said, profoundly relieved it was the truth. He looked at Thady and Eylin. "Have you?"

"Not me," said Thady. "Haven't heard word of it in the Pig, either. And I hear most things tending bar. See most things, too. More than I want to, generally speaking."

"Nor me," said Eylin. "Asher, you're the most powerful Olken mage in Lur. What have you felt?"

"Nowt," said Asher, without a pause.

"And I've heard not a whisper at Justice Hall," said Lady Marnagh. "Asher, what of Dathne? She'd tell you, Asher, wouldn't she, if she felt anything...odd?"

"Course she would, Sarnia. But she ain't," Asher said, smooth as custard. "So I can't tell you what it means, Barlsman. Sorry."

Frowning, Jaffee unsteepled his fingers and fiddled with his Barlsbraid. "No need to apologise. I suppose it's possible these Olken simply...imagined things."

"Or had one ale too many in someone else's inn," said Asher, raising an eyebrow at Thady. "Where the brew be inferior."

"It is odd, though, isn't it?" said Eylin. "Asher, are you quite sure you or Dathne haven't—"

"I told you. I'm sure," said Asher, scowling. "Reckon I'm like to keep news like that to m'self? Reckon I wouldn't run here squawkin' to you lot if I had an inklin' there were somethin' wrong with Lur?"

"No, no, of course you would," Eylin said hastily.

Pellen swallowed a groan. *Asher, Asher...if they ever find out...* "I think the thing to do is wait and see,"· he suggested. "More than likely it's nothing. Some odd quirk of nature. Lur is as prosperous and fruitful as it's ever been. There's no hint of that changing. But naturally, should you hear any more about these feelings, Barlsman Jaffee—if any of us hears something—we should convene again at once. Agreed?"

His fellow Olken nodded. Then Rodyn Garrick tapped a thoughtful finger on the table. "And if it's not nothing? What then?"

"Then obviously we address the problem, quickly and discreetly," said Lady Marnagh. "This Mage Council is charged with maintaining the kingdom's safety. I don't think the matter should be discussed outside this chamber. Nor should any of us pursue independent enquiry, for fear of alarming people. Asher—"

"Sarnia?" said Asher, exquisitely polite.

"I don't begin to understand your particular mage powers...but is it possible for you to—to seek out this—this *wrongness* of which Jaffee speaks?"

"I s'pose," said Asher. "Ain't done nowt like that afore, but I s'pose I can try if the Council reckons it be needful."

So casual, he was. So *unconcerned*...at least on the surface. Pellen found himself marvelling. *But then, he always was a good liar.*

"I think it's an excellent suggestion," said Jaffee, bestowing upon Lady Marnagh an approving smile. "For I have no doubt that if anyone can plumb the heart of this mystery, it's our Innocent Mage."

Pellen, still watching Asher, saw his jaw tighten. *Don't bite Jaffee. Please don't. One brawl is enough to be going on with.*

"Like I said, I'll try," said Asher. "Only don't get your hopes up. Sometimes things just happen and there ain't never a reason why. Guess we just got to trust that things'll work out, one way or another."

"Indeed," said Jaffee solemnly. "Faith is the wind that lifts our wings."

Asher blinked. "Aye."

"All right," Pellen said, quickly. "If there are no other matters to be raised? Then we're done."

CHAPTER ELEVEN

✳

The council chamber emptied quickly after that, until only he and Asher were left. Getting up, Pellen pushed the door closed, then turned and considered his difficult friend.

"What?" said Asher, meeting his eloquent stare. "You think I were goin' to *tell* 'em? Ha! Sink *that*."

Profoundly troubled, Pellen returned to his chair. "Asher—keeping your own counsel unprovoked is one thing," he said, toying with his quill. "But they raised the issue of trouble stirring, and you looked them in their faces and *lied*. If they find out you lied do you honestly think they'll forgive it? It's ten years since you saved Lur, my friend. I suspect your currency as the Innocent Mage is not unlimited."

Shoulder propped against the chamber wall, Asher grunted. "Don't need it to be bloody unlimited, do I? It's only got to last till Lur's sailin' sweet again."

"And how long will that be? Do you know?"

Asher said nothing. Something dangerous seethed beneath his skin. Eyeing him askance, Pellen decided to ease the tension by changing the subject. At least for the moment. "Tell me," he said, tossing the quill aside and sitting back. "Do you trust Rodyn Garrick's easy capitulation over these Justice Hall changes?"

"Ha," said Asher. "I don't trust Rodyn Garrick. I'll stick a harpoon through my right eye afore I'll believe he reckons Olken and Doranen be equals."

"Well, I'm not sure *I'd* go that far, but after the way he carried on about you censuring Ain Freidin—" He drummed his fingers on the table. "So what's behind this uncharacteristic docility?"

"Indigestion?" Asher suggested, trying to smile. And there again, that dark, unwelcome hint of dire trouble. "He's Rodyn bloody Garrick, Pellen. Who knows what he's thinkin'? I don't reckon to fret on it overmuch. Not while we got him under our noses here in Council."

"I suppose," he agreed, reluctant. "He just makes me uneasy."

Instead of answering, Asher folded his arms and stared at the floor. Pellen, considering him, felt all kinds of misgivings stirred by the disquiet in his friend's face.

"What is it?" he asked. "You've been distracted—upset—since you walked in here. What's happened?"

Asher sighed. "Reckon you really don't want to know."

"Actually, reckon I really do," he retorted. "Sometimes I think you forget who I am, Asher, and who I'm answerable to."

"I bloody don't!" said Asher, stung.

"Really? Then prove it. Tell me what's going on."

For the first time that morning Asher sat in his customary council chair. Propped his elbows on the table and scrubbed his hands across his face. He looked exhausted. Almost...defeated.

Abruptly and coldly sick, Pellen felt his skin crawl. "The diary? You read the diary?"

"Aye," said Asher, sounding tired. "And it ain't no bloody use to us. What Gar translated, it's just warspells and personal witterings. The spell that killed Morg. Nowt on the Wall or the Weather Magic or suchlike. Nowt to explain what's stirrin' under our feet. Nowt on how I'm s'posed to save us from it."

He was so bitter. And who could blame him? The weight of a kingdom was forcing him to his knees. "I agree, that's a blow," he said, with care. "But we can't fall in a heap."

"Why not?" Asher muttered. "Fall in a heap, stand on our heads, turn bloody cartwheels down the length of the High Street—for all I know that's as good a way as any to get us out of this strife."

Oh, *Asher*. Pellen slapped the table. "*No*. I refuse to believe we can't find a cure for what's ailing our kingdom. What about Durm? He was the Master Magician; he guided Borne in his WeatherWorking for all those years. Those books of his you spoke of, the ones you keep hidden in your library. Surely there's something there we can use? He must've left behind some kind of Weather Magic instructions or—"

But Asher was shaking his head again. "When it comes to Weather-Working there were only one of his books seemed it might be useful. I got Barslman Holze to look at it for me, not long after the Wall fell. But he couldn't make head or tail of it any more than me. Bloody thing's writ in some stupid code, Pellen, squiggles and chicken scratchin's. A load of bloody nonsense. Everythin' to do with WeatherWorkin' Durm kept secret. Just like he never said who he wanted followin' him as Master Magician. Him and Borne, they were spit scared of another schism. So they never shared nowt."

Pellen breathed out a slow sigh. "I suppose they never dreamed things could ever go so wrong," he murmured. "And who can blame them? Only one man ever did."

"Aye, well, that bloody Jervale didn't finish the job, did he?" said Asher, surly. "Pity he didn't stay asleep long enough to dream the rest of what could go arse over tits around here. Reckon my life might be a sinkin' sight easier if he had."

It was tempting to sympathise with him, but they'd make no progress moaning over what couldn't be changed. "There's nothing on the walls of the Weather Chamber that will help?"

"I don't reckon so. I'll look again, but..." Asher groaned his frustration. "I don't know what to do, Pellen. I know I be the only one who can fix this, but I don't bloody know *how*."

"Yes, you do," he said quietly. "It's in you somewhere, Asher. Buried deep, perhaps, but it's there. All the Weather Magic that was put into you, *somewhere* in there is the answer. It must be."

Asher shoved out of his chair. "You don't know that!" he snapped, pacing angrily, fists shoved in his pockets. "*I* don't know it and I'm the one who got that bloody magic stuffed down his gullet!"

"I know it because Barl was no fool," he retorted. "Everything the WeatherWorker needed to know she put in her magic, Asher, I'd stake my life on that. Why else would she not leave any instructions behind? All you have to do is *look* for it. Stop fighting who and what you are, and instead—embrace it. Open your heart and your mind and seek the answer inside you. You'll find it. By all I hold dear, I'll wager it's there."

"*Just like that, eh?*" said Asher, still pacing. "So you reckon it's a doddle? An easy peasy piece of piss?"

"I never called it easy," he said. "But I think you make it harder than it need be. Did anyone have to teach you how to summon the rain? How to make it snow, or stir the wind? *No.* The knowledge was in you. It's *still* in you. Asher, you can do this."

"Aye, Pellen, mayhap I can!" Asher shouted, turning. "But I don't bloody *want* to! I've spent ten years tryin' to *forget* what I know!"

"Yes, well, I think that's my point!" he snapped, nearly pushed to shouting himself. "And forgive me if this sounds blunt and unfriendly, but I'm of the opinion you've no *right* to forget it. Fair or not, Asher, you are who you are and you don't have the luxury of putting the rest of us in danger just because—"

Asher leapt towards him. Snatched the nearest empty chair and slammed it down hard on the chamber's parquetry floor. "Pellen Orrick, you're a sinkin' bloody fool! Flappin' your lips when you know nowt about *nowt!* Care to guess what I did last night, Meister Mayor? Meister Mayor who can't even sprout wheat seeds? While I were asleep, with my wife beside me and my son and my daughter but a few steps away? I summoned *warbeasts.* I nearly *killed* 'em. Dath and Rafe and little Deenie, who mean more to me than *anythin'*. I nearly *killed* 'em with the magic that's in me. All I did were read Barl's bloody diary, and that stirred me up enough that I summoned *warbeasts* in my *sleep.*

So are you really goin' to sit there and lecture me on how I don't have the sinkin' luxury of not wantin' to wake what I got sleepin' in my blood?"

Stunned, Pellen stared at him. Stared at the terror and the tears in his eyes and was flooded with pity and horror and hot, hot shame. "Asher—I'm sorry, I didn't—"

"And Deenie *felt* it," said Asher, heedless. Wrenched himself away and started pacing again, staggering almost, buffeted by a depth of feeling he had never before revealed. "And she *screamed*. Oh, Pellen, she bloody screamed. If you'd heard her, my little Deenie, screamin' 'cause of the warbeasts I called, 'cause she could feel 'em in me. I never knew she could do that, feel magic in folk. But she can. She never told us, but that be somethin' she can do." Breathing harshly, he fetched up against the chamber window. Flung out one hand to brace himself, and let his face fall into the crook of his elbow. "She can feel there be somethin' wrong in the earth, too," he said dully. "She can feel all of it. Reckon *I* poisoned her with that. Me and my bloody magic."

Pellen tried to speak. Had to clear his throat. "Asher, you don't know that."

"Course I do," Asher whispered. "Ain't no other Olken who can do Doranen magic, is there? Well, there ain't no Olken Dath's ever heard of who can sense magic the way Deenie can. Course it be my fault. Can't be nobody else's."

"All right," he said at last, not quite certain of his voice. "Perhaps that's true. Perhaps this—this ability did come from you. But why do you call it a poison? Why not call it a gift?"

"*Gift?*" said Asher and laughed, with such scorn. "If you'd heard her screamin', Pellen, you wouldn't call it a gift." Turning abruptly, shoulders hitting the wall, he let himself slide until he was sat on the floor. "It ain't a gift. It's a bloody curse."

Heartsick, he nodded. "Yes. Yes, I can see that. I'm sorry, Asher. I—I don't know what else to say."

Asher dragged an unsteady hand down his face. "There's nowt you can say, Pellen. Nowt to say, nowt to do."

"You're right. It's awful," he said. "And I hope you know I'd cut off my other leg to spare you and Dathne such grief. To spare Deenie the grief..." He looked down at the table. Hating himself, even as he knew he had to say it. "But it's something apart from what this kingdom is facing. And I'm sorry, I'm *sorry,* but you *can't* let it interfere. We've run out of *time.*"

"I know," said Asher, after a long silence, letting his head tip back against the wall. "Why d'you reckon I'm so bloody fratched?"

"We may have a little grace left to us, but we can't, we mustn't, count on much," he added. "You fobbed off Jaffee and the others well enough today, but what about tomorrow? Or next week? Other Olken are bound to confide their fears in our revered Barlsman. It's what he's there for. Or Thady will overhear something, tending his bar. And whatever it is that's churning in the earth, if it gets any worse, if it gets any louder — then could be even folk as magic-deaf as I am will start to hear it. And then —" He felt his mouth dry. "I think things will be worse even than when the Wall fell."

"Reckon I don't know that too, Pellen?" said Asher, caustic. "I do. All right? I know."

And still bitterly resented being pushed towards the inevitable. But that was just too bad. It couldn't matter that Asher didn't want this. All that mattered was that he did what had to be done.

And it's not as if this time we're asking him to die...

Thrusting aside any lingering guilt, Pellen cleared his throat again. "Asher —"

Asher looked up, his face so stark that seeing it was like a blow from a clenched fist. "I know what you reckon I should do," he said, his voice ragged. "You reckon I should go back to the Weather Chamber and WeatherWork our way out of this mess. Either fix that bloody Weather map somehow so it keeps on doin' what it's been doin' for centuries — or finish the job Morg started so Lur can start afresh, proper, like we thought it did already. Eh? Ain't that what you want, Pellen?"

Doused with fresh shame, defiant because of it, he nodded. "Yes. This land is my home. It's my daughter's home. Thanks to Morg it's the only home we're ever going to have. And I want you to save it. I'm sorry, but I do."

"Course you do," said Asher, and stared into the distance at something awful that only he could see. "But here's the thing. If I work the Weather Magic, Deenie's goin' to feel it. It bloody nearly kills me, Pellen. You know that. So what d'you reckon it'll do to her, eh? Eight years old? A little girl? If you was me, and it were Charis, what would you do? Would you kill your little girl to save this kingdom?"

He couldn't speak. Could hardly breathe. The ugly question hung between them, unanswered. Unanswerable.

"Aye," said Asher, and clambered awkwardly to his feet. "That's what I thought."

The chamber door closed very gently behind him.

Dathne sat in the garden that used to be Gar's private bower, the one he and Fane had destroyed with fury and glimfire, and tried to ease her jangled nerves by embroidering a small tapestry. The sunlight warmly caressed her skin, a welcome simplicity after the night's cold terrors. Remembering, she jabbed the needle into her finger. Sucked at the ruby-red bead of blood, softly swearing, then thrust aside the awfulness, just as she'd thrust aside so many bloodied, haunting memories.

She was getting very good at doing that.

With a sigh, she considered the tapestry. *A pity I'm not getting good at this too.* But such sedate pursuits had never been her strong point. Business and books and herblore and visions. Bossing people. Those were her talents. Or had been, once. Teaching. She was good at teaching. In the first years following the Wall's destruction it had meant everything to her, passing along to Olken children what she knew of Olken magic and its ways. Telling them their history. Making sure they knew the truth, when the truth was still new and imperfectly known.

But now everybody knew it. Lur's history was taught in every school and chapel these days. Nothing hidden. No more secrets.

Well. No more but one.

And suddenly the sunlight lost its caressing warmth and she was shivering, once more burdened with shadowed knowledge.

I thought it was over. It was meant to be over.

"Hey now," said Asher, dropping to the stone bench beside her. Appearing when he was needed most, like always. Blindly she turned to him, embroidery hoop dropping heedless to the grass, and blindly she hid her cold face against his chest.

"I know, I know," he said, rocking her. "I know, Dath. I know."

And he did know. It was her only solace, that in her pain for her children she wasn't alone.

The bower's carefully nurtured flowers scented the air sweet and fresh. Bees droned sleepily, and in the branches of the fussy tarla tree small green titbirds bobbed and chirped. Early spring was upon them, and Lur was reborn. Calming, she eased herself free of Asher's tight, almost suffocating embrace. Caught sight of his face and lost her breathing again.

"What? Did something happen in Council?"

"Aye, y'might say that." His voice was low, his eyes miserable. "Seems there be folk talkin' to Jaffee about funny things they've felt. He told the Council and now they all know somethin's wrong."

"And what else?" Because she knew there was something else. She knew every mood in him, every twist and turn of his heart.

"I lied to 'em, Dath," he said. "Told 'em I ain't felt a bloody thing. They believed me for now, but..." He shook his head. "That won't last long. Thady and Eylin ain't felt it yet, but once they do they won't believe their precious Innocent Mage can't feel it. Rodyn Garrick neither, nor any other Doranen. So..."

So. She knew what that meant. *WeatherWorking.* Frozen, untouchable by sunlight or any warmth, she slithered off the garden seat and backed away. "You can't. What about Deenie? She'll feel it. Asher, she's too young to feel that."

Instead of answering, he picked up her embroidery hoop and stared at her tapestry. A fishing boat on the ocean. Her own design; she'd meant it as a surprise. Washed in sunshine he touched her tiny blue stitches with the tip of one scarred finger. Almost, *almost,* his lips quirked in a smile.

She could have stamped her foot like a child in a tantrum. *"Asher!* Are you listening? I won't let you do it. I won't let you hurt our daughter."

"Don't be daft, Dathne," he said, and tossed the tapestry to the seat. "I ain't about to hurt Deenie."

"How can you not hurt her?" she retorted. "You hurt her last night. I know you didn't mean to, but you did. And it'll be a thousand times worse with full blown Weather Magic, you *know* it will."

He nodded. "Aye. I do."

"Well, then?"

"Well, then, Dath," he said, meeting her fury without flinching, "reckon you'll have to do somethin' about that."

"Me do something? What are you—" Choking, she stared at him. She knew him too well. "I *can't.* Have you gone mad?"

"Maybe," he said, his eyebrows pulling low. "But I can't see another way round it. Can you?"

"You want me to *drug* her? So you can do Weather Magic?"

Still his steady gaze held hers. "Time was you were willin' to murder a man with drugs, for less."

He might as well have punched her. Winded, she dropped to the neatly clipped grass. *"Asher..."*

Then he was on his knees gripping her shoulders, holding her up. "Think I *want* to, Dath?" he demanded hoarsely. "You reckon this be *easy* for me to think on? I ain't got no *choice*—and neither do you. Whatever's brewin' with the weather, woman, either I nip it in the bud, *tonight,* or what we've built these last ten years comes tumblin' down around our ears."

She could feel herself weeping, hot tears on her frozen face. "You don't know that. You can't be sure."

"I'm sure!" he said, shaking her. "And so are you." He shook her again, his face twisted with anguish and anger. "You started this, Dathne. You made me the Innocent Mage. Now *I* got to finish it. For Deenie and Rafel. For all of us."

She struck his broad chest with her fist over and over again. Nodding. Sobbing. "I know. I know."

"Oh, *Dath*," he groaned, and snatched her to him. Buried his face against her neck. "We'll be all right. We will. I promise."

She wanted to believe him, so hard she hurt. But she knew, just as he did, that where Barl and the Weather Magic were concerned...promises were no more to be trusted than glimfire in a rising wind.

"So, Rafe, how was school today?"

Shrugging, Rafel shoved his spinach round and round his dinner plate with his fork. Mama was trying to sound interested. She was trying to sound bright and happy, like there was nowt a thing wrong. It made him cross 'cause something was wrong all right. The tension in the solar's air made him want to shout and stamp.

I ain't a tiddy mouse like Deenie. I ain't deaf or blind or addled like Jed. She shouldn't pretend. That's wrong. It's like lying.

"Rafel?" said Mama. "Did you hear me? How was—"

"It was fine. It was school," he said, almost a grunt. And that was all he wanted to say. He didn't want to tell anyone about what had happened. What he'd done. The thing that made him feel small and dirty, worse even than when he was prickled with guilt for his terrible secret.

"Rafe," said Da sharply. "Don't take that tone with your ma. And you look at her when she asks you a question. And mind you eat your bloody spinach. It be food, it ain't for playin' with."

Burning with resentment, he glared sideways at Da from beneath his lowered lashes then dropped his fork to the plate. "I don't want my spinach. I'm full."

"You be full when the plate's empty," said Da. "Eat up, I said."

Mama sighed. "Asher..."

Eyes big and round, Deenie started to cry. Not a loud boo-hooing, just a few trickly tears, but still. Da threw down his napkin, shoved his chair back and stamped over to the solar window to glare down into the Tower gardens far below. He always stared out of a window when he was fratched, so all anyone could see of him was the back of his head. He didn't like it when people could read his thoughts in his face.

"Asher," Mama said again, but it sounded almost like a question. Almost like she was frighted. But why would Mama be frighted?

At the window, Da nodded. "Aye."

Rafel watched, his insides shivery, as Mama got up from the table leaving most of her roast duck and baked carrots and buttery spinach behind. She went to Deenie, her face pinched up and not saying things, and pulled his sister's chair away from the table. Then she held out her arms and let Deenie clamber into them, the way she used to when his sister was a little sprat.

"Hush, Deenie, don't cry," Mama said, as Deenie hiccupped into her sunshine yellow blouse. "Bedtime, mouse. You didn't get much sleep last night."

Remembering last night, Rafel felt his insides shiver again. Last night was horrible. Today was horrible too. *Everything* was horrible. He wanted to cry.

Mama took Deenie over to Da, and Da turned away from the window and tickled the back of her neck in the way that made her giggle. But Deenie didn't giggle this time. Instead she reached for him and tried to climb into his arms.

"No, no, mouse," said Mama, holding her back. "Da can't cuddle you now. He's got work to do. He'll—he'll cuddle you in the morning. Asher—"

Da slid a finger under Deenie's chin and tipped her head up. "Don't you be fratchin' your ma, little sprat," he said, pretending he was all stern and scowly. Then he smiled, except not with his eyes. His eyes were awful, old and sad. Bending, he kissed the tip of Deenie's nose. "Off to bed, mouse. Sleep tight. Don't you let them bedbugs bite."

More fat wobbly tears were rolling down Deenie's cheeks. "I don't feel good, Da," she whimpered. "I feel bad—" She banged her skinny chest. "In here."

"I know," said Da. It was nearly a whisper. "But you'll feel better soon, Deenie. I promise."

Mama took Deenie out of the solar, and Da turned his back on the room again. Looking at him, Rafel saw how his head drooped and his shoulders slumped like he was so sad he couldn't stand up straight. He felt his throat go tight. His nose tingled, and his eyes prickled hard. Not knowing what else to do, he picked up his fork and poked it into the hated spinach.

"Never mind that, Rafe," said Da. "Truth be told, I don't much like spinach neither."

He let the fork drop again. "Didn't meant to fratch you, Da," he said, having to choke the words out. "Didn't mean to fratch Mama, either."

Da held out one arm, an invitation. Rafel went to him, flooded with relief. Before he could blink it away a fat tear of his own wobbled out of his eye.

"What happened at school today, Rafe?" Da asked, his voice quiet, his strong arm holding him close.

He shrugged. "Nowt, Da. It was just school."

"Rafe..."

Squirming, he kicked at the wall under the window. Da's arm tightened.

"Don't do that. Just tell me what happened."

"*Nowt*. Just—poxy Arlin Garrick," he muttered. "Being poxy. Like he is. We had a brangle. I didn't touch him, Da!" he added hastily. "Promise!"

To his surprise, Da laughed a bit. "Like father, like son, eh?" he said, almost to himself. "That'd be right. So what happened, Rafe? All of it, mind. No leavin' bits out."

He heaved a deep sigh. "Arlin was doing magic. At nuncheon. In the yard, under the big tree. Meister Vyne can't see that bit from the schoolhouse. Arlin was showing off, Da, just like he always does. Da, he was calling *boggles*."

"Boggles?" said Da.

"*You* know," he said, impatient. "Frighty things. He was making 'em up with magic. Like I said, showing off." *As if he's the only one who can do it. I can do it. I've done it lots and mine are a hundred times scarier than his.* "Da, he was going to skitter them over the hedge into the girls' school next door."

Da stared down at him. "Rafel...what did you do?"

He nearly kicked at the wall again. "I—I popped 'em. Wasn't hard. Arlin's magic ain't that fancy." Feeling his father's arm go rigid, like wood, he looked up. "I *had* to, Da. Boggles are—"

"*Rafe,*" said Da, his face and voice terrible. "You tangled Doranen magic? Regular Olken can't *do* that! You *know* you ain't—how many bloody times have I said—"

"Arlin never guessed it was me!" he protested. "Honest, Da. Promise. But—" He stopped, suddenly aware that he'd said more than enough.

Too late. "But *what?*" said Da, and gave his shoulder a hard shake. "Rafel, didn't I just tell you not to leave bits out?"

He shoved his hands in his pockets. "I laughed. When the boggles popped. I couldn't help it, Da, Arlin looked so fratched. And when he couldn't make 'em come back again he—he looked like to poop his trousers, he was so cross. And doesn't it serve him right? He was going to set them boggles on the girls, he—"

"Aye, Rafe, I heard you the first time," said Da, his voice still growly. "What happened after you laughed at Arlin?"

He shrugged. "Not much."

"*Rafe.*"

This was the bad bit. The bit he didn't want to say. He didn't care if he got a wallop for popping the boggles and he didn't care if Da fratched on at him about not doing magic. He didn't even care if he got stopped giving Stag his supper apple for a week. *Two* weeks. Jed would give it to him, so Stag wouldn't miss out.

But he did care about telling Da what Arlin Garrick had said.

"*Rafe,*" Da said again, in the voice that meant all his patience was used up. "What did the pimply little shit do?"

"He just ... said things," he whispered, squirming. "Lies."

Da was silent for a long time. Then he sighed. "About me?"

He nodded. He couldn't trust himself to speak. His nose was running now, and the solar had gone blurry.

"Rafe ..." Da dropped to a crouch in front of him. "We talked on this already, sprat," he said, resting a heavy hand on his shoulder. "Folk say things. You can't stop 'em. It ain't bloody fair but there's nowt to be done about it."

Rafel folded his arms tight, shaking his head. How could Da say that? How could he not care?

If he'd heard what Arlin said, that he was as good as a murderer, getting King Gar killed like that, and how he was only an Olken, and how could an Olken destroy a great Doranen mage like Morg? Some Doranen must've helped him, and then he did something to make 'em forget, so he wasn't really a hero after all. If Da heard Arlin say all that ...

"Reckon I care what some Doranen spratlin' witters?" Da asked gently, and patted him on the cheek. "Trust me, Rafel: I don't care a bloody bit."

He sniffed. "Why not, Da? Why don't you care?"

Da fell silent, his gaze shifting sideways, which always happened when he remembered bad things. "'Cause I don't. 'Cause some things ain't worth botherin' about," he said at last. "One day, when you be older, I'll tell you the full story of what happened the day Morg died. Then you'll know why I don't care about Arlin Garrick, or his da, or any other bloody Doranen—or Olken—what snivels behind my back. And you won't neither."

"You could tell me now," he said, hopeful. "That ole Darran told me some of it, but I want to know the rest."

Da's face went all stern. "I know you do, Rafe. But you ain't ready for it."

He was, he *was*. Da had no idea what he was ready for. What he could *do*. "Yes, I am," he protested. "Da—"

"Sprat, you got to learn to swallow *no* for an answer so it don't gripe your belly," Da snapped. "I've said you ain't ready and that's the end of it." He sighed again. "So, you popped Arlin's boggles, and laughed when he were upset. That fratched him to say some things about me what riled you up. Then what?"

And then Goose had leapt to Da's defence, calling Arlin Garrick a *poxy, cross-eyed, split-arsed moo.* So Arlin Garrick's best friend Trentham Villot called Goose's da a *hop-rotted beersot,* which didn't sound awful bad unless you were Meister of the Brewers' Guild.

So *then* Goose and Trentham started brangling, fists and boots, and Meister Vyne came running out, and in the end Goose got his backside caned and so did Trentham Villot, and that wasn't bloody fair at *all.*

"Did you own up as how you started it?" said Da. "You and Arlin?"

"I tried to, Da, but Meister Vyne wouldn't listen. Arlin just laughed. He didn't care Trentham got walloped for him."

"What about Goose?" said Da. "S'pose he ain't talkin' to you now, is that it?"

That was the thing, almost as bad as the lies Arlin told about Da. "No. He said not to fratch on it. He said—he said—"

And then, just like Deenie would, he broke into sobs. *"Don't matter,"* Goose had said, his voice scratchy after yellin' from the cane, and his watery eyes red. *"One day you'll stand up for me, I know you will. 'Cause we're friends, you and me, Rafe, and that's what friends do."*

"So you learned a hard lesson today," said Da, holding him close again. "You got a friend in strife 'cause you let your temper ride you. Best you not let that happen again, eh?"

Muffled against Da's weskit, he nodded. "I won't, Da. Promise." Then he wriggled a bit, till he could see his father's face. "But I wish—"

"What?" said Da. There was the tiniest glint in his eye. "That you could smash that Arlin Garrick flat with your magic?"

It was shameful, but he nodded. "Aye," he whispered. "Aye, I surely do."

Da pinched the end of his nose. "Reckon I don't know that, sprat? Reckon I ain't had that feelin' m'self, once or twice?"

Because Da didn't sound cross, he risked a big question. "When you killed Morg, Da. Did you want to? Did it—did it feel good?"

"Sink me bloody sideways, Rafe..." Da let go of him and stood, turning to the window. "The things you ask. Aye," he said, after a long time. "I wanted to kill him. He were evil through and through. But it didn't feel good, Rafel, 'cause I weren't just killin' him. Two other men died with him...and neither deserved it. You want to think on that, sprat, when you find y'self wishin' you could pop poxy Arlin Garrick with your magic. Think on that, and think on poor ole Goose with his caned backside. Ain't nowt in the world as magic'll make simpler. All magic does is tangle things up."

"Aye, Da," he said, because he knew it was expected. But he didn't really believe it. Everywhere in the City, throughout Lur, magic made their lives simpler. If it was so terrible no-one would use it, would they?

"So here's what I reckon," said Da, looking over his shoulder. "I reckon it weren't just fratchin' with Arlin that's got you riled, Rafe. Them boggles he called...they made you think of last night, eh?"

Last night. He didn't want to talk on that. Didn't want to remember Deenie screaming. Running into his bedchamber and screaming about monsters and the twisting earth and a man with green-gold eyes and red hair, crying tears of blood in a river.

"You ain't to fret on that," said Da. "There's nowt will hurt you in this Tower, Rafe. Nowt to hurt you anywhere in Lur. You or Deenie. I won't let it. You hear me?"

"Aye," he said, nodding.

"And d'you believe me?"

He wanted to. But last night Deenie screamed that Da was frighted, that he was hurt near bad enough to die. And Deenie could feel things. He knew that now. She could feel things that were true.

If Da can't protect himself, how can he protect us?

"Rafe?" said Da. He sounded hurt and surprised. "Don't you believe me?"

"Course I do," he said quickly. "I believe you, Da. You and Mama won't let nowt happen to us."

"Aye," said Da, and tousled his hair. "That's right." He let his hand drop. "Now, I got me some work to do, sprat. Time you paddled a bit in your bath then got y'self warm and dry into bed. Off you toddle. I'll see you right as rain in the mornin', eh?"

Da had to work? But it was late. Outside the solar window the night-birds were singing, and stars were sprinkled across the sky. Da had been at work all day. It didn't seem fair he had to work at night too.

"What kind of work, Da?" he said. "Can I help?"

Da smiled. "That be a kind thought, Rafe, but no. You got your own work, I reckon — scrubbin' them sproutin' spuds out of your ears."

"I ain't got spuds, Da," he protested. "I never once had a spud!"

"Aye, well, there be a first time for everythin'," said Da. "Now off you go."

"But what about Stag?" he said, remembering. "He hasn't had his supper apple."

"I'll give it him tonight, Rafe." Again, Da tousled his hair, then reached down and swatted him lightly. "Run along."

With Deenie all fratched they'd not finished dinner. Cook's peach pie was sat on the sideboard, not a bite of it taken, sweet and ready to eat.

Da saw him looking at it, and smiled a tiddy bit. "Aye, snatch a slice. But don't tell your ma, with y'spinach not eaten. 'Cause if she finds out I'll say I ain't had nowt to do with it."

"She'll never know, Da," he said, grinning. "Promise."

Da snorted. "She'll bloody know when she sees a piece of pie missin'."

That made him giggle. But even though Da was joking, underneath that he was serious. And even though he was smiling, his eyes were still sad.

"Night, Da," he whispered, throwing his arms tight around his father. "You sleep well, eh? Don't you let them bedbugs bite."

Da's arms closed round him so hard, for a moment, all the bits inside him felt squashed. "Aye, sprat. You too."

The first bite of filched peach pie exploded in his mouth like summer. Halfway to the solar door he spun on his heel, mouth open to tell Da it was wonderful, he should have a piece. But he didn't say it. He didn't say anything. Da was turned mostly towards the window again, a thin slice of his face showing like a rind of new moon. And that thin slice of face was so grim, and so *sad*...

The peach pie turned to cold wood-ash on his tongue, Rafel trudged downstairs to his privy bathroom, opened the window...and threw the rest out.

CHAPTER TWELVE

✳

Seated in his favourite wingback chair, Rodyn Garrick watched his good friend Sarle Baden hold his brandy glass up to the warm, leaping firelight. "A fine drop," Sarle said, approving. "Your cellar is second to none."

It was true. He prided himself on the quality of his wines, his liquors. How could he not? With his vineyards and his palate, with his reputation, he could serve only the best.

Sarle swallowed heartily—it was his least attractive trait—then cast a frowning glance at the library door. "You're sure we'll not be disturbed, Rodyn?"

It was late. The house was quiet. His servants were banished to their cellar and attic, and his son knew better than to wander from his bed.

He nodded. "Quite sure."

"Good," said Sarle, relaxing in his own chair. "And so to business. Ain is making excellent progress."

"I'd be surprised if she were not," he said. "She's a talent, that woman. Not another Barl, of course, but nevertheless—she's a find. I'm thinking…" He tapped a finger to his lips. "She could well prove the right tutor for Arlin. I shall speak with her."

"Really?" said Sarle, not hiding his surprise. "Rodyn, I know the boy's gifted but he's young for—"

"Arlin will achieve the tasks set before him," he said, and took a restrained sip from his glass. "He's a child in years only. In potential, he is—" He smiled. "Ageless."

Sarle frowned. "Yes. Well. He's your son, Rodyn. I'm sure you know best."

"I do," he said. "Now tell me—is Ain certain there'll be no more trouble with her clod of a neighbour?"

"She's learned her lesson," said Sarle. "Her workshops are warded beyond all risk of leakage. *And* detection by that fool your Mage Council sent, who is still watching and waiting to catch her out." He sniffed. "A pity you couldn't over-rule Asher on that."

Rodyn kept his expression mild. To achieve his ambition he needed Sarle's assistance. That obliged him to swallow impertinence—though with far less pleasure than Sarle guzzled his brandy.

"Yes," he said. "A great pity. But given our plans, Sarle, it's prudent not to stir the bastard's suspicions. It's enough he decided not to push the matter of Barl's Laws."

"He has no inkling of what we're about?"

"None," he said, smiling. "I'm playing him sweet for now. He can think our clash of wills over Ain has put me on the back foot. I care naught for his opinion."

Wood popped and crackled in the fireplace. Sarle drained his glass and set it aside. "Quite right. But in that case, Rodyn, what's got you frowning?"

"Really? Was I frowning?" he said lightly, displeased that he'd betrayed himself. "It's not the company, I assure you."

"Then what is it?" said Sarle, holding one thin hand out to the fire's warmth. Idly stirring the flames with his mind so they leapt higher and hotter. "Was this morning's Mage Council so irritating?"

As much as he confided in anyone, he confided in Sarle. "No," he said slowly. "But I have this small suspicion Asher lied to us today."

Sarle leaned forward. "About what?"

"That old fool Jaffee made mention of Olken coming to him claiming they felt a disturbance in the earth," he said. "When asked, Asher said he'd not felt a thing." He pursed his lips. "I can't put my finger on it, precisely, but there was something about the way he said it. A look in his eye."

Sarle laughed, disbelieving. "You let yourself be disquieted by the *Olken?* Rodyn, my dear friend, are you not feeling well? The Olken are no better than infants startling at their own shadows. A disturbance in the earth? A disturbance in their bowels, more like. You know they will insist on guzzling ale by the barrel. And as for Asher—surely he's far too conscious of his exalted status as Lur's saviour to risk it with blatant dishonesty. Lying to the Mage Council?" He sneered. "The bastard doesn't have the guts."

Amused, Rodyn refreshed their brandy glasses then rested one arm along the fireplace's mantel. "I expect you're right, Sarle. I expect I imagined it. Now tell me—how proceeded your meeting with Artin Moyne?"

Sarle's affronted temper vanished. "Very well. He's interested, Rodyn. He's definitely sympathetic to our cause."

And that was *very* good news. Artin Moyne had influence. And their cause, so vital, so all-consuming, required every Doranen voice they could find. As it stood now, far too few of their people comprehended what needed to be done, or were willing to contemplate the drastic action of which he dreamed. Lur's Doranen were too comfortable. Complacent. Life in this borrowed place had softened their sinews.

But I shall change that. It will take time—but I have the time. And the resources. I do not care how long it takes—I will make this dream come true.

"Moyne expressed no hesitation? No doubt?"

"None," said Sarle, promptly. "He agrees with us, as I said he would. He'll do whatever he can to discreetly further our plans."

Rodyn felt his satisfaction expand on a warm cloud of expensive brandy. "Excellent, Sarle. Slowly but surely, we proceed towards our goal."

"We do indeed," said Sarle, and raised his glass in a toast. "Here's to our success, my friend. Here's to the day we quit Lur once and for all — and the day that will surely follow it, when we set foot in our true home. Lost Dorana."

"To Lost Dorana," he echoed, raising his own glass. "And to those of us with the wit and wisdom to find it."

Asher thought Dath would hear him, coming into Deenie's room, but she didn't stir as he crossed the threshold. Deenie, breathing deeply, was curled beneath her green-and-white striped blankets. The glimlamp on the bedside table was set to burn low. The room was cosy, comfortable, pink-frilled for his little girl. Standing beside the glimlamp an emptied glass, smeared with the dregs of the posset Dathne had brewed. *Sleep-well,* she'd called it. A promise of dreams.

"She farin' all right?" he asked, lingering in the shadows. Afraid, if Dathne looked at him, of what he'd see in her eyes.

"Yes," said Dathne softly. She didn't sound angry. That were something, at least. "If the Tower fell down around our ears I doubt she'd hear it. She'll not stir till afternoon tomorrow, at least. I made doubly sure."

"Dath..." He had to stop. Wait. His voice was a traitor. "If there were any other way..."

She shrugged one shoulder at him. *Shut up,* that meant. So she might not sound angry, but that didn't mean she weren't feelin' it.

Best he not finish what he was going to say, then. Best he tread careful, since the ice was thin between them. "Reckon I be goin' now," he said instead. "Don't know how long this'll take."

Her fingertips smoothed a lock of hair from Deenie's flushed cheek. "I should come with you."

"Ain't no need," he said. "Ain't nowt you can do, Dath. 'Sides, you be wanted here with Deenie."

"You've no business working Weather Magic on your own."

"I did it mostly on my own before. I be used to it."

"This isn't the same, and you know it!" she snapped. "Send for Pellen. Have him stand watch while you work."

"Pellen's got Charis. He won't leave her this time of night."

"He can bring Charis here. I'll care for both girls. *Asher*—" Dathne swung round at last on her stool beside Deenie's bed. There weren't enough colour in her cheeks.

"Nowt'll go wrong, Dath," he said. Trying to ease her. Trying to ease himself. "Ain't I the Innocent Mage?"

"Don't," she said fiercely, her voice low for Deenie. "Don't you throw that at me. And you're *not* innocent any more, Asher. Neither of us is. We know things now. Dreadful things!"

"Dath..." Abandoning the safety of shadows, he crossed to the bed and dropped to his knees beside her. Pressed a finger to her lips. "You *know* I got to do this. So why go on about it? Arguin' hard fact be like a dog chasin' its tail. Round and round and round, and nowt to show for all that effort but sweat."

She turned her head away. "And if you die? What am I supposed to tell our children?"

He used the same finger to turn her face back again. "I ain't goin' to die, Dath. How can I die? I ain't battlin' Morg this time. Just his leftover magic. And I got Barl on my side, ain't I? All her magic, sleepin' inside me. Me and Barl, we won't let that bastard win."

"What are you going to do?" she whispered. "Break the last hold Weather Magic has on this kingdom? Turn back time to the days before the Doranen came? Or will you try and put things back the way they were before Morg interfered?"

He shrugged. "I don't know. I don't know what be possible, Dath. I don't know what I *know*."

"You can't make another Wall," she said, her eyes hollow with fear. "You *can't*. That *will* kill you."

"We don't need another Wall, Dath," he said, gentling her cheek with his hand. She pressed against him, seeking comfort. "These past ten years have shown us there ain't nowt beyond them mountains we need savin' from. Our troubles be right here at home."

"And you have to fix them. I know." Her hand came up to cover his.

"Barl's *tits,* I know. And I hate it, Asher. You've no idea how much I hate it."

Somehow he found a smile for her. "Oh, I d'know. Reckon I might have an inklin'."

They clung to each other then, beside their drugged, sleeping daughter, and kissed as though they'd never see each other again.

"Keep Rafe home from school tomorrow," he said, as they held each other pressed forehead to forehead. "Keep him here in the Tower. No gallivantin' round the countryside on his pony. Send word to Pellen first thing that Deenie's poorly, so Charis don't come. If I ain't back from the Weather Chamber by this time tomorrow night, send Pellen to look for me. Don't you do it, Dath. Don't you leave the sprats alone."

"No, Asher, I—"

"*Please,* Dath." He couldn't bear it, the thought of her finding him dead if what he was about to try turned into a sinkin' great disaster. "I did what you wanted, last time. You can do this for me. Say you'll do this for me."

He felt her breath warm against his skin as she breathed out, hard. Felt her fingers tighten on the back of his neck. Heard her swallow a sob. "All right. All right, sink it. I'll do as you ask."

He kissed her. "Aye, but you be a fine, slumskumbledy wench."

Pulling away from him, she slid off Deenie's bedside stool and turned her back, arms wrapped around her ribs as though they were broken, and paining her. "So you'd best go, hadn't you, seeing you're so eager to throw your life away."

Feeling helpless, feeling lost, he rose from his crouch. "Dathne—"

She flung up a hand. *"Go."*

He kissed his sleeping daughter, and went.

After feeding Rafe's pony its supper apple, almost amused at its crossness that he weren't Rafe, he made his way through the darkness of the palace grounds to the Weather Chamber. Closed its bottom door behind him, summoned glimfire, climbed the one hundred and thirty stone steps to the glass-domed room at the top and closed that door behind him as well.

Alone, his heart pounding from more than the steep stairs, he brightened the glimfire he'd conjured and stared at Barl's blighted Weather map. To his ordinary eye it seemed unchanged from the other day. Dropping to one knee beside it, he rested his fingers lightly on the tallest peak of Barl's Mountains. Felt the black stirring of Morg's meddling, sickened... and beneath that felt the stirring spark of Barl's cruel and complicated magic. It was still there. Still struggling to be heard. Barl and Morgan, battling yet.

He bumped his backside to the parquetry floor and crossed his legs. Rested his elbows on his knees and dropped his chin on his knuckles, perplexed.

Fine. So what now? Don't s'pose someone'd like to give me a hint?

Unhelpful silence. The chamber was cold. He'd pulled on a warm coat before leaving the Tower, but even so the chill air beneath the glass dome ceiling nipped at his skin. Pushing discomfort aside, he bent his thoughts to matters magical.

With the Weather Orb's destruction, Barl's magic lived in only two places now. His blood, and her Weather map. And when he touched the map he could feel that magic stirring in both of them. But what did it mean? Were they connected, somehow? Could they — mad as it sounded — *talk* to each other?

Tentative, apprehensive, he reached out his hands. Laid them palm-down to the Weather map, his left on the Dingles and his right — 'cause why not? — smack dab on Restharven.

Look at me, Da. Muckin' about with this malarkey again.

Within heartbeats he felt the sizzle of Weather Magic in his blood. Felt the stirring of power, the call to wind and rain and snow. Could almost see the spells' tongue-twisting words rise before his inner eye, feel his fingers twitch to trace their burning sigils on the cold chamber air. Morg's left-behind foulness stirred too, shuddering through him, waking hard-buried memories of torment, recalling the whisper of a loathed and loathsome voice. His flesh crawled, his belly heaved.

Against his will he remembered his Guard House imprisonment and Morg the sorcerer, sheathed within hateful Conroyd Jarralt, ripping through his mind in search of people to kill. Ripping through his mind with pleasure, 'cause the bastard knew how much it hurt.

Panting, Asher snatched his hands off the Weather map. Felt himself topple until he struck the parquetry floor. For a long time he lay there, little shudders running through him. Framed by the chamber's glass dome ceiling, the indifferent stars shone down. Spark by spark his sizzling blood fell quiet — but in its place rose a high tide of fear.

Sink me bloody sideways. I can't do this. I can't.

Except he had to. For Rafel. For Deenie. For every child in Lur. If he did nowt here this night, just let Lur's turbulence run its mysterious course, well, true, things could well settle 'emselves just fine. But just as easily the world could turn upside down. How could he take that chance? If something went wrong, there weren't no place to run. Even if they could get thousands of folk over them mountains, there weren't nowt on the other side 'cept a slow, stinkin' death. And remembering how Tollin had died . . . how could he begin to think that were a choice? It never was. Pellen were right. This small battered kingdom was the only home they had.

So. Morg might be defeated, but nowt else had bloody changed.

He sat up. Scrubbed a hand across his face. Stared at the Weather map with sour dislike.

Barl, Barl . . . I'll tell you this for nowt. Dathne ain't the only slum-skumbledy wench I know.

His breathing hard and harsh, he flattened his palms a second time to the blighted Weather map. This time didn't fight the sickness roiling through him, the memory of Morg, but instead sought what little remained of Barl's miraculous magic.

Aye, there it was, a feeble candle-flicker in the dark, valiantly struggling against Morg's creeping malaise. Sweet where the sorcerer's touch and taste were poison bitter. Flavoured with hope and not despair. He heard his breathing falter, for as hard as ever he tried to deny it he'd missed this. He'd missed it. And so, for the first time in more than ten years, since he'd let the fury of UnMaking flood through him, Asher surrendered himself to magic.

And shouted wildly as the sleeping power in his blood caught fire.

Twice before—when he took the Weather magics into himself, and the time he stood before Matt in the Black Woods, so angry—he had felt the same kind of breathless unfolding inside himself. Had felt this soaring invincibility, as though he had wings and were suddenly made a new man. Even as he fought against its seduction he laughed, because now he felt whole again. For ten long years he'd been incomplete—and now he felt whole. He didn't want that to be true. He wanted that to be a lie.

But it ain't. It ain't. Barl bloody save me, it ain't.

It was the reason why he denied his power. He knew that. He'd always known it. It was why he fought so hard to make sure that power stayed sleeping in his blood. Because even in the instant his magic burned through Gar, killing him, he'd felt its savage glory. Felt a kinship with Morg.

No. No. I ain't him. It's Barl in me, not him.

Except they were both in him now. As he shuddered over the Weather map, his scarred hands roaming its ruined surface, he could feel both Doranen sorcerers battling in his blood. Every time he touched a patch of Morg's blight he felt his belly heave and bile rush into his throat. Felt Morg, vile and gloating. But when he touched an unblighted part of the Weather map he heard a different voice whisper in his mind, striving to be heard over Morg's rotten mutterings. A sweet voice, a young voice. A woman's voice he'd heard before, in his dreams. But not Dathne.

It was the voice of the Weather Orb, carving secrets in his bones.

I be here, Barl. I be listenin'. Tell me what I'm s'posed to do.

Opened fully to her Weather Magic, feeling it dance like a dagger through his veins, he could feel as well the wounds in the Weather map, more keenly than ever. Its screaming shuddered through him, slicking his cheeks with tears. His labouring heartbeat thundered in his ears.

Buried beneath its pain he could feel something else, some unravelled, unravelling link between the map and Gar's kingdom. The connection between Barl's magic and Lur's earth, not severed yet. Not quite yet. But it trembled on the brink of breaking...

And he knew then, without knowing how he knew it, that the power was in him to save the Weather map. To pour fresh life into it, fresh magic. To beat back, if not defeat, the worst of Morg's ravages and sing Lur's distressed earth back to painless sleep. He had the power to buy the kingdom some brief, precious time.

But sink me bloody sideways... this is goin' to hurt.

All restraint abandoned, all doubts and fears and resentments discarded, Asher drowned himself in magic. Drowned the Weather map, too. Everything the Weather Orb had poured into him in that long-ago moment of Transference, spells and sigils he had never looked at, let alone used, they flooded to his tongue and the tips of his fingers. Flooded out of him in cataracts of heat and light and pain.

Time melted like butter. It dripped and poured around him, golden as glimfire.

For hour after hour he shouted the ancient words, over and over and over again. Shouted their syllables and his suffering. *Aravnakai te ramakari.* His fingers burned the air. *Shas'o shas'o ahani.* Blood dripped down his face. *Tolnek rusta. Rusta tolnek. Ta rastu. Ta rastu ne.* His carved bones were dissolving. His throat was worn away. His voice grew ragged. He was shouting it to shreds.

Beneath his left hand he could feel the Weather map shaking. Overhead, through the glass dome, the stars grew shy, then one by one vanished as night fled before the approaching dawn. Hours of magic, and still he hadn't finished. Still the link between Lur and the Weather map was in danger of breaking. Morg's dark-hearted corruption was not defeated. For all his shouting and sigils, the Weather map's wounds were not cleanly healed.

He couldn't see for the blood in his eyes. He had to breathe through his mouth because his nostrils were clogged red. There was blood on his coat-sleeves and his trembling hands. Barl's Weather map was daubed wet and scarlet.

Am I bleedin' to death? he wondered. *Is all my blood on there?*

He thought it might be, but he couldn't stop. Not now. Not when he was close enough to taste victory, salt and iron mingled bitter on his tongue.

If I die doin' this I reckon Dath'll bloody kill me.

His senses had long since blunted beneath the unrelenting onslaught of magic's pain. The worst calling of rain had been nothing compared to this. *This* magic sliced him like a razor, like pitiless Dragonteeth Reef. He could almost believe he was being UnMade just as he'd UnMade Morg. Thought he was being pulled apart to specks and flecks of blood-soaked dust.

At last...at long last...as the climbing sun spilled warmth and golden light through the chamber's glass dome and onto its floor...emptied, exhausted and battered to a pulp he slumped across Barl's Weather map. Dragged his crusted eyelids open and saw, blurred and bleary, that the map was almost healed. A smear of blight here...a touch there... Hardly enough to notice. Practically nowt, compared to before.

We did it, Barl. We bloody did it.

The Weather Chamber swirled around him, and headfirst he fell into the fast fleeing night.

"Asher...Asher...for the love of Barl, man, come to your senses! Come on!"

Irritated, he tried to swat aside the wet cloth dripping on his face. "Gerroff."

"Asher! Oh, praise Jervale. Praise Barl."

He sucked in a quick breath, wincing. Dathne? That were Dath. And the other voice...that were Pellen. Pellen Orrick, pretty well the last of his friends that hadn't managed to die. Groaning, he opened his eyes.

"Here," said Dathne, her face wet with tears. "Drink this. No fratching."

Pellen's strong arm eased his shoulders off the Weather Chamber floor and held him tight so Dathne could press a wooden cup against his lips.

"*Drink!*" she said again.

It was Dathne, so he drank.

"Sink me, woman!" he spluttered, his mouth on fire, his belly heaving. The stuff was foul, worse than any potion Nix had ever forced on him. "You tryin' to bloody poison me?"

"Here, take this," said Dathne, ignoring him and thrusting the emptied cup at Pellen. "And give me that cloth." A moment later she'd taken over where Pellen left off, dripping water on him and tryin' to bathe him like a baby. Sinkin' bloody woman, did she think he'd turned feeble? "Stop *fratching!*" she scolded. "If I'd brought a mirror with me and you looked in it, I swear you'd drop dead from fright."

"How's Deenie?" he mumbled as she slopped his stubbly face clean. Sunlight dazzled his eyes, and warmed his cheeks. He was ravenous. "And Rafe?"

"They're fine," she said. She sounded breathless with temper... or fright. "Deenie woke fresh as new milk an hour ago, and Rafe's spent the day tearing the Tower down to get out into the countryside on that pony of his."

He looked up at Pellen. "Charis? How's Charis?"

"She's fine too, Asher," said Pellen. His face was carved deep with worry-lines, and his smile was half-hearted. "She said—she said—" His voice broke. "She said she heard the earth singing."

He closed his eyes. "Singin', eh? Ain't that poetical."

"Deenie said the same thing," Dathne added. "Peas in a pod, those two."

He listened to her swish the cloth in a bowl of water, and wring it out. "And what does Rafe say?"

"Ah well, you know our Rafel," she said, sounding amused now. "No poetry for him. But he said he thought the earth was happy. Which for Rafe is dancing close to poetry."

With an effort he opened his eyes again and sat up, Pellen's arm helping. Every bone ached, every muscle shrieked a loud complaint. He looked at them in turn, his wife and his friend. "How long have I been here?"

"Not so very long," said Dathne. There were still tears on her cheeks. "It'll be sunset in an hour."

That meant not quite a full day. He thought he remembered the sunrise. He did remember the magic. His head was pounding and his throat was sore.

"What happened?" said Pellen. "What did you do? Can you recall?"

Shifting on the hard floor, he turned to look at Barl's Weather map. Blotched a little here and there, but mostly whole. Mostly remade. Some kind of miracle, surely.

"You were right, Pellen," he said, his battered voice thin and scratchy. "The magic was in me. All I had to do was...let it out." He shivered, memory stirring more keenly. "So I did."

"Let it out how?" said Dathne. "What did you do with it, Asher?"

Frowning, he touched the Weather map. Sucked in a quick breath, feeling warmth and strength and an odd kind of peace. Feeling the Weather Magic soaked into its bones. The blight still tried to whisper, but it was faint. Almost killed. Encouraged, he pushed his feelings out further, ignoring the resentful pain, and felt an echo of that warmth and strength in the kingdom's earth beneath them.

"I ain't ezackly sure," he said slowly. "I reckon...could be...I fed it into the Weather map. Into Lur."

In silence they looked at Barl's amazing creation.

"And sinkin' near emptied yourself of life doing it," said Dathne, at last. "You fool."

"Don't fratch at him, Dathne," said Pellen quickly. "Not after he's nigh on killed himself to save us."

"Don't lecture me, Pellen!" she snapped. "He's my bloody husband and the father of my children and if I want to call him seven different kinds of sapskull for coming within a hair of making me a widow and his children orphans then *that's* what I'll do and *you'll* not gainsay me!"

Asher grinned tiredly at his troubled friend. "Don't fret, Pellen. Think I ain't used to it after ten years of marriage?"

Dathne slapped him. "Watch your tongue, you rapscallion."

Catching her hand, he pressed it to his dry, chapped lips. "Sink me, but you're beautiful when you be angry."

"Asher," said Pellen, as Dathne spluttered. Silenced for once, though her eyes promised retribution. "Is it enough? What you've done? Is Lur's trouble settled once and for all?"

Barl bloody save him, he hoped so. "I d'know. It better be. I couldn't do any more."

"No," said Pellen, solemn. "You couldn't. As it is you came close to doing too much. Never again, Asher. Do you hear me? *Never again.*"

"Trust me, Pellen," he said, shivering, "you won't get no fratchin' from me on that."

It was true. There was an emptiness inside him he'd never felt before. He felt almost . . . almost *broken*. Used up. Hollowed out.

"You know how we got to handle this, don't you?" he said, looking at Dathne, then at Pellen. "Total bloody secrecy. This never happened. I ain't been here for years. Same goes for you, Pellen. And you ain't never been here, Dathne. You forgot the bloody Weather Chamber existed. And we don't never talk on this. Agreed?"

Silence, then they nodded. "Agreed," they said, a Dathne and Pellen duet.

"Good," he said. If he weren't so bloody tired, and in so much pain, he'd be well-pleased. "So that's settled. Now let's get out of here, eh? Reckon there be a bottle or three of icewine in the Tower somewhere with my name on 'em. You two get ale."

Between them, Dathne and Pellen levered him onto his feet. Groaning, every inch of his body voicing new and shrill complaints, he turned his aching back on Barl's Weather map and shuffled out of the Chamber. Stumbled down its one hundred and thirty bloody steps and outside into spring afternoon sunlight.

Beneath his tired feet, the replenished earth slept.

Dathne's arm slipped round his ribs. Her warm lips pressed his cheek. "Come along, you," she whispered. "Let's see you home."

PART TWO

CHAPTER THIRTEEN

❖

Setting aside partisan squabbling—choosing to overlook the four complaints that waited to be heard in Justice Hall—Lur's oft-fractious Olken guilds joined hands with each other, and the Doranen, and held a ball in the City's Guildhouse on the high summer's night of Pellen Orrick's retirement, to thank him for twenty years of steadfast mayoral service.

The farewell gala was a grand and glorious affair. Lit broad floor to lofty rafters with golden glimfire, decorated with flowers and streamers and tricky bits of Doranen magic, the Guildhouse echoed to the lilting strains of genteel music, the swish of silk skirts, the measured tread of jewelled slippers and polished boots. Almost everyone who was anyone in Lur had come here this night to dance and flirt and gossip and drink and nibble away the frolicsome hours until dawn.

Catching her breath, Dathne snatched a glass of bubbled sweetwine as it passed her on a tray. "Look, Asher," she murmured, sipping. "Don't Rafel and Charis make a charming pair?"

Asher grunted, scowling into his tankard of spiced cider. After four dances in a row he'd had enough to be goin' on with, so now he and Dath were squashed out of the way in a corner where he could keep an eye on things without folk comin' up to natter. Out on the dance floor—the Guildhouse's meeting room, made over—his troublesome son and his best friend's daughter leapt and whirled and made fools of 'emselves rompin' through some newfangled highsteppin' jig, alongside a hundred or so other Olken and Doranen as ought to know better. Fernel Pintte was one of 'em, Barl rot his socks.

"Asher!" said Dathne, and niggled him in the ribs with her elbow. "Stop sulking. Fernel's chosen. It's done and done."

Aye, it bloody was, though it griped him something fierce to admit it. Despite he'd nigh on talked his tongue loose, and made sure to monitor the vote-counting on the day, Fernel bloody Pintte were Dorana City's new mayor. And if that weren't a sinkin' disgrace...

"So I suggest you get used to it," added Dathne, tired of his grumping. The Guildhouse's glimlight glowed on the ruby-red silk of her dress, and the ruby necklace he'd gifted her. "Like it or not, the chain of office is his."

Well, he didn't bloody like it, did he? Fernel Pintte were a trouble-makin', rabble-rousin' upstart of a jackanapes. Arrogant as a Doranen and twice as nasty. How he thought he could step into Pellen Orrick's shoes...

Right to the last moment he'd thought Goose's da could win the race for mayor. Weren't Ned Martin born and bred in the City? A lifetime in the brewin' game, with enough prize medals to sink him down a well and five turns as Guildmeister to show he could keep good order? That made up for his pricklesome nature, didn't it? Shouldn't it?

He'd thought so. He'd hoped so. But there weren't never no tellin' what folk might up and do. Three years ago Fernel bloody Pintte had arrived in the City to take over The Weary Traveller, one of its oldest and best-loved inns. Straight into the Hostlers' Guild he'd walked and the next thing anyone knew his busy fingers were dabbling in every Dorana City pie and even some beyond it. Pellen were dismayed on that too, and did his best to uncover good reason to clip Pintte's wings — but there was nowt he could find to prove the man a problem. So Fernel bloody Pintte went on his merry way, turning hisself influential, charming witless fools hand over fist, leaving 'em sundazzled so they couldn't see the jackanapes behind the smile, and telling 'em ezackly what they wanted to hear.

Not once since the day he was sent packing from Pellen's house had they heard another peep of a word from the man about chasing the Doranen out of Lur — and they'd been listening close. Anyone might reckon he'd abandoned the notion. Pellen was inclined to think it. But Asher wasn't so sure. Pintte might not be talking on it, but men like him didn't give up that kind of dream.

And then, with Pellen announcing he was stepping down, Pintte announced *he'd* be running for City Mayor.

Briefly Asher thought of tossin' his own self in the race . . . but Dathne had flat forbade it.

"You're not strong enough," she'd raged at him, tears in her eyes. *"Curl your lip at me all you like, Asher, but we both know it's true. And I won't stand for you risking yourself. For what? To be mayor? No. It's not worth it."*

That were the trouble with Dathne — she had the bad habit of bein' right. Ever since that night he'd poured himself into Barl's Weather map, poured his magic, his terror, his hope and desperation into the sinkin' thing so Lur wouldn't founder, he'd been — different. More grey in his hair. More ache in his bones. More bad dreams in his sleep . . . and less sleep to have 'em in.

"Asher," Dathne said again, softly this time. Her hand stroked his green-sleeved arm, pulling him out of harried thought. "Pellen *had* to step down."

He swallowed another mouthful of spiced cider. Pity it weren't a tad bit stronger. He needed strong drink tonight, with Pintte boastin' about the Guildhouse in Pellen's chain of office, trailing his cronies after him like a bad smell.

"I know," he said, still frowning, as Rafel galloped Charis round the dance floor with both hands clasping her slender waist. He looked mighty fine tonight, in blue silk and dark green velvet. Every lass he smiled at sparkled. "But I don't have to like that, either." ❧

An aguey chest had brought Pellen low early this past winter, turning him pale and listless, sapping his strength. By winter's end, with Kerril making dire predictions, he'd had no choice but to call it quits. *Twenty years.* Pellen were the longest serving mayor in the history of Lur.

With his friend retiring, and confident Goose's da would be Dorana's next mayor, he'd thought mayhap, at long last, he could leave the City for good and settle down along the coast with a fishing boat. Not in Restharven, with his brother Zeth still there, a cantankerous ole man, but somewhere. Him and his family, safe and happy and never havin' to think on magic again.

He'd really thought he could do it. Just over ten years had slid by since that night he'd saved Lur a second time. Ten peaceful years and no hint of trouble. He weren't old yet, but for certain sure he was getting older. Hadn't he earned the right to live his life for himself?

'Cept now here was Fernel Pintte ... and the bastard was starting to stir trouble again. Starting to make his noises about the Doranen, and who did Lur really belong to, eh?

He might be more polite about how he says so, compared to last time, but he ain't changed his bloody tune. And now he's got folks startin' to hum along with him.

And seein' as how he'd so neatly got hisself made mayor, well, that meant trouble were only just got started. The Mayor of Dorana had a lot of clout, not only in the City but most places in Lur. Folk paid attention. With Pellen that had meant trouble got sat on till it ran out of air. But he knew, he *knew,* alarm humming in his bones, that Fernel Pintte were about to start fanning flames, not smothering 'em.

'Cause that be the kind of manky man he is. And once he starts stirrin' in earnest, Barl bloody save us then. I was right. He weren't ever to be trusted.

Seeing as how Pellen weren't well enough for dancing, which he could manage well enough even with only one leg, they'd set him up all cosy and important on a dais down the far end of the Guildhouse's vast meeting room. Just this moment he was all on his lonesome, smilin' a bit watching Rafel and Charis bow and curtsey at the end of their jiggin' about, so Asher tipped the rest of his spiced cider down his throat.

"Reckon I'll have a quiet word with Pellen," he announced.

"Oh," said Dathne, disappointed. "But it's time for Meistress Choice, Asher. I was going to ask you to dance."

Again? Perish the thought. "Ask Pintte," he said, and gave her his empty glass. "See if you can wheedle him into sayin' what he's up to."

He left his wife complaining under her breath and threaded his way through the fringes of the Guildhouse throng, nodding and smiling but not stopping until he reached Pellen in his fancy chair, up on the dais.

"Reckon you'd be better off at home," he said, and hooked an empty chair closer. If it were anyone else he'd sit himself up on the dais, but 'cause this were Pellen he minded his manners. "Ain't all this cater-waulin' givin' you a headache?"

"Odd as it may seem," said Pellen, his smile inching wider, "some of us do enjoy music."

Dropping into the chair, he scowled at the fussy clot of Olkens in the gallery above them, with their fiddles and recorders and whatnot. "This ain't music, it be a herd of cats bein' strangled so a bunch of fools can prance about like drunk spring lambs, gettin' mucky with sweat."

Pellen looked at him. "You're calling my daughter a drunken spring lamb?"

"Y'know what I bloody mean."

"Almost always," said Pellen, and laughed.

Ha. As the caterwauling started up again, Asher looked at the crowd of merrymakers. Them lasses with the gumption to ask a man to dance were leading their swains out to make fresh fools of 'emselves. Rafel was picked, of course. Some sweet-faced Olken girl. Charis, bold little minx, had asked a young Doranen lad to jig with her and he'd said yes. Eyebrows were going up here and there, seeing it. Equal or not, these days, there weren't much hobnobbing Doranen to Olken and *never* a suggestion of two turning sweethearts.

It might come one day. Prob'ly will. But if it does I hope I ain't around to see it. Talk about ructions...

Fernel bloody Pintte had agreed to dance with Dathne. The usurped mayoral chain flashed and winked on his chest as he elbowed his way to the middle of the dance floor. Ten years had aged him, and too much rich food had fattened him, but that didn't stop the bastard leering at Dathne like a tomcat.

Asher felt his face scrunch tight. "Reckon I'd rather Morg put out my eyes with that poker of his afore I had to sit here and watch *that*."

"Asher..." Pellen shook his head. Not a dark hair left on it, these days. Where'd the bloody time go, eh? "It's one thing not to like Fernel. It's quite another to paint him a villain without proof."

He snorted. "Proof? We got all the proof we need. You heard him that day in your parlour. You know what he thinks *and* you know what he wants."

"Yes," said Pellen softly. "I heard him. I heard you, too. It's not what a man thinks but what he does that defines him. So far Fernel Pintte's done nothing more outrageous than win an election you wanted him to lose."

"Pellen, be you goin' deaf in your old age? He's banging that same drum again, he's—"

"Not once incited anyone to violence," said Pellen. "He's just talking, Asher. He's perfectly free to talk."

Stymied, Asher glowered at the sight of Pintte daring to laugh at something Dathne said. *Charm my bloody wife, would you? Lay a finger on her untoward, you bastard, and I'll set a wereslag on you so sinkin' fast...*

"Besides," said Pellen. "It's not just Fernel Pintte, you know. There are Doranen, too, who look longingly at the mountains."

What? He'd not heard a bloody thing. Trust Pellen to know. "Who?"

Pellen examined his fingernails. "I've been told...Rodyn Garrick. Sarle Baden's another one. Oh, and Ain Freidin. You recall her?"

Ain Freidin? Aye. And what were Rodyn Garrick up to with a Doranen? He'd ask, but Garrick weren't here tonight, of course—catch him honouring an Olken. Arlin was, though. Made Rafel's life a misery at school, the poxy little runt. Like father, like son. Sarle Baden he weren't over-familiar with. Lived mostly in the country, out beyond the Home Districts somewhere. With luck he'd bloody stay there.

And they're all stirrin' trouble, are they? Reckon I need to put my ear a bit closer to the ground.

"Perhaps," said Pellen slyly, "if they talk long and persuasively enough they'll convince the General Council to consider another expedition." His tired eyes widened in mock-dismay. "Imagine that, my friend—Fernel Pintte and Rodyn Garrick romping hand in hand over the mountains and far away. I can see why you'd object. Who would you have to bellyache about then?"

"Ha," he said, giving Pellen a sour look. "Very bloody funny."

Pellen grinned. "I thought so."

"Well, it *ain't*," he said. "Last thing we need is folk pushin' and shovin' to get back over them mountains. Remember how long it took us to pick ourselves up last time? Half the bloody kingdom frighted near to death, for nowt."

"I remember," said Pellen, sighing. "And you're right. We don't want that again."

"'Sides, ain't no reason to think anythin's changed from what poor ole Tollin found," he added. "But that Fernel bloody Pintte..." He scowled at the new mayor, still jigging with Dathne. "He's the type as won't take no for an answer. He'll push and shove and niggle, thinkin' sooner or later he'll turn the tide towards him. And if we got Doranen rowin' in his boat now..."

"I think the whispers are wrong," said Pellen. "I can't believe Rodyn Garrick would join with an Olken."

"Aye, well—" Asher scratched his chin. "Fingers crossed, eh?" He glanced up. "How you feelin', any road?"

"I'm fine. Charis takes good care of me. She's a sweet child. So much like my Ibby. Asher, don't take this amiss, but—"

"What?" he said, as Pellen hesitated.

"I'd not have her heart broken. So if Rafel's merely...dallying..."

Startled, he stared at his friend. "Rafe and Charis?"

"You didn't know?"

The Meistress Choice dance was done with, and a new dance started. Asher looked at the whirling, colourful couples and saw his son was partnering some other Olken lass now. She looked familiar but he couldn't remember her name. Girls were always buzzing round Rafel, bees to a blossom.

"Pellen—" Discomfited, he shook his head. "Rafe ain't said nowt to me on bein' partial to Charis."

"Which is why I worry," said Pellen. "For you might as well know that she's partial to him."

Oh. Then best he had a word with his rakish son, eh? *Last thing I need be him causing a brangle over petticoats. 'Specially with Pellen poorly, and such a good friend.* "I'll see she ain't dallied with. My word on it."

"It's not me thinking Rafel's not good enough for her," Pellen said quickly. "He's a fine boy. Only...I remember being young and full of hot blood. I remember—" He laughed, a little colour touching his face. "Well. As I say, I'd not have Charis hurt."

Asher had to grin. So, in his green days Pellen had been a bit of a lad, eh? Prob'ly he'd cut a fine figure in his guardsman's uniform at that. For himself, he'd only been passing interested in the lasses...leastways until he met Dathne.

"He won't muck her about, Pellen. Reckless Rafe might be, but not cruel. Not ever."

Pellen, 'cause he were Pellen, heard the rough beneath the smooth. "You and the boy are still at odds?"

He shrugged, one-shouldered. "He reckons he's hard done by, but he'll get over it soon enough."

"I know you think so," said Pellen, after a moment. "But Asher—he's not a child any more. He's a young man with a gift and he wants to explore it and you've not convinced him why he shouldn't."

"Don't need to convince him, do I? I'm his da. What I say goes."

Pellen shook his head. "Why is it so important to you that he continues this pretence?"

"You bloody know why, Pellen!"

"There's a difference between him working Doranen magic in private and showing it off in Market Square," said Pellen, keeping his voice low. "And even if he did show it off, he's in no danger. Barl's First Law is dead, Asher. We killed it."

"That ain't the point," he said, irritated. "Rafe might swear blind he won't cause a ruckus but he's my son and I know him. The likes of that Arlin Garrick'll say the wrong thing *one* time and that'll be that and you can't pour spilt ale back in the jug, can you? Won't no good come of lettin' Rafel explore his *gift*. He can bloody sit on it, like I do. Instead of frettin' on bloody magic he can make up his mind what he's to do with his life proper. I've had enough of his dabblin' here and dabblin' there and never choosin' a path to walk."

"That's not always a simple decision, Asher."

"Never said it were simple," he retorted. "But he can't keep driftin' rudderless, Pellen. And he can't keep on hopin' to make his life about magic. It ain't goin' to happen. I ain't goin' to let it."

Pellen sighed. "Well . . . I'm sure you know best."

In other words, *Asher, you're making a mistake*. But he weren't. He knew in his bones it were dangerous to let Rafel run loose with Doranen magic. "Any road," he said, "ain't no cause for you to fret on Charis. I'll see her right."

"I know you will," said Pellen, and patted his shoulder. "It's just . . . my lass is at that age, isn't she? You've got Deenie, so you know how it is."

Deenie. Gardenia. His little brown mouse. He looked for her on the dance floor, but no. She weren't there. Had she stepped out even once tonight? He didn't think so. Deenie adored her Uncle Pellen so of course she'd come to the ball, but . . .

"If I worry," he said, "it be 'cause she *ain't* a lass as flutters her eyelashes. Too quiet by far, that's Deenie. I ain't even sure where —"

"There," said Pellen, nodding. "Being persuaded by Charis to flutter a little, I suspect."

Pellen was right. Charis, all lit up like glimfire in her yellow silk gown, two Olken lads worshipful by her side, was laughing at Deenie, cajoling her to dance. Meek and shy in her own pretty blue dress, Deenie were blushing and shaking her head. Standing behind the long table of refreshments, holding a glass of lemonwater like it were a potion to ward off evil.

Go on, mouse. Have a dance, eh? Have some fun. You can't stand your whole life unnoticed in the bloody shadows.

Charis won, of course. Deenie never could resist her best friend for long. Grinning, Asher watched her take one of the young men's bent arm—Mick Greeley, that was, his da ran Dorana City's markets, a sober lad, respectable, nowt a whiff of trouble about him—and walk shyly with the lad onto the dance floor. Dathne saw her, and winked. She was all set to dance with young Greeley's da. The other lad dancing attendance, he could see now, was Rafe's best friend Goose. With luck Charis would flutter her eyelashes at him. Fall for him, mayhap, and wouldn't that be useful?

Rafel, Rafel . . . you better not be triflin' with Pellen's only child.

Where was the sprat, any road? Not on the dance floor now. Not at one of the refreshment tables. Not anywhere in the room that he could see. And neither was poxy Arlin Garrick . . .

Them two. I swear. At each other's throats from the moment they first met.

Uneasy, suspicions stirring, he slid off his chair.

"Asher?" said Pellen. "What's wrong?"

"Nowt," he said, 'cause his friend didn't need more to fret on. "Just feel like stretchin' m'legs a bit. If I take a wander, you'll be fine?"

That had Pellen pulling a face. "I'm not quite in my dotage yet, thank you. By all means run along. I'm sure I'll amuse myself tolerably well without you."

He grinned, briefly. "Aye. I'm sure you bloody will too."

Even as he walked away from the dais a handful of Olken crowded in to take his place. Pellen greeted 'em cordially and they fell into eager discussion. Heading for the nearest door to take him outside, Asher found himself waylaid by Eylin Cross, no longer on the Mage Council but still a woman of influence. Hovering behind her were Nan Mortley of the Shepherds' Guild.

"Asher," said Eylin in her brisk, no-nonsense way, "bide a moment. Nan needs a word with you about her suit in Justice Hall."

He raised both hands. "Now, Eylin, you *know* I ain't to talk on what's upcoming afore—"

"Trust me," said Eylin grimly. "And make an exception for this."

Eylin weren't the flighty type. If she said it were important, if she thought to press him on it here at Pellen's farewell ball, then..."All right." *Rafel, you'd better keep y'self out of mischief.* "We'll step aside and you can tell me quick what's amiss."

Escaped from the Guildhouse, from the overbright glimlight and laughter and warmth, from Charis, Rafel turned his face to the starstruck sky. Out here, in the small but lush Guildhouse garden, clipped grass beneath his feet, fragrant flowers in profusion around him, a cool breeze flirting like a lass with his hair, he could breathe slow and deep. Breathe out every last skerrick of tension and frustration and sorrow.

Uncle Pellen looks so poorly. And Fernel bloody Pintte—he can't even pretend to be sorry. No wonder Da hates him. How'd he ever get made mayor?

Mama and Da, they pretended their old friend was fine. But he wasn't Asher of Restharven's son for nothing. He felt what he felt, and what he felt made his chest hurt. Other things made it hurt too, but tonight Pellen's wan face and weary eyes and fallen flesh hurt the most.

And Charis, bloody Charis, dancing like a whirligig. Chatter, chatter, chatter like there was nowt wrong. *When Papa's better, Rafe, we're going to travel round Lur a bit. When Papa's better, we're going to plant a new garden. When Papa's better...* When a blind man could see Pellen was an ailing man and she was fooling herself.

Even so, you couldn't stop yourself from looking at her, could you?

Fretted raw, he could feel his magic simmering inside him. Wanted more than anything, so strong he could *taste* it, to lash out and break something. Crack stones. Shatter glass. Smash the Guildhouse garden's djelbas to splinters. Pull the stars from the sky.

Aye, and wouldn't that prove Da right and me at fault?

"Rafel...?"

He didn't turn. Didn't have to. "Go back inside, Deenie. I don't want company just now."

"Oh. All right. If you want. Only..."

The hurt in her voice stoked his anger. "Ain't no *only,* Deenie. There's just you being a nuisance. As usual. Go away."

"I will. I will, except—" Her voice was unsteady. Still hurt, but stubborn too. And wasn't that his sister in a nutshell? "Rafe, you're stirred up. All hot and gnarly inside. I can feel it."

He threw her a burning look over his shoulder. "Good for you. Now, unless you want to *see* it, *go away.*"

"You don't have to be mean," she said. "There's no call to be mean."

"Ain't no call for you to stickybeak in my business, either, but here you are anyway. Stickybeaking."

"Fine," said Deenie. "Burn yourself up, then. See if I care."

He listened to her stamp back into the Guildhouse, where music played and folk danced, most of them celebrating. He'd tried to pretend happiness too, but the lie wore him out. For all that Pellen Orrick was years older than Da and Mama, for all he'd been their friend before they were married, somehow, slowly, he'd become their son's friend too.

Like ole Darran was. An ear to listen. A shoulder to lean on. Someone who knows what Da's like, and doesn't always take his side.

And he needed that, 'cause though he loved his father, sometimes Da could be bloody hard work. Like with his magic. He was so bloody *tired* of having to hide his Doranen power, like these were the old days and Barl's First Law still ruled. What did it *matter* if the Doranen knew he was like Da? Not once his whole life had his parents given him an answer. All they did was boss him, and expect him to obey. The way Da carried on, it was clear he was *ashamed.* Ashamed of the son who'd inherited his gift.

As though it's my fault. As though I did something wrong.

So did that mean he had to leave home? Find a new place to live, and busywork that would keep a roof over his head while he learned for himself the true extent of his Doranen magic? He didn't want to. Him leaving like that would break Mama's heart. But Da wasn't giving him much of a choice.

'Cause it's my bloody life and I'll live it how I want.

Footsteps behind him. *"Deenie!"* he said, still not turning. "Sink me, *why* can't you—"

"Deenie?" A soft, unpleasant laugh. "So much for the oft-vaunted Olken talent for sensing things."

Swallowing a curse, Rafel turned. The garden's dim glimlight showed him silvergilt hair, and flamboyant striped silk, and a smile that had nowt to do with friendship. And suddenly he was a sprat again, facing down his bitter enemy in the school yard . . . or the street.

"What's the matter, Arlin?" he said, with sweetly false sympathy. "Won't any of the girls dance with you?"

"I've got the pick of any girl in there," said Arlin, eyes narrowing. "Even your drab little sister, Rafel. If I snapped my fingers—"

"Try it," he advised. "Go on. Then see how sorry you are. You muck about with Deenie and I'll show you some Olken magic. Maybe I'll show you—"

"Now, now," said Da, stepping out of the shadows. "Settle down there, Rafe. You lost your sense of humour, sprat? Arlin's teasing, is all. He knows better than to start a brangle over a lass. Not with me, any road. Not when it's my lass."

Arlin's mocking smile vanished. "Meister Asher." He took a step back—did he realise it?—and folded his arms. "You must've misheard. Me, interested in an Olken girl? Hardly. I've got my standards."

"Rafe," Da said, one hand lifting. "Let be. Not every man can hold his drink like a man. Show a little pity for them as can't."

He couldn't trust himself to speak. Could only feel some small, passing pleasure at Arlin's tight-lipped anger and bite his tongue, hard. And feel pleasure, too, knowing that for years he'd stolen spells from Arlin, and never once did Arlin suspect. He'd never understood it, how Arlin could be so arrogant about his magic when as far as he could tell, Garrick was no better a mage than any other Doranen.

"Reckon you might want to make y'self scarce, young lord," Da suggested kindly. "Have a sit down somewhere till you be sober again. Wouldn't like to see you so het up you puked your guts over that fancy clobber of yours, eh?"

"Meister Asher," said Arlin, after a tense moment. "Rafel." He favoured them both with a curt nod then made a hasty, undignified retreat.

"Poxy little shit," said Da, watching him go.

Still not trusting himself, Rafel grunted.

Da stared at him. "*Now* what are you fratched at, Rafe?"

"Wasn't any call for you to step in, Da," he said tightly. "I don't need help with the likes of Arlin Garrick."

Da's eyebrows shot up. "No?"

"No!" he said, nigh on shouting. "All you did poking your nose in was—was—" *Make me look a fool. Make me feel small and useless.* "Da, I didn't need your help."

"Oh, aye?" Da snapped back. "So you're sayin' you weren't about to lose that fine temper of yours and try magickin' the little sea-slug into the middle of next week?"

It smarted that Da could read him so easily. "So what if I was? He was smearing on Deenie!"

"Aye, but if Deenie never hears of it Deenie won't be hurt, will she?" Da retorted. "And how's branglin' with Rodyn Garrick's sprat goin' to manage that, Rafel? Do things your way and *everyone* would bloody know!"

Why didn't Da understand? Why wasn't he *angry?* "The likes of Arlin Garrick didn't ought to get away with saying muck about whoever they want!"

"Oh, *Rafe.*" Da shook his head. "The likes of Arlin Garrick's a *Doranen,* you young fool. Hundreds of years they been arrogant shits. Reckon they're goin' to stop bein' 'emselves any time soon?"

"They won't stop being themselves till we make them, Da. Nowt'll change if we don't stand up to them."

"Things have changed already," said Da, impatient. "You just be too young to see it. And they'll change more. But it takes time, Rafe, so while you be waitin' you got to learn to walk away. No good'll come of stirrin' things up. *'Specially* not with magic. Not while we be stuck here with 'em like cats and dogs in a barrel."

"Then maybe Fernel Pintte's right," he muttered, still hotly smarting. "Could be it's past time we showed them the door."

"*Rafel...*" Da turned away, hand rubbing over his face, then swung back again. "You'd side with Pintte? At Pellen's farewell you'd—"

"Aye, Da, I would!" he retorted. "If Pintte's right, then I—"

Without warning, the balls of glimfire dotted round the small Guildhouse garden flared and spluttered. Belched eye-stinging, throat-catching smoke.

"Sink me," said Da, his head snapping up. "Rafe, d'you feel that? D'you feel—"

And beneath their feet, in the deep earth, Lur groaned.

Startled cries came from inside the Guildhouse. Through its many windows Rafel saw fits and bursts of light as the golden glimfire beneath the rafters surged and spat bright sparks.

The waves of unease in the earth rolled higher and harder. Turning, Rafel saw his own shock and sickness reflected in his father's face.

"Da? What's this? I thought—"

"Aye, Rafe, so did I," said Da. He sounded strange, almost *frighted*. But that couldn't be right. "Come on," he said, starting towards the Guildhouse. "Let's find your ma and sister."

"*Asher!*" said Mama, catching sight of them, her voice lifting over the hubbub. Folk inside the Guildhouse milled and gabbled, crying out as the balls of glimfire sizzled and bounced. Even the Doranen looked shocked, standing together in little groups whispering and staring accusingly at the Olken guests. But Mama paid no heed to that, she shoved her way through the anxious throng, ignoring the folk who yelped and glared.

When she reached them Da caught her in a swift hug. "Where's Deenie?"

Mama's face was milky pale, her dark eyes wide. "She's with Goose," she said, her voice breathless. *She* sounded frighted. "Over there, in the corner." Pulling one hand free, she pointed.

Reassured, Da nodded. "Pellen? And Charis?"

"I'm sure they're fine too. Asher—"

"I don't know, Dath," said Da, still holding her tight. "Let's talk on it at home. Rafe—"

He clasped his father's shoulder. "Aye, Da, don't fret. I'll fetch Deenie."

Da spared him a swift, strained smile. "Good sprat."

For once, he didn't mind being called a child.

Leaving his parents he made his way round the edge of the dance floor, trying not to flinch as the glimfire spat more stinging sparks. Trying not to groan out loud as the waves of wrongness surged and shifted beneath his unsteady feet. He hadn't felt this in ten years. His head was spinning, pins and needles in his blood. Many of the Olken who only moments ago had been laughing and dancing, they were feeling it too. He heard their moans, saw their fear, watched them clutch at each other. Watched the tears of fright trickle down their cheeks.

If he wasn't bloody careful, he could weep with fright himself.

"Rafel! *Rafe!*"

And that was Goose, safe in a corner with Deenie huddled against him. His sister wasn't crying but she shook like a flower in a windstorm, even with Goose's strong arm around her.

"Hey," he said, joining them. "You all right?"

Goose had sprung up and filled out so much this last year, Deenie looked like a little girl beside him even though she was a young woman now. "Fine," he said, nodding. "But you're not, are you? Rafe..." His eyes were bleak. "Is this—"

"The riverpond? Aye," he said shortly, as his belly churned and heaved. "Hush up, eh? Deenie—"

His sister turned her pinched face towards him. "What's happening, Rafe?" she whispered. "I feel so bad. Lur feels bad. I don't understand, I thought—" Then she cried out, and she wasn't the only one, as another enormous wave of wrongness ripped through the earth, the air, through the blood and bones of most Olken in the room.

And outside the Guildhouse, the night was deafened by thunder.

"*Rafe!*" said Goose, as Deenie pressed her face into his fine brocade weskit. "Can you stop this?"

More thunder roared, like a rock-slide. Then screams and shouts as the Guildhouse glimfire extinguished in a shower of sparks and the room plunged black. A heartbeat later it lit up again in jagged fits as spears of blue-white lightning seared and sizzled the dark.

"D'know," he said, his blood seething. "Will you watch Deenie a mite longer? I need to—"

"No, Rafe," Deenie said. "Please, I don't—"

"I ain't going far," he said. "And Goose is with you. Don't fret, Deenie. I'll be back in a ticktock."

"Do what you need to," said Goose. "I got her."

There was something about the way his friend said it, the way his arm cradled Deenie, the look on his face. He stared. *Goose...and Deenie? He's never said a word to me.* But there wasn't time to think on it. He had more alarming things to think on just now.

Everyone in the Guildhouse was shouting. Someone had found candles—little puddles of light were popping up everywhere. Someone else must've told the musicians that fiddles were soothing, 'cause them as were stuck up in the gallery had started playing again. Over the music and the fratching he could hear Fernel Pintte trying to be mayor, but it wasn't working. Too much fright, too much upset. Too many Doranen demanding explanations. And in Pintte's voice he could hear the pain of Lur's pain. Dorana's new mayor was a powerful Olken mage.

Trying to shut out the noise and the hurt, Rafel stumbled and shoved and excused his way to the Guildhouse's open doors.

Escaped outside, he nearly fell over his mother, and Da.

"Where's Deenie?" his father demanded. "Rafel—"

"She's with Goose. She's fine. I wanted to—" When he saw the sky, his voice died in his throat. "Oh, Da," he whispered. "Da...we're in trouble."

He felt Mama's arm slip round his waist. Felt Da's hand come to rest heavy on his shoulder. "Aye, sprat," his father said. "We sinkin' well are."

The glorious summer stars were vanished, blotted out by thick cloud. Vivid forks of lightning stabbed the city like a cut-throat. Thunder rolled and rumbled, pressure against his skin, in his head. He could feel his magic roiling, boiling in his blood. The night's wildness was calling him. He wanted to leap and shout.

"Hold fast, Rafe," said Da. "'Cause this be only the beginning."

And as though Da's words were a knife blade severing a taut, restraining rope...lightning cracked—thunder roared—and a cold rain fell like hammers. Like the end of the world.

CHAPTER FOURTEEN

❊

Because she couldn't trust herself to speak, Dathne stood at the Tower's solar window and stared at the sullenly weeping world beyond it.

Since the night of Pellen's farewell ball, nearly two weeks ago, it had stormed and rained almost without ceasing. Tremors had been felt in every part of the kingdom. Countless creeks and riverlets and ponds were overflowing. There'd even been some drownings. Dorana's City Guardhouse — all the Guardhouses in the kingdom — were on the highest alert. Frightened people did silly things. Dorana's Guardhouse was full right now of hotheaded Olken and Doranen youths caught brawling in Market Square, each blaming the other for Lur's overwhelming strife. Rafe's friend Goose was one of those arrested, swirled up in the disturbance trying to save another lad from harm.

All fear and no sense, the fools, and not once stopping to think. Don't people understand anything? We survive this together or we perish alone.

Behind her, she heard Asher shift on the solar's low couch. "Dath? You goin' to say somethin'?"

"Trust me, Asher, you don't want to hear what I have to say."

"Yes, I do," he said. "I always do."

All right, my love. But don't say you weren't warned.

She turned on him. "You can't do it. You nearly killed yourself last time. And anyway, we both know this has gone far beyond fixing, even with Weather Magic. Whatever time you bought for Lur—it's spent now. And there's no more coin in that purse."

"Dath..." Asher lifted his head from his hands. "If I don't try again, them fools Pintte and Garrick are goin' to—"

"Then let them!" she snapped. "If they're so stupid they won't listen to you then *let* them. You don't like them anyway, so why should you care if they get themselves drowned?"

He sighed. "You don't mean that."

"Don't I?" She laughed, scornful. "Given a choice between your life and theirs do you think I'd choose those fools over you?"

"No, Dath," he said, pressing his thumb tips to his eyes. "Course I don't."

"Asher..." Heartwrung for him despite her frightened fury, Dathne stepped swiftly to the couch and sat by his side. Smoothed his close-clipped, badgery hair. "Stop blaming yourself. You've done everything you could. More than anyone had a right to expect."

He shrugged, unconsoled. "Ain't been enough, though, has it?"

"Asher, you bought us *another ten years*. There's not a man or woman in Lur who could've done more. And as for Fernel, and Rodyn Garrick—you've shouted yourself hoarse in both Councils *and* you've petitioned them privately and still they insist on ignoring you. I say if they're determined to be blind fools, then so be it. But you *cannot* risk WeatherWorking again. I won't have it. I won't lose you to—"

Hurried footsteps on the Tower staircase. Rafel. He strode into the solar, his face lit with elation. But Dathne, knowing him, thought she saw trepidation beneath it.

"Goose's let out," he announced. His hair and shoulders were damp from the rain. "They all are. Cautioned and fined, but no worse."

"Ha," said Asher, unslumping. "Don't tell me that Captain Mason's a soft-head. When the Council hired him in charge of the Guardhouse he promised he'd be strict."

"It was a steep fine," said Rafel. "Fifty trins, which Goose's da said he won't pay. And every offender's name noted in the record of affray. That's strict enough, seeing as how Goose did nowt wrong."

Dathne smiled. Always leaping to someone's defence, was her son. "But aside from being poorer, he's none the worse for wear?"

"Got himself a ripe black eye," said Rafe, pulling a face. "And a couple of loosened teeth."

"Well, mayhap that'll teach him not to brangle in Market Square," said Asher. "Hope you been payin' attention, sprat."

Dathne saw the flash of resentment in their son's eyes. Saw his jaw tighten, briefly, and the instinctive clench of fingers to fists.

Oh, Asher. Have a care. Don't let Lur's new troubles blind you.

"Any other news, Rafe?" she said, patting her tactless husband's hand in warning. "What's the gossip?"

Rafe looked at his father sidelong, then wandered over to the solar's window. "Word is Fernel Pintte and Rodyn Garrick are set to leave for the coast by the end of the week."

"Anyone goin' with 'em?" said Asher, eventually.

"Didn't hear that." Rafe grimaced. "Though I s'pose Arlin'll traipse along, so he can say after how he saved Lur single-handed."

"If there is an after," Asher muttered. "If they don't kill 'emselves and half of Westwailing while they be about it."

"Da..." Rafe shoved his hands in his pockets, looking so like his father. "We can't sit on our arses doing nowt. I don't see what's wrong with trying to break the reef."

"Rafe, it's *been* tried," Asher said sharply. "*I* tried." It was another cruel memory he'd worked hard to smother. "And when I failed, Barlsman Holze and the best Doranen mages Morg didn't manage to kill, *they* tried. And how did that tale end? With most of 'em dead outright and Holze ravin' witless for nigh on three months. The bloody reef's poison. There ain't no undoin' it."

Rafel was staring. "I never knew you tried to break the reef."

"Aye, well, it were a long time ago and we never did run around shoutin' it from the roof tops. Point is, Rafe, we failed."

"But Da, like you say, it was a long time ago," said Rafe. So young, so — so *cocksure.* "You said it yourself — things change. We all thought Lur was a safe and peaceful place, but it's not. It's growing more dangerous by the day. What if the rain won't stop? What if the earth tremors get any worse? There's already crops ruined and stock drowned. Much more of this and food's going to get scarce. What do we do then? How will we live? We've got to find a way out of this bloody kingdom. And if we can't go over the mountains we've got no choice. We have to get out on boats."

Asher shoved to his feet. "What boats, Rafe? Fishin' boats? They'd never stand up to the open ocean."

"Then we'll build bigger boats," said Rafe, reckless. "Better boats."

"And sail 'em *where,* sprat?" said Asher. He was starting to lose his temper. "Like as not there ain't nowhere to sail to. For as long as there's been Olken in Lur has a boat ever come here? *No.* We ain't seen so much as a sail on the bloody horizon!"

"That doesn't mean we shouldn't *try!*" Rafe shouted. "And if you won't then someone else has to. Someone's got to do more than stand around telling folk to give up hope. Barl bloody save us, Da, you could be wrong. Why don't you ever admit you could be *wrong?*"

Seeing Asher's face, Dathne leapt up. "Rafel, that's enough." Her voice was trembling. Her whole body was trembling. The hurt in Asher's eyes... "You don't know everything. You don't know —"

"I know enough, Mama," said Rafel, pale with temper. "I know Lur's broken and Da can't fix it. And if he can't *no-one* can. Now, I don't like Fernel Pintte and Lord Garrick any more than you like 'em, but at least they're trying to *do* something. So I say let 'em. I say we've got nothing to lose."

"That ain't always true, Rafe," Asher said quietly. "Sometimes we don't know what we got to lose till we've gone and bloody lost it."

Rafe's face shuttered. "Any road," he said. "That's the latest news."

"Rafe, where are you going?" said Dathne, as her son headed for the solar door. "Rafe —"

"Out for a bit," he said, not slowing. "I'll be back for supper."

She stood there, silent, listening to his footsteps fade. Then she looked at Asher. His face was shuttered too, all thought and feeling locked away. She reached out, touched his arm.

"Asher, he's young. He doesn't —"

He walked to the window. Rested his palm on its pane of glass and stared out at the rain and the waterlogged garden. "Dath, I got to go too. Down to Westwailing. If them fools are bent on doin' this...I got to be there."

She wanted to say no. She wanted to rail against his sombre certainty, hold him and kiss him until he changed his mind. But she couldn't, because down in Westwailing there was still a small chance he could make a difference. And he needed that. He needed it badly.

And whatever he does there, at least it won't be WeatherWorking.

"I'll go with you," she whispered. "We'll all go."

His head snapped round. "No, Dath. You and the sprats got to stay here. Ain't no tellin' what'll happen when they start faddlin' with the reef. Me and Holze and them others, we went at it careful. That won't be Garrick and Pintte. Them fools are goin' to try rippin' it to shreds. It won't be safe."

"Right now, nowhere in this kingdom's safe," she retorted. "Rafe's right about that much. Besides. It's time he learned a thing or two first hand, our brash son. And I don't want Deenie left behind on her own. She's fragile, yet. She needs me. And Asher, *you* need *us*."

She could feel the conflict in him. He wanted to argue, declare himself the stalwart hero. The lone wolf. But his eyes told a different story. He was hurting, because of Rafe, whose youthful arrogance was sharper than a knife. And worse than the pain, there was shame...because he'd let her talk him out of trying to WeatherWork again.

But she refused to be ashamed of that. Though they didn't speak of it, she knew there were wounds in him that hadn't healed. Might never heal. What was it Queen Dana had said once to Gar, that Gar had told Asher and he had told her?

Weather Magic is a double-edged sword, and every time you wield it you cut yourself a little.

Well. For Gar's sake and Lur's, Asher had nigh on cut himself to ribbons. She had no desire that he cut himself again. Not now, not ever. And he knew it.

But...could she trust him to honour her fear? If Pintte and Garrick failed in Westwailing, as seemed most likely, and Lur's strife made good on its threat to tear the kingdom apart—could she trust him not to try WeatherWorking their way out of trouble a second time?

Of course I can't. He's Asher.

"My love," she said. "I want your word on something. No matter what happens on the coast, promise me you're done with Weather Magic. On the lives of your children, promise me you won't touch that Weather map again."

Wearily he shook his head. "Dath—"

"*Promise me.*"

"All right," he said, after a terrifying silence. "I promise."

She smiled, tightly. *I don't care if he resents me. I don't care what he does so long as he doesn't go back to that bloody Weather Chamber.* "Good. Now I'd best get busy packing, since we're off to the coast."

"I'll see to the carriage and horses," said Asher. "And after that, reckon I'll wander down and have a few words with Pellen. He likes the company, and he'll want to know about Pintte and Garrick's plan."

She frowned. "He's supposed to be resting. If you wear him out with politics and gossip, Asher, he'll never—"

"Trust me, Dath, he'll be a sight more fratched not knowin' what's what. Last thing Pellen wants is to be left out."

And that was true too. She sighed. "Just be home in time for supper. Or you'll have Cook out of sorts and you're not the one who has to listen to her griping."

She turned to leave a second time, and for a second time he stopped her. "Dath..."

Twenty years was a long time to live with a man. She knew him as she knew herself. Too well for comfort, sometimes. Too well to lie. "You can't, Asher," she said softly. "I know you want him to think well of you, always. But ask yourself this, my love. Will it help Rafe or hurt him to know about the Weather map? When there's nothing he can do with it? When there's nothing he can do for you?" She took a consoling step towards him. "He might not admit it, but he's frighted like the rest of us. Rafe knows you. He *loves* you. You've not lost him over this. He knows better than anyone you're not a coward."

He tried to smile. "You reckon?"

"I do. Now go cheer up Pellen. Give him my best." She darted back to him and kissed him lightly on the lips. "And don't forget—I love you too."

She left him alone then, for he wasn't a man to weep easy in company. Not even when the company was his wife of twenty years.

Until the day Morg tried to destroy Dorana, the alehouse that stood on this spot was called the Green Goose. According to them as remembered, it had been the favourite watering spot for all the palace and Tower staff. Da used to drink and rowdy and play knucklebones there three or four nights a week, so folk said. But the alehouse burned down on the day Morg died, and the innkeeper had burned with it along with his family.

The new alehouse built in its place was named the Dancing Bear. Goose's da brewed the ale for it, and sometimes Goose did too now he was trusted alone with the hops and the malt barley and the recipes that won prizes at the annual guild fair.

Still fratched with his father, Rafel brooded over a mug of Goose-brewed pale ale. Two fiddles and a tambourine made cheerful music in the corner, much more to his liking than the noise at Pellen's ball. Though a lot had changed in the City, this remained an Olken place. No Doranen drank here. And most of those Olken were sneaking looks over their shoulders at the hero's son, in the corner. Looks that suggested disappointment and dismay, that the hero hadn't lifted a finger this time to save them.

Don't blame me. I tried talking to him.

"Hey," said Goose, sliding onto the bench opposite. His hair was wet. Would it never stop raining? "Got your message. What's wrong?"

He shrugged. "Nowt. Didn't feel like drinking alone, is all." Sour mood easing, just a little, he sat back. "How bad's the trouble with your da?"

Goose waved at one of the barmaids, pulling a face. "Let's just say I'm not his favourite son."

"Goose, you're his only son."

"And not his favourite, either."

"But you did nowt wrong," Rafe protested. "You were trying to help Solly."

"Which cost me fifty trins and my name writ down in the Guard-house, so—" Goose broke off and smiled at the barmaid. "A pint of strong, Flora lass."

Flora dimpled. "Yours or your dad's?"

"Mine," said Goose, grinning. "Or folk might start to talk. A brewer who won't drink his own ale? That'll get tongues wagging."

Flora's dimples deepened. "One pint coming up, Goose."

For a moment Rafe admired the saucy swing of her hips as she returned to the bar. Then he looked back at Goose. "Your da's a bloody fool. He ought to be proud of you, standing up for a friend."

"Probably he would be, if it didn't cost me fifty trins," Goose said, resigned. "You know what my dad's like about money."

"Aye," he said, and swallowed more ale. It was a touch sweeter than what Goose's da brewed. But then, Goose was a touch sweeter than his da, so no surprise there.

Waiting for his own tankard, Goose looked around the crowded ale-house. There was laughter, there was gaming, the music was loud and bright, but beneath the jollity was a bitter taint of fear. The rain didn't help, drumming harder than ever on the Bear's tiled roof, a constant reminder Lur was falling apart.

"I heard what the mayor and Lord Garrick are planning," said Goose, lowering his voice. "Is it true? Have we got no choice but to trust in them?"

The sweet ale in his belly turned abruptly sour. "Looks that way."

"But Rafe..." Goose chewed at his lip, as dismayed as all the other Olken in the place. "Your dad's the WeatherWorker, he—"

"That's what he was, Goose. I d'know what he is now."

Flora's return with Goose's tankard broke the shocked silence. "Thanks, lass," Goose said, subdued, and fished some coins out of his pocket for her. After she left them, he leaned across the scarred table. "Rafe, what's wrong?"

Rafel put down his own tankard and scrubbed a hand across his face. *I didn't mean to say that. I didn't mean to . . .* "Nowt," he muttered. "Leastways nowt I want to talk on."

"You still feelin' bad?" said Goose, all quick sympathy. "I thought things had eased off a bit. I've heard other Olken, strong mages, say how things have eased off."

"They have," he said tiredly. "You're right, the earth ain't howling so loud." *Prob'ly 'cause it had nigh on howled itself to death.* But he wasn't strong enough for that conversation. Not tonight. "So aye. I'm feeling better." *For now.*

Goose nodded. "That's good. Rafe . . ."

They'd been friends so long he didn't need for Goose to finish. "No. There's nowt I can do to fix what's gone wrong. Da won't let me."

"Rafe—" Goose rubbed his nose. "Your dad's only trying to protect you."

Rage flashed through him. "Did I ask him to?" he said, leaning across the wooden bench, fist thudding. "I never did, Goose. I never bloody asked and now, when I could make a difference? With the power that's in me?" Sitting back, he gulped the rest of his ale. "I'm no more use than tits on a bull."

"Any road," said Goose, at last, uncomfortable. "At least you're not feeling so sick." He swallowed more of his own ale. Belched. "I came past the Chapel on the way here. Blazing with lights, it was. Full of folk in service with Barlsman Jaffee." His gaze drifted around the noisy room. "Seems to me these days we're either praying or drinking."

"Those ain't our only choices, Goose," he said, and levered himself to his feet. His head buzzed muzzily, sloshing full of ale. "We can gamble, too. Let's find us a game of knucklebones. I'm in the mood to wager big."

They joined a round started up by a few lads as worked the Livestock Quarter, and soon enough one or two others, old school friends, joined them. Raucous and riotous, they hooted, hollered and traded cuicks and trins back and forth, tossed the yellowed knucklebones, accused each other of ham-fisted cheating, laughed and pretended all was right with the world.

Then Rafel looked up at the clock above the bar, and saw he was in danger of getting home late for supper. Leaning sideways, he took a deep breath and bawled into Goose's ear.

"Time's shifting. I gotta go."

Cheerfully ale-sloshed, Goose nodded. "All right. But come by the brewery first thing tomorrow, why don't you? We're shorthanded—and you've got nothing better to do."

The words were meant friendly and teasing, but they stuck him like pins. *Nothing better to do.* Aye, and wasn't that the truth? *I ain't Goose. I don't want to be a brewer. All I want to be I can't. And I still don't know what to do about that.* But that wasn't Goose's fault...and sweating in the brewery was one way to kill time and earn himself some coin.

"Aye," he said. "I'll be there."

Once outside the alehouse, he turned up his coat collar. The rain had eased to a mizzle, and the empty cobbled streets were slick and treacherous under foot. Their glimlamps sparked and sputtered, struggling as they'd struggled ever since the night of Uncle Pellen's ball, and the storm that ripped Lur out of its warm, safe cocoon.

But he didn't want to think on that, either, so he shoved his hands deep in his pockets and started walking back home. Prodded by what Goose had said, he didn't take the back streets this time, but crossed over to Market Square to find the Chapel still blazing with glimlight and folks stood on the steps 'cause they couldn't fit inside. And there was singing. Beautiful singing. Hymns to Barl. He stood in the Square's shadows, listening, and bit by bit his lingering anger faded. Soothed by sweet voices instead of Goose's sweet ale.

After a while he realised he wasn't alone. Looking sideways he saw Da standing a bit distant, listening with him.

"Been sittin' with Pellen," Da said, his own gaze not moving from the chapel. "Chewin' over this and that."

Uncle Pellen hadn't set foot out of his house since that night in the Guildhouse. Rafel felt the worry of it tickle his throat. "He feeling better?"

Da shook his head. "No."

"So Kerril's right?" he said harshly. "He's dying?"

"We all be dyin', sprat," said Da. "Just some of us faster than others, is all."

That wasn't the answer he'd been expecting. "Thanks, Da. That's right cheerful of you."

Da snorted. "Y'know you be late for supper?"

He tipped his face to the cloud-smudged night sky, feeling the mizzle harden, hinting at more rain. "So are you."

"Aye," said Da, still thoughtful. "So you and me got that much in common."

They had magic in common too, only he was s'posed to pretend they didn't. Anger stirred again — but he was too full of ale and weariness to brangle, so he held his tongue.

"I'm goin' down to Westwailing," said Da. "Your ma and Deenie are comin' too. Reckon you should ride with us. Reckon you should see for y'self what comes of faddlin' with things as are best left alone."

"*Da*—" He swung round. "Why'd you have to put it that way? Why can't you say you're going down to Westwailing to show support for the mayor and Lord Garrick?"

"'Cause that ain't why I be goin'," said Da, with a careless shrug.

"You're going so you can sneer and say afterwards *I told you so*?" he demanded, incredulous. "Da, that's mean."

Da looked at him, his face patchworked with glimfire shadows and his eyes gleaming bright and hard. "I'm goin' so I'll be there when things go sinkin' wrong, Rafel. I'm goin' so mayhap I can save them fools when arrogance looks like costin' 'em their lives. I'm *goin'*—" Da stopped. Took a few deep breaths. "I'm goin'," he said more quietly, "in case there's a chance I can talk 'em out of this afore they start."

"You won't," he said. "Their minds are made up, Da. As made up as yours."

"I know," said Da, his voice almost a whisper. "But I got to try, sprat. How will I live with m'self if I don't bloody try?"

He sounded so lost. So hurt. Shaken, Rafel stared at him. *That ain't my da. Asher of Restharven doesn't sound like that.*

"Come on, sprat," said Da, and like magic he was himself again. Brisk. Confident. Careless of the world and its feelings. "Best we tit-tup home again so your ma can crack a wooden spoon over our heads. Fierce set on tidy supper times, your ma. Nasty bad habit that, but she won't give it up."

Though he was temper-churned and restless, still he had to laugh. "All right."

Leaving the Chapel and the singing in the wet night behind them, they started walking towards the High Street, and home.

"Da," he said, as the voices lifted plaintive towards the hidden stars. "D'you believe in all that?"

"All what?" said Da, steadily tramping.

Suddenly he felt awkward. Embarrassed. But he'd started it, so he'd have to keep going. "You know. Chapel. Praying. Barl's mercy. D'you think she's real?"

"She was real," Da said, after a moment. "She were a flesh and blood woman, Rafe. She lived and breathed and walked these streets."

"I know *that.*" Why couldn't Da ever just answer a question? "But now? D'you reckon she's watching over us now? Hears us praying? Does what we ask?"

Da grunted. They'd reached the steep part of High Street, where it tilted straight towards the palace ground gates. Walking fast was a puffing business.

"Ain't that a question for the likes of Barlsman Jaffee?"

"I already know what he thinks. I want to know what *you* think. I want to know if—"

"If we be foolin' ourselves, prayin'?" Da said, breathing hard. "Fillin' our bellies with false hope like you filled yours full of ale tonight?" Da shook his head. "I d'know, Rafe. That's the truth. Mayhap we are. Mayhap them folk back there singin' their hearts out ain't bein' heard by nobody but us. But if it makes 'em feel better...if it gives 'em strength to go on when they be frighted...does it matter? Folk need somethin' to cling to when the waters turn rough."

"They are rough, aren't they? Lur's in trouble, Da. Real trouble."

"Aye," Da said heavily. "It surely is."

"So when do we leave for Westwailing?"

In the damp, ill-lit darkness he could feel his father's surprise. His cautious pleasure. "That means you're comin', does it?"

The brewery wasn't going anywhere. He could earn himself some coin there when he got back. He'd send a message to Goose. His friend would understand.

"Yes. I'm coming."

"We'll head out tomorrow, early as we can," said Da. "I want to get down there afore Pintte and Garrick and them fools they be takin' with 'em turn up. I want some time to get a feel for the place, 'specially now. I want to see if what they want to do can be done."

And that made him stare, and slow down a bit. "And if it can be? Will you help them?"

"If it can be I'll have to, won't I?"

"How? There'll be no Olken magic used, Da. Every last spell will be Doranen."

"Aye, well," said Da, suddenly cagey. "I got me a few tricks up my sleeve."

The trunk. Durm's secret spell books and scrolls. The ones he wasn't meant to know about. He nodded, careless. Trying to look innocent.

"That's good, Da. That's good to know."

They walked in silence the rest of the way home.

At first light next morning, in a steady mizzle, they loaded up their carriage and trundled out of Dorana City, heading for the coastal township of Westwailing.

It was a miserable journey. Thirteen days of patchy rain, high winds, two hailstorms and four more juddering earth tremors. The carriage bogged three times and they broke a wheel once. That happened on a lonely stretch of road between Flat Iron and Slumly Corners. Doranen magic took care of it, since it was Asher's turn to play coachman and there was nobody around to see.

Rafel watched his father mend the snapped spokes with absent-minded ease and had to walk away, so riled did it make him. One rule for Da and another for him. And his parents wondered why he was so easily fratched.

When at long last they reached Westwailing, with Fernel Pintte and Rodyn Garrick and the rest somewhere on the road behind them, they took rooms at the Dancing Dolphin, still sailing along after so many years.

After that, it was a matter of waiting.

Dismayed and disgruntled, Asher stood with his family on Westwailing's long stone pier and stared at the harbour's somnolent waters. Stared beyond them to the distant, foaming breakers rolling in over Dragonteeth Reef. Beyond the reef churned the whirlpools and treacherously random waterspouts spawned by the blighted magics left behind after Morg's destruction. The magics that had tried to kill him all those years ago. The memory was a bad one, almost as bad as what had happened to Matt and Veira... and Gar.

Never wanted to think on that again, did I?

Yet here he was, thinking. Brought face to face with a past he couldn't forget or outrun.

Two days ago, the afternoon he and his family arrived in Westwailing, he'd taken a skiff out to the reef. On his lonesome, though his family fratched at the notion. Twice a year, every year, someone from the fishing community sailed along the reef's edge to see if the whirlpools and the waterspouts were gone or growing weaker, but they never were. Three men had drownded, even, caught unawares. Dathne, Rafel and Deenie were frighted he'd make the fourth. He'd ignored 'em. Seeing the reef up close again were something he'd needed to do.

Holding the skiff hard against the drag of the whirlpools, sailed as close to the reef as he dared, he'd watched the waterspouts spiral havey-cavey from the ocean's shifting surface. Squinting, he'd felt the spouts' spitting spray sting his face. Soak his hair and clothes. Splatter the skiff's sail. The air was full of angry sound and his whole body thudded to the racing beat of his heart. Then he'd looked at the swirling, growling mouths of the whirlpools, monstrous holes in the ocean eager to suck helpless ships to their doom. Opened his mind to the rot in the reef.

It were just as bad as he remembered. He puked his lunch over the Skiff's side, feeling it. Pintte and the others were mad. He had to stop them afore it was too late. But he didn't know how.

Raised voices pulled him back to the present. Further along the pier, towards its far end, a bustle of busyness as Rodyn Garrick and his son and the Doranen mages he'd brought with him prepared to challenge Morg's creeping blight. That troublesome Ain Freidin was one of 'em—and didn't that raise some questions? Fernel Pintte bustled too, hob-nobbing with Westwailing's mayor and council and chivvying the Olken fishermen who'd agreed—for a steep price—to sail them all out to the reef. Fools, every last one of 'em.

Brooding across the harbour, he pulled his hands from his pockets and folded his arms. "I'm tellin' you this be a sinkin' bad idea."

Beside him, Dathne patted his arm. "Yes, Asher. We know."

Deenie tucked her fingers into the crook of his elbow. "The reef makes me shivery," she said, her voice low.

"Your own shadow makes you shivery," said Rafe, scornful. "Why'd you even come?"

Ignoring him, 'cause Rafel in a stroppy mood were best handled by turning deaf, dumb and blind, Asher looked down at his daughter. "The reef's bad, mouse, I know. But is that all you feel?"

"Don't, Da," said Rafel. "You'll only set her off. You know what she's like."

Pushed, he shot his son a warning look. It were a sinkin' shame Rafe had run across Arlin Garrick after breakfast, and let hisself get riled by the poxy little shit. Not that he needed much excuse right now. Dath

were right—their son might be turned twenty, but he had some growin'
up to do.

*Twenty. I were his age when I left home for the City. Were I brash like
him back then? So fearless, and bloody certain I already knew it all?*

He couldn't remember. Too much had happened since. He'd sailed
past forty. *Forty.* How were that possible?

"I'm all right, Da," said Deenie, with a trembly smile. "Don't
mind me."

Which were just like his little mouse, but didn't answer his question.
"Deenie, if you feel there be somethin' else we—"

"No, Da," she insisted. "Don't *fuss.* You'll have folk looking at us.
At *me.*"

And for Deenie there could be nowt worse than that. Rafel loved
attention. Thrived on crowds and noise and bein' noticed. But Deenie?
She weren't never happier than when she were buried up to her eyebrows in a book.

*She be a right proper mix of me and Dath. But Rafe? Sink me, Rafe
be so like his granfer. Before Ma died, Da were the village lantern
everyone followed.*

"Please, Da," said Deenie, giving his shirt-sleeve a little tug, her
wary gaze skittering to see if they'd been overheard by the Olken and
Doranen scurrying like ants about the pier.

"Deenie," said Dathne. "If you don't feel well we can go back to the
Dolphin."

"Your ma's right, mouse," he said, and smoothed a hand down
Deenie's arm. "Ain't no reason for you to doddle about here if this
malarkey don't amuse you."

Rafel snorted. "Y'should have stayed home in Dorana, Deenie. Kept
company with Charis."

"No," said Deenie. "Charis has enough to fret on with Uncle Pellen.
She didn't need me underfoot."

Reminded of the sorrow left behind them in Dorana, Asher scowled
at the pier's salt-crusted stonework. Then, taking Deenie's hand, he
flicked a warning glance at Dathne and wandered their daughter a little

ways back along the pier, towards Westwailing township where almost as many folk were gathered, hopeful of excitement, as came for the Sea Harvest Festival every year.

When they were a comfortable distance from eavesdropping ears, Pintte and Garrick and the rest of 'em, and Rafel, he let go of Deenie's hand and slid his arm round her shoulders. She looked up at him, so trusting. A plain little thing, scrawny like her ma was back when he'd first met her.

"Come on, mouse," he said gently. "Tell me what you feel."

"Da..." Deenie scrunched her face. "I don't like talking on that. Any road, you know already."

"I know what *I* know," he said. "Don't know what *you* know, do I? Come on, Deenie. Nowt much good comes of keepin' secrets."

Sighing, she wrapped her thin arms around her ribs, just like her ma did, and turned her head to stare out across the harbour. Mid-morning and for the first time in days the sky was clear of rain. The unclouded sun struck glittery sparkles off the water and a salt-laden fresh breeze ruffled her short hair, rushing colour to her high-boned cheeks.

"Does it matter how I feel, Da?" she murmured. "Won't change anything, will it."

Sadly, that were true. But he still wanted—*needed*—to know what she could sense. Ever since that stinkin' night she'd woke screaming 'cause he called warbeasts in his troubled sleep, he'd fretted about her. Not the way he fretted for Rafel, who chafed against any and all restraints. He feared for Deenie because, like him, she didn't seem to care much for her magic... and yet, like her brother, was cursed by him with something not given to other Olken.

"It matters to me, mouse," he said. "Ain't it my job to keep you safe? Can't do that if I don't know what's what, eh?"

She had a sweet smile, his Deenie, but now her lips were pressed flat. "You can't keep me safe forever, Da. You won't *be* here forever."

Pellen. "You and Charis been talkin', mouse? She got you all stirred up on account of her da? Don't let Pellen bein' poorly fright you. I be stayin' right here."

Deenie looked at him. Young, so sinkin' young, but cruelly grown-up in her eyes. "Until you go."

"Deenie...Deenie..." He caught her to him in a crushing hug. "Pellen's goin' to be *fine*. If Morg couldn't kill him no bloody cough will. Now why don't you stop tryin' to sail me off course, eh, and tell me what it is you feel."

CHAPTER FIFTEEN

᠅

The skirling cries of Westwailing's seagulls filled the long silence. Fratched voices lifted in dispute as Fernel Pintte kept doin' what he did best, raisin' hackles. Patient, Asher waited till Deenie was ready to speak.

"It's just the reef, Da," she whispered at last, her head tucked neatly under his chin. "That's what upsets me. I can feel the way Barl's magic is tangled in it still. I can feel the whirlpools and the waterspouts. Da, they're so *hungry*. They'll gobble anyone who sails near them. And I can feel—" She trembled. "*Him*. Morg. I can feel his magic. It's like a weed, Da, choking a beautiful rose. Making it feel all—all twisted and ugly. Does that make sense?"

So she did feel what he felt. He closed his eyes, sick with sorrow. *I did this to her.* "Aye, mouse."

Her arms tightened round his waist. "And I can feel you, Da. You're scared. Don't say you're not, because I *know*."

Back along the pier, Dathne and Rafel were standing side by side, keeping well apart from everyone else. He was all stiff-spined and prickly and her hand rested between his shoulder blades in comfort. Rafe wanted to be one of the mages as broke the blighted spells on Dragonteeth Reef and gave the people of Lur hope for a different future.

"Why can't I, Da?" he'd demanded. "Arlin's sailin' out to help and I'm a sight better mage than him. You know I am. So why can't I?"

"You know why, Rafe," he'd replied tiredly. "It ain't for them to see what you can do. Not yet." Not bloody ever, if he had his way. "Any road, it's too dangerous."

And oh, Rafe had bellowed about that. Kicked against being protected and being told he still had to hide. From a spratling he'd never accepted how careful he had to be. But then he never knew how closely the Doranen had watched him, waiting to see if he'd grow freakish like his da. They'd watched Deenie too. They still watched. Olken with the power of Doranen magic in their veins? One was enough. One had saved them. But more than one would be a fox loosed in the henhouse.

But Rafe ain't never wanted to believe it. He don't want to admit that bein' different ain't a blessing.

So he'd argued and argued to join Pintte and Garrick in their folly and only surrendered at the last gasp, with sinkin' poor grace. That were Dath's doing. She'd gentled him. Coaxed him to back down. Stood bridge between her son and husband, to make certain they were still speaking at the end. Which they were, but only just.

It ached him somethin' awful, to be so at odds with Rafe. But how could he love his son and not try to keep him safe? What kind of a father would he be, to trust Rafe into Fernel Pintte's unchancy keeping?

"Are you cross with me, Da?" Deenie whispered. "Did I do something wrong? If I did, I'm sorry. I never meant to."

Startled, he stared down at her. "*Cross* with you? No, mouse. I were thinkin', is all."

She laid her cheek against his chest again. "Rafe's mad now but he'll get over it. You're the sun and the moon and the stars to him, Da. He's so proud of you he could burst, sometimes. And he thinks if he breaks the rotten reef magic so's we can sail away from Lur and find somewhere to live where the earth isn't screaming, then that'll make you proud of him. That's why he's fratched."

He had to wait a moment, before he could speak. "Rafe *told* you that?"

Deenie wrinkled her nose. "Don't be silly, Da. Rafe hardly ever talks to me. I'm his bratty little sister. I just know. I can feel it."

"Like you feel I be frighted."

"Aye," she said. "Like that. I don't mean to. I can't help it."

"I know, mouse," he said, and kissed the top of her head. "I know."

She looked up at him, her eyes swimmy with tears. "Da, is something bad going to happen? Out there at the reef?"

He didn't want to lie to her—but telling the truth was worse. "Nowt's goin' to happen, mouse," he said, and tried to sound like he believed it. "Like as not Pintte and Garrick and the rest'll get wet and catch cold, is all."

Deenie nodded, but her eyes were still swimmy. She shivered again. "I don't know, Da. I'm scared something might."

And what did that mean? Were she afflicted with *visions* now, like her ma used to be? He opened his mouth to reassure her, because he couldn't stand to see her so upset—and then cursed instead.

Fernel bloody Pintte was comin' to interrupt.

"Asher," Pintte said briskly, in his expensive velvet britches and his costly silk shirt and the weskit with gold peacocks on it that made him look like a fool. And his mayoral chain of office, of course. Couldn't dare let folk forget for a heartbeat he were Mayor of Dorana.

Pellen, Pellen, why'd you go and get sick?

"Fernel," he said, leaving his arm round Deenie's shoulders. "Nice day it's turned out. You be sure you want to spoil it?"

Ignoring Deenie, Pintte looked down his nose. There was something about the man, something furtive, that reminded him of that sea-slug Willer.

Or could be it's his bloody peacock weskit.

"Spoil it?" said Pintte, sneering. Ten years later, and he'd not forgiven the way he'd been chased from Pellen's house. The burning memory was in his eyes, buried deep...but not deep enough. "I think you meant to say save it. So. Let me ask you again, Asher. Will you join us? For this is your last chance to do something for the kingdom."

Before he could answer, Deenie slipped out from under his arm and leapt at Dorana's mayor. His timid tiddy mouse, biting the mangy cat. *Bless her.* "How *dare* you say that? My da's done more for Lur than *anyone* since Barl. More than *you'll* ever do." Her fists were clenched, the swimmy tears streaming down her salt-kissed cheeks. "You ought to listen to him, Meister Pintte. You shouldn't be doing this! It's *wrong.*"

Fernel Pintte's eyes were popped wide in shock. Almost he took a step back. "Asher! Control your unruly daughter or I'll banish your family to shore. You've been allowed onto this pier as a courtesy only."

Banish my family. Aye, he would, the poxy shit. No authority here, not in Westwailing, but he'd find a way to throw his weight around regardless. Just like sea-slug Willer, Fernel Pintte were that kind of man.

"Deenie..." Swallowing temper, he touched his little girl's shoulder. "Reckon your ma might like some company, eh?" He nodded down the pier, where Dath now stood on her lonesome. Rafe had wandered away, and was talking to one of the Westwailing fishermen gettin' the chosen boat ready to sail.

Deenie looked. "All right, Da." She kissed his cheek. Glowered a last time at Fernel Pintte. Turned on her heel, almost flouncing, and swished along the pier in her new silk skirt. Glospottle blue it was, and didn't she look fine.

At his leisure he shifted his gaze back to Fernel Pintte. Looked the man up and down. Did he even have the nouse to be a little bit nervous? Or were he so puffed up with self-consequence, so sure the Mayor of Dorana could snap his fingers and command the ocean's waves, that he were convinced he and his Doranen cronies were safe as eggs in a hen?

"You plan on sailin' out to the reef with Garrick and them others, Fernel?"

Pintte's nostrils narrowed with displeasure. "Of course."

"You might want to rethink that."

"No, I don't believe I do."

"Fernel..." With an effort, Asher tamped down his temper again. "Look. Forget it be me sayin' it. Forget we don't like each other and I once made you run away like a lass and *lissen,* would you? There ain't nowt you and them Doranen can do to break the reef. You—"

Air hissed between Fernel Pintte's clenched teeth. "Asher, I'm no more interested in your arguments now than I was in Dorana. All I want to know is—"

"Forget what you want and let me tell you what you *need,*" he snapped. "'Cause I'm tryin' to save your life, Fernel. Barl alone knows why. The only thing you'll do on that bloody boat is get in Rodyn Garrick's way and then most prob'ly die along with him, his poxy son and them fools he's talked into doin' this with him."

"Barl's *tits,*" said Pintte, choking, and half-turned away. "If you're not the most *arrogant*—" He turned back again, his face red with suppressed fury. "Are you so bloated with past glories you think you'll be *forgiven* for refusing to lift a finger now, in Lur's direst hour of need?"

The urge to kick Pintte into the harbour was almost overwhelming. "I don't give a shit about the past, Fernel. All I can think on is the next bloody hour. I don't want to spend it watchin' you drown! So swallow your pride, accept I know what I'm talkin' on and do what I say 'stead of—"

"Asher, *enough,*" said Pintte, throwing up one hand. "And for the love of all things Olken say you'll come out to the reef with us. Loathe you as I truly do, I can't deny your power, or forget you're the only Olken mage who can wield Doranen magic, or that you've already defeated Morg's evil once." Pintte grabbed his arm, shaking him. "Your skills could tip the balance in our favour! You *can't* turn your back!"

Wrenching his arm free, Asher shoved his hands in his pockets so he wouldn't throttle the stupid bastard. "I bloody can, Fernel, 'cause what skills I got won't make a sinkin' bit of difference."

"You don't *know* that!"

"Yes, I do! Last time—"

"*Forget* last time!" Pintte shouted. "It was twenty years ago! Asher, you have to know how important it is that we undo the magic in that reef. With our way cleared to open water then—"

"Aye? Then what?" he said, suddenly tired. "We break the reef, collapse the whirlpools and the waterspouts, then *what,* Fernel? You herd the Doranen onto boats, like sheep, and set 'em sailin' towards the horizon? Till they run out of water and vittles or get sunk in a storm? Be that your notion, Meister Mayor? Kick 'em all out of Lur, good luck and good riddance?"

"They *want* to leave," said Fernel, his pouched cheeks stained red.

"Mayhap Rodyn Garrick wants to scarper," he said. "I heard a whisper on it, and Barl knows he's pushin' this reef business as hard as you. And his mate over there, Sarle Baden. He must want it, or like as not he wouldn't be here. Ain Freidin and Ennet Vail the same. But—"

"And if they *do* want to leave, Asher, who are you to say no?"

"All right, Fernel, so they want to," he snapped. "That's four Doranen out of how many, ezackly? And what makes you think they ain't the only ones? 'Cause I ain't heard any other Doranen clamourin' to leave. Have you?"

Fernel Pintte's chin tilted again. "That's not the point, is it? It's not their wishes I'm concerned with. It's the welfare of this land. *Our* land."

"Jervale's bloody bunions, Pintte!" he said, itching to shake some bloody sense into the fool. "How are the Doranen hurtin' Lur? I must be goin' blind 'cause I can't see any damage."

"Well, you're right about that much," said Pintte. "You *are* blind, Asher. *They are Doranen.* Conquest and domination are in their blood. They usurped us once and they *will* usurp us again now that Lur is steeped so deep in trouble. Trouble *you* don't even seem to notice."

Asher stared at Fernel Pintte. *Forget shakin' the bastard. I want to throttle him.* "You think I don't know we're in trouble, Fernel? Trust me, I know."

"Then *help* us!" Pintte implored. "Our one sure defence against Doranen magic is *you*—and what good are you? You can't fix what's gone wrong and you won't break magic's hold on that cursed reef! And it *can* be broken."

"Says who? Rodyn Garrick? You be willin' to risk your life on *his* say-so? Fernel—" He spread his arms wide. "The only reason Garrick's climbed so high is 'cause all the *good* Doranen mages be long dead!"

Pintte stepped close, salt air rasping in his throat. The gleam in his eyes was unsettling, and desperate. "Lur's time is running out, Asher. Escape from this prison is our only hope—not only against the treacherous Doranen, but against famine, flood, tremors and this ungovernable weather—calamities which I know in my heart they have caused. Why do you refuse to see it?"

"Only thing I see," he retorted, "be an Olken who's let fear and bitterness twist him so *ugly* he—" Breathing hard, he bit back the rest. "Fernel, the Doranen ain't our enemies and what you be plannin' to do here ain't the answer to our woes. You muck about with that reef and all you'll do is make things in Lur a sinkin' sight worse."

Pintte's pointed finger jabbed him in the chest. "Do you know what your problem is, Asher? You're still a lackey of that dead royal family. But the Doranen aren't our friends—and you're the only one who can't see it. You lived in their pockets for so long you've forgotten you're Olken." He stepped back. "Or maybe...you never were. Maybe that taint of Doranen magic in your blood—"

"Shut your bloody mouth, Fernel!" he said, his vision hazing with rage. "Afore I—"

"Afore you *what?*" said Fernel Pintte, scornful. "Kill me with your Doranen powers? And how would that make you any better than Morg?" He laughed, a nasty sound. "You might want to climb down out of that Tower of yours, Asher. When it comes to the Doranen you'd be surprised by how many people think as *I* do."

Sickened to vomiting, more like. "You bloody fool. You be set to stir trouble the likes of which we ain't seen for centuries. And as for that reef, I'll tell you for the last time. *Them mages won't break it.* All they'll do is get the lot of you killed."

Fernel stepped back, his face twisted with contempt. "I can't force you to help. But there will be consequences for refusing, Asher. For you *and* your family."

Asher met him stare for cold stare. "You threatenin' my wife and children?"

"I'm stating a fact," said Pintte, eyes glittering with malice. "And here's a few more for you to chew on. This working *will* succeed. It will cleanse Dragonteeth Reef of its remaining foul magics. It will collapse the whirlpools and the waterspouts and clear the way for the Doranen to leave. And for the first time since Barl and her thieving friends crossed the mountains, Lur will belong to the Olken once more."

He shook his head, disbelieving. "You're mad, Fernel."

"A final word of warning, Asher," said Pintte, oblivious. "Interfere, and you'll be banished from Westwailing for life."

"My brother tried that once. Didn't work. But don't you fret, Fernel," he said, smiling. Feeling savage. "You want to kill y'self, you go right ahead. Prob'ly I won't even shed a tear after."

With a snarling hiss, Fernel turned on his heel and stalked back along the pier to the Doranen and Westwailing's mayor and council. On a gust of breeze, the sound of pipes and drums as Westwailing's town band struck up another jaunty tune. With sudden foreboding Asher remembered the Sea Harvest Festival that had nearly drowned him and Gar. Saw dozens killed and Westwailing wrecked to rubble.

I never should've let Dath and the sprats come with me. I should've put m'foot down, and made 'em stay at home.

But there was no point moanin' over that now. They were here. Fernel Pintte and Rodyn Garrick and them other fools, they were set on muckin' about with fire. And when they got their fingers burned... when dead and dusted Morg burned 'em...

Sink me bloody sideways. I should've stayed at home too.

Rafel wondered, just for a moment, whether he should risk Da's wrath and step between him and Fernel Pintte before they came to blows. Snatches of their heated brangle blew to him on the lively breeze, words like *fool* and *dangerous* and *arrogant*. Fighting words. Jabbing fingers. Waving arms. Any ticktock they'd be rolling on the pier like tomcats, surely.

But Da won't thank me for sticking my nose in. Da ain't interested in anything I've got to say. I wasted my time traipsing all the way down here. I should've stayed in Dorana and helped Goose make his ale.

Temper simmering, he glanced around the pier. Behind him, Mama stood with Deenie, who'd done nowt but sigh and mope ever since they'd reached the coast. Arlin Garrick and his da, and the other Doranen mages, they were huddled whispering and pointing out to the reef. Making their plans to see it broken once and for all. Westwailing's mayor and his followers milled about like lost sheep, casting anxious glances first at the Doranen and then at Da and Fernel Pintte, still arguing. The other Olken on the pier, the fishermen, ignored everything save the task of getting their smack ready to brave the distant reef.

The rest of Westwailing's fishing fleet floated at rest, tucked safely out of the way of the upcoming magework. Rafel frowned at it. Funny. The family had visited the coast a handful of times in his life. He'd even been out on a fishing boat once, with some of the cousins he counted practically as strangers. Hadn't much cared for it. Found it hard to imagine Da living that life, fish and stink and guts and hard work, scales and blisters and calluses and salt. Da still talked of moving back down here, leaving the City and coming to live beside the ocean.

He can if he wants. Mama too, and Deenie. But I won't. That's his dream, not mine. I've got my own dreams and no matter what he says I'll live them. Whatever he says, I will be a great mage.

"Rafe..."

Mama. He shoved his hands in his pockets and kept on staring at the moored fleet. He didn't want to hear her defending Da, again. Taking his side, again.

Once, just once, I wish she'd take my side.

"I could do it, y'know," he said, letting his gaze stray from the tethered smacks to the reef. If he squinted, hard, he could just make out the waterspouts dancing beyond it. "I wouldn't disgrace you in front of Rodyn Garrick and his friends."

"*Disgrace* us? Rafe—" Mama took hold of his arm and pulled him round to face her. Her eyes were shocked. "This has nothing to do with Rodyn Garrick or any Doranen, or with us fearing you'd let us down. This is about doing what's *right*."

"What Da thinks is right," he muttered. "But Mama—"

Her fingers tightened on his sleeve. "No, Rafe. Not again. And you should know better. There's not a mage in this whole kingdom, Olken or Doranen, who understands the way your father does that *some* things are best left alone. How can you pretend not to know that? You're his *son*. And you've been told things denied to everyone else."

"Even if that's true," he said, "I still don't—"

"*If* it's true?" Mama echoed. Shock was burned away by anger. "You puff and preen yourself a fine mage then stand there and say *if*? D'you mean to tell me you don't feel what's out there? What your father feels, and Deenie?"

No. He couldn't tell her that. The tangle of magics in Dragonteeth Reef was *bad*. It tasted rotten in his mind, like maggot-ridden meat. And worse than that, it was strong. Twenty years, his whole life, and it hadn't grown weaker by even a breath. No doubt on it, the task of breaking it was dangerous.

But I don't care. I could do it. I know I could. The power's in me.

He tugged his arm from his mother's grasp. "I don't reckon this is about what's risky. This is about Da. He won't let me help Garrick and the others 'cause he doesn't want to be shown up as wrong about the reef."

Mama gasped. "*Rafel*—are you *blind*? Your father doesn't care about being wrong, he cares about people dying for no reason! He's come here against every opposition to try and save Fernel Pintte and the Doranen from their overweening arrogance, which puts *all* of us in danger!"

"You keep saying that, Mama, both of you do, but—"

"Because we know a little about this, Rafel," she snapped. "We've lived a few more years than you. I *know* your father, better than anyone alive. If he can't stop those fools he's going to blame himself for what happens because of them. It won't be his fault, it'll be theirs, but he'll *still* blame himself. And if—no, *when*—things go horribly wrong out at that reef, Rafel, d'you know what he'll do then? He'll risk his life for them, though they sneer and jeer and call him coward behind his back. *Coward!* When he saved every life in this kingdom. Was prepared to *die* for it. When they howled for his blood, when they—and now you, his son, *you*—"

Her angry grief doused his temper. "I'm sorry," he said, reaching for her. "I didn't mean—Mama, I'm *sorry*." He folded her against him, feeling the past shudder through her, feeling shamed and chastened. Feeling like a bad son. "Please, Mama, don't fratch yourself. It was twenty years ago. Don't—"

"It was *yesterday*," she said, wrenching out of his arms. "For him and for me. You don't know, Rafe. For all the stories Darran told you, trust me, *you don't know*. What it cost him. What it *still* costs. What your father's had to do since—"

"Mama?" he said, staring down at her. She was so *small* now. She used to be the tallest woman in the world. "What is it? Did something happen you never—"

"No. Nothing happened," she said. There were tears on her cheeks. "Don't mind me, Rafe. I'm tired, that's all."

And that was a lie. His parents were keeping secrets again. One of these days, soon, they'd have to stop treating him like a child. They'd *have* to.

Footsteps behind him. Slow. Almost hesitant. *Da*. And then a gentle hand came to rest on his shoulder.

"Rafe. *Rafe*. You think I don't know how hard you want to be part of that mageworking?" Da asked. "I do. And I know right now you don't care for me overmuch. But I can't let that fret me. Better you alive and not likin' me, than you thinkin' me the best da in Lur as you die."

His father was trying to wheedle him. He didn't want to be wheedled. Shrugging free, stepping aside, he turned. "It ain't certain I'd die."

"It ain't certain you wouldn't," Da retorted. Like Mama, his eyes were full of pain. "Reckon I'm about to risk you on a maybe?"

"What I reckon," he said, through gritted teeth, "is that you've got to let me make my own choices."

Da shook his head. "Not this time, sprat."

Sprat. "I ain't a bloody sprat, Da! I'm—"

"I know what you be, Rafe," said Da, his voice strangled tight. "You be the bloody heart beatin' in my chest. You goin' to stand there and look me in the eye and ask me to rip it out? With my own hands? Ask me to throw it on the ground at your ma's feet and say, *'There you go, woman. That's how much I love your son.'* Eh? Is that what you're goin' to do now, Rafe?"

And what was he s'posed to say to that? He had nowt to say. Da was more than wheedling, he was playing dirty, like a gutter drunk, and there was nowt he could say.

Then he didn't have to even try finding words, because there was a bustling behind them. Raised voices, boots scuffling on the stone pier. He and Da looked round to see Fernel Pintte and Lord Garrick and his poxy son Arlin and the other Doranen mages tromping down the pier towards the battered, fishless fishing boat as was set aside to take them out to the reef.

Pintte and Lord Garrick never missed a step or turned their heads. But Arlin, passing, slowed almost to stopping and smiled wide. He reeked of insolence and contempt. "Meister Asher. Rafel."

"Arlin," said Da quietly. "Barl's blessin' on you."

Arlin laughed. "As if we need it."

"You need somethin'," Da replied. "You need a bloody miracle."

"Arlin!" snapped Rodyn Garrick over his shoulder, and Arlin hurried to catch up.

Sarle Baden, Ennet Vail and Ain Freidin didn't slow, or speak. They were trying to pretend Da wasn't even here. That hurt. Did it hurt Da too?

Even if it did, he'd never let on. He's my da but at times like this . . . I don't know him.

"Asher," said Mama, joining them, Deenie at her side. "We don't have to stay here. We can go back to the inn. We can pack, and go home."

Da shook his head. "I can't, Dath." He took one step after the Doranen mages and Pintte. "Dath, I—"

Mama's fingers caught hold of his green-and-bronze striped sleeve.

"No, Asher. It's too late. They'll not let you join them now. Not even if you begged. They'd *let* you beg, and then they'd laugh in your face."

The look in Da's eyes when he turned to Mama near broke Rafel's heart. "I should've found a way to stop 'em, Dath."

Mama captured Da's shoulders with both hands. *"Don't,"* she said fiercely. "What they're doing? It's their choice. The Innocent Mage warned them and they wouldn't listen. *No* blame falls on you."

As Da held on to Mama like a desperate man, Deenie whimpered and pressed a fist against her chest. Tears filled her eyes. She was such a watering pot. "I don't feel good. Da, make them change their minds."

Letting go of Mama, Da stared at the fishing boat. Its crew was all aboard, and its passengers were climbing in after. "Can't, mouse. Your ma's right. It be too late. Dath... take her back to the Dolphin."

Mama's face was all pinched. Sunlight gleamed and glittered the silver strands in her hair. "What about you? Asher—"

"Don't start on me, Dath. Just get Deenie away from here."

"Come, Deenie," said Mama, her voice still hard, but her face gone crumply. "You too, Rafe."

He opened his mouth to protest, even though he knew it wouldn't do him a mite of good. But Da spoke first.

"No," he said. "I want Rafe with me."

Stunned, Mama stared at him. "What? Asher, no. Rafe can't—"

"He's right, Dath. He ain't a sprat," said Da, so grim. "And when this goes bad I'll need him. I can't do it alone."

"You'll have to," said Mama, her eyes terrible. "He's not ready. He's not *trained.* He—"

"I weren't trained neither," said Da. His eyes were terrible too. "I got pushed in the deep end. Was you did the pushin', as I recall."

"Asher—"

"The magic's in him, Dath," Da said roughly. Deenie was shivering. Da *never* spoke rough to Mama. "It's in him just like it's in me. And I need it. He'll manage."

"Mama—" Rafel reached for her. "Don't fret. I can—"

But she knocked his arms aside. "You're just a boy, you don't know anything! Asher, he *can't*."

Da and Mama stared at each other. Something was going on; they were brangling without words now. He looked at Deenie, who shook her head. She didn't understand either.

"Dathne, I'll fix it," Da said, his voice soft again. Sorry. "He'll have what he needs. He'll be safe. I promise."

"And the Doranen?" Mama demanded. Her eyes were full of tears. She was nearly weeping.

Da sighed, then pulled a face. "Looks like I were wrong. Looks like we can't keep him secret forever."

And Mama gave up. Just like that. She gave up, so *heartbroken*... "Fine."

"Mouse," said Da. "You sit tight. Me and Rafe'll see you soon."

Deenie flung her arms around Da's neck, and Da held on to her like they were both drowning, then released her.

"Be careful, Rafe," Deenie whispered, and patted his chest. "Look after Da."

He tried to smile at his spratty, bratty, watering pot sister. "I will. Mama—"

"*You*," she said, glaring. The tears were spilled on her cheek now. "*Both* of you." Stepping close, reaching up, she pulled his head down and kissed his brow. Reached for Da, and kissed him hard on the lips. Then she took Deenie's hand and they walked away, past the Mayor of Westwailing and his cronies, with Deenie looking back over her shoulder.

Rafel lifted a hand. Waggled his fingers at her, just once, then frowned at his father. Something was niggling. *Dathne, I'll fix it.* "Da, what did you mean, you'll fix it? Fix what? Fix *me*?"

With its yellow sails flapping gaily and its broad, light blue hull cleaving the harbour's gentle waters, the fishing boat headed away from the pier. Da stared past it towards the ruined, malevolent reef.

"Figure of speech, that was. You'll need a helpin' hand to do this. Don't fret, Rafe. I'll see you right."

"I ain't fretting," he said. "I just—" He shook his head, baffled. "I don't understand, Da. You won't help Garrick and the others break the reef, and you won't let me help them break it, but you'll risk yourself—you'll risk *me*—to save them when it goes wrong. How does that work?"

"I d'know," said Da, shrugging. "It just does."

"*Da—*"

"Rafe, it just does." Da turned then, and gently shook his shoulder. "This were always goin' to end bloody, sprat. But doin' it *my* way, that means when it be all said and done, folks'll know you had nowt to do with the blood. They'll know all you did was try to save some lives. And that be the *only* thing that matters."

Something in Da's voice, in his eyes, made his heart thud. He nodded. "All right."

"Rafel..." Da cleared his throat. "Y'know I love you, eh? Y'know I'd bloody walk through fire for you?"

They'd had a fratched time of it lately, one way or another. Snapping and snarling and glowering, all at odds. Lectures on Charis. Brangles over magic. Seemed lately they couldn't find even two sweet words to swap.

"Aye," he said, when he could trust himself. "Course I do. Same as I would for you, Da. Any day. All day."

Overhead the gulls whirled and wailed, their harsh voices smothering the cheerful music gusting to them from shore. Small waves slapped at the pier. Crawling in his blood, the rotten magic in the reef.

"So. What now?"

"Now, sprat? We wait," said Da. He sounded angry—and resigned. "And we cross every one of our fingers, besides. 'Cause there's you, and there's me, and there ain't nobody else."

CHAPTER SIXTEEN

A rlin. For the love of Barl, *must* you disgrace me?"

Belly still churning even though he'd just emptied it, Arlin wiped his mouth on his fouled silk sleeve. "Sorry, sir," he muttered. "But I can't help it. I—"

"Hold your tongue," his father commanded. "And get control of yourself. You can start by letting go of that rail. The weather's fine yet you're acting as though we're sailing through a storm."

"Yes, sir," he said, and unclamped his fingers from the fishing boat's side. Made himself stand upright, even as the cramps in his gut demanded he bend himself double and upend his stomach's lining onto the slimy, fish-scaled deck.

Casting him a last look of disgust his father walked away, rejoining Sarle Baden, Ennet Vail and Ain—Lady Freidin—in the fishing boat's blunt bow. Barl's tits, the smack stank of rotten guts. Why wouldn't he be puking with that stench fouling his nostrils and throat with every breath? And the weather might be stormless but the waves beneath the boat's hull were rhythmic and relentless, rolling...rolling...

With an anguished moan he threw himself over the railing again, as his retching body tried to turn inside out and his eyeballs strained so hard he thought they'd burst.

"Not to worry," said a nearby fisherman, coiling a tarred rope. "Ain't every man as takes to the water, young lord."

Arlin eased off the rail and glowered at him. "Who asked you? Sail the boat, clod, and mind your own business."

The Olken blinked, his face smoothing blank. "Aye. Right you are, then. Sorry to interrupt. Sir."

Ignorant fool. The trouble with Olken was they had no respect. Not any more. Not since they started considering themselves *equals*. His father was right about one thing, at least: Durm's stupidity had done more than see the Wall destroyed. It had destroyed a way of life. Destroyed centuries of obedience, of acceptance that the Doranen were naturally superior and always would be — pathetic pretensions to Olken magic notwithstanding.

Lur's ruined now. Let the Olken have it. Somewhere beyond these shores there's a land fit for the Doranen. Not our ancestral homeland. Father's wrong about that, old Dorana is surely long lost to us. But there is somewhere. And once that cursed reef's broken we'll quit this Olken-ridden wasteland and find it.

The cramps in his belly had finally eased. Turning his face into the salt-soaked breeze he sucked in a deep breath and waited, but his belly stayed quiet. Perhaps the worst was finally over. Profoundly hoping so, he made his unsteady way forward to his father, who stood in serious, low-voiced conversation with his companions, all three mages close friends and allies in the notion that Lur had nothing to offer the Doranen any more. The Olken mayor stood with them, deluded into thinking he was relevant to the morning's events. He wasn't. For all the good his magic would do, he might just as well as spit on Dragonteeth Reef.

But he's useful, so we tolerate him. His ignorant antipathy towards the Doranen plays neatly into Father's plans.

Father favoured him with a cold smile as he reached the bow. "Good. We're nearly there, Arlin. Are you clear on how this working is to proceed?"

"Yes, sir," he said, nodding. "My lords, my lady," he added to the others. "Meister Mayor. My apologies. Something tainted in what I was served for breakfast, I fear."

Indifferent murmurs from Baden and Vail, who rarely had any time for him. An affronted stare from Pintte. And Lady Freidin — Ain — nodded, unsmiling. She never smiled at him. For eight years she'd been his secret tutor, taught him everything she knew, helped him discover the length and breadth of his talents — and how better to hide them — and never once had she smiled. He was over his childish infatuation with her, of course. But still. One smile. Was it too much to ask?

Shading his eyes, Arlin looked across the stretch of water in front of them to the foam and froth of ocean breaking over the reef. Hardly distant at all now. The wind had picked up, and the fishing boat was making good time. Beyond the reef the waterspouts danced, capricious and deadly, and whirlpools yawned with deep, wide mouths. Their churning roar sounded a low, predatory warning.

He felt his guts clench again, and ruthlessly banished the fear. *I am ready for this. I am a great mage.* And he was eager, so eager, to prove that were true. He'd waited in the shadows long enough.

Fernel Pintte cleared his throat. "As you know, sirs, madam, we Olken have a particular affinity for all things natural," he announced. "Since my arrival in Westwailing I have been focusing my thoughts and feelings upon Dragonteeth Reef. I am comfortably certain that we have chosen its most vulnerable section. And as you battle the poisons Barl and Morg left behind I shall lend you my strength in prayer, so we can achieve victory."

In private Father called Dorana's mayor a shrill pipsqueak — but now he smiled, at his most frostily genial, and offered Pintte a polite half-bow. "Your help will be most welcome, Meister Mayor. The task before us is daunting."

Pintte's eyes narrowed. "But achievable, yes?"

"Oh yes," said Father, the merest hint of an edge to his voice. To be questioned over magic by an *Olken?* That was an insult keen as any sharp blade. "I assure you, Meister Mayor, our goal is quite achievable. We do not seek to destroy *all* the magic still sunk in the reef. Just this small stretch of it."

"Precisely," said Pintte. "That's all you're asked to do."

Father's lips curved again, but his eyes were chips of blue ice. "I suggest you find somewhere unobtrusive to sit now, sir, so you can lend us your prayers undisturbed. We must prepare for the working."

From the look on his face Pintte cared not at all for being dismissed, but he was truly a fool if he thought he belonged here with real mages. He withdrew, and Father beckoned everyone closer.

"Make no mistake," he said, his sweeping gaze cold with purpose, "this working will test us as we have never before been tested. Barl and Morg between them have set a challenge that doubtless would've daunted King Borne himself, or Durm. But we are equal to the task. The future of every Doranen trapped in this misbegotten backwater depends upon us, therefore we *must* be equal to it. Follow my lead. Tread where I tread. Do not let yourselves run ahead of me. Especially *you,* Arlin."

He dropped his betraying gaze to the tilting deck. Father was always doing that. Had done it ever since he could remember: diminished him in public even as he boasted of his son's prowess in private, to those he trusted. He knew why, of course. It was to preserve their secret.

But it still hurt.

"Yes, sir."

"It is vital that we maintain our focus, no matter what unfolds around us," his father continued. "Unless we press against the reef's weak spot with our conjoined wills, undiluted, we will not break through the barrier that keeps us from the world. It will take every last drop of our sweat and power to collapse the whirlpools and the waterspouts along this stretch of reef. But once we have done so—" Father's face lit with a rare, genuine smile. "Then it will be a simple matter of destroying the reef itself, giving us access to open water. And then—*then*—"

Behind them, one of the Olken sailors shouted. "Reef ho! Reef ho, Captain!"

They all pushed to the bow's railing, and saw that the sailor had not mistaken the case. Directly ahead of them lay Dragonteeth Reef, foamed with breaking water, spray spitting high into the air. Beyond it, magic-spawned waterspouts and whirlpools. Even as they stared two more towering spouts spumed into life, whipping up from the ocean's restless surface. As those two were born three others further out died, collapsing with great wet slaps across the reef and into the surging salt water. Droning ceaseless beneath them, the ravenous whirlpools.

"Lord Garrick! A word!"

Father turned. "Yes, Hayle?"

The fishing boat's captain was a young man, short and muscled and crusted with salt. Something indefinable about him was reminiscent of Rafel's father. An air, an attitude, an indifference that grated the nerves. Olken arrogance: it was a hard thing to stomach.

"Can you do what you do from here?" the captain demanded, standing before them with his fists on his hips and his booted feet spread wide. "Only this be the end of mild water we've reached. Here on in, the whirlpools and the spouts be set to rile things up. And I ain't lookin' to have my boat driven onto the Teeth and smashed to matchsticks."

Father looked back to the reef, frowning. Was it too far away for the working? Doranen magic was strong. But was it strong enough to reach from here?

"If this is the best you can do," said Father, grudging, "then so be it. We will just have to compensate for your inadequacy, won't we?"

The Olken captain's eyes squinted in a frown. "How long d'you think to take on this?"

"How long?" Father spread his hands. "As long as we require. Hayle, we seek to free Lur from the last bondage of Morg's evil. Do you mean to suggest you've somewhere more important to be?"

"We'll heave to, then," said the Olken, his face stained dark red. "And sit tight."

Father turned his back on the fool, dismissing him. Then he raised a beckoning hand. "Arlin."

As the boat's captain retreated, barking orders to the crew, he stepped close. "Father?"

"Time to prepare ourselves," he said quietly. "We're close enough. Open yourself and tell me what you feel."

Aside from seasick, you mean? But if he gave the thought a voice Father would banish him to twiddle his thumbs with Pintte. *You need me now. I'll not jeopardise that.* So he closed his eyes, ignoring the shouts and running feet of the fishermen as they obeyed their captain's orders, pushed away the lingering nausea in his emptied belly and focused on the reef. Loosened his rigorously guarded senses and reached out to taste its magic.

"Faugh!" he exclaimed, revolted, and stared at his father in shock. "That—but it's *foul*. I—I can't taste *any* of Barl's sweetness. Does aught of her workings survive?"

His father nodded. "It does." Even his intimidating composure seemed shaken. Around them, their fellow mages looked equally dismayed. "But only barely. Morg's magic has had twenty years to infect this place. Like a pestilence it has multiplied. It should've been mage-worked at the first."

"I thought Asher tried."

"He did," said his father. "He tried, and he failed. And then after Holze failed soon after, and Asher told the day's Council that it *couldn't* be done, they believed him without question." Father's face twisted. "Because he was the Innocent Mage. Because he killed Morg. Because—because—" Rage was choking his voice. "Because twenty years ago we let guilt addle our reason and turn us into *milkmaids*."

"You didn't speak out?" he said, unthinking.

The look Father gave him was so cruel and so cold he thought the blood would freeze in his veins. He stumbled backwards, bumping into Sarle Baden.

"My apologies, sir," he muttered. "Forgive me." And wasn't sure if it was Sarle he addressed, or his father.

Sarle said something excusing and stepped around him to stand at Father's left hand. Ain moved to his right hand, and Ennet Vail stood beside Sarle. Then Father turned his back, and the others turned with him. The message perfectly clear, he looked at the deck again, just for a moment, then sighed out his feelings until he was empty. Almost empty. As empty as he could make himself, with so many feelings swallowed.

"Follow me," said Father, his voice low and slow. "This working's purpose is to unbuild what was built. To destroy what was created. To purify what was poisoned. We begin with Ramin's Threefold-charm of Dissolution. *Shin'tak tak'shin. Dodek'ma ma'dodek. Shin'dodek ta'ma. Adek. Adek. Adek…*"

Reciting the spell, sketching its sigils on the salty air, Arlin forgot he was seasick… forgot his frustration, and Ain… forgot the useless Olken mayor behind him and the fishing boat's crew and Asher, cowering on the harbour's pier. Forgot Rafel, cowering with him. All that mattered was Dragonteeth Reef. All that mattered was not disappointing his father.

Opened fully to the reef's foulness, he felt bile crawl up his throat. Felt his bruised belly quiver. Heard the small sounds of disgust from his father's powerful friends as they too let down their defences and embraced in full the bitter magics sunk into the reef.

There was no sound from Father, of course, save the soft, spitting urgency of Ramin's dissolution spell.

And if he can stomach it then Barl's bloody tits… so can I.

Westwailing's mayor and most of its officials had returned to the crowded foreshore. Two men were left behind, wearing stout wooden truncheons and watchful expressions. Ordered by Fernel bloody Pintte, Da reckoned, to keep a close eye on 'em. Nosy bastards.

Stranded at the far end of the long stone pier with his father, staring across the wide expanse of harbour stretching between them and the reef, Rafel twitched as he felt the first roil of clean Doranen magic stir his blood.

Da, stamping from one side of the pier to the other, stopped still and lifted his head. "Here we go."

The dot of blue and yellow fishing smack shifted on the distant, uneasy water. Doranen magic roiled again, clashing with the reef's foulness. Rafel felt bile scald his throat, his mouth. He heard his father grunt. Saw him shift a half-step, bracing himself.

"*Sink* it."

"What, Da?" he said, alarmed. "What—"

"This ain't no bloody use," said Da, glaring towards the reef. "We ain't nowhere near close enough. This far away we be tits on a bull."

He'd wondered about that, but when his father didn't mention it . . . and he was wary of seeming pushy. He glanced at the watchdog officials. "Maybe, Da, but this is as close as we're going to get. Those two won't let us set foot off—"

"Ha," said Da. "Like they got a say in it." Turning, he raked his fierce gaze along the nearby line of moored smacks and skiffs and harbour runabouts. "Don't need nowt fancy. Just somethin' as won't sink when things get a mite frisky . . ."

Stunned, he glanced again at the officials. Suspicious now, their hands were resting on those truncheons. "Da—wait—you want us to steal a boat?"

"Borrow."

Steal—borrow—he doubted the mayor's watchdogs would notice the difference. "Da—"

Da scowled at him. "Rafe, we ain't got a choice."

Another surge of soiled magic washed through him, and through Da. Stronger this time, with a hint of bared teeth. He saw his own sickness reflected in his father's abruptly pale face.

"You're right," he said, blotting cold sweat from his forehead. "But what about—"

"I'll take care of 'em," said Da. "Rafe—"

And right then, between heartbeats, he saw Da change his mind. Saw sudden fear swamp the sickness. Saw his grim resolve fail.

He stepped closer. "Forget it, Da. I'm coming."

"No," said Da, shaking his head. "Your ma's right. I can't risk you, sprat. You ain't ready. Not for this."

"Are *you* ready?" he said, stepping closer again. "Is *anyone?* Da—"

"No," said Da. "I ain't goin' to push you in the deep end, Rafe."

"You're not pushing, I'm jumping!" he retorted. "With my eyes wide open. Like you said, Da, I ain't a sprat any more. This is *my* choice and you *need* me, so — so stop flapping your lips, why don't you? We got to get out to that reef before it's too late."

Da stared at him, furiously dumbstruck. Silver in his hair now, just like Mama. Silver in the unshaven stubble on his cheeks and chin. Lines grooved round his mouth, spiderwebbing his eyes. Older, and thinner, and more tired than he'd let on.

Then he shook his head. "Sink me sideways, Rafe, you got a bloody mouth on you. Where'd you get that mouth, eh?"

Rafel grinned, though his heart was hammering him dizzy. "I d'know, Da. Let me think on that a ticktock."

"Very funny," Da growled. "But you ain't too big for a wallop."

"Wallop me after," he suggested. "Right now we've got to go."

As though pleading his case, the harbour waters slapped against the stone pier, harder and higher. The tethered fishing fleet, agitated, tugged at its moorings. And the salty sea breeze shivered, stinking of Morg.

Da took him by the shoulder, his grip almost desperate. "Y'know this ain't a game, Rafe? Y'know we could *die?*"

It was on the tip of his tongue to say something clever, something full of bravado. And if this was Goose he was staring at, he would have. But it was Da.

He nodded. "I know. And I'll try not to. I'll try my best to see you don't, either. But Da — we're who we are — *what* we are — for a reason. And if we waste that, well, I reckon we won't like ourselves much."

Silence, as Da stared at him. And then he sighed, his eyes full of shadows. "Reckon you're right, sprat." Letting go, he pointed at a cluster of boats moored close to the pier. "That skiff there. That'll do us. Get it unhitched while I take care of them two gawpin' fools."

The fools shouted a warning, truncheons drawn, as he climbed down slippery stone steps and jumped onto the small, weatherbeaten skiff Da had chosen. Its dark green paint was faded and blistered, its single, undyed canvas sail copiously patched. As he unhitched its oiled mooring rope he watched Da freeze the two running watchdogs with a word.

"Don't just stand there, sprat," said Da, coming down the stone stairs. "Get them oars out."

"What about Pintte's watchdogs?" he said as he fitted the skiff's oars into their locks.

Da clambered into the small boat. "I'll let 'em go in a ticktock. Now come on, put your back into it. Row us away from the pier."

Only mildly resentful, he plonked himself on the splintery wooden rower's seat, reached for the oars and started pulling. Da stood by the mast and stared towards the distant, poisoned reef.

"Bit further, Rafe. Bit further. Come on. Where's your elbow grease?"

So he rowed a bit further, easing them away from the moored fleet and into open water, feeling the Doranen magic seethe and his muscles stretch, creaking. The pier and the statue-still watchdogs fell behind them. Fell further. Sweat stung his eyes. Turning, Da gave a sharp nod and pointed.

"Vardo."

"That's a good trick, Da," he said, as the watchdogs leapt and shouted. "When this is over you can show it me."

"We'll see," said Da, scowling. "All right, Rafe. Stop rowing."

Together they shipped the oars, then he turned himself round on the uncomfortable bench. They were still a long way from the blue and yellow fishing smack, and the reef.

"What now?"

Da looked down at him. "Now you hang on."

"What d'you mean hang — *shit!*"

A wave had risen beneath the shallow-drafted boat, smooth and powerful, lifting them and surging them towards the arrogant Doranen mages who thought they were strong enough to break Morg's hold on the reef.

Clutching the bench with both hands, Rafel stared drop-jawed at his father. "Come on, Da. You *got* to show me how to do that!"

"Do I?" said Da, eyebrows lifting. "After what you used to get up to in your bath?"

Jaw-dropped again, he swallowed. "You knew about that?"

"Course I bloody did," said Da, as the huge wave he'd summoned carried them swiftly across the wide harbour. "Piss poor mage I'd be if I couldn't feel that goin' on under my own roof."

"You—you never said anything."

"Every sprat needs his secrets," said Da, shrugging. "'Sides, you weren't hurtin' anyone. You were just lettin' off steam."

Tangled with difficult feelings, he stared at the fishing smack, much closer now. Stared at the whipping waterspouts on the other side of the reef, spawned by wicked, capricious magics. Thought he could hear the throaty roar of the whirlpools. Tried not to think of being sucked down to his death.

"Da—"

Da grunted, all his focus on keeping them aimed fast for the smack.

"Da, that wasn't all I did," he said, quickly, before he could change his mind. Before he could die with sins unconfessed between them. "For years I pinched spells from Arlin, and I did them. All kinds of spells. And I never got one wrong."

The skiff crashed down on the harbour's rolling surface. Tumbled off the splintered rower's bench, Rafel stared into his father's shocked face.

"I'm sorry. I was mad. You wouldn't let me—you wouldn't *teach* me—and—" Cautiously, he sat up. "I'm sorry."

Da dragged a hand over his spray-soaked hair. "Rafel—"

"There's more," he said, bracing his back against the skiff's side. "It's worse."

Groping for the mast, Da cleared his throat. "Tell me."

His courage almost failed him, then. *I shouldn't have said anything. He's going to hate me.* But it was too late now. "That trunk, in your library," he said hoarsely. "I—I picked the lock."

"You picked the *lock?*" said Da, boggled. *"When?"*

"The day I felt the earth go funny. At the riverpond. Remember?"

"Then?" Da looked like he wanted to sit down, hard. "Rafel, you were a *sprat*. You were *ten*. How did you unpick that sinkin' lock?"

"I don't know. I just did. It—it wasn't hard."

Da ran a hand down his face. "Sink me." And then he sucked in a sharp breath. "Rafe, you didn't pinch any of the spells in—"

"No," he said quickly. "No. I swear."

"Good," said Da, sagging.

"I'm sorry," he said again. "But—at least you know for sure I can do it. Doranen magic. And with the reef—I won't get in the way."

Da gave him the strangest look. Not angry. Almost—almost *guilty*. It didn't make sense. And then he turned to stare at the blue and yellow smack. "We'll talk on it later, Rafe. On your feet, now, and see how you go with a bathtub the size of a harbour, eh? Quickly, sprat. We ain't got long."

That was true. Whatever Rodyn Garrick and his mages were doing, it had stirred the poisoned reef to snarling. Pain bloomed behind his eyes. Unsteady, uncertain, he clambered to his feet, reached for his magic—then hesitated.

"Trust y'self," Da said quietly. "Like I trust you."

It was all he needed to hear.

Breathing out, like a prayer, he gathered the harbour's wild water, none of it safely tamed in a tub. And then, for the first time, no hiding, no whispering, opened himself to the power within.

The borrowed skiff sat on its stern and *ran*.

"Good, Rafe, good," said Da, as the wave hurled them onwards, malleable to his mind. Faster and faster, Westwailing vanishing behind them, the reef and the fishing smack looming ever closer.

Their business was serious, dreadful—and he wanted to laugh.

"Easy, sprat," said Da after a few minutes. "Don't want to run ourselves onto the Dragon's teeth. Let's take a breather, eh? I want to get a feel for what them bloody fools are doin'."

Regretfully he took his father's advice, letting the wave he'd conjured dwindle almost to death. The skiff settled onto the harbour and drifted to a lilting standstill, perhaps a quarter league distant from the blue and yellow fishing boat. Not so close they'd be swiftly noticed, but close enough to see its crew dotted around the deck, working hard, and the yellow heads of the Doranen mages gathered in the bow.

271

Not far beyond the smack stretched the ragged reef, with its cloud of sickening magics. On the other side of the reef six enormous waterspouts whipped their erratic way across the water's restless surface. And droning beneath their higher-pitched howl, the whirlpools. Shading his eyes, Rafel thought he could see one, groaning and grinding a hole in the ocean.

"Drat 'em," said Da tightly. "That be a bloody daft thing to do, Garrick. And here's me thinkin' you were a sight smarter than that."

Tasting the air like his father, he let out a sharp sigh. Daft was right. Poxy Arlin's father had the mages attacking the reef's magics with a Doranen spell of coercion, designed to force things apart. Which was fine if they were looking to lift buried stones out of the earth or pull down an old brick wall, but they weren't. Worse, he could still taste what was left of the first spell they'd tried, and now the leftover echoes of that compulsion spell were muddling with the coercion chant and—

"You feel that, Rafe?" said Da, one hand going to his head. "The reef's pushin' back."

"Aye," he gasped, his skin prickling with the loathsome touch of it. The pain was in him, too, spiking through his temples and deep into his chest. His belly heaved, and he spat saliva and bile mixed yellowish at his feet. "Barl's mercy, is that Morg?"

Da was bent over, hands braced on his knees. "What be left of him. Rafe, don't you give in to it. Don't let his muck in you. Could be I might need you in a ticktock or three."

"Why?" he said, and spat sickness again. "What are you going to—"

But Da wasn't listening. Dropped to his knees, one hand braced on the skiff's side, he was pouring his power towards the reef, trying to shore up what little remained of Barl's sweetness. Pouring so *much* power, Rafel could hardly believe it. What was in his father made his own powers look paltry. All this was in Da? He'd never given a hint of it. In twenty years, not once.

How could he have this and not want it? He's mad.

But even though Da was amazing, what he gave of himself wasn't enough. Morg's foul malevolence was too vile. Too strong. Not even Da's power and the power of the Doranen mages in the fishing boat combined could smother the reef's seething darkness. Letting blind instinct guide him he tried lending his own power, but compared to Da and the Doranen it was only a trickle. It was like pissing on flames let loose in a summer wheat field.

His father was breathing so hard now it sounded almost like groaning. With his belly still heaving and his mouth slicked sour, Rafel crabbed his way to the skiff's bow.

"Da! *Da!*"

Blood was trickling from beneath his father's closed eyelids, and out of his nostrils over his pressed-white lips. His fingers were bloodless on the side of the small boat, and every muscle in his rigid body shuddered.

Hunkering down, he threw one arm around his father's shaking shoulders. "Da, it's no good. We can't do it. Stop, before you *kill* yourself."

"No, Rafe…" Teeth chattering, Da cracked open one pain-filled eye. "We can. But you got to help me."

"How?" he said, hearing his voice break. "Tell me what to do and I'll do it."

Da's fingers anchored themselves in his shirt, and twisted. Tugged him close. "Rafe—" His voice was a choked whisper. "D'you trust me?"

What? "Aye, Da! You know I do!"

Da nodded, coughing, a harsh, hacking sound. His twisted fingers tugged again. "Rafe, I'm sorry. You weren't s'posed to find out. Not like this."

He stared. "Find out what? *Da,* find out wh—"

And then he gasped as his father's spread-fingered hand pressed hard to his face. A flash of heat, burning. A convulsion in his blood. A burst of power, incandescent, like a sunrise in his mind. He tried to pull away, tried to protest, but he couldn't move. Couldn't speak. Now his blood was on fire, flames pumping through him with every beat of his heart. His bones caught fire—and still he couldn't scream.

Shouting, Da snatched his hand away. Rafel felt himself fall backwards, felt his shoulders smack the skiff's wet boards. Dazed, he stared at the blue sky, at the clouds scudding across it, set to blot out the sun.

And then he realised: *I'm different.*

Closing his eyes to the blue sky and the clouding sun, he turned his sight inwards—and discovered a cauldron of power he'd never dreamed might exist. It was terrifying. Glorious. Hot and bright and hungry...and his.

First came astonished pleasure. Then came the rage.

"Rafel!" said Da, on his feet again and hauling him upright, his stubbled face ghastly behind its mask of smeared and trickled blood. "Hate me later. Hate me all you like, 'til I die an ole man—but first we got to help Garrick and them other fools afore it's too late!"

He felt so betrayed, so wounded, he wanted to vomit, or weep. Wrenching himself free, he snatched at the skiff's mast for balance and unleashed his woken senses on the world. Felt in a searing rush the unmuffled malevolence of Morg's blight, saw its claws sunk deep in the heart of the reef, saw with his newly opened eyes how it strangled the tattered shreds of Barl's miracle. Fed off them. Distorted them. Like a parasite consumed them.

Staggering, his mind reeling, he managed to keep his feet as the skiff rocked and juddered beneath them. The harbour's waters were waking. Something terrible stirred. A dreadful wave of nausea rose and rolled through him.

"Shit! What—what—"

"Be you with me, Rafe?" Da demanded, breathing hard and heavy. "I need you with me, sprat. 'Cause any ticktock now—any ticktock—"

It seemed to him then that the whole world inhaled, and time stood still, and he was crushed to a pulp. He felt the reef's magic, Morg's magic, writhe and shudder in his twisting guts. He felt his blood catch fresh fire, freeze solid then burst burning from his eyes and nose. He heard himself shout. Heard Da shout. Felt the world exhale and magic rip through the water between the reef and the skiff. Their borrowed boat flew into the air, tossing them with it, then smashed again to the harbour's wildly agitated surface.

His head smacked salty timber, knees and elbows striking hard too. Tossed beside him, his father grunted in pain. Battered and bruised, he scrambled upright and looked around. Da had the same idea. Clutching the skiff's sides as it rocked and spun, they stared at the blue and yellow fishing boat flailing too far away. Her crew darted from stern to bow and back again, answering their captain's faint shouts. Terrified in the cloud-striped sunshine, blond Doranen heads huddled close.

A heartbeat later he cried out, because a whirlpool was forming right before his stinging eyes, in the stretch of whipped-up water between the fishing smack and the reef. In *Westwailing Harbour,* where they'd always been safe. The surge was small but steadily growing, the harbour's waters spinning . . . and spinning . . . and as he watched, dry-mouthed with horror, he saw the blue and yellow fishing boat begin drifting towards it.

"Rafel!" said Da, and reached for his arm. His fingers, taking hold, felt desperate. "We got to stop that bloody thing. We can't have whirl-pools in the harbour. It'll be the end of everything, sprat."

"Stop it?" he said, the heel of his right hand pressed to the side of his head against the spike of pain stabbing through his skull. "How?"

"I don't know," said Da, teeth gritted. "But we got to *try.*"

Head pounding, he stared at his father, who'd lied to him. Betrayed him. "Da, there ain't no way we can—"

Da's fingers closed so hard on his wrist it felt like the bone might break. "You wanted to know what it were like, facin' Morg? You wanted to know how I felt that day? *This* be how I felt, Rafel. *This* be what it were like. You piss your pants. You shit y'self. *This* is why I told 'em to leave well enough alone."

With a shrieking scream a waterspout whipped into life a long stone's throw from the bow of their skiff. Another shrieking scream and there were two waterspouts—then three—then four. The skiff rocked and spun like a paper boat on a millrace as the spraying spume swiftly soaked them to the skin.

Too far away, too close, the whirlpool whirled wider.

Rafel dragged his sopping sleeve across his face. *We're going to die. Sink me, we'll bloody drown or get sucked down that thing or ripped to bitty pieces by a waterspout.* He turned to his father, not knowing what he'd find. Saw anger. Saw revulsion. Saw pity. Saw fear.

And then saw the face of the Innocent Mage.

CHAPTER SEVENTEEN

✠

Power blasted from Da's outstretched fingers in a stream of burning
light. Touched the nearest waterspout, which collapsed in a gouting
wave. Touched the next, the next, the last. As their skiff stopped its wild
lurching, Da fell across the rower's seat.

"*Da!*" Rafel shouted, reaching for him.

"I be fine, sprat," Da grunted, shoving to his feet. Fresh blood slicked
his face, muddling with the salt water. He looked like someone had tried
to skin him alive. A good thing Mama weren't here to see it. She really
would skin him. She might skin him yet.

If I don't do it first.

His newly woken powers seethed.

"Rafe," said Da, his voice rough and rasping. "You know when
Doranen mages do a working, sometimes not all of 'em say the spells.
Sometimes they just let 'emselves be used. You know that?"

He nodded, distracted. The whirlpool was maybe twenty feet across
now, roaring louder. Though the smack's crew was fighting hard, they
couldn't keep their boat from drifting towards its widening mouth.
They'd never survive the encounter. They'd be smashed to splinters.

"*Rafe,*" said Da. "Listen!"

He glanced sideways. "What?"

"Sprat, I need to use you. It'll take more power than what's in me to fuddle that bloody whirlpool."

"We can do it together," he said. "Teach me the—"

"There ain't time." Blood-slicked face twisting, Da cupped the back of his neck. "And there ain't time for me to do this gentle, neither. Rafe, it's goin' to hurt. Are you with me?"

He looked again to the fishing boat. The waterspouts had tossed the skiff a good bit closer—to the smack, the reef and the growing whirlpool. As the smack's crew fought their desperate battle, Fernel bloody Pintte dangled over the side, wildly gesturing. Rodyn Garrick, sopping, his long blond hair plastered wet to his skull, stood with poxy Arlin, tall and thin and wet through, his yellow hair short like most young Doranen wore it these days. Along with the other mages they were throwing spells at that howling hole in the ocean. For all the good they were doing they might as well be throwing flowers. Or turds.

Da's cupping fingers tightened. "*Rafe*. Are you with me?"

"Don't ask stupid questions, Da," he said, slicked with cold sweat. "Just do it while we still can."

"Right," said Da, nodding. "Might be best you sit all the way down."

So he bumped his arse to the skiff's rough floorboards, and let his hands fall loose into his lap. Kept on staring at the helpless, drifting smack. At Arlin, who was going to spit blood when he found out who helped save him.

Ha.

Da's left hand came to rest gently on his head. "Here we go. Don't fight it. You'll feed bad but you won't die."

At first he felt nothing but an oddly warm sensation, as his father pointed towards the viciously expanding whirlpool, whispering under his breath. Then Da traced a sigil on the wet-salt air, which caught fire and burned with a strong, wild scent.

Power surged. Magic stirred. Rafel took a deep breath. Da whispered again, and drew another sigil, and now he felt a kind of collapsing, as though he were a blown-up pig's bladder with a pinprick in it, slowly losing air. Another deep breath. Another fiery sigil. Then he felt a stabbing pain behind his eyes—and suddenly he was bleeding magic. And it hurt...Barl's tits, it *hurt*...

Dimly he was aware of Da raging against the whirlpool. Dimly he could hear someone moaning and realised: *That's me*. The trickle of power leaving him widened...widened further...and suddenly Da was pulling magic from him in a white-hot flood. He choked a scream in his throat.

Da was cursing the whirlpool now, cursing Morg and even Barl. Rafel cursed with him, shuddering with the pain. Then Da dropped to the floor of the skiff, retching for air, and the terrible outpouring of his magic stopped.

"It ain't workin'," Da gasped. "All them whirlpools feed on each other, and they feed off that bloody reef too. I ain't strong enough to break 'em."

So—was that it? Had they failed?

"Come on, sprat," said Da, coughing. "On your feet. We still got work to do."

He couldn't stand. His bones were hollow, his muscles pulped. He could taste iron-salt blood, thick and wet on his lips. But Da hauled him up and somehow he managed not to fall. Managed to open his bleary, burning eyes.

Oh, shit.

The doomed fishing boat tossed on the edges of the whirlpool's growing wake. The swirling defiant water was nigh on forty feet across now, thundering its hunger, growling to be fed.

"Work?" he croaked, cold with terror, as beneath their unsteady feet the skiff began to drift. "What work? Da, what can we do?"

"We can save them bloody idiots on that fishing boat, I reckon," said Da. "Afore they manage to get 'emselves drowned."

At her wits' end trying to comfort Deenie, Dathne jumped near out of her skin when someone banged a fist on the inn's chamber door.

"Meistress Dathne! Best you come quick!"

That was Silas, who'd taken over the Dancing Dolphin from his father, Hiram, dead these three years past. She glared at the closed door then bent again over her daughter, curled whimpering on the bed and shaking so hard the bed-frame's timber creaked.

"Meistress Dathne!" Silas called again. "Be you in there?"

She pressed a kiss to Deenie's brow then hurried to the door. Cracked it open a finger's-width and tried to smooth away her frown. "Silas? What's amiss? Only Deenie's not feeling spry and—"

Silas was large and red of face, just like his father. "Trouble down the harbour, Meistress Dathne," he said, his pouched eyes wide. "Seems your Asher's neck-deep in it. And Rafel. The mayor sent someone to fetch you."

Dathne swallowed a curse. Of course her men folk were neck deep in trouble. Where else would they be?

Who jumped first, I wonder? Or did they jump together, hand in hand?

She glanced at Deenie, who shivered and shook on the soft feather bed. "I can't leave, Silas. My daughter's—"

"Go, Mama," said Deenie, her voice reed thin and trembling. "They might need you. I can't help them. I'm useless."

She waved her hand in a "just a moment" gesture at Silas, shoved the door shut and returned to the bed. "Don't talk like that," she scolded, smoothing Deenie's sweat-damp hair. "You're *not* useless. If you're anything, you're too sensitive. Deenie, I—"

Pansy eyes huge in her pale face, Deenie summoned an unsteady smile. "I'm not dying, Mama. I'm just—just a mouse. Go."

A wave of angry misery surged through her. All she'd ever wanted was for prophecy to be over. She'd wanted peace and happiness for her family. Her children. Why couldn't they have happiness? Why wouldn't strife leave them alone?

Is this my fault? Has my past destroyed their hopes for the future?

"Mama..."

Fighting weak tears, she looked down. "What, mouse?"

"Please. *Go.*"

"I'll not be long," she promised, chafing her daughter's cold hand. "If you need me call me for Silas and he'll find where I am."

The *someone* Westwailing's mayor had sent to fetch her was a plump, anxious young Olken man who dithered in the Dolphin's public lounge and nearly ran towards her as she came down the crooked stairs.

"Meistress Dathne! Praise Barl!"

Curse Barl more like it. "Who are you?" she snapped, heading for the front door.

The mayor's young someone leapt after her. "Trotter. Phlim Trotter."

"And what's happened, Meister Trotter?"

"Looks like magic gone mad, Mayor Threeve says," he said nervously, his voice low, as they left the inn and struck out towards the harbour. "And Asher—"

She flicked a glance at him, walking as fast as she could along Baitman Alley without actually running. "I know. Silas said."

"But that's good," Phlim Trotter added, breathless. "If there's a man who can save us it's the Innocent Mage."

His simple faith should have warmed her. Instead she was wintercold inside. Asher... Asher...

Indifferent to Phlim Trotter's panting discomfort, Dathne swung hard left into the skinniest of laneways separating one alehouse from its neighbour, swished her way between a wall and a row of rubbish bins and shot out the other end of it into Seaswell High Street. The thoroughfare was buzzing, Westwailing's homegrown and its visitors milling and agitating, staring down the township's gentle slope towards the harbour. Ignoring Trotter's ineffectual bleating, she leapt to the top step of a handily placed baker's shop, shaded her eyes and fixed her anxious gaze on the distant water.

Oh, Jervale preserve us all.

Waterspouts were whipping across the wide harbour where the mageworkers' distance-shrunk fishing boat plunged like a mad horse, close enough to the reef's jagged teeth for the folk gathered in the street to be crying aloud their fear and consternation. Smaller still, a mere black dot, another boat. A skiff. It plunged just as madly through the harbour's wild, thrashing water.

Dathne felt her heart seize.

I'm going to kill them.

Provided, of course, that the waterspouts or something worse didn't kill her husband and son first. But perhaps they'd be all right...if Asher undid the binding on Rafel's power.

Oh, Rafel. Will you forgive us?

Pushing that fear aside, she glanced down at Phlim Trotter, fraught on the pavement at the foot of the bakery steps. "Young man, can you run?"

"Run?" he echoed, his flushed face dripping sweat from mere walking. "Ah—"

"Never mind," she said, and picked up her skirts. "And don't worry, Meister Trotter. I'll tell the mayor you did your best."

Abandoning him, she ran.

When the third screaming Olken fisherman was flung overboard to drown in the whirlpool-churned harbour, Arlin gave up any hope of surviving.

Staggering on the smack's pitching deck, furious with fear, his father was bellowing at the boat's captain. "You're the sailor, Hayle! Sail us away from here! Get us back to the pier!"

"I be tryin'!" Hayle shouted back, blood from a split eyebrow slicking his face ghastly red. He'd lashed a length of rope to the boat's mast and wrapped its end around his wrist, an anchor to help him stay upright as the boat lurched and tossed and plunged. "Why don't you help? Why ain't there a Doranen spell to save all our hides?"

There was, of course. There were several incants designed to move a boat at will across water. Ain and the other two mages were desperately reciting them now—but they weren't working. Morg's leftover magic of ruination was too strong for them. The sigils sputtered to sparks and memory almost as soon as they flared into life.

"See to your own tasks, Hayle!" Father snarled. "Leave the matter of magic to your betters!"

"Sir," said the captain, and returned to his men.

Arlin touched his father's arm. "You have to let me do something. Why did you bring me if you won't—"

"Not yet," said Father. "I won't have you revealed yet."

"But *sir*—"

His father slapped him. "*Do as you're told!* Have I nurtured you for twenty years to have you throw my efforts away now?"

Face stinging, Arlin shook his head. "No, sir."

"Then stand here out of the way," his father snapped. "The rest of us are equal to this task."

He watched his father rejoin Ain and the others. *I hope so, for all our sakes.* Then he grabbed hold of the boat's railing and stared with horrified fascination at the roaring whirlpool that had them trapped.

The dreadful thing was easily sixty feet across, large enough to swallow the fishing boat whole. And if by some miracle of magework they *weren't* swallowed whole then the chances were good that their vessel would be smashed to flotsam against the reef, because even as the whirlpool sucked them inexorably towards it, a half-dozen randomly spawned waterspouts kept granting a cruel reprieve. Towering above them, moaning and howling as though they were alive, the wickedly capricious spouts thrust them left then right then left. Whipped them in sickening circles and tossed them clear of the water completely only to buffet them back into its wet, avid embrace.

He'd already vomited again, twice.

And then he nearly lost his balance as the smack lurched and heeled over. His feet slid out from under him, and only his desperate hold on the railing kept him from falling. He sent up a swift prayer, though he'd been taught their religion was a lie.

If you're taking me, Barl, for pity's sake take me fast.

The roar of the whirlpool and the keening of the waterspouts were so loud his ears felt buffeted almost to deafness. He was battered and bruised, knuckles skinned red raw, splinters in his palms, his cheeks, and forehead after being skidded from one side of the smack to the other, face down.

Burning through the pain he felt a sudden spike of anger.

I had plans. I had dreams. I don't want to die.

Something touched his knee. Turning, looking down, he saw whey-faced Fernel Pintte huddled amidst a tangle of fishing nets. The Olken's head was split open. Blood dripped off his nose. "You said this wouldn't happen," he moaned. "You Doranen, you *swore* on Barl's legacy this—"

The Olken captain's sudden shouting distracted him. Swinging round, Arlin looked to where the man pointed. It was a small boat, rolling towards them in line with the reef, seemingly unaffected by whirlpool or waterspout. But how was that possible?

"Asher!" Hayle cried. "It be Asher the Innocent Mage, come to save us!" Then his face changed. "The bloody fool, he's like to kill hisself. I fear there ain't no-one can save us now, not even him."

What? Asher? But—but—was Rafel with him? Ignoring Pintte's querulous bleating—let the fool bleed to death or go overboard; who would care?—he let go of the railing and risked what was left of his life staggering to the other side of the boat. Flung himself onto its railing, held on tight and stared at the onrushing plain canvas sail. Two men stood in the battered shallow hull beneath it, both dark haired. One his father's age, one his own. He felt his belly clutch hard.

I think I'd rather die than be rescued by Rafel.

His father left his friends to their desperate spellcasting and joined him.

"Look at him," said Father, through tightly gritted teeth. "*Asher.* Flouting his unnatural talents."

Arlin shook his head, bemused. "How is he doing that? How is he able to control that skiff and the water so easily when you—" A sideways glance at his father stopped him. "When Ain and the others can't—"

"Wipe the admiration and envy off your face, boy!" his father spat. "No Olken should be able to wield Doranen magic. The man's an abomination."

Of course he was. But if there was any chance Asher could save them...

Because I can't. I'm not even permitted to try.

Asher's skiff was close enough now for him to make out the Olkens' faces. What could be seen of them beneath slick fresh blood was pale with strain. Father and son stood side by side in the bow, Asher's right hand anchored to Rafel's left shoulder, Rafel's left hand holding tight to his father's right. Their eyes were slitted with fierce concentration, and they rode the racing boat as easily as if they stood upon Westwailing's stolid stone pier.

Arlin felt the power coursing between them. Felt their common bond and their unity of purpose. Rafel was taller. His father was thinner. But they were two men with one heart and one mind.

Barl's tits, how he hated them.

The fishermen who'd not yet drowned were laughing and shouting, feet drumming the deck. Captain Hayle leaned dangerously over the side of his boat. Cupped his hands to his mouth and sucked deep lungfuls of salty air.

"Don't come no closer, Asher, or you'll be caught along of us!"

Neither Asher nor Rafel replied. They were too busy fighting the wild water and the coils of filthy magic still pouring off the lethal, sharptoothed reef. Magic that had been mostly sleeping, until he and Father and the others had woken it to violent life.

So this is our fault. Asher was right, curse him. We never should've attempted to break magic's hold on the reef.

"Asher!" Hayle shouted. "Go back while y'can! Ain't no point you bein' drownded along with us!"

Could Asher and Rafel even hear the man? Arlin doubted it, with waves smashing on the reef and spray flying and that cursed whirlpool roaring and fresh waterspouts keening to life even as older ones died.

Asher raised his left arm, fingers pointing at the nearest waterspout, and a stream of raw power poured out of his body. The waterspout touched by Asher's power collapsed in gouts of foam and spray.

Hayle led his fishermen in a ragged cheer. Arlin could easily have cheered, himself. He could feel the echo of Asher's power in his own flesh and bones, overwhelming. Exhilarating. The Olken might be an abomination but he'd bought them a reprieve, however short-lived. Beside him, Father leaned precariously over the railing, narrowed gaze hungry, thin lips peeled back in a furious grimace.

The skiff continued its racing progress as Asher collapsed every waterspout he could reach. How powerful was he, then, if he could foil the reef's poisoned magics and guide his boat at the same time?

Arlin gasped, understanding. *But he's not.*

Asher battled the waterspouts but it was *Rafel* who was controlling the skiff. Wrapping it in compulsion and moulding the waters beneath its hull. And that meant Rafel was — was —

Like Asher.

Sick with dismay, Arlin stared at Asher's arrogant son. *Of course.* And now he understood his immediate, persistent antipathy towards Rafel. All their lives, from boyhood, he'd *felt* the potential in the Innocent Mage's firstborn child. When his flesh crept, when his blood stirred, *this* was why.

Because Rafel is wrong. Like his father, he's wrong. Like his father he can kill us with magic.

"The liar! The filthy *liar!*" His father was trembling, bone-white with fury. "He said his son was plain Olken, but the perversion breeds true. I'll see him thrown off the Mage Council for this. I'll see him censured and sent packing as far from Dorana as can be contrived!"

Arlin's mouth was cottony dry. He had to cough and spit before he could speak. "What about the daughter?"

"How should I know?" said his father, venomous with contempt. "But I'll find out. I'll —" And then he was choking with disbelief. "Barl's mercy, what is he doing? He can't — he *can't* — surely not even *Asher* can think —"

But clearly Asher could. Asher did. Like his father, Arlin could feel it: the Olken's desperate push against the rapidly growing whirlpool.

"Rodyn!" cried Ain, hurrying to join them. Though she was spray-soaked and exhausted, still she was glorious. *Please, Ain, smile at me.*

Sarle Baden and Ennet Vail hurried at her heels. "You feel it?" she said, breathless. "Is it even possible, do you think?"

Before his father could answer, he stepped forward. "It might be, Ain. Asher is —"

"Hold your tongue," said his father, fingers biting into his arm. "You're embarrassing me."

So many times he'd promised himself he would stand against his father's unkindness. He'd not kept his word once. He'd not keep it today, either. At least not here, and not now.

But when this crisis is behind us...when we're safe again on dry land...

"Rodyn?" said Sarle Baden. His eyes were red-rimmed, the rest of his face bloodless from the effort of fighting the reef. "Is he really —"

"Yes," Father snapped. "But not even the vaunted Asher can hope to destroy that whirlpool. It's being fed dark power from the reef. Not even with the help of his gross son can he succeed."

"Yes — his son," said Ennet Vail, looking as wretched as Sarle Baden. "Rodyn, we can't permit—"

"Never mind that now, Ennet! We must help the Olken collapse the whirlpool."

"You want us to *help* him?" Baden demanded. "That upstart Olken bastard?"

Father turned on him, snarling. "I want to live, Sarle. Don't you? So let us render him our assistance, shall we? Let us save him so he might save us, so that we, at our leisure, might see him thrown down at last. Arlin! Have you the wit to join us?"

He flinched, and hated himself for flinching. "Yes, sir. I stand ready."

I always stand ready. I am always your obedient son, no matter what you do or say.

His father's smile was so fierce that even Ain and the others had to look away from it. "Then let us save ourselves, shall we? While we still can."

*　　*　　*

Thrumming with power, holding the skiff dangerously close to the reef and the whirlpool, Rafel risked a look sideways. "I don't think you should do this, Da. I don't think—"

"What?" Da unslitted his eyes long enough to glance at him. "That I be up to it? Bite your tongue." He tried to smile, but only managed a dreadful grimace. "I ain't even got one toe in m'grave."

There was no time to argue on it. All he could do was keep the boat off the reef and out of the whirlpool. Lend Da more strength, if more strength was what he needed. Breathing hard, he fought the water beneath them, struggled to hold the skiff in one place, as Da poured every bit of power and magic he possessed at the relentlessly expanding whirlpool.

Except it won't be enough. It can't be enough. He's only one man. But—

He heard Da gasp, even as he felt the slap of fresh power himself. Startled, struggling to keep hold of the water beneath them, he stared across the whirlpool at the blue and yellow fishing boat so perilously close to being sucked to its death.

"Sink me bloody sideways," Da muttered. "Do you feel that, Rafe? Or did I tumble into dreamin' unawares?"

"No, Da. You ain't dreaming."

The Doranen mages were trying to link with them in a working. Rodyn Garrick and his poxy son and the other three. It wouldn't work for any other Olken . . . but because it was Da—

And me. They know about me now. That's going to cause some ructions when this is over—if I ain't dead. Prob'ly even if I am.

"Let 'em in, Rafe," said Da. Fresh blood was trickling from his nose. "Can't hurt now. Might even help. They ain't tryin' to kill us. They be tryin' not to die."

Tightening his grip on Da's shoulder, feeling Da's fingers take a brutal hold on him, he opened himself to the Doranen mages' power. Let Rodyn in. And Arlin. Let in the other three. Pushed their strength from himself into Da, who was a crazy man, trying to tame a whirlpool.

It was odd, how he could be so hurt and angry and still feel this proud.

Da was breathing harshly, long slow drags of air that sounded like his lungs were tearing. Blood leaked from his eyes.

"Let me *help,* Da," he said urgently. "You can't do this alone!"

"I ain't alone, sprat. Got them fancy Doranen mages holdin' my hand," said Da, trying to smile. Trying to comfort him. "Just you keep the boat still. Keep it off the reef and away from that whirlpool. The bloody thing's a bastard. Don't reckon I can—"

Rafel shouted, feeling Dragonteeth Reef's poisoned magic wrench and twist and writhe, feeling it fight his father's efforts to destroy the roaring whirlpool. Morg was dead and still the sorcerer was fighting, determined to destroy what he could not steal or possess. Horrified, he felt Da sink to his knees. Felt pain blossom in him as it blossomed in himself.

The skiff's canvas sail cracked once, and the stern began to slip...and slide...

"*Hold on, Rafe!*" Da shouted, furious. "Don't you pay no notice to me! Hold this bloody boat *steady!*"

"But Da—"

"*Do it, sprat, or you'll kill us all, y'hear? You want to murder me, Rafel? D'you hate me that much?*"

Close to weeping like a girl, like his sister, he closed his mind to pain, to fear, to the imagined look on his mother's face when she learned that Da was dead of fighting the magic in Dragonteeth Reef. Instead he sank all thought and feeling into keeping the skiff steady a flea's jump from the whirlpool. But it was so hard. Morg's magic was thick like tar, trying to trap him and suffocate him. Trying to win, even though he was long dead.

Help me, Barl. Ain't you in there too? It ain't only him in there. This is your fight as much as ours, so bloody fight!

Two more waterspouts screamed into life, so close he could feel their spray stinging his face.

"Rafel—" Da groaned. "Get rid of 'em."

Get rid of 'em? How? There'd been no time to teach him the spell. Except...he hadn't known how to pick that lock, had he? And if he could pick a lock, at age ten...

Desperate, dizzy, he reached deep inside himself, summoned what was left of his newly woken magic—and threw it haphazard at the whipping waterspouts. Searing power poured out of him. Half-blinded, retching, he could see with his inner eye the dark tracings within the writhing towers of water. See the violent confrontation between his magic and Morg's.

The waterspouts collapsed.

Shocked, he nearly lost his balance. And then he felt something shift. Something *give*. Turning, he saw the whirlpool was slowing.

"Da!" he shouted. "You're doing it! Sink me, Da, it's *working!*"

"Aye," Da said faintly. His legs gave way, abruptly, and he thudded to the rower's bench. "Aye—just a bit more—a bit more—"

The Doranen mages on the fishing smack were starting to fade too. They'd poured everything they had into the working, to help Da.

But not 'cause they care if he lives or dies. Only to save themselves. Best not to forget that. Especially since they've gone and found out the truth.

The whirlpool's dull roaring had changed pitch. It was lighter now. Softer. Splashier. Holding his breath, Rafel watched the churning water slow...and slow...willed the sinkhole to collapse—to die—but that was too much to ask, even of the Innocent Mage.

But I ain't complaining. You're a bloody miracle, Da.

"Rafe..." Da's voice was the merest thready whisper. "Rafe...hurry. We ain't got long. Get us over to that smack—"

He was nearly emptied of strength himself, drained right down to his dregs. Feeling his own blood trickle hot and wet from his nose, he gathered the restless water beneath the skiff and rolled them forward again, between the hungry reef and the slowing whirlpool, heading for the blue and yellow fishing boat and the folk they'd risked themselves to rescue.

Closer...closer...his head pounded with the effort. He didn't dare look at his father, though he could hear Da's laboured breathing. *Barl, help him. You better help him.* And then they were close enough and he eased the skiff to a stop.

The fishing boat's captain was still alive, but it was Rodyn Garrick who did the talking.

"You'd best climb up here, Asher," he called down, chalky-pale from the mageworking—but strong enough still to throw his weight around, the arrogant bastard. "Then you and that boy of yours can do whatever it is you do—" His face twisted with disgust. *And there's Doranen gratitude for you. Typical.* "—so we might return safely to the pier."

Da gripped his knees, slumping, his face screwed up in pain. Rafel took one look at him and realised he didn't have the strength to speak. He barely had the strength to keep the whirlpool at bay.

Hold on, Da. Don't you let go now or we're all bloody sunk.

"Sorry," he called back, staring up at the Doranen. Rodyn Garrick, with poxy Arlin beside him, his face a white mask. The other three, hovering behind. "That ain't going to happen. You'll have to float back to shore with me and Da."

Garrick laughed, disbelieving. Nodded contemptuous at the skiff. "In *that* thing? *All* of us?"

The small boat shuddered beneath his feet, fighting his uncertain control. Magic and chit-chat at the same time . . . not as easy as it looked. He could feel the sweat pouring down his face and spine. Exhausted, hurting, he let temper have its way.

"Well if it ain't good enough for you, bloody stay where you are! Think I give a shit? My da's nigh on killed himself to save you but if you don't want to be saved, fine. Stay there and bloody drown—you and your *boy.*"

"You're Asher's son?" said the captain, voice raised strong over the mayhem, while Garrick spluttered, lost for words.

"Aye," he shouted. "Rafel."

"Hayle," the captain answered. "And we'll be down to you directly." His tired gaze flicked sideways. "Leastways, those of us who ain't got a yen for bein' drownded'll be down."

He turned away from the railing, calling for his crew. Light-headed with relief, Rafel dropped to one knee beside his father. "Hold on, Da. We're nearly done."

Da nodded weakly. "Hurry, sprat," he breathed. Scant paces distant, the swirling whirlpool growled. "It'll slip me any ticktock..."

No. No. He laid an arm across his father's shoulders. "We're hurrying, Da. Just you bloody hold on."

Looking up, his gaze collided with Arlin Garrick's narrow-eyed glare. Such fury. Such hatred. *Guess he ain't best pleased to find out what I really am.* Despite the killing effort of steadying the skiff, he grinned.

"Something you wanted to say, Arlin?"

"Arlin!" snapped Rodyn Garrick, over his shoulder.

Cringing like a kicked dog, Arlin fell silent.

Then Captain Hayle returned with his crew—what was left of them, any road—and they started tying oiled ropes to the railing. Rafel counted heads. *Six—seven—eight—* It was going to be a bloody tight fit.

"Is that everyone?"

Hayle nodded, knotting off his rope. "Aye."

No, someone was missing. "Where's Fernel Pintte?"

Hayle nodded behind him. "Mayor Pintte's senseless. Hit his head. We'll lower him to you first."

Pintte senseless? That was a blessing. "Fine, Captain, but crack on, eh? We ain't got much time before—"

"Aye," said Hayle, glancing at the whirlpool. "Can you get that skiff of yours a mite closer?"

Barl save me. Sharply aware of silenced Arlin staring down at him, feeling him use his magic, feeling his pain and exhaustion, he coaxed the water beneath the skiff to lift them—lift them—until the skiff's blunt bow kissed the fishing smack's hull.

Hayle and his men flung Fernel Pintte over the smack's side, tied up in ropes like a goose trussed for the oven. As soon as Dorana's mayor thudded onto the skiff's boards, not stirring at his indignity, Rafel shoved him out of the way, then looked again to the captain.

"You next, Hayle."

"Me last," said Hayle. "Got to see these fine folk settled first."

Thanks to Da he knew a bit about the stubbornness of fishermen. "All right."

Turning to Arlin, Hayle thrust a tied-off rope into his hands. "Go on, young lord. Hold tight, scoot quick, and if you happen to strip a bit of skin off y'palms, remember — it could be a bloody sight worse."

Arlin hesitated.

"Come *on,* Arlin!" Rafel shouted up at him. "We ain't got all day."

Behind him, Da groaned. "Rafel —"

"Arlin! Stop pissing about!" he shouted, then turned to his father. *"Da!"*

His father's face was ashen beneath its smeared coating of blood. "I be losin' it, Rafe. Get 'em down here — we got to go —"

"The whirlpool!" cried Sarle Baden. "Hurry!"

Foaming...splashing...a whisper of power. The harbour sinkhole began to spin more swiftly.

Da was close to sobbing with the strain of fighting the whirlpool. *"Rafe."*

"I *know,* Da," he said, desperate. "Just a bit more. Not long now. Just a bit."

And then he found himself fighting his own frantic battle as the water beneath the skiff surged, responding to the waking whirlpool, testing his control. As he struggled to keep the skiff steady, to keep it from sucking towards the whirlpool, as another waterspout roared into life, the fishing smack lurched violently — and the five Doranen mages desperately slithered over its canting side.

A second waterspout spewed into the air, close enough to soak them with whipping spray — and he lost control of the water, and the skiff, and was knocked off his feet completely and fell on top of Dorana's still-senseless mayor.

The clambering Doranen tumbled into the harbour like rotten apples from a lightning-struck tree.

Rafel scrambled off Fernel Pintte, not caring if he broke bones, and threw himself precariously across the skiff's side. Reached for the nearest bobbing blond head, grabbed it by the hair, and hauled.

It was Arlin.

He dragged the poxy little shit coughing and spluttering into the skiff. Arlin shouted with pain then heaved up gouts of salty water. "My father—my father—Ain—"

Rafe shoved him aside. "Stay down and shut your trap!"

Two more waterspouts howled up from the harbour. There was no time to collapse them even if he'd been strong enough—and he wasn't. Not any more. And Da was sprawled across the rower's seat, barely moving. Barely breathing. But he wasn't dead, not yet, so he had to stay where he was untended. Rafel reached down to the water for the next closest Doranen mage, locked his fingers around the man's wrist and pulled. Pulled again. Felt his shoulder trying to pull free of its socket, the pain as hot and bright as magic, and kept on pulling. Hauled the coughing, kicking Doranen over the skiff's side.

It weren't Rodyn Garrick.

The other three Doranen mages were too far away to reach. Long yellow hair plastered across their faces, they splashed feebly towards the wildly tossing skiff. Arlin was hanging over its side, shrieking, waving his arms around and getting in the way.

"Father! *Father!*"

"Bloody *stay down,* I said!" Rafel bellowed at him, and knocked Arlin on his skinny arse.

Hurling abuse, Arlin flailed to his feet. Ignoring him, hating him, Rafel reached his hand out again. But as his fingers closed on the closest mage's sodden shirt, the whirlpool ripped free of Da's magic with a rumble like thunder; an enormous waterspout, erupting, flipped the fishing smack onto the reef. Flung the skiff sideways. The stricken Doranen's shirt was torn from his desperate grasp.

No time to think. No time to feel. No time to stare in horror at the blue and yellow fishing smack, broken-backed and splintered, its captain and its crew smashed and dying before his eyes. No time to try and save the last three mages in the harbour.

They were beyond saving, any road. The whirlpool had taken them. They swirled round and round, screaming — and swirled out of sight.

CHAPTER EIGHTEEN

✵

*F*ather!*" howled Arlin. Then he leapt. "Rafel, you murdering *bastard!*"

Rafel punched Arlin hard in the gut, twice. Dropped him retching to the bottom of the skiff, clenched his fists double-handed and struck him across the face. He felt the flesh over his raw knuckles split, saw Arlin's cheek split over the bone. But he couldn't care about that. It was knock the fool as senseless as Pintte or let them all die.

With the last of his strength he reached within himself, to that place where so much power had hidden. The power Da had kept from him. *Don't think on that. It doesn't matter. Not now.* The cauldron was scraped almost bare. A few sparkings remained, nowt more.

A few sparkings would have to do.

Shuddering, he summoned them. Shuddering, he imposed his will on the water. The water resisted—resisted—and he strained to break it, strained to breaking, felt the hot blood pour from his eyes and his nose. Spat blood and saliva on the boards at his feet.

Meanly, grudgingly, the water finally obeyed. The skiff lurched as the wave he'd created retreated them from death. Half-blinded, exhausted, he clung to the mast. Turned to see if his father could help...but Da was still sprawled across the rower's seat, with only the uneven rise and fall of his chest to show he wasn't dead. Hurting so much, his head pounding, his body pounded, Rafel throttled his fear.

He'll be fine. He'll be fine.

Woken and weeping, Arlin huddled face-down at his feet. The other rescued Doranen reached for him. Who was it? Sarle Baden? With a foul curse Arlin knocked the older man's hand away. The mage recoiled then looked round — yes, it was Baden — and dragged the straggling wet hair from his face. Sat up, groaning, and stared across the turbulent harbour towards the reef.

"Barl save us," he croaked, his voice scratchy with salt. *"Look."*

The unrestrained whirlpool roared savagely wider, white foam spewing into the air. Beyond the reef dozens of waterspouts whipped and howled. And the fishing smack, ruined, fell at last to pieces and was sucked spar by sail by rigging by net, down into the harbour's depths.

Still clinging to the skiff's mast, Rafel dragged his gaze from the dreadful sight and looked back to Westwailing's pier. So far away, too bloody far...and he was so sinkin' tired...he had nothing left to give...

In the space of three heartbeats five more waterspouts burst into life around them. Then another. And another. The sluggishly moving skiff slewed hard port, then harder starboard. Rafel dropped to his knees in the struggle to control it.

"Barl save us," Baden said again, and this time he sounded helpless. "Grieve not for your father, Arlin. We're about to join him."

Trussed-up and discarded Fernel Pintte stirred, muttering. Rafel looked at him, his vision blurred with pain and effort. Looked at grief-struck Arlin. At Sarle Baden. At Da. Four lives counting on him...but only one that counted. A dreadful thought. Shameful. Wicked. And true.

Hold on, Da. Hold on.

Nauseous with terror, with feeling so much foul magic, Dathne watched the skiff desperately jink and swerve across the turbulent harbour, trying to reach Westwailing's pier. Beside her, halfway down the stone finger's length, the township's mayor was almost in tears.

"*Please,* Meistress Dathne, we can't stay here any longer! It be too dangerous. We've got to *retreat!*" Threeve's imploring fingers hovered a hairsbreadth from taking hold of her arm. "Can't you see we could be washed away any moment?"

The craven fool was exaggerating...but not by much. Whipped-up water slapped viciously on both sides of them, dangerously tossing the tethered fishing fleet. She'd lost count of how many waterspouts now ripped across the harbour...and by her uncertain reckoning three more whirlpools had formed. But what did that matter? So long as Asher and Rafel were still out there—not drowned—

"I don't care, Threeve," she said, so afraid she sounded calm. "Run if you want to. I'm not shifting an inch."

"But I can't leave you out here!" said Threeve, anguished. "*We* can't leave you. Please, Dathne, *please*—"

"*Look!*" shouted one of Westwailing's fishermen, standing with the others a respectful distance behind them. "*Here she comes!*"

Heedless of the danger, of Threeve's shouted protests and the scouring salt spray, Dathne bolted towards the end of the pier. The skiff was coming in fast but erratic, threatened at every turn by huge waves and whirling waterspouts. It was close enough now for her to see Rafel and one Doranen standing with the mast between them. But where was Asher? Where *was* he? She felt rage and grief burst from her in a single, moaning cry.

Then dimly she heard a dull thudding in her wake as Westwailing's fishermen chased her down the pier. They were risking their lives and she didn't care. It was Asher they were running to. Asher, and her son.

Skidding to a halt, arms windmilling to keep her balance, she watched the skiff wallow, losing speed, losing purpose. No, no. Not this close. She couldn't lose them this close. Not so close she could see her son's drained face, streaked with water and blood, empty of hope.

A pair of hands seized her, thrust her roughly aside. One of the fishermen. She didn't know his name. "You stay put," he ordered. He sounded like Asher. "This be our harbour."

Numb, Dathne watched the six men pound down a treacherous stretch

of stone steps leading down to the water. To another skiff tethered to an
iron ring sunk into the pier. One untied the skiff, one stood by the til-
ler, and the other four leapt for the oars. Two men on each, they dug the
wooden blades into the surging water, heading for Rafel's skiff before
it was too late. She pressed her fingers to her lips, trembling. Skittered
her terrified gaze around the fretful harbour, expecting at any moment a
fresh waterspout to rise up and smash both boats.

Rafel's skiff swung about, taking on water. Straining, she could see
another blond head in the small boat, seated and slumping. Was there
no-one else? Only Rafel and two Doranen? The skiff slewed again and
then she saw him. Saw Asher, folded over the skiff's rowing seat.

Barl save me. He looks dead.

Choking back tears, she watched the fishermen reach her husband
and son. Rafel and the Doranen mage with him caught the ropes the
men threw and tied the two wallowing skiffs together. As the harbour
heaved and the dancing waterspouts danced closer, the rescuers fell to
their oars again. Rafel eased his father off the rowing seat, gestured at
the Doranen who stood with him, and they unshipped their skiff's oars.
Started rowing with desperate strength.

When Threeve touched her shoulder, Dathne nearly fell off the pier
with fright.

"It's nearly over," the mayor said. Like her, he was soaked to the skin,
bedraggled and shivering. "You should stand back, Dathne. Don't be in
the way."

He was right, sink him. As the tethered skiffs reached the pier she
retreated, though every screaming instinct told her to run down those
wet stone steps and throw herself on Asher and Rafel.

One by one, the fishermen brought up the men from the rescued skiff.
Rafel first, staggering. The two Doranen came next — Sarle Baden and
Arlin Garrick, both looking half-drowned. Arlin's face was bruised
raw and bleeding. Then came Fernel Pintte, wits wandering, festooned
with rope, his hair and face clotted with blood from a head wound. She
hadn't seen him in the skiff. And last of all Asher, not sensible at all.
Asher they carried, and laid down on the pier.

"Mama," said Rafel. She'd never seen him so tired. So distressed. "Mama, I—"

But before she could reach him, before she could reach Asher, Arlin Garrick turned on Mayor Threeve. "Arrest this Rafel of Dorana! *Now!* He murdered my father and Ain Freidin and another Doranen besides!"

Stunned, Threeve looked to Sarle Baden. "My lord, is that true?"

"No, it ain't bloody true!" said Rafel, his voice cracking. "They drowned. We tried to save 'em but they drowned. If there's anyone to blame it's Garrick and Pintte, for ignoring my da and—"

Arlin hit him. *"Olken filth! Shut your mouth!"*

As Rafel shoved Arlin, sending him staggering, nearly sending him into the harbour, Dathne leapt for Asher, sprawled senseless on the wet pier. Threeve shouted an angry protest, Pintte croaked an objection, and Sarle Baden threw up his hands and walked away. Five of the fishermen exchanged looks then pushed to separate Arlin from Rafel.

But the sixth fisherman flung out a pointing hand. "Barl save us all! *Run!"*

Two monstrous waterspouts were heading directly for the pier, slashing through the harbour faster than galloping horses.

Dathne looked to the nearest man. *"Help me!"*

Ungainly, ungently, they hauled Asher between them by armpit and ankle and began their staggering flight towards the township-end of the pier. Threeve and the other fishermen helped Pintte, Arlin Garrick and Sarle Baden. Rafel refused assistance, grabbing his father's weskit to help.

"Mama—" he said, almost tripping. "It wasn't murder, I swear. I *never*—"

"I know you never," she panted. "Save your breath, Rafe. Tell me later."

Westwailing's harbour shore was crowded shoulder to shoulder with folk eager to see what was happening at the reef. They'd turned the day into a kind of picnic. But now, with disaster struck, with waterspouts and whirlpools whipping up what should have been safe waters, the musicians had fallen silent, the children had been sent home, and voices were raised in anxious dismay.

Then as one they cried out—a dreadful shout of fear. Heart hammering, her fingers tight and aching around Asher's ankles, Dathne risked a swift look behind her...and saw the twin waterspouts plough through Westwailing's fishing fleet. Saw them smash the wooden boats to splinters, toss them in the air like kindling, like toys. Utter ruination in a matter of moments. Wood and canvas rained down on the wave-swamped stone pier.

"Barl's mercy!" she heard Threeve sob. "Barl forgive us."

But it was far too late for that.

By a miracle they reached dry land safely, winded and shocked. The crowd backed away, helped by officials with ready truncheons. Ignoring them, caring nowt for what anyone else said or did, Dathne guided Asher to the grass and knelt beside him. Took his hand in hers and stroked his cold, bloodied face. Rafel knelt opposite, holding his father's other hand. Somewhere close by, Arlin Garrick was shouting incoherent threats. Sarle Baden was trying to calm him, and Mayor Threeve was calming Fernel Pintte. Dathne ignored all of them. Looked at her son. There was something *different* about him. Something knife-edged and newly forged, though he was exhausted.

He lifted his gaze. Pain in his eyes, and anger, burning shallow beneath the fear. And she knew.

Oh, Rafel. My sweet boy.

"I'm sorry," she whispered. "We thought it for the best. We thought—"

He looked down. "Not now, Mama."

On the grass between them, Asher moaned softly, then opened his eyes. *"Dath..."*

"Hush," she said, tears falling. "You hush."

"Rafel?"

Rafel bent low, his anger thrust suddenly deep. "I'm here, Da."

"Dath, I tried to stop 'em," Asher whispered. "I tried to save 'em. But they died."

She stroked his cheek. "*Hush,* my love. It's not your fault."

"Dath..." He coughed, weakly. "Dath, I reckon we're in trouble."

Oh, she wanted to deny it. She wanted to tell him he was wrong.

"I know," she said, and pressed her fingers to his lips. "But don't think about it. Right now you need to rest." She looked up at Rafel, on his knees, with his deep anger and his surface distress. "There'll be time to think about all of it when we get home."

"Home," said Asher. "Aye. I want to go home."

"Rafel —" She heard her voice break. "Rafe —"

But her son wouldn't look at her.

Oh, Asher, Asher. What have we done?

"Asher and his family left for Dorana this morning. Did you know?"

Seated by the window of his guest house privy parlour, Arlin nodded. Smoothed his blue silk brocade sleeve, as though its wrinkling mattered. "I heard."

"Yes." Sarle Baden cleared his throat. His coat was plum purple. No more a mourning colour than blue, but then — they'd not anticipated a need for black. "Threeve had no grounds to detain them."

"Threeve *claims* he had no grounds to detain them." He shrugged. "What else would you expect? He's Olken."

"You can raise the matter in General Council," said Baden, after a moment. "Perhaps even the Mage Council. You can call for a hearing in Justice Hall."

It was raining. Again. Beyond the open curtains Westwailing's cobbled streets were deserted, and waterspouts danced across its dull grey empty harbour.

"No. I'm not returning to the City, Lord Baden."

"*Not* retur —" Stranded in the middle of the parlour's expensive carpet, Baden stared. "May I ask —"

Because there are things I must do at home. Things that cannot wait.

"You may not."

"Arlin —"

He turned his head, just enough. The bruised cut over his cheekbone throbbed. "Lord Garrick."

Silence. Sarle Baden, Father's oldest and dearest friend, breathed in and out quietly. Stood still. Only his abraded palms gave a hint of the previous day's adventure. Briefly, the man closed his bloodshot eyes. He'd been weeping. Or perhaps it was the salt from Westwailing's ruined harbour.

"Lord Garrick," Baden said at last, "if you like, I can speak on your behalf in General Council. I can lodge a petition in—"

"No."

Baden stepped forward. "You can't mean to leave this matter unpursued. Your father is *dead.*"

Father—and Ain, who'd never smiled at him. Ennet Vail too, who mattered not at all. "Yes, thank you, I had noticed!" he said, and stood. Turned his back on the cobbled streets and the harbour. On the folly that had left him without a body to bury. "Get out, Lord Baden. Go back to Dorana with Meister Pintte. Say what you like to those fools in the City. There'll be no justice for my father there. He was murdered by a hero's son."

Baden swallowed, his eyes sheened with grief. With what he imagined was grief. The man had no comprehension of grief. "Arlin—"

"Lord Garrick!"

"Arlin, you've no-one but servants on the family estate. You need more than servants around you at this difficult time. You need—"

"To be left alone." He nodded at the closed door. "I believe I said you could go."

"What of your father's work?" Baden said, his voice hoarse. "His dream of leading our people out of their bondage to this land."

He raised an eyebrow. "Yes? What of it?"

"I intend to see that dream fulfilled, Arlin. And he'd want you to help me."

You intend? I don't think so, Sarle. "As you say, Lord Baden, my father is dead. I very much doubt he wants or dreams anything."

"I see," said Sarle Baden. Two small words, very clipped. Very tight. "Do you have any objection if I take up his cause?"

Every objection under the sun. "Sarle, Sarle..." He smiled. "You can leap into a whirlpool for all I care."

The chamber door slammed so hard behind his father's best friend that the glass in the window shivered, in danger of breaking.

There was brandy in the privy guest parlour. Disdaining the polite civility of a glass, Arlin drank it straight from the bottle. Felt its fumes sear his nose and eyes. Felt its potency fog his flogged mind.

I am an orphan. My father is dead.

Silly of him to be so surprised, really. Contrary to impressions, his father had been merely mortal. A man. No more and no less. But he was surprised. It had never seemed possible for Rodyn Garrick to die.

I should weep. Aren't I meant to be weeping? I am the bereaved. He was my father. I should weep.

But there weren't any tears. His eyes were dry. He was empty. So he drank some more brandy, to fill himself up.

For Deenie, the two-week journey back to the City was the worst of her life.

With Da so poorly, retching three or four times an hour, Rafe drove the carriage the whole way. Mama had wanted to hire someone but Rafe wouldn't let her, even though he was retching too, and Da was asleep when they talked of it so he couldn't take her side. Mama was so worried about him she let Rafe win the argument. At least — that was partly why. But there was another reason. Deenie could feel it, bubbling under the surface. She could see it in the way Mama wouldn't quite meet Rafe's eyes, and how Rafe was fretted about Da but didn't sit with him while Mama packed their things.

Rafe was so *angry,* hotter and gnarlier than she'd ever felt him. It had something to do with what happened on the harbour. With the terrible burst of power she'd felt in her brother, that had buried her face in the pillow and made her scream, and scream, and scream. With the power that was in him now, finally set free.

But nobody was talking about that.

They left Westwailing at first light the next day, even though Mayor Threeve came to the Dancing Dolphin himself and begged them to stay so Da or Mama or Rafel or *someone* could make the whirlpools and the waterspouts disappear. But that couldn't be done. She heard Da telling Mama that, his voice broken and sad, and Mama told Mayor Threeve.

He tried to argue, upset and blustery, but Mama stood her ground. Then the mayor started on about the drowned Doranen, and how there'd been an official complaint made, and how if they didn't want trouble they'd stay as long as they were wanted and then maybe—

And that was when Rafel stormed out of his chamber, crackling with so much power Mayor Threeve nearly wet himself.

"You come here *threatening* us?" said Rafel, looming over the frighted mayor. "What are you? Arlin Garrick's yapping lapdog?"

Mayor Threeve was twice Rafe's age and an important man, but he turned pale as buttermilk. "No—no—you misunderstand. I—"

"No, Meister Mayor, *you* misunderstand," said Rafe, his eyes glittering. "Only a fool would listen to Arlin Garrick right now. His da got swallowed by a whirlpool. He's half out of his mind with grief. And *my* da nigh on killed himself trying to save Arlin's da and them other Doranen mages *and* your fishermen. So in the morning we're going home. The harbour's your problem. Da told you it was a mistake to fuddle it. You should've bloody listened."

Almost weeping, Mayor Threeve gave up and left.

In the morning it was pouring rain, but Rafel wouldn't change his mind about driving. He didn't want to sit in the carriage with Da and Mama he wanted to be on his lonesome, no matter if that meant he got cold and wet and caught an ague. Mama was so hurt, but she pretended she wasn't. She put Da in the carriage, wrapped snug in a blanket and so poorly, and didn't say another word.

The rain fell for three days, unceasing. For three days in the steadily rolling carriage, with Da sleeping and heaving and Mama silent, Deenie huddled in the corner and watched the sodden world go by, silent, because her parents weren't talkative and Rafel hardly rubbed two words together, even when they stopped for the night at this inn, or that one.

They woke on the fourth day to clouds, but no rain. "Mama, I want to sit up with Rafel a while," she said as they snatched a plain, cold breakfast. "Can I? Please?"

Da roused himself. He still looked awful, his eyes sunken, his face horribly pale. Every time he breathed, it looked like the air hurt him. His lips were dry and cracked.

"Course you can, mouse," he said. "Rafel won't mind."

Except her brother did mind, she could see it in his surly eyes. She waited for him to argue. Was surprised when he didn't. Asked him why, when they were back on the puddled road home.

Rafel shrugged. "Why should I care? It's not like I'm going to talk to you. You might as well be luggage."

And that stung, like he knew it would. Days gone by since the Harbour and he wasn't one whit less hot and gnarly. She didn't bite back. She knew that would be pointless. So she sat beside him like luggage, glad to be in the fresh air. Content to enjoy the dank green countryside, the flitting birds in the hedgerows, the breeze in her face, the carriage horses, and wait for him to talk.

Because he would. She knew her brother.

Five hours later, he stirred. They'd bought pasties and cold fresh milk for lunch in Yelton, one of the tiny villages leading to the Flatlands, and he'd let her hold the heavy reins while he ate and drank, now that the worst of his retching was done. Taking them back from her, grunting begrudging thanks, he looked at her sideways.

"Why don't you bite me?" he said, sounding almost...resentful. "Why d'you let me treat you so mean?"

She could still taste her own pasty, tingly-spiced on her tongue. "You're upset. I don't mind."

"Upset," he muttered, and slapped the reins hard against the carriage horses' backs, to stir them into a faster trot. "Is that what you call it?"

Sitting beside him was like sitting next to a furnace. The power in him burned so hot, so bright. He'd never burned like this before West-wailing harbour. She thought she could find him blindfolded, in the middle of the night.

"You can feel it, can't you?" said Rafel, accusing. "Could you always feel it, Deenie? Were you part of their lie?"

"I've never lied to you, Rafe!" she protested. "Not ever."

"You never told me you could feel things. That's the same as lying. When it's about me, it's the same."

Now he sounded like a sprat. Like he was working up to a tantrum.

"Rafe, I never lied. I never knew. Not about this."

He sighed, a gusty sound full of pain. "The only reason *I* know is 'cause Da needed my power. If we hadn't gone to Westwailing, chances are I'd have never found out. Chances are I'd have died an old man, like Darran, and never known what was in me. What I could do."

The cloudy sky was getting lower. The air felt suddenly damp. Any ticktock it was going to start raining again, and once it started raining she'd get called back into the carriage. *Delicate,* Da and Mama said she was.

And I s'pose I am. But I hate it.

"I'd be angry too, Rafe, if it was me," she said quickly. "Even if I knew why they didn't tell me. Even if I understood it was 'cause they were scared for me. I'd be mad."

"Hah," he said, hunching his shoulders. "Don't you go wheedling me, Deenie. I ain't in the mood."

"I'm not!"

"You are. You never get angry." He nudged his elbow to her ribs. "You should try it, sometime. Prob'ly do you a world of good."

She didn't think so. It was bad enough feeling other people's crossness. "What are you going to do, Rafe? You can't stay gnarly forever."

"Can't I?" He slapped the reins again, and the carriage horses increased their pace. "I'm thinking I'll give it a try."

"Oh, *Rafe* . . ."

"Don't fret on it," he said sharply. "It's not your problem, is it?"

In a way it was. Because what he felt, she felt, whether she wanted to or not. And what he felt, so hot and hard, was making her feel ill.

"They love you, Rafe," she murmured. "How can you punish them for loving you? It's not fair."

He glared at the carriage horses' broad brown backs. "How can they love me and lie to me? Is *that* fair?"

Poor Rafe. He wanted this to be simple. He wanted him to be right,

and them to be wrong, and no uncomfortable middle ground between
the two. But nothing in life was ever not messy. She'd learned that much
from all the things she could feel. She let her head fall against his shoulder, and waited for him to shrug her away. But he didn't. Her eyes prickled with tears, there was so much pain in him.

And then it started to rain, and Mama called her inside.

"Order! Order! I call this meeting of the General Council to *order!*"
Speaker Shifrin bellowed, banging his gavel almost to breaking. "If you
do not come to order I shall *disband these proceedings!*"

The General Council ignored him. Defeated, frustrated, Shifrin collapsed onto his seat, tossed his gavel to his desk and sank his head into
his hands. All around him the tempest raged on, accusations and refuta-
tions and lamentations and disarray.

Asher considered shocking them all to silence with a thunderbolt or
three. But only briefly. Things were bad, but they weren't so far downhill
he had to tell these shriekin' fools the truth about his Weather Magic.
Not today.

And Barl bloody willing, not ever.

But in the meantime there were no reason he had to put up with *this*
malarkey. Two days after reaching home from Westwailing and he was
pretty much recovered from his exertions there. Kerril's mucky possets
had done the trick. He still got tired a mite easy. Still felt a few aches
and pains in his bones. And when he closed his eyes to sleep he could
hear the ravenous whirlpool, roaring...

*But it didn't kill me. Nor Rafel, neither. And them it did kill, well, we
did our best to save the poor bastards. I ain't about to blame either of us
for them.*

Others might. Others did. Not Arlin Garrick, not yet any road. Word
was he'd collapsed in private grief. But Garrick's friend, Sarle Baden. He
was makin' a fuss. Fernel bloody Pintte. Natter, natter, natter to anyone
who'd lissen. But so far they'd done nowt official, and if they changed
their minds — well, they'd best look out. Because he'd warned 'em, he'd
bloody *told* 'em, don't muck about with Dragonteeth Reef.

But there ain't no tellin' nowt to a yellow-headed mage. Or any Olken as arrogant as Pintte.

He looked at Council Speaker Shifrin, expecting him to bang his gavel again and restore order, but Rufus had given up trying to assert his authority. So he looked at Dorana's mayor, 'cause Pellen wouldn't have put up with this folderol for two minutes, but Fernel Pintte were too busy brangling with Sarle Baden, wearing his little bandage round his forehead like a bloody badge of honour.

Scowling, Asher shoved to his feet.

Down to me, again, eh? Why's it always come down to me?

Shouldering his way through clots of fratching Olken and Doranen, he fetched up at the Speaker's table and rapped his knuckles hard upon its document-crowded top.

"What y'doin', Rufus? Be you the Speaker or ain't you?"

Rufus glared. "You want to knock sense into their idiot heads, Asher? You're welcome to try." He hauled his chain of office over his head and threw it down on the meeting's laboriously handwritten agenda. "I'm done with it."

"Oh no you bloody ain't," he retorted. "'Cause if you quit, some fool's like to ask *me* to take over. Now, you put that bloody chain back on, and I'll get 'em to quit their cacklin'."

He clambered his way onto Shifrin's Speaker's table. Summoned his bell from Justice Hall, boldly using Doranen magic, and raised it clanging over his head.

"Shut your traps!" he bellowed. "The whole sinkin' bloody lot of you!"

One by one they fell silent, the Olken and the Doranen chosen by their guilds and their districts to meet in General Council once a month to thrash out issues of importance to Lur. When at last the only sound in the chamber was the bell's clamour, he put it down on the table. Raked his jaundiced gaze over them, and slowly shook his head.

"You lot, you be a bloody disgrace. Reckon the folks as sent you here want you carryin' on like *this*? Raisin' hackles and pointin' fingers and lookin' for somebody to blame? What's the use, eh? Blamin' each other ain't goin' to fix our troubles."

Sheepish sideways glances. Gazes dropped to the floor. Hands pushed into pockets and shawls tugged tight. Shamefaced the lot of 'em, and so they bloody should be.

"I can't deny we got ourselves a bad situation," he continued, staying on the table. "With them whirlpools and waterspouts springin' up like weeds everywhere between the reef and Lur's coastline, and every bloody fishin' fleet in the kingdom stuck at anchor or smashed to kindling. We got a lot of families without their livelihoods just now."

"It's worse than that, Asher," said Sarle Baden. "Without the fishing fleets' catches and not enough fish in our rivers and lakes to make up the difference, and the wheat and barley crops ruined almost to a field, stock drowned or dropping with footrot — and there's a pestilence been found in my apple orchards, I've just had word — Lur faces a crisis the likes of which has not been seen for centuries."

Agitated muttering from Olken and Doranen alike. Then Bediah Threeve, come up to Dorana from Westwailing 'specially for this meeting, tucked his thumbs into his braces and rocked on his heels.

"Are you sure there ain't a chance you can fix Lur's harbours, Asher? You and your boy?"

Me and my boy. He felt the words prick him, like spurs. He'd hardly laid eyes on Rafe since Westwailing Harbour. Days and days of silence and avoiding each other. 'Cause they had too much to say and no bloody way of sayin' it, all choked up with grief and guilt and anger and blame. Dathne told him not to push. Give it time. And he was trying. He was. Only —

"Asher!" said Threeve. "Can you fix them? We need to know."

The Council chamber was dead quiet, like a crypt. Every gaze on him, every breath held.

He stared at Westwailing's mayor. "*Fix 'em,* Bediah? No. You got told in Westwailing — ain't no-one can fix 'em, which be why I said don't fuddle with the bloody reef in the first place."

And they didn't like hearing *that,* but so what? It were the truth and he weren't about to swallow it 'cause some folk found it inconvenient. Or 'cause Rodyn Garrick and his friends had died of their foolishness.

Frustrated, he stared around the gathered faces. "You think I ain't gutted by what's happened? Y'think I don't want to snap m'fingers and make them whirlpools and waterspouts disappear? But I *can't,* so best you stop hangin' your hats on the hope I can." He raised a warning finger then. "And my boy can't, neither, so don't none of you get the bright idea of bailin' Rafel up and fratchin' at him till he says he'll try just to make you go away."

Because you bloody would, and he would, and I'll fettle every last one of you if you put my son at risk.

Rufus shifted uneasily in his seat. "Yes. About Rafel, Asher . . ."

More mutters and whispers. Exchanged glances. Fresh tension.

"Aye, Rufus," he said, sighing. "For once the City's tattlemongers be right. Rafe's got a drop of Doranen magic in him, like his da."

Sarle Baden fixed him with a piercing pale grey stare. "You kept it a secret."

"That an accusation, Lord Baden?"

"An observation."

"Aye, well, here be another one," he said, letting his temper show. "My family ain't none of your bloody business." He looked around the crowded chamber. "And that goes for the rest of you. If it be good enough that *I* got Doranen magic, you better bloody believe it be good enough for my son. And anyone who says different, you'll answer to me. Now, are we here to talk on tacklin' Lur's problems or do we turn round and go home?"

"There's only one answer to our woes," Fernel Pintte declared. "This Council must rescind the prohibition on sending expeditions over Barl's Mountains."

"Why?" demanded Sarnia Marnagh, one of the few in the chamber who'd kept her seat. "So you can forcibly eject all the Doranen from Lur? Chase us out of the only home we've ever known? Is that your intention, Meister Mayor? To start a Doranen purge, and save yourselves at our expense?"

Her angry question ignited fresh uproar, Olken shouting at Doranen, Doranen waving clenched fists at Olken. Asher, closing his eyes, felt a stirring in the air. Anger and power were a dangerous combination.

Barl bloody save us all. Reckon we'll cut each other's throats long afore we got a chance to starve to death.

No point ringing the bell again. He needed to be a bit more *definite* this time. Recalling a spell he'd read in Durm's privy notebook, he muttered its words, drew its sigils, and watched every chair in the chamber leap as though come to life. Watched them rattle and bang and make a bloody good racket, thudding and scraping against the mosaiced floor. Felt a grim satisfaction to hear the startled cries, the squeals of fright, to see the wrath of Barl put into every last fratchin' bloody one of 'em.

Wheezing Barlsman Jaffee, who'd tipped out of his seat and was frowning gently in reproof, reached up and tapped him on the knee. "I think you've made your point, Asher," he said, breaking the shocked silence. "Now take advantage of the moment and get these fools to listen. For if we don't take action quickly, I do fear Lur is doomed."

CHAPTER NINETEEN

✠

For once the wittering ole Barlsman were offering pithy advice. Still stood on the Speaker's table, he fisted his hands on his hips. "You heard Barlsman Jaffee," he said loudly. "Now sit down again, the lot of you."

Olken and Doranen stared at him, unwilling to obey.

"Plant your bloody arses or I swear I'll start throwin' the furniture!"

Eyes wide, every councilor sat. Wary now, a smidgin afraid. Remembering—and not before bloody time—that he were the man who'd killed the sorcerer Morg.

"Fernel, Fernel," he said, shaking his head. "You don't bloody learn, do you? First the Harbour, now this. Tollin proved there weren't nowt for us beyond the mountains."

"Tollin crossed the mountains *fourteen years* ago!" Pintte retorted, on his feet. "How arrogant you are, to stand on that table declaring there's no point us seeing for ourselves what's happened in the world in all that time. Or do you claim to know *without* seeing? Does this mean there's something else you're not telling us, Asher? Or are you simply making things up?"

As the Council chamber rustled with whispers, Asher climbed down off the Speaker's table. Put himself at floor level, with Pintte, and shoved his hands in his pockets.

"You sayin' I be a liar, Meister Mayor?"

Pintte held his ground. "I'm saying you're—what's your quaint term for it? Oh yes. *Frighted*. And because you're—*frighted*—you want everyone else to be frighted too."

You poxy shit, I should've let you drown. "So. I be a liar *and* a coward?"

Relishing an audience, Pintte smiled with mock-humility. "Asher, once you did Lur a great service. I don't deny it. But that great service did not make you our *king*. You don't lay down the law or issue decrees. You are one voice, no louder or more important than any other." He indicated the gathered Council with a sweep of his arm. "And we, the chosen representatives of Lur's people, *we* decide what will be done and what won't."

Asher considered him. "What? Like you decided how it'd be a clever idea to try breakin' the magic in Dragonteeth Reef? That worked out dandy, didn't it? So aye, by all means, let's go rompin' over the mountains, Fernel. I mean, what could go wrong, eh?"

"Then what do you suggest we do?" Fernel shouted above the renewed clamour. "Cling to the frail hope Barl will send us a miracle? If Barl cared for Lur we'd not be suffering now!"

"Frail hope?" said Jaffee, creaking to his feet. "I find that an unfortunate choice of words, Meister Mayor. Particularly since you are shouting at one of Barl's miracles. You've accused Asher of arrogance. The same might be said of you in declaring she has abandoned us."

Fernel's chin came up sharply. "Barl was a Doranen. It was the Doranen who brought calamity here in the first place. Forgive me if I'm reluctant to trust Lur's future to the hands of the sorceress who helped create this dilemma."

The council chamber burst into another furious uproar. This time both Olken and Doranen berated Pintte. But not all of them, Asher noted. At least not all the Olken. A handful ranged themselves beside Dorana's mayor, vigorously defending him against attack.

He slumped on the edge of the Speaker's table, not at all inclined to put himself in the middle of *this* brangle. This were Jaffee's business, him bein' Lur's senior Barlsman. But Jaffee didn't seem inclined to fight.

I miss Holze. He were a doughty man. He stood up to Morg. But Jaffee ain't got hisself much of a spine.

In the end it was Sarle Baden who called for order, and was listened to. As one of the mages who survived Westwailing, one of the most powerful Doranen mages left in Lur, he could clap his hands together and flare a bit of light round hisself and that gave folk pause long enough for him to get a word in edgewise.

"It's no secret, Mayor Pintte, that you harbour resentment towards my people," he said. "And that you wish for us to leave this kingdom and never return. Nor is it a secret that your sentiments are shared by many Olken." His eyes narrowed as he smiled without warmth. "It's time this Council knew that as many Doranen feel the same way."

Stunned silence. Then Rufus cleared his throat, and leaned forward over the Speaker's table. "You want to leave Lur?"

"You're surprised, Speaker Shifrin?" said Baden, turning, his pale eyebrows lifted. "Have you—has any Olken—never once wondered if the Doranen are happy here?"

"Of course we're happy," Lady Marnagh said quickly, and looked around the chamber at the Olken seated nearest her. "Lur is our home. Lord Baden, please don't presume to speak for—"

"Lur is our adopted home," Baden interrupted smoothly. "Forced upon us centuries ago by dire circumstances. But times have changed, Sarnia. Morg is dead...and somewhere beyond Barl's Mountains lies our *true* homeland. Lost Dorana. There are many of us who wish to return there and create for ourselves lives not circumscribed by outdated, unnecessary laws."

Asher frowned. "Laws against muckin' about with magic?"

"You'd have us abandon Barl's wisdom?" said Jaffee. "Lord Baden, that would be—"

"A choice," said Baden. "That I and many Doranen believe should be available to us. Hence our willingness to assist in breaking the reef."

"But you failed," said Jaffee. "You should take it as a sign."

"And so we do," Pintte declared. "A sign that it's time for a second expedition to cross Barl's Mountains. On this, at least, Lord Baden and I are in perfect accord."

"Pintte—" Asher shook his head in tired disbelief. "Did that knock on your noggin doddle you altogether? How many times d'you need to hear it? There ain't nowt for us over them bloody mountains."

"I don't believe that," said Pintte, his jaw clenched tight. "If Tollin had pushed on, if he'd not cravenly turned back when—"

He slid off the Speaker's table. "Cravenly? What's that s'posed to mean? Are you sayin' Tollin and his people were cowards 'cause they turned for home once folk started dyin'?"

Fernel Pintte's face reddened. "If they hadn't let their fears overcome them then—"

"Then what?" he demanded, furious. "Pintte, you be an ignorant fool. Only thing any of us'll find over them mountains be a slow cruel death. And if you reckon I'm about to stand here with my thumb stuck up my arse while you chinwag frighted folk into throwin' their lives away on *your* bloody say-so—after *Westwailing?*—then you ain't been payin' close enough attention to me."

Not giving spluttering Pintte a chance to reply, he rounded on Sarle Baden.

"And *you!* You got a bloody nerve, Lord Baden. You know in your belly how bad Morg's magic is. How long it survives. How it twists and kills. Your friend Lord Garrick just *died* goin' up agin Morg's magic. And you want to send folk out to where that mad bastard once *ruled?* What's *wrong* with you? Eh? What are you *thinkin'?*"

Pale with fury, Sarle Baden pushed his way through his fellow councilors until he, too, stood before the Speaker's table. "I am thinking that if Barl hadn't rendered the Doranen impotent there would be a chance of us defeating Morg's legacy," he spat. "For you're right about one thing, Asher—we have no hope of cleansing the world of his stain when the only magic we have is the watered-down trumpery left to us by Barl. But somewhere beyond the mountains, in Lost Dorana, lies our true magic. Our heritage. It is past time we reclaimed it. And because my friend Rodyn Garrick died for that dream, I am determined to finish what he began."

"By going over them mountains?"

"*Yes,*" said Baden. "Asher, there are Doranen who were prepared to brave the ocean beyond Dragonteeth Reef. Even though we have never been a seafaring race. Compared to those terrors, braving a mountain range is nothing. The Doranen did it once. We can do it again."

"With Fernel Pintte, who's been agitatin' against you? Stirrin' up bad feelings and creatin' ill will?"

Baden spared Pintte a brief, sidelong look. "With *anyone* who'll help us achieve our aims. Besides. What Pintte and Olken like him feel isn't new, Asher. Your people have resented mine for six hundred years." He smiled without warmth again. "As you well know. You may've been friends with King Gar, but otherwise...?"

"Don't you chuck me in the same basket as Fernel bloody Pintte," he said, his voice low. "I might not have a lot of time for your folk, Baden, but that be a long stone's throw from wantin' to see you tossed out of Lur on your arses."

Baden sighed. "This isn't about us being tossed, Asher. It's about us leaving of our own free will."

"You see?" said Fernel Pintte, triumphant. "So Asher, will you attempt to force people to stay where they have no desire to be?"

Loathing Pintte, confronted by questions he'd never asked himself and didn't want to answer now, in public, he looked at Jaffee.

"Barlsman? You got an opinion on this?"

"Not at present," said Jaffee, sounding shaken. "I would pray on the matter before passing pronouncement."

"We don't require your prayers," Baden said bluntly. "Nor do we seek the approval of a woman dead six centuries. The religion you serve holds no purpose for us, Jaffee. We look to Lost Dorana for answers now, not to a painting on your precious chapel wall."

As the chamber echoed with alarm and consternation, Asher glared at Fernel Pintte. *Now look what you started, you meddlesome shit.* "What Lord Baden believes or don't believe ain't no business of this Council," he said. "Reckon that be between him and Barlsman Jaffee and Barl. The only thing as matters to us right now is this fool idea of puttin' together another expedition. So I reckon we ought to—"

"And what *I* reckon," said Fernel Pintte, raising his voice, "is that you should tell us the truth, Asher. At last. Tell us how you've known for ten years that trouble was coming to our poor little kingdom. Tell us what your peculiar mage senses told you—that you refused to tell this Council."

Asher felt his mouth suck dry.

You bastard, Pintte. You stupid, stupid bastard.

"Asher?" said Lady Marnagh, as the silence stretched to breaking point. "What is he talking about?"

Not a sound in the chamber. Hardly even a drawn breath as thirty shocked gazes skewered him. He could feel his heart pound to pulp against his ribs. With an effort he unclenched his fists. Steeled himself for a lie that had to be told.

"Asher," said Jaffee. "Is what he says true?"

"Aye, it's true. Ten years ago I knew Lur might be in strife. I felt things. Wrong things, in the earth and the air. I—"

"But Asher," said Jaffee, frowning. "In the Mage Council—when I raised the matter you said—"

It was hard, bloody hard, but he made himself meet the old cleric's pained stare without flinching. "I know what I said, Barlsman. But—"

"So Rodyn was right," said Sarle Baden. "He told me you'd lied. Did he perish because of that lie, Asher? Did he die in Westwailing because—"

"No!" he shouted over the Council's outcry. "I tried to save Garrick down in Westwailing. I tried to save all of you! I lied in the Mage Coun-

cil 'cause I weren't sure of what I felt and I didn't want to start a panic for nowt! Turns out I were wrong, and I be sorry for that, but—"

"So you say now," said Baden. "But with Rodyn dead—"

No, no. This were all going wrong. "I ain't the only one knew somethin' weren't right, Baden! Fernel bloody Pintte knew. Why not say *he* wanted Rodyn Garrick drowned?"

"You'd smear me to save yourself?" Pintte demanded. "How typical. My friends—" He stared around the turmoiled chamber. "I had nothing to do with what happened in Westwailing. As you all know, I nearly died myself."

Choked almost beyond breathing, Asher shook his head. "I swear on Barl's bones, I tried to save everyone. I never let a soul perish, not *one*."

"We know you did," said Barlsman Jaffee, and looked darkly at Sarle Baden. "To suggest otherwise is wicked calumny. But this other business..." He sighed. "Meister Mayor—"

"Yes!" said Pintte, truculent. "I held my tongue ten years ago, it's true—because *Asher* said speaking out would be dangerous. I held it because he's the Innocent Mage, above reproach, and may Barl forgive me for that. Perhaps if I had trusted myself instead of Asher we'd have long since found what we need somewhere beyond the mountains. Then we wouldn't have risked the dangers of Dragonteeth Reef, and young Arlin Garrick and all those other families would not be in deep mourning even as we meet here today." He turned, his eyes burning with hatred and triumph. "Think of it, Asher. All those deaths avoided. Our people's terror avoided. Perhaps even famine and widespread suffering avoided... if only I had not trusted you."

He felt dizzy. Sick. "So everything gone wrong in the kingdom be *my* fault, Pintte? Is that it?"

"No, no, I hardly think so," said Barlsman Jaffee, distressed, his wheezing louder. "Certainly there are some questions to be answered but—"

"Yes," said Pintte, over-riding Jaffee. "Do you dispute me, Asher? Do you deny *anything* I've said?"

Asher stared round the council chamber. At the hostile faces and the doubts and the fears. Watched folk look down, look away, refuse to meet his eyes. So. He could argue Pintte's accusations till he were breathless, but the damage was already done.

"No."

"No," said Pintte, almost crooning. "And tell us this, Asher, since for once you seem inclined towards honesty—can you save Lur this time? Are you still the Innocent Mage?"

Sweat was trickling down his spine. "No."

"Then *I* think," said Fernel Pintte, his voice raised over the Council's loud dismay, "that you should stop interfering with those who would seek to do what you can't. Indeed—it seems to me you've done quite enough."

Feeling sick enough to vomit now, Asher stared at Fernel Pintte. Then he looked around the suddenly silent council chamber. "You want to blame me for Lur's troubles? Fine. Blame me. I can't stop you," he said, hearing his voice grate. Feeling his throat close. "You want to listen to Pintte? And Baden? You want to send your loved ones over them mountains? Then you send 'em. I can't stop that neither. But when they don't come back, or when they come back dyin', like Tollin and his folk? Don't say I never warned you. Don't you bloody dare say it. 'Cause here's me standing afore you, and I'm sayin' *don't do it*. 'Cause it'll end in blood and tears, I promise. Just like Westwailing."

The silence persisted, and still folk wouldn't meet his eyes. Pintte was smiling. Sarle Baden was impassive. So he shrugged and walked out.

Weren't nowt else he could do.

Dathne took one look at Asher's face as he slouched into the Tower solar and put aside her quill and paper.

"What is it? What's happened?"

Instead of answering, he crossed to the rain-slicked window. Rested his forehead and one fisted hand on its leadlined diamond panes, looking so defeated she had to fight herself not to run to him. But any kind of fussing would only rouse his temper. Since Westwailing he'd been prickly, quick to snap and snarl. He blamed himself for everything. Not stopping the mageworking. Not saving the lives that were lost. For Arlin

Garrick's violent grief. For Rafel and Deenie, and what they suffered. In truth she'd not yet quite forgiven him for that, either...but the rest?

The rest wasn't his fault. Sometimes people can't be saved from themselves. When is he going to learn that lesson?

Never, most likely. Because he was a good man who couldn't bear to see anyone in strife.

"Asher..." She clasped her hands on her small writing desk. "Please. Don't shut me out."

He sighed. "Pintte. And Sarle Baden."

"Not Rafe?" she said, sick with sudden fear. "They're not raising trouble because of his —"

"No," he said quickly. "Rafe's fine. They don't care about him."

"Then *what?*"

Unsteadily, he told her. When the sorry tale was finished he fell silent, his breathing harsh. His face hidden. Tormented by her own pain, her own guilt, she stared at him, silent. Then a stirring of awareness turned her gaze to the solar doorway. Deenie was standing there, her blue cotton blouse and skirt dusted with flour. She'd been downstairs in the kitchen, baking with Meistress Watt. But of course, being Deenie, her father's distress had called her like a beacon.

Dathne shook her head. *Not now.* Deenie nodded, her thin face stricken, and softly withdrew. Such a good girl. If only there was a way to — to *undo* what she could do. Life promised to be cruel if she continued to feel everything so keenly.

She looked again at Asher. His back was still turned to her. "I'm sorry," she whispered. "If I hadn't asked Fernel to come here that first time — Barl's *tits,* I knew he could be difficult. But he's one of our best mages. I thought we needed him."

"Ain't your fault, Dath," he said wearily. "I be the one who said to keep what we knew secret."

"To protect Lur! To prevent panic! Not for any other reason. Not to — to miser power to yourself, or —"

"Aye, but that ain't the point now, is it?" he said, and shifted to face her. His eyes were grieved. "The point is he's got folk lookin' at me sideways. Doubtin' me. Wonderin' what else I know that I ain't told. And Dath, I *have* got secrets."

"Everyone's got secrets, Asher."

"Not like mine they bloody haven't! The Weather Magic. Barl's diary. What I did to keep Lur steady. And if folk ever find out—"

"They won't," she said, standing. "But Asher, even if they did, I'll never believe the likes of Fernel Pintte or Sarle Baden could turn the people of Lur against you. Not after what you've suffered and sacrificed for this kingdom." She felt rage rise, scalding her blood. "And if they try—"

"Dath..." Asher rubbed at his eyes. "It ain't me you should fret on. Pintte and Baden be set on gettin' up a second expedition. Pintte's come right out and said it—the Doranen don't belong here. And that bloody Sarle Baden, he stood there *agreein'* with him. He says there be a mortload of Doranen mages as want to quit Lur fast as they can. They want to go home, to Lost Dorana."

"So *let* them," she retorted. "We won't miss them. We don't need them any more."

"Now you sound like bloody Pintte," he said, staring.

She shrugged. "Being hateful doesn't always make him wrong. Asher, Lur's broken. Too broken to fix. You *know* it. With the Doranen gone, the strain eases on the rest of us."

"You don't mean that," he said, pushing away from the window. Crossed to the solar's couch and dropped onto it as though every breath, every step, hurt him. "Dath, Pintte and Baden are goin' to get 'em all killed. Every last fool they hoodwink into goin' with 'em? They'll die."

"Asher..." Hesitant, she joined him on the couch. Left some distance between them so he'd not feel cornered. "If people choose to go, then—"

"Then I don't need to lose sleep on 'em?" he demanded. "That's what you said about Westwailing, Dathne. And in case you ain't noticed, I'm bloody losin' sleep! I can't stand back and watch the Doranen go to their deaths. How could I make that right with Gar?"

She reached for his hand. "Gar is dead, Asher. Your loyalty belongs to the living. To your people. The Olken."

It might've been true, but it was the wrong thing to say. Even as she spoke the words she knew that...but it was too late. He leapt up, and started pacing.

"There be enough folk dead, Dath. I can't—I ain't about to—" He rounded on her. "I can stop this. I can make it so no-one has to leave."

She went cold. "Asher, don't even *think* it."

He took a step towards her. "Dath, I—"

"No." She flung up both hands, halting him. "After Westwailing? After what happened the last time? *No.* Besides—even if you could pour more magic into that Weather map without killing yourself, *which you can't,* how would it solve anything? The Doranen *want* to leave. And you've no right to stop them!"

"They want to leave 'cause they be frighted by what's gone wrong in Lur!" he retorted. "And 'cause Sarle Baden's fillin' their heads full of romantic bloody nonsense. If they weren't frighted they wouldn't lissen. He'd just be some crackpot, mutterin' in a corner. And Pintte? Bloody Pintte's usin' Lur's strife as an excuse to push 'em out! And neither one of 'em wants to be told there ain't nowhere to go!"

"Then stop trying to tell them! Stop trying to save people who don't *want* to be saved!"

Incredulous, Asher stared at her. "Dathne, you ain't *thinkin'.* The Council's goin' to say yes to Pintte and Baden's expedition. And when it fails, 'cause it will, the rest of us'll be right back where we started. Stuck here in Lur, and Lur fallin' to pieces around us. So if I don't try fixin' things, what happens then?"

"I don't know," she said, defiant. Terrified. "All I know is that you promised me you'd not touch that Weather map again. Asher, you *promised.* And if you break that promise I will *never* forgive you."

And she walked out so he could think on that for a little while, on his lonesome.

Goose peered over the rim of the vast oak tub. "No," he said. "Not yet. Keep crushing."

Sweating, choking on the stink of bruised malted barley, Rafel glared.

"I've been crushing the bloody stuff for hours, Goose. My arms are about to fall off!"

"You've been crushing it for nigh on five minutes," said Goose, grinning. "You little girl."

"Little girl?" He blotted his forehead dry with his sleeve. "In case you're addled from drinking your own ale, Meister Goose, you might remember *I'm* back from Westwailing where—"

"You were a hero. I know," said Goose, still grinning. Then the grin slipped. "And came bloody close to feeding a whirlpool. So if you're still weary, then..."

He was. Not just from the harbour, but from the long carriage drive home, too—and most of all from the effort it took to keep his newly woken magic contained. It was unruly, his power. Simmering always on the edge of his mind. Teasing, taunting, demanding to be let loose. And fighting, fighting so hard, 'cause he couldn't let it. 'Cause it had to be contained.

Oh yes. He was weary.

But he'd skin himself alive before admitting it. "Weary yourself!" he scoffed, and starting pounding the malt again. "You roll them oats. That's your job, I reckon, not giving me grief."

Snorting, Goose fed another scoop of groats into the handroller and cranked its heavy handle. "Come on, Rafe. Life ain't worth living if I can't give you grief."

"Ha!" he said, and picked up his heavy wooden hammer. "Life ain't worth living upside down in an ale casket, neither!"

Goose pulled a face. "True."

Comfortably companionable, they continued pounding and rolling. Goose was experimenting with a new ale recipe he'd dreamed up, so they were making a small batch in the home brewery down the back of his family house. The air was thick with the rich smell of crushed malt and rolled oats, and damp with steam from the huge kettles of freshly boiled water standing ready to make the mash for fermenting.

Rafel, watching Goose roll his last scoop of oats, seeing the fierce concentration in his friend's face, and the carefully buried excitement, felt a pang of envy. Lucky Goose, knowing what he loved and was good at. Was allowed to be good at. No-one ogled him for being a brewer. No-one stared at him with curiosity and suspicion. As though he might erupt into dangerous magic any ticktock.

Goose looked up from his rolling. "How's your father?"

"Da?" He reached for the broad oak paddle and loosened up the crushed malt. "He's fine."

"And you?"

"And me."

"You sure?"

He scowled. "Yes."

The look on Goose's face said he wasn't convinced. These days his da wasn't Meister of the Brewers' Guild but that didn't stop him hearing every last whisper from what went on in the General Council. Three days had passed since Da's brangle with Fernel Pintte. Dorana was still buzzing on it—and City folk didn't know half of what went on.

And I only know all of it 'cause Goose told me. His da talks to him like the man grown he is. Da and Mama want to keep me a sprat. Even after Westwailing, they're trying to protect me. When are they going to realise it's too late for that?

Goose came over to check the pounded malt again. "That'll do," he declared, and fetched the large pail of rolled oats. Together they lifted the heavy tub of malt, tipped it into the oats, then shoved the emptied tub to one side. "Here," said Goose, handing him the oak paddle. "Mix them up good and proper."

"Aye, sir," he said, and got stuck in with the paddle. While he mixed the malt and oats, Goose lugged over the empty oak barrel set aside for his new ale. Levered the first full, steaming kettle off the stove and tipped the boiled water out slowly, encouraging more steam to billow. Tipped in the second kettle, and some of the third.

"Right," said Goose, smiling. He was a man who surely loved his work. "Time for the magic."

They dribbled the dry malted barley and rolled oats into the sloshing oak barrel, then Rafel stood back as Goose poured in more steaming water. When that was done his friend nodded, well pleased.

"Now we wait a bit. Fancy a tot of my last brew?"

"What was your last brew?" he said, feeling cautious. "I ain't of a mind to tiddly myself so early in the day."

"You won't," Goose promised. "It's mild as mother's milk. Weaker than what we're brewing here, which is why I had a little fiddle with the recipe."

Rafel took the cool bottle Goose offered him, plucked from a clay-and-tile lined pit in the brewery floor, unstopped it and swallowed. Liquid gold poured down his throat. "Not bad," he said, pretending indifference, and hitched his hip onto a handy oak barrel. "I'd pay for it in a pinch, if I had to."

Goose didn't bite. "So tell me the truth, Rafe," he said. "How are you?"

He sighed. *Should've known he wouldn't let it go. He never does.* The day they got back from the coast he told Goose everything about Westwailing. Told him how Da had hidden most of his magic from him for *years,* and only revealed the truth 'cause he'd been pushed to it. With Goose there wasn't any need to hide. All his pain, his rage, his bewildered betrayal—Goose knew it all. There was comfort in that.

"I ain't fine."

Goose was watching him closely. "You still not talking to your dad?"

"Not about—" He shook his head. "Not really."

"Rafe."

He swallowed more ale. "He could talk to me. He could say sorry."

"Maybe he doesn't know how," Goose said gently.

"Or maybe he's *not* sorry."

"And if he's not?" said Goose. "What then? Are you going to stay mad at him forever?"

Bloody Goose and his questions. As bad as Deenie, he was. "You saying I ain't got a right to be mad?"

"I'm saying with what's going on, maybe there's other folk deserve your anger more than him. Fernel Pintte, for one."

"Aye," he admitted, feeling his belly gripe. Fratched as he was at Da, and he was bloody fratched, what Pintte had said in the General Council... "I tell you, Goose, I wish I'd never helped save that poxy shit's life. Or Sarle Baden's."

Goose snorted into his ale. "Don't let Barlsman Jaffee hear you say that." Then he shook his head. "Sarle Baden's grieving, and Pintte's raving, you know that. Your dad—he'd never hurt Lur. Only a fool would think it. Only a mean fool would say it. Fernel Pintte's a mean bloody fool, Rafe."

"I know," he agreed. "Da knows it too. But still—he's hurt. He'd never say so but I can tell." He grimaced. "Even if we ain't talking."

"What your dad said about not sending more folk over the mountains," Goose said, frowning. "Did he mean it?"

"Course he meant it. You ever know my da to say nowt he didn't mean?"

"But..." Goose was still frowning. "He doesn't know for sure that what Tollin wrote about is still true, does he? He's not had a vision or anything. Right?"

"Right," he said slowly. "I s'pose you could say it's nowt more than a feeling."

"Do you feel it?" said Goose. "Do you think it's still death to cross Barl's Mountains?"

Rafel stared at the brewery's cool brick floor, and was suddenly five years old again. Hiding in the lampha bushes outside the palace, listening to things he wasn't s'posed to hear. Looking back at himself, a man now, remembering the sprat he'd been, his dreams of exploring, he remembered too how full of fear Tollin's voice was. How cracked and seamed with grief. And how angry Da had sounded, that good men died with nowt to show for it but sorrow.

And he remembered Westwailing, so close and so raw. The taint of Morg's sorcery. How he and Da had vomited half the way home, purging that taint the only way their bodies knew how. It meant he understood a bit better, why Da was so set on keeping everyone in Lur.

But does that mean I don't want to go see for myself what's over the mountains?

No. It bloody didn't. Even if it was dangerous he wanted to go.

He looked up at his best friend. "Goose, I hate Fernel Pintte's miserable guts... but he's right. We can't stay pinned in this kingdom. Not with its troubles, and no sign of healing them."

Goose put down his half-drunk ale bottle on the cool end of the stove. "So you think it's safe to go?"

"I didn't say that. What Morg left behind him?" He shuddered. "I ain't got words to tell you. But it ain't *living* magic. It's leftovers. And I reckon it can be beat." *I reckon I can beat it.* But he couldn't say that out loud, not even to Goose. "With enough good mages, any road."

"And Sarle Baden? He's a good mage?" Goose said, looking to his brew again. "Good enough to keep folk on an expedition safe?"

Rafel watched him add more water to the steeping mix of grains in the oak barrel. Breathed in the thick, fuggy smell of the mash. "Well, Rodyn Garrick wasn't a complete fool, and he put his life and Arlin's in Baden's hands when they were working the reef. Why?"

Goose fitted the barrel's lid back on, put the waterless kettle on the floor with the other two, then shoved his hands in his pockets. And then he pulled one hand free, and rubbed his nose.

"Rafe... I'm going."

"Going?" he said blankly. "Going where? The mash ain't done yet, Goose, and I don't know how to finish it. You're the fancy brewer here, not me."

"*Rafe.*" Goose sighed. "I mean I'm going with Pintee and Baden. It ain't been announced yet, but the Council's said yes to another expedition. Pa and I talked it over, and we decided I'm going, for the guild."

Years ago, when they were sprats, he and Goose once fratched themselves into fisticuffs. Some stupid reason or other. Maybe he'd said Stag was the better pony, no argument. Any road. Goose had punched him in the belly so hard he couldn't breathe. So hard he fell on his arse and sat there gasping like a landed fish, while Goose stood over him with his fists clenched, howling, *"Take it back! Take it back!"* So he took it back and they never talked on that again, not ever. He never said diddly about

Goose's ponies again, neither. Not the dirty cream one or the one that came after.

Now he stared at his friend, gut-punched a second time. Gut-punched so he couldn't speak, disbelieving and dismayed.

"See, the thing is," said Goose, determined, "Pa's too old. He wants to go, but his leg's bad and his chest's wheezy and there's no pother who can fix him. And see, Asher, the guild's worried. After all the bad weather the barley yield's down by more than half. So's the oat crop. And the quality of the grain? Nowhere near what it used to be. I've seen the guild records. And it's not just the rain and tremors. It's like Lur's getting *tired*. Like it's worn out with growing things. And we've got to do something. All our brewings are at stake. The whole guild's at stake, I think."

"And this is what your da came up with?" he said, finding his voice. "You joining Pintte and Baden's expedition?"

Goose nodded. "That's right."

"But — why *you?*"

"Why not me?" said Goose, ready to be offended. "If it's guild business, someone in the guild's got to go. And Gryf Macklin might be Guildmeister these days, but no big decision gets made without Pa's chinwag. And he wants it to be me."

"What about you, Goose? Do you want to go?"

"I wasn't sure at first," Goose admitted. "It's a big thing. And with what your dad said — but like you say, he could be wrong. And if I go, then I'm a part of something important. Not just for the guild, but for Lur. I'd like to do something important. I'd like to matter." His cheeks tinted. "Like you matter."

"Me?" Doubly dismayed, Rafel slid off his oak barrel perch and started pacing. "Goose, don't be bloody stupid. Ain't you the youngest brewer ever to get the Guild Medal? Ain't the strong brew you cooked up last winter the best-selling ale in all Dorana City? Goose, you've done more than I have. And you —"

"What?" said Goose. "Rafel, what?"

"You've got a future," he muttered, goaded into saying what he'd sworn he'd never confess. "And what've I got, eh? Magic nobody wants me to use. And a da as — as —"

"Asher, your dad's a *hero*," said Goose. "Your dad's the greatest man ever born in Lur. Beating Morg — and what he did down in Westwailing, he —"

"He ain't the same, Goose," he said, still pacing. "Westwailing—it changed him. Day and night he sits around brooding on them fools who drowned, and on how every harbour in the kingdom's ruined, and how he didn't stop it and how he can't fix Lur. And he broods on my magic."

"Can't blame him for that, Rafe," said Goose. "It's something to brood on."

"Maybe, but it's mine, not his," he retorted. "Mine to use, mine to ignore, mine to study on, if that's what I want. But Da's so scared of magic fuddling me, Goose, he's got me chained up like a dog!"

Goose shrugged. "Then unchain yourself, why don't you, Rafe? Do what you want. Come with me."

CHAPTER TWENTY

✦

W hat?" Rafel stepped back. "Goose, I can't. I mean, I want to, but I can't."

"Why not?" said Goose, a little hurt. A little puzzled. "After all those explorer games we played when we were sprats? I thought—" Then he jumped, turning. "Sink it. The mash."

Thoughts on the new expedition were flung aside as he pulled the lid off the oak barrel, grabbed his stout oak pole and began stirring the malt barley and oat mash, thick as porridge and twice as heavy. It wasn't a job for two, so Rafel again perched himself on the spare oak barrel and watched, his thoughts racing.

I can't go. How can I go? How would it look? And Mama? If I even suggest it, she'll never forgive me.

"Right," said Goose at last, and hoiked the oak pole out of the barrel. "Now it gets to sit for an hour or three." Sticking a thumb-tip into the hot, odorous mash, pulling it out again quickly, he stuck it in his mouth and sucked. "Not bad. Should ferment up just right after it's sat a spell, and I've yeasted it."

"Pleased to hear it," Rafel muttered, feeling gnarly. "Don't know what Dorana City's alehouses'll do with themselves once you gallivant over them mountains."

Splattered with ale mash, stinking of malt, Goose looked at him squarely. "Rafe. Are you going to bellyache forever? Until you're an old man? *Come with me.*"

"I can't, Goose," he said, feeling wretched. "Not after what happened in the Council meeting. Not after what Da said."

Goose picked up his half-finished bottle of ale and emptied it down his gullet. Swallowed, burped enormously, then tossed the bottle onto a handy pile of hessian sacks.

"Going to say something now," he announced. "You might want to punch me after, but it's got to be said so I'll take my chances. And you can sit there with your trap shut and listen, right?"

"Goose—"

"Trap *shut,*" Goose insisted. "And *listen.*"

He folded his arms. "Fine. I'm listening."

"So here's the thing," said Goose. "If a whirlpool had took your dad down in Westwailing, like it took Arlin's, or if his magic had killed him, you'd be on your own now. If he weren't here to answer to—if he'd died—would you go?"

And for a heartbeat he *did* want to punch Goose, for daring to even ask such a question. For daring to put into loud words that tiny, horrible thought lurking deep in his mind.

I would. I would. I bloody well would.

But he couldn't say it out loud. "What—leave Mama and Deenie behind? Alone? How could I do that?"

"I guess you couldn't," said Goose. "But since your dad isn't dead, Rafe, they'd not be alone. If you want to go, you should go. Like you say, it's your life. Not his." He grinned his quirky, lopsided grin. "Besides, if you don't come, Rafe, I'll be stuck on my lonesome with Fernel bloody Pintte. Call yourself my friend and do that to me, would you?"

Groaning, Rafel pressed the heels of his hands against his eyes. "You ain't fair, Goose. None of it's so easy as you make out."

"No?" said Goose, and busied himself tidying up the oat-roller. "How old was your dad again, when he left Restharven to come here?"

"My age," he muttered. "Everybody knows that."

Goose glanced at him sideways, still tidying. "So what you're saying is *he* was man enough at twenty to make his own future—and you're not."

"That be a *bastard* thing to say, Goose," he whispered, when he could find enough breath to speak at all.

"Look," said Goose, letting his roller-brush drop by his side. "If you don't want to come on the expedition, Rafe, that's one thing. I'll respect that. I will. But if you *do* want to, and you stay behind because of your dad? You'll regret it. You'll blame him. He'll *know* you blame him. And pretty soon things'll go from bad to worse between you—and chances are they won't ever improve."

He shook his head, bemused. "Since when are you the smart one, Goose? *I'm* the smart one. *You're* the one with the beer and ale."

"Bollocks," said Goose, grinning. "I was always smart, Rafe. You were just too arrogant to notice."

And that stung. *Arrogant? I ain't arrogant. I just know my own mind.* "So. Who else is going on this expedition, aside from you and Fernel bloody Pintte and Sarle Baden? D'you know?"

"There's a few names I've heard mentioned," said Goose. "But nobody definite. I heard Arlin Garrick wants to come, only Sarle Baden won't hear of it."

"Good. Arlin ain't right in his noggin. He'd have killed me soon as look at me, down in Westwailing. Losin' his da that way..." And as much as he hated the poxy shit, he couldn't help but feel sorry. The way Rodyn Garrick had been swallowed alive...

"Rafe?" said Goose. "You all right?"

He shook himself free of the memory. "Aye."

"Rafe..." Goose sighed, all ready sympathy. "It might help if you talked on it."

The one thing he'd not told Goose was the details of those deaths on the harbour. That would come too close to reliving them—and the dreams were bad enough. He didn't want to put those pictures in Goose's head.

"One day," he said. "Goose, when d'you leave? Is it settled?"

Goose nodded. "Within a week. Pintte and Baden are jigging some talking stones strong enough to work this time. They don't want to go until they're sure of that."

It was a sensible precaution. "A week," he said. "So there's time to change your mind."

"Don't want to change my mind, Rafe," Goose said quietly. "But a week's long enough for you to talk your dad round—if you want to."

If he *wanted* to? Of course he bloody wanted to. The notion of Goose crossing the mountains without him? Unbearable. But to talk Da round they'd have to be talking, wouldn't they? That meant he'd have to put aside his anger long enough to take the first step. Which meant what was more important: pride, or friendship?

How can I not go? This is my chance. Maybe my one chance to find out the kind of man—the kind of mage—I was born to be.

"I'll talk to him, Goose," he said. "I'll convince him somehow. You're right. Time's come to stand up for myself. Live life the way I see it. Besides—I don't like to think on the kind of trouble you'll find if I let you out of my bloody sight."

"Says the man who nearly got himself swallowed by a whirlpool," Goose teased, grinning. "You and me, Rafe. Adventure bound at last."

Even though his nerves were jangling, even though he dreaded the conversation to come, he grinned back. "Them mountains won't know what's hit 'em."

"They surely won't," said Goose, and they laughed, and laughed, and laughed.

Goose shoved him out soon after, with no more help needed brewing the ale and guild work needing attention, so he made his way out of the Brewers' district, on foot. His horse was lame with a twisted fetlock and there'd been no other horse to borrow. Da and Mama had taken Deenie riding out to Crasthead Moor, hoping fresh air would perk her up after Westwailing. She'd been pale and indifferent ever since they came back. *"Nerves,"* said Pother Kerril. *"She's too sensitive for her own good."*

There'd be no argument from him on that. Every time he turned around the last few days, there was his mousy sister, watching him with those big eyes. Silently urging him to fix things with Da. He wasn't blind, he could see she was feeling their upset. But it was his business, not hers. Best she get used to that.

So many folk stopped him on his way to the High Street, putting aside any fears of him to ask after his father. Matronly Olken women patted his cheek and smoothed his hand, thanking him for what he'd done down in Westwailing. They were the ones old enough to have lived through Morg and the Final Days of prophecy, who remembered life with the Doranen before the Olken rediscovered their magic. Da held a special place in their hearts.

"Promise you'll give him our love, Rafel," they said. "Tell him he's in our prayers. We left flowers for him in the Barlschapel. *We* know what he's owed, even if others don't."

The young Olken women he encountered didn't stop. They just giggled behind their hands, eyelashes fluttering as they passed him in little groups, like flocks of doves. Well. One stopped. *Charis.* Bold as brass, she was, catching him by the arm so he couldn't walk on, and shooing her friend to stand off at a distance.

Charis made him nervous. She wore long bright skirts and frivolous blouses. She pinned her hair full of flowers and smelled like flowers, too. Sweet and heady, all roses and freesias. Flirty and teasing, at her da's gala farewell she'd asked him to dance, and with the *knowingest* look in her eye.

Sink me, that seems a lifetime ago.

"Rafel," she said, dimpling. "Is Deenie feeling less poorly? I'm sorry I've not been up to the Tower to see her, but Papa, you know, he — he — " She faltered, her confidence fading along with her smile. "Well. He's still aguey in his chest, no matter what the pothers do."

He knew that. Da was fretting on Uncle Pellen's health, along with everything else. Aside from Mama, Pellen Orrick was the only friend he had left from the bad ole days. With Darran gone... and Jed, two winters past... and with him hardly speaking to any family he had left on the coast...

Me and Mama and Deenie and Pellen. That's who he's got. Ain't so many, when you think on it. And now here's me set on going over the mountains with Goose...

He shoved the inconvenient thought aside.

"Rafel," said Charis, her fingers still on his arm. "Is something amiss?"

Startled, he looked down at her. "No. Course not."

"Only with the expedition, and that flapdoddle in the Council meeting, and what happened in Westwailing—" Her fingers tightened. "I know things haven't been easy, Rafe. I'm sorry for it."

Her warm sympathy took him by surprise. Just as surprising, the comfort he felt in her hand on his arm. He cleared his throat. Couldn't help but think of Da's terse warning on the road down south.

"That girl's my best friend's daughter, Rafe. You'll not fuddle with her unless you want real trouble."

He stepped back. "Aye, well. Nowt to be done about it, is there? Charis, I've got to—"

"Of course," she said, blushing. "Only—Rafel, would you ask your father to come visit us? Soon? Papa would feel so much better for seeing him. He's not been by since you got back and—well, Papa worries. He's so fond of your da."

"I'll mention it," he promised. "And you give Pellen my best, eh? I'll be seeing you, Charis."

"I hope so," she said, with a flash of her usual bold, flirty self. Her fingers waggled a goodbye wave, then she tossed her hair and rejoined her friend. They walked off arm in arm, giggling, and he turned on his heel to get back to the Tower.

Let be to mind his own business at last, with not so many folk wandering this top end of the High Street, he stared at Barl's Mountains rising jagged against the clouded sky. Ole Darran used to talk on what they looked like, before the Wall came down. The way the magic softened and blurred their peaks, keeping Lur safe. He used to say how Barl's Wall turned the sky gold, and you could see it shimmering on the brightest bright blue day. And how at night it was so beautiful, sometimes he used to look at it and weep.

Staring at the magickless mountains now, he tried to imagine climbing over them. On *foot*. Had to be on foot. No horses could get up there. It was a daunting prospect.

Step by step, thinking on it, his pace slowed. Daunting as it was or not, he wasn't frighted. He wanted to do this, so bad his insides ached. So bad he could *taste* it. Freedom. Adventure. The chance to prove himself, alone. Da should understand that better than anyone.

But he's forgotten how he felt when he was twenty. He's frighted—and he wants me to be frighted too.

Da had risked him in Westwailing, but only 'cause he had to. Didn't want him to risk himself, though. Didn't care what his son wanted. Refused to see things any way but his. Could a man be slumskumbledy? If he could, that man was Da.

If I ask them, Pintte and Baden will take me on their expedition. They might not want me, but knowing me leaving Lur will fret Da, they'll say yes. Besides—my magic's bound to come in handy and they know that, too.

So. His decision was made. He was going. No matter what kind of fuss Da kicked up. Whether he managed to talk his father round, or not, he was going. A pity he couldn't sneak away in the dead of night, like Da had left Restharven all those years ago. It'd be a sight easier.

And I won't feel guilty for going, either.

Except...except...Da had wept, in Westwailing.

That night, with the township in an uproar, its harbour a wasteland of waterspouts and whirlpools, after he'd hunted that bastard Mayor Threeve out of the Dolphin, he'd seen the depth of his father's love. The unlimited reach of his fear, that something might happen to his only son. It was raw. Painful. Almost...too private. And he'd looked so *frail*.

Fresh resentment stirred. Love didn't excuse lying. And it could be an anchor, as well as a blessing.

If he really loves me, he won't stand in my way. So I'm going. I am.

Except...except...Da had wept, in Westwailing.

But I can't let Goose go alone. Da could be wrong about what's over the mountains, but what if he ain't? If I let Goose go alone and some-

thing happened to him? I'd never forgive myself. He's my best friend. He's like my brother.

Surely Da would understand that. After what happened to King Gar? He'd have to understand.

But if I go, and Da frets on me so much he makes himself sick... or worse... how do I live with that? If I cross the mountains and come home again a hero, only to find Da's perished of fear for me while I was gone?

The thought made him sick. So now he had to choose between his best friend and his father? Between his own freedom, and his father's life?

How is that fair?

Except... except... there was no choice.

Goose'll understand. He's got a father, too.

Resentful and resigned, he kept on walking for home.

Hearing the rap-rap of knuckles on his closed library door, Asher looked up. "Come in."

The door opened. *Rafe.* His eyes were... wary. "Da. You busy? You look busy."

Slowly, carefully, he put down his freshly inked quill, his breathing not quite steady. "No. I ain't busy." He flicked the papers on the desk in front of him. "Just gettin' ready for a case in Justice Hall. You'd reckon folk could keep 'emselves brangle-free for five minutes at a stretch, but they can't. Fools, the lot of 'em."

Rafe hesitated, then came in and dropped into the chair on the other side of the desk. "You been sayin' that my whole life, Da. You goin' to sit there and tell me you be surprised?"

That tugged a small smile out of him. "No. S'pose I ain't."

Awkward silence. Rafe rubbed at his nose. It were one of his little habits when he was fratched, or comin' to confess a misdeed. "You sure you're ready for Justice Hall, Da? You ain't too tired still?"

"Didn't fall off my horse this morning," he said, mildly enough. "Reckon I can sit in a chair down Justice Hall. Rafel—"

"Bumped into Charis, down on the High Street," said Rafel, skritching at a dried stain on his trews. "Uncle Pellen's asking after you, she says. She says why ain't you been down to see him since we got back?"

Prickled with guilt, he looked out of the library window. The clouds were coming down again. There'd be rain before sunset. "Kerril said he ain't been spry. Don't want to tire him." It was true. Well, partly true. Pellen would ask him about Rafel, and Westwailing, and he didn't have the strength to talk on it. Not yet. "I'll maybe go see him tomorrow. Or the day after."

Rafel nodded. "You should. She was fretted. More than I've ever seen her."

Oh, Pellen. "I will. Rafe —"

Rafel shoved to his feet and wandered over to the window. Stared down into the Tower's gravelled forecourt. His face, not quite hidden, was brimful of secrets. Crowded with all the things he hadn't said.

"Did you hear? The Council's told Pintte and Baden they can have their expedition."

"Aye. The bloody fools." He shook his head. "They'll be sorry."

Rafe flicked a glance sideways. "Goose is going with them."

Fright like a fist of iron, crushing his heart. "Aye? Well, you ain't."

"Ain't I?" said Rafel, and shoved his hands in his pockets. "Decided that, have you, Da?"

"That's right."

Rafe swung round, scowling. "Just like you decided to keep my Doranen magic a secret?"

He stood. He had to. This weren't a sitting down conversation. "Mind your manners, sprat."

"You never should've kept it a secret, Da," said Rafe, his chin up, his eyes hot. "Not from me."

"You didn't need to know, Rafe."

"Maybe not when I *was* a sprat," said Rafe, closing half the distance between them. "Maybe not then. But now? I'm a man now. You should've told me."

"And I did tell you, didn't I? When it was needful."

"For *you*," Rafe spat at him. Where was his sweet son? "But it's *my* magic, Da. You had no right to hide it, just like you've got no right to decide where I go or what I do with my life!"

Fright hammered him again. Fernel bloody Pintte and his sinkin' expedition. *I should've let the bastard drown.* "So you reckon you can just walk out on your family? Is that what you reckon?"

"You mean like you did, when you were my age?" Rafe retorted. "Walked out in the middle of the night without even sayin' a proper goodbye?"

Asher banged his fist on the desk, making the ink pot jump and splash. "I left Restharven for the City so I could make money to take care of my da. *That's* why I left. Why d'you want to leave? 'Cause the work facin' us here in Lur ain't adventurous enough for you? You reckon to make y'self some kind of *hero*, traipsin' about in other people's barren lands?"

"*No!*" said Rafel, hands clenching. "I couldn't care less about being a bloody hero. Reckon I've heard enough about heroes to last me the rest of my life!"

And that were a deliberate, personal stab. Sick with the thought of losing his boy, hurt by the jibe, he shoved out from behind the desk.

"You need to pin your ears back, Meister Roughtongue, and lissen close to what I say," he said, jabbing a pointed finger into his son's fancy weskit. "Them fools Pintte and Baden got good Olken killed once already. And now they be tryin' to get more good men killed goin' over them mountains. You got knucklebones in your noggin, Rafe, if you reckon what they be plannin' won't end in blood and tears. And if—"

"You don't know that!" Rafel shouted, knocking his hand away. "You're just *guessing*."

"Mayhap I am," he retorted. "Mayhap I were guessin' when I warned 'em not to fuddle with Dragonteeth Reef, too. But I weren't wrong about that, eh?"

"No," said Rafe tightly. "But that doesn't make you right about everything else. And Goose—"

"Oh, aye, Goose," he said, scornful. "Call y'self his best friend, do you? Well, if that's true you'd talk him out of this madness, 'stead of eggin' him on. Did you say you'd go with him?"

"And if I did?" said Rafel, his breathing harsh and hard. "So what if I did?"

"Then you'd best turn round and tell him you made a mistake. 'Cause you ain't goin' with him, Rafe. You ain't settin' a toe out of this City."

Rafe shook his head. "That ain't up to you, Da, 'cause I ain't a criminal and this ain't Justice Hall. You don't get to lay the law down on me. I can walk out that door and you don't get to say otherwise. If I want to, I can join that expedition *and you don't get to say I can't.*"

"No?" he said, his voice soft with anger and fear. "Best you think again, Rafe. There ain't a man or woman goin' over them mountains without the Council gives 'em leave. Now, things might be fratched a bit between me and them just this ticktock, but if you reckon they'll let you go when I say I want you here? Then, sprat, you be a sinkin' bloody fool."

Rafe's eyes were bright with tears. "You'd do that?" he whispered, his voice close to breaking. "You'd shame me like that before the Council? Before the City?"

Shaking, trying to hide it, he nodded. "Rafel, I'd do a bloody sight more than that to keep you safe. *You're my son.*"

"Aye," said Rafe, stepping back. "That I am. More's the sinkin' bloody pity."

The door slammed loudly, finally, behind him.

Adrift on the library's handwoven rug, Asher listened to his pounding heart. Told himself this were nowt, it were nowt.

Fathers and sons fratch, that's the way things be. He'll get over this. He will. It's for his own good. He knows that. He'll come back to me, by and by.

And all around him, the silence stretched on.

Dathne found her son in the hushed, glimlit stable yard, fussing over his precious Firedragon. Kneeling in the stallion's straw, he looked up from rubbing liniment into the horse's strained fetlock, pain and anger glowering in his eyes.

"If you've come to defend him, Mama, don't. I ain't in the mood to hear him defended."

She ran her hand along the top of the stable's closed half-door. "You know, Rafe, it was both of us decided to tamper with your magic. Both of us who thought it best you didn't know. You can't be angry with your father, and not be angry with me."

"Don't worry, Mama," he said, soothing the horse as it flinched. "I'm angry with you, too."

She might've smiled, if she hadn't been so close to weeping. "Were we wrong, to keep it from you? Really? With you stealing spells from Arlin Garrick? Sneaking into your father's library and fuddling with private things? *Dangerous* things? Should we have trusted you with all that power when it turns out we couldn't trust you to do as you were told? To believe us when we said it was so important for you to be careful?"

He flushed. "I was a *sprat,* Mama. Every sprat gets up to mischief."

"Mischief, yes," she agreed. "Dancing leaves and cracking stones, that's mischief. Slopping water in your bath. But Rafel—"

"I know!" he said, goaded. "I shouldn't have done those other things. I knew they were wrong when I did them, and I did them anyway, and I'm sorry. Nowt bad happened, but still. I'm *sorry.*"

The chestnut stallion swished its tail, head tossing, not liking raised voices. Rafel soothed the animal again, then reached into his grooming box for a fresh bandage to wrap around its injured leg.

"Did you really tell Goose you'd go with him over the mountains?" she asked. "Or was that something you said because you're angry with your father—and you wanted to hurt him?"

Stung, he looked up again. "You think I'd do that?"

"I don't know," she said, after a moment. "You might. You've been so—so *gnarly* since Westwailing Harbour."

"You saying I ain't got the right to be fratched?"

"Oh, Rafel." She had to blink back tears. "I'm saying what's done can't be undone. I'm saying your father and I love you very, very much, and if we've made mistakes it's *because* we love you, not because we want to hurt you. If it's a crime for parents to protect their child, then we're guilty, no argument, and you must sentence us as you see fit."

Rafel pinned his stallion's bandage in place, then stood. Stroked his hand down the horse's long, gleaming neck. Glanced up, frowning, as rain began to drum on the tiled stable roof.

"I did tell Goose I'd go with him," he said, not looking at her. "But on my way home I changed my mind."

"Why?"

"Why d'you think?" he said roughly. "'Cause I knew what me going would do to Da."

She considered him. Five minutes ago, surely, he'd been her little boy. Smiles and giggles and kisses at bedtime. Now here he stood before her, a man, with a man's anger and a man's pride. His father's pride—and his courage.

He's his father's son. And isn't that the problem?

"Not me, Rafe?" she said at last. "You didn't worry what your leaving would do to me?"

"Mama—" Pushing past the horse, he reached for her across the stable door. "Of course I don't want to fret you. But you're the strongest person I know. You're *Jervale's Heir.* And Da—what happened in Westwailing—he's not—he's not as strong as he used to be, Mama. He ain't been for years. And—and—"

She framed his dear, sweet face with her hands. Kissed him on both cheeks. Leaned her forehead to his. Smiled as his hands came to rest on her shoulders. "I know."

"He just fratched me all over again," Rafel muttered. "He didn't give me a chance to explain. When I said Goose was going with Pintte and Baden, he jumped on me with both feet. And I—I—"

She kissed him again. "It's all right, Rafe. I know what he's like."

"And now I've got to go back on my word to Goose." He sounded so *young.* There were tears in his voice. "What kind of a friend does that make me?"

"Rafe, he'll understand. He'd never expect you to choose him over your family. Would you blame him if he had to put his father ahead of you?"

Turning away, he smeared his sleeve over his face. "No. Course I wouldn't."

"Well, then."

"It's just—" His face twisted. "I'm scared for him, Mama. This expedition—"

"I know." She managed a small smile, for his sake. "We'll just have to say our prayers hard, won't we, that your father's wrong for once. Now, are you coming in? It's nigh on supper and you know how I hate it when you're late to the table."

That provoked a snort of amusement. "I'll be in soon, I promise."

"I'll hold you to that," she said. "And Rafe—" She had to wait a moment. "Make peace with your father."

He sighed. "Mama—"

"Please, Rafel. For me?"

"I will," he said eventually. "For you. But in my own time—and in my own way."

She wanted more, but couldn't ask for it. Some of this was Asher's fault, after all. And hers. So she smiled at her son, and blew him a final kiss, and left him to fuss with his precious stallion.

Most all of Dorana City and half the rest of Lur, it seemed, turned out to farewell Fernel Pintte and Sarle Baden's expedition. Dathne took Deenie and Charis to stand with her on the steps of Justice Hall, a goodly vantage point to see Barlsman Jaffee and a whole flock of lesser clerics bless the expedition members who were set to gather in the Market Square before riding off towards the Black Woods, and the mountains. Rafel was out there somewhere too, on his lonesome. Saying a private goodbye to his best friend Goose.

Asher kept company with Pellen, ailing in his feather bed. It was his second visit since coming home from the coast. During the first, his friend had taken poorly again and he'd gone home so frighted it was hard to eat or sleep. Whatever Kerril had done in the meantime, it seemed to have helped.

For now.

"I suppose," said Pellen, his face sallow and deeply lined, his voice pale and breathless, "the Council could've chosen worse than Rubin Stott to take over from Pintte as mayor. Pour me some water, would you?"

Asher half filled a glass from the pitcher on the bedside table, and watched as Pellen tried not to spill it, drinking. "Seein' as how you hired on Stott to be your deputy, reckon you ain't wrong." He took the emptied glass back, pretending not to notice the tremor in Pellen's fingers. "And seein' as how they had to nigh twist his arm off at the elbow afore he'd do it, I'd say they chose right. Any man as wants power be ezackly the wrong man to have it."

"Agreed," said Pellen, then coughed tearingly into his kerchief. When he took the linen away from his lips, Asher saw fresh blood on it. Couldn't quite hide his horror, or dismay.

"Pellen—"

"Now, now," said Pellen, gently chiding. "You can put away that long face. Kerril's potions keep me brisk enough."

"Aye, but can they cure you?"

"No," Pellen said at last, staring at the bloodstained linen. "No, I'm sorry to say they can't do that."

He had to clear his throat. "You told Charis?"

"No. Not yet," Pellen admitted. "Cowardly of me but in this, I'll gladly cling to cowardice. You and Dathne—you'll stand for her, once I'm gone?"

"Don't ask stupid questions," he snapped. Anger kept the grief at bay. "Course we bloody will."

"Forgive me," said Pellen. "I get anxious. She's a clever lass, but young to be left alone in these uncertain times."

Uncertain times. Aye, well, that were one way of puttin' it. *M'self, I'd call 'em bloody awful.*

Pellen was staring at him closely, his dark eyes clouded a little and sunk deeply in their sockets, purplish shadows beneath them. He looked a mortal sick man. Surely Charis had guessed. Which meant father and daughter were keepin' secrets from each other. But if that got 'em through each painful day, who was he to look sideways? Turned out that as a da, he weren't no sinkin' great shakes.

"This isn't your fault, you know, Asher," Pellen said quietly. "No more than Westwailing was. You did your best to stop Pintte and the others. If they choose to ignore you, the blame belongs to them. There's not a man alive or dead who's fought harder for this kingdom. You *mustn't* reproach yourself."

Pellen were a good friend, trying to make him feel better, but nothing could do that. Dread was in him, hollowing his heart.

His good friend's thin face turned brooding. "You still think the expedition is doomed?"

"Don't matter a fly's fart what I think, Pellen," he said, shrugging. "Ain't nobody interested in what I got to say."

"Asher..." Pellen shifted against his pillows. "He still won't speak to you?"

Rafel. A week since their fight, and his son was yet to say a kind word to him. It wasn't just Goose, of course. It were Westwailing and his magic, too. Everything between them a tangled, gnarly mess.

He shook his head. "No."

"I'm sorry," said Pellen. "Children. How empty our lives would be without them... and how much less painful."

Pellen's easy sympathy made his eyes burn. "I don't care," he said, knowing it was a lie, knowing Pellen knew it too. "He can hate me till the day he dies, so long as he lives long enough to die an ole man. I *couldn't* let him go, Pellen. It be true I can't prove the expedition's headin' for disaster, but—" His clenched fist struck his chest, which hurt with every breath. "I feel it. In my bloody bones, I *feel* it. So how could I let him go? If I gave in... if I said him likin' me were more important than him *livin'?* Be faster and kinder to cut his throat m'self."

He heard his voice break, and was shamed. He had no business weighin' Pellen down with his troubles. His friend were *dyin';* he didn't need more strife in his dish.

"Asher," said Pellen, and reached out his hand. "Don't. Rafel's angry, I know, but anger doesn't last forever."

He looked at the thin fingers resting on his arm. "Not for some folk, mayhap. But my family? We ain't of the mood as forgives and forgets. Look at Zeth. Hates me as much today as he did the day our da died. As he did the day our ma died. The day she bloody birthed me, 'cause he didn't reckon they needed another mouth to feed."

Pellen snorted. "Rafel is *not* your misery-loving brother. He's your son and he loves you."

"He's a man, Pellen," he said bleakly. "And I'm treatin' him like a sprat. That Goose—if somethin' happens to him...*when* somethin' happens to him..." Grief threatened to break him again, and he had to stop a moment to blink, and breathe hard. "I had words with Goose's da, y'know. Tried to talk him into stoppin' his son from throwin' his life away on Pintte's say-so. But he wouldn't listen, the bloody fool."

"And what does Dathne say?"

"Not a lot," he said. "But she cries when she thinks I be sleepin', and can't hear her."

Pellen's thin fingers on his arm tightened. "Give it more time. Rafe'll come round."

"Not if Goose dies, he won't. Not if Goose dies, and he reckons he could've saved him if he'd been there." Groaning, he pressed one hand across his eyes. "I may be younger'n you, Pellen, but I ain't young no more. And I got hurts inside me from that bloody Weather Magic. Wounds as ain't never healed goin' back twenty years." He let his hand fall and looked at his friend, for once not trying to hide a thing. "I'm tired. And this fight with Rafe—it be wearin' me down."

"I can speak to him," said Pellen. "Would it help if I speak to him?"

Touched, and shamed again, Asher shook his head. "He wouldn't pay you no mind, Pellen. You're my friend. Makes you bad as me, right now. Leastways that be how he'll see it."

"Most likely," said Pellen, sighing again, and took back his hand. "It was just a thought." Then he frowned. "These hurts, Asher. These—these unhealed wounds. Should I be worried? Does Dathne know? What have you done about them?"

Shame was burned away by anger for letting despair loosen his tongue. "Never you mind about that. It ain't nowt. Forget I said a bloody word."

"Too late," said Pellen. "You can't pour spilt beer back in the jug. That business with the Weather map. Trying to fix what was wrong with Lur, last time. That's what did the real damage, isn't it? And then with what happened in Westwailing, you made things worse. That's what you're paying for now. Am I right?"

He stared at his knees, hating himself. Not answering.

"Asher!" said Pellen sharply. *"Am I right?"*

CHAPTER TWENTY-ONE

✦

Asher sighed. "And if you are? Like you say, Pellen—ain't no pourin' spilt ale back in the jug."

"How bad is it?"

There were aches and pains in him now, gnawing at his tired bones. Aches and pains Kerril's strongest potions couldn't dull. "Bad enough."

"Well, if a stubborn frog like you is *admitting* it," said Pellen, trying to make a joke. But it weren't funny, and he knew it. None of this were funny. "I'm sorry, Asher. For all of it."

"Don't know what you be apologisin' for," he said, struggling to stay on an even keel.

"Someone has to," said Pellen. "And since Fernel bloody Pintte won't..." He shrugged, then his gaze sharpened, and he was suddenly Captain Orrick of the City Guard again. "Asher—I hope you're not thinking to do anything foolish."

"Course I ain't."

But Pellen didn't believe him. "Working that Weather map nearly killed you ten years ago. It nearly killed Dathne, to see you so hurt. Would you do that to her a second time?"

He stared at Pellen, derisive. "You sayin' that when you was our doughty Guard Captain, and some fool of an Olken took a swing at you, you never set foot in a brawl again after?"

"That's different!" Pellen retorted. "Your Weather Magic's *lethal,* Asher."

"And a brawler's knife ain't?" he said, pushing out of his chair. "Pellen, leave be. I ain't sure what I'm goin' to do. Just—don't you make it any harder on me, eh? Lyin' there all poorly and pathetic. Tryin' to use my sympathy agin me."

"All right," said Pellen, grudging. "But don't you expect me not to speak my mind."

Fetched up at the open chamber window, looking out across the City's rooftops towards Market Square, he shook his head. "I don't. Known you too bloody long for that."

Fleeting sunshine was warm on his face, the light breeze scented with blossoms from window-boxes, and tinged pungent by pigeon dung. Bloody birds nested in every nook and cranny of a house. Staring further across the rooftops he could see the distant tiles of Justice Hall, and a narrow strip of stained glass: Dorana City's Barlschapel. The bits of street and laneway he could see were empty. Nobody scurrying on urgent business, or lazily strolling to admire shop window displays. Anyone not bedridden was down to the Square or lining the main street leading to the City gates, squashed belly to arse so's they could say to anyone who'd listen after, *"I was there to see the expedition ride out."*

It were just like last time, when Tollin and his foolhardy friends got 'emselves blessed by Holze. The breeze strengthened and he caught a hint of voices raised in joyful acclaim, as folk lied to 'emselves as how their troubles would soon be over.

Laughter when they leave and weepin' when they come back. How is it folk got such short bloody memories?

"Asher..."

He turned. Barl save him, Pellen looked bad. *It ain't fair. Why do all my friends die?* "Aye?"

"Have you thought you could be wrong about things?" said Pellen, almost hesitant. "We've had more settled weather, these past days. I hear the flooding's eased. The tremors have stopped. Maybe...maybe what happened before was a false alarm."

"Pellen..." He shook his head. How much did it hurt him, to dash his friend's frail hopes? "No. I wish it were, but it ain't. What happened before were Lur clearin' its throat. Now the kingdom's just holdin' its breath. Bidin' its time."

"Why do you say that?"

Asher closed his eyes. Ignored Pellen's dismay, and the pain in his bones, let the mage in him sink deep and felt the drips and dregs of the magic he'd poured into Lur's earth. So little left now. So much heart-ache to come.

"'Cause it's true," he murmured. "'Cause I can feel it." He opened his eyes. "And I'll bet Fernel bloody Pintte can feel it too. Prob'ly it be why he's so keen on rushin' off over them mountains. He knows what's comin' and he don't want to be here."

"Well, if you're right—whatever comes, Lur will survive it," said Pellen, his eyes feverish. "We survived before there was Weather Magic. We survived the coming of the Doranen and the fall of Barl's Wall. Whatever happens, Lur will survive it too. If I believe nothing else, I believe that."

Wish I did. But he didn't say so out loud. Mayhap Pellen really did believe it, and weren't just tryin' to cheer him up. Spoilin' things for him wouldn't be very kind.

"Asher," said Pellen, still sharp. "I want you to promise me something."

Wary now, he shoved his hands in his pockets. "What?"

"Promise me you'll not do anything foolish on your own. That for once in your stubborn life you'll seek advice from those who care for you *before* you do something that can't be undone."

Pellen meant well, but he didn't understand. How could he? He weren't a mage. He couldn't feel the earth, he only walked on top of it.

"I'm wasting my breath, aren't I?" said Pellen, disappointed, falling back against his pillows. "You'll do what you think is right, no matter what I or Dathne or anyone else might say."

"I'm sorry, Pellen."

"Don't be. You're the Innocent Mage. It's not my place to—"

"Not your *place?*" he demanded. "When it's you who got Gar and Matt and Darran out of the City, away from Morg? The only reason we beat the bastard is 'cause of you." Breathing hard, he dragged a hand down his face. "Not your *place?* Sink me, Pellen, you dare say that again and I'll—I'll—"

"You'll what?" said Pellen, smiling. There was an ominous rattle in his chest. "Slap the dying man who's trying to save you?"

And what could he say to that? Nowt. But even if he'd had the words, tears were too close.

"Forget I asked it," said Pellen. "And promise me this, instead."

With a terrible effort, he made himself smile. "Sink me twice. What now?"

Leaning over, Pellen tugged open the drawer in his bedside table and pulled out a battered, dog-eared pack of playing cards. "Don't summon a horselir to eat me when I thrash you at zephyr."

Pellen, Pellen. *You be breakin' my bloody heart.* "Fine. I won't summon a horselir," he said, and returned to the chair by the bed. "But I ain't about to promise I won't make it snow down your nightshirt—*if* you beat me." Taking the cards, he began a swift shuffle. "'Cept you won't. So I reckon you be safe from snowfalls, for now."

"Goose."

Amid the hustle and bustle of the expedition's final preparations, now that Barlsman Jaffee had said his prayers over them, Goose was taking a quiet moment, it seemed, to gather his thoughts. Was sat on an upturned bucket outside his horse's stable round the back of Justice Hall, where Pintte and Baden's collected group of adventurers milled and argued and jostled.

"Goose," Rafel said again, when his friend didn't look up. "Have you got a spare ticktock?"

They'd spoken once since that afternoon of ale-brewing, when he'd told his friend he'd travel with him over the mountains. Just once he'd seen Goose, to break his promised word.

Goose lifted his head. "Rafe."

They stared at each other, silent, as around them Fernel Pintte and Sarle Baden and the other eight as were leaving, four Olken and four Doranen, fetched bridles and saddles, double-checked saddlebags and backpacks. Rafel spared them a glance, and didn't recognise one of them. Then he shoved his hands in his pockets. There were too many folk here, with big ears and flapping lips.

"Walk with me a little ways? Have you got time?"

Goose shrugged. "A minute or so. Can't walk far in a minute."

"We can walk far enough," he said, and nodded to the tree-shadowed pathway leading to the lane that ran behind the Hall. "If you want to."

Goose looked to where Fernel Pintte was in conversation with Sarle Baden. Not friends, those two, but joined in common cause. No more Doranen in Lur. "Meister Mayor!"

Pintte turned. When he saw who'd come visiting, his face collapsed in a scowl. "What?"

"Need to take a moment," said Goose. "I won't go far. Won't be long."

"And we won't wait for you if that's not the case," Pintte retorted. "Rafel—"

Rafel held up his hands. "Ain't come to cause trouble, Meister Mayor. Just need a word with Goose, here, before you go."

Fernel Pintte turned his back. So prob'ly that meant he and Goose had their moment.

Goose seemed to think so, 'cause he pushed himself off the bucket and threaded his way through the chaos towards the pathway. Guts twisting, Rafel followed. Joined him in the dappling shadows, his mouth crowded with words.

"Rafe, I ain't mad at you," Goose said, patient. Not smiling. "I've told you that once already. So if you're here to say sorry, save your breath. To be honest, I never really thought you'd come. I never thought your father would let you."

And that burned. "*Let* me?"

Goose rested a hand on his shoulder. Tightened his fingers and shook him, just a bit. "Rafe, I swear—sometimes you're thicker than a brick wall. He nearly got you killed in Westwailing. Did you truly think he'd let you out of his sight so soon after? Trust you to Fernel Pintte and Sarle Baden, when he blames them for what happened there? Don't be daft. Even if he wasn't stone-blind certain the expedition's going to go bad, he'd not risk you. And he is certain, isn't he?"

Goose's kind forbearance was worse than anger. They were the same age — yet oddly, his friend seemed older, of a sudden. And he felt younger. Like the little brother being left behind.

"It doesn't make him right."

"That's not the point, Rafe," said Goose, and let his hand drop. "The point is he *thinks* he's right. And your father's the most stubborn Olken in history. Did you know he came to see my dad? Tried to browbeat him into making me stay home?"

He stared at his friend, horrified. "Goose, I didn't know, I swear. I didn't ask him. I've hardly said a word to him since—" He chewed at his lip. "Goose, I'm sorry."

"Never mind. It doesn't matter," said Goose, frowning. "Rafe, don't you be a fool. Don't you let this come between you and him. Once we've got the way cleared over the mountains, once we've made friends with whoever we find on the other side, there'll be other expeditions. You and me can go next time."

He nearly said, *If there is a next time.* But that would sound mean, like he didn't believe he'd see Goose again. And the last thing he wanted was to make his friend think he thought that. Only...

"Maybe so, but this first expedition'll likely be dangerous, Goose. It ain't right you're going alone."

"Alone?" Goose nodded at the increased bustle in Justice Hall's rear courtyard. "With that lot?"

"Goose..."

Goose heaved a deep sigh. "You know what your trouble is, Rafe? I'll tell you. You think just 'cause you've got a dash of Doranen magic in you that you're a bit better than everyone else."

That made him blink. "What?"

"And you think I can't look after myself," said Goose, eyebrows lifted, challenging. "You think that if you're not around to save me, I'm

as good as dead already." He smiled, friendly but pointed. "That's a mite insulting, y'know."

"What?"

"Kindly meant," Goose added. "But still insulting. You keep saying as how you're not a sprat any more. Well, that makes two of us, Rafe. I don't need a nursemaid and I don't need you to save me. Wanted your company, mind. This expedition won't be the same without you. But like I said. There's always the next one."

Shaken silent, Rafel stared at him. Had Goose lost his mind? Or had he spent so much time with Fernel Pintte and Sarle Baden that he'd got himself infected by their blind arrogance? Was this how Da felt, faced with a whole Council chamber full of men and women like Goose, who'd let themselves be hoodwinked and bamboozled by hope and fear?

He swallowed. "I don't think I'm better than you, Goose. But I do know I'm different. And the ways I'm different? I know they save lives. You're my best friend, you sinkin' fool. I don't want nowt to happen to you!"

"It won't," said Goose. Then he pulled a face. "Or if it does, there's nowt to say you could stop it. Besides, *someone's* got to go. Lur's a boiling pot with the lid stuck on tight. We've got to get the lid *off*. Or there'll be brawling and worse between us and the Doranen and when it comes to worse we both know who'll win."

How could he fratch with that? Every word Goose spoke was true. But even so . . . even so . . .

"Sink me sideways, Goose," he said, and pulled his friend into a rib-cracking embrace. "You better come back safe and sound."

"I will," said Goose, pounding him between the shoulder blades. "I'm coming back safe and sound just so I can say 'I told you so.'"

In the courtyard behind them, the sounds of horses clopping out of their stables. "Meister Martin!" shouted Fernel Pintte. "If you're coming with us, now's the time! Or stay behind and stuff your belly with regrets."

Goose let go, and stepped back. "You talk to your father, Rafe. You've only got one. And he's only got you. Well, Deenie too, but that's not the same. A man's son is his *son*."

"Aye," he said, unwilling to trust his voice further.

"*Talk* to him," Goose insisted. "Or I'll kick your arse black and blue when I come back."

"Looks like you'll be busy then. Saying '*I told you so.*' Kicking my arse."

Goose grinned, a flash of his old self. "I'll manage."

The bustle behind them was growing. They were out of time — out of time — "Goose," he said, on impulse. "About Deenie —"

And Goose *blushed*. "I know. I was going to say something and then —" He glanced away. "Tell her to wait for me, Rafe? Tell her —"

"*Meister Martin!*" shouted Pintte. "Last warning!"

"Coming, Meister Mayor!" Goose called back. Then he shrugged. "Sorry, Rafe. I've got to —"

"I know," he said, and stepped out of the way. "Go."

A crowd of family and friends had gathered to bid the expedition a private goodbye, before it got swamped and swallowed by the hundreds of gawkers lining the streets from the Square to the City gates. Olken and Doranen, they wept and hugged and exchanged fervent farewells. Goose's da near picked his son up off the ground, holding on to him.

Standing in the shadows, Rafel watched as one by one the men handpicked by Fernel Pintte and Sarle Baden extricated themselves from their well-wishers, climbed onto their horses and fell into orderly line. Sarle Baden first, then Fernel Pintte, then the other Doranen, then the Olken. Goose last. He was the youngest man by far. Of course they'd stick him on the end.

As Baden nudged his horse forward, leading the group out to the Square, Goose turned in his saddle. Smiled. Nodded. Rafel nodded back, a crushing pain in his chest. Then a wave of dread, of sick foreboding, washed over him. Threatened to suck him down to darkness like the whirlpool in Westwailing Harbour. And he knew...he *knew*...

This is going to end badly. I won't see Goose again.

Heartsick, he spun round, searching the jostling well-wishers, looking to find Goose's da and make him go after his son, drag him off his horse and keep him safe at home. But Goose's da was swept up in the tide of clamouring families...and the tide was pulling out, it was pouring after the expedition. The tail of Goose's skinny bay gelding disappeared through the archway, the sight of its rump swamped by heads and backs and waving arms.

Rafel tried to shout, but his voice was lost in everyone else's shouting. And then a huge roar went up from the crowd of Olken and Doranen in the Square. They must've caught their first look at mounted Fernel Pintte and Sarle Baden and the rest, so jaunty and dauntless, ready to ride to the City gates. Ride to the Black Woods. Climb over Barl's Mountains...and horribly die.

Goose. Goose, don't go. Come back.

As the last well-wishing stragglers scurried to catch up, the Justice Hall grooms, pressed into service, went to fetch shovels and stable-forks so they could put the place to rights. But after the very last ignorant family member had passed through the archway, still one person remained.

It was Da.

"You talk to your father, Rafe," Goose said. *"You've only got one. And he's only got you."*

The bright sunlight showed him Da's weary, careworn face. Showed him threads of grey hair. Showed him slumped shoulders and grieving eyes. Some of the awfulness that had swamped him faded. He stepped out of the shadows and walked to join him.

"Where've you been, then?" he said, struggling to sound careless. As though they'd not been silently raging for days and days. "You missed all the speechifying."

Da nodded. "Borin', was it?"

"Course it was. I near bloody nodded off."

A tiny, tiny tug of smile. "Where be your ma, and Deenie?"

"Ain't sure," he said. "I left them on the Chapel steps, being yapped at by Barlsman Jaffee. Charis was with them." Somehow, he managed a swift grin. "Three women together? Like as not they've gone shopping. You'll get back to the Tower tonight to find the treasury box empty."

"Like as not," Da agreed. "I were sittin' with Pellen a bit. Let him beat me at cards."

Rafel snorted. "You *let* the City's best zephyr player beat you? Right, Da. Course you did."

"Aye, well," said Da. "He ain't feelin' too spry these days, is Pellen. Got to cheer him up somehow." He flicked a glance at the dawdling Justice Hall stable hands, who had no reason to rush about their work. "I ain't in the mood for watchin' Pintte and them fools ride out the front gates. Walk back to the Tower with me."

Just like that, eh? Typical bloody Da. And what about Goose? That was his best friend heading off with Fernel Pintte. What if he wanted to wave him goodbye?

'Cept I don't. Not again.

"Goose ain't a fool, y'know," he said, feeling his simmering temper rise. "He's trying to help Lur."

"I know," said Da. "Ain't his fault he's been steered wrong, by his da and others. He be a good lad, Rafe. I'm sorry."

Aye, but sorry for what? *For treating me like a sprat? For making sure I couldn't go with him? For knowing I ain't going to see him again?* He didn't dare ask, just in case . . .

"Right."

"Come on, then," said Da, and started walking. Rafel stared after him for a moment, uncertain whether to go on being fratched — or to plump for feeling resigned. After a brief skirmish, he settled on resigned; he'd been fratched at Da for weeks now, and all he felt was miserable.

And I did promise Mama I'd make my peace.

They eased along alleys and through laneways, so the gawkers traipsing Dorana's streets wouldn't know they were there. Halfway back to the Tower the crowd dribbled away and they risked the straight way home, up the High Street to the gates of the palace.

Da didn't say another word until they were safely in the palace grounds, surrounded by flowers and trees, well away from prying eyes and eager ears. Then he sighed, and seemed to relax a bit. Slowed his determined march to a stroll, breathing just a mite too heavy. What Rafel could see of his face was sweaty, and gloomed with dark thoughts.

"Reckon I need to tell you somethin', Rafe," he said. "But afore I do, you got to promise me you won't say nowt on it. Not to your ma, not to Deenie. Not to anyone. You promise?"

They might be talking now, but he still felt inclined to snap. "Who've I got to tell, Da? You warned me off Charis and Goose is riding out of the City and—and he ain't coming back."

Slowed almost to stopping, Da swung round. "Why d'you say that?"

"Why?" Instead of slowing, he stopped altogether. Fisted his hands on his hips and stared at his father, incredulous. "Why d'you bloody think? 'Cause I'm a mage just like you, Da, and I *feel* things. Why d'you bloody think I was so set on travelling with him? Why d'you think I never wanted him out of my sight?"

"And why d'*you* think," Da retorted, his voice husky, unsteady, "*I* made bloody sure you stayed put?"

So much for making his peace. *Goose.* He couldn't answer. Could barely breathe. Rage was a red mist smearing his vision.

"Rafel," said Da, and took him hard by both shoulders. "You think I don't know how you feel, sprat? *I know.* I spoke the words that *killed* my best friend."

"Then how could you stop me?" he said, his voice cracking. "When you know Goose needs me, Da, how could you keep me here?"

"'Cause *I* need you more!" said Da, shaking him. "I need you with me, Rafe, 'cause what I *don't* know is if I can stop what's comin'. Not without you. Just like I couldn't save them fools in Westwailin' without you. I be too hurt and worn out to do this alone. And there ain't another mage in all Lur I can ask."

"Ask to do what, Da?" he said, retreating. "What's coming to Lur?"

Letting go, Da stared at him, so intent. "You ain't felt it?"

"No. Da, I don't know what you're talking about."

"Thought you might've felt it," Da muttered. "And not said nowt 'cause you and me ain't been talkin'. What about Deenie? Has she felt it, and not told me or your ma?"

"Felt *what,* Da? What are you—" And then his throat closed. His heart, already thumping, thumped harder. Rattled his ribs. "Are you saying it's starting again? Like before? The storms? The tremors?"

"Worse than before, Rafe," said Da. "Much worse."

"How do you know? Have *you* felt something?"

"No," said Da, after a moment. "Not yet. But it's comin', Rafe. Trust me."

He didn't want to hear this. "You could be wrong, Da. Things were bad ten years ago, weren't they? And then they got better. I think they're getting better again, right now. It's stopped raining and—what? *What?*"

Da was shaking his head. Almost laughing, but his eyes were terrible. "Sink me, Rafe. The only reason Lur didn't rip itself to bits ten years ago is 'cause I nigh on killed m'self, holdin' it together."

"*You* held it—" Suddenly cold, even in the unclouded sunshine, Rafel stared back at his father. Remembered something his mother had said, about the sacrifices Da had made. He felt small, a boy again. Looking to his father to make everything all right. But from the look on Da's face... "How? The truth, Da. No more bloody secrets."

"Come on," said Da, grabbing his shirt-sleeve. "Reckon it's easier to show you than tell you."

They went to the Weather Chamber.

Awestruck, silent, Rafel stared around the sunlit room. He'd never set foot in this place. He'd wanted to, often enough. He'd even dreamed of sneaking in, with Goose, back when they were sprats. But something always stopped him. Some instinct, some deep, nameless feeling, that to come here without Da, to come here uninvited, would be to cross a line... one he could never cross back over.

Da was looking at him, almost—almost *anxious*. "You feel it, don't you? You can feel what were done here for six hundred bloody years. Even though the Weather Magic ain't burned into your bones."

The air in the glass-domed chamber was cool and dry, and it thrummed against his bare skin like a drumbeat in the distance. Echoes of power. Echoes of pain. Echoes of voices, screaming in the night.

"Yes," he said softly. "I can feel it."

"Ha," said Da, briefly pleased. "Knew you would, sprat." Then he nodded, scowling. "And that's the Weather map. Sinkin' bloody thing."

Moving closer, he stared at the map, marvelling. He didn't know much about it—Da never said, nor Mama. Darran had never seen it, but he'd known a few stories and told them once or twice. He'd called it beautiful, and he was right. A pity about the scattered patches of blight marring its intricate details.

"Touch it," said Da.

Startled, he looked up. "Me? But—"

"Touch it," Da insisted. "Then tell me what you feel."

Hesitant, he reached out one finger to the map—then snatched his hand back, gagging, and scrubbed it over his mouth as though he'd just bitten into something rotten. The map felt like Westwailing, like the magics spat out by the whirlpools and the waterspouts and Dragonteeth Reef. Diseased. Rancid. Bloated black, like a corpse.

"Morg."

Da was nodding. "Aye, Morg's in there, the bastard. But d'you feel anythin' else?"

"I don't know," he said, his belly churning. He wanted to retch.

"Touch it again, sprat," said Da. "For as long as you can stand."

That was the last thing he wanted to do, but it was Da asking, so...

"I don't know," he said again, when his guts finally stopped heaving. "At first I thought it was dead, but—"

"But you ain't sure?" Da said, watching him closely. "You reckon you might feel a tiny spark of somethin', buried under the blight?"

"I think so." Then he shrugged. "Or could be I'm just imagining it."

Sighing, Da came to stand beside him. Pressed his palm flat to the map. His tired face tightened with revulsion. "You ain't," he said at last, through gritted teeth. "There be a spark of power there. Almost burned out now. You be good all right, sprat, if you can feel it."

The compliment warmed him. The look in Da's eyes killed that warmth. "What does it mean? I thought all Lur's Weather Magic was long gone. I thought it died with Morg, when the Wall came down."

Da sighed again. "That be what we told folk, Rafe. Me and Pellen and your ma. We thought it were safest that way, see? We thought the worst were behind us, and Lur were free of Doranen meddling. We thought."

Chilled, he stared at the map. "You were wrong?"

"Aye, sprat," said Da, sounding so sad. "We were wrong."

And with a whispered word, and a tracery of burning sigils, Da made snow fall beneath the chamber's glass-domed roof.

The stunned delight in Rafel's face as he watched the snow fall made the pain of calling it not matter. Made it hardly hurt at all. Asher felt the trickling blood on his lips, tasted it on his tongue, and didn't care. Rafe were smiling. They were talking again.

Whatever else comes, at least we got that much.

"Da, it's—it's—I want to do that," said Rafe, his voice hushed, fingers reaching to touch the tiny, drifting white flakes. "Show me how to do that."

Simple pleasure died. Shaking his head, he banished the snow. "Can't, sprat."

Hurt, Rafel stared at him, snowflakes melting in the palm of his hand. "Why not?"

"The Weather Magic's lost. It be long dead and gone."

"But you just said—"

"As good as," he added. "What's left of it be in me. And when I die, it'll be dead for good."

"But that means it ain't dead now," Rafe argued. "So you could teach me. Da—"

Closing his eyes, Asher took a deep breath. *Sorry, sprat. Sorry. But I won't curse you with this.* "Weather Magic can't be learned like other Doranen magic, Rafe. I be the last WeatherWorker of Lur."

Disappointed, Rafe hunched his shoulders. "Then why did you bring me here?"

"'Cause I got to break a promise to your ma, and I don't want to do it alone."

"*Da*—" Rafe stamped about a bit, just like he used to when he were a sprat, and thwarted. "Stop turning everything into a bloody riddle, would you? Just tell me what we're doing here, simple and straight out, or I'm leaving."

He had to smile, even though he were sick with nerves. With the echoes of pain. "Sink me, you got a mouth on you."

"Sink *me*," Rafe retorted. "Look, Da! I'm walking to the door—"

He stepped in front of his son. Pressed one palm flat to Rafe's chest. "No, you ain't."

"Da..." Rafe turned away. "No more games. It ain't been a good day and—" He turned back again. "Please. No more games."

The pain in his son, for Goose, were like a knife stuck in his own heart. *Forgive me, sprat. I would've spared you if I could.* "Rafe, the last time things went bad in Lur, I came up here and I put 'em to rights by pourin' more Weather Magic into that bloody map."

Rafel's mouth fell open. "You what? But—*how?*"

So he explained. Told his son the truth of what had happened when he were a boy of ten, holding nowt back.

"So... you weren't bedridden with an ague those weeks," Rafe said, when the tale was told. "When me and Deenie were sent off with Uncle Pellen and Charis for that jaunt down to the Dingles."

He shook his head. "No, that were a taradiddle. Like I told you—I nigh on killed m'self fuddlin' with the Weather map. Your ma—" He winced, remembering. "She ain't never been so fratched at me her whole life. But I didn't have a choice, Rafe. Just like I ain't got a choice now."

Swallowing, Rafel looked at the Weather map. "You want to do it again?"

"No, I don't bloody want to!" he snapped. "But if I don't—we'll see the end of Lur. A lot of folks'll die. And if Pintte's expedition does make it back home across them mountains, what they'll find..." He grimaced. "Rafe, I got to do it."

"Da—" Rafel stamped about a bit more. "There's got to be something else we can do. You said it yourself—you're not strong enough for this."

Admitting it hurt, but his pride weren't something Lur could afford just now. "I *know*, Rafe. That be why I need you."

Rafe stopped his stamping. "Da, you promised Mama. If you do this, she won't forgive you."

"Rafe..." He gave his son a weary smile. "One of these days I'll sit you down and I'll tell you some of the things your ma and me have forgiven each other. She'll be fratched, I don't deny it...but she'll get over it. Ain't nobody knows Lur comes first better than your ma."

Folding his arms tight, Rafe started pacing again. "I still say you could be wrong. If what you say is true, Deenie would've felt something. You know what she's like. She'd be in tears all over the place or waking us all up with nightmares. So I reckon—"

"Then you'd reckon wrong, sprat," he said quietly. "'Cause for one thing, last time this happened I started feelin' things were goin' wrong long afore anyone else. And for another, I be the WeatherWorker."

"Which means what, Da?" said Rafe, challenging. "You want me to help you, then I want to know." His eyes narrowed. "No more secrets, remember? After Westwailing you owe me that much."

You owe me. The sprat was so angry. No matter how he explained why he and Dath had tampered with him, Rafe might never understand. But right now there weren't time for explanations. Explanations would have to wait.

A sudden, clutching fear. "Rafe, you ain't been trying anything, have you? You ain't snuck off to—"

"To what, Da? *Play?*" Rafe's fingers curled to fists. "And if I have?"

"Rafe—"

"Don't worry, Da. I know better. I know what's inside me is bloody dangerous."

Sick with relief, he nodded. "We'll work this out, sprat. I promise. When Lur's sorted, we'll work this out."

Rafe nodded. "We surely will, Da."

"Right. Well. About bein' WeatherWorker. It means I feel things different. Good as you are, Rafe, you can't feel everythin'. And what I feel..." He didn't try to hide his shiver. "Rafe, once things have gone from bad to worse, I'm feared they'll bring Lur to an end. Not just the land, sprat, but the people with it. I'm feared what's comin' will set us at each other's throats."

"But Da, we're peaceful," said Rafe, shaking his head. "We always have been. I don't believe we'd—"

"Rafe, *think*," he said, desperate. "We only be peaceful 'cause there ain't nowt to fight on. But with the reef's magic havin' wrecked every harbour, and no more fishin', and crops that ain't yieldin' what we need 'em to yield—d'you reckon we'll survive another calamity with the weather? More floods, more sick, drowned stock, more folk washed out of their homes? D'you reckon there won't be hunger and panic and folk branglin' in the streets? D'you reckon the Doranen won't start thinkin' on how life weren't this complicated when they were in charge?"

Rafe looked at him, uncertain. "But—we got laws, Da. They wouldn't—they couldn't—"

"Course they would. Course they *could*. Laws only protect folk when everyone abides by 'em. But if them as be stronger wakes up one mornin' and decides they don't fancy followin' them laws no more—what's to stop 'em from doin' whatever they bloody like?"

It broke his heart, stripping Rafel of his belief that life were safe and always would be. *I fought Morg so this wouldn't happen again. Gar died so none of us would be frighted again.* So were the fightin' and the dyin' for nowt, in the end? Were that the harsh lesson Lur was bein' taught?

"Da..." Rafe folded his arms, his jaw stubbornly clenched. "Say I agree with you. Say things are set to turn as bad as you think. That doesn't mean you should risk your life again. At least—not before you have to. Not before it's clear there really ain't no other choice."

"Rafel, I *told* you—"

"*No!*" Rafe said, and started his pacing. "You can wait a bit longer, Da. At least till Deenie feels something too. I heard everything you said, I did, but—but could be you can't exactly trust what you feel. I mean, you're fretted about Uncle Pellen, and you ain't over what happened down in Westwailing, and maybe doing this right now, Da, maybe it ain't such a good idea."

Oh, Rafe. "And maybe," he said, "if I can get some more power into that bloody Weather map, and stop the weather failin' on us, there'll be time for you to ride after Goose and tell him he don't need to go over them mountains. His da told me all about it, Rafe, how the brewers be worried for their oats and their barley and their bloody hops. So if I fix things here..."

Shocked, Rafe stopped his pacing. *"Da—"*

"I know you be scared he's goin' to die somewhere out there," he said. "So if I won't let you go with him—and Rafe, I never will—then I reckon I ought to try my best to keep him out of mischief."

Tears filled his son's eyes. "But Da...what if *you* die?"

"I won't," he said. "Not with you here. 'Cause that be your job, eh? Keepin' an eye on me. Makin' sure I don't die."

"That's my job?" said Rafe, incredulous. "When I don't know the first bloody thing about Weather Magic? *Da—*"

He shrugged. "You might not have the Weather Magic but you got the potential for it. You can feel it in the map. And there be all that power in you, that I might need to borrow again." He tried to smile. "If you don't mind."

"Mind? Da, don't be bloody stupid." Rafe took a deep breath. Blew it out, hard. "So, what do I do? What do *you* do? How does it work, you putting power into that map?"

"I don't rightly know," he admitted. "Just...it be part of the Weather Magic. Part of me. All you got to do is not let me go too far. Stop me afore I pour all of m'self into the bloody thing. 'Cause it'll suck me dry if I ain't careful."

"This is mad," Rafe muttered, and half-turned away. "Da—"

He took one step towards his son, and stopped. "You can do this, Rafe. You can. I got faith in you."

Slowly, very slowly, Rafe turned back. "Have you?"

The doubt in his son's eyes was a punishment. *Do I deserve it? Prob'ly.* "Hidin' your magic weren't never about trustin' you. I only did it to keep you safe."

Rafe nodded. "I know."

"But you be fratched anyway," he said. "And you don't forgive me."

A glitter in Rafe's eyes. "Say you were wrong, Da."

But I weren't. "I was wrong."

"Say you're sorry."

I ain't sorry, and I never bloody will be. "I'm sorry, Rafel."

Silence in the chamber. In the dome-filtered sunshine, Barl's Weather map gleamed, slowly dying.

"All right," said Rafe. "But you're telling Mama this was all *your* idea."

He tousled his son's short hair, in passing. "You drive a hard bloody bargain, sprat. Now let's get ourselves settled, eh? And we'll do what we can do to save this sorry bloody kingdom, afore it's too late."

CHAPTER TWENTY-TWO

❊

"Pass me the tea caddy, Deenie?" said Charis, as she swished freshly boiled water in the pot to warm it.

Deenie took the caddy down from its shelf above Charis's kitchen bench, prised off its lid, made sure the scoop was in there, then handed it over.

"Thanks," said Charis, with a half-hearted smile.

Watching her toss careless scoops of loose dried peppermint leaves into the teapot, feeling her friend's strictly concealed upset, she blinked back tears. "Mama might not be a proper pother, Charis, but she knows all about herbs and possets. I'm sure Uncle Pellen will feel better soon."

Charis nodded. "I'm sure, too."

Except she wasn't. Deenie could feel that she wasn't, just as she could feel Uncle Pellen's slowly failing spirit and Ma's terrible, wrenching grief—not only for her friend, but for her husband and son, as well. Their feelings tangled inside her, making it hard to breathe. Making her head hurt, and her throat. After weeks of Da's misery and Rafel's rage it was enough to make her burst into sobs.

I hate feeling things. I wish I could snap my fingers and turn into stone.

No-one could tell her why she was like this. Not Pother Kerril, not Pother Nix, not even Mama or Da. *He* said it was 'cause she was special. As though somehow that would make it all right. Well, it didn't. She didn't want to be special, not if it meant living the rest of her life feeling other people's hurts like they were her own. And the older she got, the harder she felt them, as though the seed of her feeling things grew as she grew.

What will it be like when I've finished my growing? I don't want to find out. I want to find a way to stop it.

Not even Charis properly understood, and she was a mage with power. She said she knew how it felt. But even when she was weepy with what she could feel in Lur, it wasn't the same. No-one was the same.

No-one is like me, not even Da.

The loneliness of that was almost too hard to bear.

With the boiling water added to the teapot, Charis swirled it round a few times then set the tea aside to draw. "I'm so glad you bought that shawl, Deenie. That shade of blue is so pretty on you."

Deenie glanced at the kitchen table, where she and Mama had carelessly dropped their parcels. "I do love it. But I wish you'd bought the green one."

"I didn't need it," said Charis, putting the lid back on the tea caddy. "I have a green shawl already. And besides —"

"Besides what?" she prompted.

"Nothing," said Charis, and made herself smile. "Maybe next time. Anyway, it's fun to look at things without buying them."

"Charis..." She hesitated. *I don't want to pry.* But they were close as sisters. "Charis, is it — is it money?"

"No!" said Charis, quickly, hotly — but then her face crumpled, and she nodded. "The possets Papa needs now, the herbs are so rare. Especially with the rain and the flooding. It's not that there isn't money, there is, but — I don't know how long it has to last, Deenie. I don't know how long —"

"Oh, Charis," she whispered. "I'm so sorry. I wish —"

With a heartbreaking effort, Charis banished her fears. Blinked back the tears, tilted her chin, and carefully untied her frilly yellow apron and hung it on its hook by the muslin-curtained kitchen window.

"I meant to ask you before, how's Rafel? I never see him around. Well, just that once in the street the other day, but—that's not the same."

Oh, Charis. Her friend tried to seem indifferent, but whenever she spoke of Rafel her heart leapt into her eyes. A few days after Uncle Pellen's farewell ball, when she couldn't help herself, she'd asked if Rafel ever spoke of her. The hurt when she found out no, he didn't—it was awful.

"Rafe's fine," Deenie said, cautiously. "Only a bit upset that Goose is leaving."

"Of course he's upset," said Charis, all swift compassion. "They're best friends, him and Goose." She reached for a cloth and dabbed the bench dry. Snuck a sly, sideways glance, looking for a moment exactly like her old self. "What about you, Deenie? Are you upset Goose is leaving?"

She felt the heat rush into her cheeks. "I don't know what you mean."

"I think you do," said Charis. "Haven't you seen how he looks at you? I have. Are you sweet on him? He's ever so nice."

And how was this suddenly about her and Goose? "Charis, you're imagining things," she said, flustered. "And Rafel is *fine.*"

The teasing light died out of Charis's eyes. "Well, good. That's good," she said, and kept on drying the dry bench.

Deenie watched her, worried. She'd never come right out and asked Rafel if he liked Charis especially. She thought he did, even though he never spoke of her. She thought it was 'cause he *did* like her that he flirted with so many other girls when there were parties and balls in the City. Girls he liked well enough, but not so much it made him uncomfortable.

Charis made him uncomfortable.

"But he's still awful cross with Da," she added. "If only they'd *talk* to each other, I know they could fix things. But they're both so stubborn, Charis. Mama's at her wits' end with the pair of them, and so am I. If we were still on the coast I swear I'd push them both in the harbour, waterspouts or not, and then—"

But Charis wasn't listening. Fresh tears had welled into her eyes and this time she didn't blink them away. And then she was slumping on the kitchen bench, her shoulders shaking. Over Rafel?

Please, please, don't let it be about Rafel.

"Oh, Deenie," Charis whispered, the tears flowing down her cheeks. "I'm so afraid. Papa—Papa, he's—oh, I can't say it. I *can't.*"

So, not about Rafel. And now she wished it was. Charis's pain for her father was a dreadful thing, as hungry as the whirlpools in Westwailing Harbour. But as her arms went out to hold and to comfort, she felt a fresh wave of awfulness crash over her. Sharp as broken glass, the pain sliced through her chest and throat, stealing her breath. She let go of her friend and ran for the scullery. Flung herself over the big stone tub, retching and retching, as her head spun and her body shivered hot then cold then hot.

"Deenie!"

And that was Mama, shaking with alarm. Charis must have fetched her from Uncle Pellen's chamber. Blindly she turned and let her mother's loving arms shelter her. Buried her wet face against her mother's shoulder and sobbed.

"Deenie, what is it?" said Mama. "What do you feel?"

Mama's hand stroked her hair, over and over. But it only dulled a little bit the glass pains in her chest and throat. "Da," she choked out. "Mama, Da's hurting."

She felt her mother tense. The softly stroking hand stopped. "What kind of hurting?"

"The magic kind, Mama," she said, squeezing her eyes tight shut. "And it's bad. It's very bad."

"Jervale spare us," Mama muttered. "I'll make him bloody sorry he ever met me. *Charis!*"

Charis was hovering in the open doorway, so scared. "Aunt Dathne?"

"We have to go, child," said Mama. "Tell your father he must stay in bed again tomorrow. Tell him I'll come back with another posset by the evening. No getting up, mind. You'll see he keeps under his blankets?"

"Yes, Aunt Dathne," said Charis, her voice wobbly with fright. "I'll tell him. Is—is Deenie all right?"

"Of course. She's just tired," said Mama. "It's been a long, exciting day. Come along, Deenie. Let's get you home. Charis—"

"Yes?"

"Run outside, child," said Mama. "Find a cart or a carriage that can take us back to the Tower. It's too far for Deenie to walk when she's feeling unwell. Use Asher's name, to be certain of help."

Deenie lifted her head, ashamed. Saw the fright in Charis's face. Felt like a fool, and so sick. "Oh no, Mama. Please. Don't make a fuss. I can walk. Charis, I'm all right. Don't fret for me. I'm only—"

"Hush!" said Mama fiercely. "You'll do as you're told. Charis, what are you waiting for? *Go.*"

Charis fled.

"Deenie," said Mama, holding her. "Quickly. While we're alone. You're sure it's your father? That he's meddling with magic?"

She sounded so raw, Deenie broke free of her embrace and stared at her. "Yes, Mama. It's Da. I know what he feels like."

The look in Mama's eyes—she'd never seen it before. Never felt this kind of frightened rage in her, not even down in Westwailing. "Where is he, Deenie? Can you tell?"

Reluctant, she opened herself to the messy, hot pain. "I—I'm not sure. But I think—yes, he's with Rafe. I can feel Rafe a little bit. He's not hurting, not like Da. But he's frighted. And I can feel—there's something else. Power. A lot of power. A lot of strong magic." She tried, but she couldn't stop the whimper. "I can't tell where they are, Mama. I'm sorry. I'm sorry."

"No, no, no, it's all right, Deenie." Mama pressed a hand to her forehead, distracted, so much fear in her eyes. "I think I know where they are. I think I know what they're doing." A sob caught in her throat, half-anguished, half-angry. "Oh, Asher. I'm going to *kill* you."

Trembling, she shrank from her mother's rage. "What's happening, Mama? What—"

"Oh, Deenie, it's all right," said Mama, and kissed her. "You mustn't be frighted, mouse. Whatever they're playing at, I'm sure Da and your brother will be fine."

Except she didn't believe it.

I don't believe it either. This is bad, like Westwailing. Oh, Da. Rafel. What have you done?

"Da!" Rafel shouted, falling to his knees beside his stricken father. "Da, what is it? What's gone wrong?"

He'd thought what he'd seen in Westwailing was something, but it was nowt compared to Da pouring power into Barl's Weather map. Fantastic, fiery sigils, setting the air alight. The chamber's glass dome had trembled, smashed shafting sunlight to rainbows. He'd felt his blood burn, his hair stir. Da's Weather Magic called to him, shuddering his bones.

But now blood was streaming from his father's eyes, as though someone had tried to gouge them from his skull with a blunt gutting knife. More blood flowed from his nose, even his mouth.

"Da!" he shouted again. "Can you hear me? Can you talk?"

Da didn't answer. Sprawled across the Weather map, he only coughed and groaned.

Barl's bloody tits, Da! Don't let you die, you said. How am I s'posed to do that?

Shaking, he pressed one hand to the Weather map then recoiled, sickened, feeling Morg's filthy magic all stirred up in there and spitting. *Don't be a coward, Rafel. Da needs you—and so does Goose.* Retching, he touched the map again, and this time caught a fleeting glimpse of Barl's magic. Stronger than it had felt before Da started pouring himself into the map...so something had happened. Something good, before it all went bad.

He bent close to his father, pressed his lips to Da's ear. "It's working, Da," he whispered. "Don't stop. Let me help. Take my magic, like you did in Westwailing. Take as much as you need. Take all of it, I don't care."

Blood bubbling on his lips, eyes closed, Da nodded. "Hold...my hand...sprat."

Barely breathing, he wrapped his fingers round Da's hand. It felt cold. Weak. Da wasn't an ole man. Why did he feel like an ole man?

His magic's killing him. This is what he meant. Weather Magic's bloody murder. Oh, Da.

Da groaned again, then opened his eyes. His face was masked in blood. "I'm sorry, Rafe. It's goin' to hurt you. Worse than Westwailin'."

"I don't care, Da. It doesn't matter. Just hurry. Let's get this done so we can see you safe in bed, all right?"

Da's ole man fingers tightened, and he tried to smile. Rafel tried to smile back at him, his heart racing. Then he breathed out, slow and deep, and gave up his magic, all of it, to his father.

Furious heat...freezing cold...thunder and lightning and snowstorms in his mind. A high, sweet voice screaming. That was Barl's voice, twisted in pain. Morg's voice, full of hatred, snarled beneath it.

Rafel choked, his blood turned to fire. And then he howled, because a whirlpool was sprung to life in his head. He could hear Da howling with him as the greedy, starving map tried to suck them both dry. The Weather Magic was pitiless. It was the worst pain he'd ever felt, like shards of shattered glass slicing him to ribbons. It was in Da, not him, but still he could feel it, storming through both of them without pause or mercy.

"Da—Da—" He was weeping, and he didn't care. "Da, stop. There's something wrong. I don't think it's meant to be like this...*Da!*"

Lost inside the Weather Magic, Da couldn't hear him.

Rafel tried to let go of his father's hand, but he couldn't. The magic had melded them. Was draining both of them dry.

Without warning, the sunlit weather chamber plunged into darkness. Eyes bloodied, vision blurring, Rafel looked up. Saw ugly greenish-black clouds boiling above the glass dome. The temperature within the chamber plummeted. Hail rattled. Rain pounded. The chamber's parquetry floor shook.

"Da! Is that you? Are you doing this?" he shouted. "Da, you've got to stop! Da, stop it, *please!*"

Beneath its wet, scarlet mask, Da's face had drained milk-white. Desperate and dizzy, Rafel struggled to prise his father's fingers loose, struggled to get free of him, to break the cruel bonds of magic before it killed them. As the sudden storm raged overhead, and the Weather map beneath his hand thrummed and sizzled and burned with power, he fought to save them...

Except he had no idea how to break a working.

But I can figure it out. I figured how to crack stones, and dance leaves, and make waves in my bath. I unpicked a Doranen lock and I collapsed waterspouts in Westwailing Harbour. I did all of that, I can bloody do this.

But before he could defeat the pain, he had to accept it. That was the hardest part—letting the pain take him and shake him like a rat-dog with a rat. Surrendering, he sank himself beneath the surface of raw magic...

...and saw the bonds of Da's working like ropes of fire, binding him and his father so tight. But the scarlet flames were blighted black, infected by Morg's lingering malice. Twisted, distorted, they tried to destroy what they were designed to nurture. Burning, they burned him. He was weeping with the pain.

I can't...I can't...

Da's strength was swiftly failing, even as the storm beyond the Weather Chamber grew more and more ferocious. His own strength was failing. He could feel himself being emptied without mercy, feel the ravenous theft of everything he had, everything he was and hoped one day to be. His mind was spinning. Fading. Within heartbeats he'd be gone—and so would Da.

Now or never.

With the scant power that remained to him, trusting to instinct, trusting himself, he ripped the binding ropes apart. Destroyed the working link. Pulled himself free from death, and Da with him. He hoped. He heard Da cry out. Felt him shudder. Felt Barl's Weather map writhing in pain. Felt the earth of Lur writhe with it, convulsing, and his body being tossed aside as the storm beyond the Weather Chamber shook its fist and smashed harder.

Rafel opened his eyes. *"Da."* His voice was shredded. His throat raw. "Da, can you hear me?"

Da was groaning, his breathing harsh and disordered. Splotches of his dripping blood disfigured the Weather map. He was still sprawled across it, still trying to give it power. Rafel could feel his Weather Magic sparking, struggling, feeding the map and the storm beyond the chamber in mean dribs and drabs.

But dribs and drabs were enough. The damage continued.

"No—Da, no, you have to stop," he said, and rolled disjointed to his hands and knees. Crawled by inches back to his father. Took him by the shoulders and tried to drag him off the map. "Please, Da—please. *Help* me. You have to *stop!*"

But lost inside the Weather Magic, lost to sense and reason, Da fought him. Rafel felt his tears fall hot, like burning embers.

This is my fault. It's my fault. I was meant to keep him safe.

"Da, please, please, come back. Please let go. *Come back."*

And with the little strength that was left to him, the miserly dregs, like cracking stones as a spratling he wrenched his father free. Tumbled with him to the parquetry floor. Held him close, as though he was the father and Da was his son, wounded and in dire need.

"I got you, Da, I got you," he whispered. "It's Rafel, Da. I got you. Don't fret, I won't let go."

No reply. Could Da even hear him? *What do I do now?*

And then the chamber door flew open and Mama burst in, raging worse than any storm, soaking wet and steaming with fury. Deenie crept in behind her. Just as wet, but not angry. Weeping. Trembling so hard her teeth chattered.

She felt us. Oh, sink me. Of course she bloody felt us.

"What's he done, Rafel?" Mama demanded as she strode across the floor. "What's the bloody fool done? Has he killed himself? Has he killed us all?"

Rafel scrambled sideways as Mama dropped to the floor beside him and hauled Da into her arms. "He—he was trying to fix the Weather map. Fix Lur. With Weather Magic. Like he did last time. He—we—the map—"

"*We?*" Mama demanded. "Do you mean you were *helping* him?"

Her eyes were so dreadful he couldn't look at her. He stared at the floor. "Aye," he whispered. "He asked me to. Mama, he practically begged me. How could I say no? But something went wrong. The Weather map, it—"

"Of course something went wrong!" Mama shouted. In the chamber doorway, Deenie sobbed. "The bloody map's *wrecked*. It's *ruined*. It nearly killed him the last time and he swore to me, he *swore*—"

"Dathne," Da said, his voice a croak, and opened his blood-caked eyes. His reaching fingers touched her tear-streaked face. "Don't fratch at the sprat. It ain't his fault. And don't fratch at me, neither, you—you slumskumbledy wench. I had to do it. I had to. I—"

"*Asher!*" Mama screamed, as Da began convulsing. Began thrashing like a line-hooked fish hauled to its slow death on a pier. "*Asher!*"

But Da couldn't hear her. And over their heads thunder crashed, and lightning cracked, and a terrible, terrible rain poured down...

PART THREE

CHAPTER TWENTY-THREE

✵

A rlin travelled to Dorana City in his father's expensive, perfectly sprung carriage. Except, of course, it was *his* carriage now. It was all his: the vineyards, the mansion, the City townhouse, the treasury. The library. The Garrick estate, to which he was the sole heir. With so much wealth gained, so swiftly, some might say he should be grateful to Asher and Rafel. He was sure some *did* say it, behind his back, where they couldn't be overheard.

But let them say it to my face.

Nine days had trudged by since ignorant Sarle Baden had departed the City, leading the expedition that should have been his, too. That would have been his if grief hadn't felled him. If Baden hadn't shoved him aside.

And now he'll fail. He'll not find Lost Dorana. The fool. If he'd not been so arrogant, so eager to usurp Father's dream as his own. If he'd been willing to be led. Then I might have helped him. Then I might have told him what Father knew, and I know, and nobody else.

Since the expedition's departure it seemed Lur was fallen to pieces, was floundering, aimless, as the length and breadth of its dire predicament finally was understood. The rain had returned, soaking into the still-soaked ground. The storms were back as well, causing fresh floods, and the earth tremors, more violent and vicious than ever. Half the

Garrick vineyards were rot-ruined already, his envied inheritance turning to slime before his eyes. And Lur was rotting right along with it. Asher's fault, all of it. No proof yet, but he knew. Every ill in the kingdom could be traced back to him. Every ill ...

My father is dead.

The carriage was slowing. They'd reached Dorana already? Well, perhaps it wasn't to be wondered at. With the miserable weather and the constant fear of not knowing where lightning might strike, when the earth might tremble, gaping and greedy to swallow men whole, not many were willing to risk journeying far on the open roads.

He pulled aside the carriage window's curtain and looked outside. They'd passed through the open City gates and were heading for the General Council chamber behind the central Market Square. He saw rain. Mud. A scattering of wet, unhappy faces. Some misguided, self-deluded Olken were out and about, trying to pretend the world wasn't drowning around them. Trying to pretend they weren't drowning with it.

Drowning. *Westwailing Harbour, whipped ferocious and deadly. The cold shock of immersion as he plunged into the water. Pain and confusion as he was dragged into the skiff. And his father ... his father ... that last dreadful glimpse of him in the whirlpool. Screaming. Spinning. Spinning, then sucked under to die.* Rafel's fault — and Asher's. He'd hardly eaten since. Who needed food with a belly full of hate?

I must have justice. Murder cannot remain unavenged.

And he would have it — but not by proxy. Sarle Baden might have had faith in the workings of Justice Hall, but he knew better. Father had taught him well. The Hall's corrupt lackeys were not to be trusted. Besides ... revenge would mean nothing if it were not deeply personal. Meted out by his own hand.

At last the carriage reached its destination, and he strode into the Council chamber building intent upon driving home to the incompetents who passed for leaders in this soaked, sorry kingdom that the great Rodyn Garrick must be remembered in *blood*. Asher might be lying on his deathbed but his misbegotten, unnatural son lived. His son could pay. His son *would* pay — or Lur's Olken would feel the weight of Lord Arlin Garrick's heavy hand.

The Council chamber was in an uproar. Pellen Orrick, grey-faced and surely deserving of his own lingering deathbed, for he looked half-dead — was raging at the gathered councilors.

"— was right! *Again!* Why didn't you listen? If you'd listened Asher wouldn't be paying the price for your stubborn disbelief! Barl save us, we don't deserve him!"

Admitted to the chamber by two easily cowed City guards, Arlin stood unnoticed as Orrick sank sweating and coughing into his chair, and the unchastened Council defended itself against his accusations. Shouted at him, and each other. He felt ill, to be witnessing his people so lower themselves as to seek understanding from Olken.

We are Doranen. The greatest mages the world has ever seen. How have we forgotten that? How have we become these meek, mewling supplicants? Father was right. I never should have doubted him. We have betrayed our proud heritage, inviting our own destruction.

Speaker Shifrin, that fat Olken fool, was adding to the mayhem by clanging his bell, which not a single councilor attended. Shifrin was useless. So was Barslman Jaffee, more concerned with Orrick's wheezing than in imposing discipline on the rabble. And Rafel? Where was Rafel? Was he even here?

Yes. There he was. Returning to the Speaker's table with a pitcher. Watching him succour Pellen Orrick, pour ale into a glass for him and steady his shaking hand as he drank, Arlin felt a wave of loathing so intense that for a moment he thought he might not keep his feet.

And then it passed, and he had himself coldly under control. That was important. Father would despise him should he allow emotion to weaken his resolve.

"Meister Speaker!" he said loudly. "Meister Speaker, I would be heard!"

But Shifrin couldn't hear him above the gabbling and his own pathetic attempts to restore order. So, uncaring that he had not been invited here, considering himself above such petty considerations, he stalked across the chamber floor.

"Lord Garrick!" said Shifrin, noticing him at last. "My lord—I'm sorry but this is a privy gathering. You've not been granted leave to—"

"I will present myself wherever I choose," he said, making his way towards the Speaker's table with a studied, deliberate nonchalance. "In case you've forgotten, Shifrin, my father was a councilor."

"What of it?" said Rafel, one hand on Orrick's shoulder. "Council positions ain't hereditary, Arlin."

The chamber was falling quiet, as one by one councilors both Doranen and Olken stilled their chattering tongues. Smiling, Arlin halted. Decided to let the incivility pass, for now.

"And yet here *you* are, Rafel."

"I was invited," said Asher's son, his face darkening. "And my father's not dead."

His smile widened. "Yet."

"Lord Garrick!" said Jaffee, his shocked protest cutting through the Council's babble. "That was uncalled for."

Ignoring the old fool, and the rest of the Council, he kept his gaze on Rafel. "Speaker Shifrin, I stand before you seeking redress for a gross injustice. My father—"

"Arlin," said Rafel. Letting go of Orrick's shoulder, he stepped out from behind the Speaker's table. "Don't do this. Don't make a fool of yourself. Go home and mourn in private. Your father wasn't murdered."

"Of course you would say that, Rafel," he replied, ruthlessly civil. "Being one of his murderers. But I prefer to—"

"Arlin, bloody accept it. Your father got himself killed," Rafel retorted. "And he near got mine killed with him while he was at it. I'm sorry he's dead, but—"

"Sorry?" Astounded, he had to wait a moment for his breath to return. "You're *sorry*, Rafel? That is a very—*small*—word. That is a word lacking weight, and meaning. It's the word you use when you tread on someone's foot, accidentally. Or when you interrupt them during polite conversation. It is *not* the word you use for stealing an innocent man's life."

"I didn't steal anything!" Rafel shouted. "I didn't *kill* anyone. I—"

"Be quiet," said Pellen Orrick, his voice hoarse, weak, but full of authority nonetheless. "*Both* of you. We don't have time for this. We have to—" And then he closed his eyes briefly, shaking his head. "Forgive me, Meister Speaker," he said to Shifrin, then nodded to another ferrety Olken seated close by. "Mayor Stott. It's not my intention to—"

Fernel Pintte's replacement glanced at Shifrin, then raised a hand. "No need to apologise, Pellen. Your experience is undisputed. Please, go on."

"Lord Garrick," said Pellen Orrick, "there's not a man or woman in this chamber who'd diminish the natural sorrow any son must feel on the loss of his father. But this is not Justice Hall. If you have a grievance, make representation to Lady Marnagh once our session here is concluded. As senior administrator of Justice Hall she will examine your complaint and—"

"Sarnia Marnagh is well known as Asher's friend," he replied, not bothering to look at the ageing Doranen woman who so failed to understand where her loyalty belonged. "I have no confidence in her judgement."

"Be that as it may, Lord Garrick," said frail Barlsman Jaffee, over the muttering Council. "Not one of us stands above the law. Now you must withdraw, so we might continue our urgent business undisturbed."

They were *dismissing* him? As though he were a nobody, an Olken? "What business could you have more important than murder?" he demanded. "More important than the slaughter of one of Lur's great mages?"

"This kingdom's *survival!*" said Shifrin. "Lord Garrick—as Meister Orrick says, this Council grieves with you and mourns the kingdom's loss of your father. But—"

"*Platitudes!*" he spat at the fat fool. "I have not come here for *platitudes*. I want—"

"No-one here gives a *shit* what you want, Arlin!" said Rafel, his face savage. "So shift your arse out of this chamber before I—"

Pellen Orrick slapped his hand to the Speaker's table. "*Rafel—*"

"No, Pellen!" said Rafel, half-turning. "I'm sick of this poxy little shit and his poison tongue. Him and Fernel Pintte and Sarle Baden, all three tarred with the same lying brush. I'm a murderer. My *father's* a murderer. You call yourself Da's friend? What you were saying before, did you even *mean* it? Or are you no better than this bloody Council, this leaky boatload of sinkin' fools?"

Orrick lurched to his feet, unsteady on his one wooden leg. "*Shame on you, Rafel. If your father was here*—"

"Well, he's *not*," spat Rafel. "He's lying three-quarters dead under his blankets with my mother—your friend—weeping over him. Because he risked his life for this kingdom, *again*." His furious glare raked the chamber. "I don't know how any of you look yourselves in the mirror."

Forgotten for the moment, Arlin retreated almost to the chamber doors where he might continue to discreetly observe the proceedings. Rafel was invited here for a reason. Whatever that was, he wanted to know.

This murderer's life is become my business. There is nothing too small about him that I would not learn. I will bring him down. I will lay him low. Before I am done with him, he shall weep at my feet.

"Rafel," said Speaker Shifrin sternly. "Your anger is excusable—you fear for your father's health. So do we. But you weren't asked here to judge us. That's not your place."

Rafel scowled at the Speaker. "Then what *is* my place? Why am I here?"

Shifrin played his gaze over the murmuring Council until it fell silent. Glanced at Jaffee, and Sarnia Marnagh, and last of all at Pellen Orrick. Then he turned to Rafel. "You're Asher's son."

Warily, Rafel stared back at him. "I know."

"Levity, Rafel?" said Shifrin, his expression tightening. "With Lur facing its darkest days, you'd—"

"Shifrin," Pellen Orrick said, touching his arm. "It's a tense time."

"What I mean," said Shifrin, through gritted teeth, "is that like your father, you can feel the earth the way other Olken mages can't?"

"So?" said Rafel, still wary.

"And like your father, you have the touch for Doranen magic?"

Arlin, closely watching, saw Rafel's fear, imperfectly concealed. Was thrilled by it. Fear was a weakness—and weakness could be exploited.

"You know I do," Rafel said. "What's going on? You ain't saying what's happened is *my* fault? Or Da's fault? Because we didn't cause this, we were—"

"No," said Shifrin, curt with impatience. "Rafel, nobody's blaming you—or your father. We know how much we owe him."

"Then tell me what you want," said Rafel, so arrogant. His father's son, indeed. "Or I'm going back to the Tower. My mother needs me."

"And so does Lur," said Shifrin, with an uneasy sideways glance at Pellen Orrick. "Rafel, with your father—" He hesitated. "—unwell, it could be you're our kingdom's only chance of survival."

"I'm not," said Rafel, taken aback. Arrogance abruptly subdued. Interesting. "It's the weather that's gone wrong, and I ain't a WeatherWorker."

"We know that," said Speaker Shifrin. "But you have power. There has to be something you can do to stop Lur falling apart."

The councilors leaned forward, all of them, even the Doranen, waiting to hear what Rafel had to say. Waiting for him to *save* them. *Rafel.* They were pathetic.

Rafel looked at them, still uncertain. "If that's true, I don't know what it is."

"When Lur faced its first great crisis, Doranen and Olken magics were melded," said Barlsman Jaffee. "And Weather Magic was born to keep us safe. Now Lur faces destruction once more, and this Council believes—"

"What?" said Rafel, incredulous. "That we should make our own Weather Magic? Or something like it? Don't be mad. It's more likely we'd make things worse, not better. Those magics—" A memory, unpleasant, shifted behind his eyes. There was fear again. *What did he know?* "You don't want to muck about with them."

Arlin bit his tongue. It galled him, but he agreed with Rafel. These Doranen were milk-and-water mages. Not a one of them was strong enough to wield that kind of power. It didn't exist here, anyway. Barl had seen to that. The magic they were after could only be found over the mountains, in Lost Dorana.

"Nothing's been decided, Rafel," said Jaffee, frowning. "Nothing *can* be decided until the meaning of every shiver and twist in this kingdom, no matter how subtle, is understood. You are the strongest Olken mage we have. Will you seek the answers for us? Will you bind yourself to Lur's suffering earth and tell us what we need to know so we might cure what ails our poor, beleaguered home?"

Shoving his hands in his pockets, Rafel stared at the floor. Paced a few steps. Paced back again, saying nothing. Then he looked up. Arlin, catching his hard stare full-face, felt himself flinch. A thought rose, unbidden: *Don't get on his bad side.* Disturbed, angered, he pushed it away. *The Olken's not been born that I will ever fear.*

"We're seeking a way to save the kingdom, so that no more tragic sacrifices are made," said Jaffee, sounding almost humble. "But we can't save it without you, Rafel. Please. Please, help us."

The council chamber was utterly silent. Every breath held, every body still as stone. Every hopeful, harrowed gaze trained on Asher's murdering son.

"All right," Rafel said at last. "I'll ride out tomorrow — *if* you promise me two things."

"Rafel..." Pellen Orrick shook his head. "You'd bargain? *Now?* With so much at stake? Your father —"

"Is a fool," Rafel said fiercely. "And d'you know why, Pellen? 'Cause whenever anyone asked him — *asks* him — for something, he gives it. No matter what it might cost him, he gives it and never once stops to think of himself. Well, that ain't me."

An uncomfortable stirring round the chamber. "What is it you want?" Shifrin asked at last.

Arms belligerently folded, Rafel treated them all to his most arrogant stare. "First off, you don't argue with me when I tell you what I find. You don't throw your hands up and say I must be mistaken. You don't ignore me, like you always ignore my da. 'Cause I know this much, what you're asking me to do? It's going to *hurt*. A lot. And I'm not much interested in being called a liar afterwards."

Shifrin took a moment to look at his fellow-councilors. Not a one of them spoke. Not a single face showed any objection.

"Agreed," said the Speaker. "Whatever you find, we will accept as the truth without argument. What's your second—request?"

Arlin swallowed his contempt. Request? Demand, more like it. Asher's thuggish son was browbeating them, twisting their weak arms—and they were letting him.

No wonder the kingdom is come to such a parlous place, with weaklings like this in charge. What use is a Council that begs, instead of leads?

Stirring from thought, Rafel turned and flung out a pointing finger. "You tell *him* to stop calling me and my father murderers. You make Lord Arlin bloody Garrick swear on oath before this Council, here and now, that he knows what happened down in Westwailing *wasn't murder*."

Aching with rage and the urgent desire to destroy, Arlin strode out of the shadows and back into the chamber's light. Halted face to face with Rafel, and let his enemy see him, really *see* him, for the first time in his life. He watched Rafel absorb the blow. Watched the Olken upstart blink. Swallow.

That's right, Rafel. I'm something else to fear.

And then he slid behind his mask again, and shifted his gaze past his father's murderer to Shifrin. "I will do no such thing, Speaker! I'll not betray my father for *him*. And that he would stand here, flouting my right to justice, my right to be publicly heard, that he'd hold a knife to this kingdom's *throat*—he proves me right in everything I've ever said." He laughed, and looked again at Rafel. "So which of us has the poison tongue now?"

Rafel turned away. A small defeat, and he relished it.

The first of many, Rafel. My word on it. The first of many.

"Rafel..." Slowly, painfully, each halting step an effort, Pellen Orrick abandoned the Speaker's table and confronted Asher's son. Rested one hand on his shoulder. "Rafel, I'm sorry. You can't ask for that. Lord Garrick may be wrong, he may be blinded by grief, disordered by it, even, but he is entitled to his challenge. Asking us to deny him justice *is* putting a knife to Lur's throat. And when your father learns of it..." He shook his head. "Do you *want* to break his heart?"

Rafel walked out.

"Lord Garrick," said Speaker Shifrin, when the hubbub at last was died down and Pellen Orrick was seated again, more grey-faced than ever. "As you can see, this Council cannot—will not—take sides in this matter. If you wish to pursue the question of your father's death, you *must* petition Justice Hall. Now kindly withdraw, my lord. This Council has business that must take precedence over your grief."

With the weight of the entire Council against him, he had no choice but to obey. So he bowed to the blind fools who'd trust Lur's fate to a murderer and withdrew from the Council chamber into its antechamber, to consider his next move.

Rafel was nowhere in sight. Which was lucky for him.

"And if I begged you not to go, Rafel? Would that make any difference?"

Not looking up, Rafel shoved a second spare shirt into his almost-full pack. *Mama, please, enough. How bad do you want me to feel?* "It's only for three days. Four at the most."

"Three days—or four—might be all your father has left to him!" his mother retorted. "You heard what Kerril said. It's a wonder he's still breathing. He could stop breathing before you've reached the City gates. Is that what you want, Rafel? To be wandering around the countryside while your father breathes his last?"

"I'm doing what *Da* would want!" he said, fumbling the pack's buckles. "I'm putting Lur first, just like he's put Lur first pretty much his whole life. He's lying in his bed like a breathing corpse, right now, for putting Lur first. And for me."

"For you?" said Mama. "What do you mean?"

He stared at her across his clothes-scattered bed. These past long days of cruel uncertainty had been especially brutal for her. Eyes shadowed and sunken, cheeks pale, everything strong about her turned fearful. It was as though a stranger was wearing her face. Rain slashed against the chamber window, filling the silence with threats of strife.

"Goose," he said at last. Hating to admit it. "Da thought if—" He had to stop, guilt burning his belly. "He thought—"

Mama dropped to the blanket box at the foot of the bed. Elbows on her knees, face buried in her hands, she looked so dejected, so small and lonely, he could've wept.

"I know what he thought," she said, muffled. So weary. "Oh, *Asher.*"

And it had been for nothing, in the end. Goose and the others were gone over the mountains, and Barl alone knew what they were facing. There'd been no word yet through the talking stone they'd taken. Between fretting on him and Da and feeling Lur's torment, it was getting harder and harder to sleep.

"Mama," he said, close to despair. "You *know* he'd want me to go."

She looked up. "And what makes you think I care what he'd want?"

He'd never seen her defeated, not like this. Not even in Westwailing, when she'd given up and walked away.

"Mama—"

"Don't," said Mama, and hid her face again. "Rafel, I can't see the point of you doing this. Barl's map is destroyed and there's no more Weather Magic. The last threads binding it to Lur are snapped. So what can you do?"

Sighing, he tossed the buckled pack aside and joined his mother on the blanket box. Slipped his arm around her shoulders and pulled her against him. "I can feel the earth. Better than anyone, even you. Well, except Da." He pulled a face. "And maybe Deenie."

"*Deenie?*" Mama pulled away from him and stood, arms wrapping tight round her ribs as though she held herself against a mortal wound. "You leave Deenie out of this madness, Rafel. You're a man now. You'll do what you want and I can't stop you. But Deenie?" Her voice broke. "She's younger than her years. Still a child, in many ways. I'll not have her dragged into this. I'll not have her life ruined by magic, by being different, by—"

"But Mama," he said, as gently as he could. "She *is* different. You can't—"

She turned on him, her dark eyes shimmering with tears and fury. *"Don't you tell me what I can't!* I am her *mother* and I will protect her till the last breath leaves *my* body! I was born Jervale's Heir and I accepted that burden. I did all that was asked of me to see that evil was defeated. But the days of prophecy are *over,* Rafe. The Circle is broken and I'll not see it mended. I'll not give my daughter to it." Fingers pressed to her lips, tears falling, she almost sobbed. "I'll not forgive your father for giving you to it."

"Mama!" Shocked, he got to his feet. "Don't blame Da for this. I *wanted* to help."

"And now you want to leave," she said bitterly. "But how does that help *me?*"

The need to hold her, to be held by her, was so sharp it hurt. But he didn't dare move. *If she pushed me away now, I'd break.* "What helps Lur helps us all, Mama. Doesn't it?"

She snorted. "Your father thought that way. Now look at him. He's a lump of flesh in his bed. And is Lur helped? No. It's suffering, worse than ever."

"Which is why I've got to go. I've got to get beyond the City walls and into the Home Districts, so I can feel what's going on without folk getting in the way. Doranen magic's so loud."

"That's what Matt used to say," she murmured. "And it killed him in the end. It kills everything. I *hate* it."

"Mama, I would *never* ask Deenie to do this," he said, willing her to believe him. "I know how much she's hurting. And that's one more reason for me to go. If I can feel what's happened to Lur, if I can understand, then—"

"Then *what?* You can't fix this, Rafel! Lur is ruined and there's *nothing* to be done."

Looking at her now, it was hard to believe she'd been Jervale's Heir. She'd given up. Did Da know she'd given up? "You can't be sure of that."

"Yes, I *can*," she insisted. "Rafe, it's *over*. At long last this kingdom has run dry of Barl's magic—and we have no choice but to endure the coming dark days. And I'm sure, Rafe, *I know,* that the Council is foolish to think you'll save us."

The derision in her voice lashed him. "Why? 'Cause I'm not the mage my father is?"

"No!" she cried. "Because what they want is *impossible*. What your *father* wanted is impossible. Nothing lives forever, Rafe. Not even a kingdom."

He stepped back. "So—you want us to do nothing? To sit in the rain with our mouths open until we drown?"

His mother stared at him in bleak silence for a long time. Then she shook her head, slowly, and turned away. "You haven't heard a word I said."

"Oh, I heard you!" he retorted. "I just think you're wrong!"

"Fine," she sighed. "Then you go. Traipse about the Home Districts to your selfish heart's content. Do the Council's bidding. Just don't be surprised that when you can't snap your fingers and make everything all right, they blame you."

"They won't do that. They understand—"

"All they understand, Rafel, is that they want the world the way it was!" she said, swinging to face him. "And when they finally realise they won't—*can't*—have it, they'll get angry. *Believe me.*"

"No. Mama, I'm not a fool," he said, his own temper stirring. "I made the Council promise to heed me. I'll be fine. I think you're—"

"Take that condescending tone with me and you'll be well sorry for it," she said, her face and eyes so cold. "Am I some ole woman in my dotage? *I have lived through this before.* Face the truth, Rafel, no matter how painful or unpalatable it might be. Lur has used up all its second chances. This kingdom's last frail hope of deliverance was Fernel Pintte's misguided expedition. And with that lost we—"

Goose. "Don't call them lost," he snapped. "You don't know they're lost. We just haven't heard from them yet, that's all. You don't—"

"I don't *what?*" she spat. "Remember Tollin and his expedition, and what happened to them? Well, my bright boy, here's something else you were never told. I sat beside that man as he *died.* I breathed in the stench and corruption of his rotting flesh as it fell from his raddled bones. Your father was right—Pintte and Baden never should've gone. They and their followers have perished, and hope is perished with them. Now those of us left behind in Lur will reap what Barl and her precious Morgan sowed."

He didn't know how to answer that. He was so angry, so disappointed... any ticktock he was going to lose his temper and say something he could never take back. That she might not forgive.

"Rafe..."

Halfway to the chamber door, his pack in one hand, his long, oiled riding-coat and broad-brimmed leather hat in the other, he stopped. Turned. The pain in her face was a punishment.

"Mama, I'm not doing this to hurt you," he said, his voice tight. His throat tight, and his chest. Breathing hurt. "I'm doing it for Lur. For Da."

"I know," she said. There was no softness in her. "Make sure you farewell him. So you'll know you've done it, even if he won't."

"Mama..." His eyes were burning. "I'll be back in a few days. No more than a week."

"You'll be back when it suits you, Rafel," she said, shrugging. "And not a moment sooner."

He left her standing in his chamber, so much anger, so much pain, and thudded his way downstairs to his parents' floor of the Tower. Dropping his pack, coat and hat on the landing he pushed the main doors open and walked soft-footed to their privy apartments.

Deenie was in there, reading to Da.

Looking up at his entrance, his sister marked her place on the book's page with her finger. "Rafel. You're leaving?"

"Aye," he said roughly, halting two steps through the doorway. "Are you going to fratch at me too?"

Deenie shook her head. Pale and trembly, she looked too small for her clothes. "Why would I fratch at you, Rafe? You're only trying to help." Her face twisted. "I wish *I* could help. But I'm useless."

"No, you ain't," he said, and walked further into the chamber. Looking at his sister, not his father, 'cause looking at Da made him come over girlish and weepy. "You're keeping Da company."

"For all the good it's doing him."

"You don't know it's not. You don't know he can't hear you."

"I s'pose," she said, disconsolate.

Looking at her closely, he saw pinch-prints of pain around her mouth. "You still feeling poorly?"

"I feel what I feel," she said, her voice low. "No point talking on it, Rafe. I can't make it go away, any more than you can."

"No," he agreed. "But you feel things harder. You always have." He pulled a face. "I wish I was like you, Deenie. I wish—"

"No you bloody *don't*," she said, suddenly raging. But Deenie *never* raged. It was like a punch in his guts. "Why would you say that, Rafe?" Tears stood in her eyes, on her lashes. "You've grown up with me screaming. You know my nightmares. At least you can go out there and try *fixing* what's gone wrong. Me? I get to stay cooped up in this Tower, drinking muck that make me feel like I'm only ever two breaths away from vomiting my guts out, and if you *were* like me then you would be too, so don't you talk that folderol. Not to me."

He walked all the way over to her and crouched by her side. "I'm sorry, Deenie. I never meant to—"

"I know you didn't," she muttered. "Don't mind me. It's not been a good morning, is all."

He smoothed a wisp of dark hair behind her ear. "Reckon I can see that."

"I'm frighted, Rafe," she said, groping for his hand. "I'm so frighted Da's going to die."

"Deenie..." Her fingers felt fragile and defenceless in his. He raised them to his lips for a kiss...and then, at last, let himself look at their father.

Oh, Da.

So still. So silent. All his restless energy vanquished. He looked *empty.* Gone away. Just a shape beneath his blankets.

"I keep remembering Darran," said Deenie, her voice thick. "I was tiddy, I know, but I remember him. I remember that last night."

"Don't," he said roughly, 'cause he remembered it too. "Darran was an ole man. Years and years older than Da. He was palsied. *Da ain't dying."*

Deenie looked to the chamber's open door, then scrunched down in her chair. "I want to tell you something," she said, so softly he could hardly hear her. "It's bad. I tried to tell Mama, but — she won't listen. She says it's 'cause I'm not well. She says it's the possets and elixirs making me imagine things. Pother Kerril says the same." She leaned close to him, quivering. "And it's true, I am having nightmares. But this ain't a nightmare, Rafe. This is *real."*

He'd never seen her so intense. "What, Deenie? What's real?"

"There's a darkness inside him, Rafe. Something bad is in there, making him sick. Keeping him asleep. Away from us."

Uncertain, he stared at her. "Deenie..."

"I can *feel* it!" She pressed his hand palm-down to Da's cold forehead. "Can't *you* feel it, Rafe? Please, *please,* tell me you feel it!"

But the only thing he could feel was misery, to see Da sunk so low. "Maybe," he said cautiously, and took his hand back. "Maybe I feel something."

She shifted away from him, disgusted. "You're just saying that to jolly me. You're as bad as Mama, treating me like a sprat." She stood, paying no heed to the book as it thudded to the carpet. "I have to take another posset now. If you're going, goodbye."

"No — Deenie, wait, don't —"

But she was gone, stamping out of Da's chamber all crooked elbows and crossness.

He looked at his father. "Is she right, Da?" he whispered. "Are you in there somewhere, trying to get out?"

Da didn't answer. He hadn't moved since Pother Kerril brought him out of his thrashing fit in the Weather Chamber. Days and days of silence and sorrow. Even his sunken eyes were unmoving behind his closed eyelids. His chest rose and fell as he breathed. That was it.

"Da..." Rafel kissed his father's raspy, stubbled cheek, then stood. "I'm leaving for a bit. Council's asked for my help. But I'll be back, so don't you go anywhere. You hear me?"

He turned for the door—and there was his mother, tears like rain sliding down her hollowed cheeks. She stood aside as he approached, and didn't lift her face for his kiss. She *always* lifted her face for his kiss.

"*Mama...*"

She closed her eyes. Held out a hand, to fend him off.

"You know where I'll be," he said, defeated. "And I've got my bit of talking stone. Call if you need me."

She said nothing. She still wouldn't look at him.

Furiously miserable, he walked past her to the landing. Picked up his buckled pack, his coat and his hat. Took the treads of the Tower's spiral staircase two at a time, his boot-heels angrily rapping the marble treads. Once in the foyer he paused to shrug into his oiled coat and button it up, tug his leather gloves from one pocket and pull them on, jam his hat on his head, and then strode outside, his pack hitched over his shoulder. The rain had eased to a mean drizzle, which was a blessing. His only one.

Firedragon, strained fetlock well-mended, was ready for him. He tied his pack to his saddle's cantle, swung himself astride the restive stallion and held him in check until they were safely out of the stable yard. Then he gave the horse its head and they galloped pell-mell, mud flying, along the tree-lined avenue, away from the Tower, and his father, to the palace grounds' main gates.

CHAPTER TWENTY-FOUR

✠

His progress after that was much slower. Despite the misting rain, folk were braving the City's streets. And since everyone knew him, and knew flame-coated Firedragon, since they knew Da was poorly, he couldn't walk the horse ten strides without someone stopping him and asking, *"How goes your father?"*

Because they loved Da, and he was Asher's son, he couldn't be rude. Couldn't jam his heels into Firedragon's wet flanks and gallop like a madman to Dorana's gates or slink his way out of the City down back lanes and alleyways. No. He had to nod and smile soberly and thank them for their concern. Tell them, *"Da's abed, which ain't a pleasure for him, but he's resting mighty comfortable. I'll tell him you asked."*

But folk didn't ask just 'cause they loved Da. They were frighted too, looking for comfort...and who could blame them? The mood in the City was dark, fear making everyone ripe for fratching and brangles and fisticuffs. The City's guards were being kept on the hop. No wonder the Council had asked him to do this. And though a part of him still resented how they'd ignored Da and his warnings, which had led to the mess that was Westwailing—though he was close to *hating* them for that—and even though they wouldn't do what he wanted, get rid of Arlin once and for all—he'd never have refused them.

If only Mama could see that. If only she could see how refusing the Council wouldn't only disappoint Da, it would give bloody Arlin rocks to throw at them. There was no telling how much trouble that poxy shit would make out of it, with the City on edge. With *Lur* on edge. Frighted folk were skittish folk, and skittish folk, like spooked horses...they didn't much care who they trampled.

But right now Mama couldn't see straight. And he understood that, he did, only...he felt like a sprat again, small and shivery inside, because his mother was fratched with him. His whole life she'd been the one who understood. Now she was turned against him. He'd never felt so lost.

But she'll forgive me when I fix this. When Da doesn't die, and I find a way to fix Lur, she won't be fratched. She'll be proud.

In fits and starts he continued through the City, until finally he reached its open gates. There was a whole crowd of folk waiting for him there. As a general rule that kind of folderol wasn't allowed, on account of not slowing down the travellers coming in and going out. But Captain Mason of the Guards stood on duty today, making sure folk behaved themselves and turning a blind eye to those who'd gathered to wish Asher's son well. As he rode past, smiling his thanks, the Captain nodded. *Good luck.*

"Captain," he murmured, half-raising his hand. And then couldn't utter another word, because Charis was one of the Olken patiently waiting to wave him goodbye.

"Rafel," she said, as he halted restive Firedragon in front of her. She'd thrown a pretty green shawl over her head to keep off the drizzling rain, but she was still damp in patches. Mud splattered her stockings and the hem of her skirt. "Rafe, can we talk?"

He'd not meant to dawdle once he was free of the City. Once safely beyond the anxious well-wishers he'd meant to give Firedragon his impatient head so they could gallop away from busy Dorana, to somewhere quiet that would let him hear Lur properly. That was what he'd meant to do. 'Cept here was Charis, in the rain and splattered with mud, looking up at him with those eyes...wanting to talk.

"I s'pose," he said, half pleased, half wary. "Go on ahead and wait for me down the road."

She tried to smile. "I won't keep you long, I promise."

As she wriggled her way out of the crowd he looked at all the solemn Olken faces gathered on either side of the wide-open gates. Could feel Captain Mason's displeasure, but knew he couldn't ignore them. Not after stopping to have a word with Pellen's daughter. He could feel their fear, a cold breath on his skin. Could feel them thinking, *"He's Asher's son. He's going to save us."*

He felt sick.

Now that he'd stopped, an ole man raised his gnarled hand. "Barl's blessings on you, Rafel. And on your father."

The fervent words were repeated, rushing through the crowd like a warm wind through a field of green corn. But before he could say anything, give these good folk thanks or hope or even a smile, frowning Captain Mason started chivvying them about their business. So he tugged his hat-brim, eased his hold on the reins and let Firedragon bound through the open gates and onto the City road.

Charis had walked just far enough to keep them private, and was standing forlorn in the drizzle with her shawl pulled tight. He jogged Firedragon to join her then drew rein again.

"What's amiss, Charis? Not your da?" Alarmed, he saw there were tears in her eyes. What? No, no, Pellen couldn't be — there'd be all kinds of noise if he was — "Charis, he ain't —"

"Dead? No," she said swiftly. "But Rafe, he's...that Council meeting...I begged him not to go, I *begged* him, but..." Her voice caught on a sob. "He's stubborn. And now he's paying the price."

"I'm sorry," he said, feeling useless and clumsy. Bad enough when Charis was all flirty and knowing, with her cheeky smile and her frivolous blouses that stirred a man to noticing she wasn't a girl any more. But now here she was all weepy and here *he* was wanting to climb off Firedragon so he could hold her and comfort her and —

Am I in love with her? I can't be in love with her. She's Deenie's little friend. And Da warned me — he warned me —

"Rafe?" said Charis, anxious. "Rafe, what's the matter? How's your father?"

"Da's fine," he said quickly. *Settle down, you fool.* "He's resting comfortable. Thanks for asking."

"Oh, *Rafel.*" Charis glared up at him. "Don't talk to me like I'm one of *them.*" Her head jerked towards the stragglers still loitering about the City gates. "You can't hide from me, you know. I've known you my whole life. And who knows better than me what it's like to have a father so poorly? And Asher is... poorly... Rafe, isn't he?"

She wanted to know if Da was dying. He couldn't answer. Couldn't bring himself to think on it or let himself feel her bright, burning sympathy. He had a job to do. If even *once* he let himself think—

"I've got to go, Charis. Give my best to your—"

She stepped into the road, blocking his way. "No. Wait."

"*Charis*—" Guts twisting, he soothed Firedragon's fret with one stroking hand, easy in the saddle as the horse pawed the cobbles and swung his hindquarters, tail swishing with temper. "What d'you want from me, eh?"

"The truth," she whispered. "The truth would be nice."

"I told you the truth, Charis. Da's in his bed, he's asleep. He ain't in pain. At least—" He cleared his throat. "Kerril says he ain't."

"But will he get better?"

I don't know. No-one knows. But if he doesn't—if he doesn't—

Staring at his gloved fingers folded tight round Firedragon's reins, he flinched as Charis's hand rested lightly on his knee.

"You know what Goose used to say about you?" she asked. "He used to say the real Rafel hardly ever showed his face."

"What?" Shocked, he looked down at her. "What d'you mean *Goose said*—when did you and Goose ever—"

She was almost smiling. "He's your best friend, Rafel. And Papa likes his ale. Every few days I'd buy a jug or two off him, directly, and we'd chat a bit."

"About *me?*"

"About all kinds of things," she said. "But yes. Sometimes we talked of you. Goose thought—"

"Hey," he said, scowling. "Don't talk on what he used to say, Charis, or like he ain't thinking anything right now. He ain't *dead.*"

"Sorry," she said, and took her hand from his knee. "I didn't mean to—I only meant—" She folded her arms. "I like your father, Rafel. I'm worried for him. I'm worried for *you*. What happened wasn't your fault."

No, no, no. He wasn't talking on that. Not to Charis, not to anyone. *Da witless on the floor of the Weather Chamber, in his arms, thrashing and grunting, his face covered in blood . . .* "I've got to go," he said, and swung Firedragon to one side.

She leapt in front of him again. "How's Deenie, Rafel? I've not seen her for days."

He couldn't ride over her, though the thought was bloody tempting. Just like Mama, she was a slumskumbledy wench. *"Charis—"*

"And don't you say she's fine!" Charis snapped. "Don't you dare say it, Rafel. She's my best friend. She's the sister I never had. And I know she's feeling the upset in the earth, worse than you are. Worse than me." Her fisted hand pressed against her belly. "It's bad this time, isn't it? Rafe? This time we really are in trouble."

It was hard to meet her eyes. "What's Pellen said?"

"Papa?" Smearing spilled tears from her cheeks, she half-laughed, half-sobbed. "Nothing. He thinks silence can protect me. But I see how frightened he is. He's so sick, and he's frightened." She looked at him, her eyes beseeching. "Rafel, can you fix this?"

Barl's bloody tits . . . He breathed out, hard. "I don't know. I don't know if anyone can. Even Da. If he—*when* he wakes."

"Oh," she said, her voice small. Then she tilted her chin. "Well, I did ask for the truth. And Deenie?"

"Ain't nowt you can do for Deenie, Charis. Ain't nowt anyone can do. She feels things and they hurt her. That's just the way it is."

His blunt words upset her, he could see that, was sorry for it, but she didn't lash out. Instead, she tugged her shawl tight again. "I'm holding you up. Perhaps when you come back from your Council business you could stop in and see Papa? He does fret so, being cooped up in the house with mostly me for company."

"He doesn't get other visitors?"

"Oh yes, but it's not the same," she said. "How can it be the same? They came to know Papa afterwards."

She meant after the Wall came down. He remembered Da saying that once, when he wasn't paying close attention to his words. After he'd downed two pints of particular strong ale. *"There be the folk as were there, and the folk that weren't, sprat,"* he'd said. *"Some things, you can't explain 'em, or share 'em. If they were there, you don't need to. And if they weren't, they won't understand."*

"Then I don't see as how I'll make a difference," he said. "It was Da knew him then, not me."

Her smile was brief, her eyes full of quiet misery. "True. But you're Asher's son, so it's almost as good. But only if you've the time, Rafel. I don't want to impose."

And that made him feel mean. *"Charis..."*

But she was walking away, back towards the City gates, and Firedragon was about ready to stand on his hind legs with temper, being made to wait for so long. So he loosened his hold on the stallion's mouth, clicked his tongue and let the horse leap into a bouncing canter, hooves pounding wetly on the soaked City road. Overhead the clouds lowered groundwards, heavy with rain. The drizzle thickened and the air swirled cold and damp. Summer, it was s'posed to be, but this wasn't like any summer Lur had ever seen. Not in a long time. Maybe not ever.

Charis, her eyes beseeching. *Rafel, can you fix this?*

Heavy with dread, he urged Firedragon faster.

The stallion's long, easy strides swallowed the open road. He passed a handful of carts and carriages heading for the City, but with his hat pulled down and rain misting thickly no-one saw it was him. And then Firedragon threw his head up, ears pricking, pace slowing without being asked. Looming out of the gloom ahead, a motionless, solitary horse and rider. Rafel didn't know the animal but he recognised the man sat unmoving in its saddle.

Arlin.

Reaching him, Rafel pulled Firedragon to a plunging halt. Dorana City was a goodly distance behind him now, just its rooftops and the old palace visible above the gentle rise and fall of the rolling green countryside, dotted with yellow-tipped wild lampha bushes and bold scarlet frantins. Arlin and his horse stood on the Home Districts crossroad. Turn right and after ten leagues or so a traveller would come across the beehive district of Rumfylde. Turn left, and the Saffron Hills sweetly beckoned. Keep straight on and after days and days and a few roundaboutations, there'd be the coast.

"Rafel," said Arlin, his pale hair darkened with rain and his pale eyes shadowed with unfriendly thoughts.

He smoothed a wet lock of Firedragon's mane. He'd intended to ride towards Rumfylde, but Arlin was in the way. Of course. That was what Arlin did. He got in the way. But he wasn't about to start something, 'cause they were alone and it didn't pay to be careless where this Doranen was concerned. Not after what he'd glimpsed in the Council chamber.

He's been hiding himself, like I have. Arlin bloody Garrick's a sneaky little shit.

"Arlin," he said, pleasantly enough. "You're a long way from home on a wet day."

Arlin lifted his bare head and stared quizzical at the clouded, weeping sky. "Very wet, yes. I wonder, can you tell me when it's due to stop raining?"

"I reckon you know I can't."

Arlin's lip curled in a sneer. "So much for being the new Asher."

"Never said I was," he replied, as Firedragon shorted, unsettled. "Only said I'd help, if I could."

Arlin laughed. "*Help?* You think you can *help?* Like you helped in Westwailing?" He tipped his head, quizzical again. "I wonder how many more men and women must die from your helping them, Rafel."

Sink me . . . "Arlin—*I'm sorry.*"

"You expect me to believe that?" said Arlin, eyebrows lifting. "To believe you're capable of remorse?"

It was no use. Talking to this blind fool was a waste of time Lur didn't have. "No, Arlin," he said tiredly. "I don't."

"Why are you out here, Rafel?" said Arlin, and kicked his brown horse closer. His eyes squinted against the relentless, drizzling rain. "Do you honestly expect me to buy this—this tarradiddle about you being able to *feel the earth?*"

Firedragon laid his ears flat back at Arlin's stallion, ready to snap or strike. Scowling, Rafel jobbed the horse's mouth in warning, not willing to back off. Arlin would see it as a victory, of sorts.

"You calling me a liar?" he said. "Just 'cause you Doranen are deaf, dumb and blind to the earth, I must be too? I thought that kind of arrogance died with Conroyd Jarralt."

"You prate to me of arrogance?" Arlin snapped. "*You?* Son of the most arrogant man this kingdom ever birthed?"

"Arrogant or not he saved your bloody life. So you might want to swallow that nasty tongue of yours, Lord Garrick."

Arlin's teeth bared. "What I'll swallow is your admission before the Council that you and your meddling father are responsible for all our current woes. You are *unnatural.* Both of you. It is *unnatural* that an Olken can wield Doranen magics. Not to mention insulting that you'd dare refer to yourselves as *mages.* The Doranen are mages. You Olken are—"

"I'll tell you what we are, Arlin," he said, as Firedragon began to dance on the spot. "We're the folk as were rightfully born to this land. The folk as paid the price for *Doranen* arrogance. Six hundred bloody years kept down by you and yours. And if that ain't enough, we're the folk as saved you from Morg. *That's* who we are, *my lord.*"

Arlin looked skyward again, the rain falling steadily onto his face. "Morg was twenty years ago, Rafel. He's dead and gone. The buried past. What can you do to save us now, you and your precious Olken magic? Can you restore the weather to its former perfection? Can you undo the damage your father wrought, interfering with Barl's brilliant workings? *Can you make this cursed rain stop?*"

He forced himself to breathe slowly, feeling the stirrings of an unwise rage. "You're full of shit, Arlin. You always were, from our first day in school. Spew it somewhere else, why don't you? I've got a job to do, as assigned by the Council."

Easing his hold on the reins, he nudged Firedragon a step sideways so he could get past bloody Arlin and make tracks for Rumfylde. But Arlin put his hand out, catching Firedragon's bridle. The horse stopped, grunting a protest.

"Lur is on the brink of chaos, Rafel," said Arlin, his voice soft with menace. "You know it. *I* know it. *And* we know you can't save it. You must stand before the Council and admit that. You must—"

"Forget what *I* must," he said, as Firedragon jerked and tussled to get free. "*You* take your bloody hand off my horse's bridle or so help me—"

"You'll what?" Arlin sneered. "What will you do, Rafel?"

Rafel smiled. Bollocks to being careful. Arlin was asking for it. *"This."*

With a snap of his fingers he severed the girth on Arlin's saddle, and in the next breath cracked three stones lying in the grass by the side of the road. The shards slapped Arlin's horse on its fat dappled rump. Squealing, the beast bucked and bolted...and Arlin, still in his saddle, tumbled to the ground.

"You *bastard!*" Arlin shouted, sprawling, his fine clothes splotched and splattered with mud. "That was assault. Assault with *magic*. I'll see you thrown in the Guardhouse, Rafel. I'll see you destroyed in Justice Hall. I'll have you charged with attempted murder *and* the murder of my father!"

Laughing, Rafel rode past him. "You can try, Arlin," he said, over his shoulder. "But I'm Asher's son, remember? And you're the son of the man who wrecked the reef in Westwailing. So maybe you might want to think on that a bit."

Ignoring Arlin's furious shouting he dug his heels into Firedragon's flanks, and they galloped towards Rumfylde leaving the Doranen lordling to catch an ague, or walk home on blisters, or both.

He didn't care.

For three long, wet days he wandered through the Home Districts. Lur was weeping. Suffering. Bleeding from the deep wounds the Weather Magic, in its death throes, had gouged in the earth. He felt its pain in the waterlogged orchards, with their ripely rotting fruit, in the beehives, grimly droning, in the fields of drenched sheep and milch cows, and in the tilled soil screaming on the edge of hearing.

At first he thought he might go mad from it. The onslaught was brutal. Inescapable. Was this how Deenie felt? Haunted? Battered? No hope of respite, not a single moment's peace?

Poor little mouse. I never realised.

But gradually his senses numbed — and he welcomed their deadening. It meant that finally he could snatch a little sleep. Everywhere he travelled he kept himself to himself. Kept his hat pulled low and didn't give his real name. Everywhere he travelled he eavesdropped, shameless. In alehouses and markets and the inns where he stayed, he minded his own business and listened to the locals gossip. Not every Olken he encountered had magic, and of those who did, not many were powerful. He didn't stumble across one man, woman or child who felt the earth's tumult as keenly as he did... but many were feeling it. Felt ill, and afraid.

On the fourth day he visited Riddleton, a village on the furthest edge of the Home Districts, sat at the feet of the Saffron Hills. The land thereabouts was prime grazing country, where some of the best cattle in Lur were raised. Riddleton was a sleepy place, tucked far from the City, mostly overlooked 'cept twice a year when the big Livestock Markets were held. Out here, with the Saffron Hills rising, a gentle echo of Barl's savagely splendid mountains, with more open countryside than the rest of the Home Districts' hemmed-in fields and clustered cottages, Lur's torment shouted loudest of all.

Weary after so much time in the saddle, worn down by the ceaseless rain, sometimes drizzling, sometimes heavy, he ambled with Firedragon along the hedge-rowed lanes leading to the village. The constant scraping of earth-distress against his nerves set his teeth on edge, muttered pain behind his tired eyes. Firedragon, sensing his disquiet, broke into a shuffling jog-trot, wet tail swishing, slapping his flanks. Every bone aching, he eased the horse back to a walk. In the fields on either side of them rust-red, black spotted Saffron cattle grazed the wet grass. If they could feel the earth's misery they gave no sign of it. He envied them their dumb beast ignorance.

Once in Riddleton village, he took a room at the Speckled Rooster. Saw bedraggled Firedragon settled in a warm, dry stable with a hot mash, then took himself off to tramp the dripping streets and boggy laneways. To bully his beaten senses into reading the sorry earth one more time.

This would be his last night away from home. He'd learned what he'd needed to learn, what the Council had sent him to learn. But he knew, his heart sinking, they'd not want to hear what he had to say...

Barl save us. Mama was right. This can't be fixed. The damage is gone too deep.

The thought bludgeoned him to a halt. He had to fall against a handy tree-trunk and wait for the shivering to pass. Lur was *dying*. He couldn't see for unshed tears.

What do I do, Da? How do I tell Mama and Deenie?

Da. The shard of talking stone sat in his pocket, but it hadn't stirred once. He chose to believe that meant his father hadn't stopped breathing. Surely Mama would call for him if Da slipped away. She was fratched, she thought him reckless, but she'd not punish him like that. And any road... if Da had died, he surely would've felt it.

He pushed off the tree-trunk and kept on walking, barely taking in the patchwork of market gardens on either side of him, carrots and corn and beans and peas. Bedraggled and wilted, but grimly holding on. Sobbing through his blood, Lur's curdling pain. Such a good thing Deenie was safe at home in Dorana, deadened with Kerril's elixirs. If Da was right, and magic was a curse, then his poor mousy sister was its worst victim.

Wandering aimless through the village, ignoring the glances from folk as were curious about strangers, he felt his thoughts slide from Deenie to Goose like rocks down a riverbank.

I never asked Deenie if she was sweet on him. Never told her what he told me. Doesn't matter. They can work it out themselves when he gets back. 'Cause he's bloody coming back. I don't care the Council's not heard from Pintte or Baden. That could be any reason. And anyway, I've been on the road for days. By the time I get home, they'll have heard something. There'll be word from the expedition by the time I ride through the gates.

There had to be. 'Cause if there wasn't...

And suddenly he was too tired to keep on walking. Too tired, too disheartened, too sick of what he felt. So he headed back to the inn. He wanted to sleep. To forget. To dream that Lur was thriving, just for a little while. For one last night. 'Cause in the morning he'd have to ride back to Dorana and tell the Council there was no hope.

Sink me bloody sideways, Da. How did we come to this?

He took to his bed soon after supper, but didn't stay asleep for long. Wrenched from uneasy slumber into storm-wracked wakefulness, he blinked muzzily at his chamber ceiling as lightning cracked like whipshot and thunder rumbled and rolled. The Speckled Rooster shuddered under the onslaught, window-panes rattling. Through the closed door he heard a young child scream.

"Meister Tamly," the innkeeper greeted him. "A wild night."

"Gamble," he said, scrambled into his damp clothes and tumbled downstairs to the shabby, glimlit parlour. "You all right?"

Gamble shrugged. He was a slight man, with grey streaks at his temples and a fondness for loudly spotted weskits. "I'm not dead yet."

Rafel stared through the parlour's bobble-paned windows at the pounding rain, at the blizzard of stripped foliage, at the torrents of water gushing through the laneway outside, all the storm's destruction lit in silvery fits and bursts.

"Barl preserve us," said Gamble, bowing his head.

"You can feel it, can't you?" he said, his stomach churning, his hands clenched to fists in his pockets, where nobody could see them. In his bones, a painful drumming. "The last tatters of power tearing loose in the earth."

"Sure I don't know what you mean, sir," said Gamble, carefully tone-less. "Sir, might be you'll feel happier in your chamber with the curtains drawn, like the other guests."

"Gamble..." He sighed. "When I told you I was Ned Tamly, a farm manager looking to buy a new bull? I lied. I'm Rafel of Dorana. Asher's son."

"Asher's son?" Gamble's eyes in the fitful glimlight were wide and full of wonder. "The great man himself?"

He'd long ago lost count of how many times he'd seen that look on an Olken's face. Once it had thrilled him. Later, grown older, he'd felt it shrink him. But now — *now* — "That's right. He's my da."

"Well, sir," said Gamble. "It's an honour." Then the pleasure in him dimmed. "Word's reached us Asher's ailing and is like to die. Is that true?"

No, it bloody well ain't. "It's true he's not himself just this ticktock, but he'll be on his feet directly. Gamble, I —"

The Speckled Rooster trembled as thunder boomed low over their heads. Strike after strike of lightning turned night into day. Somewhere upstairs, the same child screamed again. Gamble sucked in a quick breath, then risked himself close-pressed to the nearest window, trying to make out what was left of his storm-wracked world. The tiffa trees in the front garden were bent double and a bed of cheerful pansies lay pulped flat. Gamble moaned, a thin sound of distress, and turned as though the sight were too painful to bear.

"Gamble," said Rafel, seeing him properly, at last. *Feeling* him. "Seems to me you're an Olken with a rare touch of magic."

Gamble flicked him a wary glance. "And if I am? I don't use magic to run the Rooster. I'm not a Doranen, needing magic to blow my nose."

That made him smile a little, even as another crash of thunder rattled his teeth. "Got no great opinion of the Doranen, have you?"

"Hardly lay eyes on one, save maybe twice or thrice a year," the inn-keeper replied. "They buy their Saffron cattle in Dorana. No need to muddy their fine shoes in Riddleton."

"Believe me, you don't miss much," he said dryly. "We Olken poddle along pretty well without them, all in all. Gamble..." He waited for the echoes of fresh thunder to die. "I need to know — what is it you feel?"

Gamble's face was troubled as he stared out at the storm. "Mortal afraid, Meister Rafel. Mortal afraid."

The parlour lit up stark blueish-white as more lightning cracked through the storm-ridden village. Hard on its heels a dreadful growl of thunder. Somewhere close by, a dog howled in terror. The child wailed. Doors slammed.

"Last storm I saw this bad was when the Wall came down," Gamble added. He turned his head. Despite his fear, his eyes were calm. Almost resigned. "There's no Wall to come down now, young sir. So what are we looking at? As Asher's son, do you know?"

What he'd learned was for the Council first. Besides, he didn't want to make this man's night any worse. "Not for certain, Gamble. Wish I did."

A muscle leapt along the innkeeper's tight jaw. As though he heard the lie — but chose not to challenge it. "And are you afraid?"

There seemed little point in lying about that. "Aye, sir. I'm frighted shitless."

"Oh," said Gamble, and looked sorry he'd asked. "What about the Doranen? Do they know what this means? Can their magic fix things?"

Remembering Rodyn Garrick and the rest of them down in West-wailing, how helpless they'd been in the face of the reef — how Arlin's father died — Rafel shrugged. "I doubt it."

Gamble's face crumpled, just for a moment. "Not even Barlsman Jaffee can help us?"

Another shrug. "He's praying in his chapel. I suppose that's help of a sort. So far it's not made any difference but — it might do. I don't know."

"And your father?" said Gamble. "Can he get better in time to save us?"

More lightning and thunder. Once the rolling booms fell silent, Rafel looked at the innkeeper. "Only a fool abandons hope. This ain't the greatest danger Lur's faced. That was Morg, and he's long dead. Lur's our home, Gamble. Whatever ructions we've got on our hands this time, I'm going to fight for it—and so will my da."

"Fight with what?" Gamble whispered. "Sickles and spades? There's Doranen magic at the heart of this trouble, Meister Rafel. How do us Olken fight that? It's not our way."

The truth of Gamble's words struck him hard, like hammer to anvil. Olken earth magic didn't start this. Couldn't finish it. Only Doranen magic could undo the damage here. Except there wasn't one spell Durm had left behind him that might help them now. If there was, Da would have used it already. And since he hadn't...

Jervale have mercy. Don't say Rodyn Garrick was right. Don't say our only hope can be found in Lost Dorana.

'Cause that meant Fernel Pintte's expedition was the kingdom's last chance. It meant Lur's fate was resting in Sarle Baden's hands. But would Baden and his mage cronies even care? He didn't think so. They had no love for Lur or the Olken. They cared only for the Doranen. And Goose—Goose could never stand up to them and demand that they help Lur. Neither could Pintte, though the fool fancied himself some kind of authority. They'd get ridden over roughshod. Shoved aside. Ignored.

That's even if they're still alive.

Bitterness galled him. Self-contempt. Despair. As he stood beside the Rooster's innkeeper and watched the storm rage, unabating, he lashed himself just as hard.

I never should've let Da talk me out of going with them. I let him treat me like a sprat and now it looks like Lur's going to pay the price.

He left Riddleton at daybreak. The storm had blown itself out just before the sunrise, leaving behind it wreckage and ruin. Downed trees. Smashed cow byres. Scattered straw thatching and roof tiles shattered in the streets. Sorry he couldn't stay and help the stunned folk of Riddleton put their battered village to rights, desperate to get home, he kicked

Firedragon into a canter and let the horse leap the felled tree-trunks and piles of gutter-trapped debris.

Dead cattle littered the fields, the poor beasts struck by lightning. Dismayed farmers wandered among them, counting their dreadful losses, their faces pale and drawn in the glowering light. The sky was still clotted with rain-filled clouds, gauzy tendrils drifting low enough to trail through the treetops. The air was so damp Rafel thought he could wring it like a wet cloth.

Hardening his heart to the suffering because he couldn't help them, he urged Firedragon into a gallop.

Hours later, with the stallion near to dropping beneath him, feeling like he could drop from the saddle himself, he passed through the City's open gates. Home. He'd go home to the Tower first and then—

"Rafel!" said the City guard on duty. Biddle. They played knuckle-bones together at the Bear. "Can you hold? I've orders to send for Captain Mason on your return."

Mason? Why? Seized with sudden fear he nodded. Nudged Firedragon out of the way and sat waiting, silent, unseeing, as Biddle sent a runner to the Guardhouse. Mason arrived a short time later, on foot and running and hardly out of breath. A fit man, and a good one.

"What is it?" Rafel demanded. "Captain, is it—"

"No, no," Mason said hastily, standing close by Firedragon's steaming shoulder. "Your father's not dead, Rafel. It's the Council—it wants you urgently. There's word of a sort from Pintte's expedition."

Rafel felt his heart leap. "They're alive?"

"Yes," said Mason, sorrowful. "But the word's not good. You'd best prepare yourself."

Goose. "What's happened?"

Mason frowned. "By rights the Council should—"

Leaning down, he took hold of the captain's wiry shoulder. "Please, Mason. Goose Martin's my best friend. If he's—if he's hurt—"

"We don't know anyone's hurt," said Mason with rough sympathy. "But there's trouble. Barlsman Jaffee says there's been some kind of attack."

"An *attack?*" Rafel stared at him, letting go. "Who's attacked them? Twenty years the Wall's been gone, we ain't heard a peep from anyone. So who—"

"I don't know," Mason said grimly. "I don't want to think about it. We've enough trouble of our own right here. The notion there's someone skulking over the mountains, intent on doing us a mischief..." He stepped back. "I've sent word to the Council you're home. They'll be gathering. You should go."

Rafel straightened. "Yes. Thank you, Captain."

"Rafel—"

"No, sir," he said, not needing the question asked aloud. "The news ain't good out there, either."

And he rode away, leaving Mason speechless and troubled behind him.

CHAPTER TWENTY-FIVE

A scant hour later, slouched beside one of the Council chamber windows, a dull pain throbbing behind his eyes, Rafel found himself sorry he never found the warspells that Da used to defeat Morg's demons. He could surely use them to bring these fools to their senses.

Whose bright notion was it, asking Arlin to come? Bet they're bloody sorry now.

Lord Garrick was haranguing the Council, Doranen the target of his ire as much as any Olken. The offended councilors brangled over the top of him, hands waving, spittle flying. After learning the truth of the Home Districts, and the message they'd received from the expedition, the chamber stank with fear and nobody was attempting to impose order on the meeting. Not Shifrin, not Mayor Stott, not even Wheezing Barlsman Jaffee. And this time Pellen was nowhere to be seen.

"—rank *cowardice!*" Arlin was shouting, one fist pounding on the council gallery's wooden railing. "We cannot sit on our arses and do *nothing!* Sarle Baden's only hope lies with us sending help! We *can't* abandon him."

Typical bloody Arlin. Not a word to say about Lur's strife. All he cared for was saving Doranen lives—and the sound of his own voice.

Herrick Grey, Meister of the Tanners' Guild, lumbered out of his chair. "Convenient how you forget Dorana's mayor is endangered with

Sarle Baden, Lord Garrick, along with five other good Olken. Your father's son, you are. He'd be proud to see it."

Arlin's face darkened dangerously. "Do not presume to speak to me of my father. Not in this place, where his murderer is made welcome."

Now Jaffee roused. Da always said the man was a doddery ole dimster, not a patch on fiery Barlsman Holze, but it seemed the kingdom's dire predicament had finally spurred the man to decisive action.

Better now than never, I s'pose. I just hope it ain't too little, too bloody late.

"Lord Garrick, *please*," said Jaffee, angrily pained. "You *cannot* continue to make such accusations against Rafel without you—"

"And if you do not send help to Sarle Baden," said Arlin, trampling Jaffee without hesitation or shame, "that will be murder too." Richly clothed, extravagantly jewelled, doing his best to intimidate with wealth, he glared at his unruly audience. "And this Council has winked at murder long enough."

Elderly Jaffee creaked to his feet, his eyes pouched and bloodshot. He'd grown gaunt these past weeks, prayer and worry stripping him to the bone.

"My friends," he said, arms raised, shuffling around to look his outraged and protesting fellow-councilors in the eye. "The kingdom looks to us for leadership. We cannot permit our fears to overtake us, or let ourselves be distracted by a son's natural grief."

As the clamour slowly died down, Rafel tipped his aching head against the window-frame. Grief was one thing. Grief he could understand. But Arlin wasn't grieving. Or not only grieving. Arlin was set to choke himself on hate and the desire for revenge.

He won't be happy until I say it was murder. He won't be happy till Da's dead and I'm rotting in the Guardhouse... or worse.

With the chamber almost hushed, Jaffee turned back to Arlin. "Lord Garrick, I tell you plainly: this Council's patience is at an end. You were asked here out of courtesy, because Lord Baden is a close personal friend and his expedition—in part—honoured your father's dream of—"

"Really?" said Arlin, scathing. "*I* thought I was asked here so you could beg me to do what Rafel has confessed himself and his vaunted father incapable of — saving Lur."

"Lord Garrick, you're an arrogant pup," said Speaker Shifrin, and banged his gavel in a warning. "Mind your manners or you'll be asked to leave."

Rafel shoved away from the window, the dull pain behind his eyes sharpened suddenly to a spike. Stirring in the chamber air, a sizzling tang of power. The hair was standing up on the back of his neck. Jaffee felt it too, and the other Doranen.

Arlin's rage was getting the better of him, and fast.

"Lord Garrick!" Jaffee said, with surprising command. "Control yourself. Magic is *forbidden* in the Council chamber, on pain of dire retribution. Not only is this place warded, so you would be severely harmed, the penalties imposed would see you ruined to begging. Is that how *you* would honour your father?"

For a moment Rafel thought Arlin was mad enough to ignore Jaffee, ignore common sense, and invite his own destruction. He held his breath.

Go on, then. Do it. Destroy yourself, Arlin. I don't bloody care. I'm sick to death of seeing you everywhere I turn. I'm sick to death of you trying to destroy me.

Arlin breathed hard, like he was running a race. Fingers fisting and unfisting, jaw clenched hard enough to break most of his teeth, he glared around the chamber — and the councilors glared back. The City guards by the closed double doors took half a step forward, ceremonial pike-staffs at the ready. Jaffee shook his head, and they reluctantly stepped back.

"Lord Garrick," said the Barlsman, sounding tired to dropping. "Is it not tragic enough that beyond these four walls our beloved kingdom is tearing itself apart? Must we in here tear ourselves apart *with* it? How can we hold on to any hope if we do?"

"*Hope?*" said Arlin. The faintest hint of gold shimmered around him, power on the breathless point of explosion. "Did you not hear your precious Rafel? Did you not pay attention to your Innocent Mage's son?

417

There is no hope. Not in this weeping land. Lur's only chance of survival lies in the finding of Lost Dorana and its wealth of ancient magic. Help *must* be sent to Sarle Baden, so his quest does not fail. *I* must be sent to him. I should have gone in the first place. If I had—"

"You could have made a difference?" said Jaffee. "Could have saved the expedition from whatever mischance has befallen it? Lord Garrick—*Arlin*—" The Barlsman shook his head. "Such youthful bravado does not—"

"Bravado?" Arlin sneered. "Trust me, Jaffee. Not a man or woman in this chamber knows who I truly am—or what I can do." His gaze flickered sideways. "Asher's son is not the only powerful mage in Lur. And if this Council lacks the courage or the will to send me where I am sorely needed, then I shall leave it to perish in a windstorm and go alone, without its blessing."

Stabbed with pain, Rafel shook his head. *Sink me bloody sideways. This has to be a dream.* Whether or not Rodyn Garrick's son was what he claimed, one thing couldn't be argued. "Arlin's right," he said loudly. "There ain't no answer here for what ails us."

"Rafel?" said Barlsman Jaffee, disbelieving. "You *agree* with him?"

He'd rather dance naked through the streets than say it again. "The only hope we ever had was the Weather Magic. And Da—" He caught his breath. *Careful now, careful. What they don't know can't hurt him or me.* He could feel Arlin's knifepoint gaze, pricking him. "Like he told you before. It's gone, and it ain't coming back."

And that was the unvarnished truth, at least.

"Councilors, you promised you'd believe me when I told you what I felt. *That's* what I felt. If there is magic to save us, we ain't going to find it in Lur. If it's anywhere it's out there somewhere, across Barl's Mountains."

Silenced, Jaffee exchanged a look with Speaker Shifrin and Mayor Stott, then sank back into his chair and lowered his head to his hands—either in prayer or defeat. The rest of the Council buzzed like a tipped-over beehive.

Glancing sideways, Rafel saw Arlin still staring. His impulse to obliterate with magic mastered, now he was thrown a little, suspecting he was being mocked.

Don't worry, Arlin. The only fool in here is me, for putting my hand up to get tangled with you. 'Cause if you are going over the mountains, I know one thing for certain sure. You ain't going alone.

For while Lur might need him — Goose needed him more. And he wasn't about to abandon his best friend twice.

Oh, Mama. Mama, you're going to skin me.

"Councilors, we need another expedition," he said, raising his voice above their consternation. "We need to go after Lord Baden and the others. And if we can't find them — or if — if —" He paused, willing his hammering heart to ease. "Ain't no getting around it. Lur needs that lost magic. One way or another, we've got to find it and bring it back before the kingdom's done tearing itself apart. Me and Arlin can —"

"*What?*" said Arlin, with a startled laugh. "No. If it's Lost Doranen magic that's required then this is Doranen business and none of yours. As a Doranen I tell you plainly, Rafel: you're not welcome in our lands."

"Never mind him, never *mind!*" Rafel shouted at the Olken councilors, bellowing their offense. "Shut your bloody traps, the lot of you!"

As they fell raggedly silent he turned back to Rodyn Garrick's ignorant, hate-blinded son.

"Arlin, don't be pig ignorant. There ain't no way you can tell which bits of that ancient Doranen magic are needed to heal the damage done to Lur. But I can."

Arlin's lip curled. "So *you* say."

"That's right. 'Cause you ain't the one as can hear the earth screaming. You ain't the one with Lur's pain bubbling in your blood. And you ain't —"

"What I *ain't,*" said Arlin, pale with rage, "is going anywhere with *you.* If you think I'll trust my life to my father's murderer then *you're* the fool, Rafel."

He shrugged. "Fine. Then you can stay behind and I'll take another Doranen with me." He looked at the Doranen mages clumped on their side of the council chamber. "So? Who's game, eh? You're sick and tired of the Olken hero, Asher? Then find a hero of your own and let him do what my da did. Risk everything for Lur."

This time the Doranen councilors' silence was uneasy. Every gaze avoided his. And not one of them — not *one* — offered to chance him or herself. Offered any kind of help at all. Fear had them by the throats and they weren't about to fight it. He tried to understand, to forgive... and couldn't. He felt his own power stir, his own shimmer of rage.

"You bloody Doranen, you make me *sick!* I can't *abide* Arlin Garrick, poxy, arrogant shit that he is. But he's still worth more than any five of you fancy mages tied together. And you Olken, who ought to be climbing all over each other to save Lur? You make me sick too. Why ain't you speaking up with me? It's our home and you won't *fight* for it?"

And now the silence was full of shame, and anger, and sullen resentment. Face suffused dark red, Shifrin shoved out his chair. "Have a care, Rafel," he growled. "Any respect you're shown in this Council chamber comes to you by way of your father. And it has a limit."

"Like your courage?" he retorted. "Forget about finding Lost Dorana, if it frights you too much. What about Goose and the rest? What about Fernel Pintte? You don't reckon we ought to help *them?*"

Shifrin banged his fist on the Speaker's table. "We don't even know if they're still *alive!*"

"And you don't bloody know they ain't!"

Breathing harshly, Shifrin shoved the blue shard of circle stone towards him. "Then why don't you find out, Rafel? Try reaching Pintte yourself, if you're so sure we're cowards, and useless."

It was a challenge he couldn't ignore. Not only 'cause Arlin Garrick was stood there, smirking, but 'cause if he didn't then he'd lose any shred of authority he had. Lose with it any hope of getting over the mountains and finding Goose. So he stepped up to Shifrin's table and laid both hands on the blue crystal.

Intense cold. Searing heat. His heart raced, pumping his magic-scalded blood faster and faster. And then a wave of overwhelming dread. Terror that tried to drop him dead where he stood. Pintte's fragmented message, booming through his skull. *Danger. Help us. Not alone.* But when he tried to find Dorana's mayor, the fool who'd sunk so many in Westwailing, he found nothing. Felt nothing. Heard nothing but the lingering echoes of horror trapped in blue crystal. He snatched his hands from the circle stone, trying not to retch.

"You see?" said Shifrin. "There's nothing there. No-one to reach. They're gone, Rafel. Most likely dead. And you want us to throw more lives after them? Barl forgive us, your father was right. It was folly to send those men over the mountains. This Council won't approve a third expedition. Especially not when you're talking of finding Lost Dorana. Are you mad? That fabled land fell to magewar centuries ago."

"You don't know that for certain sure, Shifrin," he retorted. "You're only guessing, 'cause you don't want to take the risk."

Shifrin pounded the Speaker's table again. "I don't want to see good men die for no reason, Olken *or* Doranen. *Any* death would be a waste."

"Speaker Shifrin is right," Barlsman Jaffee added. "It would be nothing short of wickedness to send anyone in Sarle Baden and Fernel Pintte's misguided footsteps. I know your friend went with them, Rafel. You have my condolences for his loss. But—"

"You ain't asking me, Barlsman. I'm bloody offering."

"And your offer is declined," Shifrin snapped. "Yours and Lord Garrick's. Rafel, how can you even think of abandoning Lur now? We've got storms raging unchecked across the kingdom and the dregs of magic in the earth creating havoc. You're *needed* here. With your father helpless in his bed, and Barl alone knowing if he'll ever leave it, you're the only Olken we have gifted with the Doranen touch. You might be Lur's only hope of surviving."

He nearly said, *No, I ain't. You got Deenie at a pinch.* But he swallowed the words just in time. Letting that slip would nigh on ruin Deenie's life. Mama would never forgive him.

"I *told* you, Shifrin, I can't help Lur. I can't stop the storms. I can't heal the earth. And this time things won't right themselves. So we have to try something else, something desperate, or I promise you, I *swear* it, *Lur won't survive.*"

Frighted murmuring from the Council. Sickened looks exchanged between Shifrin and Jaffee. Lur's powerful men, with no more power now than spratlings.

"Whatever happens, if I die doing this, ain't no blame will fall on you," he added. "I'll sign a paper before I go, saying how it was my idea and you tried to stop me and I wouldn't listen. I'll happily do that. And I won't say anyone's got to come with me. I'll go alone. Might be better that road. But—"

Arlin snatched him by the sleeve and pulled him around. "You think *you* can decide who will or won't do this? *I am not bound by your petty pronouncements.* I am a Doranen mage, and I will claim my heritage and birthright without seeking *your* permission. Without *you*. I will—"

"Be bound by the decision of this General Council!" shouted Speaker Shifrin, slamming his gavel so hard it nearly broke. "As will you, Rafel. We will now deliberate on these weighty matters. You will be informed of our decision in due course. Until then you're dismissed. Quit this chamber at once. And do *not* talk of this meeting to *anyone*."

For a moment, just a moment, Rafel thought about arguing. Da always said the Council could talk itself to a standstill and never once find common ground to stand on. And Lur's time—Goose's time—was fast running out.

"Rafel," said Barlsman Jaffee gently. "Go to your father. He needs you, my boy...and so does your mother."

And that was playing gutter dirty—but it was also true. He turned on his heel and walked out, not looking at fuming Arlin Garrick as he passed him. The guards opened the double doors as he approached. He thanked them with a curt nod and a strained half-smile, and made his way to the antechamber beyond.

"Rafel! Stop! *Don't you walk away from me!*"

And that was Arlin, of course, who lacked the sense of a drunken flea. Chasing after him like he had the right to bark orders. Halfway down the corridor leading to the outside world, and sorely needed fresh air, he spun about.

"Leave me be, Arlin. I ain't of a mind to chat just now."

Arlin waved an impatient hand. "I want —"

"*I don't care what you want.* So unless you're looking to get dumped on your arse a second time, *leave me be.*"

Arlin's slender fingers clenched, as though they ached to strike or strangle. Raw power crackled the air around him. "Lost Dorana is none of your business. I'll not permit you to —"

Rafel brought up his fist. Ignited the cauldron of magic inside him and let glimfire burst from his blood. Flickering flames danced over his white knuckles.

"Arlin, you get older but no bloody wiser. D'you *remember* Westwailing?"

Arlin smiled, fierce and feral. Blew on his glimlit hand — and blew it out. "You don't frighten me, Rafel. You never have. You never will. And you will *never* cross those mountains."

He'd die before he'd show Arlin he felt even the smallest bit impressed. Shoving his hands in his pockets, he shrugged. "Aye, well. We'll see about that, won't we?"

Then he turned again, and walked away.

"*Rafel,*" said Charis, standing in her open doorway. She was wearing a white apron over a yellow blouse and green skirt, and her dark hair was tied back under a yellow scarf. Flour dusted her hands, her cheek, the tip of her nose. She looked flustered. Beautiful. "You're back. When did you — why are you —"

Broad-brimmed hat in his hands, he smiled at her, tentative. "I put Firedragon in your stable. Hope you don't mind."

"What? No, no of course not," she said. "Rafel, what are you —"

"I stopped by to see Pellen." *And let the Council stamp about that all they bloody like. I don't care.* "Is he here?"

The surprised pleasure died out of her eyes. "Papa? Why do you need to see Papa?"

For so many reasons, he couldn't answer. "It's complicated, Charis. And it's important." He put on his best wheedling voice. "Please?"

Beneath the smudges of flour, her cheeks tinted pink. "I don't know," she murmured. "He's awful weak, Rafe." Her fingers tightened on the edge of the front door. "It might be best if you come back another time. I can't have him upset. I can't—I don't—" Her voice broke, and she stared at him in mute misery.

Sink it. *"Please,* Charis," he said, knowing he was being selfish, knowing he was using her girlish feelings for him. *But this is bigger than her feelings.* "I ain't looking to fret him, or you. I only need a little while. And I'd not come bothering if it wasn't needful. I ain't even been home yet. I ain't seen *my* da. You reckon I'd come here before seeing him if I didn't have to?"

She shook her head, tears brimming. "No, of course not." Letting go of the door, she and stepped back. "But Rafel, when I ask you to leave—you have to leave. Don't wheedle me then."

"I won't," he said, stepping over the threshold. *Not unless I have to.* "So... I can go up?"

"Yes, go up." Her hands twisted in the apron. "He's not long had his supper. He's still awake. But Rafel—"

He paused on the staircase and looked down at her. "Don't you trust me, Charis?"

"He's all I have, Rafe," she said, as the brimming tears fell. "And Kerril says I won't have him much longer. If you—if you feel the smallest kindness for me you'll remember that. When you're talking your important mage business... you'll remember it."

So she didn't trust him. At least not altogether. *She knows me too bloody well, that's the problem.* "I'll be quick as I can. Only—"

Now her fingers were clutching the staircase newel-post. "What?"

"You're so busy seeing him a sick man, you forget Pellen Orrick lived his life doing right by Lur. He won't be sorry to see me. He'll be glad I came."

"Forget?" Tears banished by anger, Charis glared at him. "You think to school me on my own father, Rafel? It seems Arlin Garrick's right after all. You *are* as arrogant as any Doranen."

He shrugged. "Meek men don't get much done in the world, Charis."

And he kept walking up the staircase, feeling the heat of her stare scorch his back.

"Rafel!" said Pellen, as he tapped on the open chamber door. "So, you're home again. Good. Well, don't just stand there. Come in. Have a seat."

But he couldn't move. Was nailed to the floor at the sight of Da's friend. Only five days since he'd seen him in the Council chamber, but so much had changed. Pellen's face was faded blueish-grey, all its flesh consumed by fever. His dark hair was fever-bleached too and cropped to stubble, showing the vulnerable shape of his skull. Just like a babe's. Even covered by a nightshirt it was clear he'd languished to skin-and-bone, worse even than Jaffee.

"What?" said Pellen, raising an eyebrow. "Didn't Charis tell you I'm dying?"

He'd come here seeking advice. Or maybe...permission. He'd not thought to be struck dumb and close to tears.

A small, wry smile curved Pellen's lips. "So I do look worse than your da. I should be sorry to hear it, but I'm not. This is a race I'm happy to win, Rafel. You'd best tell me how he's doing today. The truth, mind. No coddling."

Rafel cleared his throat. There were tapers burning by the bedside, soaked in some kind of healing incense. Kerril's doing. She had them burned in Da's chamber, too. He never noticed them making a difference, but nobody wanted to cross Lur's best pother.

"I don't know," he muttered, the sweet smoke tickling his nose. "I ain't been home yet."

"Days on the road and you're here instead of with your father? What's the matter with you, Rafe?"

"I got called to see the Council, urgent."

"Oh," said Pellen. Then he jerked his chin at the bedside chair. "Sit down, I said. Makes me tired, shouting across the room at you."

He pushed the door to and did as he was told. "You got any word on Da?"

"I'm told he's holding his own," said Pellen, cautious. "But Charis and that bloody pother between them think to eke out a few more days for me by mouthing comfortable lies. That's why I asked you how he was looking. Can't rely on what Kerril says. If I had the strength I'd be insulted." He pulled a face. "Mind you, I think she's gone a bit sweet on me. Silly girl." Then his clouded gaze sharpened. "Speaking of sweet, you're not looking sugar plums at my daughter, are you?"

What? *Yes.* "No! Pellen—"

"Good," said his da's friend. "She can do a sight better than a fowsty young buck like you."

Stung, he felt his jaw drop. "Oh. So—"

"Easy, Rafe. I'm twigging you," said Pellen, wearily teasing. "But she's a conversation for another day. Why'd the Council want you so urgent?"

"The expedition. There's word."

Pellen snorted. "And it's bad, of course. The fools. A pity heeding your father's gone right out of fashion. So, they're all dead?"

Weary himself, and worried, he felt his belly clutch with anger. *"Pellen—"*

"Sorry, Rafe." Reaching out, Pellen patted his knee. "It slipped my mind. Goose Martin. A good lad. But they wouldn't have summoned you just for that. What else does the Council want?"

He slumped in the chair. "The impossible."

"Ah." Pellen frowned at the ceiling. "So...*these* are the Final Days your mother tried to save us from. After all we went through, prophecy got it wrong."

He sounded sad but not exactly surprised. As though he'd always known things would turn out this way. "Pellen..." No use hesitating. Best to just say it. "Me and Arlin Garrick want to go over the mountains. We want to find Old Dorana, and bring back magic as can save Lur. The Council's talking on it now, but they'll say yes. It's our only chance."

"And crossing the mountains," said Pellen, after a while. "That your mad idea, was it?"

"Arlin said it first. I said I'd go with him."

"Bet *that* put a smile on his face."

He couldn't help grinning. "Not really."

"Rafel..." Pellen heaved a sigh. "Nobody knows where Lost Dorana is. It's why they call it *lost.* You could wander for years and never find it."

"I know," he said. "But I can't let that stop me. Any road, leave Lost Dorana aside and there's still Goose."

"Rafe—"

"No," he said, and leapt up. "I don't want to hear it, Pellen. Goose ain't dead. He's with Sarle Baden, and Baden's a powerful mage. He ain't dead. None of them are. In trouble, it sounds like, but not—not dead."

Pellen dragged a hand over his grey-stubbled face. "What can I say to talk you out of this? D'you want me to tell you how you shouldn't trust your life to Arlin Garrick? Because you shouldn't. Given half a chance, that young man would push you off a mountain."

"Prob'ly," he said, shrugging. "So prob'ly I shouldn't give him half a chance, eh?"

Pellen growled. "It's not funny, boy."

"Never said it was," he replied. "Pellen, I don't know what else to do. All I know is even if Goose wasn't out there somewhere, needing me to help him, I'd still go. 'Cause Lur needs help worse than Goose and the rest of them. What I felt in the earth, out in the Home Districts...what I can feel now, here with you..." He didn't try to hide the shudder. Sat down again, suddenly close to despair. To tears. "I've got to do *something.*"

"I understand that," said Pellen, troubled. "You're your father's son. But Rafe—that boy of Rodyn's, he's—"

"Believe me, I don't want to go *anywhere* with the poxy shit. But even though it's Arlin, I'll still be safer crossing the mountains with him than if I went on my lonesome."

"You're sure about that?" Pellen asked quietly. "Because I'm not."

"Don't fret," he said, trying to hide his own doubt. "I've got a few tricks up my sleeve. If Arlin thinks to faddle with me, could be he'll get himself a nasty surprise."

"It's one thing to be confident," said Pellen, with a sharp look. "It's another to be—"

"Arrogant? Aye. So I'm told."

That earned him another sharp look. "I see you've convinced yourself there's no other way. But—"

"Pellen..." With an effort, he calmed himself. *I can't fratch at him. He's only trying to help.* "I don't know if Da's dying...but I *do* know Lur is. And it's Lur dying that's put Da in his bed like a wax doll."

"Maybe that's true," said Pellen, frowning again. "But Rafel, speaking as a father, I can tell you *your* father wouldn't want this for you. All he wants is his son safe and well."

He sat back. "Does he? 'Cause down in Westwailing, when he needed help, when folk were in danger? He risked my life without thinking twice, Pellen. Back Da into a corner and he'll use anyone. You know that. He used his own best friend. Killed him. So me going over the mountains to save this kingdom? That's just being a good son, ain't it?"

Pellen's deep sigh turned into a raw, hacking cough. Sickened, Rafel waited for the spasm to pass, gave his father's friend water from the bedside pitcher, then waited to see if he was strong enough to keep talking.

"Rafel," Pellen croaked, stranded against his bolstering pillows. "Are you sure this isn't because your father denied you the last time? Because you blame him for whatever fate's befallen your friend?"

He shoved out of the chair again. Paced the small, sweet-scented chamber. "If I don't do this, Pellen, if I don't save Lur, then every last bloody pain Da ever suffered for this kingdom? He suffered it for *nowt*. I can't have that. I *won't* have it. Lur's got to live."

"Though it cost you *your* life?" said Pellen, and dragged open his blue-veined eyelids. "Your father wouldn't want that."

"I don't care what he wants," he retorted. "Not this time."

"Well, then...since your mind's made up...what do you want from me?" said Pellen, a wheeze in his voice. "An old man with his left foot stuck in the grave?"

Good question. Halted at the foot of the bed, he found himself suddenly struggling for words. "Da might wake up after I'm gone. If he wakes up, and—and you—you ain't—"

"If I'm not dead?" Pellen shook his head and laughed, the wheeze sounding louder. "Rafel, you're bloody killing me. No, no, don't apologise. After Charis and Kerril, well-meaning as they are, your bluntness

428

is a breath of fresh air." He sobered. "Yes. I'll tell him. I'll try and make him understand. If I'm not dead by the time he wakes up."

If he wakes up. The unspoken words hung between them, loud as a shout.

"Thank you," he said. "I surely appreciate it."

"And there's nothing else you've come for?" said Pellen. "My blessing, perhaps?"

You're as bad as Charis. You both know me too well. "I s'pose," he muttered. Looked up, and met Pellen's sad gaze. "Since I can't have Da's. And I'll not get Mama's. It'd mean something, if you gave it, Pellen. You're family."

Pellen's pain-shadowed eyes washed brilliant. "Barl save me, Rafel. You and Asher. Cut from the same cloth." Then he grimaced. "About your mother..."

"She's already well fratched at me. I don't see this'll make much difference."

"Don't talk tosh," Pellen snapped. "Rafel, I've been friends with your mother close on a quarter century. Right now she's beside herself not knowing who to be more afraid for, you or your father. So if you're determined to do this, you'd best do it with your eyes wide open. You'd best face up to what you'll be doing to her, by leaving. And to your sister."

"Deenie doesn't need me," he said. "She's got Charis. But Mama..." He rubbed his face. "I already know what she'll say. She said it already, before I rode out for the Home Districts. She accused me of abandoning Da. She thought I was being reckless and selfish and cruel."

Five days since she'd shouted those barbed words, and he was still bleeding.

"I don't understand, Pellen. She used to be fierce. She fought as hard as Da ever did to save Lur from Morg. Why doesn't she — why can't she — I don't understand."

"People change, Rafel," Pellen said gently. "Women have babies and they change. She's still fierce. But she's trying to protect her family now. That's what she's fierce about. That's what she's fighting for."

"That's why I went!" he protested. "And it's why I'll cross the mountains with Arlin. How can she not know that? How can my own mother not know—"

"She knows, Rafe. But her instinct is to protect you. So you be kindly to her, d'you hear me? Don't you—"

The unlatched chamber door swung open. "Rafel," said Charis, politely smiling, her eyes coldly watchful. "It's been so kind of you, stopping by to see how Papa's faring."

In other words, *get out now.* Mindful of his promise not to wheedle, he smiled at Da's dying friend. "It was good of you to see me, Pellen. But Charis is right, you need to rest."

Pellen beckoned him closer with one crooked finger. "Rafel..."

He walked round the bed and bent low. "Aye, Pellen?"

"Barl keep you safe, boy," Pellen whispered. Pulled him down and kissed his forehead with hot, dry lips. "And Jervale watch over you too. You are your father's son, Rafel. If anyone can save Lur, I think you can."

Until Pellen said it, he didn't realise how much he'd wanted to hear that. *Needed* to hear it. Knowing that a man like Pellen Orrick believed in him...

"Rafel," said Charis sharply. "I'll walk you downstairs."

Pellen let his hand drop, and Rafel straightened. Looking down at the man he'd known as long as he'd known Da, suddenly he was a sprat again, on Darran's bed. And he knew that when Charis closed the chamber door behind him he'd have seen Pellen Orrick for the last time. Just as he'd known, waving Goose goodbye, that—

No. I was wrong about that. I'll see Goose again. I will.

Charis opened the front door so hard she nearly pulled it off its hinges. "Goodbye."

"Why are you fratched at me?" he said, staring. "You said don't wheedle you and I didn't."

"No, you didn't wheedle me," Charis snapped. "But you made Papa cry. And that's a lot worse, Rafel. I'll not soon forgive you that."

"Cry? He wasn't—"

"You think a man has to shed tears to be weeping?" she demanded.

430

"You broke his bloody heart, Rafel, and it's not strong enough. Not any more."

Silenced, he pulled a face. "Broke *his* heart, Charis? You sure on that? Could be it's another heart you're thinking on."

She slapped him. And then she kissed him, a desperate pressing of warm lips to his. Startled, he tried to kiss her back but she broke free and stumbled out of his reach.

"You don't love me," she said, her eyes accusing. "You never even *saw* me. So don't you think, just because you're leaving, don't you think you can—"

His lips were tingling. "How d'you know I'm leaving? Were you *listening?*"

"Of course I was," she said, derisive. "Did you think I'd not make sure you didn't upset him?"

"You were listening," he murmured. *Slumskumbledy bloody wench.* "And? What d'you reckon?"

"I reckon you've got no choice," she said, her voice threatening to break. "If things are as bad as you say . . . you've got to go."

She'd taken off the apron and the headscarf. Before he could stop himself, he smoothed a lock of her long dark hair and tucked it sweetly behind her ear.

"I saw you, Charis," he said, his voice hoarse. "There was never a day when I didn't see you."

Her mouth dropped open. "*Now* you tell me?" she said, almost breathless. "*Now?* When you're going across the mountains likely to die in a ditch in a strange land all alone? You—you—*sapskull.* You *popster.* Go away, Rafel. I *hate* you."

And she slammed the house's front door in his face.

Women.

Aggravated, he made his way round the back of the house, rescued Firedragon from the stable, swung into saddle and headed for home.

CHAPTER TWENTY-SIX

Asher lay so still he didn't disturb his swaddling blankets, but Dathne smoothed them anyway. It helped her to feel she was doing something. Helping him. Nursing him, as a good wife should. But the gesture felt pointless. He didn't know she sat beside him because he'd gone far away. How could he have walked so far ahead, leaving her behind? She'd always been the leader. From the day they met she'd led him where he needed to go. But then he'd abandoned her. And now Rafel was abandoning her too.

Like father, like son.

Salt water stung her eyes. She blinked it away. She was tired of weeping. Tears turned her from plain to ugly and they didn't change a thing. Her husband was stupored and her son was leaving. Soon she would be alone, save for a daughter whose frights and imaginings were just one more burden. Once there'd been a Dathne who would have fought against that. Who would have rejected such a bleak future and instead pummelled the present until the future changed.

I don't know where she is now. I don't know how to find her.

In the past, when she'd been lost and uncertain, she'd had Veira to guide her back to the path. To show her where to find her courage. She'd had Matt, as well. But her dear friends were dead and the hand that had held hers during that crushing double grief—Asher's hand—was cold and careless of her needs. She could hold it. She did hold it. But he could not hold her hand in return.

It wasn't supposed to be like this. We saved the kingdom. We were meant to have a happy ending. We thought we had a happy ending. Now we're faced with the real ending...an ending that will end us.

Unless Rafel prevailed.

"Can he prevail, Asher?" she whispered. "Or will the darkness that lies beyond those mountains swallow him, as it's swallowed everyone else who's challenged it? I know he's like you. I know there's a strength and a power in him unmatched in any other Olken. But Asher—*look* at you. You've been *defeated.* That means *he* can be defeated. He wants me to smile and wave him goodbye. He wants me to be proud of him. He wants that I should celebrate what he's about to do. But I can't. *I can't.* He's asking me to dance on his grave before he's even buried in it."

Asher said nothing. After so many years of his brash, vibrant presence, his absence was a gaping wound. The Innocent Mage had ruled her life since she was younger than Deenie. Was woven into her fabric like a thread of gold, glittering. Her touchstone. Her lodestar. Her lamp in the darkness, leading her home.

Now he's being extinguished. And I am powerless to help him.

Despair was a grey tide, lapping at her feet.

"Oh, Asher..." Weary, so weary, she let herself fold to his bed. Rested her cheek on his blankets and imagined his hand, stroking her hair. Imagined his deep voice murmuring comfort. Imagined her body loved by his. Remembered the thousand small ways he gave her joy and the things he did that made her frown.

Make me frown again, Asher. Give me reason to scold.

And still he did not speak to her. For a moment she was so *angry* with him she wanted to shriek.

You promised me. You promised. Asher, how could you do this?

His silence reproached her.

"That was different," she told him. "I was Jervale's Heir then. I was part of the Circle, bound by oaths I couldn't break. Not even for you. And we weren't married when I...misled you. We had no children. I owed you *nothing*."

Kerril kept tapers burning in the chamber. Claimed they had a healing effect. For herself, she found them revolting. But her desperation had reached such heights...if Morg himself appeared and offered to—

"I'd listen," she whispered. "I would. I don't think there's anything I wouldn't do for you. Please, Asher, come back. Deenie's hurting so badly, and I can't help her. And Rafel—oh, *Rafel*—"

Aching, she sat up. Threaded her fingers through Asher's lank, lustreless hair. Touched his closed eyes, his pale lips. Traced the length of his crooked nose. Once, only weeks ago, days, her lightest touch could stir him. Make him smile, and kiss her. And now she might as well be touching a marble effigy.

But she couldn't afford to let herself think about that. She had something particular to say. Something to ask. A question she couldn't leave unanswered.

"Jervale alone knows what dangers our son will face," she said, forcing herself to fold her hands in her lap. "And he might have power, my love, but power won't be enough. Should I..." She swallowed, feeling the heat of terror rise in her throat. "Asher, should I give him Barl's diary?"

She wanted to. Jervale's mercy, she wanted Rafe to absorb every last warspell in that book and arm himself to the teeth against whatever was waiting beyond the mountains.

"We know he's strong enough to wield those magics. You made sure of that in Westwailing. And we can't let him leave this kingdom without—without doing all we can to *protect* him. How could we do that? We're his parents, Asher. Grown man or not, Rafe's still our child."

Sometimes Asher breathed so lightly her eyes tricked her into thinking he wasn't breathing at all. She held her own breath, waiting to see his chest rise...waiting to hear that faint sighing of air as it fell...

"Asher," she said, as he breathed, *"should I give him the diary?"*

And as though he'd spoken, she heard his answer.

No.

No. Loving Rafel wasn't reason enough to reveal this last secret. The diary had to stay hidden. Because Doranen like Arlin Garrick must never learn of its existence. Once released, the warspells couldn't ever be called back. And there were other magics written there, that must never see the light of day. Because—

Because he could use it to find the way to Lost Dorana. And once there, he might discover magics that make the warspells look...safe. I can't risk it. Whatever dangers Lur faces now, they're nothing compared to unbridled Doranen magic. Asher would never forgive me if I endangered this kingdom. And I'd never forgive myself if I put Rafe in harm's way. If he can't find that lost, forsaken country—then he'll come home again. He will.

She felt sick. In protecting her child, in denying him what he needed for his self-imposed task, she was also betraying him. He believed so hard that what he planned to do was right. Was what his father would want. Was somehow his—his *duty.*

"We did that to him, Asher," she said, staring into her husband's beloved, secret face. "The Innocent Mage and Jervale's Heir...between us we made our son think he'd be shown wanting if he didn't throw his life away for Lur. Shame on us. *Shame on us.*"

Asher said nothing. She took his silence for assent. Felt the hot tears spill, and meander down her face. It was the only warm thing about her. She was so cold. And brutally alone. As a young woman, as the Heir, she'd learned to accept that her life must be solitary and would likely remain so. And then Asher had come and turned belief inside out. Shattered acceptance. Dared her to daring. She'd broken the rules. Broken his heart. Broken her own heart. And yet...they'd mended. Made a life. Made children. Found joy. Found peace.

But peace, it seemed, was nowt but illusion. Joy was fleeting. Children...left. And the man she loved more than peace and joy, more than life, was broken again—and she couldn't mend him.

Beyond the hushed chamber's uncurtained window the night sky was filling with clouds. Another storm brewing. Lur's pain taking form. In the earth, in her blood and bones, she felt its vicious echoes. But that pain was dull. Her pain for Asher was sharp.

I am in my own death throes. If he dies... so do I.

Stranded in her chamber, curled up on her bed, kept dull and quiet with Kerril's possets, Deenie felt the storm break like glass shattering in her blood. Its violence rushed through her, scouring her clean of herbs and conjured apathy. Whimpering, she pressed her hands to her temples to hold in the hurt. It did no good. Every beat of her heart pumped it through and through her shaking body. Like glass, Lur was breaking.

Am I breaking with it?

She wasn't a child any longer, to run crying to Mama. There was no comfort there anyway. Mama was almost empty these days, all the fight poured out of her. She'd spent her whole life fighting and now she was tired.

I'm tired too. I'm tired of feeling things nobody else can feel. I'm tired of not being believed. I'm tired of being alone. Of being afraid. Of being a mouse waiting for the hungry cat to pounce.

Frighted and lonely, knowing she'd most likely regret it, she sought out her brother. He'd been home a handful of hours but they'd not spoken yet. She'd heard him and Mama, though, shouting. She'd not drowsed her way through that. So much hurt and anger, pins and needles in her heart. They'd shouted about him leaving again. About Da, and Barl's Mountains. About Goose and the others who'd gone away... and weren't going to come back. Because she couldn't help either of them, she'd stuffed her fingers in her ears.

Rafe was in his privy chamber, hunched in the window-seat reading an old, tattered manuscript. Standing in the doorway, she waited for him to notice her.

"Go away," he said, not looking up. "I'm busy."

That manuscript—it was Tollin's account of his expedition, that failed. The first time she'd found Rafe reading it—out in the Tower gardens, where he'd go to be alone and where she could always find him—they were both sprats. Nearly nine, she'd been, and sure as sure he wasn't s'posed to have it. Had spied on him reading bits aloud to himself, playing parts, playing explorer, then crept away before she could betray herself, giggling. But he wasn't a sprat now, and neither was she.

"Rafe," she said softly, inching her way acrosss the carpet. "Do you really think Tollin's records will help?"

"I said go away," he muttered. The chamber's glimlight sputtered, throwing shadows every which way, echoing the earth's ceaseless unrest. "Don't make me make you."

But she persisted, because his threats didn't scare her. Even with all that power in him, straining to burst loose, churning in his blood like the whirlpools down in Westwailing. He was her brother. She could never fear him.

"The others would've seen that manuscript, you know. Goose and Fernel Pintte and Sarle Baden. If it didn't help them, I don't see it helping you."

An exasperated sigh hissed between his teeth. *"Deenie..."* And then he let his head fall back against the wainscoting. "How did you know I'm going? Were you listening too?" He pulled a face. "Bloody girls."

"I wasn't *listening,*" she said crossly, because the way he said it meant something sneaky and sly. "I *heard.* You might think on keeping your voice down if you want to talk secrets on the stairs."

"Ha. Right."

The thought of him leaving was like knife blades sliding under her skin. "Rafe...do you have to do this?"

And now he shifted his gaze to meet hers. "Aye."

If he'd shouted at her, like he'd shouted at Mama...if he'd rolled his eyes, tried to make it a joke...if he hadn't just *looked* at her, so serious, so resigned...

I can't fratch at him. I can't.

Tremblly, she dropped onto a handy footstool. *Rafe.* "So...that manuscript. Did you pinch it from Da? That time you did the really tricky magic, remember? Is that when you pinched it?"

"That was years ago," he said, letting the worn parchment slide onto his lap. "What does it matter now?"

It didn't. Of course it didn't. 'Cept he was going away and they hardly ever talked. "I know, but..." She chewed her lip. "Did you?"

"What if I did?" he said, looking out of the window where the rain was pouring and the sky flashed with lightning. "Who you going to tell?"

"Nobody. I just wanted to know. That tricky magic. Did you make it up?"

She watched a memory play over his face. Watched some small, secret pleasure ease the strain in his eyes. Sitting so close to him, almost close enough to touch, she could feel his woken power burn. Like a bonfire, flames leaping, licking her with heat.

He nodded. "Aye. I made it up." His gaze flicked sideways. "That's a secret."

When was the last time he'd trusted her with a secret? When was the last time they'd sat together like this, so cosy? The journey home from Westwailing. Those few moments she'd rested her head on his shoulder. And before that? She couldn't remember. They weren't close. They never had been. And yet she could feel him, like the blood in her veins.

"You been to see Da yet?"

In a finger-snap, like magic, his pleasure froze into pain. "Aye."

"And did you feel it?" she said, heart thudding. "What's in him? Please tell me you felt it this time, Rafe. I don't want to be the only one who can feel it."

"Sink me," he swore. *"Deenie—"*

"Please, Rafe, don't shout. Everything's awful already, don't shout."

He tossed the manuscript aside, slid out of the window-seat and thumped to his knees on the carpet in front of her. Took her by both shoulders and shook her. Not hard, not to hurt her. He was trying to change her mind.

"Deenie, you've got to stop this," he said, so earnest. "No, I don't feel any blight in Da. And you don't, neither. You've got yourself stirred up, is all, the way you did when we were sprats. Don't you remember how it was? You'd wake yourself screaming in the night, pointing at ghosts and ghoulies no-one else could see. You'd swear upside down they were real, but they never were. They were just bad dreams. This ain't no different."

"That time Da dreamed the warbeasts," she retorted, and knocked his hands aside. "That was real."

"That was one time," said her brother. "You were right *once,* Deenie. And never again. You can't—"

She scrambled to her feet, tipping the footstool on its side. "Shut up, Rafe. Just 'cause you did some clever magic down in Westwailing you think no-one else can be special? Is that it?"

"*No.* But—"

"I ain't a sprat now," she said, glaring. "And I bloody well ain't dreaming. Why won't you—"

"Can Pother Kerril feel it yet?" he demanded, and stood. "Best pother in the kingdom, she is. Cured folks as were gasping their last. What's she say, Deenie?"

She felt a single tear snail its tickling way down her cheek. "I don't care what Kerril says. I *feel* things, Rafel. That's what I do."

He stared at her, silent. Outside, the thunder boomed. Lightning lashed the sky. "I know," he said at last. "It's just... I want you to be wrong."

"Don't you think *I* want to be wrong?" she whispered. "Don't you think I'd give *anything* to be wrong?"

And then they both jumped, startled, as a deafening clap of thunder crashed overhead. All the glimfire blinked out, plunging them into darkness.

"I got it," said Rafel, and reignited every lamp. "We're fine, Deenie."

"No, we're not. Oh, Rafe, do you feel as awful as I do?" She pressed clenched fingers to her chest. "I'm all—*broken*—inside."

The earth's pain was in his eyes, bright as shattered glass. "Me too."

"It's going to be bad like this, over the mountains. Prob'ly it's going to be worse."

"I know. Deenie—"

"I'm not saying don't go," she said quickly. "I know you have to. Only... don't try to pretend you ain't afraid. If you stop yourself feeling fear, you might stop yourself feeling other things, Rafe. Things that could keep you alive."

"Like what?" he said. Fratched and grudging, yes, but at long last *listening.*

She wanted to lie, but she couldn't. "I can't tell. Lur's screaming so loud it makes my head spin."

Beyond the chamber's window rain hammered the already hammered Tower gardens. More thunder rumbled, marching somewhere distant. Prob'ly over the Flatlands. That felt about right.

"A big bloody help you are," he said, scowling. He looked like Da. "If you're going to witter warnings at me, Deenie, witter something I can use."

"I wish I could," she said. "But I don't know how to save you, Rafe. I don't know how to save anyone. Or Lur. All I can do is feel smashed to pieces."

He was her big brother and he loved her. Not easily, she knew that. His love was well-peppered with impatience. Her fears had always gritted him, like sand in his boots... just as his brash boldness always made her feel small. But he hugged her now, adrift on the carpet, and she hugged him back. Breathed in the sweat and horse of him, the faint yeastiness of strong ale, the sweet tint of sickroom incense. All the different smells that made him Rafe.

He's leaving. He's leaving. I don't want him to go.

"Rafe," she said, muffled against his shoulder. In that moment knowing everything about him. "Don't fret over Mama."

His arms tightened. "She's so fratched at me, Deenie. I thought she was scalded when I rode off for the Home Districts. But now I'm going over the mountains—" His voice cracked. "I reckon she might let me ride away without another word."

He was trembling. "No, no," she said, holding him harder. "She's frighted for you. We both are. What you're trying to do? And with nobody to help you but that Arlin Garrick? Of course we're frighted."

Rafel let his arms drop. Took a half step back. "I ain't getting lost, or worse, over them mountains. I've got power and I'll use it." His eyes were fierce. "I'll burn anyone as gets in my way. I'm saving Goose, I'm saving Lur, and I'm coming back."

She didn't know if he was right. She only knew he thought he was, and that not even Mama's rage and tears would change his mind. Not even Da lying in his bed so still and pale, with the blight in him only she could feel, poisoning his veins. Rafe thought he was born for this ... and nothing else mattered.

"You always were stubborn," she murmured, pressing her palm to his cheek. "You always did what you wanted, no matter what anyone said. No matter if you were being naughty or not." She tried to laugh. "And most times, Rafe, you were being naughty."

"True," he admitted, and covered her hand with his. Then his wry smile faded. "Deenie, I've got things to do. I want to read that manuscript again. I want to—" Hesitating, he let his hand drop. "I've got some thinking as needs doing."

He wasn't telling her the exact truth. There was a sudden tartness to him, like the scent of fresh lemons on a warm breeze. *Prob'ly he intends on being naughty again.* But since she had no hope of stopping him, best she be gracious.

"It's all right. How long before the Council gives you formal leave to go?"

"I'm not sure," he said, shrugging. "But I'll wager not long." He looked out of the window at the still-blustering storm. "'Cause Lur ain't got long. You and me know that, if nobody else does."

"True," she said quietly. "Lucky us, eh?" She tried to smile. "Don't work too late. You need your rest."

"Deenie..."

Stopped halfway to the door, she turned. "Yes?"

There were tears in his eyes. *Tears.* And he looked so young. So vulnerable.

"What, Rafe?"

He shook his head. "Nowt. Nowt. Never mind me. Off you go."

She closed the chamber door behind her, and went downstairs to the kitchen to see if Meistress Watt would let her dabble her hands in some pastry, or something else as might need baking. Maybe that would ease her troubled heart.

But she doubted it. She couldn't imagine feeling untroubled ever again.

As the door shut behind his sister, Rafel breathed deeply a few times. Waited until all he felt was irritated amusement. *Naughty,* Deenie called him. And if he was, what of it? Just like he'd told Charis—meek men never got anything done.

Still. The word echoed in his memory, niggling, as he slipped into Da's library and settled himself on the carpet in front of the trunk containing Durm's secret magics. The scrolls and the diaries Da never showed him or even spoke of, even after Westwailing and the waking of his power. So much left unsaid between them. About Westwailing. About a lot of things.

The storm had passed but it was still raining. Sheets of water running down the library windowpanes. He'd conjured himself the tiniest ball of glimfire, not enough to alert Mama, who was sitting with Da three rooms round from this one. If he was careful and quiet she wouldn't know he was here. After their shouting match on the stairs he reckoned they'd both be best off not laying eyes on each other till morning.

He rose and looked at his reflection in the watery window, the glimfire shadowing him mysterious and dark. Roiling inside him, so much pain. Lur's. Mama's. Deenie's. Pellen and Charis's, too. And his power churned. His woken, hungry, simmering power, that wouldn't obediently go back to sleep. That he didn't understand, and likely now never would.

Da should've told me. He should've taught me years ago how to control it. I don't know if I can do this alone.

Grief like a bunched fist struck hard, stealing his breath. Eyes burning, throat closing, fire roared in his blood. Guilt like a snowstorm turned his bones to ice. He wasn't naughty, he was *wicked,* to be angry with Da now, when his father was dying.

Not wanting to look at himself a single heartbeat longer, he turned away from the window and made his way back to the trunk. Dropped to sit cross-legged in front of it. Fuddled the lock, such a simple thing to do now. Easy as sneezing. Was *anything* beyond him? Easing the trunk's lid open, he let the glimfire hover and picked up the first of Durm's hoarded books.

The thing he needed most was a way to protect himself from whatever darkness lurked over the mountains. If the enemy was miasma, blight and foul enchantments, natural things turned lethal like the waterspouts and whirlpools now infesting all of Lur's harbours, then he needed some way of banishing them. Collapsing them. Or shielding himself, at least. But if his enemy was flesh-and-blood, some race of men warped and twisted by Morg's foul magics, or maybe even demons who'd not perished when the sorcerer perished, then the spells he was after would have to give him the power to kill. The way Da had killed the day the Wall came down.

I wish I had those magics. I wish they hadn't been lost.

Killing with magic . . . the thought did give him pause. Pushed to it, could he kill a man? Smash him to blood and splinters with nowt more than words? Words . . . and the power burning inside him.

Da did it. And we're the same. If it comes down to Lur and some man I don't know . . . if I had to, I could kill.

One by one, reading quickly, he worked his way through Durm's books and scrolls. He found spells of compulsion and transformation and deconstruction and repression. Magics that in the wrong hands could cause untold harm. That no Olken would have a chance of resisting, not even if they were strong in the earth like Meister Gamble of the Speckled Rooster in Riddleton. Touched by these magics, Gamble would burn like paper.

Heart pounding, Rafel saw how the spells might be used as weapons. And he needed weapons. Against the darkness, against the mountains. Maybe even against Arlin. So he snatched quill and paper from Da's desk and started scribbling down the incants, scribbling any kind of magic that might be turned to his advantage.

He found five different spells for conjuring objects from one place to another. Of course he knew the Doranen did that—he'd seen it—but it was never an incant he'd managed to pinch from Arlin, and though he'd tried to fuddle it on his lonesome he could never make it work. Odd, that Da would've kept such commonplace spells secret. And then, reading more closely, he saw that while one conjuring spell was for objects, the rest were for the conjuring of *living* things, small to large. And that would explain them being locked in the trunk. Get one of these wrong...

He felt himself turn a little queasy, discomfort that had nothing to do with Lur's suffering earth. But he scribbled them down anyway. Better safe than sorry.

Pity we daren't risk 'em to get us over the mountains. That'd save a few blisters and uncomfortable nights. 'Cept then folk would know this kind of magic exists... and we'd likely get ourselves in all kinds of bother.

The next spell he read was for seeing things over long distances. He grinned. *That* could come in mighty useful. And then he chewed his lip, so tempted. It was late. He was hungry. And he should really make certain these magics would work...

Closing his eyes, he reached for his power. And there it was, waiting for him, dangerous and beautiful. *So beautiful.*

Drifting, his blood humming, he looked at the faded-ink words of the incant scrawled in Durm's dashing hand. Let its lilting syllables sink into his mind. Breathed them out again, a whisper of words. A single sigil, caressing the air. Thought of the place he wanted to see...

...and was in the Tower kitchen. Glimlit, but empty. He could smell the spicy sweetness of fresh baking. On the wide shelf beside the window, that magical place where Rafel-the-sprat had loved to stand and sniff, a ginger cake on a pottery plate. Moist and golden brown. Still warm. A heady aroma. He heard his belly growl.

So, turning his mind to those other spells, he conjured it.

Warmth like kissing, coursing through his veins. A surge of bright power to drown Lur's constant drone of pain. Beyond the library window the constant rain poured down. Barely noticing it, stunned, he touched the conjured ginger cake with his fingertips. Felt its stickiness and touched fingertips to his tongue. The taste burst through him, like magic.

He nearly ruined himself, trying not to laugh.

Next, he conjured a sharp knife and cut himself a fat slice.

After that, his growling belly silenced, he returned to the task of sifting through the rest of Durm's books and scrolls. And even though this was serious, even though there was grief and anger and fright hovering, still…as his fingers scrawled spells, scrawled protections for his dangerous journey, whenever he looked up at the window he could see himself smile.

Word was sent from the Council early the next morning. A summons, no fancy folderol. No *Your kind attendance is requested.* Just *Come now. Jaffee's privy chapel.*

Mama and Deenie were both still abed—or not venturing beyond their chambers. Rafel left a note, saddled Firedragon and rode through the mizzling rain down to the Market Square. Gave the stallion to the Barlschapel stable lads and made his quiet way inside, where a cleric led him to Barlsman Jaffee's secluded rooms.

Arlin was there already, velvet and seed pearls gleaming gently in the glimlight. At the sound of footsteps he turned in his wooden chair, his dissatisfied expression tightening to anger.

"No need for cartwheels," Rafel said, with his own sneer. "You ain't the face I was looking for, neither."

Arlin didn't answer. Arms folded, eyes slitted, he stared stony at his knees.

Poxy little shit.

Propping himself against the nearest bit of stone wall, he lapsed into silence. Let his gaze drift about the chamber, with its plain stone floor and its plain wooden desk and chairs and the portrait of Barl in its beautiful frame. Somewhere in the greater chapel the acolytes were singing hymns. Learning, or practicing. Their sweet voices rose and fell, praising the mercy of Barl.

A short time later, Barlsman Jaffee swept into the austere chamber. He looked weary. Sleepless. His Barlsbraid was unravelling, its offering flowers fallen out. Creases and wrinkles marred his fine clerical robes.

"There will be no parade," he announced curtly, taking his place behind the desk. "No public business of any kind that draws attention to your leaving. Nor will you be going alone."

Arlin sat a little straighter. "I beg your pardon?"

"Sit, Rafel," Jaffee ordered. "And you, Arlin, be quiet. I have had enough deliberation and argument for the time being. Accept the Council's decision or go home to your vineyards. It's up to you. Rafel, *sit*."

Feeling sleepless himself, twitched with the leftovers of Doranen magic and too much ginger cake and the pain in Lur that wouldn't leave him alone, Rafel glowered at Jaffee a moment then dropped into the privy chapel's other wooden chair.

"I am not satisfied with this decision," said Arlin. "I wish to present myself before the entire Council, not—"

"No," said Jaffee, hands tucked into the opposite sleeves of his robe. More authority in him now than Rafel had ever seen. "I speak with the Council's united voice. Accept or reject these terms as you like, Lord Garrick. No other terms shall be offered to you."

"In that case," said Arlin, standing, "I shall make my own arrangements."

"That would be pointless," Jaffee replied. "Recall that Barl's Mountains are warded. Not even you are strong enough to break them. If you wish to enter the pass at Gribley, then the official wardkeeper must clear the way. And she will do so only with specific instructions from the Council."

Rafel watched Arlin wrestle with that, amused. Then he looked at Jaffee. "What did you mean, we're not travelling alone?"

"The Council has chosen three of its own to journey with you across the mountains," said Jaffee. His lips curved in a bleak smile. "It is felt your lack of friendship with Lord Garrick might prove to be a...hindrance to success."

Arlin was breathing hard with temper. "And I am to have no say as to who—"

"None." Jaffee's eyes were cold. "Lord Garrick, we stand upon a precipice which even now crumbles beneath our feet. If you would save this kingdom, save the lives of its innocent inhabitants, do such service to Barl as makes you beloved in her eyes, I implore you: do not make this a matter of your pride and ambition. You would have tens and tens of thousands perish because you think yourself better than an Olken? Because you and Rafel cannot see eye to eye? Because you chafe against the Council's authority and restrictions? If that is true—"

"Of course it's not true," Arlin snapped. "If I had no care for Lur and the lives here, would I be risking my *own* life?"

"No," said Jaffee, gentle now. "You're a good man and a brave one, Arlin, and we stand in your debt. But I urge you to set aside all personal considerations. The only thing that can matter is finding a way to save Lur and, Barl willing, the other expedition. For all your differences and difficulties, you and Rafel hold that belief in common. Let it be the start of a better, kinder understanding."

From the look on his face, Arlin wasn't anywhere near to being convinced. But he nodded. "Very well."

Rafel hid his amusement. "So which councilors are coming with us, Barlsman Jaffee?"

"Nib Hambly, Hosh Clyne and Tomas Dimble," said Jaffee. "Three good men. Dedicated, strong mages—" He cleared his throat, abruptly uncomfortable. "And unwed."

"Three *Olken?*" Arlin choked, incredulous. "Are you mad, Jaffee? What use are *Olken?* Rafel's power might be warped and unnatural but at least—"

"Have you forgotten, Arlin? No unwed Doranen might sit on the Council," said Jaffee. "Our own people's rule, and perhaps not wise."

"Then choose a *married* Doranen; send—"

Jaffee shook his head. "There is no *sending*. No-one can be forced to this undertaking. Besides, Arlin—it would seem being Doranen is little or no protection against the dangers that lie beyond the mountains. Or is Sarle Baden not the mage we believed?"

And *that* shut Arlin's trap good and tight. Rafel stood. "Seems we've a mite to do, then, Barlsman. Best we get to it, 'cause the sooner we leave, the sooner we get the good folk of Lur off that bloody precipice." He turned to Arlin. "Agreed, Lord Garrick?"

"Have I a choice?" Arlin said sourly. "It's agreed."

CHAPTER TWENTY-SEVEN

�֍

They had one day to ready themselves. One single, rainy day to breathe in the last they might ever see of their loved ones. Of home. Trying not to dwell on that, Rafel prepared for the arduous journey. Kept himself busy so there wasn't time to think. When he was done, his bulky pack was full of jerky, hard-baked biscuits and nuts, the kind of food that would sustain him in the arduous climb over the mountains. Two canvas waterskins. Two spare shirts. Spare socks and underdrawers. Heavy leather gloves. A talking stone like the one Pintte and Baden had taken with them, strong enough to reach the Council. Flint and striker. A canvas groundsheet. To go with the pack, he collected a stout walking stick, a knife, a coil of rope — and a sword. That prompted a grim smile. He'd had to dig through piles of mouldering relics in the old palace to find it. Swords belonged to the long-dead time of Trevoyle's Schism. Cleaned and sharpened, its scabbard saddle-soaped then oiled, the weapon was a stark reminder of the dangers he'd be facing.

Last, and most important, he had Tollin's parchment, folded small, and the collection of spells taken from Durm's secret library. They were rolled tight and tucked safely out of sight, for he didn't dare let Arlin get a glimpse of them. It would make learning them tricky — but he'd find a way. He had to.

The whole frantic day, he didn't see his family. Suffering, Deenie stayed in her chamber. And Mama—Mama stayed with Da. They didn't even share a farewell supper. The Tower was full of silence, and dread. So he ate alone, and sat alone, and used the time before sleeping to study Durm's spells.

Sunrise came meanly, murky behind the low clouds. Watery light seeping to the ground, seeping between the partly drawn curtains in his father's chamber. Brought to this terrible moment at last, Rafel sat by the bed.

Sweet air. Cool silence. Not enough words. More words than he could count. This man. *This man*. Who loved him. Who lied to him. Who trusted him with his life. Who put him on his first pony. Held his hand. Wiped his tears.

"Da..."

Nowt had changed. Weeks slid by since the Weather Chamber, and nowt had bloody changed. Da just lay there, not speaking, not moving. Morning and afternoon, Kerril or Mama spooned gruel down his gullet, fed him possets and potions meant to keep him alive. He swallowed them. He didn't wake. He didn't wake now, with his cold hand held so tightly.

Eyes blurred and burning, grief like a white-hot coal lodged in his heart, Rafel leaned forward. Bent low. "Da, it's Rafe. Can you hear me?"

Silence. Slow breathing. Beneath the warm blankets his father slept, still as a doll.

"Da..."

Not enough words. More words than he could count.

He kissed his father's thin, stubbled cheek... and walked away.

Mama and Deenie looked so forlorn, standing in the Tower foyer. They were saying goodbye here, since his leaving wasn't public. He hugged them both, hard. Felt the depth of their fear for him racking through them, mingling with the strident pain in the earth.

Mama fixed the collar on his long oiled riding-coat, then smoothed her fingers over his hair. "Be safe, Rafel. Be watchful. Trust your instincts." Her lips trembled. "Come home."

He felt like a sprat again, caught out in some mischief. "You do know why I'm going, Mama? You know—"

"I know, Rafe," she said. Her eyes were dry. "I'm proud of you."

And that nearly undid him.

"Don't pick fights with Arlin," Deenie whispered, her thin arms around his waist. "He can't help being a sinkin' bloody fool."

Painfully smiling, he kissed her hair. "He could try, the little shit. Deenie, take care of Charis for me. Uncle Pellen—"

"I know. I will," she said, her arms tightening. "She'll be here when you get back. You make sure you bring Goose back. And yourself."

He nodded. "Promise. Deenie—"

She pulled away. Her eyes were shadowed-smeared and trickling tears. "Go, Rafe. Just...go."

He was right to do this. He had to do this. If Da were awake they'd be doing this together. But riding away from the Tower was the hardest moment of his life.

He joined Arlin and his fellow Olken travellers in the old palace's privy royal chapel, hardly used these days, where Barlsman Jaffee was waiting with prayers and a blessing. Couldn't help a sneer, catching sight of Rodyn's son. Not even the prospect of endless toil and stark danger could prevent the new Lord Garrick from flaunting his inherited wealth. Velvet. Seed pearls. Slender gold rings. What was he thinking—that he'd dazzle the darkness beyond the mountains into submission?

Prob'ly. Arlin really is a sinkin' fool.

Done droning the daily invocation, Jaffee smudged pungent oil on the insides of their wrists so the strong pulse there could carry Barl's love to their hearts. Then he folded his hands and stared down at the five of them, kneeling humbly before him.

"My sons, you do a great thing," he said, his thready voice heavy with emotion. "Every day of your journey will see you in my fervent prayers."

Clyne, Dimble and Hambly murmured something, being grateful. Rafel heard Arlin swallow a sharp breath. Bitterly resenting these Olken intruders. For himself he didn't much care they were coming. Could be

Jaffee was right, and they'd be safer five than two. Arlin prob'ly would be. The three of them could pull him off the poxy shit when his temper finally snapped. As for the men as individuals, well, he knew Tom Dimble from his work with Da at Justice Hall. Close to middle-age, he was. Da called him trustworthy, and that was good enough for him. Nib Hambly and Hosh Clyne, a few years older again, he knew only to nod at in the street, or propping up the bar in the Dancing Bear. Whether they chose this task, or got asked by the Council, either way they had gumption, agreeing.

And it could be worse. They could be Doranen.

"Here is my final stricture, upon all of you," Jaffee added. "As you climb Barl's Mountains leave your former selves behind. When you reach the summit and descend into the unknown, let there be no more Doranen and no more Olken. Know yourselves only as men of Lur. Strive together for the saving of this poor, stricken kingdom, for should you fail in this task I fear all of us will perish. Barl go with you."

And the blessing was done.

Arlin had agreed to provide the large carriage that would carry them to the Black Woods village of Gribley, nestled at the foot of Barl's Mountains. Waiting in the old palace's stable yard as the horses' harness was checked one last time, Jaffee's written instructions on what to do once they reached Gribley safe in his pocket, Rafel looked up at the grey, drizzling sky. Remembered the day, nearly sixteen years ago, when Tollin and the rest rode out of Dorana City on their big adventure.

So much *excitement,* there'd been. In warm sunshine he'd watched them ride through the City's gates, laughing, 'cause even though Da had been dead set against the expedition he'd not stopped Mama from taking spratty Rafe to stand with the cheering crowds. Excitement too those scant weeks ago, when Goose rode off with Fernel Pintte and Sarle Baden and those other hopeful explorers. The sun had shone in the bright blue sky that day, as well. The people of Dorana had cheered.

And today it's raining, and we're leaving Dorana by the back door with only a handful of folk to know. But I ain't about to think anything on that.

The three Olken councilors were stood in a tight-knit group, talking together in low voices. Pale and uneasy, they flicked him glances that told him gumption or not, they weren't altogether sure about what they were doing, or who they were doing it with.

And Arlin? Arlin was grousing at his coachman, complaining about something that wasn't done to his satisfaction. The coachman bore the abuse stolidly, staring at the wet ground. An Olken would need to be desperate to work for that little shit.

Sink me sideways, Da. This'll be fun.

Dismissing his coachman back to the carriage, Arlin next lashed out at one of the old palace stable lads. Rafel hunched his shoulders, biting his tongue, as the rain dripped steadily off the brim of his leather hat and splattered the shoulders of his oiled riding-coat. He could've stood under shelter, like the councilors, but seeing as they were about to be cooped up in Arlin's carriage till long past nightfall he wanted as much fresh air as he could get. Behind the glooming clouds thunder rumbled, like giant marbles rolled over a wide wooden floor.

Firedragon, left to his own devices in a spare stable, waiting to be retrieved by one of the Tower lads, poked his head over the half-door and curiously eyed all the goings-on. Rafel stared at him, swamped by a sudden wave of affection. Swamped by fear he'd never see the horse again.

And then, just as sudden, the thought of travelling all the way to Gribley in Lord bloody Garrick's fancy carriage, with bad-tempered, mean-mouthed Lord bloody Garrick for company, was more than he could stomach.

"Oy!" he said, and marched over the slippery cobblestones to Arlin, who was still tongue-lashing the hapless stable lad. "Change of plans. I'm riding to Gribley."

Arlin turned. Even his travelling coat was made of the finest, most expensive leather in the kingdom. And the stitching on his gloves? That was gold thread.

"What?" he snapped, impatient of interruption.

"You heard me," Rafel said mildly, 'cause staying mild with Arlin was a sure way to fratch him. "I don't fancy sitting on my arse all day. Not in a carriage, any road. I'm riding."

"Really?" Arlin looked at him. Looked at the carriage, loaded with their packs and other equipment. Looked at the three councilors, men he loathed for no better reason than they were Olken. He turned back to the lad. "Send to my townhouse. Have them bring me my brown stallion."

"Yes, m'lord," the browbeaten stable lad murmured, and bolted.

Rafel didn't know whether to laugh or be pissed. *And there was me looking forward to riding to Gribley on my lonesome.* "Time's marching on, Arlin. We can't hang about here waiting for your horse. We've got to be on our way before folk arrive here to start work. Besides, it's a long day's travelling to Gribley."

"Then leave," said Arlin, looking down his nose. "My animal's the best-bred horse in Lur. I'll join you soon enough."

And he bloody would, too, even if he had to kill his stallion to manage it. Rafel shrugged and smiled, mildly. "Suit yourself."

Leaving Arlin to fume, he asked one of the other lads to saddle Firedragon then crossed to the clutch of whispering councilors. "Carriage is all yours, Tom. Lord Garrick and I feel like riding today."

Tom Dimble folded his skinny arms, brows pulled low. "Do you, now?" He sounded...suspicious.

"Tom—" Rafel shook his head. "Don't be a numbskull. We ain't about to leave you stranded. You know what the pass-note says. Five to travel over the mountains. If there ain't five, nobody goes."

Tom thought on that. "I suppose," he said at last, grudging. "But Rafel, the weather's foul. Why would you want to—"

"Ride all the way to Gribley cooped up in a carriage with Lord Arlin bloody Garrick?" He snorted. "I don't know, Tom. Let me think on that, why don't you?"

"Well..." Tom said, with a hint of amusement, and looked at his fellow councilors. "Perhaps it's not so hard to figure, at that."

"And if Arlin rides, you're spared him too," he added. "So we're all happy, eh?"

"Happy," said Tom, with another look at Hambly and Clyne. His amusement vanished. "Yes."

He stepped closer, and lowered his voice. "Tom, you don't have to do this. There's time to change your minds. I know the Council reckons it's safer to send all of us but—Garrick and I ain't helpless. We can protect ourselves just fine. So if you don't want to come..."

Hosh Clyne, by a whisker the oldest, shook his balding head. "Decision's made. We should go."

And that was that. So he nodded at the three men who didn't want to be here, who weren't wanted by him or by Arlin bloody Garrick, and fetched Firedragon from his stable. The councilors loaded themselves into Arlin's fancy carriage and the coachman picked up his water-slicked reins.

"Mind you don't spring those horses," Arlin snapped at him. "I'll see you sorry if there's one pulled muscle between them—and if I find a bowed tendon when we reach Gribley I'll—"

"My lord," said the coachman, touching his hat-brim. "They'll reach Gribley sound."

As the carriage-horses tossed their heads, restive, and Arlin glared his mistrust at the coachman, Rafel vaulted into Firedragon's rain-speckled saddle. "Well, Arlin," he said, his booted feet groping for the stirrups, "I'll be seeing you by and by. Ride safe, now. Don't go tumbling, trying to catch up. A nice safe, steady jog—that should do it."

Arlin's answer was a silent snarl. Rafel swallowed a grin. So, looked like Jaffee's pious prating was nowt but a waste of breath. Arlin didn't look a mite interested in letting bygones be bygones. Not that he was bothered by that. He already had a best friend. And to save Goose he'd cross Barl's Mountains with the sorcerer Morg himself.

He nudged his heels to Firedragon's flanks. The horse grunted, muscles bunching, then launched into a prancing trot out of the stable yard and into the puddled driveway beyond. He didn't bother looking back to see how closely the carriage followed. He didn't care.

Parades and cheering and the City's streets lined with excited faces...how would it feel to ride out of Dorana like that? Better than how it felt to be skulking away like a thief in the night, even though he knew why the Council had decreed they depart through the old palace grounds' privy gates, with the sun barely risen and not a soul to see them go.

But it was a forlorn hope, that they'd keep this desperate expedition secret. Word of their going would spread soon enough. With the pain in Lur's earth a relentless, grinding ache in nearly every Olken's bones, folk were frighted and talking openly of trouble. And sooner or later, Asher's son would be missed. Councilor Hambly, being a farmer—could be few folk in the City would notice him gone. But Tomas Dimble? His absence in Justice Hall would be loud as a shout. And Clyne's barber shop was always full of customers, and they'd soon be wondering where their favourite barber was gone. Besides. Someone else in the Council would talk. Someone always did. That was just people.

But that ain't my worry, is it? It's for Jaffee and Shifrin and the rest to lose sleep on. I've got my own worries.

Like the sick fear that they'd acted too late and he'd not be in time to save the kingdom or Goose. That even if he did return from over the mountains with everything and everyone he loved made safe, he'd come home to find himself lacking a father.

Wait for me, Da. Don't you dare bloody die while I'm gone.

With Arlin's coachman keeping his horses in hand, and Firedragon eager to splash from puddle to puddle, he reached the rarely used palace gates with the carriage well in the rear. Not caring for that, not caring for Arlin, neither, still waiting for his horse to be brought up to him from his townhouse, he eased Firedragon to a quivering halt. Used his burning Doranen magic to swing the gates open...then let loose his hold of the bit. Firedragon, so responsive, feeling his tension, feeling the muddled mess of his fears and hopes and griefs, flybucked twice, stretched his neck out, and leapt.

More than anything he wanted to let the stallion gallop unchecked to Gribley. But he couldn't. So he let Firedragon bolt a little way then gradually, regretfully, made him slow down and wait. At last the carriage reached them, wheels splashing fresh rainwater and mud, and they continued sedately, together, beneath the grey and drizzling sky.

Eventually, with palace and City lost to mist and mizzle, they turned off the Small City Road onto Black Woods Way, the narrower road that would take them into the forest and on to Gribley. Barl's Mountains loomed in the distance, cloud-topped and forbidding. Just as forbidding, the spreading skirts of the shadowed, mysterious forest. Wolves lived there, and bears. Some Olken. Veira had lived there. She'd left Mama her cottage, but Mama had long ago given it to somebody else.

Now, though, they still travelled through open countryside. The day was unfolding dim and soggy, no hint of a break in the lowering clouds or misting rain. There wasn't much hereabouts but rabbits and the eagles who hunted them. Even when it wasn't raining, this stretch of Lur was seldom troubled by carts and coaches. Rafel liked this corner of the kingdom. Liked its wildness and its solitude. When they were sprats, he and Goose had played explorer out here. Under blue skies and a warm sun, frighting themselves with imaginary dangers.

Goose. He felt his guts squeeze. *Don't think on him. You're doing what you can, as fast as you can.*

Hoof beats behind them, steadily gaining. He glanced round to see Arlin's cantering approach. Firedragon shied. Holding the horse steady with knees and hands, Rafel looked sideways as the Doranen mage kept on cantering, alongside the carriage then past it until he'd drawn level. Then he dropped his own stallion back to the steady trot that kept them bowling along towards Gribley. With the collar of his oiled coat turned up and his hat pulled low, Arlin's face was almost completely hidden. He offered no greeting, no comment of any kind.

Rafel sighed. *Don't see how this is going to work if we can't say two civil words to each other.* "Arlin, d'you reckon—"

"I reckon you needn't concern yourself about what I reckon," said Arlin, with the swiftest of glances. "The Council in its...*wisdom*...has chosen this path for us. I'll ride it because I have to. Because compared with finding Lost Dorana, where my people will at last be free of this pathetic, crumbling kingdom, my distaste for your company is not important. But that doesn't mean I have to indulge you in pointless conversation."

Days with this poxy shit? Weeks? *Months,* maybe? Rafel swallowed dismay. "Fine, Arlin. So we ain't friends, and never will be. But—"

Deep in the earth a soft groaning, growing louder. The dull ache in his bones grew sharp edges. Closed his throat. Nearly—nearly—

"Hold up," he said, his belly churning. "Arlin, *hold up!*" Ignoring the Doranen's protests, he reefed Firedragon round in a tight circle. *"Coachman, halt your team!"*

"What are you doing?" Arlin demanded as his coachman slowed the carriage. "You don't give orders to my man. You don't—"

"Shut your trap, Arlin," he said, one fist raised. His blood was turbulent, warning whispers rising swiftly to a scream. The rain kept falling but the world felt...still.

And then came the tremor, bursting through the deep soil and the rocks, through the skin and bones and flesh of the kingdom. Its echo burst through him and through the Olken councilors trapped in Arlin's carriage. As they cried out, and the carriage-horses plunged in their harness, as the wretched earth roiled and rippled and Arlin Garrick swore, trying to control his panicked stallion, Rafel clung to Firedragon praying he'd not fall off. Leaned over the horse's shoulder and vomited his breakfast onto the shivering road. Lur's pain was his pain, flowing in white-hot rivers through his veins.

At long last it stopped.

Easing himself upright, spitting bile-tainted saliva, small bonfires of pain burning behind his eyes and in his joints, he looked first to the carriage—no damage, no horse injured—and then to Arlin. The Doranen was pale, his eyes slitted as he wrestled his own jittery horse to a standstill.

He spat again, then wiped his mouth on his sleeve. "You all right, Arlin?"

Arlin looked at him blankly. "Why wouldn't I be?" Turning, he waved a hand at his coachman. "Get that carriage moving, you fool!

We'll not reach Gribley before midnight if we stand about here admiring the scenery."

The coachman touched his hat-brim. "Yes, my lord."

Bloody Arlin. Rafel nudged Firedragon to the edge of the road, waited for the carriage to draw level then urged the horse to keep pace with it. "Tom," he said, peering inside. "You fine gentlemen all dandy?"

Like Arlin they were pale, but unharmed. "Near enough," said Tom, next to the window. "But Rafel—"

Their blood surely continued to sizzle, just like his. "I know," he said bleakly. "And you can bet we'll feel worse before we feel better. But we ain't got a choice, eh?"

Tom glanced at his companions. "No," he said, subdued. "No, I suppose not."

And with that sobering realisation, the journey continued.

They reached the Black Woods village of Gribley nearly six hours past sunset. Long shadows stretched across the glimlit courtyard of the village's modest inn, where the Council had arranged for them to stay the night and where Firedragon and Arlin's stallion would be stabled until fetched. Brooding around them, the hushed Black Woods. Daunting above them, Barl's Mountains.

As the coachman and the inn's stable hands saw to the carriage, Arlin handed his stallion over to the stablemeister's care and stalked inside without a word to anyone else. Rafel tended Firedragon himself, unsaddling and grooming him, making sure he'd taken no unnoticed hurt in the long ride from Dorana. When the horse was clean and settled he had words with the stablemeister, then measured Firedragon's feed to his own satisfaction. Giving the horse supper, smoothing his untangled red-flame mane, he bid his private farewell. Waited until he could show his face to the world, and went in search of his companions.

He found Tom, Clyne and Hambly supping ale in the inn's plain parlour. "Where's Arlin?"

The councilors exchanged looks. "Taking his leisure alone, in his room," said Tom, indifferent. "We asked him to join us."

"Waste of good breath, Tom."

Another exchanged look. "Yes."

Staring at them, Rafel was uncomfortably aware that Tom and his friends didn't welcome his company. Why? 'Cause they had privy Council business to discuss? Or 'cause they wanted to discuss him? Because he made *them* feel uncomfortable? The reason prob'ly didn't matter. Point was, they were sitting there waiting for him to go away.

Fine. I ain't an idiot. I can take a hint.

But it didn't bode well for the rest of their journey.

"I'm a mite travelsore myself," he said, keeping his voice casual. "A bath sounds inviting. Enjoy your ale, councilors."

Wearily climbing the stairs to his room, he considered disturbing Arlin—then reconsidered the notion. Trying to make peace with the Doranen would only be a waste of *his* good breath. After his bath he ate a plain hearty meal brought up to him from the kitchen, mutton and potato and carrot stewed in thick gravy, and downed three mugs of strong ale. After that he studied Durm's spells until his eyes wouldn't stay open, then tumbled headfirst into sleep. Pain danced through his uneasy dreams, and he woke at murky first light unrefreshed.

Swiftly dressed, he joined Arlin and the councilors in the parlour, where they ate scrambled egg and bacon and drank tea in tense silence. Then they collected their packs and walking sticks and swords—Arlin, swordless, eyed the weapons with a sneer—and made their way through the deserted, rain-drizzled streets of Gribley to the village's outskirts, and the one Doranen mage living in the Black Woods.

Her cottage sat deep in the shadows of the mountains, a stone's throw from the unremarkable beginning of the pass. Looking up and up the rocky, winding pathway, Rafel felt the weight of the cliffs and crags, their brooding silence, pressing down hard enough to break his bones. Felt the pain of their climbing in him as though he'd already begun. Felt clammy fear, and a brutal, savage doubt.

And then he felt Arlin's considering, scornful stare. That was the only encouragement he needed.

Forget it, Lord Garrick. I ain't turning back.

Phena, the pass keeper, was wizened and white-haired, her thin bent body wrapped in a dark blue wool tunic. Charged with husbanding the warding hexes that prevented any unsanctioned crossing of the mountains, rumour had it she could kill a man where he stood with nowt more than a word. One look in her deep-set, pale green eyes and Rafel believed the rumour, absolutely.

"So," she said, standing in her open doorway and staring her visitors up and down. Her voice was cracked with age. "Five more brave fools, I see." She smiled. "Welcome to Gribley."

"We're on Council business," said Arlin, close to contempt even though she was Doranen. "Let down the wards so we can be on our way."

Rafel flicked Rodyn's boorish son a look, as Tom and the others shuffled, displeased. "Arlin—"

But Phena wasn't offended. "You're Asher's son," she said, ignoring Arlin. "Rafel. Last saw you as a babe in arms. You take after your father. I'm sorry he's dying."

With an effort, he managed a polite smile. "Thank you, Lady Phena. It's true he's poorly, but I'm sure he'll be fine. Please—you've been the park keeper here for many years. What d'you know of the mountains?"

Phena laughed. "Many years? Yes. I was already old when Tollin and his men crossed over. I was older still when the few who survived the journey came back, walking dead men. And I was ancient when Sarle Baden ordered me to let him go by." She sniffed, staring at Arlin. "Just like you, little lord. The same tone of voice. The same inflated conceit. They've not returned. I think it's likely they won't. The mountains are hungry. That's what I know." Another sniff. "How desperate is the Council, to feed them more men?"

Arlin's face tinted with temper. "I haven't ridden all this way for a lecture. Lower the wards, woman."

"Ah," said Phena, with a wrinkled-eye wink. "D'you hear him, Rafel? D'you hear him, good sirs? I expect this is why you Olken don't have much time for us."

Rafel offered her a respectful nod. "Lord Garrick's not got the manners of a rutting boar, but—it is true we need to be on our way."

She looked the five of them up and down again, taking in their oiled coats and their broad-brimmed leather hats and their bulging rucksacks and their long, stout sticks. The swords strapped across every back, save Arlin's.

"Barl's mercy on you, young mages," she said softly. "Though I must warn you—in her mountains, mercy is hard to find."

The damp air sizzled as she ignited four scarlet sigils. Rafel felt a crawling pressure against his skin, felt the hair stand up on the back of his neck. Heard Arlin's breath catch in his throat.

Phena raised one thin grey eyebrow. "So what are you waiting for? The way is clear. Off you go."

With a smile of thanks, not looking at Arlin or Tom and the others, Rafel crossed the lowered warding...

... and the journey began.

Within moments of them crossing the unwarded threshold onto the pass, Arlin pushed by Rafel and took the lead. The weathered path they followed, marked with Doranen hexes to guide the way, was too narrow for anything other than single-file tramping. Rafel didn't care. He had nothing he wanted to share with Arlin, and no spare breath for conversation anyway. Glancing over his shoulder at Tom and the other two councilors, he saw they'd let themselves drift back, just far enough to suggest they were in a group of their own. Just far enough so their panting, whispered comments couldn't be overheard. Uneasy, he fixed his gaze between Arlin's shoulder-blades and wished he didn't feel quite so twitched.

Are they going to be trouble? I bloody hope not.

The going was brutal tough, hexmark to hexmark, down and up scrawny, sideways-scraped gullies, over fallen trees and tumbled rocks, scrambling for purchase up sheer, rain-slippery cliffs leaving bits of skin and fingernail behind. Slowly, grindingly, the mist-shrouded village of Gribley dwindled behind and below them.

The mountains' silence was oppressive. Disapproving. As he climbed, Rafel could almost believe the ancient mass of rock and soil might in any heartbeat shrug, disdainful, and toss them downwards to their deaths. Though the Wall had fallen before he was born he could feel its tattered remnants buried in its bones. Echoes of a power he could hardly begin to understand. Echoes that reminded him of what he'd felt in Barl's Weather map, in her Weather Chamber, so far away now in Dorana City.

And he could feel other echoes, too. The black touch of Morg's blight, that had brought her miraculous Wall to ruin. That had ruined the reef, and even now tried to ruin Lur.

The cloying darkness made the climbing so much more difficult. Especially with Arlin Garrick leading the way. It seemed the Doranen was ignorant of Lur's struggle or Morg's filthy legacy. Every time he had to stop and catch his breath, not because he was a weakling, but because what he could feel in the mountain threatened to press him flat, Arlin muttered and rolled his eyes with contempt, and never once held out a helping Doranen hand. Even Tom, Nib and Hosh looked at him askance after a while, 'cause they couldn't feel it either. At least not the way he could.

He was starting to think there was something to be said for being ordinary.

After nigh on ten bruising, blistering, rain-drizzled hours, stopping only twice to eat, drink and relieve themselves, with the first day's light fast fading and what had been a constant drizzle threatening to turn into proper hard rain, Rafel called for a halt—and the others didn't argue. They'd reached a decent place to camp for the night. Not a cave, exactly, but a wide, shallow scoop in the mountainside that left just enough wiggle room for them to escape the worst of the weather. To pretend, on this first night in the wilderness, that they had a safe roof over their heads.

Weary almost beyond bearing, they set about collecting fallen branches for a fire. Well. Two fires, 'cause Arlin found his own fuel quick-smart and settled himself on his groundsheet at the far end of the miserly cave, making it clear he had no interest in anyone's company save his own.

Rafel exchanged a raised-eyebrow look with Tom, then pretended Arlin didn't exist. The wood he and the councilors collected was wet, like Arlin's, but that was easy fixed. Tom and the other two watched owl-eyed as he used Doranen magic to dry it enough for burning then ignited it with a single word of command.

And even though he'd helped them, stopped them catching an ague from the damp and cold, he could still feel his fellow-Olkens' simmering suspicions. Their reluctance to accept his mysterious Doranen power.

Sink me, Da. Reckon I'm starting to understand what you were on about.

The thought startled him. He'd been so busy being angry with his father for denying him the truth of his magical potential, he'd never stopped to wonder if the reason behind it had been a good one. But seemingly it was. Dispirited, his skinned knuckles stinging, an ominous shiver starting up now that they'd stopped battering their way over rocks and fallen trees, he left Tom and his suspicious friends toasting themselves by their fire at the opposite end of the cave and gathered more dead wood so, like Arlin, he could sit on his own.

Settled on his groundsheet in the middle of the shallow cave, warming at last as shadows danced over its walls and beyond its wide mouth the rain drummed harder and the last light drained from the darkening sky, he chewed his way through a mean handful of hard-baked biscuit and jerky. It wasn't enough to fill the hole in his belly but he didn't dare eat more. They might be able to eke out their supplies by hunting birds or small mountain creatures, but they couldn't rely on that hope. When the worst of his hunger pangs were placated, and his fellow Olken curled asleep by their fire, he tugged Tollin's parchment from his pack and conjured a small, fitful ball of glimfire to read by.

"What's that?" said Arlin.

It was tempting not to tell him. *Nosy bastard.* But since there wasn't much point starting a brangle for no good reason... "Tollin's expedition account."

Arlin held out a hand. "Show me."

"You want something to read, Arlin, maybe you should've brought a book."

"You're wasting your time with that," said Arlin, his firelit eyes derisive. "Thanks to the Doranen who travelled with him, our path across the mountains is hexed plain to see."

"Maybe," he retorted. "Maybe not. There ain't no way to be sure all the hexes have held. It's been a while, Arlin."

Arlin sneered. "You can't tell that Sarle Baden's enhanced them?"

"He's enhanced the ones we've found," he said, struggling with temper. "We ain't found all of 'em yet. Any road, there's more to getting safe across these mountains than where to put our feet, Arlin. There's where to find fresh water once we reach the first big peak, and what bits and pieces up here we can safely eat, and—"

"I don't need an Olken to tell me any of that," said Arlin, still sneering. "I've a far more reliable source of information."

"And what would that be, Lord Garrick?" asked Tom, not as asleep as he'd appeared. He sat up. "You know something we don't? Something that should've been shared with the Council?"

"What I share and what I keep to myself is entirely my business," said Arlin. "It doesn't concern you."

"It concerns me," said Tom, his voice sharp with authority. Three years in Justice Hall were standing him in good stead. "It concerns all three of us, my lord. *We* are the Council on this expedition and you are answerable to us for everything you do."

Clyne and Hambly were sitting up now too, frowning as hard as Tom. Arlin snorted. "I didn't invite your company, Dimble. And I don't feel inclined to suffer your impertinence."

"Then you can suffer the end of your journey," said Tom, so stern. "The Council won't be flouted, Lord Garrick. Answer the question or at first light go home."

CHAPTER TWENTY-EIGHT

✳

Y ou'd think to force me down the mountainside, *Councilor?*" Arlin
    laughed, the inconstant firelight warm on his still-damp hair. "You
fool, it's not in your power."

Rafel rubbed a hand over his unshaven face, stubble rasping. *I'm too
bloody tired for this.* "Maybe not, Arlin, but it's in mine," he said, letting his voice bite. "And I'm as keen to know what you're on about as
they are. Then again, I'd be happy as a pig in shit to keep going without
you, too. So take your pick. Either way I win."

Arlin sat a little straighter. "You dare threaten me?"

"Bollocks, Arlin," he sighed. "Why d'you have to make everything
a brangle? Just tell us what you're talking on. I'm pretty sure your teeth
won't fall out."

Unless I punch you, and right now that's bloody tempting.

Flames crackled in the damp silence as Arlin chewed on his chances
of defeating Asher's son in a fight. He had to know he was in danger of
losing. Badly.

"It's nothing," he said at last. "An old family tale. More like a legend,
really. Hardly worth mentioning. Which is why I never mentioned it."

Arlin's eyes were wide, his gaze steady. Too steady. Rafel felt himself
smile. He remembered looking like that when he fibbed to Darran. Or to
Da. With so much magic to hide, he'd had to fast become a good fibber.

"Lord Garrick, I don't believe you," he said. And before Arlin could blink, or think of stopping him, he conjured the Doranen's pack halfway across the cave, to his ready arms. *"I wouldn't!"* he added, as Arlin started up, ugly with rage. "Or I'll freeze you where you sit — and might well forget how to let you loose again."

Tom Dimble made a sound of protest. "Really, Rafel, this isn't—"

"Shut up, Tom. You want to know what he's hiding, or don't you?"

Tom looked at Clyne and Hambly, who shrugged. "We want to know."

Arlin's face was drained chalky-white. "You dare touch my belongings? You dare use magic on me? I swear to you, Rafel, I *swear,* there will be—"

"What's in here, Arlin?" he said, softly polite. Hefting the heavy pack. "What don't you want me and Tom and these fine sirs to know of?"

Arlin said nothing, his breathing thick with fury.

He smiled. "Tell me, or I'll tip the whole sinkin' lot on the floor and paw through it till I get me an answer. You think I won't? You bloody know I will."

"Return my belongings," said Arlin tightly, "and I'll tell you. Touch one thing in that pack and I'll burn it to cinders with a word."

"And leave yourself with nowt?" He hooted. "Not even spare underdrawers? I don't bloody think so."

Arlin's eyes narrowed. "To thwart you, Rafel? I'd do without a lot less."

"Give it back to him, Rafel," said Nib Hambly. "This is our first night and you're at each other's throats? Ain't much hope of us lasting weeks at this rate, is there? *Give it back.*"

Instead of a conjurement, he used his muscles. Threw the pack at Arlin, and smiled again when it was fumbled.

"You councilors," said Arlin, undoing the pack's buckles. "I hold you witness to this *thuggery.* When we return to Dorana City — if you're not dead from your own incompetence long before — you'll side with me and watch as this *lout* is removed from Justice Hall in chains."

Rafel rolled his eyes. "Is this where I'm meant to start shaking in my boots?"

"Be quiet, Rafel," said Tom, his own temper fraying. "Don't make things worse. Lord Garrick —"

Arlin finished rummaging in the pack and pulled out a slender, leather-bound book. "The husband of my late mother's second cousin was a member of Tollin's expedition. Vont Marbury. This is his account."

Rafel stared. "You had family on that first expedition? I didn't know that." He looked at Tom. "Did you?"

"No," said Tom stiffly, after a moment. The Council, caught napping. "It's a tenuous connection. Not a matter of blood. We had no reason to even suspect."

Seemed no-one did. He looked back at Arlin. At the diary. "Has Sarle Baden got a copy of that?"

The oddest glint in Arlin's eyes. "No."

"You *kept* it from him?"

"Yes."

"But why would you —" And then he shook his head. "You really are a miserable *shit*. You were *punishing* him?"

Hosh Clyne broke from his whispering with Tom and Hambly. "Punishing? Rafel, what are you —"

"You wanted to go with him and Pintte, didn't you?" he said to Arlin, flapping a hand at the gaping councilors. "You weren't half-witted with grief, like Baden claimed. You wanted to go and he wouldn't bloody have you."

The slowly dying fire washed Arlin's face with shadows. "He didn't need Marbury's account. He had Tollin's." A careless shrug. "Which I've read."

"Then why niggle me on it?"

"To amuse myself."

"Rafel, this is most disturbing," said Hambly. "How do *you* come by a copy of Tollin's account? It was to be kept privy, for the Council only. And it's the Council that should —"

Rafel hunched a shoulder at him. With their whisperings and their suspicions he wasn't of a mind to be scolded by the likes of Nib Hambly. "All right, Arlin." He wriggled his fingers. "Let's have a look at it."

"No, let *us* have a look at it," said Tom. "Rafel, you overstep yourself!"

He turned round. *"No,* Tom, I don't think I do. Last time I looked, *I'm* the one who sailed Westwailing Harbour. Don't seem to recall any of *you* three helping out." He turned back. *"Arlin.* Give me the bloody diary, would you?"

With a contemptuous smile, Arlin floated Vont Marbury's expedition diary across the cave, to his hand. Rafel plucked it from mid-air, opened it carefully, and started reading its scribbled pages. The writing was cramped and crabby, the ink faded with age and blotched with strange stains.

"I don't see there's any difference between their tales. His and Toll-in's," he muttered eventually. "They both talk on taking care with the same stretches of the pass. Where to find water. Which lizards and birds' eggs are safe to eat. They even describe the mountains the same way—two sets of teeth set close together. So I don't—"

"What?" said Tom, breaking the taut silence. "Rafel, what have you—"

"Sink me," he breathed, and looked up at Arlin, whose tired, stubbled face was tight-drawn now . . . 'cause he knew, he bloody knew. This was what he'd not wanted to be found. "You didn't think to *mention* this?"

"Mention what?" Tom demanded. "Rafel, what have you—"

"Pipe down, Tom," he said, his skin crawling. "And I'll read it to you."

Tom's expression was as tight as Arlin's. Clyne and Hambly, seated on either side of him, glared. "I don't care for your tone," said Tom. "I'll thank you to—"

"You want to hear this or not?" he snapped, still staring at Arlin. *You poxy, poxy, poxy little shit.* " 'Cause if you do, *pipe down.*"

When Tom said nothing, he took silence as an invitation to continue. Cleared his throat and tipped Arlin's family diary towards the sputtery glimlight.

"Over three weeks of travel into these desolate new lands, and we have encountered a dreadful, lingering evil. A terrible malevolence. The very air we breathe is poison. And Vesty—Vesty swears he hears a voice. In his dreams, he hears it."

Nib Hambly was a brawny man, muscled from hard farming work, but he looked shaken. "Barl save us. What does that mean?"

"Vesty," said Clyne. "That's one of the Doranen who died on Tollin's expedition, isn't it?"

Rafel nodded. Anger was stirring, and with it his power. The glim-light he'd conjured flared and spat sparks. "According to Tollin, he swelled up and turned black and rotted to pieces before he stopped breathing." The way Tollin himself had died, according to Mama. It was one of the gruesome expedition details that had so delighted him and Goose, as sprats.

Goose.

He scrambled to his feet, the diary discarded. "You're a sinkin' bloody bastard, Arlin. You knew about this and you didn't say a *word?* So you're pissy with Sarle Baden. So *what?* That's your shitty trouble; that ain't to do with anybody else. But you're so sinkin' selfish, you don't care who gets hurt just so long as *you* get what *you* want. And when you *don't...*"

Eyeing him warily—and he was bloody *right* to be wary—Arlin uncoiled gracefully. Stood lightly on the balls of his feet, tensed. "Calm yourself, Rafel, you—"

His clenched fist came up, and the sparking glimfire flared hot. "*I ain't finished, Arlin.* You kept your mouth shut to punish Sarle Baden and now there's Goose out there somewhere in the wicked dark, and that Fernel bloody Pintte, and them others who never hurt you, and from what we heard through their talking stone it sounds like they've been punished right along with Baden. And for what? *For what?* So you can have *revenge?"*

The damp night air in the cave was shivering, shining golden. The ball of glimfire glowed like a small captive sun. Eyes glittering, Arlin stepped back.

"You're wrong to blame me, Rafel," he said. "You said it yourself,

Tollin's account also spoke of the gruesome illness that befell them. How can you blame me when—"

"Tollin never said a bloody word about voices!"

"Most likely because he knew he'd be laughed to shame!" Arlin retorted. "These are the mindrotted ramblings of a dying man, you fool. Who would give them credence? No-one with a whit of commonsense!"

"Da would've!" he said, so close to breaking, so close to smashing Arlin flat with his power. "After what he survived with Morg? *Da* would've known to take those ramblings serious. And if you'd given him the bloody chance, Arlin, if you'd told him, told *someone,* then—then—"

Then Goose wouldn't be out there alone. Maybe dying. Maybe dead already. None of them would.

Arlin stepped back again. More than cautious now. More than wary. The poxy shit was afraid.

And so he bloody should be. He should be pissing himself.

"Rafel—" Arlin held both hands out. No shimmer of power in him, all his magic locked away. "It was a mistake. You're right. I was angry with Sarle. My only thought was to deny him success. I didn't believe the diary. I didn't think anyone would get hurt. We still don't know for certain that anyone *has* been hurt. For all we know their talking stone was damaged. For all we know we'll stumble over them in a day or two. *Rafel.*"

Slowly, so slowly, the roaring in his mind faded. His burning blood cooled, and with it the urge to slaughter. He breathed out, hard, so dizzy he nearly staggered.

"As the official Council presence on this expedition," said Tom Dimble, "I tell you, Lord Garrick, that we are heartily displeased." He looked at his companions, and they all clambered to standing. "The Council should've been told of Marbury's account before it allowed Mayor Pintte and Lord Baden to lead their expedition. Before *we* were sent in their footsteps. You might well have put us all in grave danger!"

Recovered most of his arrogance, Arlin shook his head. "And you wonder why I never mentioned this. You *Olken* . . . you start at your own shadows and somehow you've managed to turn the Council's Doranen as cowardly as yourselves. If I'd shown you Marbury's diary you and those other timid fools might not have allowed—"

"*Might* not?" said Hosh Clyne, his voice uneven with temper. "*Would* not. Permission for this expedition would *not* have been granted had we known—"

Arlin smiled, so unpleasant. "But it was. And we're here. And—"

"We'll not be here beyond tonight," said Tom flatly. "This expedition is over. Mysterious, malevolent voices in the dark lands beyond these mountains? It's too dangerous to continue. Not until this matter has been discussed by all the Council and prayed on by Barlsman Jaffee and—"

"*Prayed* on?" said Arlin, incredulous. "Discussed in Council? There's no *time* for that. We must—"

"The decision's made, Lord Garrick," said Nib Hambly. "No point you arguing. You're not the authority here. Come first light we'll—"

"Keep on going," said Rafel, stirring. *I can't bloody believe it. I'm agreeing with Arlin. Again.* Much more of this and he'd drop dead with a brainstorm. "He's right, Meister Hambly. Lur's running out of time. And Goose and the others, they're running out of time too, even faster. Dangerous or not, we've got to keep going."

All three councilors were staring at him, dismayed. "You'd side with the *Doranen?*" said Clyne. "But Rafel—you *loathe* him."

He shrugged. "No. Loathe is much too mild a word. But it happens I agree with him on this. I can loathe him and agree with him, Clyne. It ain't that hard, 'specially with so much at stake."

"*Rafel*—"

"Save your breath, Tom," he said, suddenly so bloody tired. "If you want to turn tail, you go right ahead. I won't stop you. Truth be told, I'll prob'ly cheer. But *I* ain't turning back and neither is Arlin. Any of one of you try to stop us and—" Another shrug. "Well. Ain't no point in you trying to stop us, is there? We all know you might as well try spitting against the wind."

The looks on their faces answered him.

"Good," he said, nodding. "Now I'm a mite weary—and we need to be on our way again come dawn. Reckon I'll get some sleep." With a snap of his fingers he extinguished his glimlight, plunging their meagre cave into flame-flickered darkness.

As Tom and the others huddled close, muttering, he dropped to his groundsheet. Felt the abandoned diary under his arse, tugged it free, then held it out to Arlin. "Here."

Arlin was staring at him, half-lit by the dying fire. "You think this makes a difference? You think because you strut and puff your bravado like a cock on a dung heap I'll *forget* Westwailing?"

He grinned, not kindly. Lightly sleeping in his blood, all that power. "I don't want you to forget Westwailing, Arlin. I want you to *remember* it. Every bloody time you're tempted to do me a mischief, I want you to remember it. Now take this sinkin' diary before I use it as bloody kindling."

Tight-lipped, Arlin took the leather-bound book. Shoved it safely back in his pack, then hesitated. Looked up. "What happened to Vesty and the others. The way they died. You're not . . . concerned?"

"Afraid, you mean," he said, curling up beside his fire. "I've known since I were a sprat how Morg's magic killed them."

Arlin finished shoving the diary away and dropped cross-legged to his canvas groundsheet. "That doesn't answer my question."

"No?" he said, yawning. "There you go. Fancy that."

Tom and his Council friends were still huddled. Then their whispering stopped, and in the faint firelight their mingled shadows separated.

"We'll continue," Tom said coldly. "But Speaker Shifrin will hear of this, and the rest of the Council. You can both expect to be severely censured on our return."

Arlin didn't bother to reply. Rafel just sighed. Grunted. Let them make of that what they would. Tom and his namby-pamby friends chose to decide he'd accepted their authority, and all three settled themselves down to sleep. Beyond the cave, the rain continued.

And that was the first night.

A sodden dawn woke them, and the journey continued.

The long, wearisome days passed slowly. By their third sunset the constant rain had dribbled and died, along with any pretending that they were five men with something in common. Tom and his fellow-councilors even stopped their private whispering, all complaints exhausted. Strength was needed just to keep going. The Doranen hexes on the rocks and trees made sure they never once took a wrong step, and thanks to Tollin and Vont Marbury they knew where to find the natural springs bubbling through cracks and crevices in the mountains. Knew that the bright green lizards with the blue eyes were safe to eat, provided the sac of poison was cut from each scaly armpit... and that the stub-tailed brown lizards with the orange tongues were instant death. Knew that the dull blue berries on the scraggly vines wrapped around the mountains' stunted saplings tasted bitter, but would help them stay awake... and the pale, foamy-headed fungus that fed on rotted logs would make a man vomit till he turned his insides out.

As they fought their way over the unforgiving mountains, hating them too much to care for their wild beauty, they stumbled across signs that Fernel Pintte and his group had journeyed ahead of them. Boot prints dried around this water spring, and that one. Recently broken branches. Charred embers where a campfire had burned. Roasted animal bones picked to ivory by small, busy ants. The going continued cruel. Phena hadn't lied: Barl's Mountains were merciless.

Lying each night on hard rock, or gathered leaf-litter, staring at the tree-latticed sky or hiding from rain and mist beneath his broad-brimmed leather hat, Rafel thought about Barl and the terrified mages she'd brought with her from the Lost Dorana he and Arlin were so desperate to find. Thought of the children. *Children.* It was a bloody wonder all the sprats didn't perish. And babes-in-arms. There'd been babes-in-arms too, according to Doranen history and stories.

Hundreds of Doranen, starving and terrified, running for their lives from Morg. Hard to imagine. Though they brought such trouble with them, hard not to feel sad.

How can I blame them? You'd be crazy not to run.

With the unknown lands beyond the mountains crawled closer with every sunrise, the pain writhing in his blood and bones darkened. Grew more intense. As though now he didn't only feel the echoes of bitter magic in the mountains . . . but also in what lay beyond them. The ruined lands Tollin and Vont Marbury had run from. That Da had said would never change. But still, still, he clung to hope.

Da could be wrong. He's got to be wrong. Or we've come a sinkin' long way for nowt.

And that was all he'd let himself think of his father. If he let himself think any deeper he'd stir his fears to waking. Start to wonder if . . .

Even his body's constant thrumming of pain was more bearable than that.

Conversation continued scarce. What did any of them have to say to one another? The councilors were friends, true, but exhaustion had silenced them. Of the three men only Hambly, the farmer, was used to such relentless physical toil. Tom and Clyne, City folk both, suffered for their comfortable lives. He wanted to feel sorry for them, but it was hard.

I bloody told you not to come.

As for Arlin, he was showing the strain of their travelling, too. Like all of them he was scraped and cut and bruised from clambering over boulders, over fallen trees, into gullies and out again. No Doranen magic to ease his way — it was too dangerous. Could start a rockslide, or worse. Even he could see that. Did he still mourn his father? Watching him sideways from time to time, Rafel found it hard to tell. The way Rodyn had snapped and snarled, the way Arlin never stood up to him . . . had there been love there? Was there true grief? How could any son love a father who treated him so cold?

But that kind of thinking sailed him too close to dangerous waters. Better to dwell on less difficult distractions, like his never-ending pain.

Once he spoke to Arlin on something personal. Something not to do with trapping lizards or finding water or making sure a guiding hex wasn't corrupted. On the nineteenth night of their brutal journey, wrenched and skinned and too tired for sleep, he sat propped against the scorched trunk of a lightning-struck tree and struggled to breathe through the seething agitation in his blood. His small fire, carefully walled with loose rocks, threw a little heat and light. Better than nothing, but not enough to chase the deep-seated chill from his bones. He was used to it now. Had glumly accepted he'd likely never be properly warm again.

Beneath him, around him, the poisoned earth whispered. Here in the wilderness, just like in Lur's Home Districts, there was nothing stood between him and what he felt.

A good job Deenie ain't here. She'd be curled up screaming right about now.

Spikily aware of nearby Arlin's brooding gaze on him, he opened his gritty eyes. "You don't feel a sinkin' thing, do you?"

Stubbled with beard, his blond hair dirty, matted with sweat, Arlin looked as battered and exhausted as he felt. Unhealthily thin, the flesh fallen away in his face, 'cause the jerky and nuts and hard-tack biscuits, the lizards and berries and occasional birds' eggs, they kept starvation at bay, and no more.

I'd bloody kill for a ginger cake.

"What? What are you talking about?" said Arlin, croaky with weariness. Snappish that he'd been caught staring.

Rafel let his head bump against the rough dead bark behind him. "No. You feel nowt. Reckon this is the first and last time I ever felt jealous of a bloody Doranen."

Arlin snorted. "That you'll admit to."

Sitting well apart, like they always did, Tom and his friends fed twigs to their own campfire. Pretending they were the three of them alone. Just as thin, just as filthy and stubbled. Regretting their predicament, now it was days too late to change their minds.

"You still insist that as an Olken, you're special?" said Arlin, prodding. Even parched and croaking, he managed to sneer. "That your mage senses are superior to mine?"

"Not superior," he said wearily. "Different."

"And what is it you claim to feel that I don't?"

He should've kept his mouth shut. "Nowt," he muttered, letting his eyes drift closed. "Leave me to snore, Arlin. Sunrise comes bloody early this high up."

"Rafel..."

Startled, he opened his eyes again because Arlin had thrown a stone at him, hard. "Don't bloody do that!"

"Then answer me!" snapped Arlin. "What do you feel?"

Beneath the arrogant belligerence—was that a whisper of fear? He thought it was. He thought maybe Arlin was frighted. *So maybe I'm wrong. Maybe, at long last, Arlin is feeling something.* Could be the darkness had finally touched him. He rolled his head, just a little, and met Arlin's resentful stare.

"I feel the mountains, Lord Garrick." The young night's silence deepened, as though every unseen bird and tiny animal was holding its breath. Listening. "They're alive with the memory of what happened here. They suffer. They hold grudges. They remember the Wall, and what brought it down. They remember Morg and all his wickedness, six hundred years of hurling dark magics into their stones and buried bones. The mountains are weeping. That's what I feel."

For a long time Arlin said nothing. Then he laughed, scornful. "Fanciful nonsense. You're lightheaded, Rafel. Raving. Westwailing addled you. I've never heard such tripe."

"No. He's right," said Tom, stirring beside his fire. "I can feel it too. Not as deeply—he's Asher's son, after all—but I feel it."

"So do I," Nib Hambly whispered. "My dreams...my dreams... they've been cruel and cold these last few nights."

Surprised, unsettled, Rafel squinted at them. "What about you, Meister Clyne?" It was too dark to see the barber's downturned face, but he could hear the man's unsteady breathing. "What do you feel?"

"I don't know," said Clyne. "But my dreams have grown fearsome. And my spirits are low."

"Of course they're *low,*" said Arlin, scathing. "Look around us, you fool. Look where we are. You can't give his claims *credence.* You may be Olken, Clyne, but you're surely not so stupid."

Rafel scowled. *Shut up, Arlin. You ain't bloody helping.* "Tom? How long have you been feeling like this?"

"For certain?" Tom exchanged a cautious glance with his companions. "A few days. Before that?" He shrugged. "There's much of what we're doing would give any man bad dreams."

Arlin shoved a broken branch onto his dwindling campfire. Kicked the flames higher with a snap of his fingers. "This is *nonsense*. The four of you frighten each other like little boys."

"Do we?" Rafel pulled a knee to his chest and wrapped his arms around it. Rested his chin, the dull throb behind his eyes threatening to sharpen. "But you're feeling bad too, Arlin. You've got to be. A mage like you? You might not feel the earth, like we can, but don't tell me you can't at least feel Morg's presence here."

With four pairs of Olken eyes on him, Arlin busied himself thumping his pack into a lumpy pillow. "What I feel is my business."

"And what *I* feel is *your* business?"

"You started this, Rafel," Arlin retorted. "Not me."

"I asked one bloody question! You're the one couldn't leave it alone." Frustrated, he snapped his other knee close. Was glad of the tree-trunk behind him, a bolster. "You're the one sitting there calling me a—"

"I'm the one who'd like to get some rest," said Arlin. "And instead I'm being kept awake by Olken bedtime daffydowns." He settled onto his groundsheet, curled tight to hold in any meagre warmth. "Morg is dead. His magic's dead. There are no voices. Go to sleep."

Bemused, Rafel shook his head. *Just when I think he can't get any more arrogant.* Then he rolled his eyes at Tom and the others. "You heard Lord Garrick, sprats. Beddy-bye time."

Muttering, the councilors bedded down. He bedded down too, but sleep came slow and fitful. No voices, true. Just the earth's keening cry, moaning through the empty places inside him.

The next day they continued, and did not speak of darkness and bad dreams again. But Rafel kept an eye on Tom and the others, every instinct telling him to beware. *But beware of what? Maybe Arlin's right. Maybe it's 'cause I'm worn down. Worn out.* And he was. No point denying it.

Except Arlin's fear remained, too. Ruthlessly buried. Not spoken of. But there.

Another three days of punishing travel, another three nights of restless, painful sleep. Hour by hour he felt more and more beaten, more and more bruised. The air thickened around him, so that walking in sunlight was like swimming in the dark. His blood felt like molasses, his heart struggled to pump. He wanted to pull Arlin aside, to whisper, *Can't you feel it?*

But letting Arlin see weakness would be a sinkin' mistake. Arlin wasn't Goose, a shoulder to lean on. Arlin would smell uncertainty and move in for the kill.

Tom and the others were feeling it, he could see that. He could see the pain in them, slowing them down. Tom he did take aside. Tried to make him see sense. "I know it's risky, but you should turn back. It's only going to get worse."

"We can't," said Tom, his voice thinner than it had been, his eyes sunken and bloodshot. "We have a sworn duty. We'll see this through."

He sighed. "You're a fool, Tom. It's not worth your life."

"You think it's worth yours," said Tom, shrugging. "And you're not the only Olken willing to fight for Lur."

"Hosh and Nib might see it different," he said. "They might think—"

"They agree with me," said Tom. "Give over, Rafel. Save your strength for climbing the next bit of cliff."

What could he do? No law said they had to listen. "Fine," he said curtly. "But don't blame me when you're broken, and can't be fixed."

The twenty-fifth day since their leaving of Gribley dawned cool and cloudy. According to Tollin's expedition account, they were nearly four days slower in their crossing. But even so, they should be quit of Barl's Mountains before sunset.

Worn to a thin edge, as he chewed a leathery mouthful of jerky he found himself comforted and frighted by the notion. He was more than ready for this part of the journey to be over. But come so close to Morg's abandoned domain, his heart thudded hard against his ribs. He felt bad enough now. How much worse would he feel walking through the lands Morg used to rule?

Don't think on that. You'll feel what you feel, and whatever you feel, *you'll bear it. You ain't got a choice. Goose is relying on you.*

Close by, Arlin was choking down cold, charred lizard meat. He felt the Doranen look at him, as though he'd spoken his fears aloud. Met the poxy shit's stare unblinking, daring him to speak.

Arlin looked away.

Breakfast finished, they shrugged into their much lighter packs, morosely silent, and trudged on. Soon enough the path tumbled downwards, steep and treacherous, shrouded so thickly with foliage they couldn't tell how close to the ground they were, or what waited for them beyond the mountains' blotting blanket of trees. One mis-step, one stumble, and there'd be broken legs — or necks. Sweating and swearing, clutching at low-hung branches and saplings, unbalanced by packs and swords and stout walking sticks, they struggled to stay on their feet as they wended their way down the lower slopes of the mountain. There was no birdsong. No lizard skitterings. No sense of any life. This close to Morg's old kingdom, everything felt dead.

And then a burst of daylight, blinding, as at last they emerged from the forested gloom.

"Barl's mercy," said Tom Dimble, panting, his face contorted. Running sweat. "We've done it. We've escaped Lur."

They had. Before them, a new stretch of mountain, this time split in half by a wide gap. Clinging to the edge of the weathered left-hand peak, a man-made stone staircase, narrow and crumbling. Years and years old. Treacherous: one careless step and a man would plummet to his death. And through that wide gap, bathed in cloud-filtered sunlight, glimpses of a land they had never seen before.

Tom, Clyne and Hambly were clasping hands, patting shoulders. Wearily celebrating despite their undisguised discomfort. Even now they remained their own privy expedition. Arlin, stood apart and disdainful, picked at the worn stitching on a finger of his leather gloves. Seemingly unmoved by what they'd achieved.

Rafel smeared his forearm across his filthy, sweaty bearded face.

Sink me, Da. We crossed the mountains.

So... what next?

Though he was exhausted, and the stench of Morg's magic rose unleashed within him, burning his blood and scalding his bones so he could easily weep from the torment, he broke into an unsteady run. He heard Arlin curse and follow, battered boots loud on the uneven rocky steps, desperately trying to overtake him. Of course. Further behind Arlin came Tom, Clyne and Hambly, gasping and wheezing. He heard his own harsh, laboured breathing as he staggered up the staircase on lead-heavy legs. Nearly. Nearly. He was nearly at the top. One more step. Another one. Just one more. He thought he could feel Arlin's ragged breath hot on his neck.

There.

Hand flung against the bare rock wall beside him, perilously close to tumbling, he took a deep breath. Took another. Another. Tried to subdue the sick churning in his guts. But before he could blink away the sweat and properly see the new land spread before him, he heard an agonised, choking moan.

Turning, staring past clumsy, crowding Arlin, he saw Tom Dimble's legs buckle and drop him sprawling on his back. His staff hit the stone steps and rolled away. Further down the staircase Hosh Clyne and Nib Hambly were struggling too, fallen against each other, barely staying on their feet.

Tom's eyes were anguished in his sickly grey face, blood seeping like tears. His chest heaved for air, every muscle twisted with pain. *"Rafel—"*

Tossing aside his own staff he shoved by Arlin, ignoring the Doranen's furious protest, and plunged back down the staircase.

"Tom—Tom—what is it?" he said, dropping to the ground beside him. "Can you talk?"

Eyes rolling, nostrils bubbling a bloody froth, Tom shuddered. "You don't—feel it?" he gasped. "Darkness—*darkness*—" A dreadful moan. "Hosh...Nib..."

Rafel glanced up. Saw Tom's fellow-councilors, sprawled now like he was, writhing in pain.

"What is this?" Arlin demanded, keeping well back. "An Olken affliction?"

"No," he said tautly, holding tight to Tom's hand. Looked behind him at Rodyn's unlovable son. "It's this place. It's Morg. Can't you tell? You're ice-white, Arlin. Don't deny you can feel it."

Arlin's eyes narrowed. "I may feel it but *I'm* not dying. Why aren't you?"

Still holding on to Tom, he shuffled round awkwardly, the stone steps bruising his knees. "Don't sound so sinkin' disappointed. I'm sickened. It's just—I'm stronger than them. And they're *not* bloody dying!" *Not if I can help it.* "Tom—" He bent low. "I'm sorry. I should've kept on at you until you turned back."

"They can turn back now," said Arlin, as Tom heaved for air. "They have to. They'll only slow us down."

"Turn back?" he said, disbelieving, and waved a hand at all three men. "Arlin! For pity's sake, *look* at them!"

"I am looking," said Arlin, and took a cautious step closer. "They stay here or they turn back, Rafel. That's it. That's the choice."

Hate for Arlin was sharp as a stab wound. Fear for Goose stabbed sharper than that. Had this happened to Pintte's expedition? If they kept walking would they find their bodies? Black and bloated and running with pus?

"Sink that. There's got to be something else."

Arlin shrugged. "There isn't. Stay and perish with them, Rafel, or guide them back to Lur. It's up to you. But I'm not wasting any more time on this."

Letting go of Tom's hand, sparing a look for Clyne and Hambly, suffering as horribly, he lurched to his feet.

"You're going to abandon three stricken men?" *You bastard, Arlin, you sinkin' bastard.* "You can't. That's—that's *wicked.*"

Pale and filthy, stinking—as they all were—Arlin smiled. There was no pleasure in it, only a cold and calculated cruelty. "I've crossed the mountains to find Lost Dorana. I've no interest in mollycoddling three sick Olken who were forced upon me against my will. And if you attempt to stop me, Rafel..." Power seethed, swift and lethal. Boiling through the tainted air. "This isn't Lur. Get in my way and I'll kill you where you stand."

Tom was making strangled noises in his throat. Hosh Clyne and Nib Hambly had started to shake. Remembering Da on the floor of the Weather Chamber, the blood and the convulsions, Rafel had to close his eyes. And then he looked back at Arlin.

He doesn't mean it. He can't.

"If you walk away what am I s'posed to do? Snap my bloody fingers and—"

"Rafel?" said Arlin, suspicious. "What are you doing?"

Sweat prickling, Morg's hate darkly whispering, he ignored poxy Arlin Garrick. Finished shrugging out of his pack, let it and his sword fall to the stone staircase beside Tom, then dropped into a crouch to fumble at its buckles. He didn't dare try to do this from memory. He'd read the incants a number of times since copying them in Da's library but he was a long way from trusting himself to know the words and sigils by heart.

I can do this. I have to.

But this was such a poisoned place. Tollin and the others, they'd struggled with their magic here. What if he struggled too? What if the dregs of Morg's blighting magic tainted the spells? Tainted him? What if—

I have to try.

Tom was weeping now, little sobs of unbearable pain. He and Nib Hambly and Hosh Clyne—they didn't have much time. Morg's malevolence was crushing them. It was trying to crush him. He'd die before he let it.

"*Rafel!*" Arlin stepped closer again. "What are you—"

Tugging the folded papers out of the pack, Rafel looked up, knowing his eyes were terrible. Knowing rage and power burned in his stare.

"Shut up and stand back. I ain't got the first sinkin' idea if this'll work."

And if it doesn't I really will be a murderer.

But he couldn't think on that. Leave Tom and the others here, send them back across the mountains on their lonesome, or kill them by try-ing to conjure them home. Whatever he did they'd be just as dead, and he'd be to blame. But at least this way the poor bastards stood a chance.

Finding the scribbled page he was after, he folded the others and shoved them back to safety in his pack. Then he read the conjuring incants quickly, looking for the one that would best suit his purpose.

"Rafel, what are you *doing?*"

He almost laughed, he felt so frighted. "I'm sending them home, Arlin. Now bloody *stand back.*"

Scowling, Arlin retreated three steps. *"Sending them home?* Rafel, have you lost your mind?"

Shutting out Arlin's nagging voice, shutting out fear and doubt and every scent and sound around him and every hurt in his body, Morg's insidious magic, Rafel tucked the sheet of paper under the toe of his boot...rested his left hand on Tom Dimble's lolling head...read out loud the words of the incant...said *"Dorana City"* in a clear voice, holding in his mind's eye an image of the Council chamber...wrote burning sigils on the curdled air with his right forefinger...and waited.

Nowt happened. Nowt happened. He nearly wept with despair. Then the power inside him stirred, hugely and hotly. He felt dizzy. Felt vomit-ing sick.

A twist of pain...a flare of tarnished gold...and Tom Dimble disappeared.

CHAPTER TWENTY-NINE

❈

Stunned silence. Then Arlin stirred. "What was that? Rafel, *what did you do?*"

Fingers trembling, head pounding, that pulse of pain still burning, he retrieved the sheet of scribbled incants. "Don't you bloody listen, Arlin?" He glanced up. Wished there was time to enjoy the look on Lord Garrick's face. "I sent Tom home. Now shut your trap so I can send Hosh and Nib after him."

Leaving Arlin gaping he climbed down to Hambly and Clyne, tumbled like Deenie's childhood dolls on the narrow stony stairs. Almost as still as dolls now. Dangerously close to death. Twice more he recited Durm's conjuring spell. Twice more seared flaming sigils into the air. One after the other, the Olken men disappeared.

A heartbeat later he sat down, hard enough to rattle his teeth. Bright with pain and oddly emptied, he put his head between his bent knees. Waited to see if the spasm would pass, or if he'd just pass out.

I did it. Da, I did it. Even in this filthy place. The spell worked, I could feel it. What does that mean? What else can I do?

A scraping of boot-leather, heels hammering stone steps. Then brutal fingers tangled in his hair. Dragged his head up and back till he was staring into Arlin Garrick's furious face.

"Where did you get those incants, Rafel? That magic is *unknown*."

No matter what happened next, this would be worth it. He smiled. "Not unknown, Arlin. At least not to Durm."

Shaken, Arlin let go of him. Stepped back and nearly tripped onto his own arse. *"Durm?* That's not possible. Durm's library of magic is — it's —" His voice died in his throat. "I have read the Council library, Rafel. Every book, every scroll. The conjuring incant you just used —"

"Ain't there," he said, and pinched the bridge of his nose between thumb and forefinger. A bonfire was burning unchecked behind his eyes. "For bloody good reason, it turns out."

"Your father," Arlin whispered. "He repressed the knowledge? He *dared* to decide what the Doranen shall know of their own *heritage?*"

Rafel looked up. For the smallest, swiftest moment felt a twinge of sympathy. Could see his own remembered rage echoed in Arlin. And then he recalled who and what this man was, and fleeting sympathy died.

"Durm decided it first, Arlin. He's the one who kept those magics hidden. Him and every Master Magician since Barl's time. Da took their advice, is all. You want to complain? Complain to them."

Arlin flung out his hand. He was shaking with his fury. "Give those pages to me. *All* of them. They are *nothing* to do with you, Olken."

"No," he said, pushing unsteady to his feet. "And I'm warning you, Arlin — try taking 'em off me and I'll send you home, too. Only it won't be the Council chamber you wake up in. Try anything mucky on me and I bloody swear, I'll drop you smack dab into one of those whirlpools you and your meddling Da helped make."

"My father was right," said Arlin, his voice low and choking. "You're an abomination. The midwife should've drowned you at birth."

"And *I* should've let *you* drown in Westwailing."

And there it was. The ugly truth. A lifetime of rivalry, resentment and bitterness, of petty cruelties and secret revenges stripped bare.

Arlin's fingers were fisting and unfisting, aching to strike out. *"Rafel —"*

"Y'know," he added, in a mood to twist the knife, "since it seems we're upending all our dirty little secrets? On the day I turned eleven I pinched a spell from that book you liked to flash around at school. Remember the one, full of clever Doranen magic? That was my birthday present to me.

And every bloody day after, Arlin, *every bloody day*—I pinched another one. Right under your nose. And you never knew." He smiled again, wider this time. Nearly laughing at the look on Arlin's face. "So in case you get any clever ideas, Lord Garrick? Now that Tom and the others are gone? I ain't green when it comes to Doranen magic. And that conjuring spell is only the start of what I know."

For a long time, Arlin was silent. Whatever his feelings now, he had them well hidden. Then he stirred. "That spell. Can you use it to conjure us to Lost Dorana?"

"If I could, don't you think I might've mentioned it already?" He shook his head. "No, Arlin. It only works if you know where you're going. And since we don't... we'll have to get there the hard way."

Leaving poxy Lord Garrick to stare at thin air, he returned to his abandoned pack. Shoved the scribbled page of incants inside, shrugged it on, his unused sword awkward in its scabbard, then retrieved his walking staff. Stared up the steep stone staircase in front of them.

"Well? Are you coming?"

Arlin answered by pushing past him and taking those steep stone steps two at a time. Rafel shook his head, and followed.

Let him take the bloody lead. I don't care. And I'm safer with him in front of me than I am with him behind.

The stone staircase continued down the other side of the mountain. A hairsbreadth from a fatal fall, they took each weathered, rocky step slowly, one at a time. Who had built the staircase, and why, Rafel couldn't imagine. Didn't care. It meant there'd been people here once. Barl willing, they'd find them. Barl willing, they'd find Goose and the others, too. Alive.

'Cause if they ain't...

But he couldn't think on that. He had enough trouble to fight without thinking on Goose dead, with Arlin for company and the sickening remains of Morg's magic sullen in his blood. And in these new lands. It was a puzzle, why Tom and the others had fallen to it and he hadn't. Arlin was mostly all right. 'Cause he was Doranen? Was that the key? And was it his own Doranen magic that saved him? He thought it must be.

So I guess that makes me lucky, Da. Bloody lucky I got you for my father.

Of course, that didn't solve the biggest puzzle of all: how it was he and Da could do Doranen magic in the first place. With Da hating his magic, they'd never talked on it. Prob'ly now they never would. Unless he and Arlin managed to stumble across Lost Dorana. Could be he'd find his answers there.

If it even exists. If this ain't a bloody great waste of time...and our lives.

At last they reached the bottom of the stone staircase, without mishap. Took a moment to catch their breaths, get their bearings. Stretching before them, a wide expanse of open country. No trees. No animals. No dwellings, or even ruins. Everything was silent and still. Shadowed in the distance, at the furthest limits of sight, a vague hint of...something.

Arlin pointed. "There."

"I agree."

"And I could care less if you agree or not."

"Arlin..." Sighing, Rafel looked at him. "Like it or not we're in this together. Like it or not we need to trust each other, 'cause—"

"*Trust* each other?"

He watched Arlin stamp a few paces, then spin round to confront him. Beneath the dirt and sweat and stubbled beard, the Doranen's face was livid.

"That's right, Arlin," he said quickly. "*Trust.* Which ain't got a sinkin' thing to do with *like.* I *don't* bloody like you and you don't like me. But this ain't Lur, where that doesn't matter. Barl alone knows what we'll run into out here. Could be there'll come a time when I'm the only thing standing between you and a grisly death."

Arlin laughed. "And you expect me to believe you'll *stay* standing between us?"

"Yes."

"Prove it," said Arlin, eyes glittering. "Give me those spells you stole."

Bastard. He shook his head. "I can't."

The anger died out of Arlin's face, leaving it cold and white. "Fend for yourself, Rafel. From this point I travel alone. Follow me? Hinder me? *Trust this.* I'll make you sorry."

Almost, *almost,* he let Arlin walk away. Let the poxy shit go and if he died, good riddance. But he couldn't. He needed to find Lost Dorana, and to find Lost Dorana he needed Lord bloody Garrick.

One day I'm going to choke on needing him.

"All right!" he shouted. "Arlin, all right! I'll show you!"

Arlin slowed. Stopped. Didn't turn round. Stifling a groan, because he was so tired, so ill-at-ease, Rafel forced himself into a jog-trot until he caught up.

"I'll show you," he said again, as Arlin stared at him in hostile silence. "I will. But not now. Tonight. When we make camp, wherever we make camp. I'll show you then."

Arlin started walking. Groaning again, Rafel followed.

They trudged for hours across the greyish-green, unwholesome turf. Even in the thin, unclouded sunshine the air felt dark and dangerous. Smelled... wrong. These lands were oppressive, steeped and soaked in the most perverse of magics.

Arlin glanced sideways at Rafel, walking two good arms' length distant. As much as he wanted to disbelieve the Olken, to disbelieve he had some special connection to the earth, it couldn't be denied the man looked... unwell. There was something more at work in him than mere weariness from their arduous crossing of the mountains.

He's right. This place is poisoned. And while I can taste it, while it gripes in my belly, it isn't eating at me. Not like it eats at him.

If this was anyone else, even any other Olken, he might feel something. Feel sympathy. Offer help. But this was Asher's son, the great Rodyn Garrick's murderer, and a thief besides. Remembering Rafel's mocking smile, he felt his belly gripe tighter.

For years, he stole from me. Made a fool of me. I will punish him for that. Perhaps not today, or even tomorrow. But I will have my vengeance. When I no longer need him, I will make him pay.

Stolen magics...

If he let himself, he'd still be reeling from the shock of those three conjurations. Three living, breathing men banished home by magic. By Rafel.

What else does he know? What else did Durm hide from us that Asher's son can do... and I can't?

He'd grown up on tales of fantastic Doranen magics. Fallen asleep to his father's railings against Barl and her betrayals, to his lamenting the loss of their heritage because she'd been weak and afraid. If Father and Ain Freidin hadn't perished, perhaps they'd have discovered what Barl had thrown away. And then Ain would have taught him those magics and he would have become the greatest mage in Lur.

And Ain would have smiled at him.

"Arlin?" said Rafel, slowing. "What is it?"

They'd not spoken a word since starting across this wasteland. Barely looked at each other, each pretending they walked alone. And now here was Rafel, genuine concern in his voice. How much did it *gall* him, that Asher's son could sense his disquiet?

"Nothing."

Shading his eyes, Rafel stared ahead. After so many hours' steady progress they at last were close enough to make sense of the smudged shadows they'd glimpsed from the stone staircase.

"I can feel it too. I think it's a village. Likely the same village Tollin found." The Olken shivered. "It feels bad, doesn't it?"

Yes, it felt bad, but he wasn't about to admit it. Wasn't about to do or say anything to give Rafel the impression they had even that much in common.

"I wonder if we'll find Fernel Pintte there. And the others," Rafel added. "Sarle Baden. Goose."

There'd been not a sign of them yet. If they did find their missing men in the village, most likely it would be as rotting corpses. Their message to the Council had been discouraging, at best. He couldn't find it in him to grieve. Baden alive would only be an obstacle. His blind determination to steal Father's dreams proved that.

The day was dying, sliding towards twilight, but if they picked up their pace they should reach the village before dark. Never mind his exhaustion, he'd happily run the rest of the way. It was hard to think beyond the promised chance to look at Durm's spells.

"We should pick up our pace," said Rafel, glancing at the sky. "Night's coming, and I'd rather not be out in the open when it does. For all we know there are creatures here who shun the light, and feast in the dark."

What a charming thought.

He started walking again, leaving Rafel to follow or stay behind or drop dead. After a few minutes he broke into a shuffling jog. When his chest hurt too much to breathe comfortably, he slowed. Walked until his breathing eased, then shuffle-jogged some more. Walk, jog, walk, jog. Rafel kept up with him. The bastard was nothing if not stubborn.

When at last they reached the village the world was swathed in a purplish dusk. Like Vont Marbury before them they found old bleached bones, empty ruined cottages, cracked and weed-wrecked cobbled streets, and dry wells. If the mountains had often been silent, this place felt like a tomb. Was cold like a tomb. Smelled like one, dry and musty and drear. And like a tomb it held nothing of life.

They stood in what had likely been the public square, where naked, yellowed skeletons dangled from sagging, half-rotted gibbets. The rust on their chains spoke of infrequent rain.

"They're not here," said Rafel, and rasped a gloved hand down his face. "I don't understand. Where could they be?"

He shrugged. "Anywhere. This can't be the only village."

"Maybe not, but it's the first one," said Rafel. He sounded dismayed. "They'd have stopped here. Why isn't there some sign?"

"Stopped here for what?" he said, impatient. Irritated by the man's distress. "The place is barren."

"I can see it's bloody barren, Arlin. I ain't blind."

He stared at Rafel, silent, until the Olken dropped his gaze. "We should make camp. Come dawn we can inspect the place more thoroughly."

"Aye," Rafel muttered. "Aye, we might as well."

"Rafel—"

"I said all right! Don't you start with me, Arlin. I ain't in the bloody mood."

That was better. A dispirited Rafel was more likely to limp than leap between him and a grisly death.

"I'll find some firewood," he said. "You pick somewhere for us to sleep. *Not* inside. If there are...creatures...in this blighted place, we must be able to see them coming."

Leaving Rafel to his task, he went foraging for something, anything, he could get to burn. Fuel was scarce. By the time he'd gathered enough half-rotted, splintered wood—cottage shutters, doors, window-frames—to keep them warm for an hour or two, the Olken had settled on the remains of a tumbledown hovel one street behind the square. The shelter it offered was meagre, at best. The roof was long gone, which meant there was no *inside*. Two of its stone walls remained upright; the other two had half-collapsed. But at least if it rained, or if a wind came up, they'd be a little protected.

Provided the other walls don't collapse, and crush us in our sleep.

"I'm glad you find this amusing, Arlin," said Rafel, scowling. The glimfire he'd conjured lit the paltry hovel with a fitful, reluctant glow. "How much food and water have *you* got left?"

"Enough," he said, and busied himself getting the fire started. Once it was burning, the only cheerful thing in the whole wretched village, he spread his groundsheet and sat. Ate and drank sparingly, trying to ignore the queasy churn in his guts. Morg's leftover magics had smeared these lands like old, rancid oil, leaving nothing untouched. He could almost imagine himself breathing in the foul incants. Could almost feel them coating his bones.

Under cover of throwing more wood on the fire, he looked at Rafel, leaning against a bit of wall, hunched and miserable. Feeling their surroundings, yes, but moping for his missing friend as well. Sentimental fool. And then the Olken felt himself being watched, and looked up.

"I didn't bring all Durm's spells with me, you know," Rafel said, defensive. "Just a few. And not a single one my da used against Morg. Those spells don't exist anymore."

Carefully, he sat down again. "So your father claimed. But we know now your father was a liar."

Rafel's face darkened. "*Is* a liar, Arlin. He ain't dead. And he ain't a liar, either. He danced around the truth a bit, to protect Lur. It ain't the same thing."

"Danced around the truth?" he said, incredulous. "He said there was nothing out of the ordinary about you. *Lie.* He told Jaffee he never once felt unrest in the earth. *Lie.* He said the Council had seen all that was left of Old Doranen magic. *Lie.*"

"Like I said," Rafel muttered. "He was protecting Lur."

"What else has he lied about? And don't tell me *nowt,* because I know that's not true." He leaned forward, the fire's heat caressing. "Tell me, Rafel. What can it matter now? Lur's far, far behind us."

"Maybe, Arlin, but once we've found Lost Dorana we'll be going back there, won't we?" Rafel retorted. "D'you think I'm going to tell you anything as'll hurt him?"

"Do *you* think he'll be alive to care?"

Rafel shook his head. His shadow-smeared eyes were wide, and shocked. "You are a sinkin', poxy bastard."

And you murdered my father. Don't think I'll forget.

"Fine," he said, shrugging. "Keep your little secrets, Rafel. I don't care." He held out his hand. "Just give me those spells."

"In the morning," said Rafel. "I'm tired now. I want to sleep."

"You're *tired?*" He had to wait a moment. Had to subdue the urge to strike. "I see. So that was a lie too? A shining example of like father, like son?"

Rafel didn't quite manage to hide his flinch. "Those spells are dangerous, Arlin. They're weapons. And like I said, I'm tired. I'll show them to you when I'm feeling more rested."

"You think I'll *attack* you?"

Rafel smiled. "I think you think I murdered your father." He snapped his fingers, and the glimfire went out, plunging his hollowed face into shadow. "Get some sleep, Lord Garrick. Morning'll be here soon enough."

Long after Arlin had surrendered to his furious exhaustion Rafel sat awake, too tired to sleep, listening to the night's relentless silence. Feeling its emptiness. The deadness of this land scraped his nerves raw. Even Lur's discordant music was better than—than this *nothing*.

And underneath the deadness, a dreadful, rank disease. The blight he'd felt in Dragonteeth Reef, in the Weather map, unchallenged here and left to flourish. Sour and knotted, twisting everything it touched.

Will it twist me too, if I stay here long enough? Will it twist Arlin?

Although in Arlin's case, it might not be possible to tell the difference.

The fire was dying, their supply of wood run out. But he didn't want to risk hunting for more. Arlin might wake. And if he woke alone, he'd go after Durm's spells. And that wasn't—

"You hear that?" Arlin whispered, in the dark. "There's someone out there. In the street."

Yes. There was.

He heard it again, that peculiar, snuffling grunt. Almost like an animal, but the shape of it felt *wrong*. The sense, the presence. It was a man. Or almost a man. Heart thudding, raw nerves thrumming, he cautiously unsheathed the sword he'd hoped never to use and stood in one smooth motion, tension obliterating his loud aches and pains. Arlin was on his feet already, easing close to what passed for the tumbled cottage's door.

Joining him, Rafel touched his arm lightly. "Wait. *Wait*."

A stealthy, shuffling sound. Another snuffling grunt. Whoever—whatever—was coming, it was close to them now. Close...closer...

"Now!" he shouted, and pushed Arlin into the street. Leapt right after him, and as he leapt conjured enough glimfire to wash night bright as day. The man's—the creature's—snuffling grunt slid into a panicked scream. Half-blinded himself, Rafel raised the sword ready to maim or to kill.

And then he caught sight of their attacker's terrified face.

"Goose?"

Flinging the sword away to clatter on the cobbles, he rounded on Arlin. Shoved him hard, both hands to the chest, as the Doranen prepared to strike with magic.

"Don't! *Don't!* Can't you see, Arlin? *It's Goose!*"

Arlin stepped back, for once surprised out of his customary self-contained arrogance. Leaving him to fend for himself Rafel turned again, to his friend.

Blinking in the glimlight, Goose shuddered like a shambled ox. Clothes near to rags. His filthy hair wild and unkempt, his face scabbed, his sparse beard straggled. Thin, so bloody thin. Worst of all, the dumb terror in his eyes.

Sickened, Rafel took a step towards him. "Goose? It's all right. It's me. It's Rafel." He took another step, reached out his hand—and stopped as Goose raised an arm, whimpering.

"He's lost his mind," said Arlin, his contempt like a knife. "His wits have wandered."

Poxy bastard. "Shut up, Arlin. You'll fright him." Gentling his voice, he eased another step forward. "Goose...Goose...don't be frighted. I ain't going to hurt you. You're safe. I promise. It's me. Rafel. Remember?" He heard his voice break, felt tears sting his eyes. "Arlin—fetch Durm's spells from my pack. I'm sending Goose home."

"No," said Arlin. "You can't. He has to stay."

"Stay?" Even though Goose whimpered again, this time he didn't gentle his tone. "He can't *stay.* Look at him, Arlin. Something's happened to him. He's *hurt.* He needs help. Pother Kerril."

Arlin shrugged. "And he can have Pother Kerril—but not yet. We need him, Rafel, even if he can't find his own pizzle to piss with."

"Need him?" he said blankly. "Arlin—"

"Are you as witless as he is?" Arlin demanded. "Rafel, we've got to find Sarle Baden and the others. We need all the mages we can get, in this place. And your friend here might be our only chance of finding them."

What? "Arlin, how can he? *Look* at him. Look at his *face.*" Like poor ole Jed's face, the eyes vacant. The wits—yes—wandered. "The only place he'll lead us is over a cliff."

"So I was wrong about you, Rafel," said Arlin, coldly. "You're not your father's son. You're a pathetic, mawkish dolt. You'd let a kingdom perish to spare one man."

Arlin might as well have picked up that ole sword and shoved it right through him. Thrust it in one side of his heart and out the other. Spare Goose or lose Lur. Were those his only choices?

You think I don't know how you feel, sprat? I know. I spoke the words that killed my best friend.

Da's words to him before he poured himself into Barl's Weather map, and nearly died.

He was weeping, he could feel it. He didn't care that Arlin could see. *Hating* Arlin, for being Arlin, for being right, he tried to smile at his best friend.

I've got to do it. I've got to use him. Or I'm not my father's son.

"I know you're frighted, Goose-egg," he whispered. "I know you want to go home. And I'll send you home. I will. My word on it, man to man. Just...help us a little bit, and then I'll send you home."

"Get him inside," said Arlin. "He might bolt, out here."

Tentative, he risked reaching out to Goose again. This time his friend didn't whimper or pull back. Instead, flinching like a bear cruelly tamed to do tricks, he let himself be led into their tumbledown shelter. 'Cause a part of him remembered? Or 'cause he was so addled and worn out he had no fight left? He didn't know. It didn't matter. All that mattered was this time, Goose listened.

Arlin followed them inside, picking up the discarded sword first, then tugging the glimlight behind him with one snap of his fingers. Propped the sword in one corner and stood beside it, arms folded, closely watching. What, did he think Goose might suddenly attack?

Bastard. Poxy bastard. I don't care if he's right. Before this is over I want him broken and weeping.

Rafel dropped to a crouch on his groundsheet. "Here, Goose. Sit here."

Oh, and it nearly killed him, to see Goose stranded there, uncertain, barely able to understand such simple words. His best friend the gold medal–winning brewer, sure to be his guild's meister one day, just like his da. Funny and wise and amiable and loyal. Goose, who loved Deenie. Goose, who loved him.

Goose. Goose, I'm sorry. Forgive me.

He glowered at Arlin. "He's all right. He won't run. He knows me, Arlin. He knows he's safe."

"Really?" With another finger-snap, Arlin dimmed the ball of glimfire almost to darkness. Enough light to see by, barely. Enough darkness to sleep. "Then he knows more than I do, Rafel. *I* don't think any one of us is safe."

But that didn't stop the poxy shit falling back to sleep. Soon after, Goose slept too, huddled against the stone wall. And then, though he tried to stay awake, just in case of danger, exhaustion claimed him... and he was plagued by terrible dreams.

Screams. Howling. Violent, bestial faces. Blood. So much blood. Flames and agony and feasting carrion crows. Wolves creeping out of the shadows, devouring corpses and the wounded and babies starving to death.

He woke at the first weak touch of sunlight, aching and sick. Full of misery and dread. Woke to see Arlin up and watching him, his expression disdainful, his eyes without warmth.

"We might need your friend, Rafel, but he's your problem. Not mine. You can feed him, water him and wipe his arse, for I won't. And make sure he walks downwind of me. He stinks."

Rafel nodded, not trusting himself to speak.

Broken and weeping, Lord Garrick. Broken and weeping.

Goose stirred awake then, so frighted, so lost. Soothing Goose, trying to ease his fears, wiped Arlin Garrick from his mind completely.

Helping Goose, he couldn't keep the tears at bay.

I'm sorry. I'm sorry. This is all my fault, Goose.

Eventually, their bellies teased with miserly mouthfuls of food and water, they left the desolate village behind. Took the overgrown road leading away from the ruined buildings, trusting—hoping—that soon they'd stumble upon a larger, living village, or Baden and Pintte, or both. Goose still hadn't spoken, but he was calmer, and seemed content to follow them like a dog.

Rafel kept him close by. A dog. A bear. And his nickname was Goose. *Is that what he is now? Just a beast? No more a man?* The thought was enough to start him weeping afresh.

If he wasn't careful, he would weep himself to death.

They walked and they walked, athwart the rising sun, and saw no sign of Fernel Pintte or Sarle Baden or any member of their expedition. Saw no sign of any man or woman, or any hint that one had passed this way in days or even weeks. Perhaps longer. Rafel asked his friend again and again, *"Where's that Fernel bloody Pintte got to? D'you remember where you left him, Goose?"* But Goose only looked at him, mouth slackly open, eyes dull. No-one home.

They did come across rabbits, though. A sign of life, at last. Rafel, his mother's hunting son, killed six. They broiled them over a fire, devouring the stringy, poorly skinned carcasses like starving men...which they were. Goose tried to eat the bones as well, and cried when Rafel stopped him. Then they found an odorish, sluggish stream — and drank from it anyway. Filled their waterskins with the brownish sludge and trusted it wouldn't kill them.

When night fell, they slept. In the morning they woke, ate cold rabbit, drank foul water and started walking again, in silence. There was almost nothing to say. Rafel waited for Arlin to mention Durm's magic. Demand again to see the spells. Curse and rail against interfering Olken. But Arlin never did. *Perhaps he doesn't care anymore. I know I don't. All I care about is Goose. Show me the spell to fix him and then I'll get excited. Then I'll care.*

Their journey continued through barren wastelands, through shallow rivers, into gnarled copses and out the other side. Three more villages they came to, all of them deserted. All of them dead. They caught enough game that they didn't perish from hunger. Found enough wood to burn that they didn't freeze to death. They walked for nine days seeing no-one. Learning nothing. No sign of Pintte's expedition. No sign of any life but the animals they killed to survive. And the tainted earth tormented them, gifting them with bad dreams.

Then on the tenth day... it all changed.

"Hold up!" said Arlin, his clenched fist lifting. "Do you smell that? Wood smoke... and roasting meat."

Sunk into a mind-numbing stupor, barely aware of his body, its pains, his thoughts drifting homewards—*Are you still alive, Da? Please don't be dead*—Rafel staggered to a halt. Shambling Goose halted beside him, anxious, a whimper building in his throat. They were deep within another straggled copse, the afternoon sky criss-crossed with unhealthy branches, its light fractured and mean, their ankles held captive by brambles and blackweed and sickly foxfoot. Odd, to recognise such foliage so far away from Lur.

"Aye," he mumbled. "I smell it. Arlin—best be careful. We don't know if that's Sarle and—"

Arlin bit off an impatient curse. "Stay here if you're afraid. With your witless friend. I've no fear of strangers. They'll do well to fear me."

So bludgeoned was he by nine unrelenting days of the blight soaking these lands like old, rotten blood, Rafel had no strength to argue. To caution arrogant Lord Garrick that he might not be the only bloody mage in these parts.

Arlin started towards the strong smell of wood smoke, and out of exhausted habit he followed. Goose stumbled along with him. He was beginning to wonder if it wasn't a cruelty to keep his sick friend here. He was beginning to fear that if he left it much longer, they'd be too far from Dorana City for him to send Goose home. For all he knew they were already too far. And if they were, and he tried Durm's conjuring spell, Goose would die for sure.

Tomorrow. I'll decide tomorrow. I will.

Up ahead, the crackle of woodfire. A horse's whinny, cut short. Voices, low and carrying. The copse thinned to a clearing. Without hesitation Arlin strode out of the shadows. Stinking and filthy, weeks and weeks unshaven, still he stamped about the place as though he owned it. *Poxy, arrogant little shit.*

Slowing, almost halting, one arm out to bar Goose's way, Rafel took in the scene.

Three horses, ungroomed, common-bred and ribby, tied in a line. A fat-sputtered fire, with spitted venison roasting above it. Twelve men on their knees, rope halters round their necks, yoked together and staring at the damp, leafy ground. An open fronted tent, tattered, but opulent once. A long time ago, surely. A man on a rickety chair alone in that tent, clothed in mothworn red velvet and a tarnished tin crown. He had silvery-blond hair...

"Sarle!" cried Arlin, striding towards the seated man. "Sarle Baden!"

Blinking, Rafel stepped a few paces closer. *Sarle Baden?* But—but—

Instinct stirred, a sluggish warning. Something was wrong here. Dreadfully wrong.

The blond man raised a hand in greeting and laughed. "Yes. Yes, I am Sarle. I was Sarle. I might be Sarle again. And you are Arlin Garrick, my dear friend Rodyn's son. You've found us! Excellent. We were coming to find you. As soon as we felt you, we turned back. *Welcome, Arlin.* Welcome to my court!"

The yoked, kneeling men jerked up their heads. Rafel felt himself stagger, seeing their faces. Felt the dark sickness, his constant companion, rise up in bile and disbelief to his throat. 'Cause there was Fernel Pintte, and the other Olken as travelled with him and Goose and Sarle Baden. No sign of the Doranen. The men yoked with them had red hair. He'd never seen a man with red hair before. But why were they yoked like that? What was going on?

Tugging at Goose's sleeve, he took another step closer. But Goose wouldn't budge. Turning, Rafel saw his friend was shaking like a wind-blown leaf, tears running from his terror-haunted eyes. Then Goose's knees gave way, and he dropped limbs akimbo to the patchy grass.

Goose, Goose, I can't stay here. I've got to see.

So he left Goose behind, praying his friend would be safe, and crept a little further out of the trees. But the closer he got to Sarle Baden the more his belly churned. The more his blood bubbled, burning. Couldn't Arlin *feel* it? Why wasn't he *running?* And then he had to bend over, retching, 'cause he knew what this was. He'd nearly choked on it in Westwailing. Crossing the mountains. Crossing this land. The foul stench of Morg's blight, grown so thick now that if he had a knife he could cut it...

Arlin was staring down his nose at his fellow Doranen. "Sarle," he said, his tone so dismissive. So *arrogant.* So bloody typically Arlin Garrick. "What do you mean, *your court?* What—"

Sarle Baden came out of his shabby tent, walking towards Arlin with both arms outstretched, a wide, welcoming smile warming his thin Doranen face.

Something was terribly wrong with his eyes.

Arlin fisted his hands on his hips. "*Sarle.* I won't ask you again. What is the meaning of these ridiculous theatrics? The General Council—"

"Has no power in my court," Sarle said gently, and rested his hand on Arlin's travel-stained shoulder. "But as I say, *you* are welcome. Sarle has been...a disappointment. Competent but not brilliant. Makeshift, you might say. One does what one can. And now *you* are come, Arlin. Oh, I *am* pleased. It's not a moment too soon."

Closer now, Rafel could see that Pintte and the other men weren't just yoked, they were hobbled and gagged with wooden balls in their mouths. Their eyes were wide with terror and most of them were weeping. *Fernel Pintte* was weeping.

For the first time in his life, Rafel felt sorry for the bastard.

Arlin shrugged off Sarle Baden's hand. "Lord Baden, clearly you're unwell. Too unwell to continue. You should return to Lur immediately. I will continue the search for Lost Dorana. I will—"

"Ah...Dorana..." breathed Baden. "A name to pierce this exile's heart. But I cannot go home. I am sundered, Arlin. I am forgotten of myself. The pain—it is unbearable. I am—I am—" The Doranen mage's face twisted. "I am Sarle Baden. I was Sarle Baden. I—I—" He let out an animal howl, half agony, half madness. "I am burning out this inferior creature. Oh, the depths to which my people are *fallen.* Arlin—"

Rafel swallowed. *I have to. I have to.* "Arlin, best you get away from him," he said, soft as he could. "I don't—I reckon he ain't safe."

Irritated, Arlin turned his head. "Shut up, you fool. He's sick, that's all."

"Yes, yes, I am sick," crooned Baden. His hand stroked Arlin's filthy hair. "But you can heal me, you beautiful boy. You're strong. I can feel it. Perhaps you're the one I've been searching for..."

"Arlin!" Rafel said again, making his voice snap. On the grass behind him, Goose whimpered and moaned. "Are you bloody blind? Look at his eyes! Barl's tits, you fool, he ain't—"

"Barl?" whispered Sarle Baden. "The bitch, the slut, the treacherous whore." His hand shifted from Arlin's shoulder to the back of his neck, fingers curving. His teeth bared in a smile. "Yes. Yes. No more Sarle. I shall be Arlin. And Arlin Garrick shall take me home."

"No!" Rafel shouted, as waves of blighting blackness boiled around Rodyn Garrick's arrogant son. "Arlin—get away from him—"

With the last of his strength he reached deep inside himself for the magic that wasn't Olken. That had burst from him in Westwailing. That had helped collapse waterspouts and hold a whirlpool at bay and sent three good, suffering men safely home.

Sarle Baden gasped. His hand fell away from Arlin. Shoving the younger mage aside he took a step forward. Another. His terrible eyes were wide with wonder. With rage. Head tipped to one side, he stepped closer again.

"Do I *know* you, boy?" he whispered. "Little mage, have we met?"

Snared by that burning gaze, like a bird caught in quicklime, Rafel blinked. "You don't remember?"

Baden reached out both hands. His touch was fire and ice. Rafel felt himself weeping. Felt his strength stolen. Could hardly breathe.

Baden could breathe. Eyes closed, he breathed in deeply and slowly. "I do know you..." he murmured. "I know your scent. It is familiar. I know the taste of your magic. I know—" His crazed eyes flew open. "I know your father. You're *his* son."

Behind him, yoked to helplessness, Pintte was yelling round the wooden gag in his mouth. In front of him Arlin was staring, at last—too late—an awful suspicion dawning in his arrogant face. "Rafel—"

Sarle Baden was smiling. "Rafel? That's your name? Oh...the power in you, Rafel. Have you any idea? Do you know what you are? What you could have been? What you will never be? I have been searching twenty lonely years for you..."

He tried to speak. Tried to break free. Tried to drop dead on the spot.

Sarle Baden pulled him close until they rested brow to brow. Deep in his eyes a black flame leapt high.

"Say goodbye, Rafel..." the Doranen whispered. "Say goodbye, little mage..."

He felt a battering of darkness. His heart pounding in terror. Revulsion and fury and grief and despair.

No — no — no — no —

The sun went out. His heart stopped. The screams died in his throat. And then, a lifetime later, he opened his eyes. Looked around himself, a new man. Looked around himself.

Morg.

ACKNOWLEDGEMENTS

Tim Holman, who rode this one with grace and patience right down to the wire.

The Orbit team, without whom I'd be a sadder, sorrier author.

Ethan Ellenberg, agent and wise counsel.

Mary Webber, Peter and Elaine Shipp, Glenda Larke and Mark Timmony, whose courage in throwing themselves onto early draft manuscripts is worthy of a silver star.

The booksellers, writing's often unsung heroes.

The readers, who make all this possible.